The Storm Protocol

By

Iain Cosgrove

First published in 2013 by Iain Cosgrove

Second edition published January 2014

Front and Rear Cover Images © Rolf Zaska, 2013

ISBN: 978-0957417502

DEDICATION

To my family; the bedrock on which my foundations are built.
To Jane – Always.

ACKNOWLEDGEMENTS

I would like to acknowledge the support and encouragement of my wife Jane, who repeatedly told me that all I needed was a work ethic and a healthy dose of luck!

This is a novel and as such, it is a work of fiction. Therefore, certain liberties have been taken with real locations, events and places so that they fit with the story. The interpretation placed on them is mine and mine alone; hopefully the finished story will be worthy of the subtle changes.

PROLOGUE – THE GATHERING STORM

10th May 2011 – The night of the Storm.

Sorrows gather around great souls as storms do around mountains; but, like them, they break the storm and purify the air of the plain beneath them. – Jean Paul Richter.

A storm was coming, I could feel it. The air was charged with particles of electricity that crackled with unspent energy, portents of the thunder and lightning to come. A patchwork of uneasy stratospheric alliances danced overhead, woven into the very fabric of the atmosphere. The moisture hung like a fog in the humid air; heavy and overpowering, like the purple velvet curtains that were pulled roughly closed across the large French doors of the ballroom behind me.

The swing seat was creaking softly as I rocked myself imperceptibly backwards and forwards. The veranda had been the main selling point for me, the final seal on the deal. I'd lost count of the number of modern houses I'd viewed, but as the car had glided down the long unkempt driveway, the huge white mansion had emerged from the early morning mist in all its pomp and colonnaded splendour. She'd hooked me from the start. She was a faded princess, decaying and slowly dying, but I didn't care. She was a bit like me really. She had seen a lot of life, and her well worn patina showed on every wall and floor.

Louisiana was about as far removed from my normal sphere of operations as it was possible to get, and this had been the other hook to reel me in. It had been very expensive, but money was about the only thing I had in plentiful supply.

My mum had loved *Gone with the Wind*, especially the grand and ostentatious *Tara*. She had made me promise, almost as many times as we'd both watched it, curled together on the battered leather sofa, that I would buy her a place like that when I was a millionaire. A couple of times, especially toward the end of her life, when our communication was as distant as the ocean that separated us, I made the promises again. Advanced senility had made her a

1

stranger, but even so, I clung to those promises like a life jacket, and even began to believe them myself.

In the half light of the dusk, I could just make out the family cemetery that had come with the property. Apparently, it had put off a lot of the potential buyers, but I loved it. Generations of the Roussel family were buried in the plot, differentiated through the decades by nothing other than the dates on their simple granite headstones. I chuckled slightly as I remembered the look on the face of the local stonemason.

I had commissioned a new headstone.

Mary O'Neill, beloved mother, died 21st March 1990.

It sounded silly, but I felt by that one act, I had kept at least a tiny bit of my promise to her.

I would often wander through the vibrant flower filled plots, watching the sun set in the distance, remembering happier times. Occasionally, if the impish mood was upon me, I would also speculate on the relationships between the many deceased, and try to guess at their causes of death.

But it was my own death I was contemplating tonight.

At first, the anxious thoughts had been easy to dismiss. I was not a coward and never had been. But now, in the cold light of a May evening, I knew it was only a matter of time before they found me.

Looking back on it, I would not have done anything differently. In truth, I couldn't have done anything differently. I was a marked man, simple as that. I knew better than anyone that the Mancini brothers did not have a retirement plan. I used to action their pension arrangements myself. You couldn't just stop working for them. And I had been their most trusted lieutenant, welcomed into the inner circle, party to all manner of unsavoury and dangerous information.

At first I had thought this would save me, would make me untouchable. The note I'd left Guido had outlined my reasons for leaving and why I would not be a threat. The following day, I'd been sitting on a mottled and musty bedspread in a run-down motel, just off interstate 95. I'd been intently reading the plain white folder that was my only luggage, when an image had flashed into my head. It was a picture often repeated during my long employment, an image of a man in the grip of unrequited anger and intensity. Only then did I realise the plain unequivocal truth. In writing that simple note, I had signed my own death warrant and sealed it with my own blood. They did not do rejection.

I had been an enforcer for the brothers for two decades, so I knew where people would instinctively hide, and conversely, the best ways to stay hidden. They had called me *the Street* or *Street* for short; as stark, brutal and uncompromising as the neighbourhoods we ruled. It was a moniker that stuck with me throughout my career. It had originally appealed to my youthful and impetuous ego and I'd loved it. It implied status and power and pretty soon people forgot my given name and I didn't encourage their memories of it.

So the new owner of *Augustine Mansion* had been registered as Thomas Eugene O'Neill, hiding in plain sight.

The young Thomas had been a bright eyed and innocent twenty year old, when I'd first docked in New York all those years ago. Kathleen had begged me to stay in Ireland, and when that hadn't worked she had begged me to take her with me. I'd promised that I would send for her when I'd made my fortune, both of us realising that the likelihood of either happening was extremely slim.

I'd taken any and every job that I could, all of them unskilled, low-paid and rarely guaranteed. But just when I thought that weeks of breadline existence would turn into months and then years, a savage beating at the hands of a Latino gang ultimately changed the course of my life.

Guido and his brother Ernesto happened upon my inert body, lying in a pool of blood in an alley in Brooklyn. They intimated a way that I could get revenge and then provided the means and the opportunity for me to do it. And in that one action, they inextricably bound us together for eternity, the holy trinity. I never once questioned aloud how they managed to be in a position to find my badly beaten body so conveniently.

I already knew.

Not that I minded.

I gained immediate respect and wealth beyond my wildest dreams. But I was always respectful, to my employers and to my targets. I was a professional. I did not do torture, it was not my thing. I would calmly explain what it was that the brothers wanted, and what would happen if they did not get what they wanted. Most of my targets understood and most of them complied. The ones that did not, died, it was as simple as that. And not in a hail of bullets either, always a single shot to the head. In New York, it was known as *the Street shot*; my very own urban legend.

So, who would the brothers send to tidy up this particular loose end? Even though I could almost feel the white heat of their anger, I knew how realistic they were. They didn't have anyone in their current stable that was as good as me, and they knew that I knew it too. They would not make a mistake and they would make sure the job was done properly. I was forty five years old, not the enforcer of old. It would be someone I didn't know; a man from the outside, a new recruit to do their bidding. One thing I did know. He would be a twenty-something mirror image of me, of that I was certain.

My hand strayed to the underside of the table. I had duct-taped my favourite 9mm in place, hidden from casual view by the dainty lace table cloth, a delicious irony. If he found me, it would be a case of the best man winning, and I would not go down without a fight. I wasn't afraid; I had long ago said any goodbyes that needed saying, and I was sick of running.

Forked lightning lit up the sky, followed by a tremendous rolling roar of thunder, jerking me out of my sentimental reverie. Huge drops of rain started splashing down on the driveway. You could hear the staccato beats on the roof of the veranda, like a thousand manic drummers. But as I watched the celestial lightshow play out, I glimpsed a different type of light on the horizon.

A car was moving steadily up the driveway, the headlights flickering as it passed the willows that lined the long ornate lane. The driver was uncertain of the lie of the land; the car was moving very slowly, and it only speeded up when the driveway opened out onto the gravel parking area in front of the house.

As the young man got out of the car, I immediately knew he was the one; the angel of death. He had an aura of invincibility about him, an arrogance that only youth and supreme self confidence can bring. It was indeed like looking into a mirror that faced back in time.

He reached into the back and removed his light linen jacket, making no attempt to shelter from the massive raindrops. By the time he had shrugged himself into the suit and made his way slowly to the veranda, he was literally dripping wet. It was a sublime performance of machismo.

He was trying to impress me.

'Hi there,' he said slowly, and I suppressed a smile.

They'd even sent a Paddy. It fitted in with the twisted sense of humour that the brothers often displayed.

'Hi there,' I said in reply. 'Lost?'

'Maybe,' he replied.

I gestured to the chair opposite me.

'Please sit down,' I said, my newfound southern hospitality kicking in. 'Can I get you a drink of anything? Iced tea? Coffee? Something stronger?'

'I'll take a beer if you have one,' said the stranger, settling himself into the chair opposite me, watching the drips pool on the polished teak of the veranda floor.

I headed for the kitchen and returned in a couple of minutes with two bottles.

'Domestic okay?' I asked him, as I handed him the chilled Miller.

He laughed.

'Not domestic where I come from.'

'No, right enough not,' I replied. 'And where would that be exactly?'

'Oh come on,' he said, giving nothing away. 'Same place as you; Ireland for sure, no?'

I nodded an affirmation. He was quick, I'd give him that.

'So, what can I do for you?' I asked.

'I think you know who I am,' he said.

God, he was brazen. And there was something else behind the eyes. It was well hidden, but it seemed to be almost a sense of joy, even exaltation; like he had finally arrived, or was about to.

'So, I think you know well why I'm here,' he finished enigmatically.

He wasn't holding back, that was for sure.

I decided to play him along for a while.

'You have the better of me, young man,' I said. 'Maybe introductions would be in order first?'

He seemed to relax slightly.

'My name is Alan, Alan Murphy,' he said, tipping his beer bottle toward me in a substitute for a handshake.

I held up my own beer in a silent return salute.

'Pleased to meet you Alan, my name is Thomas,' I replied.

'I know who you are,' he said.

It was not the answer I had been expecting.

'Ok,' I said, finally relenting as I sat back down directly across from him. 'We both know why you are here. I'm not going to beat around the bush any more. But let's be adult about it. You can walk away now and neither of us will get hurt.'

'I'm not walking away from this,' he said slowly. 'After all the effort I put into finding you? You've got to be joking.'

He put his empty bottle deliberately on the table and then in an instant his hand darted inside his jacket.

So, it comes down to this, does it?

For a split second, I contemplated a future without running; being able to walk down a street without constantly scanning the crowd; a normal life. But it was only a split second.

Two decades of mental training kicked in and almost before I was aware of what I was doing, the gun appeared in my hand. A flash of lightning lit up the tableau, and I saw a flicker of uncertainty on the young man's face, before the impact of the single shot sent him backwards out of his chair. He tumbled awkwardly down the veranda steps to land in an untidy and ungainly heap.

I walked down to where his body lay, unheeding of the lashing rain. He was stone dead; after two decades as a harbinger of death, I recognised it immediately. But this time it seemed unfair somehow.

I felt cheated.

It had been too easy.

I opened his jacket to extract the weapon, but instead, his hand was grasping a plain white envelope. I gently prised his fingers off it. The outside was stained and greasy, easy evidence that the contents had been removed and replaced over and over again.

I extracted the letter and smoothed it open. Small sections of it leapt out at me. *Dear Mr Murphy*, it began. A sentence further down the page had been highlighted. *We think your search may be over.*

As the rain started smudging and blurring the ink all over the paper, I realised that there was another document still left in the envelope. I pulled it out and as I did so, I immediately knew what it was. An Irish birth certificate, with its ornate harp logo at the top, was unmistakeable. I looked across at the name of the mother, already half guessing what I would find; Kathleen Murphy.

I stood there as the rain obliterated the documents in my hand. I had seen the name of the father, standing out in stark capital letters, mocking me. I felt nothing. I was numb. The lightning crackled and the thunder roared, and still I stood there; unmoving, unyielding.

I didn't see the dark suited figure sidle up behind me, as agile, nimble and silent as a cat. I only felt the pressure of the barrel on the back of my neck, as the lightning lit up the body at my feet for one last time.

'Guido says goodbye,' he whispered in my ear, as the thunder roared overhead, punctuated only by a single, sharp crack.

CHAPTER 1 – AWAKENING

10th April 2011 – One month before the Storm.

Death; the last sleep? No, it is the final awakening. – Sir Walter Scott.

I placed the steaming mug gently onto the kitchen table. I was always careful to centre it onto the white ring, a mark that had etched itself indelibly into the soft veneer of the cheap pine. I often idly contemplated cleaning it off and then always managed to find something better to do.

I was a creature of habit.

I took my first sip, and winced at the heat and the taste; I had forgotten the sweetener again.

What an idiot.

As I pulled the sugar bowl over and stirred in a couple of spoonfuls, I turned my attention back to the job in hand. The shoe box had already been removed from the closet, a daily eight-fifteen obsession.

I emptied the contents gingerly and then carefully unfurled the soft cotton cloth that wrapped the items. The heavy material folded out and spread over the surface, but fell short of the edges, like a table cloth that was slightly too small.

I arranged the metallic objects, newly liberated from their daily slumber, creating uniform patterns on the table. It was always the same pattern with no deviations.

I surveyed the finished display, truly a work of art. A stunning triumph of design and functionality, each individual part crafted and machined to perfection. And yet, perfect as each individual piece was, it could not function individually. It could only contribute to the balanced and lethal whole.

I set to work with the cleaning solution and oils. I flipped the egg timer over; tapping it gently to make sure the sands of time started flowing.

Seated in my favourite chair, I proceeded to clean, oil, and assemble at the same slow and steady pace I always used. And just as the last grain of sand dropped into the lower vessel, I pulled the slide back with an abrupt metallic clunk.

Gently increasing the pressure on the trigger, I felt the slight buck in my hand and heard the satisfying click of the hammer. There was something primeval about a gun, something only men could relate to; a reflex buried deep in our primitive warrior subconscious.

My first daily ritual was over, a habit born out of two decades of paranoia. I held a lifelong superstitious belief that I was the architect of my own survival or destruction. I always worked that way; it was one of the primary reasons I was the best at what I did. I left nothing to chance. I made my own luck; there was no lady present.

I engaged the safety and laid the weapon aside. Picking up the box of ammunition reverently, I selected nine rounds at random. As I looked at them, glinting in my hand, I went through my other morning routine.

Carefully inspecting each round for signs of warping, I checked for suspicious markings or scratches on the sides or bottom, laying them in specific piles, left for rejection and right for selection. As I rejected, I selected another from the box and repeated, until I had nine items in a neat row to my right.

I scanned them visually, before hefting each one in my hand, to check for overall balance and feel. You'd be surprised at what you could ascertain, just by hefting a bullet in your hand for a few seconds.

I had seen the effects first-hand at a local firing range, once. Mr Ego behind me in the queue had scoffed and laughed at my superstition. As he'd loaded my rejected rounds, he'd winked to his girlfriend and his mates; he was going to make his point. And make it he did; bullet number three jammed, blowing his hand clean off. It had not been a pretty sight. So, the discarded ones were routinely disposed of. I wouldn't allow rejected ammunition back into circulation.

Once I'd finished, and only when I was completely satisfied with each individual item, I pressed each round carefully into the magazine. I only ever used nine bullets; even if the gun could take more, nine was my limit. It was my talisman and I had no intention of ever changing it.

For me, it was always about the numbers. How many targets are there? How many shots to kill? How much will I get paid?

But it went deeper than that.

I always regarded the numbers one through nine as pure. Anything higher than nine was a combination of numbers and my superstition wouldn't allow combinations. If I needed more than nine bullets on a job, then the time had come to retire.

Once the magazine was fully loaded, I visually inspected it one last time, and then I laid it softly next to the gun. Like love and marriage, you couldn't have one without the other.

I picked up the mug again and drained the bitter sweet liquid in a long final swallow. I snatched the two items from the table and slammed the magazine into the gun with a gratifying click. I eased the weapon into my shoulder holster, shrugging on my two thousand-dollar linen suit jacket. It was specially tailored for me so that it would not show any embarrassing bulges. Guido and Ernesto had immaculate taste in clothes and expected the same of their employees.

I walked over to the CD player, repeating the same two albums over and over again. I smiled at the line that was playing as I approached; it was prophetic really.

I'm a book keeper's son. I don't want to shoot no one.

I clicked off the stereo. He had been a solicitor, not a book keeper.

I trotted briskly down the stairs and out of the front door of my sleek brownstone, located in one of the better areas of Midtown; a fringe benefit of my job. I took the steps two at a time, replaying the orders from the previous night; going over in my head what I was expected to do today.

#

'There is a pharmacy at 630 Lexington Avenue,' said Guido softly.

He glanced at me and then muttered to himself under his breath in annoyance.

'Hey Street,' he shouted suddenly and with venom. 'Are you listening to me?'

I jerked in surprise; irritated at myself for drifting off. My mind was somewhere completely different; certainly not in this room. It had been happening a lot recently. Too much for my line of work, and especially where the brothers were concerned. I was a detail oriented person.

Details were the difference between life and death.

I needed to pay attention. It was shit like this that would get me killed.

'Sorry boss,' I said. 'Long day, I guess. What were you saying?'

He coughed.

'Do I have your full attention now? Good! Focus, for fuck's sake.'

He exhaled in disgust.

'Anyway, as I was saying, there is a pharmacy at 630 Lexington Avenue,' he repeated.

'There is a dude working the prescription counter, name of O'Reilly; John O'Reilly. One of your lot I think,' he said, directing the comment towards me with the beginnings of a smirk.

I nodded to indicate my understanding.

He had an Irish sounding surname. Big deal, he was probably Irish-American, so way more Irish than a real Paddy like me. But it did make it easier for me sometimes; if they were ethnic, it gave me an in.

9

'He owes us a lot of money. We know people don't carry that kind of cash around with them, and we know he doesn't have it in any of his checking or savings accounts. We know his credit rating and circle of friends; we know his share portfolio and what assets he owns. In short, we know every godamn thing about him, so we also know that there is no way on God's green earth that he can pay us back.'

He smiled at the last statement.

'So, normal persuasion job, then,' I replied. 'Lean on him a little, let him know the lie of the land?'

'No, not this time,' said Guido, surprising me. 'Normally it would piss me right off. I would love to lean on this little fucker and show him he can't fuck with the Mancini family. But in this case, lucky for the little SOB, his debt is the very thing that makes him useful to us.'

He stopped to compose himself; eyes closing briefly as he brought forth the memories.

'He has racked up a huge gambling tab which he can't pay. We were about to send some heat over to him; these suckers normally crumble like shortcake. But before we could send anyone over, he made direct contact with us. It surprised the shit out of me, to be honest.'

Ernesto nodded curtly, silently corroborating the information.

'So, we have temporarily sanctioned his ongoing debt, with the proviso that it does not get any bigger, and we are going to collect in a different way.'

Guido paused for breath and to assemble his thoughts. His hawk-like stare pierced the picture window as it framed the Manhattan skyline, the buildings shimmering in the late evening sunlight. His eyes moved constantly, darting left and right, taking everything in, as though he was searching for prey. Nothing got past Guido.

'So, lucky for him, he thinks he has something we would be interested in,' he continued, 'and much more importantly for him, we *know* we would be interested in it. Otherwise, the little cock-sucker would be in Bellevue by now.'

He grinned at me.

'I *think* you might be able to persuade him to part with it. If it is as valuable as he thinks it is....'

He left the statement lying there and looked across at me quizzically. He was almost impossibly tanned, with a face unlined by life, miraculous for one of sixty two with his type of lifestyle. Botox and UV lamps played a big part in Guido's daily routine. But his cobalt blue hawk-eyes were fierce in their intensity, set off against the dark eyebrows and framed under a sleek shock of slicked back silver hair. He was the archetypal mobster and even if he wasn't, you would instinctively assume that he was seriously connected.

You didn't fuck with Guido.

'Any hints as to what I am supposed to ask him for?' I asked, a tad shortly.

The brothers exchanged a quick glance. Ernesto's eyes darted to me for a split second and then flitted away again as quickly.

I studied him as he gazed out of the same window that his brother had moments earlier. He was slightly taller than his sibling at six feet even, with the same shock of silver hair. But his eyes were green, and his complexion was lighter and less tanned. He didn't go in for the same cosmetic treatments, so consequently his face looked like well worn leather. His eyebrows were white, and the overall effect made him look softer and more serene than Guido. I had only ever made that mistake once. I subconsciously rubbed the large circular scar on the back of my hand; I always learnt from my mistakes. But I did know one thing. The brothers were hiding something from me; I could always tell.

'It's a white ring binder,' said Ernesto quietly.

His eyes snapped back to me and his stare never left mine, his demeanour suddenly deliberately threatening. I was equal to the challenge, holding his eyes and daring him to take it further. He nodded eventually and looked away.

'Street, this means a lot to us,' he said, and I was surprised at the earnestness of his statement. 'So please don't fuck it up, for his sake and for yours.'

He didn't elaborate and I didn't expect him to.

'So how do I recognise this binder?' I asked. 'How do I know he isn't pawning me off with some old newspaper cuttings or baseball stats?'

Guido pointed to the picture behind his desk. The photographer was either brave or foolhardy, traits Guido loved and loathed in equal measure. The image revealed a tornado that had just touched down, literally carving a house in two. Guido's favourite piece of the picture was the three cattle you could just make out in the top left of the wind funnel, swirling about, legs and tails flailing. He had a bit of a twisted sense of humour.

He glanced at me and saw the confusion on my face.

'Storm,' he said. 'The word *Storm* will be on the cover and watermarked across every page.'

As I left, I failed to see the look that passed between the brothers. If I had, I would have known exactly what it meant.

#

John O'Reilly was nervous, without knowing exactly why. He was always getting premonitions. It had been that way since his early teens, and he always obeyed his subconscious. But this was different; this wasn't directional as much as a sense of foreboding.

'What the fuck am I supposed to do with these?' asked the middle aged lady at the front of the queue, holding up a packet of laxatives that he had absently thrown into her prescription bag.

He muttered an apology under his breath. She looked long and hard at him for a few seconds, opened the package slightly to check the drugs she really wanted were inside, and then snatched it off the counter with a flourish. As she stalked out of the door on a wave of self righteousness, he exhaled the breath he didn't realise he'd been holding in a big stream.

He tried to catch Cathy's eye, eventually having to resort to waving his arms like an idiot, while the Latino man at the front of the queue swore and muttered under his breath.

Cathy hurried over.

'Listen Cathy,' he said rapidly.

She put her head on one side as she listened.

'I just got a call from the school,' he continued, lying seamlessly. 'One of the kids is being sent home, and Anne is out of town this week at a convention.'

He saw the light of concern in her eyes, and for a brief second, felt a tiny bit guilty at his little white lies. He remembered the words of the Mancini brothers and the guilt dissolved like an early morning mist on the beach.

She nodded her understanding, making the universal signal for *get out of here and do what you have to do* and took his place at the counter. She smiled brightly at the annoyed Latino customer, diffusing his anger immediately with her charm and poise.

He slipped down the corridor and out onto the rear fire escape platform, which they also used as a makeshift smoking area. As the fire door closed behind him, he extricated the cigarette packet and lighter from the breast pocket of his smart white lab coat. It was crisply starched and ironed *every* day. Anne was as exacting in her standards as his mother had been. It was a pity the two of them never got to meet as they would have liked each other instinctively.

He shook a cigarette into his hand, marvelling at the perfection of shape, texture and colour. There was just something about cigarettes that made them so aesthetically appealing to him. He slowly passed the sleek white cylinder under his nose, revelling in the sweet tobacco smell.

The harsh scraping of the flint animated the small lighter. As he held the blue and orange flame to the unfiltered end, he heard the faint crackle, a bushfire in miniature, as the cigarette flared into life. He always went through the same routine, delaying the surrender; that beautiful moment when the nicotine was dragged deep into his lungs.

As he exhaled the thin stream of smoke through his nose, he contemplated both the burning tip and his current predicament.

#

The fourth child had been their downfall. They had been marginally ahead until that point; up one month and down another, but always just about even at year end. But this had been the tipping point for their perilously poised scales, delicately balanced for years, until a tiny increment in one direction had set off a chain reaction. Their household bills exponentially increased to the point that, even with their two salaries coming in, they could not cover all their outgoings.

In the middle of all this upheaval and chaos, he'd been invited to a mid week poker night at a local club with some old frat buddies. He never went out, never socialised with work or old friends, but the pressure was getting to him. It was Anne who'd suggested it might be a good idea to release the valve on the pressure cooker for one night at least.

He'd gone into the evening filled with trepidation. He hadn't been out as a *single* man for years. He was not a big drinker or a big gambler, but the sense of freedom he'd felt was amazing. The release from the bounds of his closeted life made him feel like a million dollars. The more he'd drunk, the more he'd wanted to drink, and his rising debt situation had made him bold at the tables. At the end of the night, he'd ended up taking home the guts of three thousand dollars in winnings from a one hundred dollar stake, and the telephone numbers of two different women.

It had paid off a lot of bills, and his earnest headshaking at the initial disapproval and anti gambling lecture had seemed to pay dividends in the bedroom, too.

For a while, he left it alone; the tonic of that one visit seemed to be what they needed as a couple. Lady luck had visited and bestowed her gifts of plenty. But it couldn't last and after a period of about three months, the bills started to increment with such renewed ferocity, that one night after work, he found his feet directing him past the Metro stop and back outside the self same casino club.

He should have realised; he was a stable middle aged professional man, the type who worked through his problems, not a reckless, feckless idiot. But they seemed so nice. They remembered his name at the door; they even remembered the type of drink he liked. And the first few bets were on the house; that was the only hook they needed. From then on he was theirs.

He was an addict.

He found his feet beginning to stray toward his new mistress more and more often, as dangerous and insidious as any femme fatale. The excuses over the pressures of work mounted and Anne bought them hook, line and sinker. She had no reason to doubt him; he was a genuinely hard worker.

For the first few weeks or so, he won and won big. It seemed like the sun was starting to rise, casting a warm glow over the slightly sick and guilty feeling he always carried into the club. But then, about a month into his newfound shadow life, the tide turned like a tsunami.

Rather than cut his losses, as most normal non addicts would do, he decided to wait it out; to play through the slump and win big again. But even here, the club were most obliging. They seemed to understand his needs and started him with a hefty line of credit. He was one of their most valued clients, they told him. It would be their pleasure to accommodate him. And accommodate him they did; over a six month period, he managed to rack up a debt to the tune of one hundred thousand big ones.

He'd been escorted into the manager's office, high above the gambling pit, with its line of security monitors, acres of mahogany, and plush leather chairs. His teeth had been chattering as he sat down. He knew what happened to people who accumulated large gambling debts; he may have been self deceiving, but he was not totally stupid.

Two older gentlemen sat in the corner and watched as the manager poured him a coffee. The manager's smile never wavered, but it was clear that the words coming out of his mouth were not his own. John could see it in his eyes, could almost read in the man's mind what he really wanted to say. The ferocity of the delivery, the spittle flying out of his mouth like little bullets of water gave the game away. There was plenty of intimation and lots of flowery language, but it was made crystal clear to him that the debt had now reached a level where it was unsustainable. It was *imperative* (the manager's word) that the debt be scaled down to a more manageable level.

He was given a month.

As he'd walked out, numb to the core, the two older gentlemen had smiled serenely at him and then at each other. It was like printing money for them, a guarantee of another hundred grand in the bank. John and all the other middle class pricks like him had no real fight in them. They would rather put their families out onto the street than risk losing a pinkie finger. P T Barnum had been right; there truly was one born every minute.

CHAPTER 2 – SALVATION

10th April 2011 – One month before the Storm.

The greatest enemy to human souls is the self-righteous spirit which makes men look to themselves for salvation. – Charles Spurgeon.

John watched the smoke rings, practised over many years, and allowed himself a small smile. A lifeline had been thrown to him soon after, and from a very unusual and unlikely source.

#

Glenn Collins was a self serving hypocrite, who ordinarily would not even have made it onto John's tolerated acquaintances list. Unfortunately, he'd had absolutely no control or influence over who he'd got for a brother in law, despite plenty of subtle and not so subtle hints.

John despised the very ground that Glenn walked on, but Glenn would never have suspected it. John was always civil for the sake of Sandra, his sister, but even if he had been openly hostile, Glenn would not have noticed. He was the most self-absorbed person John had ever met. He only ever thought of himself, no exceptions. Even his wife and children were outsiders in Glenn's world.

Tonight was different though. Even for a self important idiot like Glenn, he was acting really funny. Requesting a clandestine meeting in the lane at the back of John's house; asking him not to tell Sandra (John's sister, his own wife) that he was there. None of it made any sense. Glenn was always a bit eccentric, but this was different; this was bordering on paranoia. John had sensed something else this time, a small, barely vocalised hint of real fear.

John dropped the sparkling silver coins into the slot on the vending machine and extricated the evening paper, part of his home bound routine. He had a ten minute walk to his house from the Metro stop, and he liked to spend a few minutes reading the news.

He flipped the paper around to read the back page; like most American males, he headed straight for the sports section. After a brief and depressing perusal of scores, he flipped it back to the front page a few moments later. He froze for a couple of seconds, as if the gaze of medusa herself had fallen upon him. He stopped dead and read the article in detail, his mouth moving as he silently spelled out the words.

The two old dudes from the casino manager's office were pictured outside a courthouse, smiling the same supercilious smiles he had personally witnessed less than a week ago. In the article, their lawyer had outlined to the journalist why the prosecution's case against them had failed. It hinged on a lack of physical evidence and also, critically, no witnesses had been persuaded to come forward.

He read on, swallowing hard with every new revelation. Drugs, prostitution, racketeering, gambling, you name it, they were in it. Fuck! He threw the paper away from him like it was alight; he could almost feel the information burning his fingers. He had known he was in deep, but this was Titanic deep.

Fuck, Fuck, Fuck.

The Mancini's; how had he not recognised them?

The entrance to his laneway put paid to any additional rational thought on the matter. He would listen to whatever whine was in season for that week, and then get Glenn the hell out of the way. After that, a little research was in order, to see what kind of a shit storm he was really inside.

As he approached the house, he could see Glenn hiding behind the fence, looking more conspicuous and obvious than if he had been standing in front of it. Jesus, the man really was an insufferable idiot. Anne, John's wife, was bound to see him if he stayed there, and she would mention it to Sandra and then all Glenn's attempts at subterfuge would be for nothing.

John gesticulated wildly for the cretin to step into the garage, clicking the automatic door opener that he always carried in his pocket as he did so.

He entered the garage, noticing Glenn was in a strangely subdued and silent mood. John sat heavily on the fender of his car next to Glenn, who wordlessly handed him a plain white folder.

'What's this?' asked John, thrown for a second by the sudden change in focus.

'A whole heap of fucking trouble for me,' said Glenn softly, his normal bravado in temporary abeyance. 'I was a bit distracted a couple of nights ago; problems between me and Sandra.'

He looked up at John and quickly flashed a humourless grin.

'That's not what this is about by the way,' he said shortly. 'Anyway, once a month we are instructed to clean the inner offices; the ones that are normally locked. I picked this up by mistake in one of the restricted areas.'

'How the fuck did you manage that?' asked John, forgetting his own worries for a second. 'You can't exactly mistake it for window cleaner,' he added sarcastically.

'I wasn't stealing it, if that's what you're thinking,' said Glenn, a little hurt. 'I honestly thought it was a copy of our health and safety statement. I had a new employee starting that day, there are some additional steps for the restricted zones, and we use plain white binders. It was only when I got outside that I noticed the different content.'

Glenn was a contract cleaner for the US government. But sometimes, in certain company, his role became embellished to the point where it was not mops and brooms he was trained in. At these times, there were normally crowds of young women and lots of alcohol involved.

'It looks very medical and very confidential,' he said furtively. 'I had a brief look, but didn't want to probe too deep. And the name threw me for a second,' he finished, a little lamely.

So now it's starting to make sense, thought John. Go over to see my brother in-law the pharmacist; the medical guy who will do my dirty work for me. See if I really am in trouble, or if I can go back to the lazy, sloppy way I normally conduct my business. If he can, John will save me, if only for Sandra's sake.

'I should hang you out to dry, you fucking idiot,' hissed John, and then his tone changed. 'Why not just give it back and apologise?'

'Either way, I'd say my contract is gone at the very minimum,' said Glenn. 'They'll either spin it that I stole it on purpose, or they'll say I was using untrained, or worse, unregistered staff in a restricted facility.'

'Which you were,' said John sternly.

Glenn shrugged his shoulders dismissively.

'Everyone in the cleaning business does it,' he said. 'It's the only way you can keep the margins down and stay competitive.'

'Why not just chuck it away and wing it?' asked John. 'Why bother finding out what it is?'

'Two reasons,' said Glenn. 'One is natural curiosity. I've always been a bit of a nosey devil and if I'm going to potentially lose my livelihood, I'd like to at least know why.'

He looked at John straight then, and for the first time, John saw a brief glimpse of the old self important swagger.

'But the second reason is pure greed,' he said, with a glint of steel in his eye.

He tapped the word *Storm* on the front cover.

'I have a hunch that it might turn out to be a very valuable commodity indeed.'

\#

John examined the butt closely; he always smoked them as close to the filter as he could to get the last drop of satisfaction. Happy that the nicotine was all used up, he threw the stub to the floor and ground it under the sole of his boot. He was a cautious fellow and always mashed them into dust; you couldn't be too careful with fire.

He turned and his heart jumped. A stranger was standing in the now open doorway, wearing an immaculately tailored suit that was obviously very expensive.

How the fuck had he managed to get there so silently?

John tried to compose himself, and some of his natural bravado returned.

'This is a restricted area, staff only,' he said formally.

The stranger just stared at him.

'Can I help you?' he asked weakly after a while, wilting under the unrelenting gaze.

'For your sake, I really hope so,' said the stranger, in a soft and slightly peculiar accent. 'I have come to collect something that does not belong to either of us.'

John blinked at the slightly ambiguous statement, and then his confusion cleared and the beginnings of a smile creased the corners of his mouth.

'Ah, the messenger,' he said.

Without a word, he brushed past the stranger, slipped through the doorway, and reappeared about a minute later with a plastic carrier bag. He handed it to the stranger, who wordlessly accepted it.

The stranger opened the bag and extracted the single item, a white ring binder with the word *Storm* written in small diagonal letters across the front. He flicked through the individual pages one by one, concentrating more on the watermark than the contents. Satisfied that he'd got what he came for, he dropped it back into the bag and looked up at John.

He was about to open his mouth, when he saw a small kick of brick dust to his left. At almost the same instant, he heard a sound. It was so faint as to be almost unintelligible to a normal human, but it was as loud as an ambulance klaxon for him; silenced high velocity rifle fire.

#

The milliseconds ticked by in slow motion. I dropped the folder to the floor and spun John around so that his back was against my chest. Grabbing him around the neck, the 9mm sprouted from my hand as if by magic as I pulled him backwards as fast as I could, heading for the sanctuary of the passageway. As I moved, I frantically scanned the rooftops, fire escapes and windows across the street. I could see a brief flicker of movement, a glint of sun on scope, and in that second, I felt John buck slightly in my hands.

I dragged him back through the doorway as far away from the street as I possibly could, just as a burst of machine gun fire splintered the door frame. I left him on the floor in the hallway; I could tell he was badly injured, but I had other things to take care of.

I could hear screams of panic inside the pharmacy, so I decided to add to them. Running into the body of the shop, I fired off two rounds, the sound amplified hugely in the confined space.

'Run, he's got a gun,' I shouted into the confusion, before turning back to the job in hand.

Carefully approaching the back entrance again, I could see it was a fire door, and had been clicked open to stop the wind banging it closed. I drew myself up short and slid into place to the left of the opening with my back against the inside wall. I needed to know what I was up against. My first job was to neutralise the cover, and that meant the rooftop.

I had some rough co-ordinates on him based on my first glimpse. I removed the small dental mirror from my pocket, the one that I always carried, and manoeuvred it around the door jamb, hoping the reflections would not give my position away. Sure enough, I could see the tripod on top of the wall, with a black shape moving slightly behind it.

With a sniper at such close range, you do have a chance, but only one. I made sure the safety was off and I had a round in the chamber; one is all I would be allowed if he was any good.

I knew he would have his sights trained on the centre of the door. It was common sense really. I closed my eyes and visualised the scene outside, until I could literally see where he was. I counted to three, and then making myself as slim as possible, I threw myself through the door as far as I could in a sideways motion. I heard the muffled crack and felt the impact in the concrete of the floor beside me.

I rolled head over feet in combat style and was up in a second. I aimed, squeezed the trigger, crack. I saw the shape slump forward, knocking the tripod over the edge of the building parapet.

One target neutralised.

I felt movement to my right, and instinctively threw myself backwards through the open doorway as another burst of machine gun fire whistled over my head. As I fell, I could see the sparks and splinters of brick as the bullets found their mark. I rolled sideways and was on my feet like a cat. I dived forward through the opening again and spun slowly in mid air, hands held out to the side. I kept low and started firing as soon as I cleared the door jamb.

I saw the surprise on his face as he struggled to lower his aim. I felt the thud of each round as they drove him backwards over the railings. As he plummeted to earth, his finger jammed on the trigger and I heard multiple crashes as he took out windows on the way down. He screamed once and then there was a tremendous crunch. There was a small period of intense silence, punctuated almost immediately by a car alarm, and then suddenly the air was filled with the screams and shouts of pedestrians and bystanders.

I knew there would be others, so I retreated and waited. They didn't have their covering support now. The next couple of minutes would see if I was up against professionals or amateurs.

I moved back to the cover of the door, eyes scanning the horizon; nothing. As I settled back against the wall, I regulated my breathing to the extent that it was completely silent. I strained to block out the normal everyday noises; the screaming and panic on the street below was subsiding, and the pharmacy had been abandoned. And then I heard it; the imperceptible rise and fall of disguised breathing. Someone was approaching the door.

I saw the blade before the hand. Someone was pitching a knife against a gun. They were foolhardy, overly confident or supremely skilled; it does happen. I waited until the arm was extended halfway through the doorway.

I dropped my left hand across the forearm and spun violently, driving my elbow with precision into his kidney. I heard a grunt of pain as the knife dropped. Seizing the advantage, I slid sideways slightly and reached my right arm across his throat, throwing him downwards across my extended right leg. He hit the ground with a thump, and I followed up with a knee to the solar plexus. He jerked upward in a reflex and then collapsed back. He wasn't going anywhere fast.

I was just about to rise, when the hairs on the back of my neck stood up. I trusted my body implicitly, so I threw myself backwards and rolled away as a bullet thudded into the cheap plywood panelling of the fire door. I was up and aiming as the second bullet struck the solid concrete of the floor, sending up sparks and chips of floor paint. As the shadow filled the doorway, I fired three times in quick succession, feeling the satisfying recoil on each. I heard a thud and then another, followed by a sigh. I waited a couple of seconds, index finger increasing the pressure on the trigger, until the dark suited figure dropped to the ground a few feet in front of me.

I walked over and felt for the carotid artery, nodding in satisfaction when I found no pulse. I waited a further minute, my senses on high alert until I was satisfied that no one else was coming.

It made sense; most of the Mancini cleaning squads operated as quads and I had definitely seen at least one of these guys before.

I walked back to the prone assailant, kicking away the knife that his scrabbling fingers had been reaching for. He must have been in agony, but he didn't show it, just a healthy dose of bravado. They were always the same, these lads.

'Who sent you?' I asked pleasantly.

'Fuck you,' he coughed, with some venom and some blood too.

I brought the butt of my gun down on the centre of his mouth like a hammer. I felt a few teeth go, and saw a nice fountain of blood from his lip.

'Who sent you?' I asked again, softer this time.

'Go to hell!' he spat in my direction, along with some blood and the remainder of one of his teeth.

With those two defiant actions, he had told me what I wanted to know.

'After you,' I said quietly.

I placed the gun barrel between his eyes and pulled the trigger in one fluid motion. He barely had time to register surprise.

I quickly walked over to John and knelt beside him. His breathing was coming in agonising rasps rather than breaths and the carpet under his back was stained a deep red. I felt for the pulse on his neck; it was erratic and skittish, like a kitten at play.

His bloody fingers plucked loosely at my sleeve. I silently cursed the dry cleaning bill, but leant closer. He was flailing at my arm wildly now and I could see in his eyes the panic; he knew he was dying.

'Stop them,' he stuttered, so low that I could barely hear him.

'Stop who?' I asked, puzzled.

He shook his head weakly in annoyance.

'It's all about *Storm*,' he said. 'You have to stop them creating it or there will be a perfect Storm.'

'What do you mean?' I asked, puzzled, but then realised it was too late.

The light had gone out from his eyes; I could feel the spirit vacating his body as it relaxed and slumped further to the ground.

I closed his eyelids and made the sign of the cross. Old habits did indeed die hard. I holstered the 9mm and picked up the carrier bag; some light reading.

I was going to find out what the hell was going on, even if it was the last thing I did.

I pictured the two brothers, apoplectic with rage, and realised I had another chore. I had a resignation letter to write.

And all the while, the words echoed in my ears from old.

'Be careful what you wish for, Thomas.'

CHAPTER 3 – ENIGMA

11th May 2011 – The morning after the Storm.

It may well be doubted whether human ingenuity can construct an enigma, which human ingenuity may not, by proper application, resolve. – Edgar Allan Poe.

Something was bothering him. He had not been sleeping too well of late, but a six pack and a heavy night had seen him slip into one of those intense and overriding sleeps.

Deep in his subconscious, there was an agitation in the soporific splendour of his dreams; a fly in the ointment. Even though he was not aware he was asleep, he didn't want to wake up, but the annoyance wouldn't go away. It was like an inspect bite; easy to resist the irritation at first, but once scratched, the flood gates would open.

Eventually, awareness penetrated the soft grey tissues, his eyes opened, and he saw the blue LED flashing on the side of his phone. Someone had been looking for him. He checked the display. Ten missed calls; someone wanted him really badly. As consciousness flooded back like a rip tide, the phone resumed its strident ringing.

He glanced at the slightly garish glowing green digits on the ancient clock radio. It had been a purchase for college to ensure he was never late for classes; when his ambition still glowed as brightly as the luminous numbers. He sighed and then scowled with real venom; six forty am, this had better be damn good. He banged around on the bedside table with his hand, searching behind the clock radio until his scrabbling fingers gained purchase on the elusive instrument. He stabbed the green button and thrust it up to his ear.

'Roussel!' he barked into the microphone.

He heard a chair scrape in the background; someone had hastily pulled themselves upright, as if they hadn't been expecting him to pickup.

'Sorry to wake you sir,' said the disembodied voice.

It was Granger, the duty officer who covered the night watch.

'But we've got a report of suspicious activity out at the old mansion on highway eighteen.'

'Which one?' Roussel asked, suddenly interested, rubbing the sleep out of one eye while trying to stifle a yawn.

Granger chuckled to himself.

'That's right,' he said, elongating the word *right* in his peculiar southern drawl, legacy of a misshapen bottom lip, acquired during a street fight in his delinquent youth. 'There sure is a lot of em to chose from ain't there.'

He paused and Roussel could hear the rustle of paper.

'Ah, here it is,' he said finally. 'It's called Augustine mansion, near Vacherie. The person who reported it said it was on highway eighteen, the great river road. I dispatched uniform and they've already been out, but they came back to me with a request for a detective.'

Granger waited for almost a minute for a response. The only sign that someone was still at the other end was the sound of breathing coming from the receiver.

'Sir, are you still there?' asked Granger hesitantly.

'I'll be there in about forty minutes,' said Roussel gruffly.

He stabbed the red button on his phone and tossed it roughly onto the bed. He looked around at the devastation that sufficed for normality in his small apartment. As he peeled the hot and sticky sheets away from his body, he noticed a semen stain. He tried to remember the last time he had sampled the delights of intercourse. Was it that long ago he had last washed them?

Swinging his legs out of the bed, he noticed the humidity level had dropped from *barely able to move* to *just about tolerable, but your shirt will look like you've swam in it after an hour.* He figured the scant weather-based relief must have been courtesy of the storm that had raged all night.

He picked his way gingerly across the debris of his life and into the small bathroom. The large stainless showerhead pumped cold water onto his body, making him start and shiver. It was the only time he would feel cold until the same time the following morning.

He stepped out of the shower and dried himself off. He studied the tattoos on his upper arms. Celtic designs had seemed like a good idea at the time but now he was not so sure. He pulled on a two day old white cotton shirt, wrinkled and creased from prolonged exposure to the floor and clicked his tongue; a remembered imitation of his mother's annoyance. Still, in his defence, the shirt would be dripping wet within the hour. It hardly seemed worth the effort to iron it.

He pulled on his light brown chinos, and slipped his feet into heavily polished tan moccasins, the ones with the double tassels, his only sartorial extravagance. They were so heavily buffed you could literally see your face in them. He grabbed his phone and stuffed it into his pocket; he couldn't forget that.

As he picked his way toward the espresso machine, he pressed the play button on the large silver faced stereo system, smiling at the first refrain of the song.

Agents of the law: luckless pedestrians.

He pressed the requisite buttons on the coffee maker. The machine hissed and clicked as he opened the cupboard under his bedside locker and removed his gun and wallet. Shrugging himself into the shoulder holster, he casually opened the wallet and studied it for a second. There was a *St James Parish Sheriff's Department, CID* logo on one side and a silver shield with *Detective Charles Roussel, 6566* below it with his picture.

The portrait had been taken when the smile still extended to his eyes, something that his jaded and disillusioned mind refused to allow his face to do anymore.

The espresso machine bleeped loudly, interrupting his self indulgence. He snapped the wallet shut and slipped it into his pocket. Grabbing his thin cotton jacket from the bottom of the bed, he eased himself into it before dispatching the bitter liquid in a single fluid motion. He banged the cup down on the counter in the kitchenette and then grabbed the keys as he went.

He rushed through the screen door and then the front door, slamming both of them closed behind him in quick succession. Making his way across the parking lot towards a battered Ford Taunus, he noticed the weird shadows cast by the early morning sunrise. He slipped on his Oakley sunglasses, a spur of the moment birthday present from his then girlfriend seven years earlier, and slipped a spearmint gum into his mouth. It would have to do; a trick he'd perfected in lieu of brushing his teeth on early morning call-outs.

Traffic was sparse on the great river road, and he was thankful for the shades. The sun was dead ahead, and made it pretty much impossible to see where he was going. He almost missed the turn. It was a long time since he had made the journey; too long.

He pulled off the main road onto the verge and parked up, partly to investigate any possible tyre tracks or footprints for himself, but mostly for other reasons.

He walked about a hundred yards up the track and turned to his left. He pulled lightly on the wrought iron gate, and it swung towards him, not a hint of creaking on its well oiled hinges, his first surprise. The familiar twin emotions of guilt and annoyance threatened to overwhelm him.

Moving through the graveyard, he marvelled at how well tended it was. He thought about the smooth operation of the entrance gate. Someone was looking after it very well.

He spotted the grey and the pink granite stones, standing side by side like soldiers. He had been hoping against hope that they wouldn't be there, that he had the wrong house.

He moved in front of them, his lips silently recounting the words. He already knew what was carved into the stones; he had written both of the inscriptions himself. He smiled without humour. He had referred to them as *Beloved Father* and *Beloved Mother*. And even through his deep sadness, sitting in the lawyer's office listening to their last wishes, he had blessed their foresight.

They hadn't wanted an eighteen year old to be saddled with the twin burdens of a decaying plantation and a decaying plantation house, so they had ordered its immediate sale, with all proceeds going to a trust fund for his education and subsequent living expenses.

He looked back down the lane toward the main road. The last time he'd walked this strip of driveway, he had been sadly whistling his father's favourite tune, with more than a little touch of melancholy. The death of his parents had been hard, but he couldn't have stayed in the house; not close to so many shared memories.

He smiled in spite of himself. God, he'd been a bright eyed and naive little fucker. He'd managed to get himself a set of grades in high school that enabled him to get into Yale to do law. And boy had he been ready to change the world. He'd been the hardest worker in his class, but his earnest southern boy mentality had tended to alienate him from the rest of his classmates, mainly WASP's from East Coast money and privilege. Even so, he'd kept to himself, head down into his studies and had managed to emerge top of the class.

The inevitable bun fight had ensued between the best firms over the top graduate. With hindsight, he should have gone south, but his instincts told him that the money, and ergo the real power, was on the East Coast. He still hadn't given up his idealistic roots, so he'd figured it was also the place that he could make the most difference. He'd eschewed all the approaches from firms in the south with silent regret and had accepted a position with Warner, Updike and Partners, the most prestigious law firm in Boston.

Initially it had been great; the money had been good and the kudos had rolled in. He'd been feted as the most successful rookie in the practice. But then the cracks had slowly begun to show. He'd been regarded as a bit of a trophy; a southern show pony for the amusement of the Yankee gentry. The slight misgivings he had felt at first began to crystallise into huge disappointment. He'd felt he was always on the periphery.

He'd been the butt of jokes; they were always laughing at him rather than with him. And the last straw had been an overheard conversation in the gents toilets that had definitely not been for his consumption (he had been given the executive washroom key only a day previously and word had not got around.)

It had been like an epiphany. The role he'd been playing was peeled away like a badly fitting overcoat and the fiery southern boy had at last been let loose. He had downed half a bottle of Jim Bean at lunchtime. This had provided the impetus and drive to barge into the managing partner's office during a case conference, helpfully providing the man himself with a concise and honest opinion on his lineage and sexual preferences, to the widespread amusement of the folks gathered around the table.

His last act had been to drop his executive washroom key into the nearest storm drain and he had then gone on a five day bender. He'd woken up in Shreveport with his belongings piled into a battered Ford Pinto.

Curiously, his calling to the law had still been as strong as ever, maybe more so, as he was finally among his own people. So he'd found a small apartment in Convent and considered his future. He'd decided to approach law enforcement from the other end; the gritty and realistic end. He'd applied to join local law enforcement and after a spell at police academy, he'd joined the parish of St James as a patrolman. He'd worked hard keeping the neighbourhood safe, but there had still been a small vestige of ambition left in him. He'd studied hard over the next couple of years for his detective's exams, and it was the proudest moment of his life when he was given his badge and asked to join the CID.

But that had been five years ago; his trust fund had bled dry the day he'd graduated from Yale and he'd found the constant dealing with the flotsam and jetsam of society harsh and dehumanising. He also felt adrift in the community; he was effectively a ship without an anchor. And coming here to his childhood home had not had a positive effect on him. It had only served to highlight what was missing in his life. He had no roots and now, here, tonight, he realised where he needed to be. He needed to be on this land; his family's land; his land.

'Penny for them, Peeshwank?'

He chuckled in spite of himself. The county coroner always had a way with words.

'Hey Guilbeau, enough with the pet names already,' he said. 'I'm no runt; not that I can say the same thing about you, little weasel man.'

Guilbeau was a small wiry Louisiana Cajun, who liked testing his fellow men on their knowledge of Louisiana Creole. He had a shock of white hair and leathered sun-beaten skin, the colour and texture of old shoes. But his eyes twinkled with a mischievous cobalt blue and there was genuine affection in his comments. He liked Roussel; they were kindred spirits.

'What are you hanging around here for?' he asked.

'Paying my respects,' said Roussel softly.

'To whom?' asked Guilbeau.

'My Mom and Pop,' Roussel said.

Guilbeau guffawed, but his laughter awkwardly trailed off, as he caught sight of Roussel's face.

'You're serious, aren't you?' he said.

Roussel nodded.

'And all of this?' asked the coroner.

He indicated the mansion and the land.

'Sorry, don't mean to pry,' he added quickly.

'No problem,' said Roussel. 'No need to apologise. Put simply, I was born here. When my parents were killed in a boating accident, their will stipulated that the house and estate be sold to pay for my education and welfare for as long as the corresponding trust fund could afford it.'

Guilbeau clapped Roussel on the shoulder.

'I am truly sorry if I offended you, my friend,' he said seriously. 'I genuinely did not know.'

He looked around at the faded splendour of the plantation.

'But I will say one thing. I think they did you a favour, those parents of yours; these places become an obsession. One chap I know, the estate destroyed his marriage, his family and then bankrupted him; all in the name of what, tradition?'

He paused.

'No, I think you had a lucky escape, Peeshwank.'

Roussel thought about that statement as the older man looked at him earnestly. Was his life any the less self destructive? At least that man had a passion and a drive for something. What did he, Roussel, have? An empty apartment filled with pizza boxes and half fulfilled dreams. He nodded at Guilbeau to let him know he understood and there were no hard feelings.

'Any left?' the coroner asked.

'Any what?' asked Roussel blankly.

'The money; is there any of the money left?'

Roussel grinned at the question.

'After my education was all paid for, I had enough for a round of tequila,' he said. 'The estate was sold at auction and the reserve was low.'

He paused for a second to catch his breath.

'I don't particularly care, it educated me after all, but if the executor had held out, he could have got a lot more.'

Who was he kidding? He did care it seemed; a lot more than he would have thought before tonight.

'Money doesn't give us riches, Peeshwank,' said the coroner sagely.

'Too true, my friend,' said Roussel.

But he couldn't shake the feeling, and he wasn't sure that he wanted to; he was home.

They turned to leave but a flash of white caught his eye. He gestured to the coroner that he would follow shortly and walked over to the object in question. As he approached the item, he realised that it wasn't just one, but two new headstones. They were in a relatively uncultivated part of the plot. He tried to identify the unusual emotion that came flooding into his mind, and then realised what it was; jealousy. He was annoyed and affronted. This was his family plot; interlopers were not welcomed.

He took out his small leather-bound notebook. He ignored the first headstone. It was new all right, but he knew exactly who it was and why it was there. Jeremiah Bell had bought the place from his parents, so if he was gone, it must have a new owner now. He'd had no relatives to leave it to; he had always been just a bitter and twisted old man. Roussel made a note to look into the current ownership of the house.

He dated the next blank page and jotted down the name on the other headstone. He didn't know why, but he had a feeling that it was important. Or maybe it *was* just plain old jealousy.

He tried to empty his mind of the conflicting personal emotions and wondered briefly if he should call the CID chief and let him know of his personal ties to the place. He dismissed the idea almost as soon as it was formed. He didn't even know the scale or type of problem he was dealing with. The chief was a reasonable man; he'd understand.

He walked to the exit and closed the gate behind him, trying to use the closing action to stem the flood of his childhood memories.

Initially it didn't seem to be working. All he could see was a younger and happier version of Charles, running, laughing and playing without a care in the world. All the while, his eyes were moving, and his mind was trying to focus on the job in hand, scanning the ground in a seemingly random way. He was just about to give up and move on to the house, when he saw them; faint semi-circular patterns in the mud, running in a zigzag pattern across both sides of the drive.

His training clicked in and his mind emptied, concentrating purely on the problem in front of him. He bent down and inspected one of the marks. He noticed the diamond-like pattern, reminiscent of the back of a rattlesnake, and knew immediately what they were; tyre tracks.

He made a quick sketch of the pattern, even though he knew that the forensic team, who were probably already there, would do a much better job than he could. He liked to be thorough though, so he kept walking and scanning and then stopped again a few hundred yards further up. This time it was parallel markings he saw.

He crouched down and compared the pattern to the sketch in his book; it was not to scale and slightly different, but only due to his level of skill as an artist. These were also tyre tracks, and not only that, but made by the same vehicle. His reasoning kicked into overdrive. It was raining heavily last night, so the tracks had to be pretty new; all traces of other cars seemed to have been washed away by the storm.

There were two other sets, but these were different patterns from the drawing he held in his hand, and at a guess would be the coroner and the forensic team. He thought some more; one set were dead straight, right down the centre of the driveway, while the other set moved randomly from side to side.

An idea struck him; he started moving from one side to the other, and as he did so, he moved his arms as though he was steering a car, and then it became obvious to him. He snapped his notebook shut and continued on his way. He noticed more vegetation broken and flattened on the verge to the right and left; more fuel for his wild driving theory.

He didn't know why, possibly too much speed, maybe a bit of panic, and a series of over corrections. But he did know one thing; the car that those tyres belonged to did not leave in the same manner that it had come.

CHAPTER 4 – PRESUMPTION

11th May 2011 – The morning after the Storm.

God does not suffer presumption in anyone but himself. – Herodotus.

His breath caught in his throat as he saw it; the first glimpse of his childhood home in what seemed like a lifetime. She appeared unchanged in over ten years. It looked like someone had been maintaining the old girl well, but he knew appearances could be deceptive.

He tore his gaze away from the house and focused on the scene. He was a great believer in first impressions. His eyes swept the tableau, imprinting the picture in his mind like a photograph. He saw two body bags on the ground, two fatalities, and wondered what had been going on in this normally sleepy backwater.

He heard footsteps behind him, and turned sharply. A uniformed patrolman was heading towards him, notebook in hand. His head was down and his face was a study in concentration, making Roussel smile.

'Hey detective,' he said to Roussel, looking up. 'What do you need?'

'Hey Cooper,' said Roussel. 'Just give me a rundown on progress to date if you would.'

'Sure thing,' he replied eagerly.

He licked his lips and consulted his notebook.

'Neighbour called us out to a potential disturbance. Even though it was very stormy, they were adamant that they heard three gunshots in quick succession; their words'

'Who reported it in?'

The patrolman flicked back through his notebook.

'A Mrs LaTour, she lives in the house over there.'

Roussel remembered the shouts echoing behind him, as he ran from the orchard with his early morning bounty. He and *Miss* LaTour were very well acquainted, and the old girl would certainly recognise gunshots too.

'Ok, go on,' he said.

'My partner waited in the car at the bottom of the lane. I walked up slowly; I thought it was a wild goose chase to be honest, and then I saw the two bodies here. I didn't touch anything, and the first thing I did was to ring it in and get the coroner on route. Then I organised the forensic team, and also requested a detective.'

He said the last sentence a trifle defensively.

'So that's where I come in,' responded Roussel with a smile.

'If you need me for anything else, give me a ring, otherwise we're heading home.'

'Yeah no problem,' said Roussel. 'Take care of yourself Cooper and thanks; good job!'

As the patrolman turned and walked away, Roussel sought out Guilbeau again. He found him sitting on the tailgate of his car, enjoying a sneaky cigarette.

'I thought you'd given up,' Roussel said indignantly.

'I have, so don't tell my wife. I have the odd one, especially on these early morning call-outs.'

He showed off the latex gloves.

'Hides the smell of the tobacco on your fingers,' he added with a wink.

'Throw me one, will you,' said Roussel, as he pulled on his own gloves.

'I didn't know you smoked,' Guilbeau said, tossing over the packet and then the lighter. 'But I'm learning there's a lot about you I don't know, Peeshwank!'

Roussel extracted one of the perfectly cylindrical purveyors of death and ran it under his nose, savouring the smell. Then he inserted the filter end into his mouth and spun the lighter flint with his thumb, dragging deeply into his lungs. He heard the crackling as the paper and tobacco mixed with air and ignition was attained.

'I have a very ambivalent relationship with cigarettes,' he began. 'I can go months, if not years, without the desire to smoke and then suddenly; wham; I'll spark one up.'

He studied the glowing tip.

'Like now I suppose. But I could go another year without smoking another.'

'Wish I had your willpower,' said Guilbeau, 'and I expect my wife does too,' he added sourly. 'Anyway, you didn't drag yourself over here to talk about the relative effects of nicotine.'

'Walk with me,' Roussel said. 'Want to get a feel for what you think happened.'

They approached the colonnaded entrance to the house, and Roussel had to suppress the childish desire to run through the front door and straight up to his old room like he used to.

They passed the second body without stopping; he wanted to take a look at the one closest to the house first. He didn't know why, but he'd immediately assumed that it was the primary. He had a gut feeling that the first fatality was the key one, and the same gut feeling told him that the first fatality was the one nearest the house.

He never ignored his gut.

They ambled over to the front steps, where a couple of white suited forensic technicians were painstakingly sweeping the area. A cane and wicker garden chair was lying upturned on the ground near the body. There was also the outline of a person drawn on the ground in white spray paint. They studied it in silence for a minute. It looked like an invisible puppet that someone had dropped, limbs splayed everywhere.

Roussel indicated the body bag, and the coroner unzipped the top carefully and pulled the sides back. The face of a young man was revealed, blood spattered and with an alarming looking entry wound in the middle of the forehead.

'Cause of death?' asked Roussel, trying to suppress a smile.

'You're kidding me, right?' said Guilbeau.

He sighed.

'Alright, let's do this by the book, as per usual.'

He paused, as if accessing and then reciting a pre-written speech.

'Subject is an adult male in his early twenties; Caucasian with very pale skin, so maybe a visitor to the state rather than a local? Cause of death, single GSW to the head, looks like a 9mm, but I'll confirm. There is a very neat entry wound, but exit wound a different story. Death would have been pretty much instantaneous; there's not much grey matter left in there to be honest.'

'Have you got an estimated time of death for me?'

'Have to verify this, but all indications at present put TOD at about ten pm last night.'

Guilbeau resealed the body bag with a loud zip, and stood up quickly, banging his thighs to get the circulation back into them.

'Damn this old age,' he said. 'It gets to us all in the end.'

He pinched the cigarette between thumb and forefinger and dropped the stub into an evidence bag.

'Don't want to contaminate the scene,' he replied, in answer to Roussel's unspoken question.

He stuffed it into his pocket.

'Don't forget to get rid of your own evidence before you get home,' said Roussel with a smile.

He tossed a chewing gum to the coroner and whistled with admiration as his hand snapped it out of the air.

'Hey, not bad for an old man,' he said.

Guilbeau removed the bag containing the butt from his own pocket and as Roussel walked past, he stuffed it into the pocket of Roussel's jacket, patting it affectionately.

'Thanks for offering, Peeshwank,' he said fondly, slipping the gum between his lips.

Roussel waved to one of the forensic technicians, and made a gesture around his foot. The tech looked at him blankly for a few seconds, before comprehension smoothed the lines on his face. Two minutes later, the detective and the coroner had blue elasticised booties over their shoes and were walking up the steps of the veranda. There was a swing seat and a table, nothing else.

Roussel beckoned to one of the technicians. The man ambled over.

'Can I sit down?' he asked, feeling very peculiar.

He was asking a stranger whether it was okay to sit down on the veranda of his childhood home. The tech looked at him warily.

'I'm not asking your permission,' snapped Roussel, a little crossly. 'I'm trying to get a sense of what happened and just want to make sure you've processed the swing seat before I sit on it.'

The man's face cleared in relief.

'Ah yes, I see,' he said. 'Yep, that's okay sir, but could you pop into one of these first, just in case.'

He returned in a minute or so with a white forensic over suit.

'While I have you, did you also process the chair at the bottom of the steps? I might want to bring it back onto the veranda,' said Roussel.

'All clear, sir,' responded the tech, before excusing himself back to his real work.

As he shrugged himself into the garment, Roussel started talking out loud, trying to verbalise the scene for both of them.

'So, our victim is lying in a heap at the bottom of the steps,' he said.

Guilbeau nodded in the affirmative. Roussel screwed up his face in concentration before continuing.

'We can probably say with certainty that he was sitting down, judging by the overturned chair.'

The coroner nodded once more; again positive.

They circled the table slowly and Roussel pointed out something on the veranda floor; four slight scuff marks arranged in a square, where the varnish had worn off the planking of the deck. He scampered down the steps and used his hands to get a rough approximation of the distance between the upturned chair legs. Then, keeping his hands apart, he returned and measured the shape. Perfect fit, give or take.

'So, our chair was here,' Roussel concluded.

He got down on his hands and knees to study the marks from a closer angle and made another discovery. The two nearest the steps had slight concave indentations in them. He gestured for Guilbeau to come nearer and made a rocking motion with his hands.

'Whoever was in this chair may have been sitting on it in a very relaxed manner.'

He remembered the way he had sat on the veranda when he was a child; the shouts his mother had made when she'd caught him, and the thud as the front legs of the chair had hit terra firma again.

There was a puzzled expression on the face of the coroner, so Roussel pointed to the metal bar that ran under the table, between the two end panels. They both noticed the muddy marks at the same time; not quite footprints but almost. Roussel gestured the same tech over to take a sample of the dirt.

For the second time that night, he ambled down the stairs. Grabbing the overturned chair, he returned and placed it on the marks; definitely a perfect match. He sat in the chair and placed his blue booties on the patches of dirt under the table. He pushed back with his legs and the chair slipped into the concave indentations on the floor, rocking gently backward and forward as he tensed and relaxed his calf muscles. The coroner's face cleared; now he understood.

'So, as I said before, if our victim ends up in a heap at the bottom of the steps, then he must have been sitting here; does that make sense?'

'I'm tentatively agreeing with you so far,' said Guilbeau.

'We seem to be fairly certain that the chair was facing this way; you wouldn't sit on a chair with your back to the table, would you?'

'Unless you were looking at the view,' said the coroner. 'But following it through, I think we can discount that in this case, as time of death puts our victim here on the veranda at ten pm; nothing to see at that time of night.'

'What about the stars?' asked Roussel. 'Where's your romantic side?'

He hesitated for a few seconds.

'But wait a minute, aren't we forgetting about the storm last night? There's plenty to look at when a southern storm is raging, especially if you are a stranger to the area, and we don't know where our John Doe is from yet?'

'Even if I accept all that, I still have a problem with the way your back would be facing me,' said Guilbeau. 'If I shoot you from here....'

The coroner sat on the swing seat, made a gun shape with his hand, and pointed it at Roussel.

'Then you're going to fly down the stairs, especially with a powerful weapon like a 9mm, but....'

He elongated the word for emphasis.

'....the entry and exit wounds wouldn't match up; they would be back to front.'

He paused.

'But if I shoot from here....'

He gestured for Roussel to turn the chair around and then walked back down the stairs. He stopped.

'It can't have been from here,' he said with finality. 'See how I'm pointing up at you. Even if you were facing me, the shot was not point blank, so it would have come from down here, no question. If so, the exit wound would be in the top of the head and not directly out of the back, as it is on our John Doe.'

'You're positive about that?' asked Roussel.

'As positive as I can be without witnessing it myself.'

'Ok, so we have John Doe shot and killed as he sat facing his killer on the veranda. He got as far as sitting down, so must have been known to his assailant. That, or he came across as posing little or no threat.'

He got up from the chair and moved around to the swing seat. He noticed the initials CR carved into the side of the armrest nearest the house. He patted his pocket surreptitiously; he still had the penknife that had done the deed.

'We know our killer was here in this seat. So the next question becomes, who is Jack Doe, and is he the killer of John Doe and if so, who killed him?'

'That's three questions,' said Guilbeau with a smirk, 'and a lot of Doe's!'

Roussel ignored him and headed for the second body. The coroner waited for him at the bottom of the steps before trailing behind.

'So, what can you tell me about this guy?' asked Roussel.

The coroner went through the same speech again with a few modifications.

'Subject is an adult male in his early forties; cause of death, single GSW to the head. Again, it looks like a 9mm, but I'll confirm. There is a very neat entry wound, but exit wound a different story. Death would have been pretty much instantaneous, same as before, ditto the grey matter.'

Guilbeau opened the body bag and using his gloved hand, gingerly lifted out and supported the subject's right arm. As he watched, fascinated, Roussel could see that the hand was practically severed from the body.

'But this is where it gets curious. This is an interesting wound, and not something you see every day,' said the coroner. 'Almost point blank GSW to the wrist. This would not have been fatal, unless the subject had been allowed to bleed out, but it seems almost extraneous. Like something you'd see in a punishment shooting, if that makes sense?'

'None of this makes sense,' said Roussel, massaging his temples.

He closed his eyes in an effort to concentrate, working to try and clear his head.

'Have you got an estimated time of death for me? Presumably it's roughly the same as the first victim?'

'Again, I'll quote that this is purely preliminary, and has to be verified, but all indications point to roughly the same time, yes.'

Roussel stood stock still for a second. His eyes scanned the ground and suddenly it hit him; the niggling question that his mind had been juggling, since they moved to victim number two. He squatted down on his haunches.

'Look at the ground here,' he said, pointing to the area around the body. 'Even allowing for the storm, the wind and rain last night would have eradicated shallower markings. The ground has been seriously churned up here.'

The confusion on the coroner's face cleared and he snapped his fingers.

'Signs of a struggle?' he replied, half question and half statement.

'Exactly,' said Roussel. 'And it can't have been a struggle with victim number one, as he was already dead at the bottom of the steps.'

He paused.

'Unless he killed this guy, walked back up the steps, sat down with his back to the garden and then shot himself in the head.'

'No gun,' said Guilbeau.

'What do you mean?' asked Roussel.

'There would have been a gun lying next to the body. No firearm has been found.'

'So the person who killed one or both of these men is still out there?' ventured Roussel tentatively, almost as if he was trying to convince himself.

'Could be more than one person, but sure seems that way, Peeshwank.'

'The tyre tracks make more sense now anyway.'

'Tyre tracks?' asked the coroner blankly.

'There are two sets of tyre marks on the driveway; both made by the same car, or at least the same type of tyre. I was trying to work out why they were so different. Makes sense now.'

'In what way does it make sense?'

'One set of tracks, like the set left by you for instance, go directly down the centre of the drive. This would indicate to me that the driver was going slowly and carefully, especially if the layout and terrain were unfamiliar.'

He paused for breath, rather than effect.

'But the other set go wildly from one side of the lane to the other. Like someone was driving at speed and over correcting constantly. So, if I was a betting man, I'd say someone drove here carefully, but the same car left in a tearing hurry; does that have any bearing on the case? Your guess is as good as mine?'

'We also haven't answered the fundamental question?' said Guilbeau thoughtfully.

'Which is?'

'Why were they killed?'

'When we can answer that, I think we'll have found our killer or killers,' said Roussel.

Suddenly, he glanced sideways and motioned for quiet. From beneath the white forensic suit, a ringtone started, softly at first, but getting progressively more strident with every ring. Roussel fumbled under the clothing and came up with the phone, just as it stopped. He listed the missed calls; Captain Moreland.

He dialled the number and gave Guilbeau the sign for *ring me*. He winked at the coroner and turned away just as the phone was answered.

'Hey Cap,' he said. 'You're not going to like this one little bit....'

CHAPTER 5 – DISCOVERY

21st February 2009 – Two years before the Storm.

The real voyage of discovery consists not in seeking new landscapes, but in having new eyes. –
Marcel Proust.

The rats were feverish, scrabbling at the bars of the cage like demons. They were deeply unsettled and snappy. Something about their behaviour was odd, or maybe at odds with normal would have been a better way to look at it.

James couldn't put his finger on exactly what it was, but after almost ten years of observing animals in lab conditions, he knew something was not quite right.

He glanced up at the lights above the door. The *lab currently occupied* sign was illuminated a deep red, a signal to let any casual corridor walker know that they had better stay out. The *testing in progress* sign had yet to be lit; his finger was hovering over the button, he was just waiting on the single word to come through his headset.

He studied his reflection in the mirror opposite. He looked like a character from *Star Wars*; the wrap around protective goggles, stiff white coat and protective hat gave him a feeling of anonymity that he knew was naive and foolhardy. He was in no doubt that all of the individuals gathered in the conference room behind the one way glass knew exactly who he was and why he was there.

Before he could ponder too much on that thought, he got the command that he had been waiting on expectantly for the past seven minutes.

'Go!'

The gloved finger that had been hovering over the button dropped sharply and he heard the mechanical clunk as the contacts engaged. The lights came on, illuminating an extremely large maze constructed out of Perspex.

The maze was his personal triumph, designed and built by James over a five year period to develop a testing suite for his rats. The company had wanted an apparatus that would be able to benchmark with certainty how much effort a given rat would expend in response to certain sensory stimuli.

However, his creation had been ambushed by the faceless men behind the mirror. He looked at his invention now with something hovering between distaste and full-on horror. All over the maze, terrifying other-worldly machines were starting to power up. It now more closely resembled a torture chamber than a scientific experiment. There were pools of acid, deep pits bottomed out with razor sharp spikes, all manner of spinning and whirling blades and even one area where pressure sensors would trigger hydraulic rams, turning it into a compactor.

He shuddered; normally the rats would smell danger and avoid these types of hazards like the plague (a vague smile creased his lips at his unintended pun), but this was different; their behaviour was different, it was....frantic. The word came to him as the second phase of the test sequence began.

At the far end of the maze, beyond all the traps and devices, was an area of safety. In the centre of this space, a Petri dish was fixed to the floor. Above it, suspended vertically, was a stainless steel cylinder with a very small diameter.

As he watched, there was a small metallic click and a tiny white disk dropped from the end of the cylinder and into the dish, with a rolling rattling sound. He knew it was a pill of some kind; part of the facility they were attached to did nothing else except the testing of new drugs.

Almost before the tablet came to rest in the bottom of the dish, the squeals of the rats reached a crescendo. It was extraordinary, like gang mentality in miniature. The rats were rioters, baying for the blood of the establishment. An electric motor whirred into life, and the door separating their place of confinement slowly slid back.

The passage from the holding area to the maze was designed to admit only one animal at a time. He had been expecting them to file through in an orderly fashion like they normally did. This time, he watched as their nostrils flared, and then all hell broke loose. The holding pen became a seething mass of writhing bodies. Blood drops started spattering the sides as they used claws and teeth to try and create an advantage, and if anything, the smell of the blood seemed to raise them to ever more manic levels of behaviour.

Eventually, the first battered and bloodied rat was ejected into the passageway. As James watched in horror, the creature didn't stop at the first hazard. There was no shred of self preservation and as the creature hit the acid, the pungent smell of burning flesh assaulted his nostrils. The rat kept moving until the meat had been scorched from its bones and at one stage, James thought he could see the heart beating behind the exposed spine and rib cage, before it too melted away to nothing.

Another rat had found a different way to go; it jumped into a pit and to a watching James, it seemed deeply annoyed as it struggled to move forward, impaling itself ever more deeply on the sharply pointed spikes as it did so. Watching with ever increasing horror, James saw another rat use the skeletal remains of the first one to leap the acid pit. It ran into a set of whirling blades at full speed, the kind you would see in a food processor. The walls of the maze went instantly red, like tomatoes in a blender.

One by one, the rats continued their headlong drive for the safety of the other side. The smell of death seemed to drive them on, their squeals getting more strident, almost panic stricken. In less than five minutes, it was all over.

James knew he looked impassive to the watchers on the other side, but as he surveyed the battlefield, because that was what the maze had become, a tear formed at the corner of his left eye. Blood was dripping from almost every section of the maze and the stench of burnt flesh and death hung in the air.

He blinked the tear furiously away. He did not want his employers to see him getting emotional, but the anguished cries of the rats had affected him deeply. And it wasn't just their suffering that had affected him; their screams had seemed to have one thing in common. Maybe he was being paranoid after what he had just witnessed. They were only rats after all, but to a creature, he could have sworn that their last tangible emotion was not despair, but a deep seated and overwhelming frustration.

And then, as his finger hovered over the kill switch, to his amazement a bloodied and broken rat started shuffling toward the entrance to the sanctuary. It had managed by some miracle to elude all of the doomsday devices.

As it got further down the passageway, its nostrils started twitching and a new urgency energised its movements. The rat crawled toward the Petri dish and even as it was still moving, swallowed the pill whole.

As he watched, the creature's blown heart gave out, and within a couple of seconds it was dead. But the funny thing was, and he knew this would sound strange to anyone else. He knew that the rat had died happy.

He stabbed down on the button, killing the lights, and all sounds and motion ceased, turning maze into mausoleum.

#

The agent tapped a button in the middle of the table and the one way mirror instantly went opaque. He tapped another button and the main central lights came on, making the other occupants blink suddenly. There were four people in the room including him.

He looked at their expressions.

'Now maybe somebody will take me seriously,' he thought to himself smugly.

'What the fuck is this? Some two-bit circus trick?' asked Winston Nickelson.

The CIA director was a huge man, six feet five, with a shock of curly brown hair which made him look like a teddy bear (according to his wife anyway.) He was the most laid back director the CIA had ever had; an affable man who was completely at his ease in most situations, you just had to make sure you never pissed him off. His steel grey eyes burned a hole into the agent, as he waited for a response.

The experiment had seriously rattled him.

'I'm sorry sir,' said the agent blankly. 'This is about as far removed from the circus as it is possible to get.'

The director exploded.

'Just what the fuck was that all about? You've got about a minute to tell your story, before I personally throw you out of that window!'

The director was shouting now, but it seemed to have little effect on the agent.

Carl Grant, the deputy director, put his hand on the director's arm. The antithesis of the director in every way, Carl was small, bald and immaculately groomed. His brown eyes radiated concern, as he addressed the director directly.

'I think we are all in a little bit of shock, sir, after what we have just seen,' he said in a conciliatory tone.

'But....'

He slipped his steel rimmed glasses up onto his forehead and rubbed his eyes, before focussing directly on the agent.

'I do think we need to get a thorough history of this....'

He searched for a suitable word.

'....*project*, before we decide what to do.'

The agent nodded once, comprehension smoothing the lines of concentration on his face.

'I understand now, sir,' he said. 'Apologies for my thoughtlessness; I forget the effect it has on people when they first see the level of its efficacy. I do agree; a thorough background description would level set for everyone, I think.'

He fixed the deputy director with an unblinking stare.

'And thank you sir, for allowing me to present my project. It has been a bit of a personal crusade for me and I would love to further develop it into the effective weapon I know it can become.'

The deputy director nodded, to show he understood. The director also nodded, and grunted his uneasy assent, as he sat back in his chair.

'So, how's your history?' asked the agent.

'How long is this going to take?' asked the director, with a hint of impatience.

'How long have you got?' asked the agent with a smile.

He noticed the flashed look of warning from the deputy director and was immediately conciliatory.

'Sorry for being flippant, sir, but it's not often you are in a meeting with such hallowed company. Anyway, where best to start....'

He glanced up at the ceiling for a minute and clacked his tongue, before launching fully into the story.

'In the early to late thirties, before, but especially because of the Second World War, the government was always looking for what we would call a game changer today. For instance, Oppenheimer gave them the Manhattan project and ultimately, *fat man* and *little boy* scorched the earth and ended the hostilities. But, alongside the big ones and the well-known ones, there were a huge number of projects that never saw the light of day.'

He paused and noticed with vague amusement that he had their full attention now.

'It may interest you to know that one of these side projects was resurrected during the Reagan era. It was ultimately a failure; the neutron bomb was more of a flight of fancy than rude science, but it does show that some of the modern ideas came from humble pre-war beginnings.'

He paused again and this time noticed that the director was leaning ever so slightly towards him. His interest had been piqued for sure.

'In rural England, a man named Nigel Stafford-Bowles was working on his creation. He was an interesting character, our Nigel. He was born into a titled family near a village called Orlestone in Kent. His family home was a Jacobean manor house, which boasted a moat among other features. Nigel was a bright lad and got a first in biology at Oxford. He simultaneously maintained a childhood interest in chemistry, and took his PHD in industrial chemical applications, planning to combine the two disciplines for any future career.'

He stopped and drained his glass of water before continuing.

'But it was at Oxford that he reached a defining moment in his life. He started reading the works of Marx, Lenin, Trotsky and Mao among others. He devoured the works of the leading socialist writers, leaders and thinkers of the times. No book or pamphlet was too extreme or off limits, no left leaning idea or scheme was too far to the left. It became his creed, his mantra, his dogma; in short, it became a religion for him.'

'Nothing unusual about that in the early thirties,' said the director.

'No, you're right; on the surface, another spoilt rich kid from a wealthy background, assuming someone else's doctrine to assuage the accumulated guilt of a privileged upbringing. But for Nigel, it was more than a doctrine. He was easily led by all accounts. Given his ruthless scientific brain, the type that refuses to believe anything without irrefutable proof, it seems bizarre in the extreme that he would adopt a half baked creed like socialism without a shred of corroboration. But he cloaked himself in his new religion like a new set of clothes, a tight fitting skin. Given his upper class childhood, or maybe because of it, he became more convinced than ever that all men could and should be equal. And the more he got into the notion of men as equals, the more he became convinced that it was possible to biologically create equality.'

'How did he hope to accomplish that?' asked the deputy director with interest.

'In 1912, Henry Dale isolated a substance called Acetylcholine, and identified it as an agent for the chemical transmission of nerve impulses. This discovery was further expanded by Otto Loewi in 1921, when he showed the importance of the substance in the central nervous system. Incidentally, the two men were collectively awarded the Nobel prize in physiology / medicine in 1936.'

'How is this relevant?' asked a female voice from the shadows at the far end of the room. 'All you're doing at the moment is quoting techno-babble at us. When are you going to cut to the chase?'

The voice moved forward out of the shadows and into the harsh direct lighting.

Christine Browne had joined the agency straight out of college. She was now well into her fifties, but was still a striking woman. She had ignored the beauty treatments and cosmetic enhancements espoused by her peers, and at fifty three, she looked her age. But she had a grace and charm about her that men instantly found attractive. Her hair was long and contained no colour, but didn't have the harsh steel wool look that a lot of grey hair did. Her skin was pale and unblemished and her eyes burned a cruel icy blue, an unfortunate physical trait that belied the cheery side of her personality. She was the director of communications, possibly more important even than the deputy director and arguably the most powerful woman in the world.

'Bear with me, please,' said the agent. 'It will start to make sense soon, I promise.'

The communications director smiled; the agent noticed a distinct coolness in the response. He marshalled his thoughts again.

'Scientists had long been trying to identify the areas of the brain that controlled freewill, or more specifically, how to artificially or chemically mimic or inhibit personal choice. Nigel, given his background in both biology and chemistry, was a voracious reader of medical periodicals. I have been to his house; it is pretty much unchanged from the way it was when he died in the mid forties. You can barely move between the piles of magazines. Anyway, whatever it was about the specific research that Dale and Loewi conducted, Nigel seized on their joint discovery as the basis of his direction forward. Given what we know now about Acetylcholine, the way he managed to join the dots was truly remarkable. Whatever it was that prompted his interest in that set of discoveries, he zeroed in on Acetylcholine specifically.'

He glanced around the room, and noticed with vague amusement that he had their complete attention now. Even the communications director was starting to look interested.

'At this stage, in the late thirties, Nigel had inherited the family home and a modest income from a number of large rented small-holdings in the vicinity. He also had a minority stake in the old family brewery in nearby Tenterden. As an only child who'd never married, he could indulge his passion to the full. He converted the stable block into a full industrial specification lab and set about turning his socialist utopian dream into a physical reality.'

'The first results were not convincing, but he never gave up, and as he approached the middle of 1939, it seemed that his reasoned methodology, along with a couple of intuitive leaps of faith, might be about to pay dividends. And that is when the story takes a slightly sinister twist.'

'In what way?' asked the deputy director.

'Toward the end of 1939, the British war office set up a unit with the grand title of Military Intelligence Research or MIR for short, which eventually became known as MD1 or more colloquially *Churchill's Toy Shop*. Now, all scholars, students and historians believe that the work done by MD1 was on weapons and hardware; for instance did you know that they developed the limpet mine? No, neither did I, but what all the scholars and historians don't know was that in late 1939, an Oxford graduate called Major Geoffrey Walker joined the staff of MD1. He was a direct appointee of Churchill himself, who didn't bother to record the information anywhere. Our Major Walker was your original and definitive shadow operative.'

The agent stopped for a second to pour himself another glass of water from the crystal decanter in the middle of the table. Even the formerly belligerent director was waiting patiently for him to continue. But he had to admit, even though he was telling it, the story was a good one.

'Major Walker was recruited specifically for one purpose; chemical and biological weapons.'

There was a collective drawing in of breath around the room. The agent held his hand up.

'Yes, I know the public think it is a new thing, but we know better. We only have to think back to the first Great War, to the chlorine, phosgene and mustard gases that were used. But Major Walker was not looking for mere gases; he was looking for a magic bullet. And he found it in the most unlikely of places.'

He took another sip of water.

'Even though they were only vaguely aware of it themselves, both Nigel and Major Walker were alumni of the same alma mater in Oxford; Christ Church college to be precise. At this stage, Nigel had become a lonely, virtual recluse. His experiments were not as successful as he'd first anticipated, and he didn't seem to be able to make the longed for breakthrough discovery. He seized on the invitation to the reunion; a chance to interact with fellow intellectuals. Major Walker just happened to be billeted close by and thought it would be worth a few pints of free ale.'

He drained the last of the water.

'By the end of the evening, by his own account, Major Walker was pretty the worse for wear and feeling no pain. The only person in the room feeling less pain than him was our Nigel. The two of them ended up together and one of them (Major Walker doesn't divulge who in his accounts) managed to snag a two thirds full bottle of Johnnie Walker Red Label. By the time the bottle was half empty, Major Walker had just about had enough of the pinko-leftie bullshit. By the time the bottle was a quarter empty, he had miraculously sobered up, and by the time the bottle was empty, Nigel was passed out on the floor, snoring like a trooper, and Major Walker was making lots of phone calls.'

'So this whole thing came about by accident?' asked the communications director.

'Don't all the best discoveries?' asked the agent. 'Anyway, once Major Walker had hooked his fish, he had no intention of letting it go. When Nigel woke up, he found himself back at his house with an unexpected guest. Over the next week, Major Walker managed to convince Nigel that he was a died-in-the-wool communist; it was the only way he could think of to keep Nigel onside. And besides, just because Nigel was a communist, didn't mean he was a pacifist, or worse, a fascist sympathiser; far from it in fact, especially later in the war. He wore his patriotism openly, another anomaly of his adopted doctrine.'

'So what happened then?' asked the director.

'The whole operation from then on was scaled up. The lab at Nigel's house was retained, but the building became MOD property. Nigel was delighted when they offered to buy the place from him; at that stage, he cared only for his compound, his drug, his baby. Their offer, ostensibly to free up capital to pump back into the research, seemed too good to be true. They had offered way over the market value. But the real reason was obviously control and containment; they just wanted to keep a lid on things. Major Walker moved himself in and brought a staff of research graduates with him. Both men were careful to let those graduates only work on isolated aspects of the drug, for confidentiality and safety reasons. And then, one day in late 1944, they made the breakthrough.'

CHAPTER 6 – CONCEALMENT

21st February 2009 – Two years before the Storm.

Truth fears nothing but concealment. – Proverb.

He let the sentence hang in the air for a while before continuing.

'They spent the next six months or so honing and improving. All the tests they did on lab animals with the new drug seemed to be positive, but the ultimate test was obviously on human subjects, and that meant human clinical studies. Now today, we have so many regulations around clinical studies; good clinical practice is ruthlessly enforced by agencies like the FDA around the world. But this was a country at war, remember?'

He stopped again to take a breath.

'So here again, they had a spot of luck. There was a German POW camp just down the road from the lab. The majority of the POW's were working on farms and in factories, but given his war office connections, Major Walker was able to divert a number of men to the lab, ostensibly to work on the small kitchen gardens they had, but ultimately as human subjects.'

'Were they aware of their role?' asked the deputy director.

'An interesting question, and one where you would have thought the answer would be no. But both Nigel and Major Walker were extremely open with the men; seems they wanted them to know exactly what it was they were taking on, so they could give some honest feedback. And having read the contemporary reports from the time, it seems they were remarkably co-operative. To a man, they wanted to give something back; maybe do their bit to accelerate the end of the war, who knows?'

'So what happened then?' asked the communications director.

They could all hear the slight catch of excitement in her voice.

'The six men were treated simultaneously; four subjects were given the drug, with two getting a placebo each as a control. They were then monitored in a special surgical ward adjacent to the lab, one that had been constructed specially by Major Walker. All the observations were reported in six separate journals, and were recorded by six individual technicians. Each monitored their subjects from specially constructed isolation booths above the ward. I have read each journal and the reports are quite startling.'

'Don't leave us hanging man, spit it out,' said the director.

'Oh, the expected results were indeed quite amazing; the drug worked beautifully. Each of the subjects in the first test became compliant almost immediately. They could be directed to do things they normally would not do quite easily, generally with little or no knowledge that they had just done them. And obviously the two with the placebos noticed no change. But there was a side effect that had not been immediately obvious in the animal tests.'

'Was it bad?' asked the deputy director.

'Completely the opposite,' said the agent. 'It gave the four men who took it an immense and almost overpowering euphoria; so much so that they begged for more almost immediately.'

'But not addictive?' asked the deputy director.

The agent held up his hand and studied his fingernails carefully, as he considered his answer.

'They continued the tests and the subjects all reported the same thing; they were not aware of their compliancy, all they wanted was to experience the high.'

This time, he turned to the deputy director.

'But you're right, after three or four rounds of the trial, the subjects wanted it, and wanted it really badly. But here's the kicker; it was not chemically addictive. There were no unpleasant withdrawal symptoms or anything like that. This was a real and total mental craving; they lived, slept and ate their next dose; literally dreamt about it.'

The agent stabbed his finger, to make his point.

'They didn't realise it at the time, but this was the nirvana for modern day drug dealers, the zenith of drug development. Think about it; the ability as a drug user to attain unimaginable highs. No chemical addiction, no painful withdrawal, no risk at all really, with the only craving being mental, the most difficult one to overcome. Imagine controlling the supply of that drug in today's market; a sobering thought.'

'So what *is* the issue?' asked the communications director.

They all looked at her.

'Come on, think about it, gentlemen?' she said. 'Would we be here if there wasn't an issue?'

'Very astute of you, ma'am and quite right too,' said the agent. 'Let me explain. About three weeks into the trial, Nigel and Major Walker decided to up the ante and do the last big trial before declaring it a qualified success, or a successful first step at the very least. This was going to be a volume test; to see if the amount of the drug taken had any negative connotations.'

He paused and licked his lips for a second.

'Unfortunately, none of the subjects survived; I've actually visited their graves. There are six of them, still marked with simple wooden crosses.'

'But you intimated....' said the director.

'Yes I did, and indeed in the early tests, it looked like they were onto something.'

He looked at them carefully, one after the other.

'But on that last test, the fateful test, something went badly wrong. Incidentally, it was the only volume test done on humans to date, and at around the seventh hour mark, things took an unexpected turn. The four men became agitated at first. This escalated through annoyance and then, within five minutes, had transformed into full scale rage. They trashed the ward in seconds, rampaging around the room like miniature hurricanes, with the two placebo takers cowering in the corner.'

'It was frightening and so out of character,' he continued, 'that Major Walker was about to send in the troops to subdue them, when all motion ceased.'

The agent selected a cookie from the plate in the middle of the table and snapped it in two. The crunch was surprisingly loud, but then you could have heard a pin drop in the room.

'Then, as one, the four men turned to a bedside locker halfway down the room. A nurse had inadvertently left a single pill on the table.'

The director snapped his fingers.

'The rats from earlier; the pill dropped into the dish....'

'Exactly,' said the agent. 'The rats were dosed seven hours ago with a large volume of the drug.'

He absently brushed cookie crumbs from the front of his shirt.

'But here is the odd thing. In the individual recording journals, all four of the recorder-stenographers who were tracking the men used the same word. They did not write *saw* or *smelt*, they wrote *sensed*. We don't know which sense it is, maybe a combination of all of them, but after a split second, the room became a bloodbath. The men literally ripped each other apart, and turned on the terrified placebo takers too, who they seemed to regard as competition. Major Walker was the first of the observers to react, managing to tear himself away from the macabre spectacle. He ran to the entrance of the ward and threw open the door.'

The agent reached for his attaché case and extracted a single printed foolscap sheet.

'I'd like to quote from the major here,' he said, before clearing his throat.

'Facing me was a creature that would not have been out of place in Hell. The face was a bloodied mask, one eyeball pulped, the other hanging down from the empty socket like a grotesque ornament. The creature's breathing was coming in agonised rasps; I think some ribs were broken, and it was shuffling toward me. One foot was turned out at an impossible angle, multiple broken bones for sure. As I watched, it smiled a self satisfied smile, more a bloodied grimace really, and slipped the prized pill into its mouth. And then, without warning, it sprang. I had my Enfield service revolver drawn, and I had to empty the full six rounds before the creature dropped. I have not been able to stop the nightmares since that day.'

The agent looked at the faces. They were slightly shocked, but only slightly. It looked like his decision to run the demonstration at the start had elicited the results he was looking for. They could picture the effect on humans, for they had already seen it in action.

'What happened then?' asked the communications director.

'It was the last hurrah,' said the agent. 'Fate intervened and the Axis powers surrendered. The old guard in Britain was swept aside by post war elections, and the new government had no need for a magic bullet. The project was hurriedly closed down and shelved, but not before Major Walker and Nigel were both tragically killed in a road accident; the major's Morgan sports car was involved in a head on crash with a petrol tanker. There was nothing left that could be identified, apart from the chassis number.'

'Was it a hit?' asked the deputy director.

The agent snorted and turned to face him.

'Of course it was; the Allies were getting very nervous of any suspected communists, and Nigel had been a marked man for a number of months. Also, from the middle of 1944, the American Office of Strategic Services, or OSS, was jointly involved with MD1. The closure of the project seems to have been almost their last shared act; both MD1 and OSS wanted to get rid of the loose ends, and Churchill was more than happy for us to take responsibility for what he felt was a useless waste of resources. He also did not want anyone to know of his or MD1's involvement in chemical or biological weapons.'

The room was silent for a long time, each wrestling with their own thoughts. And then a single word was spoken.

'Destabilisation,' said the communications director into the silence.

They all looked at her.

'What?' she asked defensively. 'I'm only putting words to what everyone else is thinking. Imagine being able to get a substance like this into Osama Bin Laden's compound. The only thing you would need to clean up the mess is a hose.'

'We have only perfected the tablet form at the moment,' said the agent, seemingly aware of where the communications director was going. 'But initial indications are good for gas-airborne versions.'

'So, an addictive death sentence,' said the director. 'A cheery thought, if ever there was one.'

'That is its fatal flaw,' acknowledged the agent, 'or as Major Walker states in his report, *a sinister and unexpected result*, but I think I prefer the term fatal flaw. And isn't it ironic that the *fatal flaw* is the very aspect of the drug that we can use and exploit. Because, once the drug reaches a certain tolerance level, either in the quantity you take, or in addition to the residual amount left in your body, then two things happen. As I said before, it is mentally addictive rather than physical, but a trigger in your brain fires, and the substance and the desire to acquire more of it becomes overwhelming; you've seen the effects yourselves first hand. The second thing....'

He indicated the opaque two way mirror.

'It is as you say, literally a death sentence. You will do anything, and I mean anything, to get more, even if you die in the process. It does more than just remove your freewill, it removes your humanity. You become feral, savage and ferocious, and the process is irreversible. Once you are there, you are never coming back to conscious humane thought.'

The silence stretched on for a bit longer this time, as the room digested the rest of the information.

'So who owns the technology now?' asked the director, vocalising what everybody else was thinking.

'Good question,' answered the agent. 'The long answer is that the patents were registered in Nigel's name originally. These patents were transferred, along with all the documentation and resources associated with the project, to OSS. When OSS was dissolved, the project reverted to the Central Intelligence Group, or CIG, after it was created by Truman in 1946. It then reverted to the agency that replaced it in 1947.'

The agent paused for effect.

'The short answer is that you do, sir.'

The silence in the room was deafening.

'Who else has seen this?' the director asked.

'Only the four of us in this room have seen the demonstration. No one else has even a whiff of its potential. James White, the lab technician who has been helping me with the refinement of the drug, has also seen the full potency of it now, but I already have measures in place to neutralise any likely leaks. And a contract lab have been synthesising the drug compounds, but they have no idea what the substance is or what it does, and all documentation has reverted to me.'

The director was never a man to stand on ceremony; he was famed for making quick decisions.

'Here's what we are going to do,' he said. 'This is now a formal CIA project, but on a strictly need to know basis. I want all the usual protections established. The only people in the know at the moment are the people in this room. You mentioned a contract lab and a lab technician....'

'The contract lab is owned and run by one of our ex staff members sir,' said the agent. 'He has been involved in most of our black projects. He is extremely trustworthy, even if he had the faintest idea of what this drug does, which he doesn't. You don't have anything to worry about there.'

'What about the lab technician?' asked the communications director.

'White?' responded the agent. 'He's just a harmless company man, trying to make his reputation. I'll make sure he is handled in the correct manner.'

The agent indicated the three white folders, arranged in a star in the middle of the table.

'I have only given you a potted history today. I would like everyone to read the story for themselves. And I have removed the section about the unexpected result number two, the *fatal flaw*, from your copies; I don't want to cause widespread panic, if any leaks should occur.'

He looked at the director and handed him one of the folders personally.

'Apart from yours of course, sir,' he said hastily.

The director banged the table with his fist, making everyone jump, including the agent. He thought he was about to be reprimanded for suggesting there might be leaks, but his face relaxed as he listened.

'Remember,' said the director forcefully as the other two reached for their binders. 'If this drug gets out into public circulation....'

He left it hanging; he didn't have to say any more.

The agent paused and considered carefully, before asking his final question.

'So what do we call it sir, this new project?' he asked.

'It's a perfect storm,' said the communications director.

'Storm,' said the Director. 'Let's call it the Storm Protocol.'

#

James White was not happy. He knew he was only a lowly lab technician; not exactly high up in the food chain, but he was still smarting about the demonstration. On the way to his car, he passed the compactor and scowled. He had worked long days and nights designing that maze, and after years of graft on the periphery of the lab, his efforts had been spotted, or so he'd thought.

The agent who had sought him out was able to quote back to him all of the second rate projects and protocols he had been involved in. Looking back on it, he should have known something was wrong; should have realised his ego was being stroked. But the agent was very persuasive, especially when he said that he had something big; something so huge, that it required a demonstration to the director himself. Something that would have such an impact, it would bring both of them to prominence. Even better, the agent was prepared to share the recognition that would accrue from such a high profile success. The only caveat had been some proposed changes to the lab equipment.

The demonstration itself had sickened him. He had an affinity with his lab subjects and he had not for a moment realised they would all die. The agent had not explained his experiment in any terms, other than a vague outline. James was naive in the extreme, but somehow he had put two and two together and got five. He was not an animal rights campaigner, but he did care about his animals, even if they were only rats.

The agent had not even tried to describe his meeting with the director. He had come back to the demo room and had been unable to make eye contact. The agent had instructed James to remove all traces of the maze and had then left the room. He'd returned a few minutes later from the janitor station with a cleaning trolley. James had already dismantled the maze into its component parts.

The agent had watched dispassionately, as James had slipped on a pair of rubber gloves from the trolley. He'd removed the eviscerated corpses of the rats and dropped them into individual bags, leaving long streaks of blood and flesh on the insides. James had then started to stack the dismantled maze onto the trolley, as the agent had picked up the bags.

'Where are you going?' James had asked quietly.

'Incinerator,' the agent had responded.

He'd returned, just as James was placing the last piece of maze onto the trolley. The agent had then pushed the trolley out to the car park, and the two of them had raised a sweat tossing the metal and Perspex remnants into the compactor. James couldn't help but wince at the memory. The mechanical whir of the large machine had drowned out the cracks and snaps, as the last five years of his working life had been crushed into oblivion.

So, he was understandably pissed off as he passed the compactor; a metaphor for the destruction of his hopes and dreams.

As he approached his car, he removed the alarm fob and pressed the button. Nothing happened. He shook it and pressed the button again, then pressed all of them in frustration; again nothing happened. He sighed and put down his bag. He removed a small jeweller's screwdriver from his breast pocket and quickly undid the two small screws. He turned the device over and the back panel dropped neatly into his palm. He went to prise out the battery and then stopped; the battery compartment was empty.

He pondered the probability of the battery disappearing by itself, and as the synapses fired and the logic gates started making the leap from interest to caution to realisation to danger, he was just slightly too late.

Too late to prevent the gloved hand coming around his neck from behind and grabbing his chin; powerless to resist the savage twist, which his body had no choice but to involuntarily follow. Too late to prevent himself from smashing into the solid concrete of the floor, forcing the wind from his lungs and leaving him fighting for breath; powerless to stop the knees crashing into his chest, expelling the last of his air with a thin scream. Too late to stop a gloved hand stifling that scream with a gag, whilst the other reached into an inside pocket and removed a long handled screwdriver.

Suddenly, his body went rigid; all the muscles and tendons strained to breaking point, as the nerve endings tried to vocalise their pain through his rag stuffed mouth. The screwdriver had intersected his heart neatly down the middle, and it was with a kind of detached disinterest that he felt the warm sticky fluid bubbling up and out of his chest cavity. How ironic that the very action that had kept him alive for thirty two years, the rhythmic cardiac pumping at a steady seventy beats per minute, was the very thing that would kill him.

He felt the pressure ease on his chest; he was not going anywhere, and his body began to relax as the blood spread out in an ever widening pool. He looked up at his assailant, but could see nothing except a grey silhouette. He had the vague feeling his eyes were filling with blood, which his basic medical training told him was nonsense. He felt like he was sinking, or rather shrinking; like an airbed that was being slowly deflated.

This must be what it feels like to die, he thought to himself. And then he slowly did just that.

The attacker watched silently and dispassionately. There was a point where James gave an almost inaudible sigh, and then all motion ceased. The exception was the slow and steady enlargement of the blood pool. The attacker waited and watched, until the pool stopped growing.

Looking down, the motionless killer nodded in satisfaction; the edge of the outgoing crimson tide had stopped barely an inch from the heavy black work boots.

CHAPTER 7 – BROTHERS

11th May 2011 – The morning after the Storm.

A friend loveth at all times, and a brother is born for adversity. – Proverbs 17:17.

The house was set back slightly from the others in the street, giving it a gloomy, almost sinister appearance. It had been bought by Mr Mancini senior just after the great depression; around the mid thirties, along with half a dozen others in the same row.

Up until then, a lot of the brownstones on Mulberry street had been little more than ghetto's for Irish and Italian American families, scraping together a living during the post depression period. Francesco Mancini had been a new breed of immigrant, a man who hadn't believed in the depression. A man who hadn't believed in luck either, rather he made his own.

He'd spent thousands of dollars renovating both the houses and the area, taking hundreds of people out of poverty and giving the community back some work and some pride. If half of the jobs he'd provided were on the seedier side of life, so what? Even if they'd merged into the murky world of criminality, those jobs had still put food on multiple tables and had made him a working class hero.

Guido smiled to himself as he reminisced. He used to stand at this very window, waiting for his father to come striding down the sidewalk with his bodyguards slightly behind him on either side. His constitutional, he called it. Some people actually used to cheer and applaud him as he made his way home.

The room darkened as he pulled the heavy curtains across the window, obscuring the dusk gathering along the gloomy Manhattan skyline. The outer margins of the room were in deep shadow, courtesy of the single light. A weird reflection was cast across the large, low-level coffee table that was set right in the centre of the room.

As he passed by his desk, he reached out to touch the old fashioned green banker's lamp, recoiling at the heat of the shade. It had once been owned by WR Hearst, the newspaper magnet. In fact, most of the furniture in the room had historical connotations; the brothers were avid collectors and had the means and opportunity to do an extreme amount of it.

At each end of the coffee table, a large leather wing-back chair had been moved as close as possible to the edge without making it uncomfortable for the occupants to sit. Each chair had individual mahogany trays built into the arms. On the left hand tray of both chairs, a Waterford crystal shot glass sat proud and ready.

Guido picked up the elaborate crystal decanter and poured the amber liquid until the nearest glass was a quarter full, and then walked around the table to do the same with the other one. It was always the same amount and always the same distiller. They had been introduced to twenty-one year old Bushmills single malt whiskey by a colleague and friend.

He felt a brief twinge of sadness as he stood the decanter to one side of the table, ready to provide top ups should the need arise. Ex-colleague and friend; he kept forgetting.

Placed carefully on the table between the two chairs was an oversize checkerboard, but not just any board. The sixty four squares were made up of individual tiles of ebony and ivory. Each tile measured about four inches square and fitted into an eight by eight grid of eighteen carat gold. The playing area was bordered by a mahogany trim, and inlaid with mother of pearl. The playing pieces were polished amber and polished jade; not strictly the black and white required in tournaments, but the protagonists in this match didn't care.

The value of the set on the open market would have been about half a million dollars, and had been commissioned by old man Mancini himself from the finest Italian craftsmen.

Guido sat down and took his first sip of whiskey. Ernesto was always the last to arrive at the table, fittingly almost, as he was the younger brother.

He sat in the corner of the room, in the smoking chair once owned by Capone, and read the New York Times until his eyes became too tired to focus in the gloom after the drapes were closed.

Guido and Ernesto had been playing checkers with each other since around the age of ten; there were two years difference in their ages and they couldn't remember who had been ten when they'd first played. It didn't matter now. Since the date of their first game, they had not missed a single day, even if they had to play by telephone on separate travel boards.

The day their father had died had been particularly poignant, but even on such a sad occasion they had played through the evening, each slowly coming to grips with the realisation that they now jointly controlled the largest and healthiest criminal empire on the eastern seaboard.

The following evening they'd also played. The journey back from the warehouse had been quiet and reflective. He had begged for mercy, as they all did, but neither Guido nor Ernesto had been in a forgiving mood that night. He'd told them it had been only business; nothing personal. They'd told him that it had been completely personal for them and the East River had become his final resting place.

Given how they made their living, it was not surprising that they needed an *out*. What was surprising was the pastime they chose. Checkers just worked for them, helped them to relax after the combined stress of their days. Neither of them had ever married and unusually for men in their position, neither of them had a large libido. Occasional trips to upmarket and discrete brothels took care of the odd times they needed a distraction. So while others watched TV or went to the theatre or to bars, the brothers played each other at checkers, all the while sipping the best whiskey money could buy, and sometimes smoking the best Havana's that money could buy too.

They were strong because they were together on everything. They had to present a united front to their legion of lieutenants; if you spoke to one of the brothers you spoke to both of them. But when the heavy oak door of their penthouse apartment closed behind them, they needed a release.

Playing the game was the only way they could ever fight; they were too close and had never resorted to physical violence with each other. In fact, they had never lifted a finger to each other, another unusual situation in the criminal underworld between brothers.

For them it was more than a game, it was war. It was their way of taking out the frustrations of the day on each other in a civilised and constructive way.

It was about attack and defence. It was about strategy and superiority. This way, they could bloodlessly prove their manhood to each other. They could prove who was superior, at least for that particular night.

'King please,' said Ernesto.

'I didn't see that, you fucker,' said Guido with a smile.

'I know you didn't,' replied Ernesto, deadpan.

He took a sip of his whiskey, shuddering as the neat spirit burnt a track down the centre of his gullet. For a few more minutes, all you could hear was the clack of counters, the breathing of the brothers and the clink of decanter on glass as tumblers were topped up.

Ernesto lifted the last of his opponent's counters from the board.

'Victory is mine,' he said without emotion.

'Bastard!' said Guido forcefully.

They regarded each other over the rims of their whiskey tumblers for a few moments.

'He should have rung by now,' said Guido, breaking the silence, his voice bearing a serious edge to it.

'He's a professional,' answered Ernesto. 'He knows what he's doing.'

'Still,' said Guido, 'it's not like him; he normally checks in.'

Ernesto swirled the last of the liquor around the bottom of the glass.

'Does he?' he asked. 'Are you sure you're not thinking about someone else?'

'Maybe I am,' said Guido shortly. 'It does seem weird though, doesn't it?'

'We're waiting for someone to call us and it isn't Street?'

Guido nodded at his brother's assertion.

'He did break the code though, Ernesto, he has to pay.'

'I know that, I wrote the code.'

There was a flash of steel in Ernesto's eyes.

'I'm not trying to be sentimental, I don't love him like a brother or any of that shit. But I thought he was different; I truly thought he was one of us.'

'He was never like us,' said Guido with disdain. 'We both ignored it because he was so useful, but we both knew what the issue was. He had a conscience.'

He thought about his statement for a while, before knocking back the last of his whiskey. He picked up the decanter and slanted his eyelids at Ernesto, who nodded briefly. Guido half filled the two glasses again.

'I'm surprised he lasted so long before revealing his true colours to us. At least now we know he really can't be trusted. And certainly not with the information he has about our various operations.'

'Don't forget the file?'

'Yes, and the file of course,' responded Guido.

Ernesto sat forward with his elbows on his knees and his head cupped in his hands.

'I need to stretch,' he said, before getting up and walking stiffly around the room.

'If you think about it though,' he stated slowly. 'It's really not such a surprise after all. It's only the last few jobs that have made us question his loyalty. Over the years, he has cleaned up a lot of mess for us.'

'True, but if you ponder for a second the kind of targets he went after, most of those guys were scum suckers. Pretty much all our....'

Guido searched for the appropriate word.

'I was going to say enemies, but I think *competitors* is a much nicer word. Anyway those were guys that even Mother Theresa wouldn't have hesitated to whack.'

He laughed at his own joke.

'You wouldn't bat an eyelid erasing that garbage from society,' agreed Ernesto. 'All our early *opportunities* were drug pushers, pimps, armed robbers, you name it; hardly model citizens.'

'So you're saying it's only in the last couple of months, with some of our more *corporate* issues, that has made him a little squeamish. That doesn't wash; he's not afraid of anything.'

'I never said he was afraid. It's more a personal choice with him. He seems to have developed a strict moral code that is fairly useless in our line of work. But cowardly, no, you are correct. As you say, Street is not afraid of anything.'

'Except God, maybe,' said Guido. 'He's been getting a little strange in that department recently; around the time of his mother's anniversary.'

Ernesto snapped his fingers.

'You're right,' he replied. 'What was it? Twenty years, if I recall correctly. Remember that time a couple of months back? He was off the grid for a few hours; we couldn't contact him by any of the normal channels. And then one of the guys phones in to tell us he found him in the back row of the church of St Mary immaculate.'

'It's a terrible thing, guilt,' said Guido. 'As Catholics, we know that more than most. And I think he was shouldering his fair share of it, in fairness; the guilt I mean. He's done a lot of bad shit in his time, most of it in our name. Maybe the church was starting to give him some of what he was missing.'

'Oh come on, Guido,' snorted Ernesto. 'That's enough of the Dr Phil bullshit already. He wasn't married because it didn't fit in with his lifestyle. He dedicated the last two decades, no, almost twenty five years, to becoming the most lethal of lethal weapons. The karate, the tae kwon-do, the constant honing of skills on the shooting ranges, the knives, the advanced driving courses; all channelled into one goal. To be the most calm, most disciplined and most restrained lieutenant we had. Hell, I was afraid of him sometimes; he could be so....'

He searched for the word for a second.

'....focused'

It hung in the air between them like an accusation.

'In fairness, we did sort of select him,' said Guido eventually. 'Big thick Irish Paddy, straight off the boat and Catholic to boot. How could we resist?'

'We were lucky, is all,' replied Ernesto. 'Nine times out of ten, they don't survive a beating like that. But boy was he tough.'

'Being tough only gets you a certain way in this business. He had a keen intelligence; you know as well as I do that half the deference he showed to us was just so much lying bullshit. You could see it in his eyes sometimes. But I think the church was making him question his life maybe more than he should have.'

'Respect comes before church; family comes before church,' stated Ernesto forcefully.

'Maybe *respect* and *family* didn't come first for him, maybe that's what happened,' said Guido. 'He probably knew his days with us were numbered one way or the other. That's why he saw the squad coming for him; he was expecting it.'

'I bet he never expected us to find him in Louisiana,' said Ernesto. 'I hope he didn't anyway. A tense fugitive is a difficult target.'

'The CIA has its uses,' said Guido. 'We just have to make sure we don't pull too many favours; they tend to get a bit too interested if we do. And the one thing we don't want is a lot of CIA heat at the moment.'

'True,' added Ernesto, 'but that greedy double dealing bastard is always useful to have onside. It is amazing what money can do, especially when the recipient is a public servant. It really does loosen the tongue.'

'Anyway, let's forget about Street. He had his uses, but all weapons fail eventually.'

'I already have,' said Ernesto. 'Street; who the fuck was he?'

He walked behind Guido and pressed the button on the intercom next to the solid oak door frame.

'Yes, Mr Mancini?' asked a disembodied voice, half statement and half question.

'Can you send up our usual please? And make sure it is hot this time. We wouldn't want a repeat of last night, would we?'

Even through the metallic disguise of the intercom, you could hear a distinct swallow. Ernesto smiled with not a trace of humour.

'Certainly not,' said the voice a little shakily. 'It will never happen again Mr Mancini.'

'See that it does not.'

Ernesto returned to his seat. The leather was literally creaking under his backside as he sat, when there was a discrete knock on the door.

'Come,' said Guido quietly.

Two middle aged men entered the room, the second one pushing a large silver trolley. They were dressed as waiters, immaculate in black tailored trousers, crisp white shirts with black bow ties and red and white check waistcoats.

Both Guido and Ernesto considered any facial hair a character flaw and regarded both beard and moustache wearers with deep suspicion. As a consequence, any man who worked for them was clean shaven with tight, close cropped hair.

The two servants made their way to the large dining table by the window. One of the men switched on the standard lamp in the corner, while the other re-opened the full height velvet drapes and then moved two exceptionally large candelabras to the centre of the table. One removed a cantilevered box from the bottom tray of the trolley. He opened the lid and extracted two knives and two forks, buffing and polishing them until they were gleaming. He then removed two red leather tablemats from the trolley and set a place deftly at either end of the table; there were only two chairs, so it was impossible to lay them in the wrong place. As he added two napkins and two drinks coasters, his colleague was just finishing the task of lighting all twenty four candles before placing a chilled ice bucket carefully to the left of each chair. Two large bone china dinner plates and two large crystal champagne flutes completed the picture. The two waiters bowed deeply and exited quickly before even receiving the brief nod of dismissal.

The individual flickering lights of the silver centrepieces cast oddly moving shadows against the window, combining with and reflecting the late evening Manhattan skyline. The two men got up and ambled over to the table before sitting down at their respective places; Ernesto nearest the door with Guido facing it.

They smiled at each other; another part of the ritual had been played out.

CHAPTER 8 – DOMINATION

11th May 2011 – The morning after the Storm.

There is no such thing as liberty. You only change one sort of domination for another. All we can do is to choose our master. – David Herbert Lawrence.

There was another discrete knock at the door.

'It's open,' Ernesto shouted.

A small man in his late forties entered the room with a large bag over his shoulder. He was wearing a red nylon uniform with the legend *Rudino's* on the left breast pocket. The same moniker was visible on his baseball cap, which was pulled down over his face. He smiled as he entered the room, making the gap in his front teeth obvious.

'Mr Ernesto, Mr Guido, how are you two gentlemen this evening? Or should that be very early morning?' he asked expansively.

'Fine, Sam, just fine,' said Ernesto. 'But we are very hungry.'

'Good job I'm here then, isn't it,' he said with another smile, removing a large Pizza box from the bag.

He took the plates and opened the box, extracting three large slices onto each. He brought the plates to the brothers, who regarded him with interest as he removed two bottles from the bag. The bottles had been chilled; the condensation was still visible, and there was an audible pop as the cork was released from each one.

'May I?' he asked Ernesto first, pouring half a glass at the silently mouthed reply.

He dropped the bottle into the bucket and retrieved the second bottle, repeating the process for Guido. He then stood back and waited.

Both brothers took a huge bite, large pepperoni and salami with a sprinkling of parmesan. They delicately mopped their mouths with the crisply starched virgin white napkins, and washed the first mouthful down with a sip of the sparkling white wine.

'Mmm, this is perfect,' said Ernesto.

'Absolutely top class; and hot too this time,' added Guido.

Sam pushed the cap back from his head, breathing a sigh of relief. The black eye was clearly visible now, as were the row of stitches going from the corner of the eye to the ear on the left hand side.

'You don't know how relieved Papa will be,' he said.

'Give our regards to Mr Rudino,' said Guido. 'And no hard feelings, I hope? In our defence, you know how finicky we are about our food.'

He wagged his finger in Sam's direction, like a teacher admonishing a wayward pupil.

'None taken, Mr Guido,' responded Sam.

He hopped from one foot to the other, almost nervously.

'But I do need your approval on something. We are down to our last few bottles of the Prosecco. We've organised for a special shipment of the one you like, directly from Treviso. We just need to get your say so.'

'Talk to Antonio downstairs, he'll give you what you need,' said Guido.

Sam waited for another couple of minutes; until he was certain his services were no longer required. He then headed out, closing the door softly behind him.

'He showed a lot of balls,' said Ernesto, with a mouthful of pepperoni.

'What else could he do?' asked Guido.

They spent the next couple of minutes in companionable silence, punctuated only by the sounds of chewing and the occasional clink of glass on crystal. They finally sat back together almost on cue; as if they had been choreographed. Ernesto raised his glass and Guido did likewise.

'So, how are the negotiations coming?' asked Ernesto.

Even though the brothers had worked together since their teens, from the start, they had made the decision to manage separate parts of the operation. That was why their evenings were so important to both of them. It gave them time to catch each other up on all of their diverse businesses and holdings.

'I've setup the holding company like we discussed,' replied Guido. 'That particular company in turn owns a second company, which in turn owns a third company that I have just incorporated in Ireland. All of the ownership transactions are offshore and virtually untraceable.'

'What about the negotiations on the facility?'

'That really is good news,' said Guido with a smile. 'The IDA is desperate to get direct foreign investment. So much so that they are proposing to grant-aid us to the tune of almost full staff cost for first year, *plus* they are willing to get us a sweet deal on the real estate. A major Pharmaceutical company pulled out of an R&D facility in a rush last year, and all of the hardware and tooling is still there apparently. It should be possible to re-use a significant portion of it, saving capital and start-up costs.'

'IDA?' asked Ernesto quizzically.

'Industrial Development Authority; the body tasked with getting investment into Ireland.'

'So, what's the catch?' asked Ernesto.

'Not so much of a catch,' said Guido. 'Obviously, I would have preferred it if we were in Dublin. It's the capital city and is where most of the imported equipment and goods are landed. But this facility is in West Cork; a couple of hundred miles from Dublin, miles away even from the city of Cork and really not that easy to get to.'

'So, when is the cut off point; when do we have to make a final decision?'

'In the next couple of weeks; we haven't spent a lot of money yet, but if....'

Guido paused briefly before resuming.

'....no, *when* we decide to go ahead, the floodgates will open.'

'Hmm,' said Ernesto, leaning back in his chair. 'I'm still not really sure about this. I know *you* go on gut instinct most of the time, but we don't have a lot of information to make an informed decision. A lot of promises, a lot of ifs, buts and maybes, but nothing concrete; at least not that I have seen.'

'I know what you're saying,' said Guido. 'If I was in your shoes, I'd be asking those questions too and rightly so. And if it makes you feel any better, it was the way I felt up until recently.'

He held up his fingers and began to curl them over one by one as he spoke.

'Firstly, if nothing else, my informant is very trustworthy. He has made us a lot of money.'

He stopped momentarily at Ernesto's upraised eyebrow.

'Okay,' he laughed, 'he has made himself a lot of money too, but the point is that we can trust him.'

He gathered his thoughts for a second or two.

'It's a pity about that whole messy business with Street. That idiot O'Reilly, the one with the gambling debts, had no clue what he really had on his hands. If we had managed to get our hands on his copy of the folder, it would have enabled us to cut out the middle man and saved us a lot of money in the process. As it is, we'll have to stick with our original informant and plan.'

'Maybe we should have come clean with Street? Cut him in on the action?'

Guido shot Ernesto a cold look.

'You know what he's been like recently where drugs are concerned. He gets really jumpy; doesn't like it at all. Self deception is not a happy place to be. We did the right thing; he was outliving his usefulness anyway. Let's face it, he managed to persuade himself that drugs were not a big part of our operation and it suited us at the time to let him believe that.'

'Do you think he knew what we were planning to do with the Storm Protocol when we got our hands on the folder?' asked Ernesto.

'Not at the time,' said Guido. 'But he's not stupid. I think after the pharmacy situation, he would have read the file from cover to cover. He'd have an inkling after that of what we intended to do, if not to the level of where and why.'

'What do you think he did with the folder?' asked Ernesto.

'Knowing Street, he put it somewhere safe as an insurance policy,' said Guido.

'Will it come back to haunt us?'

'Not a chance; certainly not given the retainers we pay our fancy city law firm.'

'Do you think he is still alive?' asked Ernesto.

'No I don't,' said Guido. 'He would have contacted us to negotiate the return of the folder, in return for an amnesty.'

They both pondered that statement for a few minutes.

'I've also recruited a couple of staff,' said Guido, into the silence.

Ernesto looked blankly at him, his face registering the beginnings of surprise.

'Ok, it's like this,' stated Guido. 'We have a product that we want to manufacture. We know what chemicals and compounds we need to produce it and what processes we need to pass it through. But that is high level; we are not chemists and don't pretend to be. We also need a cover story.'

He wiped a morsel of pepperoni from the corner of his mouth.

'Something that is viable and feasible and believable. So I got Max to do some background checking. He read the file from cover to cover, then went onto the internet and did a huge amount of research with particular relevance to the universities and specifically ones with post graduate courses. After a month or so of searching, he came up with a couple of mature students who were working out of New York; a complete stroke of luck. They were investigating the very same area of the brain, or at least the area that our drug compound targets. It wasn't difficult to persuade them to come and work for us; Max gave them edited sections of the folder and they were very excited. And it gives us a great cover story; these guys now work for G&E Chemicals, on new treatments for diseases of the elderly.'

'We're not exactly anonymous,' said Ernesto. 'You didn't talk to them directly, did you?'

'I'm not completely stupid,' said Guido, affronted.

'And also, G&E Chemicals?' asked Ernesto. 'Although I'm sure I'm going to be sorry that I asked.'

'Guido and Ernesto,' said Guido with a smile.

'What?' he asked, at Ernesto's pained expression. 'It was the best I could come up with at short notice.'

'So these guys have no idea what our real purpose is?' asked Ernesto.

'None at all; as I said, I had their research checked out by Max, and he was very pleased.'

Max was one of their trusted lieutenants, an industrial chemist, whose special skills had come in handy in a number of the Mancini business lines.

'I gave the file to Max and asked him to put the stuff through its paces. We're going down to see him tomorrow for a thorough briefing. I installed him as the current CEO of G&E Chemicals and he has been checking out the work of our two student friends. He confirmed what our CIA pal told me; that I wasn't just a deluded old man wasting my time.'

'My, you have been busy behind my back.'

Guido shot Ernesto a pained expression.

'Some things you have to keep to yourself till the time is right to bring them out,' he said. 'Anyway, Max was astonished to find that their research was very similar to what is in our file. However, the truly surprising thing is that the results *they* have been getting are derisory. They cannot get it to work; just goes to prove how good our friend Nigel was. Max thinks it's the reason they jumped at the chance to work for us; they can see an opportunity to make their own research successful too.'

Ernesto sighed, roused himself out of the chair momentarily and then slumped back down, studying the back of his hands for a couple of minutes.

'So, explain it to me again,' said Ernesto. 'How is this scheme going to make us some serious money?'

'Have you not read this file?' asked Guido incredulously, waving the Storm Protocol dossier. 'We have a drug here that seems to give its user an incredible high without the drawbacks of physical addiction. The addiction is mental, a much harder nut to crack, and one which works massively in our favour. I even thought of a slogan to use; *all of the highs with none of the lows*. This drug seems to have *no* risk at all to people's health, and because the addiction is mental, there is no physical trigger to remove. The more people want it, the better for us. We can sell more and make bigger profits at the end of the day.'

'I understand all that,' said Ernesto dismissively. 'But I still don't see why we have to manufacture the stuff ourselves.'

'Simple,' replied Guido. 'It all comes down to the principle of supply and demand. At the moment, we are completely at the mercy of our suppliers. Most of our merchandise comes from South America or the Middle East. Those guys can jack their prices as much as they want and there is very little we can do about it.'

'Okay, I'm with you so far,' said Ernesto. 'But the reputation, and thus the demand for these drugs have been built up over many years. Cocaine, Heroin and Speed have all been around for a long time. We are talking about an untried and untested product here. In the real world, there is no knowledge of it. There is no rumour, no urban myths, no history, not even any marketing done. People are not aware that it exists.'

'True,' said Guido, '*at the moment*. But that's where we've already started to try and be clever. I have put the word out that there is something coming down the line; something big. The rumours will spread like wildfire; the jungle telegraph will do its job. If the drug is as potent as we think, then we have nothing to worry about. It will sell itself.'

'Okay,' said Ernesto. 'So let's assume it's successful and the demand is there. Where does that leave us? I personally don't see the difference.'

'The difference is, my brother, that at the moment we are reliant on criminality. Our merchandise is illegal and therefore we have to pay what our suppliers think it is worth. This new drug is synthesised using regular compounds. We can buy them on the open market; in fact, the prices are heavily regulated.'

'But they're not going to let us produce this drug in broad daylight are they? That would be stupid and obvious.'

'That's where we need to be clever,' responded Guido. 'And that's where we are being extraordinarily clever.'

'How do you mean?'

'Well, you know the poker game that I host on a Saturday.'

Ernesto nodded.

'Well, we generally don't talk about what we do for a living. It is just a few guys getting together to drop some big money on a high stakes game. But one of the guys started talking the other day, and turns out he is the chief operating officer of AllDax Ralston.'

'You mean ADXR, the pharmaceutical giant?'

'Yep; turns out they are looking for an investment opportunity. He slipped it into the conversation very casually, so I got talking to him afterwards. I used our cover story, the one I told you about earlier, and let slip that we were looking at developing a set of therapeutics aimed at slowing down and eventually curing Alzheimer's through our G&E Chemicals brand.'

'I explained to him that we were merely elderly philanthropists, helping some post grads realise a dream, but that we were also looking for professional guidance and backing. I also advised him that we were looking for a partner to share the start-up cost and obviously the profit. And the last little crumb of bait for him; I told him that we were a long way down the road on MHRA and FDA approval on our therapies.'

'And he believed you?'

'Why wouldn't he? We moulded that story carefully and it isn't a million miles away from the truth. G&E Chemicals as a company exists and has employees. The clinical area that was being developed for the Storm Protocol is the same area that other companies are targeting for Alzheimer cures, and it would appear that ADXR is one of them.'

'So how does it help us? How are we being clever, as you so eloquently put it?' asked Ernesto.

'It is very difficult for a company like ours to get approval to manufacture. It is doubly difficult if your name is not known in the pharma industry. The tie up with ADXR would work in two ways for us. They already have approval to manufacture in Ireland, so we can potentially piggy back off that. I mentioned our negotiations with the IDA and he was very excited. We can also legitimately stockpile all of the chemical compounds required to produce the drug. We have legitimate backers and legitimate employees. I've already dropped their name in my negotiations for the plant in Cork, and so far the response I've gotten has been extremely positive. All we need now is to get the remainder of the money over there, get some more local staff hired, complete the fit out of the building and get the raw materials warehoused.'

'How are we going to keep our real intent secret?' asked Ernesto.

'Why would we?' asked Guido. 'It wouldn't be the first time that a drug manufactured for one thing turned out to have alternative uses; does Viagra ring any bells?'

'Ok, I'm with you now, I think,' said Ernesto. 'So, we don't attempt to hide what the drug is supposed to do.'

'Certainly not; for FDA and MHRA approval, we will need to conduct clinical trials, and for the clinical trials we will need to manufacture large quantities of the drug. That will be our starting point. We will falsify the trial results, get the approval and then; big time production.'

'By which time, the quantities we have produced will go onto the open market as loss leaders, to get the junkies and dealers interested,' finished Ernesto. 'I like it a lot; it's hiding in plain sight.'

'Yep,' said Guido.

'So are we going to run this operation?' asked Ernesto.

'We are,' replied Guido. 'But I already have someone in place in Ireland, referred to me by one of our European colleagues. A person who is prepared to run a facility like the one we propose; who already knows the real intent and who can be trusted as far as any criminal can be. He's young and eager which helps too, and he loves making money. He has also invested a lot of his own cash and has already started on the building refurbishment.'

'A man who is motivated by money is the best type, I always think; whose only scruple is how much of the profit we cut them in on,' said Ernesto.

'Here's to capitalism,' said Guido.

Ernesto raised his glass, and Guido saluted him. They settled back in their chairs and enjoyed the silence for a while. Then they heard the sounds; slow measured footsteps coming down the hall toward the door. There was a discrete knock. The brothers looked at each other. It was a deviation from the norm.

'Come,' said Ernesto quietly.

The door opened and he walked into the room. Antonio managed the Mancini household. An enormous man, he was almost six feet five, and like all Mancini employees, he wore an immaculately tailored two piece suit, one of the perks of the job. He had been with the brothers for twenty years, joining them when his parents were killed in a gas explosion.

He walked over to Guido, bent down and began to whisper something in his ear. As he talked, Ernesto saw Guido's face harden.

'Are you sure?' asked Guido.

'That's what he said, sir,' replied Antonio in his clipped, almost upper class accent.

'Ok, thanks Antonio,' said Guido, flashing him a smile of gratitude.

Antonio nodded, and left the room.

Guido turned back to Ernesto.

'Change of plans,' he said, shortly and vehemently.

CHAPTER 9 – WHISPERINGS

11th May 2011 – The morning after the Storm.

Goodness speaks in a whisper, evil shouts. – Tibetan Proverb.

Even as he wrote the words, he knew it was an exercise in futility. He read back over what he had written, furiously crossed it out and tried again. After an hour of fruitless head-scratching and eye popping concentration, he came to a sharp realisation; he couldn't keep up the pretence any longer.

He sat back sharply and threw away the pen, his eyes stinging with un-spilt tears of frustration. And then, as he tasted the bitter aftertaste of bile in his throat, he had to smile wryly. His mum used to have a phrase for it. She called it *putting lipstick on the pig.*

He looked at his watch; it was way past midnight and everyone else in the office had long since gone home. It shouldn't have to be this hard.

Special Agent Dale Foster had always been an overachiever, or put it another way, he had always tried too hard to achieve. There was a fine line between getting it just right, and doing that tiny little bit too much, and Dale had never managed to differentiate between the two.

All through his school years, it had been the same. He could never leave something alone. He always had to add one more statement; ask one more question. People laughed it off at first, but as he'd got older, they'd found it more and more irritating and annoying. Classmates thought he was sucking up to the teacher; the teacher thought he was just being a smart-arse.

In university, things were little better. He had graduated from high school with an excellent diploma, but in university this counted for pretty much nothing. He had to start from zero again.

And start from zero he did. He'd put his head down into his studies and despite managing to alienate the entire teaching faculty, and most of the student body, he'd still graduated with a first class honours degree in history and philosophy. Sure, he'd pissed a lot of people off along the way, but he'd never bothered about things like that. For him, it was all about the result, not the impact of his actions, and consequently he'd been very much a loner. Strangely, he was not lonely; there was a subtle difference between the two, and Dale flourished in his own company.

The one thing that he had felt passionately about was the law. He'd a hugely developed sense of right and wrong. He'd been particularly outraged at the swathe that hard drugs were cutting through communities. For him, they were the ultimate in indiscriminate evil.

Drugs did not recognise creed or colour, religion or marital status, age or gender. Drugs were unheeding of social status and uncaring of financial situations.

Dale had really wanted to do something that made a difference.

It was one of the many contradictions about Dale; he didn't care about an individual as a person, but he really cared about *people*. So when he'd been walking down the street from his graduation, still wearing his college finery, and saw a recruitment poster for the Drugs Enforcement Administration, he'd thought, why not?

He dragged his attention back to the present and massaged his temples in an effort to concentrate. He only had himself to blame, but that wasn't making him feel any better. It was just another botched raid, another half baked job that he had to somehow try and spin to his superiors as positive. It didn't matter to them that it wasn't his fault; it didn't matter to them that the information he got was wrong and the tip off was flawed.

It all went back to the golden period; to the time when he'd had all of their attention.

Something huge is going down, he had told them. And he had been right, something huge had gone down. His entire career had gone down; crash and burn, baby.

He should have seen it coming. It's not that he wasn't an intelligent young man. He had underestimated them, he could see that now. He was not a *people* person, so consequently he was not in tune with the nuances of the way his snitches expected to be treated. He had also underestimated the sheer street-smart intelligence of some of his informers.

One of them in particular would always stand out. He would never forget the name; James Temple-Hill. At the time he had thought it was quite prophetic. It was almost biblical in its resonance; a sign from God. It was a name that was going to get him something; information that was going to get him somewhere. But unfortunately for Dale, James had a long memory, was easily insulted and had a huge and unhealthy thirst for vengeance.

Dale had been a rookie, barely into his first year. He'd been assigned to a divisional task force, looking at innovative ways that the DEA could maximise the benefit from the busts made by uniformed PD. Part of the role was to interview drug suspects, to see if they could be pumped for information. And that was when he'd first met James Temple-Hill.

James was not your average drug addict or pusher. Originally from England, he had grown up in a closeted world of wealth and affluence. He was Harrow and then Cambridge educated and had graduated with a first in applied mathematics. He and Dale had hit it off from the start. For some reason, he seemed to have an easy superiority and honour system that the other addicts just didn't have. James looked down on them as needle fodder looking for cheap fixes. He regarded himself as a very uncommon addict; searching instead for spiritual enlightenment. Dale was sceptical of his motivation, but not of his methods of providing information, or the quality of the end product.

James was more than happy to share his opinions with Dale; he was a very opinionated and patronising person and liked to demonstrate his intellectual superiority. In turn, Dale had identified early on that by pandering to his ego, he could extract a huge amount of potentially useful information.

James provided a steady stream of tip-offs. He gave Dale a lot of information that he could use, and boy did he use it. One of the tips resulted in the earliest successful bust that Dale could remember in his DEA career. He had been over the moon. It had brought him to the attention of his superiors, and had marked him as a rookie to watch.

The unfortunate thing was that Dale had made a fatal mistake; like everything he undertook, he failed to pay attention to the small *personal* details, and this was to be his undoing.

Dale had negotiated a reward for James; it was only a small amount, a token really, but these things were important. To a snitch like James, where his life was literally in the balance, they were part of the honour system. More than that, they were part of *his* honour system. So, when he didn't get his reward, he took it as a personal insult and vowed revenge.

Of course, Dale had been oblivious to this; it was a different section that looked after the payments. He'd neither asked, nor if the truth be known, cared whether James had been paid. But as far as James was concerned, Dale had deliberately slighted him, and when he saw his opportunity to get his own back, he'd grasped it eagerly with both hands.

Dale had to admit it was a sting that Robert Redford would have been proud of. James behaved ostensibly like nothing had happened and his tip-offs led to a number of significant busts. Then, a few months into his plan, James intimated that a huge transaction was going down. Dale was fed line after line, all of them seemingly authentic. He followed up every one, and when he'd checked out a suggested warehouse on a given night, he saw what could only be characterised as suspicious activity.

So, he'd bitten the bullet, and brought in the big guns. His boss had seemed as convinced as he was, and because of Dale's track record, he'd been given access to all the resources he'd needed.

He smiled wryly at the memory. At this stage at least he could laugh at it a little bit. He did have to applaud James for his sense of humour. After an operation involving twenty agents, and costing twenty five thousand dollars, the DEA succeeded in intercepting four container loads of toilet seats from Taiwan; their only crime the evasion of import duty. Some would argue that it was a fitting epitaph to his career; flushed away.

A ringing phone interrupted his reverie. He snatched it off the rest.

'Yes,' he barked.

'Guess who?' said the voice.

'I don't fucking believe it,' said Dale. 'I was thinking about you less than five minutes ago, you little turd.'

'Ah, come on Agent Foster,' answered James. 'Where's your sense of humour? We're even now. No hard feelings.'

'Says who,' said Dale. 'You've got some nerve calling me, do you know that?'

'It was for your own good, Agent Foster,' replied James. 'You're only as good as your last snippet of information. We are a rare breed, good dependable snitches. We just need to be looked after properly.'

'Jesus, that kind of bollocks is melodramatic, even for you,' said Dale.

'Agent Foster, I don't like being jerked around, simple as that. You jerked me around and I retaliated. That's done, it's over. I'll never call you again, you can be sure of that.'

Dale heard the conviction in his voice.

'But this,' he stopped, and Dale heard him swallow distinctly. 'Man, this is going to be bigger than both of us. Way bigger than any petty misunderstanding and bad blood between us.'

Dale laughed shortly.

'Do you know what, James? I'm sitting here wondering. I'm sitting here thinking, *what is his angle?* And do you know what, I just can't figure it out, other than it is brown and comes out of an arse.'

'There is no angle, Agent Foster,' said James. 'This is serious; certainly not bullshit.'

Dale sat forward slightly. Something had penetrated the childish outrage of his fragile ego. There was a genuine quaver in James's voice. He was openly frightened of something. Dale still went on gut instinct, even since the issues with James and the lack of trust. He knew there were few less trustworthy individuals in the world than drug addicts and drug pushers, but for some inexplicable reason, he had an intuitive belief about James this time; it made him uncomfortable, but it was undeniable.

James truly believed that what he was saying was the truth.

'Okay James,' said Dale with a sigh. 'Give me your information. I'm not making any promises, but....'

'What, you think this is about money?' asked James. 'If half of what I am hearing is true, this is going to spread like the plague. This is scary stuff. I don't want anything to do with this. You guys need to take some action; get this stuff off the market, *before* it hits the streets.'

'Get what stuff off the streets?' asked Dale. 'I've heard nothing.'

'You wouldn't,' said James. 'Since you made such a balls-up over the *toilet raid,* you are persona non grata. Nobody talks to you anymore; I made sure of that, remember? But I'm hearing things, and I'm making sure you know what they are. You may not be a lot of things, Agent Foster, but you are honest, I'll give you that. You just need to look after your snitches a little better, that's all.'

'Can you be more specific?' asked Dale, ignoring the implied superiority.

'Something big and I mean gigantic, is going down soon. These rumblings are coming from all quarters,' said James. 'The only concrete thing I can give you is this. One of my contacts told me that there's a *Storm* coming. It's unstoppable, will cut through the city like a scythe through wheat, and will make anyone lucky enough to be involved in it, very rich indeed. Those were his words verbatim; there's a storm coming.'

Dale heard a click and realised James had hung up on him. As he tried to rearrange the sensory input into rational thought, he got a strange and unsettling sensation; he believed every word that James had just told him. It was just what he fucking needed though, another potential nowhere bust. Just because James believed it, didn't mean it was true.

He turned back to his computer and tried to block it out. A new distraction wasn't going to get his report written any faster, but the words kept cycling around his head and coming back, like echoes in reverse. He could see the thunder and lightning of the storm in his imagination, lashing the road as he tried desperately to get to his destination. The rhythmic tapping of his fingers on the keys started blurring the letters together on the screen. He felt his eyelids become heavy. They became so heavy that he could not keep them open, so he no longer resisted.

CHAPTER 10 – PROOF

11th May 2011 – The morning after the Storm.

A fact in itself is nothing. It is valuable only for the idea attached to it, or for the proof which it furnishes. – Claude Bernard.

He started awake, his head banging off the desk in front of him. For a second, his befuddled brain didn't know where it was. His eyes opened and focused slowly on the trail of drool across his notepad. He saw heavy, ink-filled doodles and it was only then that he remembered his location.

He slapped his cheeks a couple of times and then clicked on the stereo. *While the music played, you worked by candlelight.*

He smiled; twilight more like.

He rummaged around in the desk drawer behind him, his hands coming up with a packet of Lucky Strike and a lighter. Lucky strike, there's a laugh. He was just about to spark up when he realised where he was; tobacco free workplace.

Dale was a secret smoker, so secret that the entire office knew about it. Of course, he had no idea that he had been rumbled almost from the start. He thought the level of his subterfuge was amazing; worthy of the CIA itself. He went to complicated extremes so that he wouldn't be spotted, little realising that the reek of tobacco on his clothes and on his breath gave it away instantly.

Half the problem of course, was that he had never wanted to give up in the first place. He had done it to impress an old girl friend; a relationship that had been built on lies and half truths, and which had perished in the dying embers of half heartedness on both their parts. But the inescapable truth was that he loved everything about smoking. It seemed no matter how hard he tried, neither his mind nor his body were ready to capitulate.

He took the fire escape to the ground floor and rounded the corner to the smoking hut at a fast walk. As he sat down heavily on the single bench that ran along the back wall, he flicked the lighter to life. The flame danced and flickered in the still night air and wisps of smoke curled towards the roof of the hut. Just like my career, he thought; straight up in smoke.

He dragged his way through the cigarette in about five pulls. He ground it out savagely under his foot and went back up to his desk, taking the stairs two at a time. He slipped his bounty back to its rightful desk, not his own, and then retrieved the toothbrush and toothpaste from his top drawer. Even though there was nobody around, he still liked to keep up the pretence.

His mouth was full of toothpaste when he felt the iPhone vibrating on his hip. At least this time it was an actual phone call. He hated these so-called smart phones, with their e-mails and their apps and their texts. All he wanted to do with a phone was talk to someone. He spat out the toothpaste quickly.

'Foster,' he answered briskly.

'Agent Foster, its Ryan,' replied a disembodied voice.

Ryan was about the only one of Dale's informants left, proving there was some shred of loyalty in the criminal fraternity. He had always been regular and reliable with information; small time stuff mainly, but just about keeping Dale in a job for the present.

'Hey Ryan, what can I do for you?' asked Dale, suddenly animated. He liked Ryan.

'Can we meet, Dooley's downtown, in about an hour?'

Dale looked at his watch. Four thirty; that would make it at least five thirty in the morning before he could get there.

'Sure,' he said to Ryan. 'Sleep is overrated anyway. I'll be there by five thirty, no problem.'

He retrieved his car from the multi-storey car park and stopped at a coffee shop a couple of blocks from the office. As he waited for his normal order, a large black coffee, he smiled to himself. He knew it was a broad generalisation, but the place was filled with uniformed patrolmen. To a man, they were ordering coffee and doughnuts; different flavours of coffee and different shapes and styles of doughnuts maybe, but coffee and doughnuts nonetheless. Maybe there was something in that urban myth after all.

Walking back to his car, he felt the first few drops of rain. It was not the normal drizzle, but an absolute thundering downpour; rain that could actually hurt when it hit you. And even though he sprinted for his car, a distance of twenty yards or less, he was completely soaked to the skin when he finally wrestled his key into the lock. It was like someone had pushed him into a swimming pool, fully clothed. He pulled out onto the road, turning the heater up to full blast to try and stop the shivering.

As he slowly dried out in the warmth of the cabin, he strained to remember when he had last had a full night's sleep. He counted back for seven or eight days, and then realised he didn't even know what day of the week it was.

He really needed to get a life.

Pulling up outside the diner, he noticed with a vague kind of disinterest that the torrential downpour had stopped. It had eased back as suddenly as it had begun into a soft misty spray. He grabbed his jacket from the back seat and shrugged it on, struggling to pull the dry material over his wet clothes.

The old fashioned bell-push jangled loudly as he turned the handle and pushed open the door. There were only a handful of customers in the diner. They looked up as one as he entered. He brushed the sheen of drizzle from his jacket and returned their stares. All of them turned back to what they were doing; all that is, except one.

Ryan Howard was the caricature of a drug addict. He was impossibly thin, with an acne riddled complexion. His unkempt hair was long and unruly and it sprawled in a dank and tangled mess down the back of his neck. His teeth were black and irregularly spaced and his lips were thin and bloodless, giving him a permanently unimpressed look.

The surprising reality was that Ryan had never taken drugs in his life. His had been a tougher fall from grace. He had lived the American dream and lost. An investment banker by training and trade, he had gambled everything away by the early eighties. A few bad investments followed by a messy divorce had seen him completely wiped out. Consciously or unconsciously, he had opted out of society for a while. It was easier to drink his share of hard liquor and do his share of stupid and pointless things than face the awful reality.

There were a myriad of broken promises behind him; debtors and creditors, countless things he was ashamed of. But in all his years of hard uncompromising living, he had never done drugs.

Opting out of life had enabled him to slip into a way of existing. He never again had the drive or ambition to drag himself back into so-called civilised society. He preferred to live on the outskirts, on the periphery, looking in, but not belonging. He was not judgemental; he made and kept good friendships. It made him sad to see so many of the people around him slowly try to kill themselves.

He hated drugs and those scumbags who dealt them, but he was not an idiot. He had developed a healthy sense of self preservation, living on the margins as he did, but he liked to think he had a small social conscience too.

So, he became an informant; nothing too serious, nothing too big, nothing that could really come back to bite him in any painful way. In fact, he was never specific at all, which was why he liked working with Dale, who understood his conflict and co-operated with him. He didn't try to make him feel guilty. It was enough for Ryan to know that he was doing his bit without drawing undue attention to himself.

Dale slid into the booth and settled his rump onto the leather bench opposite Ryan.

'Good to see you, man,' said Dale. 'You're looking good.'

'No I'm not, but thanks for the compliment anyway, Agent Foster.'

Dale picked up a menu and glanced over.

'Do you mind?' he asked. 'It's just that I haven't eaten in about twenty hours.'

'Knock yourself out,' said Ryan.

Dale scanned the menu before beckoning the waitress over.

'I'll have two helpings of the pancakes with bacon and maple syrup,' he said. 'Oh, and a large coffee too, if I can?'

He looked across at Ryan and raised an eyebrow.

'You okay?'

'I'm fine,' said Ryan.

The waitress nodded, and dropped the cheque on the table.

'It'll be about five minutes, love,' she said.

She looks tired, thought Dale to himself.

She looks like I feel.

'Are you still living in that hotel?' he asked, facing Ryan again.

'No, I moved out of there about three months ago,' answered Ryan. 'I've got my own place now,' he said, a little proudly.

'That's great,' said Dale enthusiastically, finding that he actually meant it.

'I got a job too,' said Ryan. 'Cleaning dishes in a place called Rudino's. The pay's not great, but it keeps me out of mischief, and gives me some spare cash after all the bills are paid; enough for a few beers at the weekend, anyway.'

Ryan sat back as the food was deposited. He watched with interest as Dale dug into his pancakes with gusto.

'Jesus, Agent Foster,' Ryan exclaimed. 'You weren't kidding, were you? Slow down, you'll give yourself heartburn!'

'That was good,' said Dale, about two minutes later, throwing his knife and fork onto the empty plate with a clatter.

He grabbed his coffee, took a sip, sat back and eyed Ryan levelly for a few seconds.

'So Ryan,' he stated again. 'What can I do for you?'

'I'm hoping we can do something for each other,' replied Ryan. 'You know, a little bit of back scratching.'

'I'm listening.'

'Well, you know I told you that I had a job,' said Ryan.

'Yep'

'Well, it turns out the place is connected,' said Ryan.

Dale looked blankly at him.

'Made, connected, do I need to spell it out for you?' said Ryan.

'You mean Mob?' asked Dale loudly, causing a few heads to swivel in his direction.

'Christ, Agent Foster, I didn't propose that you should actually shout the word out in a crowded diner, but yeah that's what I mean,' said Ryan exasperatedly, keeping his voice low. 'For a clever guy, you can be awfully dumb sometimes.'

'Sorry,' said Dale, suitably chastised. 'Anyway, go on.'

'You know the way I always listen out for anything interesting, any little titbits. Well, there are a couple of waiters, general dogs-body types working in the place. They can't keep their mouths shut. About a week ago, one of them told me that something big was about to go down.'

Dale's heart sank. It was just what he needed; the next fucking big thing.

'That's what I thought at first,' said Ryan. 'It's okay Agent Foster; I saw that look on your face. You think, *this guy is bullshitting me* and to be honest, that's what I thought too. I said to myself, these guys are trying too hard. They just want to impress me, to show me what big, connected men they are.'

Ryan paused for a few seconds.

'But here's the thing. They were adamant, both of them. Their stories never wavered. And then I started hearing little snippets all over the street. Some of my Junkie pals are nearly salivating at the prospect.'

'Prospect of what?' asked Dale.

'Nothing concrete, Agent Foster, but the word is definitely getting out. In fact, there are two words getting out; it's going to be big and it's going to be new.'

'I don't think there's much there I can use,' said Dale.

He sighed.

'There's too much conjecture and nothing really concrete of any description.'

He looked at Ryan.

'But do you know what? It's been good to see you.'

He drained the last of his coffee and made to stand up.

'That's a pity,' said Ryan. 'I thought it would give you some pointers. Especially when they said it was going to be so big; like a hurricane, they said.'

Dale was halfway out of his seat when he heard the word *hurricane*. He sat back down heavily.

'What did you say?' he asked slowly.

'Which bit?' asked Ryan. 'That something big was going down.'

'No, no, after that,' replied Dale. 'What did you say after that?'

Ryan thought about it for a moment, his eyebrows furrowed in concentration and then his face cleared.

'Now I remember. The words he used were *there's a storm coming*. Both of them used that phrase. I remember, because I automatically associated it with Desert Storm. A lot of my street buddies are veterans of the first gulf war.'

'Are you sure about the words?' asked Dale. 'This is important now.'

'Yep, absolutely, they both used the word *Storm*. To be honest with you, it didn't strike me as odd until you mentioned it just now,' answered Ryan.

Dale held out his hand as he got back up and shook Ryan's warmly.

'Take care of yourself man,' he said.

He dropped a fifty dollar note on the table.

'And have yourself a beer on me at the weekend, you hear me?'

'Thanks, Agent Foster,' said Ryan. 'And you look after yourself too. These connected people, these made guys. They are not nice fellas, if you get my drift.'

Dale left the bar quickly. He walked over to his car, his mind in turmoil. James and his story of big things; he would have discounted it without hesitation, but Ryan's corroboration changed the game completely. And the use of the word *Storm*; it was way too much of a co-incidence to be a co-incidence. Something big was definitely being planned. Now he just had to work out what it was.

He looked at his watch. It was six am. Who needs sleep at all? He jumped into his car and headed back across town.

When he got back to the office, he changed into his emergency shirt, the new one he always kept in the bottom drawer. He pulled all the records related to drug misdemeanours for the previous two weeks.

Within five minutes, he had a stack about a foot high on his desk. He wasn't sure what he was looking for, or even if he was looking for the right thing. As the minutes ticked past, the stack of processed files grew bigger, but he was none the wiser.

Then, just as he was about to throw in the towel, he saw the single lonely word he was looking for, scrawled in barely legible handwriting; *Storm*.

CHAPTER 11 – ADVERSARIES

12ᵗʰ May 2011 – Two days after the Storm.

No prudent antagonist thinks light of his adversaries. – Johann Wolfgang Von Goethe.

Dave Keegan was an exceptionally observant man. He had joined the Irish defence forces when he was just eighteen years old. His adventurous spirit had refused to contemplate a life stacking shelves in the local supermarket; much more of a wild goose than a contented farmyard rooster.

The Irish were amongst the most well-known and well respected of the UN peacekeeping forces and Dave had learnt very quickly that being observant saves your life. He had spent twenty years as a peacekeeper; twenty years wearing the light blue beret in war-torn dictatorships; twenty years of slow boring routines, punctuated by intense periods of adrenaline fuelled action.

He was decommissioned out of the army at thirty eight years old; an exceptionally young age to be drawing a pension. When he'd moved back to Cork, he couldn't settle. The army had given him a purpose. Boring though it was most of the time, the army had given him a routine, a reason to get up in the morning. Most of all though, he missed the camaraderie, and strangely enough, he missed the action too. Even though it had been hazardous at best and downright dangerous at worst, he had to admit it to himself; he missed the thrills.

He wasn't religious and he was pretty ambivalent when it came to morality, so as the legitimate employment opportunities dried up, and he ended up *on the social*, he found himself increasingly drawn to the seedier side of Cork city; the distasteful and disturbing underbelly.

He had been standing alone in the line for the nightclub, when his life had changed forever. An indiscriminate punch, thrown by a drunk in the general direction of his not particularly attractive girlfriend, had inadvertently hit Dave on the side of the head. It had not particularly hurt; more of a sting really, but it had triggered a deeply buried and suppressed reaction. Without him even realising it was happening, twenty years of rigorous self defence training kicked in.

Before Dave knew it, the guy was on his back on the floor and Dave's fist was raised to strike. He blinked and smiled; it had been a year since he had felt so invigorated. The bouncers quickly intervened and as he was led away, he heard an affronted scream.

'That guy's a fucking nut job!'

Dave didn't object or put up any resistance; he had learned years ago to never needlessly provoke. And anyway, he thought wryly, at least he was getting into the club for free.

He was led down a darkened corridor and up two flights of stairs, and that was when he found himself face-to-face with his destiny; the man they called *Black Swan*.

The office was dark. The two bouncers brought him to the centre of the room. One kept a grip on his arm, while the other leaned across the expanse of mahogany and whispered something into the shadows. Both men then assumed positions on either side of the room. The man seated at the desk leaned forward. He was dressed head to toe in black Armani. Dave guessed his age at around forty five; slightly older than himself.

'Anto says you were causing a disturbance outside,' said the man distinctly.

Dave couldn't place the accent; not yet at least.

'I was just minding my own business, when some idiot in front of me started swinging his fists,' responded Dave indignantly. 'He tried to hit a girl.'

He highlighted the word *girl* in his distinctive Cork lilt.

'I don't like fighting outside my club,' said the man, ignoring the remark. 'It brings down the tone of the place. I'm trying to cultivate a high class clientele. I don't need this kind of shit.'

With that, the man imperceptibly nodded and sat back in his seat; like he was an observer or part of an audience.

Dave had been waiting for them to make a move on him. He'd been expecting it since they'd escorted him into the office, in fact. As the roundhouse came at him, he blocked it high and countered with a palm strike to the man's temple. He managed to get a huge amount of rotation and speed into the hit, and it dropped the bouncer like a sack of potatoes.

He whirled to face the other man, who was watching open mouthed. He held his hands up as he had been taught, and kept unblinking eye contact with the second bodyguard. As he suspected, the confused and bewildered bouncer looked toward the man behind the desk for some direction; he was ushered out with an impatient wave of a beautifully manicured hand.

The man behind the desk leaned forward again and regarded Dave with a kind of bemused indifference.

'So, you know how to look after yourself, anyway,' he said quietly, and with a slight tinge of annoyance.

'In fairness, he did attack me,' replied Dave with a smile. 'And anyway, wasn't that the point of this charade; see how the local gombeen reacts to some aggression?'

A groaning sound started to emanate from the prone bodyguard. Dave was secretly relieved; it had been a long time since his skills had been called into use, and a palm strike to the temple could kill. He helped the bouncer up and sat him in one of the chairs as he started to come around.

'You're a cool customer, I'll give you that,' said the man behind the desk, ignoring the previous comment.

'Thank you,' said Dave. 'I'll take that as a compliment.'

'Can you drive?' asked the man suddenly, the turn in the conversation taking Dave completely by surprise.

'That's an unusual question in this day and age,' said Dave. 'I thought everyone could drive?'

'How would you like to come and work for me?' asked the man, ignoring his response.

He was the sort of guy who drove a conversation. He was not part of the talk, he controlled it.

'I'm looking for a driver; someone who can ferry me around, but also somebody who can take care of himself....'

He stopped for a minute or so.

'....and also take care of me, should the need arise. Are you interested?'

He placed huge emphasis on the word *me*.

Dave considered the question for a second.

'What kind of work are you in?' he asked.

The man smiled.

'Let's just say, it pays for me to be discrete in all my business dealings,' he said.

'Is it illegal?' asked Dave.

'Would that bother you?' countered the man.

Dave thought about his response for a couple of minutes. He thought about the adrenaline that was coursing through his body, the slightly raised pulse caused by the release of the endorphins, the natural high that combat and danger always released. He hadn't felt as alive in months.

'No, I don't believe it would,' he said, a slow smile spreading over his face.

Dave dragged his attention back to the present. His eyes scanned the road, taking everything in. He hated this place and what it stood for.

With the army, he had visited many war-torn countries; the Lebanon, Liberia, Chad, Somalia. He had witnessed the devastation of war; buildings levelled by high explosives, half destroyed houses, vandalism and looting on a widespread scale. He had seen the destruction that war could wage on innocent civilian populations, poor dirt farmers and fishermen. He had seen at first-hand the annihilation of communities to further the selfish aims of despotic dictators. But those had been developing economies, so called third world countries. This was first world. This was the supposedly developed and civilised west.

He looked at the row upon row of burnt out houses. Homes boarded up against vandalism and arson, some with half inch steel plate to protect the windows. The scorched and twisted wreckage of cars littered every intersection, and rubble and garbage were strewn across the streets like confetti at a wedding.

It was easy to see how the boss made money, how his business flourished. These communities were decimated; where hope was nothing more than a different name for drugs, and the worst of it was, he had no sympathy for them. The kids were out of control, parents caring more for how much booze their social welfare would buy on a Thursday night than where their children were and what they were doing.

Society had well and truly broken down, apparently because there was nothing for the kids to do. Dave spat forcefully out of the window. Try growing up on a farm in West Cork, scratching a living from a few meagre acres. Bring back National service. That would give them something to do. He hadn't done so badly out of the army life, and if there was anything he was afraid of, it certainly wasn't hard work.

He looked around the interior of the car; his opulent surroundings couldn't have been in starker contrast to the devastation outside. He was in a black Mercedes CLK 500, an extremely luxurious car even at the base model. But this one wasn't exactly as it had left the factory. A month in Saudi Arabia getting some bespoke modifications meant it could withstand an assault from anything up to and including anti-tank rounds. His boss had shrugged at the added expense.

'Goes with the territory,' he'd said levelly.

The first time he'd heard it, Dave thought Black Swan was a very odd name for a drug boss, or for any crime boss. Surely, your nickname was supposed to strike terror into the hearts of your opponents, not conjure up images of Hans Christian Andersson fairy tales. But the more he worked with his boss, the more he realised what an apt description it really was. For a start, his boss wore only black. Not just any old dark colours, but always Armani black, nothing else. His shoes were handmade Italian leather, imported from Turin, again only black.

In almost two years of working closely with him, Dave had never seen his boss lose his temper. Even in the most stressful of situations, he exuded a calm professionalism. He had a deep serenity like a swan, combined with an exceptional work ethic; peaceful and composed above the water, with legs going like the clappers under the surface.

The part that no one ever saw was the internal conflict. The only signs that gave him away to people who really knew him were his eyes. The Japanese called them the *windows to the soul*. Whatever they were called, if you caught sight of the glint, you didn't argue. They became empty and expressionless; showing no emotions of any kind really, just a black nothingness.

He glanced up at the rear view mirror. His boss was engrossed in paperwork. Meticulous and fastidious were the only words you could use to describe his attitude to book keeping and accounting.

'Dave,' he'd said once. 'Just because what we do is illegal, it doesn't mean we don't treat it like any other business. I've got suppliers, I've got demand, I've got profit and loss and I've got staff cost. In fact, I've got the same challenges as any other business. But do you want to know the difference between me and all the little get rich quick gangsters? Those disrespectful punks, who think they can make a few bob? I'll tell you; the difference is that I can account for every penny I make, every single red cent. That is the differentiator and that is why I am top dog.'

Dave's phone rang. It was *the ride of the valkyries.*
Da dan da da da da dan da da da da dan da da da da dan da da da.

He smiled secretly to himself; he'd always loved Apocalypse Now, especially the Robert Duvall character.

'Yes,' he answered.

'The eagle has landed,' said a tinny, disembodied voice.

CHAPTER 12 – ENFORCEMENT

12th May 2011 – Two days after the Storm.

All that makes existence valuable to anyone depends on the enforcement of restraints upon the actions of other people. – John Stuart Mill.

Dave smiled at the code word as he hung up, quickly becoming serious again as he cleared his throat.

'They've secured the package, boss,' said Dave. 'What do you want me to do?'

'Yea, great, let's head over there,' answered Black Swan, 'and don't forget to stop at Mocha-Mocha and pick me up a skinny latte on the way. Oh, and whatever you're having yourself of course,' he added as an afterthought.

Twenty minutes later, and with coffees safely procured, they pulled up outside an abandoned warehouse, deep in the countryside above Cobh. As he got out of the car and held open the rear door, Dave could smell the sea, could detect the faint aroma of salt in the air. He could almost feel the sand being blown onto his face as he listened to the harsh shrieks of the seagulls competing for the tastiest scraps of garbage.

The warehouse itself was a small industrial unit. It had been built at the height of the Celtic Tiger and had never actually been used for storage or gainful productivity; it was utilised now for rather more unseemly activities.

At first, the violence required from him in the course of his work had shocked and appalled Dave. Even when no violence was involved, the levels of threat and menace required to get anything done had been incredibly unsettling.

It was never nice to observe humanity at its most base level.

But as the months had passed and blurred into years, he was shocked to discover that he was becoming used to it; no, had *become* used to it. He was numbed to the brutality and terror, almost unfeeling in some respects. It was a safety device; he knew that all too well. You couldn't think about it that much; there but for the grace of God....

The Warehouse was completely empty, apart from a cheap IKEA desk that sat in the middle of the floor. Two chairs faced each other across the expanse of cheap oak veneer. The muscle duo, Anto and Kevin, stood at either end of the table. Dave's friends of old from his first encounter with his new employer, now colleagues rather than adversaries.

Sitting at the table on the cheap plastic chair that faced the entrance, was a terrified young man. He was trying to look hard and nonchalant and failing miserably. He was dressed in the regulation Adidas three stripe top, G-Star Raw jeans and Nike high tops. His hair was shaved at the sides, spiked on the top and dyed a heavy shade of peroxide blonde. But any trace of bravado that may have existed on the street, the shape throwing for the benefit of his customers and his mates, was gone. At that moment, he looked exactly what he was; a small frightened teenager.

Black Swan ambled in behind Dave. He pulled out the remaining free chair and sat down opposite the callow youth.

'Do you know who I am?' he asked evenly.

The youth gulped twice, but contented himself to just a single nod of understanding.

'So, you can probably guess why you are here?' said Black Swan.

The youth nodded again, this time with a guilty flick of the tongue onto his lips.

Black Swan clicked his fingers towards Dave, a signal to bring his things over to the table. He unzipped his bag and extracted a laptop. Opening the cover and hitting the power button, he waiting patiently as the machine executed all of its start-up routines. He clicked a few random buttons and then started typing; surprisingly fast and accurate for a man with such large fingers.

'Do know how much you owe me?' he asked.

The youth shook his head and dropped his eyes down, the universal acknowledgement of a guilty conscience.

'Well I do,' said Black Swan.

He pointed to his laptop.

'Do you know what? You should really get yourself one of these,' he said conversationally. 'That way, you'll never be in this position again.'

He stared at the youth unblinkingly for a minute or so, before shaking his head sadly.

'You guys never learn. Don't they teach you anything at school?'

The youth looked at him blankly. Black Swan remembered the schools he passed everyday; crumbling edifices rife with graffiti and decay; gangs of children in uniform, hanging around on street corners, smoking and drinking when they should be learning.

'I'll take that as a no,' he said, answering his own question.

He shook his head sadly.

'Anyway, so here's the story,' he continued. 'You owe me two thousand, one hundred and seventy six euro and twenty three cent. You've got until Friday at three pm to deliver that money to me personally, do you understand?'

The youth nodded vigorously, like an ornamental dog on a parcel shelf in the back window of a car.

'Ok, you're free to go,' said Black Swan. 'Remember, Friday at three pm.'

He extracted something from his pocket, as the young man got up to leave. It was a black leather glove. He slipped it on deliberately, making sure all the fingers were fully inserted and comfortable. The youth saw none of this; his attention was firmly fixed on the two bouncers, and on how quickly he could traverse the ground between the table and the exit. As the teenager came around the side of the desk, Black Swan flexed his fingers, regarding the moving digits thoughtfully.

'Just one more thing,' he added, as the youth drew level.

Black Swan got up and waited; he could sense the hesitation and the fear as the young man slowly turned towards him. He saw the angry blobs of acne; the immature flecks of hair on the upper lip. Christ, this guy was only a kid.

The punch, when it came, was so fast that the young man barely saw it. It caught him full in the centre of the face and lifted him clean off the ground, to land with a thud on the solid concrete floor. Black Swan walked over, and as the teenager writhed in pain, measured a savage and accurate kick into one of the boy's kidneys for good measure.

The youth contracted into a moaning foetal position on the floor. The blood from his broken nose pooled out onto the dark green painted concrete surface, reminding Dave obscurely of traffic lights.

Black Swan leaned over and lifted the boy's chin. He stared into the bloodshot and tear-stained eyes.

'Nobody steals from me,' he stated softly.

He said each word slowly and distinctly, emphasising the pause after each one. He took off the glove, put it carefully into a zip lock plastic bag and slid it back into his pocket. He then indicated for Dave to follow him.

'Anto, dump this crap where you found it,' he said, 'and make sure it doesn't get any more damaged than it is now. I want to make sure I actually get my money back.'

#

They had been driving for a while in companionable silence, when Black Swan looked up from his newspaper. Dave could see he was forming his thoughts, and it was no surprise when the relative tranquillity was broken.

'Dave, do you think I'm too hard on them?'

'Not my place to say, boss,' said Dave.

'But do you?' he asked. 'I know it may not seem like it at times, but I do value your opinion.'

'I think you'll do what you wanna do, regardless of what I think,' answered Dave with a smile, hoping to rob the statement of any offence. 'But to be brutally honest with you, boss, if you *do* want my opinion then, no, I don't think you're too hard on them. Without you, the snivelling little pricks would have to work for a living. If they want to try and steal from you, then they know what's coming.'

Black Swan nodded, as if satisfied by the response.

'What is the date today?' he asked, completely changing the tack of the conversation.

'Twelfth of May,' said Dave.

'I knew it was,' said Black Swan. 'When were we supposed to get an update from the Louisiana operation?'

Dave considered his answer.

'That would be yesterday, boss,' he responded at last.

He had forgotten all about Scott; shit.

'That's what I thought. You said he was reliable and you said he was good. That little cock sucker better not be holding out on me. Your neck is on the line on this one, Dave,' said Black Swan.

It was a promise not a question. Dave knew that from old.

Dave glanced at his boss in the rear view mirror and held his gaze for a couple of seconds; long enough for Black Swan to break the connection first.

'You can hold me accountable all you want, boss,' he said. 'But the simple answer is that if he hasn't checked in, there must be a good reason for it. This guy is good, and I'm not just saying that. He knows what side his bread is buttered, if you get my drift. He's looking for a long term contract.'

'So, where the fuck is he?' asked Black Swan. 'Send him a text or ring him. I need an update by tonight. I've been waiting for this for twenty five years. I shouldn't have to baby sit these fuckers, or you for that matter.'

Ten minutes later, Dave pulled into the garage of Black Swan's townhouse in Montenotte. It was part of an old Georgian terrace; four storeys over a basement, massive high rooms, classically proportioned and decorated to the absolute highest specification. No expense had been spared in the renovation of the house or the mews property at the back, which had been converted into a four car garage. Dave parked the Mercedes next to the Ferrari F430 and Porsche 911 Turbo; boy's toys that were rarely taken out and used. They were status symbols of wealth and success, just there for show really.

Dave held the rear door open like he always did. Black Swan got out and walked over to the corner of the garage. Pressing the recessed button on the wall, a subtly hidden down-arrow illuminated above what suddenly became recognisable as a set of lift doors.

When Black Swan had bought it, one of the major modifications to the house had been the installation of an underground passageway between the mews and the main living area.

The lift arrived with the traditional *ping*. The stainless steel doors glided noiselessly open and Black Swan got in. Dave waited until the lift was on the subterranean floor. He could picture his boss ambling along the stark and brightly lit passageway, like the baddie out of a James Bond movie. All he needed was the white cat.

Dave smiled to himself, as he walked across to the small kitchen area in the corner of the garage. He filled the kettle and switched it on. Then, extricating his phone from his pocket, he got down to the business in hand.

He thought about texting, *okay you little cock sucker, where are you?* Then he thought, no, that is probably taking the boss just a little bit too literally. He eventually decided on *where are you, we need a sit rep?*

When he felt stressed, Dave tended to resort to army speak. He hit the send button, put the phone down on the kitchen counter and started making a cup of tea.

While he crushed the teabag against the side of the cup, he was oblivious to what was happening to his message, as it silently streaked across the mighty Atlantic Ocean, borne on celestial motorways of copper and fibre. As he threw the used tea bag into the sink, and extracted the milk from the fridge, he had no idea that the message was nearing its destination, zipping from cell to cell as it triangulated the position of its target device. And as he poured the milk into the golden liquid, he was unaware that the message had reached its final target.

The two evidence clerks looked at each other in surprise; the received message was making the smart phone buzz liked a trapped wasp in the bottom of the sealed evidence bag.

CHAPTER 13 – COLLECTIVE

12th May 2011 – Two days after the Storm.

I'd like to believe that we've learned something from our collective past and that, at the end of the day, good will always outweigh evil. – Anon.

James Murray was an eternal optimist, but on days like these, the pessimistic side of him returned with a vengeance and he wondered why he bothered. He was hunched down low in his seat; not that it really mattered, these idiots would never be able to spot him. They were about as observant and aware as a group of primary school children.

As he watched, another exchange took place, surreptitiously hand-to-hand, money one way, small packet the other. That was the problem really, the sheer quantity. He had been sitting there for about four hours and in that time he had seen thirty four transactions. Thirty four packets of misery, disguised as temporary release. Thirty four families exposed to heartbreak and potential bereavement, and all in the name of profit.

It was around this time in an operation, generally about half way through, that the activist in him became awakened. He always wondered to himself; what was the point in eliminating supply? That was just treating the symptoms. You needed to eliminate the demand; that was the cure.

He smiled fondly as he remembered back to the time when his rampant optimism could barely be contained; before the drab and squalid reality threatened to drain his spirit away. His first interview for the drug squad, after two years in uniformed patrol, had been a good case in point.

'So just for my benefit, how precisely do you propose to eliminate demand?' the inspector had asked, dangerously softly.

James had stumbled from one badly thought out scenario to another, his face reddening by the minute. The inspector had allowed his embarrassment to build and continue, giving him no quarter under a relentless gaze, until at last he held up his hand decisively, stopping James in mid sentence.

'We are the Gardai,' he'd said. 'We deal in facts and not in conjecture. We deal in cold hard reality, not in supposition. We focus on what we can do, not what we'd like to do, or what we can't do. So, we go onto the streets and we eliminate the supply, because that is all we can do by law.'

After his ineffectual performance, James had been convinced that his interview had been a wash out, and that his drug squad career had effectively ended before it had begun. So it had been with shock and some small measure of surprise that he'd been notified of his new assignment.

'He very much admired your principles and your passion,' the female drug squad officer had advised. 'He said he wished his other operatives had more of both.'

What she hadn't mentioned was the inevitability of it all. How the principles and passion seeped slowly away, and the full extent of the constant and never ending battle with the ugly underbelly of society became abundantly clear. The dealers they removed from the street corners of the estates were like Russian soldiers at Stalingrad; for every one gone, two more stepped up to take their place.

But in the constant battle for control of both the streets and neighbourhoods of the south, he held onto something that some of his more jaded colleagues had long since lost. The inspector had seen it, but had not commented on it; he didn't have to, it shone out of everything that James did. He had pride; personal care and attention to whatever he did, no matter how trivial or inconsequential it seemed to others.

He glanced down at his watch; after half a day, he'd had enough of this. Sufficient evidence had been collected over the past few hours. As usual, he had painstakingly catalogued and noted every transaction, accompanying each full handwritten page of text with at least three photographs. His reports were detailed and accurate novellas. When he made an arrest, it always stuck. All he needed now was to execute the bust. He saw another customer approaching.

'May as well bust the two of them at the same time,' he said quietly to himself, under his breath.

His hand was on the door handle, when the radio sprang into life in a burst of static.

'Six-six come in, this is control,' said a disembodied male voice; almost impossible to place out of the half dozen radio operators.

James thumbed the microphone.

'Hey control, this is six-six,' he responded quietly.

'Six-six, you are requested to return to base immediately.'

'Control, can it wait?' asked James. 'I'm in the middle of a bust.'

He heard a couple of short bursts of static and then the bellow.

'Murray, get your arse back here now!'

The first voice had been unrecognisable, but he knew the second one immediately.

He let go of the door handle, settled back in the seat and took a few deep breaths to calm himself. He hated leaving a job unfinished. Switching the ignition on, he watched with interest as the new transaction continued. Unfortunately, it seemed that demand was as high as ever.

He drove back towards base through the post apocalyptic streets of the large sprawling estate. When he'd started working this particular beat, the socialist liberal in him had been outraged. As far as he'd been concerned, the state had a duty of care to these people. And yet the powers that be seemed to have abandoned these housing estates to lawlessness and mob rule.

The more he worked amongst the people though, the more he started realising that it wasn't necessarily the fault of the state. Yes, the social welfare system both encouraged and fostered a lack of work ethic and ambition in people, most of whom accepted their cheques with a weary fatalism. But the urban decay; buildings set alight and cars burned out. That was all down to the populace; these people were doing it to themselves. And they weren't doing it for high ideals, views and principles. They weren't trashing their community because of a cause that they believed in. No, this was just mindless vandalism and intimidation.

The young men and women were accepting the *social* in one hand, while they smashed their own homes and their community with the other, and for what? As far as he could see, it was for no reason other than boredom. He just couldn't understand that type of mentality.

He pulled into his assigned parking space, noting with interest the increased number of cars in the car park. The drug squad was based in Anglesea Road Garda Station, not the most salubrious area of Cork, and he idly wondered where the extra vehicles had come from.

He smiled at Janice on the way in. They had been flirting on and off for a few months; since the last Christmas party, in fact. They were both afraid to take it further. They were reaching that age; not yet desperate, but not wanting to cast off potential relationships as casual and carefree either.

'Hey Janice,' he said. 'What's the story?'

'Boardroom, third floor, they're waiting for you,' she said curtly, without looking up.

He walked past the desk, wondering what he had done to offend her, when he heard an exclamation.

'You can't go upstairs looking like that,' she gasped, as she tore off her headset and ran around the desk.

To his chagrin and horror, she proceeded to style his hair with her fingers, smoothing down his locks the way his mother had done when he was a child.

'That's better,' she said, standing on tiptoes, before kissing him on the tip of his nose.

She winked.

'Knock them dead, tiger!' she added with a smile.

As the lift ascended to the third floor, he thought about what had just transpired and realised there was still a huge amount about women that he didn't understand. Maybe he needed to start finding out. He made a mental note to ask Janice out on a date as soon as was reasonably possible, and then parked the information in the non-work recesses of his brain; he had other things he needed to concentrate on right now.

He didn't know what to expect, but *boardroom* sounded unsettling at best and ominous at worst. He had the feeling that he would need to be alert and switched on.

As he walked, a slow measured plod like a condemned man toward the gallows, the carpet on the third floor deadened the sound of his heavy workman's boots. At the end of the corridor, he stopped. Raising his hand to rap his knuckles on the heavy hardwood door, he was startled to find it fly open in his face.

'Ah, Detective Murray, there you are,' said Inspector Ryan. 'At last we can get this show on the road.'

The only thing that had changed about Inspector Ryan in the three years that James had been working in the drug squad was his lack of hair. He had lost none of the drive, passion or determination to make a difference. He was a whirlwind; a man whom it was genuinely hard to keep up with, even if he was precisely double your age.

James followed Inspector Ryan into the room; nobody ever got ahead of him. His eyes scanned the outer reaches of the large boardroom table. He could see all his colleagues, members of both the Cork County and Southern Region drug squads.

They were seated along one side of the table. There were no free spots in their ranks, except for the place at the far end, which was obviously reserved for Inspector Ryan. He glanced to the other side; two seats free among the unrecognisable suits.

Maybe it was not obvious to outsiders, but to James it was as plain as day that they were Gardai. They exuded that slightly imperious confidence and presence so common in police officers; possibly visitors from another jurisdiction?

This could get interesting.

James took his seat, nodding politely in turn to the sharp suited gentlemen that were sitting either side of him. He waited with interest, as Inspector Ryan resumed his place at the top of the table. The man next to James passed him a marker pen and a thin cardboard strip that was pre-folded in the middle. He glanced around, realising that names and ranks had been written and placed as nametags in front of each person. He dutifully scribbled down his own and was just placing it in front of him, when the lights dimmed slightly and the projector came on.

All the heads in the room swivelled toward the bright square of light. James fervently hoped it wouldn't be death by PowerPoint. In fairness to the inspector though, he generally used the projector only for items of criticality. James hoped the visitors were of the same vein.

'Ok, I think we have everybody we need,' said Inspector Ryan. 'Before we kick off and for the benefit of everyone involved, I'd like to give all of you the background as to why we are here. Then I will hand over to Chief Inspector Brown from Dublin to see if he has anything to add.'

He indicated the man sitting to his right.

'Just in case there is anything I've missed,' he finished.

He paused and then clapped his hands once. He then hit a button on his laptop and the first slide appeared. *Welcome to Cork,* it said simply, in large letters.

'Is everyone happy with that?' he asked, into the body of the room.

'Inspector Ryan, if I may just say a brief word?' inquired a plumy voice, halfway down the right hand side.

James leaned forward and peered at the nametag; Fergal Lynch, secretary at the Department of Justice. He remained hunched forward, immediately interested. It was not often they had a representative from the Department of Justice. It would be intriguing to see what he had to say.

'Gentlemen,' said the secretary loftily, as he stood to address the assembled throng. 'As you are all well aware, there is a distinct separation between the Gardai and the Department of Justice.'

He surveyed the room quickly.

'And rightly so,' he added hastily, noticing some of the expressions.

'But as you also know, the Department of Justice holds the budget for the Gardai, and as such, I would like to think we have even a minor influence over some of the policies and operations,' he finished briskly.

Assuming a much more sombre expression, he continued speaking, as the politician lurking just below the urbane surface slowly emerged.

'Drugs are a scourge, eating into and undermining the very backbone of our state. Nowhere in the country is this highlighted more starkly than Cork.'

He said this with added emphasis on the last word.

'I don't think I need to remind anyone in this room that the current minister for Justice was elected from Cork South-Central.'

He had their full attention now.

'I'm not saying it's critical that this operation should succeed, but I think it would be politically expedient to make this a triumph of co-operation.'

He paused and you could have heard a pin drop in the room.

'Make no mistake,' he said emphatically. 'In the current climate, our budget is being ruthlessly and forensically analysed; the minister needs to see results.'

He looked around with a slightly amused smile for a few seconds, almost daring a response.

'Thank you, Secretary Lynch,' said Inspector Ryan, inviting Lynch to sit down.

He looked steadily at each of the assembled men before continuing.

'I think that has put things nicely into perspective for us,' he finished evenly, and with no trace of humour.

James smiled inwardly; Inspector Ryan was no mug. He knew exactly what the secretary had been saying.

'Get results, or I'll get somebody who can,' would have been a much less subtle way to put it.

The silence was deafening.

CHAPTER 14 – RIVALS

12th May 2011 – Two days after the Storm.

I embrace my rival, but only to strangle him. – Jean-Baptiste Racine.

The inspector allowed the tension to ratchet up a couple of degrees, before cutting through the silence.

'Let's crack on,' he said. 'As Secretary Lynch alluded to, I don't need to tell anybody here in this room what a problem drugs are in Irish society. Unfortunately, we live it and we live with it every day.'

He indicated the man sitting to his right, who nodded an acknowledgement.

'When Chief Inspector Brown was appointed, he decided almost immediately that the best way to tackle the issue was by setting up regional taskforces.'

He glanced at his own men then.

'And that is why you are all here. There are a lot of reasons why drugs are so prevalent; there are yet more reasons why they are so prevalent in urban areas. A significant number of state agencies are focused currently on the *demand* side of the drugs problem. What do I mean by that? Well....'

He paused.

'....there is an inordinate amount of time and money put into things like social services, education, drop-in centres and addiction clinics. All these are absolutely required; don't for a second think that I'm saying they are *not* worth the money and resources put into them, *but....*'

He heavily emphasised the word.

'....they could easily be seen as *after the fact*, cures if you will.'

He stopped to let that sink in.

'I have always been an advocate of *do what you can do, not what you would like to do*. That is why I am in complete agreement with Chief Inspector Brown. In his first public speech after his appointment, he stated that we are in the business of prevention, not cure.'

The Chief Inspector nodded unconsciously at another name check.

'This task force is going to target the supply,' said Inspector Ryan. 'Our aim is to coordinate everything into a single country-wide operation. To do that, we need an enormous amount of intelligence. We need to coordinate and cooperate in a way that we've never done before.'

He stopped briefly, picked up the bottle of sparkling water, twisted the top and drank deeply.

'Anything you'd like to add, Chief Inspector Brown?' he asked.

'Only that I am fully behind this operation, and will provide all the resources that are necessary to get the job done,' said the chief inspector.

James was amused and secretly pleased to discover that he spoke with a broad inner city Dublin accent; a huge contrast to the secretary who had gone before him. He didn't like the secretary, didn't trust him at all. Conversely, he immediately liked the chief inspector; a man of the people? Go figure.

'At this point,' Inspector Ryan said, 'and especially for the benefit of the Dublin contingent, I'd like to handover to Detective James Murray to give us a briefing on one half of the Cork supply line. James?' he asked.

James blinked; he had not been expecting to be personally targeted to speak. He had nothing prepared. Not that it mattered; after three years, he was bordering on obsessive. He lived and breathed his subject, he didn't need a presentation.

James stood up. Unlike the inspector, he couldn't talk sitting down. He started pacing slowly around the room, assembling his thoughts as he went.

'You can basically divide the supply and sale of drugs in Cork the same way as the city itself is divided; with the River Lee. One side is controlled by one organisation and one side is controlled by another. There are no other smaller groups or bit players; they have all been ruthlessly and systematically stamped out.'

He paused for emphasis.

'There are only two gangs, but as in most hotly contested and profitable markets, they are bitter rivals and interestingly for us, intense enemies.'

He paused again.

'Personally, I'm going to focus on the north side of the city, because that's the one I know,' said James. 'The man at the top is a guy called Eoin Morrison, but everybody knows him as *Black Swan*.'

'Why Black Swan?' asked one of the Dublin detectives, before James could continue.

'There are a lot of rumours,' said James. 'I personally believe it's because of his educational background and his fashion sense.'

There was a chuckle around the room. James held up his hand with a smile.

'Let me explain,' he said. 'Eoin came from a very well-to-do family. His father Michael was a successful solicitor, managing partner of one of the biggest firms in Cork. Young Eoin was an only child; he never wanted for anything, except maybe attention from his parents. Dad was always working and Mum was a society girl; more likely to be seen in the social diary pages than on the school run. Eoin was sent away to Clongowes boarding school after he finished his private prep, and that's where he completed his secondary education. He then did accountancy and business at UCD. When he graduated with a first class honours degree, he headed straight back to Cork.'

'So, how did a qualified accountant become a drug lord?' asked one of the other Dublin detectives. 'Or more importantly, why would he want to?'

'That's two very good questions,' said James, 'and no one is really sure. What we do know is that he initially went to work for Pat *The Bull* McCabe. Pat ran a string of bookies shops on the north side, and used them as a very effective cover for the distribution and supply of drugs. Eoin was employed initially as the accountant for the legitimate bookmakers businesses, but he had a keen forensic auditor's eye, and it soon became apparent to him that *out-of-the-ordinary* activities were taking place.'

He stopped to select a Coke from the trolley in the corner, before resuming his slow measured pace. The small explosion of the escaping gases as he lifted the ring pull made the room jump. He smiled to himself; at least he had their full attention anyway.

'It is only conjecture at this point,' he said, 'but it does give us a glimpse into the type of character he is. Anyone I have interviewed who has been on either side of Eoin, will tell you that he is completely amoral. He seems to have no scruples whatsoever, but yet he lives by a rigid code of behaviour. He surrounds himself with very faithful lieutenants, whom he rewards handsomely for advising and protecting him. They reciprocate with fierce and undivided loyalty.'

He paused briefly.

'Make no mistake, gentleman,' he said. 'Eoin is not a common street thug. He is cold when he needs to be, he is brutal when he needs to be, but he is always calculating. He will do whatever he needs to do to stay where he is; top of the pile.'

'Is he married?' asked the same Dublin detective.

'Never married, no children,' said James. 'He is completely self-centred and I don't say that in a blithe way either. His only focus is on himself and his ambitions.'

'Does he have any weaknesses?' asked another detective.

'None that we have been able to ascertain,' said James. 'Financially, he is rock solid as you would expect from an accountant. Physically, he is fit and healthy, goes to the gym and believes his body is his temple. Emotionally; as I said, no wife, no kids, both his parents are dead. No brothers or sisters, no significant other. His house in Montenotte is a fortress, his lieutenants loyal and virtually incorruptible.'

James nodded at Inspector Ryan, who pressed a button on the laptop in front of him. An indistinct black-and-white photograph replaced the welcome message on the screen.

'Why are all surveillance photos so blurry?' asked James.

Inspector Ryan guiltily adjusted the lens on the projector, and the image snapped into sharp focus. James waited for the chuckles to die down before resuming a more serious tone.

'So, this is our man,' he said. 'As you can see, he is dressed head to toe in black; always Armani. I know you can't see his eyes properly in a photograph, but that's what makes him so dangerous. They are cold and dead; like most of his opponents. Thank you.'

He stopped his pacing and sat back down at the table, finishing his can in one gulp.

'Thank you, Detective Murray,' said Inspector Ryan.

He signalled with his head at another guy across from James, sat in the middle of the ranks of Cork detectives.

'Detective Fitzsimons, would you mind continuing?' he asked.

James's ears pricked up. As well as being one of his best mates, Sean Fitzsimons was also one of his rivals for the upcoming sergeant's position. It would be interesting to see how the two pitches compared.

'Thank you, Inspector Ryan,' said Detective Fitzsimons.

He pushed his chair back a little from the table, and relaxed. His style was much more laid back, but he always needed a bit of room as he tended to use his arms a lot when speaking.

'Detective Murray mentioned a man called McCabe in his presentation,' said Detective Fitzsimons. 'Well that is where the other side of the story picks up.'

He took a sip of his cranberry juice; a bit of a health nut was our Sean.

'McCabe senior was a successful businessman; self-made and ruthless. But within a year of hiring a young ambitious accountant, he had been forced out of all of his businesses. Not only that, but within a year of being deposed from his position of power, he was shot dead while sitting at the bar of his local pub. No one has ever managed to pin it on Black Swan; no one ever could, but even the dogs in the street knew who ordered it.'

'McCabe left behind two teenage sons; identical twins in fact, David and John McCabe,' he continued. 'Their mother had passed away years previously of ovarian cancer. They were seventeen when their father died, and both struggled to come to terms with their changed situation. David was the stronger of the two, but John really went off the rails by all accounts. David had a hard time reining him in.'

'One night, about four months after their father's death, John and David were standing outside a nightclub. They had gone to Limerick for some reason, instead of staying where they were known and feted, and John got into an argument in the line outside the club. Because of his family background, he was used to getting his own way; used to being able to push people around. The problem for him was that in Limerick, he was essentially a *nobody*. He ended up with a switchblade in the chest, which transected his aorta; he was dead before the ambulance made it to the hospital.'

'All this made David intensely angry and all the more determined to get revenge,' he continued. 'You can understand how he blamed Black Swan for his father's death; in all likelihood he *was* responsible for his father's death, but in David's head, Black Swan had killed both of them, and that is what makes it personal for David.'

'Don't get me wrong. Revenge is a very powerful emotion in itself, but young David was also intensely greedy *and* ambitious. He wanted a slice of what his father had, only much more so. He wanted the whole of Cork united under his rule, with Black Swan dead into the bargain.'

'So, he targeted the other side of the city; the weaker side; the side where Black Swan had much less of an influence. Through ruthlessness, bloody mindedness and sheer hard work, he built his business up from virtually nothing. He didn't do it by facts and figures; by calculation and accountancy.'

He stopped briefly to let his next words sink in.

'Make no mistake, gentlemen,' he stated distinctly. 'Black Swan may be ruthless, but David McCabe makes him look like Snow White. He uses threats and intimidation; stabbings, beatings and punishment shootings. That's how David McCabe rules his Kingdom; absolutely. Thank you for listening.'

James looked across at his colleague admiringly. It had been a confident and assured presentation.

'Oh, and by the way,' said Detective Fitzsimons, as he settled himself back at the table. 'McCabe also has a nickname. He is known as *the Bullock*.'

Across the table, there was a single guffaw of laughter. Detective Fitzsimons held up his hand for silence.

'I know it sounds faintly comedic,' he added, 'but his nickname is based on the character *the Bull* McCabe.

He paused.

'Which is also incidentally where his father's nickname originated too,' he finished.

One of the Dublin detectives clicked his fingers in recall.

'That film *the Field*; Richard Harris played him, if I'm not mistaken. Set in the west; Galway somewhere, John B Keane wrote it.'

'That's the one,' said Sean. 'And I don't have to tell you how driven, focused and downright scary that character was. He was almost psychotic in the range and scope of his behaviour. In short guys, let's just say the nickname of *the Bullock* is well chosen.'

Inspector Ryan let the murmurs of chat grow into a hubbub of conversation for a few minutes, before holding up his hand for quiet again. As the noise died away, he spoke into the ensuing silence.

'So in summary,' he said. 'We have two very powerful and equally vicious gangs, vying for the supremacy of our streets. Secrecy is paramount to both organisations. It is incredibly difficult to get intelligence on either of them.'

He paused.

'In short gentlemen, we have a very tough job ahead of us.'

CHAPTER 15 – SURVIVAL

13th May 2011 – Three Days after the Storm.

To live is to suffer, to survive is to find some meaning in the suffering. – Friedrich Nietzsche.

The first thing that struck me on landing back in the country of my birth, was the duality of language. I had completely forgotten, being so long in the US, but it was strange and vaguely unsettling to see the Irish words on the airport signs, as well as the English.

I wasn't sure what to expect, but Dublin Airport certainly wasn't what I had expected. I knew I was Irish; my birth certificate said as much. I remembered the tears that had fallen as the Emerald Isle had receded to a dot on the horizon. I remembered all the rebel songs; the ones I had sung, emboldened with one too many pints of Guinness in the ludicrously overpriced and maudlin Irish bars of New York. I even remembered a smattering of the hard learned *patois*; prided myself on it in fact.

But somehow this airport, this gleaming cathedral of steel and glass, just didn't feel like the gateway to my home country. I knew some of it was me. I'd been away for twenty four years, so some things were bound to have changed. I was certainly different, but some of the Irishness, the *ceol agus craic,* seemed to have been stripped from the place.

Walking down towards the baggage reclaim, you could have been in any airport in Europe. The two employees I'd met so far were both of eastern European origin; I'd had difficulty understanding what they were saying. In fact, the only Irish person I'd encountered so far was the guy at passport control.

The official had been very stern and had fixed me with an unblinking stare. For a second, I'd felt as though he could see right through me. My first instinct had been to run away. Don't be stupid, I'd said to myself, he doesn't know anything. Just as the doubt was forming in my brain, the man had relaxed and smiled.

'Coming home?' he'd asked with a welcoming grin.

I'd smiled back in return.

'Something like that,' I'd said. 'We'll see how it goes.'

Walking on through the baggage claim and straight out through the green *nothing to declare*, I continued on. Travelling light, with only a rucksack, I headed out of the terminal building and down to the coach park.

I hopped onto the *train-link*, the coach that connects the airport with Connolly and Heuston railway stations. The journey was long and uneventful. I recognised none of the roads or buildings as we drifted inexorably onward toward our final destination. Dublin wasn't my place; it wasn't where my particular angels and demons dwelled.

As the coach pulled up outside Heuston station, I felt the first jolt of familiarity, like a reconnection of sorts. Small though it may have been, it was definitely there. I walked through the grand colonnaded entrance and was reminded briefly of my last visit to Dublin; my one and only visit, in fact.

I had come up with Mum on the train. The eighth of December was the day when the country people converged on the capital, *the big smoke*, to do their Christmas shopping. I remembered the jostle of the crowds, the large tree with lights strung across the street like a mantle of stars, and the Christmas decorations in Switzer's department store window; a regular treat for the kids.

After buying my ticket, first-class, I couldn't relax until I was safely on that midday train to Cork. I jumped from leg to leg and only finally started to calm as the leviathan slowly enlarged from the dot on the distant horizon, and glided to a stop with a reptilian hiss. I placed my bag on the rack above my head, sat back in padded comfort and closed my eyes for a few minutes.

The brakes suddenly released and the train jerked a few inches forward, startling me, before slowly building speed.

Inevitably my mind strayed back to the night of the storm. My god, I'd gone through the emotional mangle that night, and suddenly I was standing back in that spot; I could even feel the rain on my body.

#

I experienced the feeling again; the distinct and immediate euphoria I'd felt, after I read the words written in the box marked *father*: Thomas Eugene Mary O'Neill.

Almost immediately afterwards, I received the proverbial kick to the solar plexus. There was a sinking feeling in the pit of my stomach; the sick realisation that I'd probably killed my own son. I felt myself descending into a gnawing chasm of hopelessness and despair, but something at the back of my mind refused to let me fall into the abyss; kept telling me that something wasn't right.

I forced my wounded brain to seize on the practicalities and then, in an instant, I knew what it was that was wrong. Kathleen had never known my confirmation name. It had been a standing joke between us. Apart from the fact that I'd been embarrassed to have a woman's name, she hadn't told me hers either, so it had been pure stubbornness on both our parts.

I tried to make sense of the discovery, tried to make sense of its significance. If she hadn't known my confirmation name, then she couldn't have added it to the birth certificate. If *she* hadn't added it, then it followed logically that she hadn't had anything to do with the it at all.

Seizing on that suddenly empowering information, my brain started connecting all of the dots. If she hadn't been party to it, then in all likelihood it was a fake and in all probability, Alan Murphy was the assassin after all.

My brain started recalibrating; I could feel the cogs working. I could hear them whirring, as the emotional baggage was ruthlessly dumped out, and the cold calculating killer slipped effortlessly back into place. I could feel the anger rising, but it was a cold hard edged anger; I could sustain this for days if I needed to.

As I stood there, gazing up at the sky, I'd felt the pressure of something on the back of my neck. As I thought about it now, with the benefit of hindsight, I realised that all the pent up emotions I'd experienced in that fateful minute or so had been funnelled into that split second.

At last, my subconscious seized on something; at last it could react in a way it was trained to do. The truth was simple; reaction to danger was like breathing for me, it just happened naturally.

I heard the first part of the whispered statement.

'Guido....'

The rising wind whipped the rest of it into the driving rain. While the O was still forming in his mouth, I whirled around, instinct and experience telling me I had the benefit of surprise, but only milliseconds to act.

As I spun, I caught the outstretched hand of my attacker with my left hand, just below his weapon. My right hand, still holding my own gun, came around in a blurred arc of speed, hitting the would-be assassin square on the side of his neck.

Still keeping hold of my now dazed assailant, I stepped in and whipped my hand across his chest. I swept my right heel backwards through the base of his ankle, taking the leg completely out from under him, and his balance with it. As he lost his footing, I kept up the pressure of my arm across his chest and he passed the point of no return, hitting the floor with a bang; I could hear the whoosh as the air was forced from his lungs.

Following up my advantage, I dropped my knees savagely into his chest. I heard a couple of cracks and a sharp, injured intake of breath. Grabbing my assailant's weapon hand and holding it tight, I placed my own gun against the sinews of his wrist and fired a single shot.

I felt the hand go limp, and at the same moment heard the agonised scream.

'Arrrgghhhhhhhhhh!'

I let go of the arm, and watched dispassionately as the gun dropped out of the now powerless fingers. Getting up off his chest, I waited until the agonised shrieks had dissipated and had been replaced with shouted profanities; he was now ready to talk, even if he didn't want to.

I knelt beside him. He was frantically trying to stem the blood loss from his shattered stump.

'Who sent you?' I asked conversationally.

'Suck my dick,' said the man, in a voice strained with pain.

'Who sent you?' I asked again, more pleasantly and conversationally this time.

'Are you fucking deaf?' asked the man.

'Piece of advice,' I said pragmatically. 'In future, never give your target any chance at all.'

I placed my pistol to the man's forehead and pulled the trigger, without even pausing.

Most people when they fire a weapon close their eyes instinctively. I had trained myself to do the opposite. I didn't want to miss a millisecond. I saw in an instant the expression change from panic to realization to acceptance. I felt rather than saw the track of the bullet; saw the explosion from the back of the head, the blood spraying like paint carelessly slopped out of a tin. The faint rustle of clothes as the already lifeless body settled back onto the ground.

This was not some grotesque killing ritual. I did not do it through any sadistic pleasure, but purely because it could be the difference between life and death; my life and death.

The survival mechanism started to kick in. I glanced at the house, filled with my meagre personal belongings, overlaid on someone else's past. I glanced at the gleaming rental car and a plan started forming, the same instant reaction to situations that had kept me alive for twenty odd years. I caught a glimpse of the future, of myself strolling into New Orleans Airport and booking a one way ticket to Dublin.

Ireland was as good a place as any to find out who I was.

#

I watched the green canopy flash past the carriage windows in a blur of movement and I realised that I was back in the present again. I picked up the bottle in front of me and took a swig. I wasn't even sure why I'd got myself a beer. I didn't like drinking during the day, but there was a strange and unfamiliar feeling in the pit of my stomach. I thought about what it could be. It took me a while to work out what it was, and then it struck me with a slow realisation; it was anxiety.

In my game, if you were anxious, you didn't live very long. But this was different. As the countryside unfolded past my window, I knew that I was getting closer and closer to old memories; ghosts that maybe should be allowed to sleep easy and undisturbed.

Extracting my hand from my jacket pocket, I placed my keys on the table top in front of me. I picked up one and looked at it. This key had been on my key ring since I was fifteen. It had born witness to my first serious kiss, my first serious relationship, and later, my first killing. I wasn't even sure why I had kept it for so long, or the house it belonged to for that matter.

I'd never been able to bring myself to sell it, but I'd never been able to bring myself to rent it out either, so I had a management company look after it for me. They checked it out on a regular basis, made sure there were no leaks or disasters, forwarded on the mail and kept it clean and tidy.

In a sense, I think I'd mothballed my previous life. It was easier to wrap it up and preserve it, ring fence it if you like, than it was to come face to face with something unsavoury or unsettling about my new life.

Mum had a way of making me face things, even in death, that I really didn't want to know or recognise about myself. I hadn't dealt with her leaving me; I didn't want to get rid of anything from her life, but I didn't want to face up to her death either. It would be an interesting reunion.

CHAPTER 16 – HOME

13th May 2011 – Three Days after the Storm.

Where thou art, that is home. – Emily Dickinson.

I picked up the beer bottle and turned to look out of the window, trying to forestall the memories. I took a long swig, shuddering as I swallowed, and watched the forty shades of green flashing past in an emerald blur. It wasn't just tourist bullshit; it really was a very lush and green country.

The further I got from Dublin, the further back in time the countryside seemed to regress. The names of the towns resonated from my youth; Portlaoise, Templemore, Thurles, Mallow, town-lands of an earlier time.

Where I'd found Dublin modern and soulless (it could have been any modern European capital city), I found these towns timeless in their Irishness. The old-fashioned shop fronts, the whitewashed stone cottages; for every mile of track I travelled, I found the republican rebel spirit seeping back into my bones. I knew why I'd come back, but I also knew why I'd been reluctant to come back. I knew the pull would reassert itself, but I had to find out. I had to know for certain, and the only place I could think of to start my quest was where it had all began; where I had begun, in fact.

I leaned back in my seat and closed my eyes again. I couldn't remember the last time I'd had a decent night's rest. Sitting there, feeling the rhythmic clacking of the train on the rails, a metronomic lullaby that would normally send me to sleep, I just couldn't make the leap from the conscious to the unconscious world.

Somehow at the last minute, the questions would shake me awake and assault my impending dreams. Sitting on this train on my way home, I knew why.

It was the spectre of family.

A small ghostly tendril was reconnecting me to the past, a past I had tried to forget like it was a dream.

Of course, I'd never had a family, never married, never even had a serious relationship. How could I? I killed people. Yes, maybe they were low life scum-bags who deserved it, but they were people too. They were sons of mothers.

I would not have been able to regularise the two lives. I would not have been able to co-habit the pleading entreaties of my victims with the soft, innocent laughter of my children. The two were just incompatible, and yet the unspoken question was out there.

The thing was, fatherhood was a mystery to me. I had no frame of reference. My own father had been austere and distant.

Richard O'Neill had been a man of his time. And he had died before the possibility of a relationship between us had even emerged. So most of what I knew about fatherhood, I'd learned from my mother, possibly not the best seat of learning for a boy to become a man. I thought then about Kathleen; I wondered if she had ever married, and then chided myself for my first thought of her being a jealous one.

I knew I was torturing myself. I knew no good would come from idle speculation. But then, there were very few *good* thoughts in my head. Happiness to me was experienced in brief diversions; it wasn't a state of mind.

An image of Kathleen started to form. Sixteen years old, bouffant hair, shoulder pads and rainbow legwarmers. She was not conventionally pretty. She was not doll-like and petite. She was a big girl, certainly larger than average, but there was an attractiveness about Kathleen. It was something she wore, like an aura or a cloak. Call it vivacity or maybe sexual energy, but something had called to me on that very first night.

We had gone out together for a couple of years, but Ireland and especially Cork were too economically ruined to support two completely unskilled teenagers. I stuck it out for as long as I could, taking jobs in fast food joints and on building sites, but inevitably at the end of the month, my expenditure always exceeded my income.

At the time, there was a lottery for visas to America. It was like having your very own Wonka's golden ticket; a key to unlock the country where the streets were literally paved with gold, or so they said. There were fifty thousand of these lifelines available, and I became one of the lucky ones.

When I'd first broached the subject with her, she had been so excited, and it was only halfway through the conversation that I'd realised why. She thought I was talking about both of us going.

It was one of those conversations where both of you are sharing it, but yet it seems to be going in two different directions, at completely crossed purposes. The further it went, the harder it was for me to steer it back and eventually I just had to tell her out straight.

We had shared a lot over those months; relationships are about the only things that flourish in adversity. So when I told her that I'd got the green card and that I was going alone, I was prepared for the shrieks, the screams, the anger and the hurt. But I had not been prepared for that look. It was empty and devoid of hope, with a tinge of shock and hurt; like a loyal dog that has just been savagely kicked.

It had been impossible to retrieve our relationship from the ashes of that conversation. She had tried once to dissuade me, and when that hadn't worked, she had begged me to take her. I had shaken my head sadly; at that stage of my life, I could barely look after myself, let alone someone else.

I had half hoped she would be there to wave me off at the docks, but was not surprised when she wasn't; it was a lifetime ago.

I felt a shiver run through me, as I remembered the house. That was another ghost I had to confront; another spectre I had to lay to rest. My father had been a successful solicitor; killed in a car accident when I was five. Luckily, he'd had an exceptionally good life insurance policy, as well as a decent pension set aside for my mother.

We had been forced to move from south to north; from a crumbling but substantial property on Merchants Quay to a much smaller house in a less affluent neighbourhood. Even when I had gone to America and she had been moved to sheltered accommodation, there had still been enough money left from the policy to pay for the nursing home. It had helped to assuage my guilt and it had also enabled me to hold onto the house. She'd posted me a copy of the will that she'd made on the day I left, leaving the whole of her estate to me; before the Alzheimer's took over and she didn't even know who she was.

Yes, there were a lot of ghosts to lay to rest.

With a jolt, I realised we were pulling into Kent station. As I dragged my bag onto the platform, I felt a strange wave of youthfulness wash over me; it was like I was twenty again, which in a sense I was.

I had never experienced Cork as a mature adult. As I walked out through the doors and onto the Lower Glanmire Road, a wave of memories and nostalgia hit me like a tidal wave. I hadn't expected to feel so reconnected with the place. I thought about who I was, and then forced myself to think about the situation I found myself in. Certainly over the last month, there were a lot of dangerous people out there who wanted me dead; I needed to focus.

I joined the queue at the taxi rank, surprised at how many people had been on the train. There had certainly been many more than I'd expected.

I watched as the line slowly dispersed. I wasn't racist; how could I be living in New York, the most cosmopolitan of all cities? When I'd left Cork, you would barely find an Englishman on the streets, let alone a black man, but now every second taxi driver seemed to be coloured. It seemed that Ireland had indeed come a very long way in twenty odd years.

It was more by luck than judgement that as I came to the head of the queue, I heard a familiar refrain and smiled at the greeting; this one was definitely Irish.

'How we doing, boss?'

'Great thanks, you?' I replied.

I could almost feel my own accent flooding back; it had been so long since I'd heard the Cork lilt and if I was truthful with myself, it felt good. I settled myself into the front seat with my small bag stuffed between my legs.

'Where to boss?' my new friend asked.

'Grattan Hill,' I said, the words feeling alien in my mouth.

'Sure, you could walk it from here,' said the taxi driver.

He noticed the look on my face.

'You're the boss,' he said, holding his hands up in mock surrender.

The driver pulled out onto the busy road, leaning on the horn and swearing meaningfully out of the open window.

'Jesus, where did this arsehole get his license?' he asked loudly, gesturing ahead. 'And look at this fucking guy. You could drive a bus through there, boy!' he shouted angrily.

I tried to suppress a smile; it seemed taxi drivers were the same the world over.

'So, what has you in Cork, boy?' asked the driver, seemingly oblivious to the fact that I was at least ten years his senior.

'Just visiting,' I said.

'From America, is it?' said the driver.

He pronounced America funny; the first three syllables, and then a pause before the last one, with his voice rising all the time. To me, it sounded quite comical; to an American, probably less so. In the US, they took their country name very seriously.

'Yes, I got a green card; I was lucky and left during the eighties,' I replied. 'This is my first time back in about twenty five years. I even missed my mother's funeral,' I continued softly.

'I wouldn't hang around, if I were you,' said the taxi driver, either ignoring me or not hearing the last remark. 'This country is fecked. Half the place is living on welfare and the other half is paying for it. On top of that, the Blacks, the Indians, the Chinese and the eastern Europeans are all coming over here. If they don't work, they're claiming welfare, and if they do work, they're pricing all of us decent people out of a job. This country is fecked,' he said again, as if emphasising it.

I smiled; yep, definitely the same the world over.

'This is you, boss,' he said, pointing ahead.

I'd been paying attention to the driver, not my surroundings. I looked straight ahead and drew a sharp breath inwards. It was as if someone was playing with the zoom on a camera. Everything was blurry and then; wham, suddenly all brought into sharp focus.

I paid off the driver with a healthy tip.

'Thanks mate,' he shouted, as he drove off; gratuities were a way of life for me now, legacy of living in New York.

My hands shook as I tried to get the key in the lock. I could feel my knees knocking. I was just about to turn and push, when I heard a loud clearing of throat to my left. I looked across, suppressing the urge to run. It was Mrs Walsh, my mother's neighbour. I was not in the mood for small talk; not now anyway.

I didn't have a mirror, but I didn't need one. I knew at that moment that the man standing beside her was unrecognisable from the teenager she used to shout obscenities at.

'Are you from the management company?' she asked.

I moved my head noncommittally, hoping it would cover either a positive or a negative response.

'It's just you're not the normal guy,' she said, stating the obvious.

'I'm not from the management company,' I answered. 'I'm moving in for a week or so.'

'Oh how nice! It will be lovely having somebody next door again,' she said. 'It has been so depressing, living next to an empty house for so long. Don't get me wrong, he makes sure it is kept lovely, but it's not the same without someone living in it.'

She held out her hand.

'Maeve Walsh,' she said by way of belated introduction. 'But you can call me Mrs Walsh,' she added, with an impish grin.

I had to think for a couple of seconds.

'John O'Reilly,' I replied in return, 'but you can call me John.'

'Welcome to Grattan Hill, John,' said Mrs Walsh.

'Thanks,' I said. 'But if you don't mind, I'm going to get myself settled inside. It's been a long journey; a long flight.'

'Off you go, young man, don't let me keep you,' she said. 'Just remember, if you need anything, I'm just next door.'

I darted inside, maybe a little too quickly. I closed the door and leant back against the cold wood, closing my eyes as I did so. That had been really weird.

Even though I'd known she wouldn't recognise me, it was still peculiar to talk to my old neighbour like she was a stranger. Even if she could be a poisonous old busy-body sometimes, she had been very good to my mum, especially towards the end of her tenure in the house. I would tell her later who I really was, when the tiredness had abated.

The house itself was like a time warp. I remembered everything. I'd seen a documentary once, where they re-created rooms for celebrities in their childhood homes. I felt like one of them at that moment; it was uncanny how familiar it felt.

I threw the keys on the table and sat down heavily so I didn't fall down. I pulled my iPhone out of my trouser pocket, selected camera mode, and then the camera roll. I flicked through the pictures till I came to the one I wanted. I'd taken it at an angle to try and block out the bloody and jagged hole in the forehead. I turned the phone on its side and tapped thoughtfully with my forefinger on top of the case.

'Who are you, Mr Mystery Man?' I asked in a whisper.

CHAPTER 17 – GLIMMERINGS

13th May 2011 – Three Days after the Storm.

Two qualities are indispensable: first, an intellect that, even in the darkest hour, retains some glimmerings of the inner light which leads to truth; and second, the courage to follow this faint light wherever it may lead. – Carl Von Clausewitz.

'Hey Dale, get the fuck off my couch!'

He felt the hands grab his clothes roughly, before he was viciously spun towards the ground. He dropped about a foot and a half, to land with a thud on the hard laminate floor. Dazed and disoriented, he staggered to his feet. A large coffee cup was thrust into his bemused hand.

'Stop fucking sleeping on the job, Foster,' his boss said. 'It pisses me off. I have to kick my drunken slob of a student son off the sofa every second morning. I don't see why I should have to do it at work, too.'

'Sorry sir, it won't happen again,' said Dale groggily.

'Anyways, seeing as you are here, go and get a shower, and then hook up with Dodds. I'll tell him to wait for you; he's checking out what came in last night.'

Dale walked slowly back to his desk, ignoring the polite round of applause. As he headed for the showers, he gave them the finger, prompting lots of kissing noises and shouts.

'Bring that over here, baby!'

He smiled to himself; where would you be without friendly office banter.

He returned to his desk, refreshed, a few minutes later. It was amazing how something as basic as a stream of cold water on the skin could affect such dramatic changes.

'Sobered up yet?' asked Dodds.

'I wasn't drunk,' replied Dale defensively.

'What a waste of the boss's couch,' said Dodds disgustedly.

'Don't start on me, Dodds, I'm not in the mood,' snorted Dale shortly.

'Come back to me when your PMT is over,' said Dodds gruffly.

'Just let it go, Dodds, will you,' said Dale resignedly.

'Sure, just give me back all those cigarettes you stole from me over the last two years and we'll call it quits,' replied Dodds, with a thin smile.

Dale looked at him, stunned.

Dodds said nothing more and went back to his files, as if no bad tempered exchange of words had ever happened.

'Are you going to join me or what?' he asked at last, in exasperation.

Dale studied him surreptitiously across the desk, as he put away his shower things and draped his towel over the radiator. He had a brief flicker of déjà vu; that feeling that he'd been in this moment before.

And then he realised it wasn't déjà vu. Dodds was him, just older, greyer and more alone. It was a depressing thought. His body craved a fix; was screaming for nicotine, but he couldn't feed the craving without giving away his secret, which wasn't a secret anyway, it seemed.

What a pointless existence.

He really needed to get something into his life, other than work.

'Ok, pass a few of those over here, will you,' said Dale.

Their field office was based in Westchester, NY, but as part of the task force they were assigned to, Dale and his team had temporarily moved to the DEA New York divisional headquarters on 10th avenue. They co-operated very heavily with local law enforcement.

As part of that teamwork and co-operation, Dale had helped broker a deal with the local law agencies. If any cases came in to them that were remotely drug related, they would pass them along to the DEA task force. Dale and Dodds, as the task force liaison officers, would go through all the files that had been flagged to them. If any of the referrals led to further busts, the credit was shared between the DEA and the referring agency. It was a good system and so far it had been working very well. Both Dale and Dodds were special agents, but both preferred to refer to themselves as just agents; *special agent* tended to get up the backs of their peers and colleagues.

Dale flicked open the first file and started scanning down. After reading the top couple of lines, he knew this one was a no hoper. He recognised the perpetrator; a lonely delusional man, who had quite literally blown his brains out long ago. Apart from the obvious physical addiction, he had so many mental issues, paranoid schizophrenia, manic depression, you name it. He was the sad and depressing face of the fight they were losing on the streets. Dale cast the file aside, much as the addict had done with his life. They wouldn't be getting any information from this one.

He picked up the next file; two students this time, arrested for possession outside a nightclub. It was highly unlikely that they would be able to provide anything of any value. He was just about to pick up a third, when Dodds threw a file across the desk at him.

'Take a look at this one,' he said. 'It could be interesting.'

The arrest was for a violent altercation outside a bar; the officers had been particularly struck by it, as it appeared the originator of the aggression had been a recent victim of violence himself. In a subsequent search, they had found a significant quantity of cocaine, certainly more than was required for personal use.

'Yep, that looks like a good one,' said Dale. 'Is there anything else in your pile?'

'Nothing else worth looking at,' responded Dodds.

Dale took the remaining four files on his desk and split them in two.

'Here you go,' he said, handing one half to Dodds. 'Have a skim through these and then we'll check this guy out.'

An hour later, they were heading towards the 5th Precinct headquarters. Dodds generally drove. He'd told Dale once that he was a very nervous passenger. Dale had only experienced it a single time, but didn't ever want to go through it again. He had never seen terror etched in such precise detail on someone's face before. He was no great passenger himself, but he'd live; he didn't think Dodds would survive another journey riding shotgun.

They drove in silence, but a surprisingly companionable one. Their occasional spats were part of the fabric of working closely together and quickly forgotten.

Halfway to the station, Dodds flicked a button on the centre console, and the next thing, Tony Bennett was telling them that he had left his heart in San Francisco. Dodds was a sucker for the old crooners. It was still early morning, so the sun was quite low. Dodds pulled the visor down to shield his eyes and slipped on a pair of mirror shades. Dale noticed a picture of a young woman stuffed into the webbing of the sun visor.

'Who's the girl?' he asked, subtlety never having been one of his strong points.

Wordlessly, Dodds extracted the photo from its nylon nest and handed it across.

'She's a looker ain't she,' he said.

For once Dale had to agree; she most certainly was a looker.

'Obviously not related to you,' responded Dale, with a smile.

'She's my daughter,' said Dodds seriously.

Dale was taken aback.

'I didn't know you were married?' he queried.

Even though they had been working closely together for over a year, they never discussed personal business.

'I'm not,' said Dodds.

Dale waited, sensing there was more to come.

'We were very young,' he said at last. 'Both of us were. We had been going together less than a year, when she told me. Of course, I immediately offered to marry her, but she was having none of it. Even if I'd loved her, she didn't love me. So, we decided to bring our daughter up together, sharing the responsibilities.'

His expression softened, as he became caught up in the memories.

'Her mother married when Joanie was about seven. She gets on great with her step-dad. Don't get me wrong, I wouldn't have it any other way; it's important for her that there is no conflict in the home.'

This time he smiled broadly.

'But I make sure every day that she knows who her father is; that she is my little girl.'

He paused.

'Her step-dad is very well off; I could let things slide if I wanted to and she would still be well taken care of, but probably because of that, I make sure I pay my way and then some. Steve understands and respects me for it, I think. He knows me and he knows her; she is my daughter, after all.'

Dale handed the photograph back.

'She's gorgeous,' he stated truthfully.

Dodds looked at him for a few seconds, searching for the punch line and eventually finding none. Putting the photograph back in its place, his expression softened as he patted it gently.

'You know something, Dale,' he said.

He rarely called Dale by his first name.

'In this job, I don't think I could have been married. It hardens you; desensitises you. But do you know what? There is not a day goes by that I don't think about that girl. I have absolutely no regrets; to be honest she's kept me sane. She is the one person who accepts me for who I am and lets me be me; if you can follow that and understand what I mean?'

Dale nodded; he understood it alright, and wished fervently that he had something like it too.

They pulled up across the street from the station. As Dodds parked, Dale managed to get across the road with only two horns and one hand gesture from the rush hour drivers. Oddly enough, his older and slower partner got none; it seemed Dodds was more nimble than he looked.

As they walked into the foyer, they happened to bump into Detective Dempsey, their liaison officer from the fifth. As Dempsey ran past, he held up his hand with his fingers apart, and mouthed the words silently; the universal gesture for the phrase, *give me five*.

The two colleagues waited patiently, shuffling their feet and looking down at the floor. Dempsey catapulted through a door on the other side of the station and rejoined them, just before the five minutes had elapsed. He shook their hands vigorously as he always did.

'Agent Foster, Agent Dodds, good to see you,' he said, as he indicated an ante room.

Dodds and Dale settled themselves down into their chairs and Dempsey busied himself at the coffee machine. He placed two mugs of steaming black liquid in front of them, without asking whether they wanted anything to drink; they were policemen after all. He banged the sugar, sweetener and creamer in the middle of the table and then sat down opposite them.

He eyed them thoughtfully across the rim of his own mug, as they busied themselves with the ritual of coffee preparation, sipping occasionally as he did so. Dale placed his copy of the file, the one he and Dodds had discussed earlier, on the table in front of him. He gently slid it across to Dempsey, who picked it up and scanned it quickly.

'Ah yea, this dude,' said Dempsey. 'I thought I might be hearing from you fellas on this one.'

'So, what's the story?' asked Dodds. 'Anything more you can give us, other than what appears in the file?'

'Yea, interesting one this,' replied Dempsey. 'He gave his name as Sam Balboni. He was causing a scene outside a bar-nightclub; throwing his weight around, but apparently not exactly Mike Tyson, if you get my drift. To be honest, our guys, the patrolmen who were called to the scene, were of a mind to let him off with a caution. But our friend jerk-off continued to mouth off to them, and coupled with the fresh injuries to his face, it just made the patrolmen bloody-minded. They brought him in, routinely searched his car and, bam, one kilo of cocaine.'

Both Dodds and Dale raised their eyebrows.

'So, definitely not for personal use,' stated Dale. 'I always wonder when it says that in a report. How much is too much?'

'Anyway, we figured we definitely had him for possession, and maybe intent to supply, too,' said Dempsey. 'So we left him stewing in the cells for a few hours. He didn't seem to be the most robust of criminals, if you get me. We thought it might soften him up a bit. But when we eventually got around to processing him, we realised very quickly that the little weasel had given us a false name.'

'Really?' inquired Dodds, his eyebrows coming together in the middle.

'Well, not so much a false name, as a misleading name,' Dempsey finished. 'Balboni is his mother's maiden name. His real name is Rudino.'

They collectively let that statement lie fallow for a minute or so, until Dale broke the silence.

'So, why lie about your name?' he asked. 'That is, unless you have something to hide.'

'That's exactly what we thought,' said Dempsey. 'So we took a look into his background, and that's when it all started to make a little bit of sense to us.'

Dale raised his eyebrows in a questioning manner; almost a carbon copy of his colleague moments earlier. Dempsey reached behind him for the plate of cookies. He placed the dish in the middle of the table, took one and bit it clean in half.

'Yea, he flagged up as being a known associate,' said Dempsey, through a mouthful of crumbs.

He swallowed hard and took another swig of his coffee.

'Or rather,' he continued, 'he flagged up as being related to a known associate.'

He accentuated the word *related.*

'It's his father who triggered the flag.'

'Associate of who?' asked Dodds interestedly.

'Guido and Ernesto Mancini,' said Dempsey.

Dodds and Dale stared at each other, coffee mugs pausing in mid air.

CHAPTER 18 – CORROBORATION

13th May 2011 – Three Days after the Storm.

There can be no theory of any account unless it corroborate with the theory of the earth. – Walt Whitman.

They watched him closely through the one-way glass. The first thing that struck Dale as odd was his general demeanour. Normally, the guys they interviewed were jumpy and nervous. This guy, despite his injuries, had an aura of casual self assuredness. As far as this guy was concerned, he had nothing to fear.

'Do you mind if we rattle him a little?' Dale asked Dempsey directly. 'If we can, that is?'

'Like I said,' answered Dempsey. 'We've already got him on the possession and maybe intent. If you can pin something else on him as well, and we get some of the credit, so much the better.'

'Do you want to sit in?' asked Dodds.

'Yea,' said Dempsey, 'but not because I don't trust you,' he finished quickly. 'It's just that station protocol demands it. You know how it is?'

He shrugged dismissively and opened the door, allowing the two agents to go ahead of him.

As they settled into their seats, the suspect regarded them curiously. Dempsey switched on the recorder.

'Interview started with suspect Sam Rudino. Date is thirteenth May, 2011.'

He glanced at the clock on the wall.

'Time is approximately eleven fifteen. Interview is being overseen by Detective Dempsey 56227. Also present are agents Foster and Dodds of the DEA.'

Dale couldn't be sure, but he thought the suspect's self-satisfied smile slipped just a tiny bit, when he heard the letters DEA. Dale made a show of shuffling the file on the desk.

'So Sam,' he said at last. 'Looks like you've got yourself in a bit of a jam.'

'Depends what side of the table you are on, I suppose,' answered the suspect.

'Listen carefully,' said Dale. 'I'm not going to beat around the bush, it's not my style. How do you know the Mancini's?'

As he spoke, Dale's eyes never left Sam's face. If he hadn't been looking for it, he'd have missed it, but he saw it; plain as day. A slight frown appeared between Sam's eyes. He recovered it well, but he was definitely rattled.

'I don't really know them,' said Sam. 'I am only acquainted with them as customers.'

'What type of customers exactly?' asked Dodds sharply.

Sam ignored the comment.

'My father runs their favourite restaurant,' said Sam. 'I deliver their order to them pretty much every night; nothing more, nothing less. No law against that is there?' he sneered.

'You expect us to believe that,' said Dodds incredulously.

'I don't care what you believe,' said Sam. 'The facts of the matter are that my father owns Rudino's restaurant. The Mancini's like our food and I deliver it; simple as that.'

Dale sat back slowly, as Dodds and Sam kept talking. A fragment of speech wafted into his brain; Ryan at the diner.

'I got a job too, cleaning dishes in a place called Rudino's.'

And further on in the conversation.

'Well it turns out the place is connected.'

Suddenly, everything clicked into place.

'Is your father a gangster?' asked Dale.

Sam looked at him and laughed at the old fashioned phrasing. The other two smiled as well, but Sam quickly realised that Dale's expression wasn't changing.

'You're serious, aren't you?' sneered Sam incredulously, a slow mocking smile spreading over his face.

'Well I fail to see how else you could get your hands on a kilo of cocaine,' said Dale. 'I am in the DEA and I couldn't. So if your father didn't give it to you....'

This time he looked at Sam directly. Sam couldn't hold his gaze; his stare broke and his eyes flicked away guiltily. Dale suddenly clicked his fingers and slapped his forehead.

'You stole it from the Mancini's, didn't you?' he stated softly.

Sam said nothing, but his Adams apple bobbed a couple of times.

Dale pressed home his advantage.

'Do you know what, Sam?' he intoned slowly. 'I thought you were in a bit of a jam, but if you stole from the Mancini's, you're fucked.'

'I didn't steal it,' Sam blurted out suddenly.

Dale tried to hide his delight; he was getting better at this interrogation lark.

'So what would you call it, Sam?' asked Dodds, joining in as he realised what Dale was doing.

He emphasised the word *Sam*.

'You now have a kilo of cocaine that belongs to them.'

'I....' Sam's mind blanked.

His eyes flickered, as he searched for the words.

'....I borrowed it,' he said finally. 'I was going to sell it and give them the profits, honestly I was. I wanted to prove to them that I wasn't just a pizza delivery boy.'

'So, where did you get it?' asked Dodds.

'A couple of the guys who work in the kitchens,' said Sam. 'Outwardly, they are waiting staff and kitchen porters, but they are also delivery mules. They take a package, hold it for a couple of days, and then deliver it onwards to its destination. These guys think they are in an episode of *the sopranos*; made guys, what a laugh!'

Sam spat the words out with vitriol.

'They are so pathetically eager to demonstrate how mobbed up they are, it makes me sick. One of them showed me his latest stash. Stupid prick even left it in his locker, unlocked.'

The cogs in Sam's head seemed to be whirring slowly; finally they caught up.

'You're not going to tell them, are you?' he asked, the tremble audible in his voice. 'I'm a dead man if you do.'

'I'll tell you what,' said Dale. 'I'll arrange a bust on the kitchens of Rudino's Restaurant. We'll take the two guys in and we'll *pretend* to seize the stash in the raid. In return, you're going to tell me everything you know about Storm.'

Sam stiffened.

'How do you know about that?' he asked.

Dale was silently exultant. He glanced across at his two companions. Dempsey was looking at him with interest, but Dodds was leaning forward intently.

'It doesn't matter how I know,' answered Dale.

He could feel Dodds eyes boring into him, but he ignored the stare for the present.

'The problem for you is that I know. So tell me what I need to hear; and don't give me this garbage that I've been getting off other people.' said Dale. 'A storm is coming; crap. Something big is about to blow; shit. I want specifics.'

Sam thought about it for a brief instant and then seemed to make up his mind.

'There are only two things I know. They are not certainties by any means; I overheard most of it at the dinner table and they talk very softly, but I'll tell you anyway.'

He composed himself before continuing.

'The first thing that I am pretty sure I understood; *Storm* is a drug. How it works, what it does and how it is made, I have no idea.'

He stopped to gather his thoughts, lids closing and eyes flicking from side to side.

'The second thing I heard is that it has something to do with Ireland; a place called Cork specifically.'

Dale blinked in surprise; the first time he had shown emotion of any kind. He had been expecting to hear a lot of things, but that wasn't one of them.

#

'And you were going to tell me this when?' hissed Dodds, through clenched teeth and compressed lips.

The annoyance drifted palpably across the partition separating their desks. They were both back in the office after a very strained car journey.

'I'm not hiding anything from you Dodds,' said Dale. 'You need to listen to me; I'm trying to tell you what happened. I only learnt this stuff myself last night.'

'We can't be partners with no trust,' said Dodds flatly.

'I know that,' said Dale.

He ushered Dodds into a side room and told him the whole story. The tip offs from James and Ryan, and the subsequent putting of two and two together in the interview room. Dodds sat back and thought about it for a couple of minutes. He finally gave a small flicker of a smile.

'So, did you corroborate this stuff in any other way?' he asked.

Dale breathed a sigh of relief; even though his story was true, it was good to have Dodds back onside. He hated petty rivalries between partners. He was glad Dodds believed him.

'Yeah I went through some of the files. The word *Storm* was sort of mentioned in passing in a few places; nothing concrete. When Sam mentioned the delivery guys, the same dudes that Ryan was talking about, I took a punt. Honestly, I wasn't expecting his reaction; he was genuinely scared.'

'Even so,' said Dodds. 'The link is tenuous at best and extremely slim at worst. Given your recent history, is it worth going to bat with a few half baked rumours? Apart from anything else, this is the Mancini's we're talking about here. These guys are bullet proof. You're going to have to be seriously solid in your evidence to try and take them down.'

'But that's just it,' said Dale. 'I don't have any evidence yet. I'm just looking for approval to collect the evidence; approval to start an operation.'

'Well, you know what I think,' said Dodds evenly. 'I think you're mad.'

Dale turned to his computer and started typing. The words flowed out of his head and straight into the report.

Two hours later, Dodds had proof-read the document with nothing more than a raised eyebrow at the end; what could he say?

Thirty minutes after that, Dodds watched with a mixture of amusement and pity as Dale came out of the office of the special agent in charge. While he didn't actually slam the door in frustration, Dodds could see the intent written all over his face.

'So what did he say?' asked Dodds, already knowing the answer.

Dale sat down heavily opposite him.

'To use his exact words and I quote, *a tissue of half baked rumour and conjecture.* He actually laughed out loud when I mentioned the Mancini's. He literally couldn't stop; I had to wait for five or six minutes to continue.'

'Anything else?' asked Dodds.

'Apparently, the only case to answer in this half baked report is lodged deep in my *paranoid and delusional imagination*, and that I need to take an immediate two-week leave of absence, starting right now.'

Dodds got up and patted him on the shoulder as he walked towards the coffee station.

'Probably not a bad idea, my friend,' he said. 'It would do you good to get away from this place for a while.'

Dale watched Dodds retreating back. Maybe the boss was right; maybe he did need to get away for a while. He opened the drawer of his desk and pulled out his passport. He'd got it when he'd joined the DEA. His head had been filled with images of drug busts in exotic locations; a heady mix of glamour and danger. But he was lucky he had done it in some ways. Most Americans didn't own a passport. He glanced down at the discredited report in front of him. He made his decision, twirling the Rolodex on his desk to the letter T. He dialled the number and waited three rings.

'Yes, good afternoon,' he said, 'I'm looking for a flight to Cork in Ireland. What's that? Oh, sorry, from New York; any of the major NY Airports will do. Yes, I can hold.'

He cradled the receiver and waited. He never did anything spontaneous; maybe it was time to start.

CHAPTER 19 – RESURRECTION

13th May 2011 – Three Days after the Storm.

It is not more surprising to be born twice than once; everything in nature is resurrection. –
Voltaire.

The beads of sweat glistened on his forehead like stars in a cloudless
night sky. He didn't notice the small sprinkles of perspiration on his upper lip, or
the way his tongue was stuck out to one side of his mouth, so intense was his
concentration.

For years, Max had regarded himself as an *in-between*. He had a sliding
scale in his head of what he should be earning; his true net worth. At this precise
moment of his life, he was definitely the wrong side of the middle. In other
words, he was not happy.

He had done moderately well in his career, but nowhere near as well as
he felt his talents deserved. He lived in a *nice* area, not in a private and
fashionable new resort with celebrity neighbours and twenty four hour security.
He drove a *nice* car, not a self-indulgent, Connolly leather bound Italian sports
car. His kids had gone to a *nice* school, not the best and most exclusive school
that money could buy. In other words, in Max's eyes, his reward was in no way
commensurate with his ability.

Then to top it all, one day he had come home early from work to find
the impossibly tanned and handsome gardener, completely at odds with the white
of the living room couch, and the naked, writhing paleness of his wife.

He didn't complain; in all honesty, he had been getting bored with home
life. He didn't contest the divorce, and his wife got half of everything. He didn't
mind that either; he'd hidden the majority of his income from her for years. He
never really saw her again after that and his relationship with his two kids drifted
into a resigned acceptance, and then almost boredom. He rarely spoke to them,
and when they both hit college age, he only really met them at special occasions.
Even then, they only spoke in the stilted code language of related strangers.

Max had moved to a small apartment downtown, which he rarely graced, apart from sleeping and the occasional takeout. But it was here that his true personality began to take hold. Divorce and hard work combined to create a fertile breeding ground, and he inhaled the toxins gladly; greed and resentment, the twin pillars of corporate America.

He kept it well hidden, especially from his employers. A man with a chip on his shoulder is dangerous. A man who feels superior to the people he works for is slightly more dangerous. But the man who feels he has something to prove to himself; he is the most dangerous of all, a viper ready to turn and strike.

Max was always looking for the angle. He didn't see things in black and white; he didn't see things as legal and illegal, he just saw things as opportunities. If he thought he could get away with it, he would exploit those opportunities to the maximum. In his eyes, that is what made him a danger to his employers. He secretly saw himself as superior. To him, it was all about intellectual power, an area where he had always excelled.

He did not realise how focused and ruthless his employers were. Their street smart intelligence trumped his Walter Mitty dreams, and although he didn't know it, he was becoming a liability to himself.

He looked up as the entrance to his office darkened. His eyes flicked back to his watch; it was a quarter to nine, another late-night.

'We're heading home now, Max,' said Jerry, one of his post-grad students.

'Are you coming, or are you going to stay a little longer?' asked Ben, the other one.

Max waved the two of them away.

'No, you guys head home,' he said. 'I've just a couple more things to tidy up and then I'll be off myself.'

As he heard the outer door to the office bang shut, he was unreasonably reminded of ice cream. Then he realised what the ongoing tickle in his mind had been; his two students were called Jerry and Ben; Ben and Jerry. He smirked and then his stomach gave a little rumble. All this thinking about food was making him hungry. He checked his watch again. He had to be nervous as he had already checked it numerous times; it was a quarter to nine.

He slid the photocopied page into the front of the folder. He'd tried to make it look as authentic as possible, or as authentic as a Photostat could. The butterflies in his stomach told him he had done the right thing. Keep hold of the real one for insurance. He took the other folder back to the safe in the corner of his office. He closed it firmly and spun the dial. You could never be too careful.

Ten minutes later, his cab pulled up outside Rudino's Restaurant. He'd picked Rudino's purely because of its association with the Mancini's; hiding in plain sight they called it.

He'd thrown the taxi driver fifty dollars; the man had kept up a steady stream of conversation since he'd got into the cab, but Max hadn't understood a word of it. The drivers face brightened and a broad smile cracked his dark African features. Money talks, thought Max with a smile. Everyone understands the language of cash.

The Maitre D nodded towards Max as he walked through the door; Max was a regular customer, well-known and respected in the area. He gestured toward the corner and got a thumbs-up; his normal table was free.

When he got to the booth, he slid sideways into the seat and immediately busied himself, laying his attaché case beside him before checking his BlackBerry for text and phone messages.

He was so engrossed in what he was doing that it took a polite cough to make him look up. He blinked in surprise, a surprise that was compounded by the head waiter running across the room toward him while trying to disguise it from the other diners.

'Glad to see you are on time,' said the stranger. 'If you remember, punctuality is one of the tenets by which I judge character.'

'I'm terribly sorry Mr Max,' said the head waiter a couple of seconds afterwards, and slightly out of breath from his fast glide across the floor. 'I had quite forgotten that your guest had already arrived.'

'No problem,' said Max distractedly, as he waved the waiter away.

'Do you always stare like that at old acquaintances?' asked the stranger, interrupting his train of thought.

'I'm sorry,' said Max, closing his mouth with a snap. 'It's just I was expecting someone....'

He searched for the appropriate word, before the stranger found it for him.

'Different, maybe? I'll take that as a compliment,' offered the stranger. 'I like being different. Or have I changed that much?'

Max shrugged. The waiter brought the menus over, which they studied in a slightly stilted and awkward silence.

'I'll have the Caesar salad to start,' said the stranger, 'followed by the seafood tagliatelle.'

The waiter nodded his understanding.

'And for Mr Max?' he asked.

'I'll have the bruschetta to start,' said Max, 'followed by the Italian mixed grill.'

'Any drinks or wine?' asked the waiter.

Max flicked a stare at his companion, who declined to comment. Max glanced quickly at the wine list.

'Give me a large bottle of still and a large bottle of sparkling water. And bring me a chilled bottle of the Pinot Grigio, too,' he said.

'An excellent choice, Mr Max,' said the waiter. 'Enjoy your meal.'

'Long time, no see,' said the stranger, as they watched the retreating back.

'I only make contact when it's something good,' responded Max.

'I'll be the judge of that,' said the stranger.

'Have I ever let you down?' asked Max.

'I don't know, have you?' asked the stranger.

Max leant forward across the dimly lit gloom of the corner booth.

'I think you are going to like this,' he said with a smile.

He reached for his attaché case, but was interrupted by the arrival of the first course. They both sat back as the waiter placed their dishes in front of them. Max dribbled some olive oil onto the corner of his plate, and picked up his bruschetta. He dipped and ate methodically, groaning inwardly at the perceived effect the oil would have on his cholesterol. He could hear the crunch and snap, as his companion slowly dispatched the Caesar salad.

'So, what's this amazing thing that has you twirling your Rolodex to my number after fifteen years?' asked the stranger through the last mouthful of salad.

Max laid his plate aside and placed his attaché case in front him on the table. He extricated its sole contents, a black ring binder, which he handed wordlessly across the white tablecloth and then he sat back and waited. He knew it would take a while. The empty plates were collected and the main course was deposited. Max tucked in with gusto. His companion, using a fork with one hand, eagerly digested both the tagliatelle and the black file. The main course went, with espresso and grappa replacing the empty plates.

Eventually, the stranger sat back, grabbed the small shot glass of colourless temptation and knocked it back in one go.

'Where did you get this?' asked the stranger.

'From you, obviously,' answered Max, with a smile.

'Don't try to be smart, it doesn't suit you,' said the stranger.

Max's own expression hardened.

'Let me worry about where it came from,' he said.

'This is a photo copy,' stated the stranger. 'If we do business, it has to be all of the copies.'

'If I get what I want, you'll get what you want,' said Max.

'Your original source?' asked the stranger. 'How can you be sure they don't have a copy?'

'Who are *they*?'

'Yeah, right!' snorted the stranger. 'Like you found this idly discarded in the trash.'

'I am certain of it,' said Max eventually, ignoring the slight. 'They came to me because I have particular talents in this area. They trust me implicitly.'

'Do they?' asked the stranger. 'Well I don't. I need hardly remind you what will happen if you cross me.'

'If I get what I want, then so will you,' repeated Max emphatically.

The stranger nodded, as if making up their mind about something.

'Okay, meet me at the normal place,' said the stranger. 'If you can remember back that far, that is.'

Max smiled; he remembered.

'What time?' he asked.

'Midnight,' said the stranger. 'And you better have all the copies with you.'

Max watched dispassionately as the stranger got up to leave. He waved away the offered money which was wordlessly withdrawn.

'You can reimburse me later,' he said under his breath, to the fast retreating back.

#

The hotel was exactly as he remembered it. The dingy yellowing foyer, the movie posters on the walls, the battered leather sofas next to the old fashioned payphones; it was like a snapshot from his memory. In fact, the only thing that had changed in the last fifteen years was the man behind the desk. He was slightly uneasy at the unfamiliarity, but he needn't have worried. He handed over the plain white envelope with the word *MEETING* written in capitals on the front.

The desk clerk slid the envelope around to face him, read the single word and stared up at him for a minute or so.

'Room six-sixty,' he said unblinkingly.

The familiar sights, sounds and smells of cheap hotels assaulted his eyes and nostrils as he made his way up the rickety stairs. The lifts had never worked, so he was quite out of breath when he made it to the sixth-floor landing. He made a mental note to check out his fitness level. Maybe this time he would last the full year of his gym membership renewal, without letting it lapse.

The light bulb was blown at his end of the corridor which made it seem gloomy and almost sinister. He gave himself a couple of minutes to recover his breath as his eyes became accustomed to the artificial twilight.

As he shuffled past the rooms, counting down the numbers, he could almost visualise what was taking place inside them. The rhythmic banging of a headboard on a flimsy partition wall, the chink of glass on glass, a TV blasting the best of the days sporting highlights, the screams and thumps of flying words and objects; all the facets of human behaviour playing out.

At last, he came to the door in question. He knocked once and then tried the handle. The door was open, but unusually there were no lights on. He stepped quickly into the room, cautious but not overly scared. Suddenly, he heard a click behind him as the lights came on. The room was completely empty.

He whirled around; the only thing his panicked brain could think of was the word *giant,* before a familiar voice spoke to him.

'Hello Max.'

He barely had time to register the blur of movement. He didn't even feel the impact of the cosh on the side of his head, as he slumped to the floor in blissful ignorance.

#

He came around slowly, disoriented at first, but gradually realising that he was lying on his side. He could also feel the cold metallic embrace of the handcuffs that were fastened around his wrists and ankles. As consciousness flooded back, he realised his body was bent backwards around something; a large cube of some kind. There was a chain between the shackles that bound his ankles and his wrists; a chain that maintained the tension in his oddly curved body, making it impossible for him to straighten from the imposed banana shape he was being forced to endure.

As full understanding returned, he realised that as well as contending with the painful bindings, he was in a completely unfamiliar place. It was most likely a warehouse. He could smell the vigorous saltiness of the sea and hear the harsh shrieks of the gulls; probably somewhere on the docks.

'Max, Max, Max,' said a familiar voice.

Max swallowed hard.

'We really don't like our employees stealing from us,' stated Guido simply.

Max gave an involuntary cough, as the boot thudded into his lower abdomen. He lay on the floor, retching and gasping as Guido turned to the man beside him; the not so gentle giant, who would always do his masters bidding.

'Thank you Antonio,' he said. 'You have done very well tonight. I think that will be all.'

'As you wish, Mr Mancini,' replied Antonio.

He dragged two chairs to the centre of the warehouse in front of the prostrate and slowly recovering Max.

Guido and Ernesto sat and watched, as Antonio's retreating footsteps echoed loudly off the empty warehouse walls. They regarded Max with rueful interest, but didn't speak again until they heard the double clang, as the warehouse door was opened and then closed again.

Ernesto tapped the attaché case he was holding.

'These are only the photocopies,' he said. 'You were told to bring the originals.'

Max opened his mouth and screamed as hard as he possibly could. The two old men watched him dispassionately and with a slightly bemused amusement. The fear in his eyes was palpable, as he shrieked and cried until his voice finally cracked; their expressions never wavered.

'Feel better now?' asked Guido.

He got up and kicked Max; a light contact compared to the last one, the mental impact not helped by Guido immediately wiping the toe of his Italian loafer on Max's clothes in distaste.

'Nobody's coming,' he said, as he sat down again. 'So you need to focus and answer our questions.'

'As I was saying,' said Ernesto, continuing the train of the conversation. 'These are only the photocopies. You were told to bring the originals.'

'Go to hell,' responded Max quietly, without any trace of aggression.

It was a simple statement.

'It's such a pity,' said Guido, addressing Ernesto directly, as though Max was no longer in the building. 'He was such a good worker; very useful.'

'Just like any other tool,' Ernesto replied. 'They get blunted and broken with use. You either mend or re-sharpen them or you....'

He left the rest of the sentence blank.

'Still, a pity all the same,' said Guido.

The two men got up heavily and walked around behind Max. He could hear their soft footfalls retreating. From his prone position on the floor, he had to strain his neck to try and see where they were going.

'Please, I can explain,' he started to beg.

The tears were coming in floods, the self pity well and truly engaged.

'Too late, I'm afraid,' Ernesto shouted back sadly. 'Once the worm has turned, he can never go back to his original hole. The time to talk is over.'

'Do you think this is far enough back?' asked Guido. 'It's where Antonio told us to stand.'

'There's only one way to find out,' said Ernesto.

Max heard a click.

The explosion was deafening in the enclosed space. Antonio had wired the hinges of the safe as well as the dial that controlled entry. The simultaneous detonation of the concentrated high explosive at the three points had blown the door clean off.

As the ringing in their ears diminished and the smoke and dust cleared, they could see the door, lying a full thirty feet away from the initial source of detonation. They walked back from their place of concealment, a hastily erected shield of steel plate that Antonio had bolted to a couple of concrete filled oil drums.

The scene resembled a grisly and gruesome butchers shop. Max's torso had taken the full concentrated energy of the explosion. The flying metal square had ripped his chest completely out of the middle of his body. It was missing; just not there anymore.

His disconnected legs twitched and danced in a macabre tango, while the blood poured from the shattered blood vessels like a gruesome fountainhead. They could see the pain etched on his ravaged features, the crushed bones and tattered flesh of his blood soaked rib cage trailing off to nothing.

His heart and lungs had been ripped away, so he could not speak, but the involuntary muscle contractions in his arms made his head and neck jerk like a badly controlled marionette. It seemed to Guido and Ernesto, watching and regarding the spectacle impassively, that this was almost the final insult. No matter whom they were or what they had done, everyone deserved a little bit of dignity in death.

Ernesto removed his personal weapon. It was a small twenty-two calibre pistol; a ladies gun, as Guido often teased him. He fired three shots in quick succession, easing Max on his journey to Hell.

'Now that is quite remarkable,' said Guido, with a hint of wonder. 'Antonio said the structure of the safe would not be compromised, but I wouldn't have believed it, had I not seen it with my own eyes.'

He stepped across the scene with distaste and swivelled his head around; peering into the shadows for the item he wanted. He grunted in satisfaction when he saw it and removed it quickly, so that he could step back and out of the ghoulish tableau. He flicked open the folder, quickly showing Ernesto the lack of grey smear-marks on the paper, consistent with original printing rather than photocopying.

As they walked away, whistling, they failed to see the bloody smear of bones and flesh in the shadows to the right of the safe door. As they clanged the door open and then shut behind them, the cardiac rhythm of the still beating heart got slowly weaker. It pumped the remainder of the blood from within the transected torso into a slowly expanding pool on the floor. Then, the heavily muscled organ seemed to give a sigh and a hiccup, before stalling into rest; almost at the same moment as the second explosion ripped the warehouse apart.

The back draft cremated the heart instantly to ashes.

CHAPTER 20 – NOSTALGIA

14th May 2011 – Four days after the Storm.

Do not dwell in the past, do not dream of the future, concentrate the mind on the present moment. – Budda.

I stretched and yawned. I hadn't bothered to set the alarm; I knew that I couldn't function without sleep, so I'd deliberately let my body recharge itself. Now I felt ready to face anything.

Even though she had been dead a long time, even though her room had been completely redecorated with new carpets, curtains and furniture, I couldn't bring myself to sleep in it. I could actually sense her presence there, a very unsettling, but strangely reassuring feeling.

I looked at my current surroundings and smiled. It was the only room in the house that I hadn't had redecorated. It was a little bit freaky really; exactly as I had left it all those years ago.

I had been a great fan of red; the holy trinity in Cork when it came to sport were Munster rugby club, Cork GAA and Manchester United football club. It was amusing as an adult to rediscover how diligently I had decorated my bedroom. Then I noticed at the bottom of one of the posters scribbled in permanent marker; *Thomas loves Kathleen.* Not all the memories were light-hearted. I threw aside the Manchester United bed sheets and headed into the bathroom.

A shower and a shave later, I was sitting at the kitchen table. The management company had done what I had asked them to do. There was milk, bread, tea, coffee and marmalade, oh, and butter of course; the real stuff, not the fake polyunsaturated crap that you got in America.

As I crunched into the second slice of toast, I started making notes on a small A5 writing pad. I had always been a prolific note taker at school, and for the line of work I was in, it was essential that mistakes were not made. I was rarely specific though. It was surprising what could be written down without giving anyone else a clue what it alluded to, while making sure it contained enough direction to prompt you back into the right train of thought.

I was always orderly and neat. There could be no loose ends in my line of work, as the Mancini's were finding to their cost.

I looked down at the creased and dirty rags that now adorned my body. Thousand dollar suits, especially ruined ones, were not the normal uniform of choice where I would be going. The first item on the list would be a visit to a clothing store.

I stood my phone on its end, and flipped it from top to side to bottom to side as I was thinking. I also really needed to get a positive identification on my lead. The second item on the list would have to be finding somewhere to print the photographs.

I thought about the birth certificate. I really needed to verify whether that was genuine or fake. The third item on the list would therefore have to be getting access to the register of births, marriages and deaths. At least it would tell me for certain if my hunch was correct; whether it really was counterfeit or not.

I thought again about the photographs I needed to print, and the reason I needed to print them. The last item on the list would have to be finding someone who recognised my mystery man. I really needed to generate a name.

As it transpired, I had the first two ticked off by mid-afternoon. I hadn't been clothes shopping in years; all my suits were bespoke personal designs, which were then tailor-made. I found it strangely therapeutic, strolling through clothes shops and finding bargains on the clearance rails.

As I exited the final shop, my arms weighed down with bags, I caught sight of myself in the plate glass window and stopped. I was unrecognisable, even to myself. I was glad in a way; it would make it much harder for my adversaries to track me down. I was glad too at how easy it had been to slip back into my Irish persona. But I was also a little sad. The person that I'd been in America, even though it had been a shallow masquerade, carefully constructed over a period of twenty years, was gone forever.

The second item on my list had been easier still. I'd slipped the memory card out of my phone and taken it to the local supermarket. They had a machine for printing photographs; I even managed to get the large size prints.

The third item gave me pause for consideration. There were a number of uncertainties in my mind. I was inclined to just walk in and ask for a copy of the certificate. I had my passport with me, which contained my full name; the name that had been used on the potentially fake document. I had imprinted the date of birth and the hospital; committed them to memory on that fateful stormy night, before the sodden paper had dissolved into a mush of pulp in my hands. It was these three pieces of information that I would need.

However, there were two nagging fears in the back of my mind.

The first was that whoever had faked the certificate had access to the original official blank documents. Granted, they may have been forgeries, but with my experience of criminality, it was generally easier to bribe than to forge.

My other worry was that whoever had faked the certificate had gone to great lengths. It was part of a hugely elaborate sting, not a schoolboy prank.

So I was torn; torn between the need to know, while also being wary of giving myself away. In the end, bravery won the day; I reasoned it might get me noticed by whoever had set up the whole complex operation, but I badly needed a lead and could take care of myself.

As I walked towards the office in Adelaide Street, I marvelled again at my new persona. I was about as far removed from my old self as it was possible to get.

I entered the office and took my ticket in line, and marvelled again at the beautiful idiosyncrasies within the Irish public service.

It took over an hour of fruitless waiting for my name, or rather my number to be called. I was not nervous; I was more interested to see what their reaction would be. They could find no record of the birth, even though they were thorough in their search, and if I was looking for the remotest sign of interest in me, I was sorely disappointed.

Even when they could find no entries, they didn't even raise an eyebrow at my spur of the moment excuse for confusing my child's birthplace; that I must have got muddled. I told them that we'd moved around as a family between Dublin and Cork, and that half the kids had been born in the capital. They seemed to accept this explanation without question.

As I walked out of the office, I felt vaguely disappointed. I was no further along in my quest, and then I thought, hold on a second, maybe I am. I knew for certain that the certificate was a forgery, which meant that I also knew that it wasn't the Mancini's who had set me up. They wouldn't bother to send two people to kill me, when one would adequately do the job.

If that was the case, then I had other adversaries.

This came as quite a shock to me. Don't get me wrong, when you're on the wrong side of the law, you tend to make a lot of enemies, but for me, they were generally on behalf of someone else.

A lot of people had cursed and sworn vengeance as I'd *educated* them. Strangely enough though, it was never directed against me personally; always my employers. It was a puzzle and no mistake, and it made identifying my mystery man even more critical. He would definitely lead me to the heart of the spider's web.

I walked home to let the fresh air clear my head. I had eliminated three out of my four tasks for the day. That was ordinarily a good return from my to-do list. But I was going for one hundred percent.

One of the items I bought on my way home was a Street map. Even though I had lived my entire juvenile life in Cork city, I was now like a stranger; a tourist. Fragments were coming back, but that was all they were; small dimly remembered shards.

As I sipped the cup of tea at my table at home, I pondered my last task. I was fairly certain that my mystery man was from Cork, and on the wrong side of the law. I needed to start thinking like a policeman. If I was looking for criminality, or a specific criminal, where would I start? How would I break-in to that circle, especially in an unfamiliar city? I applied that logic to my own background, and then it hit me; the world's oldest profession.

Vice, prostitution, call it what you like, but there was a red light district in every major city in the world. Wherever there was a red light district, there was criminal activity. Wherever there was criminal activity, there were criminals. And wherever there were criminals, there were specific individuals who could be persuaded to part with information. My only problem; I had no idea where the Cork City red light district was.

Again, using my newfound detective mentality, I pulled up a web search on my phone. I typed in *Cork red light district* and hit enter. The first link that came up gave me an address; it couldn't be that simple, could it? I went back to my map and cross referenced the links on the web to actual streets. Pretty soon, I had an area staked out. With a good sense of direction, even with my sketchily returning street memory, I would easily be able to find this place in the dark.

I walked up the stairs to bed and set my alarm for one am; I would need all my wits about me. If I was tired, I would be unprepared; after five hours sleep, I would be able to do almost anything.

#

I wandered down the street, feeling a twinge of nostalgia. Don't get me wrong, I knew from that very first day that my chosen profession was criminal. I was not floating on some flowery cloud of self-deception. My first assignment had been protection; not as in protection racket, but protection of the merchandise.

I never saw it that way. I never saw the girls as merchandise, as objects. I always saw them as people. Observing the way the other guys, the other protectors, behaved, with their brutality and forcefulness, I always thought of my mum. I remembered the lecture she'd constantly given me on the proper treatment of girls and ladies, so I always treated the girls with the utmost respect. They in turn, respected me and in fact, it came to the point where I wasn't protecting an item or an object, I was protecting a friend and a colleague. It was a method of protection that got results. I started to get noticed.

I didn't judge what they did, and they didn't judge what I did, but by god, if anyone messed with one of my girls, there was hell to pay. It was where I leaned what I later termed, *detached ferocity*; my emotions were never linked to my actions. I had already separated them and bundled them into violence.

If I thought dispassionately that someone deserved a beating, then that is exactly what they would get. Word spread quickly about this strange, quirky Irish guy who didn't take any shit, but who behaved like a gentleman. Pretty soon, girls from other districts and other territories moved over to my patch. The results brought me to prominence, but I never forgot that first lesson. No matter how deep you are in the quagmire of criminality, you have to have some standards. There has to be a line you do not cross, and if you treat people with respect, you can do anything.

I chuckled to myself. The accents were different and so were the fashions, but other than that, the environment just seemed so familiar. I stood on a corner and waited for the inevitable approach. Less than a minute later, a girl teetered over to me on almost impossibly high heels.

'Are you looking for some company, love?' she asked, fluttering her false eyelashes in my direction.

'No, but I am looking for him,' I said, showing her the picture, which I had carefully cropped to exclude the excesses of his death.

'Took a bit of a beating, did he?' she asked.

'You could say that,' I said, trying to keep a straight face.

'What is he, your brother or something?'

'My cousin,' I lied.

'Sorry love, never seen him before in my life.'

I watched her face carefully as she answered me. She was telling the truth.

'Sure I can't tempt you?' she asked slyly. 'You're very cute.'

I smiled.

'No I'm not, but thanks all the same.'

Moving further down the street, I couldn't help noticing how the girls began to look classier; better dressed or groomed, maybe? I couldn't put my finger on it. I was in the shadow of Connolly Hall, and it made me smile to think that a bastion of the working man was utilised during the night by working girls.

I struck out six or seven more times and was just about to move to my next identified location, when I was approached again. I noticed the slightly lower heels, the style and cut of her clothes, even the way she talked; this girl had much more....

I struggled to find the right word for a minute, and then one popped into my head; *decorum*.

That was definitely the right word; decorum.

She had more charm and poise than the other girls I'd encountered that night.

'You look lonely,' she stated in a voice like honey. 'Would you like some company?'

'No,' I said. 'But I would like to find this guy?'

She took the picture and studied it. If I hadn't been watching her intently, I would have missed it, but there was the merest flicker of recognition, before she masked it with her cleverly constructed charm.

'Sorry,' she replied, 'but I can't help you.'

'I think you can,' I said, making her blink in surprise.

'I told you,' she said, with a trace of annoyance in her voice. 'I can't help you. Now leave me alone.'

'I don't believe you,' I responded flatly.

Her mouth dropped open. She wasn't used to the punters talking back to her, obviously.

She inclined her head slightly, and I felt rather than saw the dark shape detach itself from the shadows of the building behind me. I turned and he stepped around to face me. He was a very large man, and I detected a trace of an eastern European accent as he addressed me.

'I believe you are bothering this young lady,' he growled.

The menace in his voice was unmistakable.

'I'm not bothering anybody,' I said evenly, smiling at him.

He telegraphed the punch from a mile away. My eyes never left his as I deflected the intended blow to one side, putting him off-balance for a second.

'I really wouldn't do that again,' I said pleasantly.

If anything, the retaliatory fist was signalled from even further away this time. Using the impetus of his forward movement, I deflected his forearm again, this time with a bit more snap, so he spun around unsteadily with his back to me. I inserted two fingers into the open gap between his neck and his collar and pulled smartly backwards. He fell awkwardly onto his backside with a crunch, prompting an involuntary giggle from the girl, which didn't help my cause.

This time when he got up, there was a new purpose in his eyes and a switchblade in his hand.

'Not so tough now, are you,' he said, waving it around in front of him.

'We'll see,' I responded, matter-of-factly.

Too late for him, I saw a shadow of doubt flitter across his face as he lunged towards me. I had anticipated nothing less and stepped forward to meet him. He was not expecting it and tensed up. I parried the knife hand easily and with the same arm, moved it up around his neck. At the same instant I pulled my right leg back, sweeping his leg from under him as I used the elbow around his neck to throw him towards the ground.

He landed so hard that I heard the concrete paving slab crack, or maybe it was his back, I couldn't be sure. The knife clattered harmlessly to one side. He turned his head toward me, his eyes misting with pain as I picked up the knife and hefted it in my hand.

'Nice weapon,' I said conversationally. 'Good balance to it.'

I threw it into the air suddenly, the blade glinting in the soft amber glow of the streetlights. It seemed to arc and tumble in slow motion. I caught it cleanly by the handle and jammed it deep into his throat, right up to the hilt, in one fluid motion.

I stood up and brushed myself down.

'He won't give you any more trouble,' I said to the incredulous girl, as the man scrabbled weekly with his fingers to try and extract the knife.

It was like watching a fish out of water. The gurgling cough got weaker and the thrashing of his limbs and torso became ever so slightly less energetic with each passing minute until all movement and sound ceased. I stooped to check his pulse; nothing. I turned back to the girl.

'Now, where were we?' I asked pleasantly. 'Oh yes, this man; tell me who he is please?'

I handed her the photograph again. She looked at me, this time with real fear in her eyes.

'They'll kill me,' she whispered.

'And you think I won't?'

I was lying of course, but she didn't know that. I indicated the body on the floor and she shuddered. I almost felt sorry for her before I heard footsteps behind me and turned quickly. As he skidded to a halt, his incredulous gaze took in the scene.

'What the fuck?' he said forcefully and I could see the rage in his eyes.

'You bastard!' he shouted, throwing himself at me.

Bad move. I easily sidestepped and caught him on the side of the head as he went sailing past. Palm strike; much more effective than a punch. He was unconscious before he hit the ground. I might even have killed him; I wasn't exactly sure how much power I had put into the blow.

I turned back to the girl, realising that I'd made my first mistake of the evening. I saw the vaguest flash in my peripheral vision and a shape rounded the corner. I looked down at the discarded heels; clever girl.

I broke into a run and skidded through the junction, trying desperately to keep my feet as I turned into the curve. I saw her about fifteen yards ahead. If she had kept her head down she would have got away, but she turned and caught sight of me.

Whatever happened, she seemed to momentarily slow down or freeze. She wasn't looking where she was going and her bare toes seemed to connect with an uneven part of the pavement. I was gaining with every stride, and as she tumbled, I hit her from behind with a rugby tackle, pulling her to the floor as gently as I could.

As I lay there on top of her, I could feel the soft feminine curves beneath the flimsy material of her dress, and for a second I felt a wave of desire. It had been a long time since I'd benefited from a liaison with a member of the opposite sex. She must have sensed this, because she grabbed my head and pulled it down, kissing me savagely, almost frantically, as she guided my other hand under her blouse.

As my fingers closed around her breast, and I felt the nipple harden through the silk of her bra, the small sensible area at the back of my brain, the one that had kept me alive for twenty years, hauled me back to reality.

I removed my hand and made to get up, but she tried ever more ferociously to keep me down.

'I'll be good to you,' she whispered huskily, trying to convey sexy with the rest of her body, her frightened eyes giving her away.

'I won't hurt you,' I said softly. 'I just need to find out who this man is. It's very important.'

She looked at me directly for a long time, her eyes scanning my face implacably from her prone position. Eventually she broke the silence.

'You might not hurt me,' she said resignedly, brushing herself down. 'But they certainly will,' she said, indicating the corner she had just run around.

'They won't hurt you, I promise,' I said. 'You've seen what I can do. I guarantee they will not touch you.'

She got slowly to her feet. I could not interpret what was hidden behind her expression and for some reason I desperately wanted to be able to do so.

'Do you trust me?' I asked.

She thought about it for a few seconds and then nodded.

'Scott Mitchell,' she answered eventually. 'He was a drug mule; used to supply the working girls with anything they wanted.'

I secretly rejoiced. At last I had a definitive lead.

'But you need to be careful,' she said. 'He works for Black Swan; when he finds out what you've done....'

She left the sentence hanging.

'Thank you,' I said softly and genuinely.

'What did he do to you?' she asked, her hand gently brushing my cheek.

'They won't hurt you,' I repeated, ignoring her question. 'I chased you; I tried to rape you. Before I could get too far, we were disturbed by the police.'

I ripped her blouse open suddenly, making her jump. For some reason, the sight of her bra made me feel light headed for a second.

'I truly am sorry,' I said with a sad smile.

She smiled back, the fear diminishing in her eyes. Mercifully, she didn't see the strike to the neck with the edge of my hand; she just collapsed onto the floor with a sigh. I stayed with her, dialling the emergency services.

'There's been an attack, back of Connolly Hall, a girl is unconscious,' I shouted into the phone.

I waited until the last possible moment; until the sirens were inches from the corner, and then ducked behind a car.

The squad car and ambulance skidded to a halt, and it was only when I heard them working on the girl that I was satisfied. At least she was safe; bruises would heal.

I melted into the shadows of the night.

CHAPTER 21 – SOOTHSAYER

15th May 2011 – Five days after the Storm.

Men may know many things by seeing; but no prophet can see before the event, nor what end waits for him. – Sophocles.

'I don't know why I'm doing this,' squawked Dodds voice into his ear. 'I'm only a couple of years away from retirement; I don't need this kind of crap.'

Dale blinked, as awareness slowly returned. He was in bed and by the look of the time, he had gotten about fourteen hours of unbroken sleep. Amazing how something so simple could make you feel so good. He tried to rub the sleep out of his eyes, as his brain struggled to catch up. He held the receiver a little closer to his ear.

'Hold on a second, Dodds,' he responded slowly. 'Give me a bit of time to wake up. What are you talking about?'

'It's in light of your *conversation* with the special agent in charge last night,' said Dodds. 'Regardless of what I believed, I said to myself, just drop it; he'll come back after two weeks of vacation refreshed, invigorated and ready to concentrate on his next obsession.'

He paused for a second for breath.

'So, imagine my surprise, when I'm talking to one of the vice guys; Gerry, you know Gerry? He has the three kids and almost got the divorce last year.'

Dale grunted.

'Yeah, that Gerry,' said Dodds.

'What about him?' asked Dale.

'So, Gerry says to me; did you hear about the explosion last night? No, says I. Well get this, he says, as he pours me a coffee; apparently, one of the Mancini's warehouses was blown up last night. Down on the docks, by the East River.'

'When was this?' asked Dale, sitting bolt upright in bed.

'It was no gas explosion either,' continued Dodds, either ignoring or not hearing the question. 'Preliminary finding from the forensic boys is that a large quantity of high explosive was used, and what's more there's a victim,' he finished triumphantly.

'No ID and they couldn't tell Gerry whether the John Doe was killed pre or post explosion, but all the same, I said to myself, this is very coincidental, *especially* in light of my partner's assertion to the boss yesterday. So against my better judgement, I rang you.'

Dale had been feverishly getting dressed, but as he slipped his jumper on, he sank heavily back onto the bed.

'Thanks for the info, Dodds,' he said, 'but it doesn't really mean anything. I need something more than this.'

'Jesus, Dale,' said Dodds sharply. 'Am I the only one in this partnership doing any thinking? What happened to the gung-ho, totally committed special agent I was talking to last night; the one who put his career on the line for a hunch.'

'What do you mean?'

'What I mean is this,' said Dodds. 'I am a great believer in signs; always have been. This is a sign. At the end of our interview with Sam, you took down the names of his two buddies, the waiter/kitchen porter types, didn't you?'

Dale nodded vigorously, even though Dodds couldn't see him.

'Franco Totti and Mario Massa,' he recalled from memory. 'It's all in the report.'

'Well then,' said Dodds. 'We go down there, ruffle their feathers a little bit, and see how many of the downy little bastards fall out.'

'You'd do that?' asked Dale in astonishment.

'Don't sound so shocked,' said Dodds. 'Believe it or not, I can be a conscientious law enforcement officer occasionally.'

Dale laughed.

'You'd better be ready to go,' said Dodds.

'Why?' asked Dale, as he slipped his shoes on.

'Because I'm sitting outside your apartment in the car with the engine running,' said Dodds, 'and I hate wasting gas.'

#

'Have you ever eaten in this place Rudino's?' asked Dale.

'I have actually,' said Dodds. 'I used to take my daughter there a lot, especially when she was younger. She just loved Italian food.'

Dodds looked across at Dale and laughed at his expression.

'You really need to get out more Dale,' said Dodds. 'Just because my kid used to like pizza, you automatically think I'm connected.' he said.

He started laughing until the tears were streaming down his face.

'It's not that funny,' protested Dale, inwardly breathing a huge sigh of relief.

He knew Dodds was not connected; he was just glad he hadn't taken offence. He needed to be very careful with the relationships he had. His sense of isolation and paranoia was beginning to dominate his life. He needed to wrestle control back again.

'So what's our in?' he asked, as Dodds managed to stem the guffaws.

'Oh you are too funny,' said Dodds, wiping his eyes with the back of his hand.

'Glad I can provide some amusement for you,' said Dale, stony faced.

'Lighten up, Dale,' said Dodds. 'Anyway, I was thinking about our in, as you put it. I took these out of evidence this morning.'

He slipped something from his inside suit pocket. Dale could see that it was a small plastic bag full of white pills.

'We'll play it softly-softly,' stated Dodds. 'We got an anonymous tip-off that someone employed in the restaurant was storing or handling drugs. We just want to talk to the two gentlemen, so that we can clear up any misunderstandings.'

'So, softly-softly,' said Dale. 'Show our ID badges, shake the tree a little and see what falls out?'

'Now you've got it,' said Dodds. 'Hopefully a good shake will dislodge some nice rotten fruit.'

Five minutes later, they arrived at their destination. Dale waited on the pavement outside, as Dodds parked the car. He peered over the dark red drapes that were hung at eye level inside the plate glass windows. It looked like any other restaurant. He wondered what secrets and lies lay hidden behind the heavy velvet curtains.

Dodds tapped him on the shoulder and the two of them entered in single file.

'Can I help you, gentlemen?' asked the head waiter.

'I certainly hope so,' said Dodds pleasantly, showing the head waiter his federal credentials.

The man took them and studied them closely; maybe a little bit too closely for Dale's liking. It was definitely not the first time the head waiter had studied law enforcement ID. He clicked his fingers in Dale's direction, like he was directing a servant. Dale handed over his own credentials, secretly seething.

'So, what exactly does the DEA want with us?' asked the head waiter.

'We had an anonymous tip off,' said Dodds. 'One or two of your restaurant employees are handling or harbouring drugs. We were in the area and we are just so conscientious....'

Here he winked at Dale.

'....so, we just had to come down on our lunch break and check it out.'

'And of course, you have a warrant for this,' said the head waiter pleasantly, with an odious smile fixed on his face.

'We thought we would do this on an informal basis,' said Dale.

'Nice try, gentleman,' said the head waiter, 'but I think I'll bid you good afternoon.'

He opened the door politely and indicated they should leave.

Dodds made no move; indeed made no sign to indicate he had even heard the waiter.

'We could leave now,' agreed Dodds. 'We could go and get a warrant,' he continued, 'but I think if we were forced to do that, then we would make that warrant as open-ended as we possibly could.'

'We would then come down here with an army of law enforcement officials,' continued Dale, 'both local and federal. We would shut this place down and then dismantle it brick by brick; tile by tile. When we were finished with that, we would then hand it over to the NYC department of health on suspected hygiene and food handling issues and let's not beat about the bush here,' he finished flatly. 'They would close you down.'

The head waiter looked from Dodds to Dale and back again with a pained expression.

'Are you threatening me?' he asked carefully.

'I would hate to use the word *threaten* in this case,' said Dodds with a smile. 'That gives it such a negative connotation. I think *giving options* would be a much more positive way to look at the situation.'

Dodds smile hardened.

'Now where are Franco and Mario?' he asked.

'Through the double doors at the back,' said the head waiter sullenly. 'Turn to the left and you can't miss them; they are both on duty today, you're lucky.'

'That wasn't so difficult now, was it?' said Dodds sweetly, patting him on the shoulder.

As they walked toward the doors, Dale heard a muttering behind him. In some ways, he wished he knew Italian better, but in other ways, he was probably better off that he didn't. In fact, he was concentrating maybe just a little too much on trying to make out what was being said. He looked forward, just in time to prevent one of the swing doors whacking him in the face. He hurried his pace to keep up with Dodds.

He entered the kitchen; his partner was already talking to a pizza chef, who was kneading balls of dough, as he listened distractedly to what Dodds was asking. When some ID was flashed, the pizza chef reluctantly looked up.

'Franco and Mario, where are they?' Dodds inquired.

'What have those idiots done now?' asked the pizza chef truculently, and then brusquely nodded over his shoulder.

Both Dale and Dodds followed the direction of his nod. Two young guys were heatedly arguing in Italian.

'Mario and Franco?' asked Dale, as they approached the two men.

'Who wants to know?' responded one.

Dale handed over his ID card; it was getting a lot of use that day.

'What does the DEA want with us?' asked the other.

'Are you Franco or Mario?' asked Dodds.

'I'm Franco, and he's Mario,' the guy replied. 'So what does the DEA want with us?' he repeated.

'Well Franco,' said Dodds, as Dale watched the furtive exchange of glances between the two men. 'We've had a tipoff; seems that you and your buddy Mario here have been slightly naughty boys.'

'And just who might that source be?' asked Mario with some bravado; spoiling the effect by licking his lips nervously a second later.

'We don't care who it is; that's why they call it anonymous. It shouldn't matter to you guys either. The point is, we are trying to establish whether the information is true or not,' said Dale.

'Enough of this crap,' said Dodds.

He glanced around the room.

'Which ones are your lockers?' he asked, pointing to the steel cabinets in the corner.

Mario walked over and pointed out two of them, which helpfully stated *Franco* and *Mario* on the front, in stylised black and white writing. Dodds flicked the first one open with a ballpoint pen and proceeded to search it thoroughly with one latex gloved hand.

'Well-well,' he said, his hand coming out holding a plastic bag full of white pills. 'What have we here?'

Dodds closed the locker slowly, so he could read the name on the front.

'Franco,' he said. 'It seems our informant was right.'

Franco looked flabbergasted.

'I have no idea how they got there,' he said. 'I've never seen them before in my life.'

'Are you accusing me of planting them?' asked Dodds, his face hardening into a scowl.

'No-no,' replied Franco hastily. 'But someone is definitely trying to set me up.'

'You wouldn't believe how often we've heard that one,' said Dale. 'Looks like you are going to have to accompany us back to the office.'

'Hold on a second,' said Franco. 'Let's not do anything hasty.'

Mario shot him a warning look, which he chose to ignore.

'I'm sure we can come to an arrangement,' he said.

He searched for an alternate phrase.

'Smooth over this problem,' he added finally.

'Are you trying to bribe a federal officer?' asked Dodds.

'No-no, not at all,' said Franco quickly. 'Just merely enquiring if there was any other way we could come to a mutual understanding.'

Dale looked at Dodds, who nodded. It was time to up the ante a little bit.

'What do you know about Storm?' asked Dale.

Neither answered, but he caught the flashed look between them and recognised it for what it was; anxiety and a little guilt in equal measure.

Franco looked at them levelly for a couple of minutes and then seemed to make a decision.

'Okay,' he replied finally. 'I'll tell you what I know.'

'Shut up, Franco,' said Mario. 'They'll look after us, you know they will.'

'Who will?' asked Dale with interest.

'It's not your locker they found the stuff in,' said Franco, with eyes only for Mario. 'Someone's trying to stitch me up. How do I know it's not them?'

'You're making a big mistake, Franco,' stated Mario.

He made as if to leave.

'You ain't going anywhere,' said Dodds, barring his way. Dale pulled over some chairs and the four of them sat in a huddle, like alcoholics at an AA meeting.

'Look, I'll tell you what I know,' repeated Franco. 'It ain't much, I'm warning you now. Most of this stuff is just rumours and conjecture; titbits that we pick up from some of the jobs we do.'

Mario shot him a warning glance.

Franco threw up his hands.

'Hey, I'm just being honest here,' he added.

'Go on,' said Dale, anxious not to break Franco's train of thought.

'How do you guys know about Storm?' asked Franco suddenly. 'Was it from your mysterious snitch?'

'Him, among others,' said Dale. 'I have my sources.'

'It seems to be working then,' said Franco with a smile.

'What does?' asked Dale.

'We were told Storm was a new drug,' said Franco. 'We were told to get the word out on the street that *Storm* was coming.'

'Were you given a timescale?' asked Dale. 'Were you told any details; what type of drug it was maybe?'

'No, nothing that specific,' said Mario, joining in. 'Just that a new drug was going to hit the streets. It was going to blow everything else away.'

'We *were* told something,' said Franco suddenly. 'We were told that with this drug there was no risk. They even wanted us to use a particular slogan; *all the highs with none of the lows.* I thought it was kind of catchy.'

'Did you believe it?' asked Dale.

Franco thought about it for a second.

'I'd no reason not to believe it,' he said.

'So, Storm is a drug,' said Dale, almost to himself. 'We've no idea of the timescale; do we know where it's coming from even?'

'No,' said Mario. 'We were just told it was coming.'

'So, anything else?' asked Dodds.

'On Storm, no,' said Franco. 'But there is one other piece of information you might be interested in.'

'Go on,' said Dale.

'Well, two pieces of information really,' stated Franco, correcting himself.

'We're waiting,' said Dodds, nodding impatiently.

'I heard the first piece this morning,' said Franco. 'Apparently an East River warehouse was blown up. Everyone knows who it belongs to of course, but the speculation on the street is focusing on the motive.'

'How so?' asked Dodds.

'Did they destroy it themselves; covering their tracks if you will, or is there some sort of feud or vendetta starting against them?'

Dale and Dodds looked at each other. Dodds raised his eyebrows and Dale nodded, but neither of them spoke.

'The other thing I heard about two or three days ago,' said Franco. 'According to the rumour, someone has gone missing; someone very high up in their organisation.'

'Can you stop talking in riddles,' said Dodds in exasperation.

Franco shot him a look.

'This may be off the record,' he responded slowly, 'but I ain't incriminating myself to no one.'

He waited to see if he would be interrupted again, before continuing.

'All I can give you is a name.'

Franco paused and then corrected himself.

'No, in fact, all I *will* give you is a name.'

'We don't even know if this guy exists,' said Mario, directing himself to Franco. 'The guy is an urban myth; a ghost.'

Franco looked hard at Mario, who shrugged and backed down.

'It's your funeral,' he said.

'The name is *The Street*, sometimes shortened to *Street*,' said Franco. 'He's rumoured to be their top *internal security* man, if you get my drift?'

'Is that it?' asked Dale. 'Is that all I get?'

'Like I said,' stated Franco, ignoring the outburst, 'that's all I know. How you choose to use that information is up to you.'

He turned back to Dodds.

'Are we cool now?' he asked.

Dodds looked at him for a second.

'Yeah, we're cool,' he said at last. 'But look at it this way; we now know who you both are and where you are hiding. My advice would be to keep your noses clean and out of trouble.'

Franco indicated the bag of pills in Dodds hand.

'Any chance I can get my property back?' he asked with a straight face.

'Nice try,' snorted Dodds.

He got up and slipped the bag into his inside jacket pocket.

'It's been a pleasure doing business with you guys,' he said with a smile.

#

Dale sat at his desk. He looked slightly depressed.

'So, we're no further along really are we?' he asked morosely.

'At least your hunches are confirmed,' said Dodds. 'You should be happy about that; those were some intuitive leaps of faith you made there.'

'But they rejected the whole scenario before,' responded Dale. 'The special agent in charge laughed at me, remember? Just because a couple of self serving kitchen porters rubberstamped it, I don't think it's going to make a whole hell of a difference to my case.'

Dodds threw him a Twinkie across the desk.

'Well shit, Dale,' he said. 'I wasn't promising anything concrete. I just thought it was a lead you might like to follow-up on, that's all.'

'Hey, I'm sorry,' said Dale. 'I appreciate it, I really do.'

A thought suddenly struck him.

'Anyway, there is that other stuff they told us, isn't there? The one piece of info that we didn't know before.'

Dodds clicked his fingers.

'Yeah, you're right,' he said. 'What was his name again?'

Dale closed his eyes and massaged his temples as he concentrated.

'I should have written this stuff down,' added Dodds. 'I'm not a rookie after all.'

'They wouldn't have disclosed everything they did if we were recording it in any way,' said Dale.

'You may be right,' replied Dodds.

'The name was *Street*,' said Dale eventually. 'They said the name was *The Street*.'

'Well, look it up then,' said Dodds through a mouthful of Twinkie.

Information technology was one of the areas where Dale truly excelled. He signed on to the federal portal. It was a reporting interface; he had been one of the volunteers to test and develop it. You could query and cross reference any of the federal databases with simple searches. He typed in *Street*, because he knew the search would strip words like *the* from the sentence.

After two pages of fruitless searching, he realised it was probably going to be a little more difficult than he had first anticipated. All that was returned from his search was a list of federal agency locations.

'All it's giving me are addresses,' said Dale morosely.

He sat back in his chair with his hands behind his head.

'Yeah, you need another word to give it context,' replied Dodds.

Dale shot him a look of surprise.

'I may be old, but I'm not completely stupid,' said Dodds.

He thought for a second.

'It's just that the word escapes me for a second. What was that show? It was a cowboy show; late sixties or early seventies.'

Dale looked at him blankly.

'Smith and Jones,' responded Dodds at last. 'Alias Smith and Jones.'

'Of course,' said Dale, slapping his head. 'Alias; why didn't I think of that?'

The word prompted another phrase into his memory; a.k.a, also known as. He typed *alias Street a.k.a.* and then hit the return key. As Dodds watched, he sat forward intently.

'Maybe not an urban myth after all,' added Dale.

'So he is real,' said Dodds.

'According to this,' said Dale, 'not only is he real, but he is extremely dangerous; a known associative of guess who?'

'The Mancini's maybe?' offered Dodds.

'Dead on the money,' said Dale.

'Anything more?' asked Dodds.

Dale scrolled through the lines.

'This guy is positively Teflon,' he said. 'Suspected of homicide; suspected of double homicide; suspected of racketeering; suspected of another homicide.'

He kept scrolling down.

'Jesus, this guy has killed more people than I have friends,' he said; and then he stopped and stared for a while.

'What?' asked Dodds impatiently.

Dale picked up his airline tickets; the envelope had been dropped into the office about an hour previously. He tapped them thoughtfully on the back of his hand. At the end of the database, one phrase stood out in flashing green; *real name Thomas Eugene O'Neill.* There was no address entered in the birthplace section, just a city and country, but as he absorbed the impact of those two words, it appeared to him that all roads seemed to be leading to Cork.

'Looks like I'll be taking those two weeks of vacation after all; just like the boss suggested,' he said thoughtfully.

CHAPTER 22 – DIVERSION

14th May 2011 – Four days after the Storm.

A man is hindered and distracted in proportion as he draws outward things to himself. –
Thomas à Kempis.

Roussel sat back in his chair and regarded the whiteboard on the wall of his office. It had been an exceptionally frustrating three days, not least because neither of the victims appeared to be local.

If there was one thing about the southern states that still annoyed him, it was that politics and law enforcement were still very parochial.

Ordinarily in a homicide, the captain would come under ruthless pressure from both the mayor and the local council, but this case was different. This was just two out-of-towners killing each other; an annoying loose end rather than a vote-loser or vote-getter.

He went back through the events chronologically, scanning the board thoughtfully to make sure he had made no mistakes.

The coroner had been as good as his word. He had autopsied both bodies that same morning, with the results sitting in a file on Roussel's desk by mid afternoon. Victim number one had died, as suspected, of a single gunshot wound to the head. DNA and blood samples had been taken. There had been no matches to any of the locally stored files, so the coroner had sent them off for comparison with the major federal databases on Roussel's behalf.

Victim number two was also confirmed to have died of a single gunshot wound to the head. The complicating issue in that particular case for Roussel was the injury to the wrist. It was impossible for Guilbeau to tell him whether the injury was pre or post-mortem. At this stage, he was going on the assumption that it was some type of punishment shooting, for no other reason than he could not work out what else it could be.

The lead he'd picked up himself, the pattern of strange tyre marks, yielded as little satisfaction as the coroner's findings had. All of his colleagues, including the captain, had agreed with his deduction of erratic driving to explain the differences in the tracks, but he'd had less luck with the maker of the tyre. Pirelli fitted their P series tyres to so many makes and models of cars, most of them non-American, that it was impossible to narrow down the search.

Strangest of all was the house. They had done a full and comprehensive sweep of the building and grounds; Roussel himself had co-ordinated it. He knew that no shortcuts had been taken, because he knew the house like no one else. It was as thorough a search as he had ever been involved in, but they had found nothing. He smiled humourlessly to himself, especially when he saw the word in capitals and double underlined on his board; *nothing.*

They had found lots of furniture. They had found suits, clothes, underwear, consumer electronics, but arranged as you would find in a show property. There was not one shred of personal information in the house. No bills, no photographs, no driving licences, credit cards or passports. No books, no magazines, no recent history of any kind. But there was one thing that had surprised and shocked Roussel the most. Any vaguely personalised items attached to the house, seemed to be derived from his family's belongings, some of which were still dotted occasionally amongst the more modern furniture and bric-a-brac.

The forensic technicians had gone through the place with a fine tooth comb. They'd found five sets of prints in the house. It had been a difficult conversation to have with the chief.

Captain Moreland had listened in stony silence, as Roussel had detailed four of the five sets they would find, including his own.

In fairness, the captain had been more annoyed that Roussel had not told him at the start of the investigation. He hadn't cared that Roussel had a personal tie with the house, he'd been more pissed off that Roussel had felt he couldn't confide in him.

However, the captain was not a man to hold grudges or stay annoyed for long, and at least it meant they could eliminate Roussel, his parents, and Jeremiah Bell, the second owner of Augustine Mansion, from their enquiries.

Then, just when all appeared to be heading for a dead end, he seemed to get the breakthrough he was looking for. The last unidentified set of prints did not match the two victims. Whoever owned the house had not died violently that night. They'd also got a hit from one of the two DNA and blood matched samples they'd sent for evaluation against the federal databases.

He'd been excited as he'd driven into the office that day. He'd opened the envelope like a child at Christmas. The slip of paper told him only two things. Firstly, he was able to identify the sample from the information provided as that belonging to victim number two. Secondly and more importantly, it informed him in large black letters that it was from a *restricted federal database; authorisation required.* He'd thrown them on the floor in anger and had then passed them on to the captain in frustration. He'd been fruitlessly waiting ever since.

He'd also been trying to track down the ownership of the house. He had exhausted all the solicitors, banks and financial institutions, both in the town and the wider locality. He tipped himself forward and thumped the desk in frustration; nothing but dead ends.

There was a discrete knock on the door and then it opened without him saying anything. It had to be the captain; nobody else came into his office like that.

'Got a couple?' asked the captain, parking his backside against the window-sill.

'Sure boss, what's up?' asked Roussel in turn.

'That stuff you asked me to follow up on,' replied the captain shortly. 'You ain't gonna like the answer.'

'I take it that's a no then,' said Roussel resignedly.

'I don't understand it,' said the captain with genuine bemusement. 'This has not happened to me in twenty years of law enforcement. A request to the Feds! Hell, this type of thing doesn't happen in a town like ours.'

He paused.

'Not only was I told to lay-off, but I got a personal call from the CIA, detailing the effect it would have on my career if I decided to continue with my line of investigation.'

Roussel looked at the captain, his jaw dropping.

'The CIA: Jesus, Captain, what happened here? None of this makes any sense.'

'If the CIA is involved, all I can tell you is that it is way out of our jurisdiction,' said the captain. 'I must say it does piss me off, these arseholes telling us to back off. They think we're just a bunch of good ole boys, only useful for traffic tickets and parking violations.'

'We just need one break,' stated Roussel thoughtfully.

'Good luck,' said the captain, patting his shoulder as he made to leave.

'So you're not asking me to give up, Captain?' asked Roussel, with a roguish twinkle in his eye.

'They told me to back off on the databases; maybe good old-fashioned police work is the way to go on this one,' he said with a wink.

Roussel smiled. He really liked the captain. He looked again at the board. The man was right though; books, notes and shoe leather were the way forward. That's where the breaks were going to come on this one.

He got up and moved to the empty half of the whiteboard. Maybe he was looking at it all wrong. Maybe the victim's identities were not the key to the house; rather the house was the key to the victim's identities. He sketched the front of the house, a basic drawing. He'd followed up with every lawyer, every bank and every mortgage and finance company in the local area, but something was gnawing at the extremities of his subconscious.

He didn't know why, but he twirled his Rolodex and dialled the number without thinking.

'Yeah, can I speak to Tony Williams please?' he asked when the phone was answered.

He heard a few clicks and then Tony's big booming voice.

'Williams,' he said, in his flat southern drawl.

'Hey Tony, its Charles,' he said. 'Charles Roussel.'

'Charles Roussel!' Tony exclaimed excitedly. 'Charlie, how are you doing? As I live and breathe; I was only discussing you with Marlene the other day.'

'How is Marlene?' asked Roussel.

'She told me that she hasn't seen you anywhere near enough,' said Tony. Roussel could hear the slight hurt in his voice.

'Especially since you got back from Boston a few years ago,' he added.

'Sorry Tony,' he said. 'It's just I find it very difficult to revisit some of that stuff.'

'So, is this business or pleasure?' asked Tony, changing the subject.

Roussel didn't answer and Tony snorted.

'Thought so,' he said. 'What exactly can I do for you, detective,' he said, putting huge emphasis on the word *detective*.

'I was just wondering if you've had any dealings or correspondence relating to the old house?' asked Roussel, trying to ignore the emotional blackmail.

'Are you kidding me?' said Tony, his annoyance temporarily forgotten. 'That's what I was talking to Marlene about. It was sold again, about a month back. The guy who was buying it contacted me directly; said he knew I had some history with the place and wanted me to handle both sides of the sale.'

He chuckled to himself.

'He paid cash; a lot of cash.'

'Any reason why he would choose somebody so far away?' asked Roussel in surprise.

'It's only a couple of hundred miles,' said Tony, half-accusingly.

'Even so, you'd think he'd go with one of the local firms, especially if he was an out-of-towner?' responded Roussel, ignoring the slight.

'What made you say that,' said Tony, and Roussel could imagine his lawyer's eyes, narrowing in suspicion.

'Lucky guess,' said Roussel speculatively.

Tony wouldn't be drawn; the consummate lawyer.

'Anyway,' he stated. 'I *was* local, remember. We only moved here since the old house was sold; after you went north. We moved to be nearer Marlene's parents. I guess the vendor told him about me. Old man Bell was always a bit of a gossip.'

'He was dead,' said Roussel flatly.

'Of course he was, it was an executor's sale,' said Tony. 'How could I forget that, I handled the sale; knew all the history.'

He chuckled again.

'Old age is a cursed thing.'

Roussel's heart rate increased slightly and he could feel the beginnings of excitement.

'So you have all the documents from the sale?' he asked.

'Sure do,' replied Tony. 'Tell you what. Marlene gets you over to sample her cooking, I get a warrant, and you get your docs.'

'Deal,' said Roussel, without even thinking.

'Tonight,' said Tony. 'Don't be late.'

Roussel smiled for the first time since the call had begun. They always ate at nine; no exceptions.

He dropped the phone and spun back to the drawing of the house. He drew two stick men in front of it, with a further stick man inside it. Under the two in front of the house he wrote *victim1* and *victim2*. Then he drew a question-mark next to victim1 and wrote *CIA* in big letters next to victim2.

He wrote *owner* under the stick man in the house and wrote *not old man Bell* next to it. He folded his hands and studied it and then cursed; he'd managed to draw all over his clean white shirt with whiteboard marker. He was trying to remove the stain with a combination of his fingers, spit and a handkerchief when there was another knock on his door.

'It's open,' he shouted.

'Hey, Peeshwank,' said a familiar voice. 'Fancy a beer?'

Roussel looked from his marked shirt to the clock; four forty five.

'If you're buying, I'm talking,' added Guilbeau, peeking around the door.

'You got something for me?' asked Roussel.

'No beer, no talk,' answered Guilbeau with a smile.

#

Guilbeau waited until the two beers were sitting on the bar in front of them. He poured his bottle into the frosted glass, the amber liquid making a chugging sound as he did so. He wiped the condensation away in a circular motion, an old habit, and then took a deep draught.

'That's better,' he said.

Roussel ignored his drink, using his finger to write letters in the condensation on his glass. He didn't say anything; he knew Guilbeau would talk when he was ready.

'About five years ago, I went to a conference in Basel, Switzerland,' said Guilbeau. 'I'd never been out of the country before. I remember because I had to get my passport; I was so excited. Turns out it was a really good week.'

He took a sip and then continued.

'Very informative, some good science, but the best things about it were the friends I made.'

He lifted his glass and it clinked gently against Roussel's.

'It's amazing what friendships can be formed over a few beers,' he continued. 'Anyway, on the last night of the conference, all of the delegates put our business cards into a large hat. One of the guys volunteered to create a distribution list, which he forwarded around to all the others. It's like having our own private global network.'

Roussel waited for the punch line. He was nothing if not a patient man.

'The coroner's collective, we called it,' said Guilbeau with a smile. 'Anyway, I had previously been very dismissive of the power of networking; I think we all were, but knowing that the guys are out there has been the equivalent of having an extra tool in the armoury. If they have questions about US policies and procedures, they can just ask me. If I have questions about any of the European nuances, I can ask them in return.'

Roussel couldn't contain himself any longer.

'Your junket memories are very nice,' he said. 'But what has this got to do with my case?'

'Patience, Peeshwank,' said Guilbeau. 'Anyway, I thought about your issues with the federal database and the DNA sample restrictions, and the next thing I'm looking at the fingerprint kit on my desk, and the two drawers in the morgue. I'll admit, it's not exactly sticking to established directives; its old school. So I fingerprinted John and James Doe, scanned in the results, and e-mailed them to the collective.'

'Now, one came back blank, as I pretty much knew it would. If it's in the FBI restricted database, then there has to be a reason why, and it's unlikely to be anywhere else. But I got a hit on the other one.'

'Really?' asked Roussel eagerly.

Guilbeau pushed a folded sheet of paper across the bar and swallowed the rest of his beer.

'Good luck, Peeshwank,' he said. 'Let me know how it goes.'

Roussel nodded.

'Say thanks to the collective from me,' he said distractedly.

Back at his desk, he unfolded the scrap of paper. One piece of the puzzle had finally fallen into his lap. Victim1 was called Scott Mitchell, and that is where he got another big shock; place of residence was Cork, Republic of Ireland.

Even though Guilbeau had hinted early in the investigation that he thought one or both of the victims might have been foreign, it still came as a bit of a surprise to see it in black and white. A couple of calls later and he had some more information. Scott Mitchell had entered the country on the eighth of May, on a standard ninety day tourist visa. He had flown from Dublin to JFK, and then onwards to New Orleans International; his final destination.

Another couple of calls later and he couldn't help but chuckle to himself. Scott had hired himself a Honda Acura from Hertz in New Orleans. Not only was it showing as having a full set of Pirelli P series tyres, but it was dropped back to the gold return area with a full tank of petrol on the twelfth of May. They had found no cars at the house, only a large Harley Davison that was not registered to anyone, so it stood to reason that the owner of the house had fled in the rental car. He was either severely panicked or a very cool customer, reasoned Roussel.

He tried to think of the reasons why Scott would have gone to the place where he was ultimately killed. The most obvious one would have been tourism, but it was a very specific location. It was near to New Orleans, that much was true, but very much off the main roads and tourist haunts. He must have had a specific reason for going.

For the time being, Roussel was going to assume his reason for visiting had something to do with the owner of the house. He rubbed out the question mark next to victim1 and replaced it with the name *Scott Mitchell*. He then absently added the question mark again. He still didn't know the motives, but one out of three wasn't bad.

His phone rang again suddenly. He snatched it up and before he could bark a reply, a stream of words hit him. He had to ask the caller to calm down and speak slower. When he eventually ended the call, after much profuse apologies from the forensic technician, he smiled a grim triumphant smile. A text had been received by Scott Mitchell's cell phone, a day after he'd died; someone wanted some information from him; someone from Cork in Ireland.

#

The car thundered along the road. He contemplated switching his siren on and then thought better of it. The last thing he needed was to be stopped outside of his jurisdiction by a fellow law enforcement officer. It had been so long since he'd journeyed to Tony and Marlene that he'd forgotten how long it actually took. Tony was a sticky old bugger. If Roussel was not there on time, he wouldn't get his info, police officer or not.

They were the nearest thing he had now to parents, Tony and Marlene. As well as being his lawyer, Tony had been his dad's best friend. When his parents had died, he hadn't had to think about a thing, Tony and Marlene had made all the arrangements. During those college years, they had been the ones ringing and visiting. They had been the couple sitting proudly in the second row, eyes shining with unshed tears and glowing with southern pride, at his graduation ceremony. They had not wanted him to go north, but of course, he'd known better, and the enforced distance between them had started to make things awkward and stilted.

Since he'd come back, he'd found it too difficult. He loved them both as people, they just reminded him too much of the loss of his parents. He knew it wasn't their fault. If he got there in time, this time, he would try and explain it to them.

For the next hundred miles or so, he anxiously juggled brake and accelerator, his eyes nervously scanning the clock. An hour and twenty minutes later, exactly seven and a half minutes before dinner was always served, he shot through the gates and up the gravel drive, coming to a skidding halt outside the modern ranch style property.

#

It was two o'clock in the morning before he got home. He felt emotionally drained; no, drained wasn't the right word. Purged was a better one. He'd told them how he really felt. The confusion over his parent's death and the feelings of resentment he'd had towards them for stepping in to take the place of his mum and dad.

Even though he knew that wasn't what they'd been trying to do, he explained how he had ignored those feelings and blamed them anyway. He described the emotions and insecurity that the failure of his law career had triggered. How he'd wanted to run away and yet had gone straight back to his childhood town. And most of all, he told them how he wasn't even sure where his home was any more.

In return, they told him of their displeasure at what they termed his abandonment of his legal career, and to a lesser degree, his abandonment of them. There had been a lot of tears, a lot of words, and strangest of all, a lot of laughter. He couldn't remember the last time he had genuinely laughed at shared memories of his parents. He knew he would be back to see them again soon, and they knew it too; a healing of sorts had begun.

Tony had walked out with him to the car at the end of the night. They had shaken hands and then mutually and spontaneously hugged each other tight.

He'd handed Roussel a letter-sized manila envelope. Roussel could see it was bursting with documents.

'I hope you find what you are looking for, Charlie,' Tony had said gravely.

He'd tapped the brown envelope gently.

'And I'm not talking about this, either.'

'I know,' Roussel had responded. 'Thanks Tony; for everything, I really mean that.'

'I know you do.'

He looked at that self same envelope now, sitting in front of him on the kitchen table. He extracted the bundle of photocopied documents; Tony had retained all the originals like all good lawyers. He opened his leather bound notebook and clicked his pen into action.

He read every document, methodically cataloguing the salient points one by one, sipping his coffee and making the occasional notation as he went. It took him a full hour to read the stack, but strangely, even though it was two am, he did not feel in the least bit tired.

He looked at the name and address he had written down; *Thomas Eugene O'Neill, Cork, Republic of Ireland.* He compared it to the name he had written down on that first night; the name from the gravestone.

Damn, now he knew why he followed his hunches. The name stared back at him. *Mary O'Neill.*

He wondered if the captain felt the same way as he did about coincidences.

CHAPTER 23 – REBIRTH

15th May 2011 – Five days after the Storm.

The beginning of compunction is the beginning of a new life. – George Eliot.

The double doors of the master bedroom were the closest point in the house to the sea. He always slept with one door very slightly ajar, so he could hear the lapping of the waves. He always felt, as he was getting up, that you could reach your hand through the gap and touch the ocean. It was as close as that.

He glanced back to the large king-size bed. The satin sheets were pulled tight around a softly snoring mound. He personally never cared for covers; he didn't feel the cold.

At this stage, he couldn't even be bothered to learn their names. They were the lucky ones as far as he was concerned, removed from the stable to live with the stallion in luxury for a while. Truth be told, he wasn't that interested in sex and the girls knew it. For them, it was only a temporary reprieve, but they grasped it willingly with both hands. For him, it was the chance to be near another human being; to feel the heat radiating from their bodies without having to get too close. He didn't like close; he didn't do close.

He left her to her dreams, and wandered out through the doors and down onto the shore. He picked up a handful of stones, flat ones, and started skimming them out across the small breakers.

His father had built the house, literally with his own hands.

David's grandfather had been a stone mason and master craftsman, and Pat *the Bull* had inherited a love of working with his hands. Simple and honest toil, he used to call it.

He'd built the house just before the twins were born; just after his legitimate business had begun to flourish. The time of contentment, before greed and the need for material possessions and massive wealth had overtaken his original requirement for simple comfort and happiness.

The Bull had been a tough man, and an even tougher father. He'd come from harsh roots; so much so in fact, that he used to call himself a *common* man.

He'd been a worker from the working-class. He'd been fiercely proud of who he was and where he came from, and no amount of money and riches could make him forget that. He'd never let anybody else forget it either, least of all his two sons.

David himself was now as rough and tough as they came. You had to be to survive in his game, even if so much of it was a performance; an act. But it had not always been that way.

Being twins, himself and John had done everything together. Like all working men made good, his father had wanted the absolute best for his boys. David had always thought that it was his *class* that separated him from his classmates. He spoke the same, dressed the same, thought the same, but they always held something back; always kept something in reserve.

He remembered distinctly overhearing a conversation between two sets of parents in the car park of the school as he waited for John to come down. He was always a nosey and inquisitive kid. They had used the word distasteful to describe his family. It didn't sound like a compliment, but at the time, he did not really know what it meant. He had looked it up in the dictionary. He could still to this day recall the exact words he had read; *unpleasant, offensive, or causing dislike.* Years later, he'd had it framed in big letters, and it hung on the wall of his home office; it still provoked some very comical reactions.

It had been about two months after that comment that his universe had shifted completely on its axis. His attitude to the world had completely changed. His father had been killed, and he'd realised he was rich. It had never occurred to him before, but back then, it had opened up a whole new vista of opportunity. He had never looked back.

And then John had been killed.

He'd immediately cloaked himself in a shell of impenetrable hardness. Over time, the urbane exterior he had built up during his school years rubbed off. Like any hastily applied paint or varnish, it eventually wore off, leaving the surface exposed and open, so he'd had to encase himself in concrete. When you got down to the core, he was still the same lonely frightened teenager.

He never allowed people to see the vulnerable side of his personality, and he consequently wrapped the concrete in a blanket of hate. Pretty soon that was all he was; the man who was solely driven by rage.

You have to have money to make money. His was the ultimate case in point, the proof of the pudding. He used money as another weapon in his arsenal; to bribe, to open doors, to purchase the stuff of his dreams and to buy trinkets he didn't want. He was still basically that spoiled teenager; whatever he wanted, he got and there was nobody to say no to him. Sometimes, early on in his bereavement, he'd wished there had been. Now, nobody dared and nobody would.

There was a discreet cough behind him.

Ben Collins was standing on the private beach, keeping a polite distance away. As well as being his most trusted business adviser, Ben was about as close as David got to a friend.

Of course, Ben was paid exceptionally well, but David knew he wasn't in it for the money. That was why he was still alive and still working in his current position; they both understood who the boss was, and where the lines were drawn. Strangely enough, despite all of that or maybe because of it, Ben actually liked him.

David nodded curtly behind him, toward the patio doors.

'Get me a new one,' he said. 'I'm bored with this one. Make sure she's gone, by the time I get home. I want another installed in her place. And blonde this time; I'm fucked off with all the brunettes.'

Ben nodded his understanding.

'And get the car brought round in about half an hour,' he said. 'I'm going to have a shower, a little bit of breakfast and then we'll go and take a look; see how the site is shaping up.'

'I'll make sure we are ready and waiting,' responded Ben smartly.

Twenty nine minutes later, he was refreshed and eager to face the day. Breakfast was always the same; a cup of decaffeinated coffee, a glass of orange juice and a bowl of Alpen muesli (the cheap ones just weren't the same somehow.)

He bounded down the steps and his driver, Tony, hopped out and opened the door. David slid into the back next to Ben; he always sat on the left side of the car, furthest away from the nearside and possible attack.

He noticed with some amusement that Tony wouldn't engage drive until he had clicked his seatbelt into place; the true mark of absolute authority.

'I know the timescales have been tough,' said David. 'But what's the story on the facility. Will I be impressed?'

More by luck than judgement, the holiday home that David's father had built all those years ago was less than five minutes drive from the proposed new manufacturing plant. David was keen to impress his new business partners. He had put a third of the money upfront from his own stockpiles, with virtually no guarantees. But given who his new business partners were, he supposed that guarantees were not something you came upon easily. And property was not giving the returns it had; time for him to try something new.

'First things first,' answered Ben. 'I took the limited documentation you gave me, and ran it past a couple of specialists; guys we already have on our payroll. Obviously, seeing as the data is mostly blinded, they couldn't synthesise anything, but they could confirm that it would, in their opinion, act on a specific area of the brain.'

'So, it's good stuff, right?' asked David.

'Well, that remains to be seen,' said Ben. 'I don't like talking out of school, boss, but you're putting an awful lot of your own money into this. Do you really think it's worth it?'

David looked across at Ben.

'I appreciate what you're saying, Ben,' he said. 'But there are two reasons why I'm doing this. The first reason is because I can, and the second reason is because I can potentially screw over that cock-sucker Black Swan; destroy his life the way he's destroyed mine.'

'Why not just have him killed and be done with it,' said Ben.

'Because it would be too quick and he is too well protected,' replied David. 'I want the bastard to suffer.'

'You're the boss,' stated Ben, without a hint of irony.

'Yes I am,' said David with a smile.

'So, based on the information in that same set of documentation,' Ben continued. 'I selected and engaged a reputable firm of chemical process consultants and engineers. They basically compared the tooling and processes that were left behind in the factory, with what we want to produce. The end result was not as good as we'd hoped.'

He paused.

'Given they only stopped manufacturing about a year ago, we thought a large percentage of the production equipment would be available for re-use. Unfortunately, it turns out we can't use a thing. Not a nut or a bolt.'

David scowled.

'Before you get too downhearted,' said Ben hastily, 'it actually accelerates, rather than delays the schedule.'

'How so?' asked David, with a puzzled expression.

'Think about it,' said Ben. 'It's like anything really. If you are trying to fit new stuff in around old stuff, it can be very fiddly and time consuming. This way, all we have to do is rip everything out and build up the production lines from scratch. Okay, on the capital side and the equipment side, it will end up costing us more, but on the manpower side, the project will come in significantly less, which will balance our budget nicely.'

'So what about the facility itself?' asked David. 'You still haven't answered my original question. Will I be impressed?'

'You'll see,' said Ben.

They made the rest of the short journey in silence. The BMW M5 slipped through the front gates. David was amused to see the sign.

G&E Chemicals, in partnership with ADXR Corporation.

They glided into the spot marked *managing director.*

David waited for Tony to open his door as he always did. They walked through the automatic revolving entrance, and into a plush and opulent reception area.

David nodded his approval.

'This is a big change since last time,' he said, acknowledging the transformation.

It had been an empty shell when they had first viewed the building.

'A bit of a reversal really,' agreed Ben.

'What do you mean?' asked David.

'Come with me,' said Ben, and led the way down a small corridor.

A security ID system with a corresponding pin code now existed on all of the main doors within the facility. Ben wordlessly handed his boss a proximity card which also had his name and photograph on it.

'Can I?' asked David eagerly, indicating the reader.

He loved gadgets and technology.

'Sure,' said Ben.

'What's my pin?' asked David.

'See if you can guess,' replied Ben with a smile.

David smiled in return. Ben knew him too well. There was only one pin number he ever used. He was lucky it was so memorable. He flashed his badge and punched in the digits *8384*. The door clicked open. He thought of John a little sadly. Even though they were twins, they didn't share a birthday. He'd been born at two minutes to midnight on the eighth of March; John at seven minutes after, so John's pin would have been *9384*; much more difficult to remember.

Ben had walked ahead of him into the main production area, so David didn't get a clear view until he was well inside. As the igniters started firing up the rows of fluorescent strip lights, he whistled quietly under his breath.

'Jesus, you weren't joking, were you?' he said.

The last time he had visited the site, it had been full of equipment. Now, there were dismantled machines and industrial skips dotted across the expanse. David was just about to ask a question, when Ben started talking.

'I know it doesn't look like we've done much,' said Ben. 'But....'

He started curling over his fingers, one by one.

'We've ripped out all of the old machinery. We have ripped out all of the wiring and electrics, and completely reinstalled all the cabling with all the requisite ancillaries, including battery backup, generator and multiple incoming supplies. An air conditioning system has been installed, and we have fully insulated the building, which is also fully re-clad, redecorated and painted. All the office blocks, toilets, everything else has been done, down to fresh concrete paint on the floor.'

They walked over to a pillar with cables sticking out, in a neat labelled bundle.

'All we need to do literally,' he said, 'is to drop the machines into place, screw them into the ground, cable them up and we are golden.'

David nodded; he was actually very impressed.

'Do you want to see your office?' asked Ben suddenly.

'Is it ready?' asked David.

'The first thing I worked on,' said Ben, with a straight face.

David didn't know whether he was trying to be funny or deadly serious.

They went back out the way they had come. Ben directed them through the lobby, and up a modern steel and glass spiral staircase. There was only one door facing ahead of them, and David chuckled. It already had his name on it.

David walked in. He'd always based himself at home. It sounded stupid, but he'd always felt more at home, at home. This was a huge departure for him. To base his business out of an office, was something he had never done before. It was also a big gamble, moving the control of his operation to West Cork, when the majority of his action was in the city centre. It was a calculated risk. David prided himself on his balls of steel; all or nothing was his motto.

As he settled himself into the high backed leather chair, he realised that all the important items from his study had been relocated. He needed to revisit Ben's salary again; he really was priceless.

#

It was well and truly dark as the car pulled out of the car park on the return journey. David was contented, and at times like this, he liked to go back and talk to them.

Ben had stayed at the facility; he'd cried off with the excuse that he had a lot of things to organise. Truth was, he found it uncomfortable being there and David understood that, promising to send the car back for him later.

People had been surprised at the time, but David could never understand why. For him, it had seemed a natural thing. As a family, this is where they had enjoyed their most intimate moments. It was the only place he would have dreamed of interring them, and he had already given Ben a discrete envelope containing his own instructions.

Tony dropped him at the entrance to the graveyard; it was the only time he never opened the door. David stepped out and the car moved off and stopped a polite distance away; near enough to be summoned, yet far enough away to give him a little bit of privacy.

It was a wild night; David did not feel the cold, and relished the rain as it drove horizontally into his face. He struggled through the old stone gates, and made his way slowly to his first stop. He was literally dripping wet when he finally made it over to the other side.

The monument was without doubt the biggest in the cemetery by at least a factor of two. His old man did not do things by halves, and he and John had wanted something to stand-out in death the way she had in life.

The tears formed, and on these visits, he never stopped them; never tried to suppress the emotions. That's why he always came alone.

His mother had died when he was very young. She had been a force of nature, but she remained to David like a dream; an ideal of what a parent should be. He didn't remember her in harsh reality. It was like looking at something with your eyes almost closed; blurry and indistinct. She was perfect, because he couldn't remember her not being that way.

The temperature was dropping rapidly, and the wind was tracking the tears all over his face. He moved on from the relative perfection of the ostentatious monument, to the simple plot that lay next to it. There were three spaces, three small and simple black granite headstones. The middle one was his father, the one to the left was John, and he had reserved the other side for himself; at the right hand of the father.

He supposed it was a bit macabre, erecting your own gravestone before you were dead, but he had experienced his father being shot dead and his brother knifed to death. He lived in a dog eat dog world, and he fully expected to get eaten one day very soon. He had never seen himself living beyond thirty. He didn't know why, maybe he just couldn't see that far ahead. He had the arrogance of youth, but some part of him was already dead.

Twins have a rarely understood and very close bond, especially identical twins. He saw it very clearly in black and white that they came from the same genetic blend. As far as he was concerned, he was half dead already. He knelt at the foot of John, the indistinct mound in front of the black granite, and imagined his brother's skeleton lying just below the surface. He kissed the peaty earth, tasting the darkness and remembering the inscription.

John, brother, rest peacefully for soon you will.

He moved on to the middle space; he could almost feel the plot swell as he stood in front of it. He remembered every defect, every line and mole on his father's face, as his emotions took physical form. Nose to nose, they would scream abuse at each other, neither backing down. And then, on the sofa in the living room at night, he would snuggle up to his father, praying for the moment that the arm would come around, feeling the warmth of the fire and his father's embrace.

He had not been an easy man to love; respect yes, love no. But he and John had earned both. His father had respected few men and loved none; not even his own father. But the twins had got under his skin, and broken down the barriers early, especially after his wife had passed away.

He was never violent; he was vigorous and forthright in his views, but so were the boys and it led to some furious rows. But in all those years, they never once ended the day on harsh words. They always made up, and if he was wrong he would admit it; a big step for such a powerful and opinionated man.

David made the sign of the cross and blessed himself, just as an icy gust of wind made him shudder. If he felt it, it must be really cold.

He'd heard it said that revenge was a dish best served cold. He was going to ensure it was sub zero.

The Bullock had come of age; had come full circle and become *The Bull.*

CHAPTER 24 – QUEST

16th May 2011 – Six days after the Storm.

The terrible thing about the quest for truth is that you find it. – Remy de Gourmont.

Dale stretched his legs as far as the economy seat would allow. He wouldn't like to be any taller. As he shifted his position, he smiled at the recollection of Dodd's scowling face, as he'd looked sourly across the desk at Dale.

'Do you have your tickets?' he'd asked.

Dale had nodded.

'Do you have your passport?'

Dale had nodded again.

'Do you have your phone?' he'd asked.

Dale had nodded a third time.

'Then what the fuck else do you need?'

Dale had thought about it, and realised that Dodds was right; the time was now.

Dodds had driven to JFK as though his trousers were on fire. Dale had hung on grimly. He had been deposited at set-down; literally ejected, as the car was still moving. Dodds had shouted a salutation and then Dale had been left alone with his journey.

The girl at check-in had eyed him suspiciously, as had the Department of Homeland Security officials, especially when he'd said he was going for pleasure. They had eyed his lack of luggage with jaundiced eyes, and he had been about to show this DEA identification, when for some reason, a small voice inside his head had stopped him. He'd had a strong feeling that his anonymity might be an advantage; he'd also been fairly certain that the Department of Homeland Security knew exactly who he was.

'Can I get you anything, sir?' asked the Stewardess, interrupting his reminiscence. 'Tea, Coffee, Beer?'

'Coffee,' he said automatically, and then changed his mind. 'No, I'll have a beer actually, if I could?'

He smiled at her.

'Here you go, sir,' she said, handing him a very small can, and a plastic cup. 'Enjoy.'

As she turned to go, she winked at him, and he recognised something in her expression. Maybe Dale was mistaken, but it wasn't the normal, painted on, have a nice day facade that stewardesses normally presented to the world. Maybe a working holiday was exactly what he needed.

He closed his eyes, and as he drifted off to sleep, his investigators mind kept subliminally reminding him that the stewardess had worn no engagement or wedding ring. His subsequent dream had been all the more pleasurable for that information.

Fifteen rows back in one of the standby seats, a man was furiously typing on his laptop. The battery indicator had already told him that he only had twelve and a half minutes left. He was also a government employee, but unlike Dale, he was aware of the existence of his fellow federal agent. In fact he knew a huge amount about DEA Special Agent 2897.

Dale slept soundly until landing. The captain, who was an old Delta veteran, kissed the plane onto the tarmac at Dublin airport with barely a judder. The stewardess had to shake him awake. She handed him his coat and his bag, and he was halfway down the steps into the terminal building, when he realised she had slipped him a piece of paper, too. He was astonished to find her number written on it in neat handwriting, and a single simple exhortation; call me! He patted the thankfully tri-band phone in his pocket; maybe later he would, he said to himself.

As his leather heels clicked a steady beat off the marble floor of the newly completed terminal two, he silently marvelled at his newfound personal spontaneity. Even Dodds had been secretly impressed, Dale could tell.

Dodds had also promised to provide any backup or information that Dale might require via local access to the official DEA and other federal systems. It would look suspicious if his ID was discovered to be live while he was away on vacation. Any time, day or night, Dodds had said. He was probably going to regret that statement.

Dale encountered his first delay in the passport hall. The Irish customs officials had decided to only open two kiosks to cope with a large planeload of American business people and tourists. It was over an hour and a half before he was able to step through the green channel and into relative freedom.

At that point, he walked to the nearest cafe. One black coffee later, he was sitting at a table for two with his notepad open. For the previous ten hours, he had been running on hunches and adrenalin, now he needed to regroup. He was in a foreign country; one he had never visited before, and he was unsure of where it was he needed to be going. His first priority had to be transport.

He contemplated going to the information desk and asking them what was the best way to get to Cork, but rightly or wrongly, he felt it would have portrayed him as a stupid American tourist. He reasoned to himself that he could fly to Cork, but then he would have the same problem with transport when he got there. Ditto the train and ditto the coach. He drove everywhere in the US, so why not here.

Twenty minutes later, and with his wallet five hundred dollars lighter, he was the proud owner of the smallest automatic transmission that Hertz could rent him. He could cope with the wrong side of the road, but not a stick shift on the wrong side too.

In the US, he had continually kept his phone up-to-date with all the new GPS maps and releases. He'd always felt he would need them eventually; now he was glad he'd done it.

The journey from Dublin airport to Cork city took him about three hours. He could summarise it as two and three quarter hours of boredom, and fifteen minutes of sheer terror.

American freeways were all pretty lawless places, but the motorway ring road around Dublin, with cars flying in all directions doing at least seventy miles an hour, was not a happy place to be learning to drive on the wrong side. It was like driving through downtown Manhattan at speed. The other thing that struck him as he entered the outskirts of Cork, was how small Ireland actually was. He had driven across literally half the country in three hours; some folks in America would regard that as a commute. He'd heard the differences between America and the English-speaking countries in Europe described as being divided by a common language; having now seen some of it at first hand, he suspected there was slightly more to it than that.

As he drove into Cork city, he ignored the entrance to the port tunnel. Pulling into the car park of the first large hotel he saw, the Silver Springs, he got out and stretched his legs. He needed somewhere to base himself and get his bearings.

Ten minutes later, he was in a business suite, reeling from the price he'd had to pay. He wanted to stay in the room, not buy it. Seemed there were other differences apart from just the language.

He put on the kettle, and made a cup of tea, mainly to give himself some time to think. He made a decision quickly and opened his notepad; he needed a computer badly.

The hotel Internet cafe was deserted. He checked the page in his notepad. He had a name, *Thomas Eugene O'Neill,* he had a pseudonym, *the Street,* and he had a place of birth, *Cork city.* His index finger lightly tapped the return key without actually pushing it as his brow furrowed in concentration. He quickly typed *how do I get more info?* and then deleted it in disgust. He sat looking at the screen, hoping the information would leap off the page by itself. In the corner, the timer was ticking off the minutes; he needed to focus.

He typed in *next of kin?* First thing he needed to find out was whether the elusive Mr O'Neill had any family left in the city. Thinking about it in the cold light of day, it seemed such a tenuous link, but Dale remembered a phrase his father used to say when considering coincidental information.

'It's like this, Dale,' he would say. 'Take a compass and set it down; see which way it points. Set another one next to it, and then add another and another. Check which way they point. If they all point in the same direction, then pretty soon you know where north is.'

Dale smiled at the memory. It did seem a tenuous connection, but he'd seen the compass needle point to Cork too many times. If it all came to nothing, then at the very least, he'd have a nice holiday. He patted his pocket; he had a number after all. Thinking about the stewardess prompted his next leap of faith.

He'd tried a number of Google searches and they had all come up negative. If he couldn't get the information online, he'd have to go old school, and where was the best place to get information about family? He typed *find family in Cork* and found the address he was looking for; the office of the registrar of marriages, births and deaths, as good a place as any to start.

He still had two further challenges. How did he get there, and how did he get the information he wanted when he arrived there. The first was easily solved; the second, he suspected, would be less so.

As Dale wrote down the address, an image floated to the front of his mind. He clicked his fingers; he had himself an in.

An hour later, and his own mother wouldn't have recognised him; the transformation from Dale to tourist was complete. He parked in a multi-storey near the registrar, and then used his GPS to locate a department store nearby. He had bought the most hideous pair of brown check golf trousers that he could find. He had teamed these with a vertical striped green rugby top, and a multicoloured Guinness cloth cap. A cheap Nikon SLR camera around his neck completed the look.

As he walked the five minutes to the office block that was his destination, he practised his southern accent; it would complete the effect he was hoping for.

At first, the ticketing system confused him, but an elderly lady showed him how you had to rip off the ticket, and how your number would appear in garish red digits above one of the service hatches. He waited patiently for his turn to come.

He noticed with relief that the kiosk displaying his number was staffed by a homely looking middle-aged woman. Being the possessor of useless, investigation based information, he knew that he had a higher statistical chance of convincing her to give him the information he wanted than if she was young and pretty.

'Howdy,' he said in his best southern drawl, with a smile painted on his face. 'I'm hoping that you can help.'

'I'll certainly try, young man,' she answered brightly.

'I'm trying to trace a long lost cousin,' he said.

He handed her the sheet he had printed in the hotel an hour and a bit earlier. He had taken the homepage of one of the American genealogy websites, and amended the search with the details he knew about Thomas Eugene O'Neill.

'This is all I know,' he said truthfully.

He handed her the sheet.

'The only other thing I can tell you, is that he would be in his early forties.'

She looked from the paper to him and back again. He noticed a slight hesitancy in her manner.

'Do you have ID?' she asked.

He slid his Passport across the table.

'Well Dale,' she added, after studying his Passport closely. 'We can't normally give out this type of information without....'

For the briefest of seconds, he contemplated sliding his DEA identification across the desk, but he instinctively knew in this case that it would be the wrong thing to do. Instead, he slipped his hand into his pocket and pulled out some large denomination bills, and leaned confidentially across the desk. He beckoned her in closer.

'I'm under cover,' he said. 'I'm a private detective, working for a woman in the US who is trying desperately to trace her runaway husband. He skipped the jurisdiction without a forwarding address and owes a huge amount of alimony....'

'It's okay young man,' she said. 'And before we go on, you didn't need to go to all that trouble and subterfuge. I was merely going to say, that we would normally need a bit more information, that's all. But private detective; sounds very exciting.'

She was grinning broadly; playing with him. It was no more than he deserved for being so stupid, but Dale cursed his rash action; it could come back to haunt him.

'So, let's try and find this mystery man of yours.'

She turned her screen around so they could both see it. Dale had been holding his breath, and realised just how difficult it was to silently breathe a sigh of relief.

She slid his piece of paper over so that it was between her and the keyboard.

'Let's see,' she said, her fingers dancing at speed across the keys. 'Ok, we've got seven returned.'

She then seemed to mumble to herself as she went through the list systematically.

'Too young, too old, too old, too old, maybe, maybe, too old.'

She hit the print button on her screen and the dot matrix beside her clacked into life.

'Ok, love,' she said, placing the paper between them. 'Looks like we have two here; one is forty five, the other is fifty two.'

Dale pointed to the first one.

'It's got to be him,' he stated with certainty.

She pulled up the detailed record.

'You're lucky. We moved all this stuff to electronic records only a year or so ago. It makes it much easier to cross-reference. The other way, everything was in huge individual ledgers.'

Dale said a silent prayer of thanks to the god of computerisation.

She looked at the details thoughtfully.

'Hmm,' she said, 'I don't think the address here is going to help you. There is a shopping centre on that area now; it was heavily redeveloped in the late eighties. I'll note it down anyway, but don't hold your breath.'

She wrote the address in a neat copperplate script.

'Now, according to this, his father was a man called Richard O'Neill.'

She tapped a few more keys.

'Now, this is interesting,' she said.

'In what way?' asked Dale.

'There are no records linked with the father's name. That means there were possibly too many of them to investigate at the time, which is feasible. However, it's more likely to mean that they couldn't find any records to match.'

'So, no record of the father's birth or death?' replied Dale, half statement and half question.

'That's right,' she said. 'Now, let's have a look at this; mother Mary O'Neill. Okay, yes, we have two records here. Birth; probably not relevant.'

She pulled up the details for the death certificate.

'There is an address listed here alright, but bear in mind, this lady died about twenty years ago.'

'It's a start,' said Dale. 'Thank you very much, you've been most kind....' he glanced at her nametag, '....Margaret.'

'You can drop the phoney accent too,' she said, with a wink. 'We're a little bit more sophisticated here since the days of *the Quiet Man*. We do have access to televisions.'

Dale couldn't help smiling. It had been pretty bad, and at least now he had another lead. He looked at the two handwritten addresses; one of them would pay dividends, he was certain.

#

Special Agent Ray Fox was going through his budget; the part of his job that he least enjoyed. His nametag said *special agent in charge*, but he didn't consider himself that way. He had been the boss for about a year now, and he liked to think he still had the respect of his men. He was their colleague and peer, as well as their superior. It was why he found budgets particularly hard. He was being told to squeeze. They hadn't used the word redundancy, but he felt that it was only a matter of time before they did; not a prospect he was looking forward to. For the bean counters, these men were numbers; to him, they were friends.

He was locking his screen for lunch, when the phone rang.

'I've just had Langley chewing my ear off,' said an irate voice.

He didn't need to expand on what *Langley* was, but it was a surprise to Ray nonetheless.

'Maybe you can explain to me why you sent a DEA agent to the Republic of Ireland.'

Tiny alarm bells started ringing in Ray's head.

'Apparently, he is about to cock up a large global operation.'

The doors clanged shut. Dale; it had to be.

'But sir,' he started to explain. 'This was not a....'

'I don't care what it was or is,' said the voice, cracking with the strain of not shouting. 'You find this idiot and you stop him.'

The phone went dead in his hand. As he replaced the instrument in its cradle, fragments of the meeting with Dale started clanging back into place like vault doors. Ray jumped quickly to his office entrance and scanned the room.

'Dodds!' he shouted above the melee. 'In here, now!'

He sat back down at his desk and waited. A shadow appeared in the doorway.

'You wanted to see me, chief?' asked Dodds.

'Come on it, close the door,' said the chief, jovially.

He waited for Dodds to get comfortable, before dropping the bombshell.

'Where is Agent Foster?' he asked, dangerously softly.

He watched Dodds. His eyes flicked away for a millisecond. Dodds knew his boss, so he said nothing.

'You know where he is, don't you?'

Dodds nodded.

'He could be in big trouble,' said the chief. 'You need to tell me everything you know.'

'Did you read the report?' asked Dodds, a trifle disdainfully. 'It was all in the report.'

'Are you saying this is my fault?' said the chief, finally exploding.

Dodds cast his eyes up to heaven for a second.

'God give me strength,' he muttered under his breath. 'No boss, what I'm saying is that it would be easier for me to explain it to you if all the information is to hand, and to do that you'll have to read the report.'

Dodds sat in silence as the chief skimmed the two pages.

'Ok, I've read it, now what,' he said, throwing it on the desk between them.

Dodds indicated the window of Ray's office.

'Dale reckons a new drug is due to hit the streets,' he said. 'I personally think he's put two and two together and made six, but he seems to believe that the common link is Ireland.'

He paused.

'The whole thing is tied back to the Mancini family, and it's going to be huge.'

'Well, do you know what,' murmured Agent Fox thoughtfully, stroking the stubble on his chin. 'He may well be right. The call I got was from the section chief, who had just got a tongue lashing from the CIA. I think he's stumbled into something and unfortunately for Dale, I think he is well out of his depth as usual.'

'We need to warn him,' said Dodds, a look of concern appearing on his face. 'You know what the CIA is like when it comes to collateral damage.'

'Do you have a way of contacting him?' asked Ray.

Dodds shook his head.

'He was going to contact me if he needed anything.'

'And you were going to get it for him?' asked the chief incredulously.

'That's what partners do,' said Dodds defensively, 'or have you forgotten that from the comfort of your leather chair?'

The chief let the remark slide.

'Just promise me something Dodds. If he contacts you, then you really need to let me know.'

'Is that all?' asked Dodds stiffly.

'For now,' said the chief.

He watched his agent leave, drumming his fingers thoughtfully on the desk as he did so.

CHAPTER 25 – UNMASKED

16th May 2011 – Six days after the Storm.

Time's glory is to calm contending kings, to unmask falsehood and bring truth to light. – William Shakespeare.

I was in one of those cafes; the real greasy spoon places that they didn't have in America. Diners they had in abundance, cafes, no. I looked at my plate; sausage, egg, bacon, mushrooms, fried tomatoes, black and white pudding, toast, and a steaming mug of white milky tea. What better way to start the day.

I had my notebook open as I ate; going through and validating the information I had gleaned over the past thirty six hours. I had a positive identification on my so-called *son*, which had been the intention. Alan Murphy had become Scott Mitchell.

After I'd made sure the girl had been treated and taken to hospital, I'd done a bit more digging around. For the rest of that night and a small bit of the following day, I'd gleaned little more in the way of information. Other than his name, it transpired that Scott Mitchell was not a very nice fellow, but that was about all I learned.

I looked at it another way. Scott Mitchell would have been very much a product of his age and his environment. Like many a teenager before him, Scott would have seen the drug dealers, driving past in their tricked out German cars with their fancy lifestyles, and he'd wanted a piece of the action. By all accounts, he'd started as a small-time dealer, working his way up to become a transporter and mule; trusted to distribute the drugs to the dealers and take the money back to the centre of operations.

No, I could understand all that. What I couldn't understand was how Scott Mitchell, a small-time wannabe criminal, had ended up on the veranda of my house in Louisiana?

I took another mouthful of bacon, marvelling at how different it tasted the closer you got to the source.

No, I could understand where Scott was from; I just couldn't see his motivation to be where he was when I shot him. What was his motive in relation to me? He'd known a lot about me that he didn't read in any book, and I didn't share that information lightly.

And that brought me to the second piece of information that I had gleaned, this time from the girl. She had given me a name; *Black Swan*. The junkies and hookers had looked at me suspiciously when I'd mentioned this man. I'd pretended that I was an Irish-American journalist, working on an expose of the drug scene in Ireland.

It was a symptom of our reality TV and celebrity drenched lifestyle, but as soon as I'd mentioned the words *journalism* and *confidentiality*, their defences had come down and they'd become positively verbose.

Black Swan was one of two kingpins who controlled the drug trade in Cork. I smiled to myself as I ate a large section of beef sausage; the other being the appropriately named *Bullock*. According to everyone I spoke to, there was no love lost between the two men. Both were extremely well protected, but both had also lost foot soldiers in the campaign; gang members killing each other on the periphery of the power struggle over silly squabbles.

Again I could understand all of it. Every bottle of milk has cream floating on the top. Every organisation has somebody running it. But the question I had to ask myself was; what did one half of the controlling interest in the drugs trade in Cork, want with a forcibly retired ex-mob enforcer living in hiding in Louisiana? It just made no sense.

I picked up the toast and mopped up the runny yellow mess of the egg yolk. There was one person who could possibly tell me. It was dangerous, but worth the risk, even if she could tell me nothing. I had an irrational desire to see her again that had nothing to do with information.

I didn't know where to start, but suspected the hospital might be a good place. It was only a day and a half since our previous encounter. I might have inadvertently hit her harder than I'd originally intended, and in most jurisdictions, concussion victims are kept under observation for at least twenty four hours.

Thirty minutes later, I stood outside the entrance to Cork University Hospital. I walked up to the reception desk.

'I'm wondering if you can help me.' I said to the austere middle aged lady, accompanying it with my brightest smile. 'A friend of mine was brought in last night; a young lady with concussion. You wouldn't be able to tell me which ward she might be in, would you?'

'Certainly sir, you go through this door, left and to the end of the corridor, up two flights of stairs and through the double doors in front of you. If she's still here, that's where she will be.'

I smiled my thanks and headed off. As I approached the ward, I became increasingly nervous. I was not a naturally apprehensive person, so it was a very unsettling feeling.

I scanned the beds as I walked through the central corridor. She was in the last one on the left, sitting up with her eyes closed. As I approached, I realised she was asleep, her breathing shallow and even. I sat noiselessly in the chair and studied her.

She was wearing a regulation hospital gown, and her face had been cleaned of the outlandish and garish makeup that most men looking for *ladies of the night* seemed to think was attractive.

Even with the large bruise on the side of her face, and the deathly pallor of her skin, to me she looked beautiful. Must be going soft in my old age, I said to myself. I realised then that her eyes were open and focused exclusively on me. To her credit, she hadn't jolted or started or even screamed; there was just a wan smile.

'You sure know how to show a girl a good time,' she said weakly.

I laughed in spite of myself.

'It worked, didn't it?'

'Thank you,' she replied earnestly.

Then she seemed to realise something, and her eyes darted up and down the room in panic.

'You need to leave,' she said. 'My....'

She searched for a word.

'....*manager* is due here any second. If he sees you here, you are dead. Especially after all they have been saying about you over the last day or so.'

'I can look after myself,' I said evenly.

'I'll be dead too,' she said.

'Don't worry,' I replied soothingly. 'If he turns up, I'll think of something.'

I could see she was about to argue and then thought better of it. She appeared to be very tired. I went to the end of the bed and pretended to be studying her notes. When I was satisfied that I'd memorised the name and address that were written in tightly spaced biro, I sat back down again.

'So, what can you tell me about this Black Swan guy?' I asked.

'Only that you don't want to mess with him,' she answered quietly.

'Have you met him?' I asked.

She shook her head; negative.

'Do you know where he lives?'

Her brow furrowed in concentration.

'North side I think,' she said. 'That's all I know.'

She closed her eyes again.

'You're a strange man,' she stated suddenly.

I laughed abruptly.

'You're not wrong, Kate Howard.'

'And lonely too, I think,' she said, ignoring my use of her name.

I was just about to answer, when I saw him loom large in the porthole windows at the end of the room. He would be through the double doors and into the ward in seconds. I had to protect her; I was the one who had put her in this position.

I sprang off the chair and grabbed her around the neck with both hands. Her eyes flicked open in genuine fear. I winked at her and increased the pressure slightly. I saw comprehension flit across her face for a second, before she started making choking sounds.

I heard the shout.

'Hey you; what the fuck are you doing?'

I looked up and tried my best to fake panic. I let go of the girl and dashed out through the double doors at the far end of the ward. I could hear her hamming it up, choking and coughing; good girl.

The door flipped closed behind me. I was just deciding which way to go, when there was an almighty crash. I heard the whistle of the bullet and the thud as it hit the far wall and then, a second later, it started raining glass and metal reinforcement.

I'd recognised this guy from the street last night. As they'd been driving her away in the ambulance, he'd stayed aloof and watchful; obviously a handler. I chastised myself silently; I hadn't realised these guys would have weapons. I don't know why it hadn't occurred to me; when I was running protection, I always carried a piece.

I ran for the stairwell and threw myself through the door. As it closed behind me, I felt the glass shatter. I threw myself to the outside of the stairs, using the banisters to steady myself, and took them two at a time to try and minimise any target area. I heard the bullets fly; feeling and sensing the zings as they ricocheted dangerously off the steel stairwell fittings that enclosed the small confined space.

I crashed through the bottom doors and raced across the car park as though the hounds of Hades were upon me. I reached the car, lungs burning and legs pumping. I jabbed the unlock button on the alarm and hurled myself into the driver's seat. I slid the key smoothly into the ignition and fired it up in one fluid motion.

The hairs on the back of my neck were doing their job. I ducked instinctively and slid the gearshift into reverse, just milliseconds before the windscreen exploded out with a crash. I buried the throttle, glad I didn't have to worry about gears; the girl who'd upgraded me to automatic at the rental desk was now worth her weight in gold.

I hand braked the machine savagely through ninety degrees, causing him to dive for cover. I slicked the gear lever into drive and then floored it. The car bucked like a stallion as the front tyres scrabbled furiously for grip, gravel kicking and spitting in all directions.

'Come on!' I shouted and slapped the wheel in frustration.

Without warning, the front tyres suddenly bit into the exposed tarmac and the car rocketed forward. I kept my foot down as the vehicle gained speed. I ducked as there was another crash and the side window came in, but at last I was moving ahead of him.

I raced through a gap, flicking the wheel left and right as the tyres screamed in protest. We were now in parallel lanes within the car park.

At the end of my lane, I kept my foot planted to the floor and hung on grimly as I hauled the steering to the right. The tail stepped out savagely, to smash side-on into the line of cars at the end. I steered frantically in the opposite direction to the skid and managed to over correct, smashing into another two or three cars with the nearside front wing. I ignored the tearing rending sound; like a car in a junkyard crusher.

Two more bullets thudded into the side, deadened by the door padding and the air bags. My thigh and calf muscles were straining with the effort of keeping the accelerator at its maximum.

After another two or three slight wobbles, the car straightened and I wrestled it back under control. The speed started building again, and I felt the danger diminishing slightly. I dispatched the next obstacle, the car park barrier, with a crash, wincing at the additional damage; there was my excess gone.

I watched in the rear view mirror with interest. I saw him tuck the gun into the waistband of his jeans as he started sprinting as fast as he could after me. An idea formed, growing and maturing as it took shape.

I let the speed of the car drop slowly, infinitesimally almost; I wanted him to think he was gaining on me. As the distance between us decreased by degrees, I saw his expression change gradually from despair, to hope, to grim determination, and then I saw the anger on his face. He was letting his emotions take over.

He suddenly veered off the footpath and onto the road until he was running full tilt behind me, gaining with every stride. I watched him in the wing mirrors rather than using the rear view. I wanted it to appear as though I was frightened and distracted. I needed to try and disguise what I was going to do next; my timing had to be absolutely perfect.

Even in the bright sunshine, I could see the beginnings of a crooked smile. In his head, he was turning slowly from potential loser to potential winner. In his own mind he was starting to get the upper hand.

As the distance closed between us and his features became more discernible and real, he reached for his waistband; the signal I'd been waiting for.

I flicked the car into reverse without even a dab on the brakes. There was a rending and crunching sound; like someone was stirring a bucket of marbles with a golf club. The tortured tyres screamed their outrage, bellowing clouds of noxious fumes into the atmosphere. Milliseconds later, their grip was restored.

Too late, he saw the intent, but by that stage he had closed the gap between us himself. I finally glanced in the rear view mirror and his eyes held mine. I saw a flash of fatalism and then fear. His muscles bunched for the leap to safety, but the distance was not quite enough. I had judged it to perfection.

The bang, when I heard it, was still pretty shocking; it sounded like a melon that had been dropped from a height onto concrete. The impetus of my continued speed as it built steadily backwards kept him pinned to the rear of the car.

Even in his badly injured state, the survival instinct took over. He must have had a dozen broken ribs at least, but he managed to weakly wrestle the weapon fully from his waistband, and extend his arm through the shattered back window. A ghastly smile of bleak resolve twisted his features, his arm trembling almost uncontrollably as he fought to steady the gun. I closed my eyes and braced myself back into the seat.

The impact jarred my spine to the core. The car following us had been day dreaming; not expecting another vehicle reversing towards it at high speed. I slipped my own into drive again and what remained of the gearbox engaged the ripped and shredded tyres.

The gun dropped from his lifeless fingers as his body slipped off the trunk of my car. As I shot forward, I saw the impetus of the vehicle behind carry it up and over his prone body as the energy of the crash continued to diminish. It lifted clumsily into the air, dropped, and then lifted again to the limit of its suspension travel. I watched with a kind of detached disinterest as it swerved off to the side after running him over. His lifeless body lay sprawled and broken, like an abandoned puppet.

I shuddered, not with horror, but more a grim realisation. I had the feeling that things were only going to get more dangerous. It was a good thing I had put contingency plans into operation. I extracted the shipping notification from the inside pocket of my jacket.

'It's about time we evened up the odds a little bit,' I said to myself softly.

#

Back at the house that night, I stared at the large DHL box that I had earlier placed on the kitchen table. I was still a little bemused at how easy it had been. It was the largest box that DHL provided for personal air freight. It was pretty big, yes, but it was exceptionally heavy, too. The waybill noted that it contained machined car parts and a selection of nuts and bolts. I had also estimated a value of one thousand dollars for insurance purposes, and had noted that the parcel was *very heavy, caution required.*

The guy behind the counter at the DHL collection point at Cork airport had looked at me strangely.

'What's all this shit then, mate?' he'd asked.

'Parts for cars; I restore big American cars for a hobby,' I'd said. 'I collected all this stuff over the last twenty odd years. When I decided to come home, I thought I'd bring all this stuff with me too. Worth a good bit to collectors and the like; it's a niche market.'

I'd noticed the stickers on it; it had already gone through the customs X-Ray machines.

'Oh right,' he'd said, completely disinterestedly. 'The customs guys have estimated the duty at sixty five Euro and seventeen cent.'

I'd handed him the cash and smiled at him, but his interest was already elsewhere; shouting at his mates to turn down the radio, so he didn't hear the football scores.

I made myself a cup of tea; how glorious it was to be able to taste real hot tea again and real milk too, after what seemed like a lifetime of coffee.

I worked systematically, first removing the packing tape, before stacking the contents on the table. When I'd finished, I had a pile of about a hundred small boxes on one side, and a large single box on the other. I always believed you needed to set out your stall properly to do anything well.

I picked up one of the smaller boxes and studied it. Ostensibly, it was a container of M14 bolts. They even had the photograph and description on the outside of each box. I slit the tape and opened it, extracting what looked like a standard mild steel bolt, finished in *iron* grey. I hefted it in my hands; it was the right weight too. I extracted a nut from the same box, and screwed it half way down the shaft of the bolt; it worked.

I attached my portable vice to the table and inserted the bolt, thread down, and tightened it into position so that only the head of the bolt was visible above the jaws. I took two very thin custom made spanners and placed them over the head of the bolt, facing in opposite directions. I took hold of the spanners, one in each hand, and twisted them with all my strength in opposing directions.

There was a sharp crack. The top of the bolt split open as I started to unscrew it like a lid. I removed the spanners and finished the job with my fingers, placing the lid to the side. I removed the bolt from the vice and tapped it into my hand. When I lifted it, a 9mm bullet dropped neatly into my palm.

The bolts had been custom manufactured to my specifications to move ammunition freely around the country and across borders. I had never used the method before, so it was pleasing to see that it actually worked.

Placing the gleaming bullet aside, I turned my attention to the larger box. It was filled with an assortment of springs, rods, tubes and an array of oddly shaped brackets.

I extracted the pieces one by one, and laid them in piles. Each was labelled with both a letter and a number, and also labelled with the type of car; Mustang, Charger, Challenger etc.

When the piles were finished, I made another cup of tea, and then worked quietly and methodically until I was done.

At about midnight, I sat back and looked at my handiwork. I now had five 9mm automatic pistols, two semi automatic rifles and two fully automatic machine guns. The odds were looking infinitely better already.

I looked at my watch; it had been a long day, but there were still a couple of things I needed to do.

I drove the car to a secluded industrial estate, stopping on the way to buy a plastic fuel container which I filled with petrol.

I parked in a shaded area, devoid of security cameras and lights. I doused the car, a little sadly, in petrol and stuffed a soaking rag into the tank so that it trailed out of the filler point and along the floor. I then dribbled a trail of petrol from the rag about twenty yards behind the car.

Flinging the can away, I lit the trail of petrol, hearing it go up with a whoosh. Even though I was expecting it, the explosion made me duck and jump as I walked briskly away.

As the flames crackled, and what was left of the glass cracked, I pulled my phone out of my pocket and dialled the pre-saved number.

'Hello, is that Hertz? It is; oh good, I'm wondering if you can help me? I think someone has stolen my rental car. What do I need to do?'

#

The iPhone made camera noises, as the button was clicked repeatedly. As Thomas Eugene O'Neill walked up his path and inserted his key into the door, another barrage of clicks could be heard.

The car was parked under a defective streetlight, casting the occupant in deep shadow. He was staying well hidden, as he had on the plane. For him it was a waiting game; not now but very soon, he would make his move.

CHAPTER 26 – HAPPENSTANCE

15th May 2011 – Five days after the Storm.

Coincidence, if traced back far enough, becomes inevitable. – Hindu temple inscription.

Roussel had dragged a kitchen chair out onto the veranda of his apartment. Of course, it was labelled an apartment block, but it was really one of those glorified motels; a suite would have been a better way to put it.

Most of his meagre belongings were packed ceiling high in boxes, some still with Boston shipping labels on them. The suite was supposed to have been temporary accommodation, but that had been five years ago. On the plus side, it was cheap, it was close to work, and he didn't need to worry about getting on with his neighbours; they changed pretty much every week.

He tipped the chair back, his bare feet braced on the top of the balcony railings. He knew he'd have to shift position, especially if anybody wanted to get to the rooms further down. He also reasonably surmised that no one would need to at three o'clock in the morning.

He swirled the amber liquid around the bottom of his glass, the ice cubes tinkling against the expensive and ornate crystal. The tumbler had belonged to his father, part of a set, one of the only things he had kept from the old house.

He took a sip, and rolled the spirit around on his tongue in anticipation of the heat and the bite. He shuddered with satisfaction as it burned its way to his gullet; warmth spreading out in tendrils, like the venom from a viper.

Picking up the bottle, he studied it closely. A true caricature of a southern man would have been drinking Jack Daniels, Jim Beam, or most probably Southern Comfort. Not this southern man. Powers Gold Label was his poison, a taste he'd acquired courtesy of a late-night mutual support session with Guilbeau. It had been a particularly difficult case, one involving a mutilated child and a deranged father. Off his head on some hallucinogen, the man had believed his infant son possessed by malevolent demons.

As a policeman, he knew for a fact that evil never slept; it was always alive and well in the world, and could be found in the most peaceful and quiet of places.

He poured himself another couple of stiff fingers. He rarely drank, and even less rarely drank heavily. Good job really, as his supply of Powers was beginning to dwindle. He'd bought a case on eBay when the dollar had been favourable against the euro. But now he was down to his last two bottles, so he was using them wisely and judiciously.

He couldn't sleep; his head was buzzing and his brain was alive with different thought patterns, most notably Tony's cryptic comment.

So what exactly was it that he was looking for?

He'd already tried acquiring wealth and success; the dusty boxes from Boston, stacked three high in his tiny suite, were testament to how important that had been to him.

Was it companionship he craved? He didn't think so. He was alone, yes, but he wasn't lonely; there was a difference. It was a long time since he'd courted a woman, but in fairness it was a long time since he'd wanted to. He didn't feel ready, and it wasn't one of those masculine, petrified of commitment scenarios. It was deeper and more fundamental than that.

At the present moment, he was a vagabond, a vagrant if you preferred; a gypsy with no roots. Seeing the old family place had brought it all home to him, but he'd also recognised something else; something equally as important. Not only did he now have a burning desire to belong, but it was a burning desire to belong to this land; this community.

It was said that from tiny acorns, great oaks would grow. At this stage of his life, he was well past an acorn. He was a seedling, desperate to take root before he withered and died.

He was starting to be recognised on the streets. He was getting nods and smiles from the middle aged, and even the older ladies. Children laughed and smiled with him. Maybe Tony was wrong. Maybe he had found what he was looking for already, and it had been under his nose all along; a sense of place.

He heard the faint refrain of *hanging on the telephone*, the song by Blondie. He time checked his watch, before taking the phone out of his pocket. Who on earth would be calling at three am. Certainly someone he didn't know anyway, the ringtone gave it away. He contemplated hanging up, but then thought; fuck it, what the hell?

'Roussel,' he barked.

'The guy you want, Thomas Eugene O'Neill, aka *the Street,* aka *Street,* is currently residing at 30 Grattan Hill, Cork City, Republic of Ireland.'

Roussel almost dropped the phone in astonishment.

'Who is this?'

'Let's just say we both work for similar organisations, and we both have similar reasons for catching him.'

Iain Cosgrove

'Oh come on,' laughed Roussel. 'You'll have to do better than that. Hello, hello....'

He tapped the phone in annoyance; the caller had hung up. He dropped the instrument into his lap and glugged back the whiskey. What the hell was going on?

The phone rang again. He snatched it up, and pressed the answer button savagely.

'Listen, who the hell do you think you are?' he asked forcefully.

'Easy, Charlie, easy,' said a voice.

He had to think about it for a couple of seconds.

'Captain?' he asked hesitantly.

'Yeah, sorry about that,' he said. 'I wanted to leave my phone free, so I rang you on my wife's phone.'

He paused.

'I just got a very interesting call.'

'Let me guess,' said Roussel, reciting the information he had been given.

'This is too weird,' agreed the Captain.

'What do you think we should do, Cap?' Roussel asked earnestly. 'What do you really think?'

'Are you still at the suites?' asked the captain.

'Sure am,' said Roussel.

'Still got that Powers Gold Label?'

Roussel smiled.

'Sure have.'

'I'll be over in ten.'

Seven minutes later, they were both settled back in chairs on the veranda. The captain took a long slow sip of the amber fluid. He held the glass up to the light to study it closely.

'That gets better every time I taste it,' he said.

He paused and puffed up his cheeks, and then blew out his breath with a whoosh.

'So, you asked me a question,' he said. 'Okay, here's where I am.'

He took another sip.

'We've a double murder. We know the identity of one victim; we also know someone is looking for him, and that person is in Cork, Ireland. We also know that the identity of the second victim is restricted in some way, and therefore linked to some as yet unnamed Federal Agency. We know who the owner of the house is, and we also know that in all probability, he was there the night of the murders.'

Roussel nodded, and resumed the recap.

'Don't forget the gravestone. The name *Mary O'Neill* must have some significance for him. The date in the past is a mystery, but it does tie him to the property, and she shares the same surname. Wife? Mother? Who knows?'

'True,' said the captain. 'But we also now have more corroborating evidence; cryptic maybe, but corroborating evidence nonetheless. So, we have to assume he is indeed in Ireland. We even have an exact address.'

'So what should we do, Captain?' asked Roussel.

The captain looked him in the eyes for a full minute.

'You know me, Charlie,' he said. 'I'm not an impulsive man. But this federal agency angle is really pissing me off. So, here's what we do. Get some sleep, pack a few things, and get to the airport at first light. First off, see if you can get any information on passenger movements to Ireland over the last few days. He'll have used a passport; maybe the only one he has?'

The captain paused.

'Don't worry if you find nothing. Catch the first flight you can to Ireland anyway. Contact me when you get there, by which time I should have made contact with a local liaison officer in Cork. If I haven't made contact, you might have to present yourself at the local police station and call me from there.'

A thought occurred to the captain.

'Do you actually have a passport?' he asked.

Roussel extracted it from the side pocket of his Bermuda shorts.

'Never thought I'd ever get to use it, mind,' he said with a smile.

'Thanks for the drink,' said the captain, knocking the rest of the whiskey back and making to leave.

Before he descended the steps, he turned to Roussel.

'Just remember, Charlie. This guy ain't no girl scout. Be careful over there.'

'I'm on it,' said Roussel grimly.

#

The first thing he saw, as he walked from the skyway to the baggage reclaim, was a sign advertising *Powers Gold Label*. He supposed he should have made the connection; Irish whiskey, you would generally assume, was made in Ireland.

He cursed his decision to check his bag onto the plane. It had caused him nothing but trouble. No amount of ID had persuaded the Department of Homeland Security that buying a ticket to Ireland and leaving immediately was anything other than suspicious. In fact, in some ways, it had annoyed them even more.

Once he had cleared the security area, there was yet more drama. The plane had sat for two hours on the tarmac at New Orleans waiting for clearance, and then another hour's delay at JFK. Still, as a man not used to travelling, it was very odd to think that only the previous morning, he had been drinking whiskey on his landing in Louisiana, pondering the mysteries of home, and here he was now, three thousand miles away; the miracle of modern travel.

He had a moment of brain fade as he was clearing the baggage hall. There was a green channel, a red channel and a blue channel. It took his weary mind a second to work out which one he needed. The automatic glass doors opened in front of him, like the star ship enterprise, and he was home free, straight into the main body of the arrivals hall.

As he stopped to adjust the shoulder strap on his holdall, he noticed, like in all airports, people were holding up signs. They were bits of card really, with names scribbled in black marker. His eye was drawn to one in particular. He read it once and then read it again. It said *Charlie Russell*. No, he thought to himself, it couldn't be. He looked at the young man holding the sign, bored looking, about the same age as himself. He had brown hair, spiked up in an effort to look younger maybe? He was early to mid thirties, with pale blue eyes, but it was his world weary expression that gave him away. This guy was a policeman, no doubt about it.

As Roussel approached, the man studied him with interest.

'Charlie Russell?' he asked, in what seemed to Roussel to be a very soft and melodic Irish accent.

'Charles Roussel,' he answered.

The man's face relaxed and he smiled.

'Charles, nice to meet you,' he said. 'James is my name, James Murray. *Detective* James Murray,' he added, with the emphasis on detective.

'So, you must be my liaison?' asked Roussel.

'Your captain rang through last night,' said James. 'He spoke to our station superintendant. Based on the information supplied, and some brief follow-up, your boss was transferred to my boss, Inspector Ryan.'

'Any particular reason?' asked Roussel, as they started walking.

'We were hoping you could tell us a bit more,' said James, glancing at Roussel. 'But the major reason you were referred to us was the drugs connection.'

'Drugs connection?' asked Roussel, in genuine surprise.

'Scott Mitchell,' said James, handing him a photo which Roussel recognised. 'Petty criminal, extortion, protection, and latterly drug dealing.'

Roussel thought about it.

'So Scott Mitchell is a dealer?'

'*Was* a dealer,' corrected James. 'A very small time petty criminal and dealer. But it's not necessarily Mitchell we had the major interest in. It is more the man he works for. Or should I say, the guy he ultimately works for.'

Roussel digested that for a couple of seconds.

'Ok, that's a potted history of Scott Mitchell,' he said. 'So, what can you tell me about the other guy? Thomas O'Neill, the man they call *The Street*.'

'Yeah, we checked him out; not much of value on him at all. The only thing we could find out, was that he left Ireland in about 1988 as a legal emigrant to the US; got a visa in one of the lotteries in the eighties. No indication of any police record or illegal activity up to that point. But we did a bit more digging.'

At this stage, they had reached the entrance to the airport.

'Shit,' said James quickly.

Roussel could see where he was pointing and laughed. Airport police had stopped and were just about to clamp his car. James ran over and showed them some ID. A heated exchange ensued, which made Roussel laugh even more. It seemed that inter-agency cooperation was the same in any country and in any jurisdiction. The airport cops finally drove off, after trading insults with James.

'Sorry about that,' he said. 'Fucking jobsworths! Where were we?'

'Left Ireland in 1988,' said Roussel, prompting him.

'Ah yes,' responded James. 'Oh, and by the way,' he asked. 'Do you have anywhere setup to stay while you're here?'

Roussel shook his head, as he replied.

'No, thought I'd leave that to you,' he said. 'Or at least, get a local recommendation,' he continued hastily, in case the first part was misconstrued; didn't want the guy thinking he regarded him as a servant.

'Sure, we'll get you fixed-up,' said James. 'But no check-in means we can go straight round to the place.'

'What place?' asked Roussel, as they pulled out into the traffic.

'That's where it gets interesting,' said James. 'We traced Thomas's mother. She's dead; died in 1990 I think, I don't have my notes with me, sorry.'

'1990 would make sense,' said Roussel, thinking back to the simple yet tasteful headstone.

'Yeah, and her name was Mary; same as the name you found, so another loop closed there, I think.'

James paused to collect his thoughts.

'We checked out the arrangements after the funeral. He was an only child. She left everything in her will to Thomas, including the house and all the contents.'

'So, I'm guessing he never sold it,' said Roussel.

'How did you know that?' asked James quizzically.

'Well, the gravestone for me indicates guilt; I'm guessing he couldn't come back for the funeral. Maybe he kept the house, so he could eventually make peace with a few memories.'

'Very insightful,' said James, studying him thoughtfully.

'Personal experience,' said Roussel. 'Don't ask.'

'Okay, you're the boss,' said James.

'So, following this through,' said Roussel, ignoring the comment. 'If Thomas flees the US to come back home, and he's fairly certain that nobody is looking for him....'

He paused.

'....or would be able to find him,' he qualified.

'Then he would probably stay in a house that he already owned,' finished James with satisfaction.

'Which just so happens to correspond to the address we provided?' ventured Roussel.

'Exactly,' said James. 'Confirms the story even more, wouldn't you think?'

He slapped his forehead in sudden remembrance.

'Also,' he said, 'I forgot all about it with the arrival of the dickheads, but we checked incoming flights for the last few days. Nothing into Cork, so we widened our search. Bingo, he flew into Dublin on the morning of the thirteenth of May.'

Roussel felt a small swell of satisfaction. He loved it when cases started coming together.

'So, what's the plan?' he asked.

'Well, by all accounts,' said James, 'this man at the very least witnessed a double murder; may even have perpetrated it. We've got to assume he's pretty dangerous, so we should try and play it a little bit clever.'

'How so?' asked Roussel.

'I was thinking a story about a hit-and-run on the road into the estate; a dealer got hit by a car, hence the drug squad are the ones doing the snooping. Case the neighbour's each side, see if we can find out anything and then call on the house itself. See how cool a customer he really is.'

'Do you carry?' asked Roussel.

'I'm sorry, what?' asked James.

'A piece; do you carry a piece?'

James looked at him with a puzzled expression.

'A piece of what?'

'A gun; do you carry a gun?' asked Roussel in exasperation.

James's expression cleared and he smiled.

'Oh, no,' he said. 'Generally, we only carry weapons in restricted situations; very few and far between really. Very isolated incidents, when we know there is a real danger, both to us and the public.'

Roussel raised his eyebrows.

'Do we not think there's a fair chance of that here?'

James laughed.

'You're in Ireland now; it's not the Wild West. No offence, but we do things a little differently here. Anyway,' said James as he glided into a parking spot and pulled up the handbrake. 'We're here; too late.'

'Would you mind?' Roussel queried, pointing to his shorts and sandals.

'Sure,' said James. 'Hop in the back there.'

Five minutes later, with Roussel changed into much more suitable Irish summer clothes, James rang the doorbell at number twenty nine. They could hear loud music pumping from the inside. Roussel stood back a bit and glanced up at the house. There were no curtains, just bed sheets, and in some cases, newspaper taped over the windows. He was thinking, definitely a rental property.

Eventually they heard the click and clank of multiple locks and bolts being undone. The door swung open, and Roussel and James were simultaneously assaulted by the unmistakeable aroma of burning cannabis.

The man in front of them was dressed in black jeans and a black Metallica T-shirt. His greasy greying hair was pulled back in a ponytail, exposing the skull and cross bones earrings that were glinting in the midday sunlight.

'What do you want?' he asked roughly.

'Drug squad,' said James. 'We'd like to ask you a few questions.'

Roussel could barely contain his amusement. The man had gone from hero to zero in about a second. It looked like he was shitting himself on the spot. His mouth worked for a few moments, but nothing came out.

'It's not mine I swear,' he eventually managed to croak.

'Relax,' said James. 'We're not here for you or your junk. We're looking for information.'

The man's face cleared and the relief was palpable.

'Certainly officer, whatever you want!' he said enthusiastically.

Roussel heard the sound of multiple toilets flushing in the background, and he could see the man groan slightly.

'There was a hit-and-run on the main road,' said James, indicating the way they had come in. 'A dealer was killed. Did see anything?'

'What day was this?' asked the man.

James looked back at Roussel; his mind had gone blank.

'Sunday,' Roussel mouthed silently.

'Last Sunday,' said James turning back to the man. 'It would be this day last week, in fact.'

'Sorry mate,' he said. 'I was in Dublin all last week visiting friends.'

'What about next door, would they know anything?' asked James.

'Next door,' said the guy. 'I think there's somebody in there now, but I couldn't be positive. I've seen a guy going in the odd time. If he's there, he certainly keeps to himself. The old biddy next to him; she can probably tell you the car registration number of the vehicle that hit your man, and what the driver had for breakfast too,' he said.

'Thanks for your help,' said James, extracting his notebook and making a big show of writing down the address. 'You may be hearing from us again.'

'Was that a threat, officer?' asked the man, some of his lost bravado returning.

'Merely a statement of fact,' said James.

They both turned on their heel and walked away, collectively flinching as the door slammed behind them. They walked past number thirty; at least for now anyway.

'I didn't say it before,' said James. 'But leave the talking to me.'

'I kind of figured that,' said Roussel, accentuating his southern accent.

James smiled, and rang the doorbell of number thirty one. They heard the sound of at least two chains being put on, before the door was opened a tiny fraction.

'Can I help you?' asked a frail voice.

'Police, ma'am,' said James.

'Let me see some ID,' she demanded.

All signs of frailty were gone from her voice, as James reached for his pocket. She studied his credentials closely, before handing them back and opening the door wide.

'What can I do for you, detective Murray?' she asked.

'We're investigating a hit-and-run. A drug user was killed on the road last Sunday.'

She shook her head sadly.

'I'm sorry, young man. I rarely go out these days, but on Sunday I leave early for morning mass, and then round to the parish centre for lunch and bingo; I don't normally get back till about eight pm.'

'That's okay ma'am,' said James. 'What about your neighbour; number thirty?'

'Who, Thomas?' she said and smiled.

Roussel and James looked at each other.

'I'm not sure he would have seen anything. I don't think he was even here on Sunday. He's just come back from the US, you know,' she couldn't help adding. 'He lived in this house as a child; I didn't recognise him. He came over the following morning to apologise; said he had been a little bit short with me. He really has matured into such a delightful young man.'

She thought about it for a second and giggled.

'Maybe not so young anymore,' she said, 'but he'll always be that naughty lad to me.'

'Is he likely to be there now?' asked James.

'Well, his car's not there, so I doubt it,' she said.

'You've been a great help, Mrs umm....' said James.

'Walsh,' she answered automatically. 'Mrs Maeve Walsh.'

'Well thanks very much Mrs Walsh, have yourself a good day now,' said James.

'You too officer,' said Mrs Walsh.

They rang the doorbell of number thirty and peered in the windows, but it seemed Mrs Walsh was right; there was no one at home. They looked at each other; they didn't need to say anything.

'Come on, let's get you somewhere to stay,' said James. 'Thomas Eugene O'Neill doesn't look like he's going anywhere soon.'

CHAPTER 27 – GENESIS

17th May 2011 – Seven days after the Storm.

It is not death that a man should fear, but he should fear never beginning to live. – Marcus Aurelius.

I closed the door and leant back against it, my mind racing. I was fairly certain that he hadn't realised I'd spotted him, just as I was completely certain that I was being watched. There could only be one explanation.

It wasn't these amateurs I'd encountered locally. If it was, I wouldn't even have made it to the front door; I would already be dead in a messy and wasteful hail of bullets. I knew this new breed of criminal; they weren't subtle and they weren't clever.

No, this was different. This was watching, waiting, monitoring maybe. This was careful, calculated and professional. This had to be the Mancini's; I couldn't think of any other way the facts could possibly fit together.

I'd known all along that I wouldn't escape either their notice or their reach. They knew I was Irish after all, and it wouldn't have been hard to put two and two together.

Pity; I'd always thought that I'd have a little more time to play with.

Still, at least I knew two things. One, this guy was no amateur, and two, I now had the element of surprise. I just had to be careful about when I made my move.

If I considered all the angles, I knew the best policy was to sit tight and wait. I was on home turf; I knew where everything was and I knew the terrain, an advantage in any battle. Let them come, I was ready.

I had to assume, given where he was parked, that he had some kind of surveillance technology. I was fairly certain that he hadn't gained access to the house. Apart from anything else, it was almost impossible to get past Mrs Walsh.

My guess, then, was some kind of listening device. He would at least be able to hear what was going on; any phone calls I'd made, people I'd spoken to within the house. I thought back over the previous two days. I had made no calls, nor had I spoken to anybody, either inside or outside for that matter, other than Mrs Walsh.

I looked down at my hand still holding the bag full of Chinese takeaway. I checked the foil packages for warmth. They didn't need reheating, so I slopped them out onto a plate and then sat in front of the television, watching American cop show re-runs. NYPD Blue had always been a favourite, but the locations, the streets, the people made me home sick for a place that wasn't even my home.

I made a huge show of switching off the television. I then clattered into the kitchen, washed up the plates, put the waste into the bin, and clomped up the stairs, making sure the front door was closed and locked. I turned out the lights as I went, until the house was in complete darkness. I took off my shoes and socks and then reached under the mattress. I pulled it out silently; it was already fully loaded.

I knew the darkness inside the house was impenetrable, so I had a curtain of black to assist me. I relaxed completely and made my breathing silent. I was wearing cotton, so there was no heavily starched material to rustle. I moved slowly and silently down the stairs and positioned myself behind the door in the front room.

I stood there like a statue. On the face of it, you'd think it would be really boring, standing in one place. But when you are concentrating so hard on breathing silently, focusing every fibre of your body on keeping still, resisting the natural temptation to tense up, then boredom doesn't even come into it. Unfortunately fatigue does. It was tiredness more than anything else that was almost my undoing.

Like a weary driver that has spent too long at the wheel, but refuses to admit it to themselves, my eyelids kept slowly drooping and then my eyes would suddenly snap open. I was forced to readjust my focus each time. This happened two or three times and then, on the fourth, I realised I was no longer alone.

The merest click of the front door gave it away. I strained my senses, and could almost feel a gap in the air opening up. The gun was tucked into the waistband of my jeans, at the small of my back. There was no way I would be able to reach it without giving myself away. I would have to do this the hard way.

I strained my heightened senses still further. I could smell the faint odour of stale sweat; could hear the tiniest inhale and exhale of air. He was good, but not as practised as me. I felt the ripples again; the disturbance of air as he advanced through the doorway. My eyes, now well adjusted to the gloom, made out an angular metallic shape. He was armed.

The fact that he had a gun surprised me, and I made my second mistake of the last three days. My body tensed from the shock of the discovery, and a single intake of breath became barely audible. It was the only trigger he needed.

He didn't even think; he just reacted. The gun swung around in a wicked glinting curve. I ducked as it whistled harmlessly over my head to hit the solid stone wall with a crash. I grabbed the wrist that held the gun, praying that his finger was trapped inside the trigger guard, and smacked it repeatedly off the exposed stone. He howled once and then I felt grasping fingers, nails long and sharp, as he scratched for my eye sockets. I bit down on the soft tissue between forefinger and thumb, at the same time dragging the heel of my shoe down his left instep, to stamp savagely on his foot.

I smashed his hand against the wall one more time, and as I pulled it back, the gun flicked out of his grasp to land with a clatter on the coffee table. I reacted milliseconds before him, and dived for where I thought the gun had landed. The coffee table splintered like matchwood, as I fell heavily through the middle of it. He'd guessed my intent from the second I'd launched myself; he jumped after me, but not to go for the gun. He made no attempt to brace himself for landing. His elbows were down, and they hit me square in the kidneys, knocking the breath out of me.

He rolled upright, as I fought to get my breath. I felt another disturbance in the air, and then sensed the toe of his shoe coming toward me at speed as I frantically jerked my head out of the way. The foot whistled harmlessly past; I wouldn't be so lucky again. I turned sideways, and spun my legs towards him as fast as I could propel them, like a gymnast on a pommel horse. I caught him at the end of the rapidly accelerating swing, hitting him just behind and below the knee, sending him flying backwards. He fell awkwardly against a chair, the solid wooden arm catching him square in the back. He cried out and dropped to the floor, as I laboured to bring my breathing back under control.

I scrambled up and grabbed for my gun. It was not there; it must have slipped out of my waistband as I'd smashed through the table. Changing tack, I leapt for the main light switch. He used the noise of me traversing the room to disguise a pincer movement. As the light came on, I felt a vicious impact to the kidneys. I whirled around, just in time to awkwardly block the second punch.

I could see he was in pain too. We stood away from each other for a second, inhabiting that safe area where you're not completely invading your opponents personal space. He spoke for the first time.

'It appears I underestimated you,' he said, as we circled wearily.

Both sets of eyes kept flicking toward the two weapons, almost casually discarded amongst the wreckage.

'Even though I read all about you, I was hypnotised by the words describing what you did. Mob enforcer; I was expecting some unskilled thug.'

I nodded in acknowledgement, refusing to break the stare. I suddenly threw a sidekick which he blocked, following up with a roundhouse kick of his own. We traded techniques, each of us looking to exploit the weaknesses in the other. He was reasonably skilled, but he wasn't as good as me. His stance was too narrow for a fighting stance, leaving him open. I went for the kill.

I feigned a front kick, turning it at the last second into a vicious foot sweep. He'd stepped back to block the kick; too late, he saw the change in direction, the speed and the trajectory of the sweep literally lifting him off his feet. I winced as he hit the floor. His head had connected with the edge of the hearth.

At first, I thought I'd killed him; that kind of impact would dispatch many a lesser man. I knelt beside him. He was out cold, but he had a pulse; strong and steady. I searched the house. The only thing I could find was a nylon clothes line; not ideal for restraining prisoners, but in this case it would have to do.

I tied him up as securely as the nylon would allow. It wasn't great, but it would be good enough, I hoped.

Retrieving both his gun and mine from the devastated floor of the front sitting room, I made sure his gag was secured, and then sat down to wait. I had a feeling it would be a very interesting conversation.

#

Dale looked at the tourist clothes that he had carelessly discarded on the floor of his hotel room. He didn't have the greatest taste in the world, but he hoped that within his own wardrobe, he would never stoop to the fashion faux pas of checks and stripes together. He glanced at the recently delivered gleaming silver tray with renewed interest; it was only when he'd got back to his hotel room that he'd realised how hungry he was.

Five minutes later, he'd dispatched a very large club sandwich and a large portion of chips. Amazing how a full stomach could make you feel so much better. He studied the two addresses that Margaret had written down for him. He was mildly anxious that he'd had to use his private detective story. He was positive that Margaret was the kind of employee who would have noted date, time and name. There was probably even CC TV footage of him. He knew it had been worth it to get the information he wanted, but he couldn't dodge that uneasy feeling. It could come back to haunt him.

A thought occurred to Dale, as he sipped on a cup of tea; he hadn't checked in with Dodds since he'd arrived. He punched in the digits from memory and got the number unobtainable tone. He kept forgetting that the international dialling code was different from everywhere other than the USA; the arrogance of America, maybe? He dialled the number again, this time getting the unmistakable US ringtone.

'Detective Dodds,' said a voice.

'Hey Dodds, how's it going?' asked Dale, quickly realising that for some inexplicable reason he was whispering.

'Who is this?' asked Dodds.

'Hey Dodds, it's me, Dale,' he replied, this time in his normal voice.

'Hold on a second,' said Dodds softly.

Dale realised with amusement that Dodds was now the one whispering. He heard a couple of clicks and then the sound of movement and doors opening and closing. The next thing he heard was the flare of a match. Dale smiled; Dodds was in the smoking area. It was then that it occurred to him. During all the activity over the past few days, the times when he had been in serious stress, not once had he even thought about smoking. Go figure.

'Where are you?' asked Dodds, and then quickly added. 'No, don't tell me; not yet anyway. I'll feel impelled to tell the boss otherwise.'

'Why, what's wrong?' asked Dale.

'Boss got a phone call earlier,' said Dodds. 'Apparently you're stumbling around like an idiot, unwittingly stepping on all sorts of federal toes.'

'Really?' asked Dale, sitting up with interest.

'Yep, apparently the top floor got a call directly from the Medusa's head; that nest of snakes over in Langley. The Boss made it very clear to me that I needed to let him know the second you made contact.'

'I got an address,' said Dale.

'Good for you,' said Dodds. 'But whatever you're going to do, I would do it quick. I'm on a tightrope here. I'll give you as long as I can, but I'm going to have to tell the boss in the next twenty four hours.'

'I understand,' said Dale. 'And thanks Dodds; thanks for everything.'

'Good luck,' added Dodds seriously. 'And Dale; don't do anything stupid.'

Dale thought about that last statement as Dodds hung up. Stupid wasn't the word he'd have used. He'd certainly been impulsive, impetuous even, but not stupid.

Dale dropped his tray outside the door of his room and headed out. He'd been told that it rained all the time in Ireland, but he hadn't experienced rain once since he'd arrived.

It was a glorious evening; no clouds and actually quite hot too. As he walked, basking in the still warm sunshine, he studied his surroundings with interest. He realised as he walked that he'd answered the nagging question that had inhabited his head since he'd arrived in Cork. The houses, the streets, the architecture; it was all untidy and old. It wasn't laid out in neat rows and intersections like the US. It was chaotic and muddled.

He kept walking, occasionally asking directions to his first address. Some people looked at him quizzically, some with an amused indifference. It was only when he neared his destination that he could understand the reactions.

The first address he'd been given, the birthplace of the man he was looking for, had been turned into a shopping mall.

'This is more like it,' he said to himself. 'This is what I remember. This is the American legacy abroad; shopping centres.'

He walked slowly back the way he'd come. He paused halfway across the bridge that spanned the river; the Lee they called it. He watched as the silvery blackness of water roared through the arches of the bridge. It was like a metaphor for his job, the river. You could stand in it with your hands out in front of you and push with all your might, but it would find a way to flow around you. Drugs, like water, would always find a way.

So engrossed was he in his thoughts, that he almost tripped over a couple of homeless guys, pathetically jangling empty coffee cups full of coppers. He caught sight of the familiar paraphernalia. One of the men was watching the direction of his gaze, and flicked it out of sight under a blanket. He nudged his companion and whispered something. Dale shrugged and moved on.

He often wondered, in idle moments, where the huge demand had come from. The liberals would have you believe it was all down to the marginalisation of society; the evils of capitalism, creating a multi-layered and multi-tiered society, where the poor were forced into ghettos. Boredom and unemployment made willing bedfellows with experimentation and addiction. It certainly wasn't a new problem; it might have been a different substance in the modern era, but there was still the same desire for escape. Before the widespread availability of drugs, how many previous generations had succumbed to the relative evils of alcohol?

The problem that Dale had with all the theories was not from a liberal bias, not socio-economic, not even socialist. Communism, more so even than capitalism, had shown what a flawed dogma it really was. The issue Dale had was down to pure and simple economics. Drugs, like alcohol before, were not cheap. He couldn't help but think, naively maybe, that people would have far fewer problems if they used their money to actually escape the bonds of poverty, rather than fund some kind of temporary artificial escape. He was too black and white; that was his problem and he knew it.

On impulse, he turned and strode back to the two startled men.

'They don't work you know,' he said, throwing a Euro coin into their cup. 'My advice; buy yourself a coffee instead. Make this the start of the rest of your life.'

He felt strangely elated on the way back to the hotel, but he couldn't understand why. He asked directions at the hotel reception to the second address. When he realised it was literally up the road, he decided to go into the bar for a quick drink, and then put his head down for ten minutes.

After a slow pint of Guinness, the waves of tiredness threatened to overwhelm him. He thanked the barman, put it on his tab, and headed for the room. The last thing he remembered thinking was that he must remember to set the alarm. His internal body clock was scrambled.

He woke up with a guilty start. It took a couple of minutes for full consciousness to return; before he realised, with rising panic, that he'd forgotten to set his alarm. He looked at the clock radio. It was ten minutes past three in the morning. He glanced down at himself; he didn't even have to get dressed, he'd fallen asleep fully clothed.

He saluted the night watchman as he walked out the front door. The man looked at him with a puzzled expression.

'Can't sleep,' said Dale, feeling he had to justify himself.

The city streets were eerily silent. The only cars on the roads were taxis, most of them with their signs illuminated; obviously a slow night tonight. As he headed off the main road towards Grattan Hill, the predominant sound was the click of his heels on the pavement. He had memorised the address, and as he walked, he repeated it like a mantra. He didn't know why; maybe to convince himself that he wasn't alone.

He turned in to Grattan Hill, cursing his shoes, as the sound of his footsteps echoed off the solid stone walls. As he neared number thirty, he realised lights were blazing in the front room. At least someone was home.

He approached as cautiously as his shoes would allow, cursing his decision not to change into his trainers. As he got closer to the house, he noticed movement and shrank back beside the frame of the window. He peered around slowly; a body was lying amongst splintered shards of wood. There was a man with his back to the window. Dale couldn't see exactly what he was doing, but he was bent over the prostrate body.

Dale's heart rate quickened; he didn't know whether the man on the ground was alive or dead, but he knew he needed to involve the local authorities as soon as possible. He extracted his phone and started to dial, but then froze with shock, as the man got up quickly and spun towards the window.

Dale breathed a huge sigh of relief as the curtain was roughly pulled across; looked like he'd got away with it. He continued with what he was doing. He hit the dial button and got a strange triad tone, each note higher than the last. He looked at the number he had dialled; it looked right.

He didn't see the blur of silver-grey as he started turning; didn't hear the swishing sound, as it moved through the air like a crack of lightning. He barely felt the impact before his eyes rolled up into his head, and he hit the path with a thud; knocked out cold.

In his unconscious state, he was oblivious to someone grabbing him around the ankles and pulling him none too gently up the steps and into the hallway of the house. He was oblivious to being roughly manhandled into a prone position on the ground. He was unaware of the nylon washing line, as it was lashed around his arms and legs, binding another victim. He was oblivious to the gag, as it was securely fastened into place.

The sole conscious occupant of the room threw his gun onto an easy chair. He checked Dale's phone; the guy had tried dialling the emergency services, but had added an extra digit in his haste.

One thing was certain, anyway. Street chuckled, before throwing the phone onto the chair next to the gun. Dale would have one hell of a headache when he woke up.

CHAPTER 28 – CONVERGENCE

17th May 2011 – Seven days after the Storm.

Thirty spokes converge on a hub. But it's the emptiness that makes a wheel work. – Lao Tzu.

Roussel copied his companion and watched with interest as the cream coloured liquid slowly settled and separated; until the bottom of the pint was jet black, with a white unblemished head.

'Slainte,' said James, clinking glasses before taking two big gulps.

'Whatever you said,' said Roussel, doing likewise.

'It means cheers, good health,' explained James.

'They say *cheers* where I come from,' said Roussel, with a hint of devilment.

'And where is that exactly?' asked James interestedly. 'I mean I know America obviously, but whereabouts. Would you be a Yankee, for instance?'

Roussel smiled.

'Definitely not a Yankee,' he replied. 'No, I'm from the south; I suppose you could call me a son of Dixie. I went north in search of my fortune, only to discover how deeply rooted in the south I really was.'

'So, Lynyrd Skynyrd then,' said James. 'Sweet home Alabama, Dukes of Hazard and all that other stuff.'

'Pretty close,' said Roussel. 'What about yourself?'

'Oh, I'm from the south too,' answered James. 'But we're talking different sides of the same city, rather than country; the other side of the Lee.'

'Do you have the same divide?' asked Roussel interestedly.

'Not really,' said James. 'It's a bit like America, only you call them states and we call them counties. Where I'm from, we regard ourselves as infinitely better than the Jackeens, the Dubs. Cork is the real capital of Ireland; don't believe any of that other crap you hear.'

'I'll bear that in mind,' said Roussel.

They paused to take another couple of swallows.

'So, are you married?' asked Roussel.

James shook his head.

'Girlfriend?'

'Working on it,' said James with a smile. 'In fact, I've got a date next Saturday.'

'Good luck,' said Roussel, with a twinkle in his eye, taking another sip.

The Guinness was growing on him. It seemed he had a penchant for Irish alcohol.

'What about yourself?' asked James. 'Do you have a wife or Girlfriend?'

Roussel shook his head.

'Never seemed to happen for me,' he said. 'Too busy doing other things.'

'Funny how that happens when you're a policeman,' said James.

This time he wasn't smiling. Both of them knew why, and they could feel their collective spirits sinking a little.

'What kind of music do you like?'

The question from James came suddenly from left field; a concerted effort to brighten the mood.

Roussel blinked. He'd been expecting another type of question.

'Anything and everything really,' he replied, thinking about it. 'I've got pretty eclectic taste, as it happens.'

'Give me a band,' said James. 'Think of your favourite one. I'd personally say you are a Black Crows, Doobie Brothers kind of guy.'

He smiled, to rob the statement of any perceived offence.

'You'd think so wouldn't you, me being a southern boy an all,' said Roussel, heavily accentuating his accent.

James waited patiently.

'Steely Dan, they would be the band for me.'

'Reeling in the Years,' said James, nodding appreciatively. 'Good choice.'

They spent another few minutes drinking in the bitter black liquid and the early evening atmosphere.

'So, how did you get into this game?' asked Roussel.

It was more for something to say than genuine interest.

'Family tradition,' answered James. 'My father was a Garda, my grandfather was a Garda. There were no choices in my house, only expectations.'

He paused for a second.

'And yourself?'

'I originally wanted to be a lawyer,' said Roussel.

James grimaced.

'I know, bloodsucking vampires,' said Roussel. 'But as I said before, when I realised that I was being treated as little more than an object of Yankee amusement, I decided to pursue other alternatives.'

'Any regrets?' asked James.

'Not yet,' said Roussel. 'Ask me in thirty years.'

A thought suddenly occurred to Roussel; something that had been nagging at the back of his mind.

'Did you get anything on the number?' he asked James, who looked at him questioningly. 'The last one that we forwarded you; the cell phone that sent the text to Scott Mitchell's mobile; when the evidence clerks were bagging and tagging the phone.'

James face cleared.

'Ah, the *phone* number,' he said. 'Well, we had mixed results on that one. I can tell you that it was definitely sent from Cork, but that's about all I can tell you. It's a pay as you go; one of those unregistered to a specific individual. There is no billing system address database to tie back to.'

'So, no way to tell definitively who owns it?' asked Roussel.

'We can only track it as part of an active high profile investigation,' said James. 'But I would need to get some serious sign off to do that. I don't think we are anywhere near that stage yet, do you?'

Roussel shook his head.

'I think you're probably right.'

James drained the remainder of his pint.

'Come on,' he said. 'If we are going to check this guy out we had better move now.'

They drove in companionable silence, Roussel laughing inwardly as the local radio station played *Ricki don't lose that number.*

'That's Steely Dan, right?' asked James with a chuckle.

They pulled into Grattan Hill. All lights were off at number thirty.

'Looks like it will have to wait till the morning,' said James, turning the car around.

As he pulled back out onto the road, he was unaware of his licence plate number being written down.

When they got back to the hotel, James declined Roussel's offer of a Guinness for the road. As he drove away, he shouted out.

'Be ready at nine thirty tomorrow morning!'

Roussel looked at his own watch. There was just time for another pint of Guinness before catching up on some much needed sleep. He ordered his drink, and also a burger and fries; memories of home. He took them both up to his room on a brown tray.

When he had finished eating, which didn't take very long, he was shocked to belatedly discover how hungry he'd been. He sat on the bed and started flicking through the hotel TV channels. Coming from the US, he was amazed to discover there were only six in the hotel. As he surfed, he didn't register that his eyelids were getting heavier, and eventually his eyes finally closed altogether, and the remote control slipped from his unconscious fingers.

He awoke with a start; an explosion from an old rerun of *the A team* had jerked him awake. He shivered; he had literally slumped to the side of the bed in his clothes, and the hotel heating had long since switched off. He checked the bedside alarm clock and then his watch; according to both it was four am. He pulled down the bedspread and got into bed. After ten minutes of fruitless tossing and turning, he cast aside the quilt in frustration; he was wide awake now.

He swung his legs out of bed, re-laced his boots and shrugged himself into his leather jacket. He'd committed the address to memory, so it was the easiest thing in the world to type it into Google maps and hit *get directions*.

Before he left the hotel foyer, he phoned the captain.

'Hey Charlie, what's up?' asked the captain.

'Couldn't sleep,' said Roussel. 'I figured you'd still be up.'

'The night is young, Charlie Boy, it's only ten thirty here,' said the captain.

'That's kinda what I figured,' said Roussel.

'Any developments?' asked the captain.

'Didn't get as much on the cell phone as I'd have liked,' said Roussel. 'They have to jump through hoops, paperwork wise, to get a trace, apparently.'

'Pity,' sighed the captain.

'But I have confirmed something; the address that both of us were given is where our boy is actually living,' said Roussel.

'So not a wasted journey,' said the captain in amusement.

'Certainly not wasted,' said Roussel. 'I've started to get a taste for Guinness, among other things.'

'Just be careful,' responded the captain. 'If you're going to question this guy, don't go it alone. Apart from anything else, you have no jurisdiction; you are their guest and observer, nothing more, you hear me?'

'I hear you,' said Roussel. 'Take care, Captain.'

He hung up and then walked straight out through the automatic door, whistling tunelessly, disobeying his superior's direct order.

The navigation was a doddle; where would modern civilisation be without Google? He found himself at the entrance to Grattan Hill at approximately four thirty am.

Roussel was an accomplished detective. On his first pass, he strolled past the row of houses nonchalantly, behaving he hoped, like any pedestrian would. He paid no attention to any particular house, noting that the curtains were drawn and the lights were out at number thirty. He didn't know for certain, but he was fairly sure that houses this old would have a back way in, and at the end of the street he was proven to be correct. He found an alleyway, which led around to a laneway behind the houses.

His first issue was the lack of numbering in the lane; he had to retrace his steps back along the street, and then count backwards to eventually arrive at number thirty. He tried the gate; it wasn't locked and had a simple latch mechanism. He opened it gingerly, nodding with satisfaction as it swung soundlessly inwards on well oiled hinges. Someone was definitely looking after the place.

He briefly contemplated heading back to the hotel, but at this stage he was as curious as a cat, and anyway, he was a trained law enforcement officer. There wasn't much he was afraid of.

He moved as silently as he could through the gate. The rear of the property was in darkness, but the moon was full and bright. It was a typical old terraced house with a single storey return. The back door was set into the side of a small extension that looked much younger than the rest of the house. He tried the handle; he hadn't expected it to be anything other than locked and he wasn't disappointed.

He extracted his small Mag light and selected the slimmest beam that he could. Luckily for him, the rear door was half glass, so he could see straight into the kitchen. The internal doors at both ends were closed; presumably one was to the downstairs bathroom and one connected the kitchen to the front room. He flicked the thin beam around the interior briefly, noting how smart and pristine everything was; it was maintained to a very high standard.

He turned his attention to the back door. There was a large glass panel set into the top half; clear single glazed, rather than the double glazed opaque you would expect. There was also a small animal flap set into the panel in the bottom half.

He clamped the torch between his teeth, knelt backwards with his elbows supporting his body, and just about managed to squeeze his head through the flap. By moving his jaw from side to side, he could illuminate the area above his head. He could see at least two deadbolts, a chain and two Yale locks. He extracted himself gingerly.

He could break a window. In fact, breaking a window was the only way he would be able to get in, but he had to think of a way to deaden the noise. He glanced around the small yard, his eye taking in the clothes on the line. The pencil thin beam continued its circumnavigation, picking out a small lawn bordered with very large earthenware plant pots.

An idea suddenly came to him. He had probably seen it on *MacGyver*, but it was worth a try. He took all of the clothes off the line and stuffed them through the flap. He spread them out underneath the door onto the cold stone floor of the kitchen, trying to create a small area of sound deadening padding.

He walked over to one of the plant pots. He put his finger in and sampled the soil. It wasn't too peaty; nice and sticky, the perfect consistency. He proceeded to dig out the material, packing the window area with the clay-like soil, until he could no longer see through the glass, and the earth was level with the wooden frame-edge of the door. He wrapped his arm a couple of times with a woollen jumper. Standing with his back to the door, he said a couple of *hail Mary's*, and then jabbed his elbow backwards into the soil packed pane as hard and as fast as he could.

He heard a soft crump as he drew in his breath, waiting for all hell to break loose. Miraculously, nothing happened. He made the sign of the cross, and then spent the next ten minutes painstakingly removing the individual shards of glass, until he had a space large enough to fit his head and shoulders through.

Stretching his arm to the limit, he managed to undo all three deadbolts, and slide off the chain. It was then just a matter of turning the keys in the two Yale locks.

He was careful to open the door gingerly. He moved inside and closed it slowly behind him; there was still a chance that some shards could fall.

When he was safely inside, he checked out the kitchen. As he had seen before, there was a door directly in front of him, and one directly behind. At the far end, to his rear, there was a small rudimentary bathroom, just as he had suspected. He peered inside briefly. It was immaculately presented and very sparsely furnished. No feminine touches of any kind.

He moved to the door at the other end of the kitchen. He pressed his ear to the panelling; he could hear nothing. He opened the door soundlessly and stepped through. He flicked the Mag light quickly around the room and took a further step.

He didn't see the obstruction on the ground until it was too late; his knees buckled, and he fell on top of the object with a dull thud. It was soft and warm and he recoiled in horror. His torch was rolling in a circular motion, weirdly illuminating the two prone bodies on the floor.

He grabbed the light and examined both quickly. One was groaning and semiconscious, but breathing steadily and with a strong pulse. The other man regarded him with wary eyes, but did not seem overly scared, which surprised him. Both men were hogtied; it was the only way they would have described it, back home in Louisiana.

There was a muffled sound from the conscious man. Roussel flicked his light back to the man's eyes; he was motioning them to the right and then up. Roussel turned milliseconds before the onrushing kick would have connected. He managed to parry it with a wildly flailing arm, but his assailant spun through three hundred and sixty degrees, and caught him square in the stomach with another kick. Roussel doubled up as the air was forced out of his lungs. He never saw the *coup de gras* coming.

His assailant sighed for a third time as Roussel slumped to the floor. Luckily, it had been a very long washing line. After seeing to Roussel, he dragged the three men to the couch and sat them upright, making them as comfortable as their bindings would allow. He waited till they were all conscious, seemingly mesmerised as he rhythmically waved his weapon backwards and forwards. The gags were all still securely in place, so he could tell he had their full and complete attention; their expressions were all he needed to see.

'So gentleman,' he said pleasantly. 'Who wants to go first?'

CHAPTER 29 – DIFFUSION

10th January 2011 – Four months before the Storm.

The advancement and diffusion of knowledge is the only guardian of true liberty. – James Madison.

He sat outside the office on a cheap plastic chair. The admin complex was located in a prefab in the middle of a combat zone, so he couldn't really complain. At least he had something to sit on.

He tried to concentrate on not looking conspicuous and only managed to look more so. He wondered for the hundredth time what the general had in mind for him as he received ever more suspicious looks from comrades walking past. Discipline was the normal reason for being static on a chair, waiting for the commanding officer.

He prayed for the door to open and end his misery, and yet in another way, he wanted to stay outside; he was a little apprehensive of what awaited him.

'Kelly!'

He jerked to attention instinctively and then realised he was still sitting down.

He jumped up, marched in and stopped. He had expected an ante room, but had also forgotten how hands-on the general was purported to be, especially in combat situations.

The general looked up as Kelly entered.

'At ease, Sergeant,' he said. 'Take a seat.'

'Yes sir, thank you sir,' he said, saluting and babbling in equal measure.

'Relax, Sergeant Kelly,' he said, indicating the chair. 'I won't bite.'

Kelly sat down and waited expectantly. The general continued to write expansively on the notepad in front of him and Kelly was not stupid enough to interrupt.

General Marty *Bubba* Bradford was a heavily decorated three star general. He had started his combat career in Vietnam, and both his reputation and his rank had risen through the various campaigns in between. He had been involved in everything from dirty little skirmishes in war-torn third world countries, to large scale conflicts between UN sovereign nations, so he knew what he was about.

He was a surprisingly small man for one in such a powerful position, but he more than made up for it in presence and charisma. His was not the typical small man syndrome. He was a genuine leader of men, and both his officers and enlisted soldiers treated him accordingly. They loved him.

Even in the Rifles, Sergeant Kelly's UK regiment, they had heard of Bubba Bradford, so when Kelly had been approached by his company commander to act as a special liaison with the US 101st Airborne Division, he had jumped at the chance. The Screaming Eagles had an illustrious history.

Sergeant Kelly was not a career soldier; it was not something he'd dreamed about since he was a boy. Soldiery was not in his family, but he had found it a surprising release from the endless quarrels and arguments with his mother. He hadn't seen it at the time, but the lack of meaningful work had been eating away at him; poisoning his soul. Men were meant to toil and he hadn't realised that. He had become lazy and complacent. He had been furious when his mother had come home from work, after a particularly vicious morning disagreement, and told him she had enrolled him in the army.

He could have refused to join-up, but he hadn't, and he distinctly recalled the millisecond that enlightenment had come to him. They'd been on the killing fields, the bleak bayonet training grounds, and had been told to put on their war faces. As he'd looked around, the youthful clean-shaven visages had morphed into unrecognisable masks of hate.

He'd looked ahead at the sandbag hanging from the gallows. It had been filled with bags of pig's blood, and as he'd chanted the same words as his comrades, *kill, kill, kill,* he'd felt a red mist descend on him. He'd charged for the object of his hate, and as the bayonet had slammed into the target, he'd realised that a man had to work for a living, and this was the work that he, Sean Kelly, wanted to do. And as the blood had spurted onto his face, he'd truly become a man for the very first time.

'Do you know what he wants me for, sir?' he'd asked Major Sherry, his commanding officer.

'No idea Kelly, but it is a big honour. The only problem for most of the men when these postings come up is that they tend to be non-combative; that could be the case here, so just bear that in mind.'

'I'll take my chances, sir,' said Kelly, not realising how prophetic those words would be.

Up close, Bubba was surprisingly anonymous for a career army man. He wore plain unadorned fatigues just like his men, but his voice, when he started speaking, was loud and commanding.

'Sergeant Kelly, you and your guys in the Rifles have a problem in Helmand province. It is echoed across all of the battlefields in Afghanistan and

Iraq, and unites us as soldiers. Your comrades are dying and so are ours. Your comrades are being maimed and losing limbs on a daily basis, and so are ours.'

'Yes sir,' said Kelly.

He was not sure there was any other response he could offer. It was the truth after all.

'Well, here in the US army, we are getting sick of it. As a general, I have a bit of clout, so I started asking questions of the secretary of defence, who started asking questions of other agencies.'

Sean did not offer a comment. He could only imagine what Bubba meant by other agencies. He read thrillers and went to the movies. His active imagination told him they had letters in their names, rather than words.

'So what has all this got to do with me, sir?' he asked.

'The military campaign to drive Saddam Hussein and his Iraqi forces out of Kuwait, if a young man like you can remember back that far, was called operation Desert Storm. You, and others like you, will be leading the vanguard of a new offensive that we're calling simply *Operation Storm.*'

'So, this is not a desk-based position?' queried Sean.

Bubba chuckled.

'About as far removed from a desk as it is possible to get,' he said. 'Is that a problem for you? I need a hundred percent commitment on this, Sergeant. If that's going to be an issue, you need to tell me now.'

'No issue, sir,' said Sean.

He really meant it.

The general narrowed his eyes and looked at him for a few seconds. Sean didn't flinch under the ocular assault. Eventually the general seemed satisfied and grunted to himself. He picked up the handset on his desk and hit the top redial button; the most used of the buttons on the phone, judging by how faded and dirty it was.

'Major Thompson,' barked the general. 'Could you join us in here for a few minutes please?'

As Sean waited, the general busied himself with other tasks. For those few moments, he was oblivious to Sean even being there. He was a man used to working around distractions; it was the only way you could survive and thrive in combat situations, and he had done that for a very long time.

Eventually, there was a discreet knock on the door.

'Enter,' shouted the general.

The visitor stepped smartly into the room and saluted with precision. The general returned the salute.

'At ease, Major,' he said.

As the newcomer pulled over a chair, Sean studied him surreptitiously. He was a tall man, but not particularly wide at the shoulder. He reminded Sean of a skyscraper in the midst of construction. You could see how tall it was, and how large it could be, but the framework hadn't yet been filled in.

His face, as he pulled the chair up to the desk, was drawn and reserved. He had angular and pointed features, rather than soft and fleshy ones. The light blue eyes sparkled with a keen intelligence, and Sean could see the muscles and sinews honed and taut on the major's forearms. He was obviously exceptionally fit, even for an army man.

'Major Thompson is in charge of the team that have been tasked with operationalising our new weapon,' said the general carefully. 'He'll give you a full briefing of what is required in combat situations, from both you and your men.'

The general nodded at Major Thompson, who resumed the conversation. Sean was struck by how deep his voice was too; it wasn't what he'd been expecting.

'Your team will be the first we have operationalised from the British army,' said Major Thompson, 'so it's important that we get this right for future deployment.'

'Yes sir,' replied Sean, nodding in acknowledgement.

'The primary use of this weapon,' stated Major Thompson, 'is in siege and stand-off situations; where a direct assault would mean serious loss of life due to terrain, solider numbers or other considerations. The weapon can be deployed in one of two ways; either in a standard tear-gas canister or in a diversionary smoke canister. We have adapted both these means of deployment, so they can be fired from launchers, but I'll come to that later.'

'So, would it be safe to say that the weapon is biological, sir?' asked Sean.

'It's a gas,' acknowledged the major carefully.

'Okay, so deployment method is smoke or tear-gas canister of some kind,' said Sean. 'But you said there were two parts to the weapon.'

'I did,' said the major. 'The other part relates directly to troop safety and is the key to the deployment. You'll all have your standard issue equipment, but in the Operation Storm deployment team, we have developed a specific canister for the gas masks. When out in the field in a combat situation, this canister must be worn at all times.'

The major held up a bright orange object about the same size as a half tin of beans, with holes in the top and bottom, like a pepper shaker.

'We have made it easy to see if an individual soldier does not have the canister deployed,' said the Major, indicating the garish colour. 'I cannot state enough that in any deployment situation, the canister must be worn by every single member of the unit. Failure to do so puts not only the individual at risk, but the entire team.'

'So, is this gas contagious?' asked Sean.

The general and the major exchanged a glance, the meaning of which was lost on Sean. There was definitely a meaning though, he was sure of that.

'Let's just say exposure is highly dangerous,' said the major bluntly, 'and leave it at that.'

'So, those are the component parts,' stated Sean. 'What's the deployment strategy?'

'Good question,' said Major Thompson.

He exchanged another look with the general. Sean was not good at reading people, but he thought he might have detected a look of relief passing between the two men.

'Hypothetically, the deployment scenario would look like this,' said Major Thompson.

He cleared his throat and took a swig from his water bottle before continuing.

'You and your team are on patrol somewhere in Helmand province. You're on the lookout for snipers, IED's and fortified positions. When you encounter a fortified position; one where the enemy has dug in and you can keep him pinned down, this would be the ideal deployment situation, and you would execute the following steps.'

The major took another long swig of water, to lubricate his vocal chords.

'First off, you would instruct all of your team to deploy their gas masks. You would personally check their masks and their utility belts to make sure they were using the right canister, before going on to any further step.'

Sean nodded.

'As I said at the start, the gas and smoke canisters were specifically developed to be deployed from rocket launchers. As part of the package, each team will get two launchers and a small GPS rangefinder device. These are standard parts of the equipment inventory you will be given.'

Sean nodded again.

'You will plot the estimated coordinates for the enemy position. The device will have the four points of the compass embossed into the plastic cover. You will need to make sure it is oriented with the built-in compass. The device will beep continually if it is not aligned correctly. On one side, there is an airflow meter. The rangefinder device will measure the prevailing wind, and will then accurately calculate the best spot within the enemy position to deploy the weapon. Once these coordinates are locked into the rangefinder, they are uploaded automatically to the guidance system on the primary launcher. Are you with me so far?'

'Seems straight forward at the moment, sir,' said Sean.

'Once the guidance system is primed, you will load one of the specially adapted canisters into the launcher; they look like mini rockets. Pull the trigger to the first position on the launcher, and it will download the coordinates to the rocket. It only takes a second or two and once the download is complete, it will release the trigger. You then aim the launcher at the specific target, and pull the trigger all the way back.'

'Can you miss?' asked Sean.

'The missile is GPS guided,' said the major. 'It's impossible to miss once the coordinates are uploaded. It's just safer to point the launcher at the target than in another random direction.'

Sean nodded his understanding.

'As part of the missile deployment solution, there is a sensor that measures the concentration levels of the gas within the target area. This is identified on the rangefinder as an amber warning light. You will need to fire one missile every minute until that amber light goes out.'

'So what happens then?' asked Sean, expecting more.

'Then, Sergeant Kelly, I'm afraid you wait.'

Sean blinked at the unusual pronunciation of sergeant. He'd almost forgotten that Major Thompson was American.

'For how long, sir?'

'Approximately seven hours. That's why it's critical that you identify fortified positions that you can contain. Once the weapon has been deployed, no one can be allowed to leave or escape.'

'So what happens at the seven hour mark, sir?' asked Sean.

'You wait for a further hour,' said Major Thompson.

He and the general exchanged that same look again.

'No matter what else happens,' he added cryptically, 'you must wait that extra hour. Then you go in, still wearing your masks and secure the area.'

'What happens if there is any resistance?' asked Sean.

Major Thompson and General Bradford exchanged their first smile of the conversation.

'Son,' said Bubba, 'and trust me on this. There will be no resistance.'

#

Almost exactly a week later, Kelly assembled his team under one of the training tents in Camp Bastion. They were fresh off a four day vacation, and it had been decided, further up the chain of command, that it was the ideal time to equip and train the team with the new weapon.

Sean watched them critically out of the corner of his eye. It was the same picture you would get watching any gathering of men from eight to eighty. They were all jockeying for position; all trying to establish themselves as the alpha male.

He knew they regarded him with some suspicion, and they also collectively thought that sometimes he was a little too easily led, but he'd been working on those qualities. He knew he was becoming a better solider and a better leader. But most of all, he knew from long experience on the battlefields, that once those helmets went on and the doors of the compound were opened, they would do anything for him and for each other. They were, in short, just an ordinary bunch of lads who had become moulded into a superior fighting force by an extraordinary situation.

'Quiet!' he shouted suddenly, into the melee.

He laughed at their discomfiture as they came shuffling and muttering over to where he stood.

'Right ladies,' he said, as he started handing out the simple operational manuals. 'Gather round, we've got some work to do.'

CHAPTER 30 – ANSWERS

18th May 2011 – Eight days after the Storm.

It is easier to judge the mind of a man by his questions rather than his answers. – Pierre Marc Gaston de Levis.

I was dog tired, and I knew it wasn't over. The death squads always came in fours, so there was another one out there somewhere, maybe watching me right now. This would be an interesting conversation; I'd have to keep my wits about me.

'I think we'll start with our most recent party crasher first,' I said, indicating my latest captive.

I screwed the silencer carefully onto the end of the 9mm.

'Let's be perfectly clear about one thing,' I added. 'No one speaks unless invited to do so. I have killed many times before, I am on the run and I am very tired, so I will have no hesitation in killing again, do I make myself clear?'

As I removed the gag from the last captive, I studied each man closely. Without the benefit of speech, their eyes were the next most expressive communication tool they had. My initial snap judgement looked like it was proving to be correct. All three of them were fearful certainly, but not afraid; there was a subtle difference between the two emotions.

As I finally freed the gag, I put a hand over his lower face, placing the silencer to my lips and raising my eyebrows. He understood my meaning; he didn't like it, but he understood it. I removed my hand slowly from his mouth, and sat back down in the chair. He looked at me with a baleful stare; he was not happy.

I opened my mouth to speak, but before I could formulate the words, he made his first error.

'You're making a big mistake,' he said softly.

I didn't let him finish the sentence. The vase on the window ledge, behind and slightly to the right of his head, exploded into a thousand pieces. Mum had loved it, but I'd never cared for it; an expedient choice of target.

'The instructions were very simple,' I said. 'The next one will be six inches to the left.'

He nodded, but again there was something controlled about his demeanour; grudging acceptance, rather than blind panic.

'Do you know who I am?' I asked.

'You are Thomas Eugene O'Neill, a.k.a *The Street*, a.k.a. *Street*,' he replied without hesitation.

I acknowledged the delivered statement without surprise. He would know who I was all right.

I studied him closely, prior to moving on. He was good-looking, tanned and well built; lots of work in the gym, I suspected, but very little martial arts or combat experience. His defence had been instinctive, rather than trained. His southern US accent was the only surprise. Guido and Ernesto tended to avoid the Confederacy; another one of their many foibles.

I removed the gag from the second man. He regarded me with wary and watchful eyes, but didn't make the same mistake as his predecessor. He waited for the question.

'What do you want from me?' I asked.

He looked at me and held my gaze.

'Storm,' he said eventually and with finality.

Yet again, it was no surprise to me; they wanted their folder back.

I turned to the last of the men; the older one, the first one I had apprehended. He had a swagger, an aura of self assurance about him that made me assume he was their leader. I removed the gag from his mouth. He spat a couple of times and coughed.

'Who are my former employers?' I asked him.

He smiled at the word *former*.

'Guido and Ernesto Mancini,' he answered, without pause.

'So this question to all of you,' I said, tapping the silencer to my temple and pointing to each of them in turn. 'Where is your buddy, your colleague, the last member of the team?'

I watched them closely as they exchanged quizzical glances. They were either extremely good at faking it, or they had absolutely no idea what I was talking about.

I transferred my attention back to the first captive.

'Okay, let's try a different tack,' I said. 'Give me your name and occupation.'

'Detective Charles Roussel, badge number 6566,' he answered immediately. 'I work out of St James Parish CID in Louisiana.'

'I know where it is,' I said softly, to hide my surprise.

I turned my attention away from Roussel to the second man.

'And you?' I asked. 'Same question.'

'Special Agent Dale Foster, Drugs Enforcement Administration,' he said, with emphasis on the *Special*. 'I'm normally based out of Westchester, New York, but I'm currently task force liaison with NYPD, based on 10th avenue.'

This time I couldn't hide my surprise.

'DEA?' I inquired incredulously.

'Absolutely,' he said. 'Although I'm not here in an official capacity,' he added, his voice trailing away.

I shook my head a couple of times, and then turned my attention to the last man.

'Don't tell me,' I said sarcastically. 'FBI right?'

'Almost,' he said unsmilingly. 'Let's just say it's the other one and leave it at that, shall we?'

I looked at him wordlessly for a few minutes. I then whipped out the small Swiss Army knife I always carried, and cut their bonds quickly and cleanly. As they sat there, rubbing their wrists and ankles to renew the circulation, I spoke up again.

'Well gentlemen,' I said. 'This changes everything.'

I showed them the weapon I held, and then slowly and deliberately laid it to one side. As fellow armed professionals, I hoped they would interpret it as a sign of trust.

'You,' I gestured at Roussel as I spoke. 'Can I call you Charles, by the way?' I asked.

'Sure,' he nodded.

'So, Charles,' I continued. 'I'm guessing that you eventually managed to find a paper trail; maybe a set of documents that attested to my ownership of a certain Plantation house, even though I tried to hide the transaction as best I could, by using a lawyer from well outside the normal parish boundaries? And because of that, you believe I'm implicated in at least one, but more probably, both murders that happened on that evening of May tenth, am I right?'

'That just about covers it,' he said.

'You see, Charles,' I said. 'I get you. I understand why you are here. I thought it would take law enforcement longer to find me, but I do understand the logical route you travelled to get here, and the assumptions you made about my innocence or guilt.

I gestured at Foster.

'But you....' I said.

I gestured at the nameless CIA agent.

'And especially you....' I said.

I paused to let it sink in.

'I have no idea what possible interest you guys could have with me?'

'If I may,' responded Foster.

I nodded at him.

'Sure, go ahead,' I said.

'For me, it started about a week ago,' said Foster. 'All I got at first was a vague indication, then some more specific rumblings about something big about to go down. I started to take notice, especially when a particular duo of unrelated informants gave me roughly the same information, but from wildly differing standpoints and for wildly different reasons.'

I inclined my head briefly, inviting him to go on.

'We then got lucky with a bust; a man called Sam Rudino.'

My eyebrows arched up in the middle.

'Really?' I asked. 'He was always a meek and mild one. So what trouble has young Sammy got himself into?'

'He was involved in a fight outside a nightclub,' said Foster.

'His ego was always grossly mismatched with his personality when he had a few drinks on board.' I said. 'But unfortunately for him, he didn't have the fists or the fight to back up his mouth. Go on.'

'When we brought him in, or rather when we interviewed him, it transpired that he was in a spot of bother.'

Foster smiled at the memory.

'Let's just say, he misappropriated an amount of something that didn't belong to him.'

I whistled softly.

'I was always telling them,' I said. 'That place was just far too relaxed. It was full of more holes than a Swiss cheese, but they never listened to me.'

I clarified the statement.

'Not on that, anyway,' I finished abruptly.

'Who didn't listen?' asked Foster interestedly.

'It's your story,' I said. 'But you know exactly who I mean; Guido and Ernesto, of course.'

Foster acknowledged my remark with a flash of triumph; obviously some personal vindication of some sort.

'Anyway,' he said. 'Sam confirmed to us, or at least as far as he could corroborate, that this ghost we'd been chasing; this big one.'

'Storm,' I offered.

'Exactly,' he said. 'As far as Sam could ascertain, Storm was a drug; a new drug that was going to be coming out of a place called Cork, in Ireland.'

He stopped to scratch the side of his face absently.

'Because he had decided to be so helpful,' continued Foster, 'we decided to cut him some slack. We went back to Rudino's, and in an effort to cover Sam's light fingered indiscretion, we interviewed two more individuals that he'd indicated might be able to provide us with a few more leads.'

'Let me guess,' I said, 'Mario and Franco; more gossip between them than a couple of Neapolitan Nonna's.'

Foster laughed in spite of himself.

'You know them?' he asked, half a statement really. 'So it wouldn't surprise you to know that it was them who gave us your name?'

'Not in the least,' I replied.

'So....'

Foster reddened slightly.

'....here is where it gets slightly tricky. At the start of my career, I was desperate to be noticed and to get ahead.'

'Aren't we all,' I commented.

'Maybe so,' he acknowledged. 'But in this case I let it cloud my judgement. Due to some over exuberance and under investigation on my part, I may have inadvertently encouraged my superiors in an ultimately expensive and fruitless investigation.'

I smiled at the description.

'You were sold a pup,' I stated flatly.

He nodded.

'So when I presented them my latest evidence, as circumstantial as it comes I think you'll agree. Let's just say they were not overly enthusiastic, to put it mildly. Firstly, there was the linking of *Storm*, the new drug, with Ireland, and the rumours of its manufacturing base being established in Ireland too. Secondly, there was the name *the Street*, given to me during an interview, also linked with both Ireland and the Mancini's. In their eyes, I'd added two and two and got a hundred. You can imagine their response. I was politely told that I really needed to take a break. So here I am.'

'Okay, I can see how you got my nickname,' I said. 'But how did you find me, once you got here?'

'The FBI reporting portal gave me your real name,' he answered.

'But how did you find the house, if you are here unofficially?' I asked.

'The register of marriages, births, and deaths,' said Foster. 'I drew a blank on you, but your mother's death certificate lists this address.'

'Very resourceful,' I said, actually genuinely impressed.

'What about you?' I asked Roussel, turning back to him. 'How did you find me?'

'Same method, slightly different route,' he said. 'I didn't have to rely on the register of marriages, births, and deaths. I had a tip off and the local police did the rest of my digging for me.'

'Very commendable,' I said.

The third man was watching me with a slightly superior smirk.

'And what about you?' I asked the anonymous agent. 'You've kept very quiet; what's your story?'

'I don't have one,' he said. 'You, on the other hand....'

He paused and closed his eyes. They flickered under the lids like computer hard drives seeking information.

'July seventeenth, 1993,' he said at last.

213

I blinked in surprise.

'An NYPD team was closing in on an extremely large shipment; heroin I think, but that's the only thing I'm hazy about. Just before the team received the order to go, a man strolled out into the middle of the deal. Even though there were five heavily armed gang members, they seemed afraid. Unfortunately, one of them panicked and they all ended up dead. But here's the kicker....'

The agent looked directly at me as he spoke.

I glanced at Foster and Roussel; they were mesmerised as to where the story was going.

'Once the arrest team recovered from their shock and surprise, they shouted an order to surrender. The unknown assailant merely holstered his weapon, and slipped unseen into the dark. The thing is, while they were searching that wharf, the police officers got a bit jumpy. They were firing live rounds in all directions into the night. Even though he must have had officers in his sights during that time, he never once fired a shot. All they found were five dead bad guys and five shell casings.'

'My beef is not with law enforcement; never has been,' I responded, by way of explanation. 'They are just doing their job. I'm doing mine, and no hard feelings as far as I'm concerned.'

Roussel and Foster exchanged a glance; from where I was sitting, I couldn't tell what it was about.

'September eleventh, 2001,' he continued. 'The date will live long in the memory, for other more obvious reasons. But well outside the downtown area, shots were reported in a neighbourhood in Yonkers; officers were called to a boarded-up Food Lion. Six Colombian males were found dead, sprawled around twelve pallets of cocaine.'

I inclined my head in brief acknowledgement.

'There was a handwritten note on top of one of the pallets,' said the agent. 'It was written all in capitals. It said simply, *just taking out the garbage.*'

'Computers are to blame for that,' I said. 'I've lost the ability to write joined up.'

They looked at me in surprise, but I knew they understood what I meant.

'Just a little freelance work,' I said. 'I used to do the odd job myself, especially if the Colombians were involved. Let's just say, we didn't necessarily see eye to eye.'

'On June the first, 1988,' said the agent, 'a young Irish immigrant was beaten senseless and left for dead in an alley in Brooklyn. Unusually for the time, he was legal; came over from Ireland on a green card he won in a lottery. The perpetrators were a bored and restless gang of Colombian youths. The young Irish man just happened to stray into their path at the wrong time; he survived against all the odds.'

'Approximately three months later,' he continued, 'a young Irish man ended up outside a particular bar. He walked inside, shouting and brandishing a gun. The eye witnesses that were in the lounge at the time all swore on oath that they didn't believe he originally meant to kill, he just wanted to shake the gang up a little. It was indicative of his early naivety that he didn't think they would be armed. They started pulling their weapons, leaving him with no choice. Five out of the six Colombian men were shot dead where they sat.'

Foster and Roussel were watching me with intense interest.

'The last one, the leader of the gang, was mortally wounded. He managed to crawl out from under the table. The young Irish man walked over to the stricken youth. As he readied his weapon for the *coup de gras*, he was heard to whisper, *live by the Street, die by the Street*, before a single shot rang out and a legend was born.'

'Not so sure about *legend*,' I said, with a wry smile.

There was a period of intense silence, as the information was digested by all.

'Do you mind if we turn the tables a bit; ask you some questions?' asked Roussel.

He cast an anxious glance at the pottery shards behind his shoulder.

'If I can answer them, I will,' I said in response.

'On the evening of the tenth of May 2011, were you present at Augustine Mansion?'

'I was,' I replied with a smile.

I couldn't help it. He sounded so much like a policeman.

'And did you kill Scott Mitchell and another as yet unknown person on that same night?'

'I did,' I answered, making him blink in surprise.

I'm not sure if it was my honesty that put him off, but he shouldn't have been shocked. If he was worth his salt as an investigator, then he should have already suspected the answer.

'It was in self-defence,' I stated, 'if that makes a difference. At least I thought it was at the time.'

I added the clarification, which sounded slightly lame, all things considered.

'We didn't find any weapons,' said Roussel.

'Probably in the belly of a gator by now,' I said. 'I threw them straight into the middle of the river, both of them. You don't know how much I hated doing that. One of them was my favourite weapon; perfectly balanced.'

'Who is the other guy? The one we weren't able to ID?' asked Roussel.

'No idea,' I said.

'You did say you would answer all the questions,' said Roussel.

'I also said that if I knew the answer I would,' I replied. 'This time I don't.'

He tried a different tack.

'Well if you don't know who he is,' he asked, 'any guesses as to why his criminal records are classified?'

I thought about it for a second.

'Guido and Ernesto decided that I was no longer on the payroll,' I said. 'They asked me to do one last job, then sent a cleanup squad to tidy up after me and take out the trash, me included. I hadn't suspected at all, but they had decreed that I too was destined for the dumpster. Luckily for me, the team they sent were just slightly too green and I managed to neutralise them all. Unfortunately, the gentleman I was meeting wasn't so lucky; even though I tried my best to protect him, they managed to kill him. Don't ask me how they tracked me to Louisiana, but track me they did, have no doubt about that. In answer to your question....'

I thought about it for a second.

'He was an assassin; a mercenary, plain and simple. Probably freelance, but angling to get on their books. What better way to make a name for yourself than eliminating your predecessor.'

'But why classified?' asked Roussel. 'I get everything else you're saying, but I just don't understand why his identity would be considered secret?'

'His connection with the Mancini's, I would guess. Anyway, does it matter?'

'I don't know,' said Roussel. 'I have a feeling it does.'

'Why did they want to get rid of you?' asked Foster suddenly, switching the direction of the conversation.

'I'd developed a conscience,' I said. 'No, in fairness, I already had a conscience. More correctly, I rediscovered my conscience. That would be a better way to state it.'

I laughed at their expressions.

'I know, it sounds pathetic doesn't it, coming from the mouth of a professional killer. But I came to a realisation; something that should have struck me years ago really. In those warehouses, all I normally saw were stacks of merchandise, pallets of square bricks wrapped in polythene. It only occurred to me recently that it wasn't just the scumbags who were dying. Those polythene bricks were killing innocent people. Don't get me wrong, I take full responsibility for every time I've pulled the trigger, it just came to the point where I couldn't deal with the unseen casualties, and the Mancini's knew it too.'

'But they have always dealt in drugs,' said Foster. 'They are one of our biggest targets.'

'Oh, I know that,' I said. 'Call it self-delusion, call it self-denial, call it what you like. To be honest, all the other stuff I did, I was fine with. The prostitution, the protection, the racketeering; all of the guys that I killed during those times, would have done the same to me at the drop of a hat. It was dog eat dog. The drugs were different. No matter how I tried to rationalise it, at the end of the day, I was culpable; as guilty as if I was injecting the gear into the addicts myself.'

'So, would you describe yourself as anti-drugs?' asked Foster.

'Strangely enough, I think I would,' I said.

'So, what is Storm?' he asked.

I thought of the white folder and the myriad open loops it would close for him.

But it was too soon.

'It's a drug,' I said. 'It was originally developed in the 1920's as a pharmaceutical tool to enforce human compliance with communist ideals, and was later developed into a biological weapon.'

'So, what is the modern significance?' asked Foster.

'I'm no expert,' I said, 'but from what I understand, it removes the power of free will. You will do whatever you are directed to do without question. However, there are also unforeseen side-effects. Apart from making the user compliant, it gives them a glorious and almost unimaginable high, without any of the nasty physical side effects normally associated with addiction.'

I nodded at their expressions.

'Yes, imagine it,' I said. 'No cold turkey, no withdrawal symptoms, nothing to complicate the enjoyment. The addiction is purely mental, which makes it all the more difficult to resist.'

Foster sat back and drummed his fingers on his chin.

'Can you imagine what would happen if a drug like that was to hit the street?' I stated flatly.

'Something big, something huge,' muttered Foster, under his breath.

'Sorry?' I said.

'Nothing,' he replied, shaking his head and rousing himself. 'But sometimes it is nice to be right.'

He said this more to himself than anyone else, allowing a small smile to crease his features.

'So, what's your story Mr CIA man?' I asked, turning to the anonymous agent. 'Have you got any questions for me?'

'Oh, don't worry,' he said. 'You've given me all the answers I could possibly ever want to know,' he added cryptically.

I looked at him quizzically, but he just shook his head. A small Mona Lisa smile briefly flitted across his lips. Enigmatic, isn't that what they called it? I was just about to say something else, when my sixth sense kicked into overdrive. I caught the merest flash of movement beyond the window. I didn't hesitate.

'Down,' I shouted, as the window came crashing inwards in a shower of glass and cordite.

CHAPTER 31 – AMBUSH

18th May 2011 – Eight days after the Storm.

Then ye shall rise up from the ambush, and seize upon the city: for the lord your God will deliver it into your hand. – Joshua 8:7.

'Is everyone okay?' I whispered into the intense silence, as the last shard fell to the ground with a tinkle.

They all nodded dazedly and I realised what was wrong. I could see them. I rolled sideways, grabbed the gun, turned onto my back, and shot out the light, all in one smooth, fluid motion. I felt the gossamer pinpricks on my face as the hot bulb fragments fell like snowflakes.

The dark was much more comforting.

I unscrewed the silencer, turned and fired two shots out through the open window. In the confined space of the small room, the bark of the reports was temporarily deafening.

'That should give us a couple of minutes,' I muttered softly.

I turned my attention to the front panel of the couch.

'What the hell are you doing?' whispered Roussel savagely.

I put a finger to my lips and then grabbed the panel with both hands. I jerked it towards me forcefully. There was a sharp popping sound, and then the panel dropped free, revealing the small storage cavity behind it. I grabbed two more pistols and associated clips.

The agent was in the process of retrieving his weapon from the easy chair, so I thrust the brace of newly liberated guns at Roussel.

'Here,' I whispered to him sharply. 'Take one of these and give the other one to Foster.'

As Roussel worked, I continued whispering.

'I presume everyone knows how to handle a gun?' I asked in a low stilted voice.

All I could hear in response were the abrupt metallic clicks, as clips were loaded and chambers were primed. I considered the professions of my erstwhile colleagues and allowed myself a small smile; silly question really.

I beckoned them all near so that I could keep my voice down.

'Roussel,' I whispered. 'Seeing as you came in via the lane and through the yard, you'll have the most familiarity with the back of the house. Take Foster with you and cover the rear.'

'You,' I whispered, pointing at the agent. 'You stay with me and we'll cover the front.'

'Hold on a second,' whispered Roussel questioningly. 'How do we know these aren't police?'

I picked up a shard of glass from the shattered window and showed it to him.

'Since when do the police shoot first and ask questions afterwards?'

His face contorted as he thought about it and then formed into a grimace of apology. I motioned them towards the kitchen and Roussel crawled out slowly, picking a route gingerly through the broken glass. Foster followed him on his hands and knees, equally carefully.

The door frame through to the kitchen was splintered, where some of the bullets had found their mark, but the equally damaged door still swung open noiselessly enough. I waited until they had both passed through, and what was left of the door closed behind them.

I strained my ears to catch the whispered shout.

'In position!'

I gestured to the agent and we both sat back against the base of the couch. We were directly underneath the window sill, the one that faced the street. It was definitely the safest place in the house at that particular moment.

I glanced across at the CIA man. He blinked his eyes a couple of times in response. He'd heard it too; uncertain and forceful whispering, wafting through the damaged window. I strained my ears again, elongating the sense to its maximum reach. And then the shouted question, as the agent looked across at me in surprise.

'Thomas?'

The name was loudly yelled, and I almost didn't recognise it. I still wasn't tuned back in to the local dialect, and people had not called me Thomas in a long time.

'Or should I call you Eugene?' shouted the stranger. 'Which is a pretty shit name, if you ask me? Are you shit, Thomas? Or shitting yourself maybe, like the snivelling little coward you are?'

I said nothing. I didn't think he would be able to help himself and I was right.

'We know you're in there,' he shouted. 'And don't think your little pop gun frightens us. We've got some serious weaponry out here.'

I flinched in surprise rather than fright as another burst of automatic gunfire came through the shattered window. A wound magically appeared on the opposite wall. I watched with a detached disinterest as the scar opened and spread, consuming everything in its path. A picture and a mirror disintegrated under the relentless assault.

I glanced across at the agent. His eyes were closed, but his face was relaxed. His grip on the gun was firm, but not tense. He had definitely been under fire before.

I wasn't sure about Roussel and Foster. As long as they stayed low, they should be fine. Foster was an unknown quantity, but Roussel and guns would definitely not be strangers.

'So what's it to be, Thomas?' shouted the mystery voice.

The agent opened his eyes and looked at me. I gestured for him to move to his side of the window frame. The walls of the house were a foot thick. Unless they had cannons, there was nothing coming through them. We slid around each side of the couch with our backs to the walls, and used our knees to slowly inch our way up, until we were both standing.

When I had redecorated the house, I had specified a heavy full length drape curtain. I was now seriously glad that I had. I motioned to the agent with my hand, trying to demonstrate what I was about to do, and then slipped between the drapes and the wall, relieved when I saw the agent doing the same. I crept as close to the outside edge of the frame as possible, trying to get a sense of what was happening outside, and how many assailants there were.

We were lucky in some ways, even though we were the ones purportedly trapped. Since I had shot the bulb out, we had the slimmest of advantages. We would be able to see out, but they would find it very difficult to see in. Unless we made any silly sudden moves, we would be able to keep our positions camouflaged and thus retain a slight superiority.

From my place of concealment, I positioned myself slowly and carefully, trying to manoeuvre the scene outside as far into my field of vision as I possibly could, without giving myself away. My eyes had long since adjusted to the gloom. I let them wander over the tableau, building up a slow and steady mental picture.

There were two high-sided panel vans parked on the other side of the road. I could make out the barrels of three machine guns. As I watched, two other men came briefly out of cover. One of them was signalling to another group of men further down the street. The signals were fairly easy to interpret, and if I was reading them right, four guys were being sent down the lane and around the back.

I made a sharp and loud *psst!* sound under my breath. The agent's face slowly materialised from the gloom between the drape and the wall. I signalled with my hand below the level of the wall. Five men were out front and four were heading around the back. He silently confirmed that he'd understood.

'What's it to be Thomas, time's running out for you?'

I inched back behind the relative safety of the solid masonry.

'Fuck you,' I shouted. 'You want me? Come and get me!'

I knew that he couldn't afford to wait much longer. The amount of gunfire had been too great. Knowing who they were, I would have taken bets that my neighbours on both sides were already jamming the local emergency switchboard. There were only so many car backfires you could rationalise away in a given night. No, his time was running out. He would have to try a full frontal assault. That's when the balance of power would shift. I knew it and the agent knew it too. I inched back into my position of surveillance. It looked like the two men I'd glimpsed before were readying themselves for the charge.

We shrank back behind the walls again as the three machine guns laid down covering fire. The room literally exploded in a shower of wood chips, pottery fragments and plaster dust. I heard activity on the front step. They had made it that far at least.

'Roussel, there are four coming around the back! Be careful.' I shouted.

'Roger,' came back the muffled acknowledgement.

I threw myself across the room to lay prone in the opposite corner. The agent shrank further into his place of concealment, and there was a split second of unnatural silence.

The next thing, the door seemed to explode inwards. I could see the muzzle flashes and the next thing I saw was the toe of a boot, as someone kicked away the splintered remains of the door.

I saw the agent tense from his corner, and as the doorway filled with shadow, neither of us hesitated.

As if unconsciously connected, we started firing at exactly the same time, matching each other bullet for bullet, report for report, until the clips were exhausted. It was the first time I had emptied a full clip in anger.

The time for superstitions was over.

We waited a couple of seconds. The agent crawled over and knelt down next to where the bodies had fallen. He felt for a pulse on one then the other, shaking his head slightly twice; two dead, seven to go.

No sooner had silence descended, than the shooting started again, this time from the kitchen. We waited, more tense than we had been during our own action. It was over in about ten seconds.

'Roussel?' I whispered hopefully; expectantly.

'Still here,' he replied softly, and I could hear his voice cracking. 'We're coming back in.'

The two of them crawled back, keeping below the level of the window. They were covered head to toe in dust and debris. They appeared like war-painted warriors.

'It was a turkey shoot,' whispered Roussel, his plaster mask cracking with a smile.

'As easy as shooting fish in a barrel,' said Foster, but he was shaking a little.

'Good job,' I said.

'One managed to crawl away, but he won't be making any more attacks.'

'So you can handle a gun.'

'Me and Foster both,' said Roussel.

'I have shot a gun the odd time,' acknowledged Foster with a fleeting smile.

He surreptitiously covered his gun hand with the other to stop it trembling.

The agent scrambled over to where we lay.

'Sorry to butt-in on this NRA reunion, ladies,' he said, 'but there are still armed men outside this house who want to kill us, and I'd say they are seriously starting to get pissed right about now.'

As he spoke, there came a hesitant shout.

'Boss, are you all right?'

When no one answered, he tried again.

'Boss, are you in there?'

'I'm afraid he can't come out to play again, on account of his being dead,' I shouted.

I heard a strangled cry, followed by a car door opening and slamming.

Then a shout rang out.

'Jimmy, what the fuck are you doing? Not that, you fucking madman.'

I heard rather than saw the object; the swish as it sailed through the gaping hole where the window had been. The agent had seen it too; the unmistakable profile against the glow from the streetlights.

'Grenade!' he shouted.

Foster and Roussel were up and through the kitchen door like greyhounds. I was right behind them, smashing my way through the frame. I made a dive through the shattered remains of the back door, and landed heavily on the concrete tiles that lined the back yard.

Just before I hit the deck, I felt the ground swell of the explosion lift the air under my body, and then the garden became a seething mass of dust and debris.

As I hit the ground again and rolled away, the force of the explosion seemed to collapse the house in on itself. It appeared to shrink and fold inwards, before the sound of the detonation reinforced what my other senses were telling me.

It seemed to last for minutes, but in reality, it was over in seconds. There was no sound; not even the tweet of a bird. A dangerous calm descended on me; the white heat of anger.

'Is everyone okay?' I asked matter-of-factly, as I allowed the rage to course through my body.

'As well as can be expected, given the circumstances,' coughed Roussel.

'Same here,' said Foster, gently feeling himself for broken bones.

'Has anyone seen the agent?' I asked.

They shook their heads collectively.

'I think he went the other way,' said Roussel. 'Towards the explosion....' His voice trailed off.

'Give me your gun,' I said to Roussel.

He looked at me and then looked at the weapon, and then back to me again, before handing it over reluctantly.

'You're not going to do anything stupid, are you?' he asked.

I stared at him for a second, but didn't answer. I ejected the spent clips and loaded another two with venom. I walked into the ruined house, through the gap where the rear door had been. Continuing on into the sitting room, I noticed that the couch was completely and miraculously untouched. The centre of the house had taken the worst of the blast. There was no ceiling anymore, and I could see all the way to the sky.

I marched into the hallway and kicked the front door cleanly off its hinges. The crash as it hit the pavement startled the three men into silence. They had been laughing, joking and high-fiving only seconds earlier. One of them actually swallowed hard as he saw me.

'That was my mother's house,' I said, loudly and distinctly.

One of them tried to bring up the muzzle of his gun. A single shot took him down. As the other two tried to bring up their weapons, I fired with left and right hands, not stopping until both weapons clicked on empty chambers.

'That was my mother's house,' I whispered to their prone bodies.

All those memories and ghosts destroyed, before I had a chance to face them. Somebody was going to pay dearly for that.

I walked back into the house and made a very brief search of the ground floor. There was no sign of the agent. Maybe a good thing; maybe he survived.

Foster and Roussel joined me in the ruins of the sitting room. I spotted what I wanted and pulled the holdall out from under some wreckage. I extracted the rest of the guns and ammunition from their place of concealment in the couch, zipped up the bag and threw it over my shoulder. I didn't wait to see if the guys were following me; to be honest, I didn't really care.

At the spot where the three guys lay dead, I turned and glanced back at the ramshackle ruin. I was only vaguely aware of Foster and Roussel either side of me. When Roussel patted me on the shoulder, I looked at him.

'That was my Mother's house,' I said, as if it would answer all his unspoken questions.

'Come on,' he said gently. 'We need to get out of here.'

We rounded the corner briskly and onto the main road, just as the first squad car went tearing in, sirens wailing.

I waited until we had got about a kilometre away. We stopped and sat on a low stone wall to get our breath back. We had been moving fairly briskly.

'Gun please,' I said to Foster, holding out my hand.

He hesitated.

'Have it your way,' I said.

I took another gun from the bag and thrust it into the hand of a surprised Roussel. I dropped the bag of weapons on the floor in front of me and put my hands up theatrically.

'You win, you got me. I'll go quietly. I won't cause any trouble.'

Foster studied me evenly for a minute or so.

'And what if we don't want that?' he asked. 'What's the alternative?'

'How about we pool our resources; find out about this *Storm*. Find out who's trying to kill us. Find out who blew up my mother's house and kill them all.'

Roussel and Foster exchanged a look. They seemed to come to a decision, and as one, wordlessly handed their weapons back. I smiled humourlessly; I wasn't feeling amused.

'Let's find out who these fuckers are?'

CHAPTER 32 – REBELLION

18th May 2011 – Eight days after the Storm.

Repression will provoke rebellion. – Hugh Williamson.

The sweat dripped down his nose and formed a large tear shaped bubble. Ordinarily, it would annoy him intensely, but when he was on the exercise bike, he didn't even notice it. When he was in the zone, nothing mattered.

Exercise was his leveller. It was his drug, his weapon of choice in the fight against stress and modern life.

He was acclimatised to the political bullshit at work; the constant schmoozing of colleagues and peers, knowing who to talk to and when to talk to them. So it always felt brilliant to expend the maximum effort on honest endeavour, a cleansing of the soul. It also gave him pause to think, to neatly order his thoughts for the coming day.

His thigh muscles and calf muscles begged for mercy, but his response to their inadequacy was to push them harder. Eighteen point six km; he wasn't anywhere near finished yet.

He was working more intensely this morning; there was always a reason. He was annoyed and pissed off. He always pushed harder when he was irritated with himself; it was a punishment of sorts.

The problem was that Ray had let Foster get under his skin. Dale had a way of doing that with people.

He glanced at the odometer on the bike. Nineteen km and his body really wanted to stop now, was literally screaming for mercy. No fucking way. He pushed harder and the units started counting down; nineteen point two, nineteen point four.

So how had Dale got under his skin? Ray had given him every chance, and had backed him to the hilt on his first big operation, but things hadn't worked out as they should have done. Everyone had told Ray that as a boss, he hadn't been unreasonable. Even Dale had told him out straight. He would have expected nothing less than the severe reprimand and permanent mark on his record that he ultimately received.

After the latest *report*, Ray had not surprisingly over-reacted, and when he'd told Dale to take a two week vacation, he'd been surprised at how easily he had surrendered. Instead of the normal histrionics, Dale had given him resigned acceptance; like a dog that has had the fight kicked out of it.

So why would that bother him? Why had he found it so hard to sleep last night? Why was he awake at four am, with his hands tensing into fists involuntarily?

It wasn't that Dale was even a likeable guy. He had no social skills and got on people's nerves. He rubbed them up the wrong way, and yet there was a small character trait that made you like him despite everything.

Ray's father used to tell him that the truth was the moral barometer of a man. If his father knew he had been lying or deliberately misleading, he'd always given Ray the opportunity to redeem himself; the truth will *always* set you free. And that's what it was with Dale; a single-minded, relentless pursuit of the truth.

The exercise bike bleeped twice to tell him his assigned distance was complete. He pushed his legs harder for another kilometre, just to prove to himself that he could do it. He eased his tired limbs to a stop and grunted in satisfaction as he checked his heart rate monitor.

He slid off the bike, and as he did so, he took the plain white towel from around his neck and vigorously rubbed the sweat from his face and his torso. He always exercised in just a pair of shorts. He didn't see the point in adding to the burden of washing, especially in his home gym.

Aside from the exercise bike, there were only two other pieces of equipment in the room. It was quiet and austere, with plain wooden floors and whitewashed walls. There were no TVs and no stereos; no distractions.

The last couple of conversations about Dale had shaken him; he didn't mind admitting it to himself. To a certain extent, he'd let his ego become a diversion. The truth had got lost and gone astray. He'd allowed the personal dressing-down he'd got from his own senior management to get in the way. He didn't like that. Since when had Ray Fox let his ego get in front of earnest endeavour and truth?

He thought back to the conversation he'd had with Dodds. Pairing them up had been a gamble. He couldn't imagine two agents less likely to strike up a partnership, but Dodds was approaching retirement and Dale had needed a bit of a toning down. They were both unassigned, so he'd brought them together. Even though all of his motivation had not been benign, he'd been pleased and surprised at how protective Dodds had become towards his partner.

He punched the keypad on the rowing machine in front of him; the only piece of electronics in the room. The screen lit up, displaying a stylised icon of him in a canoe next to two other boats. He always set it for the same speed; one below the maximum. He knew it was achievable and he never wanted to fail.

As he rowed, he tried to clear his mind, but the images kept coming back. The questions were haunting him, because deep in the recesses of his mind, the eager field agent that he concealed under the *special agent in charge* veneer had the distinct feeling that something was not right.

Dodds' barbed words had hurt him too. He didn't think he was that far removed from the street. He glanced at the screen; he was halfway there and just ahead. The second half was always harder, a metaphor for life.

Everything about the evidence as it had been presented to him was circumstantial. The informants, the name of the drug, the place, the link to the Mancini's; not a shred of it would stand up to even a mild cross examination in court. But that wasn't what had pressed his hazard lights.

He glanced at the screen again; the finish line was in sight and he was thinking too much. He had dropped way behind. He bunched his muscles and pulled with renewed vigour. He inched back into contention, but was beaten across the line by inches. He sat back and allowed his breathing to regularise. The problem must have been bothering him more than he'd thought; he had never lost before. He sprung up and roughly towelled himself down.

Heading up the stairs from the basement, he was passing the front door on the way to the kitchen, when he was startled by the loud pealing of the Westminster chimes. Ray's wife was a bit of an anglophile, but personally he hated that particular ring.

He threw open the door to find Dodds standing on the doorstep with his finger poised over the Bell.

'Don't,' said Ray.

Dodds blinked, and then blushed and looked away.

'Never seen a man in shorts before?' asked Ray.

'Seen plenty of them,' answered Dodds.

Ray glared at him for a second and Dodds muttered an apology.

'Coffee?'

Dodds nodded, and then realised his boss had already gone. Dodds was unsure if it had been an invitation or a statement. In his defence, he could argue that the boss had left the door open.

He pushed it further ajar and stepped into the house. It was light, airy and modern; uncluttered was the brochure word, and exactly as he had imagined his boss's house would look. He was just about to guess which door, when he heard the shout.

'Are you coming or what?'

He followed the sound, his footsteps echoing in the empty corridor. The hall was strangely homely, but as he pushed open the door at the end, he was greeted by a sea of white, high-gloss kitchen cupboards and a huge white island unit with built-in breakfast bar. It was stark and a bit too clinical for his taste.

A mug already sat steaming above a comfortable leather-finished bar stool. He sat and sipped, as his boss banged around in some large open drawers, eventually holding the can opener triumphantly aloft. Dodds peered at the label on the can as Ray opened the tin with practised ease.

'Baked beans,' stated Dodds, squinting hard.

'Not just any baked beans,' said Ray. 'These are Heinz baked beans. Got a taste for them as a student in London; been hooked ever since.'

He pushed a fork over to Dodds.

'You wanna try some?'

'Yeah, not bad,' said Dodds. 'But you do know Heinz is an American corporation?'

'You're kidding!' said Ray.

'I jest not,' said Dodds in amusement.

'So, how did you find out where I lived?' asked Ray eventually through a mouthful of beans.

'I'm an investigator boss, what can I say,' replied Dodds.

Ray looked at him gravely and then his face cracked into a smile.

'Good answer,' he said.

Behind Dodds, a clock chimed and a cuckoo leapt out, making him jump in his seat. Seven thirty in the morning. He glanced at his boss and his state of undress. It probably was a little bit early to make a house call.

He looked behind him and studied the clock. It was incongruous against the swish, stylishly modern interiors in the rest of the kitchen. It didn't belong.

'Yeah, I know,' said Ray, following the direction of his gaze, and the unspoken question. 'People wonder why I put that up. Well, it was given to me by my grandfather. He brought it back from Switzerland, or maybe it was Austria; a parting gift to himself when he left Europe at the end of the hostilities. I loved that clock as a kid; never missed a day winding it and it's incredibly accurate as you can see.'

Dodds compared the time on his BlackBerry. The boss was right.

'So, I've been doing a lot of thinking about this,' stated Ray.

He walked over to the clock and fiddled underneath it. Dodds could see that there was a key hanging below it on a hook.

'You and me both then,' responded Dodds.

'The one thing that doesn't ring true for me,' said Ray, as he turned the key methodically. 'The one thing that switched my radar from circumstantial to clear and present danger....'

'The call from the CIA,' finished Dodds.

'How did you know?' asked Ray.

''Cause I've been wrestling with the same conundrum,' said Dodds. 'Don't get me wrong, he can make some howling mistakes, and when he makes an error, he can get it seriously fucking wrong. But in this case, I think he got it right.'

'I think so too,' said Ray. 'And by the way, that comment stung. I'm not that far removed from the street you know?'

'Just trying to get your attention,' replied Dodds. 'No offense.'

'Well, you got my attention,' said Ray, 'and incidentally, so did Dale. But the question remains, what do we do?'

'He rang me yesterday,' answered Dodds, expecting a backlash.

The answer he got surprised him.

'Yeah, we need to have something for him,' said Ray. 'Hopefully, he'll work with us and give us anything he has too.'

Ray threw his plate and mug into the sink.

'Listen, I'm going to grab a shower now. I'll meet you back in the office. If there are any developments in the meantime, give me a shout.'

Dodds realised he was being dismissed.

'Thanks for the coffee, boss,' he said.

'Anytime,' said Ray distractedly.

#

Afternoon; Dodds was finding it very difficult to focus. If someone had asked him whether Dale had made any difference to his professional life, he would have said no, but it appeared that Dale had more influence on him than he'd realised.

Thinking back, it was always Dale that did the organising. It wasn't that Dodds was lazy or stupid; he was more than capable, it was just that Dale preferred to do it. He had a methodology, a system, and in fairness to Dale, it had worked well for both of them.

Dodds opened his top drawer and the packet of cigarettes stared back at him. He was trying to quit, or cut back at the very least. He was debating the relative merits of will power, when the red light blinked on his phone and the buzzer sounded. He picked it up.

'Hey Sandy,' he said.

'Boss wants you in the office now,' she said. 'He sounds quite flustered.'

Dodds glanced up to see the boss beckoning him energetically. He walked briskly across.

'You are not going to believe this,' said Ray under his breath. He had his headset on and un-muted the microphone.

'Sorry to keep you waiting sir, I'm just heading back to my office now.'

He motioned for Dodds to step in and close the door.

He moved back around behind his desk. He switched his conference phone into speaker mode, but kept the microphone audio routed through his headset, so that Dodds could listen but could not say anything. Ray scribbled something on his pad, and passed it across to Dodds. It said *Director of the CIA*. Dodds raised his eyebrows and then scribbled back, *you're kidding me*. Ray shook his head.

'Okay, I'm back at my desk now, sir, and the doors are closed; sorry for keeping you.'

'So no chance of anyone overhearing?' asked the director.

Ray placed a finger to his lips, and then brought it across his neck with a slashing motion. Dodds understood exactly what he meant.

'No chance at all, sir,' said Ray.

'What do you know about Storm?' asked the director.

Ray instantly liked him. He didn't beat around the bush. Not a man to mince his words.

'We are not sure that we know anything,' answered Ray. 'Most of what we have heard is rumour and conjecture. But from what we've been able to ascertain, Storm is a drug of some kind.'

'You have a quality for understatement, Agent Fox,' said the director. 'What I'm about to tell you is on a strictly need to know basis, do you understand what I'm saying?'

'Yes sir,' said Ray.

'About two months ago, a folder went missing from a secure government facility. There are only four of these folders in existence. They should have been kept under constant lock and key, within a secure restricted area, but in this particular case, all the procedures were not followed.'

'And this has something to do with Storm?' asked Ray.

'That folder *is* Storm,' said the director. 'History, background, protocol, chemical compounds, manufacturing process, clinical trials, testing results, everything.'

'So, if someone were to get their hands on that folder?' ventured Ray.

'They would be potentially an extremely rich man or woman,' finished the director. 'Make no mistake; this has the potential to be bigger than heroin, cocaine, ecstasy, all of those. If you went out of your way to design the perfect drug, you couldn't come up with a better one.'

'So, where is this folder now?' asked Ray. 'Do we know?'

'All the intelligence we have points to the document being in the possession of the Mancini brothers.'

Ray and Dodds looked at each other.

'So Dale was right,' said Ray, almost to himself.

'If you're referring to Agent Foster,' said the Director, 'then yes he was. But if you can contact him, you need to get a message to him. He is in quite a bit of danger.'

'How so?' asked Ray, with the beginnings of concern.

'I mentioned the existence of four folders,' said the director. 'I have one of them and certain key individuals within the Storm Project group have the other three. One of those individuals has become a ghost and their folder, and thus Storm itself, has vanished with them.'

'Rebelled you mean?' asked Ray. 'Gone rogue?'

'Actually yes, rogue would be a much better way to put it,' said the director. 'I'm not at liberty to discuss who the individual is. To be honest, that information is way above your pay grade. Suffice to say, they are eminently aware of the value of what they have. I believe they are selling the drug to the highest bidder. Why they engineered two folders to be removed, one in such a clumsy and haphazard way, I don't yet know or understand? Maybe they did it so they could compare the two and make sure there were no anomalies from folder to folder; we do that sometimes to protect ourselves.'

He laughed briefly and sourly.

'Unfortunately, that is not the case here. Each folder contains an identical and full disclosure.'

'So, where does the danger come from?' asked Ray.

'Given the vast sums of money potentially involved, I have to believe they are prepared to kill anyone with any knowledge of this project; certainly anyone isolated and vulnerable.'

'Does that include me, sir?' asked Ray.

'No, they would have no knowledge of you.'

'So, how did you find out about Agent Foster?' asked Ray, reading the scribbled question that Dodds had thrust across the desk. 'And more to the point, how did the rogue agent find out about him?'

'We pulled the last few records accessed by our rogue agent from the CIA database,' said the director. 'The second to last record he accessed was that of one *Agent Dale Foster.*'

'What was the last one?' asked Ray curiously.

'A man called *Thomas Eugene O'Neill.*'

Ray and Dodds looked at each other as they realised the call had been terminated.

'What do you make of that?' asked Dodds.

'I don't like it,' said Ray. 'I can't tell you why, but I have a feeling we are being played. We need to proceed with the utmost caution.'

CHAPTER 33 – ALLIANCE

19th May 2011 – Nine days after the Storm.

War makes fright, fright makes alliances, alliances make war. – Anon.

Our journey together, especially after the destruction of the house, had been a little surreal. The other two hadn't spoken at all. I had just mumbled half remembered directions. All of us were lost in our individual musings.

More by accident than design, my aimless recollections brought us back to Roussel's hotel. It transpired by complete coincidence that both he and Foster were staying in the same place.

We agreed to meet in Foster's room; he handed me one of his pass keys and we entered via the back door at five minute intervals, so we didn't arouse any suspicions.

I was last in and headed straight for Dale's room, glad that the number was printed on the card; I had forgotten to ask him where it was. When the lock opened with a green light and a click, the other two were together inside. Roussel had gathered all his things and had already cleared out his room.

There were three beds, so we collectively decided to get a little bit of sleep. I set my alarm for seven am. For my line of work, I had perfected the art of the deep catnap and it appeared my new colleagues had too. When the bell jangled on my iPhone, and brought us all back to the living, both of them appeared as refreshed and wide awake as I felt.

Roussel went down first to pay his bill. I went down next, as I had no account to settle, and the two of us waited outside in comparative silence for Foster to join us.

'What now?' asked Roussel.

His breath was condensing as his words broke the peace and stillness of the dawn.

'I have just the thing,' I said.

An hour later, I pushed the plate away from me. The all-day breakfast rarely defeated me, but this time it had.

'I told you that you'd both feel better after that,' I said.

They both sat back and smiled; neither of them had been defeated the way I had, and their plates were almost forensically clean.

'So, what now?' asked Roussel, echoing his earlier comment.

We sipped at our coffees as we studied each other.

'First things first,' I said, 'and I'm going to get this out of the way up front, because you guys are tiptoeing around it.'

They looked at me; Foster even blinked, but they allowed me to continue.

'I'm not on the same side of the law as you guys, and I've killed a lot of people.'

I paused to let that statement sink in.

'All of them were scumbags and all of them deserved it, but then, I'm trying to justify my behaviour, especially to myself, so I would say that, wouldn't I?'

I turned to Roussel directly.

'The point is,' I said, 'not only am I the number one suspect in a double murder, *your* double murder, but I freely confess to carrying both of them out, which puts you in a bit of a quandary.'

'You think?' he said with a smile.

'So, here's the decision as I see it, for you guys.'

I stated this flatly and with no emotion.

'I have no idea why Scott Mitchell a.k.a Alan Murphy, was searching for me. I have no idea how he succeeded in tracking me down. I have *absolutely* no idea what his motivation was. All I can assume, from what I've managed to find out about him, is that he was up to no good.'

I curled a finger to illustrate another point.

'The second guy who was after me; I know exactly what he was and I know exactly who sent him, and I make no apologies for that one. It was pure self defence.'

I curled another finger.

'And gentlemen, I don't think I need to remind you of the attack on all of us in my mother's house. Somebody is definitely going to pay for that.'

I curled my hand into a fist.

'So, in summary, I *am* going to find out who tried to kill me, I *am* going to find out who trashed my mother's house, and I *am* going to find out why this guy Scott Mitchell was sent to find me. Those are certainties. You can work with me or you can work against me, it's up to you. Either way, it's now personal for me. But if you do choose to work with me, I have considerable advantages that you guys don't have. I can work outside the law, which you guys can't. I have access to information and resources that you guys don't. And possibly the strangest statement of all; I'm an honourable man and you can trust me.'

Roussel made to speak, but Foster got there first, holding his hand up in a pausing motion.

'I don't know about Charles,' he said, looking at me, 'but I'll give you my take on this.'

He sat back and smiled.

'I can't believe I'm saying this,' he continued, 'but I am actually relieved that I was shot at yesterday. I've been chasing shadows for the last week, but shadows don't fire live rounds. It was nice to get some cold hard evidence that I'm headed in the right direction. I've been going on hunches and intuition for too long and like you....'

He pointed a finger in my direction.

'....I'm operating in an unofficial capacity. So, it depends what Charles says, but I think we should pool our resources. There's a lot of mutual benefit, and besides....'

He said this with a smile.

'....I think we make a good team and yes, I do believe you're an honest man.'

We collectively let that statement ring in the air for a few minutes.

'My turn?' asked Roussel, a faint smile creasing his face. 'Well, unlike you two, I am very definitely operating within the law. I have an official liaison with the police here in Cork, requested through official channels. Any deviation from those procedures could look bad, not only for me and my career, but also for my department and ultimately my whole Parish.'

He took another sip of coffee.

'Having said all that, somebody is jerking our collective chain. I don't like it and my Captain doesn't like it, so I'm prepared to work with you guys.'

Here he pointed his finger at both of us.

'This is based on the proviso that we have no secrets, and also on the proviso that we stay within the law as much as we possibly can.'

He fired the last statement directly at me.

'Works for me,' said Foster.

'Me too,' I echoed.

I lifted my mug.

'Slainte; to us!'

The pottery chinked, as they silently pledged their allegiance to our unholy trinity. Roussel extracted his notebook and pen, causing Foster to laugh.

'You are such a policeman, do you know that?' he said, still laughing.

Roussel shrugged off the throwaway remark, as he tore a page out of the notebook and put it in the centre of the table.

'If the cap fits,' he said. 'Anyway, as I see it, we have two focus areas. We have *Cork* and we have *Storm*.'

He wrote Cork in large capital letters.

'So, for Cork,' he began, 'we have you.'

He pointed at me with an easy smile.

'We have Scott Mitchell, drug pusher with purpose unknown, but a native of Cork; too much in common to be a coincidence. Anything I've missed?'

Foster shook his head and so did I.

'So, then we have Storm,' said Roussel, and wrote Storm in capital letters, as he had done previously.

'We have all the circumstantial evidence I was getting,' said Foster, pointing to the word Storm.

He then pointed at me.

'And then there's the evidence I was given, linking you to the Mancini's, and linking the Mancini's back to Storm.'

'It's a tenuous link,' I said, 'but I was told that Scott Mitchell was a drug dealer.'

'True,' said Roussel, 'but only very small time by all accounts; nothing on this scale.'

'So, we've concrete links to Storm and concrete links to Cork,' said Roussel. 'What about your two stooges from Rudino's; didn't they link Storm with Cork?'

'But I want concrete,' replied Foster. 'That's what we're missing. All we currently have is a tenuous link from a couple of restaurant kitchen porters.'

'There is one thing we've missed,' I said suddenly.

The others looked at me expectantly.

'Our friend from the CIA; where does he fit in and how does he fit in?'

'The guy who you killed,' responded Roussel excitedly, snapping his fingers. 'The second guy; the one sent with a specific purpose. It was bothering my captain and me why his information was classified. If it's as simple as you say; that he was sent purely by the Mancini's to kill you, then it makes no sense. But if he was there with a higher purpose than just to kill you? Maybe the classification was justified.'

'Still circumstantial,' I said. 'But, yes I agree with you certainly, it warrants looking into.'

'I think it's more than that,' said Roussel doggedly. 'Why would information on hit-men specifically related to the Mancini's be regarded as classified? It's almost like someone is trying to protect them; shielding them maybe?'

'To what purpose?' asked Foster.

'I don't know,' said Roussel. 'But everybody knows what the Mancini's are into. Why bother to hide it, especially from other law enforcement agencies.'

I shrugged.

'Okay, you win,' I said. 'I agree; we should certainly look into it.'

'So, what do we do now?' Foster asked. 'What is our next step?'

'Two things,' I replied. 'We need a place to stay and we need transport.'

'I still have my rental,' stated Foster.

'Do you?' I asked interestedly. 'I'll still need to add myself as a named driver, so I'll look after that and the accommodation. I have the means, the ability and the local knowledge. I don't think it's safe for either of you guys to go back to the Hotel. We can't assume that it was me they were after at my Mother's house.'

'I think we can,' said Roussel abruptly. 'They were shouting your name.'

'They could have followed one of you,' I said.

'Shit,' said Roussel, suddenly looking at his watch. 'What time is it?'

I glanced at my watch.

'Eight o'clock, why?' I asked.

'I'm meeting my liaison at the hotel at nine thirty,' he replied.

'Ok, here's what we'll do,' I said. 'We'll head back over to the hotel. You can wait there for your colleague. Foster will come with me and we'll sort out the car and a place to stay. Give us a shout when you're finished, and I'll come back and pick you up.'

'I would if I knew your number,' said Roussel.

I scribbled a number on Roussel's piece of paper.

'Don't forget, it's a US based number same as yours,' I said with a wink.

#

Roussel sat on the railings outside the hotel. Precariously balanced, he used his legs to keep from falling. When he was a kid, he used to try and stay perched on the veranda balustrade for hours. And then he realised; all his thoughts were doggedly guiding him back to the plantation.

He heard the beep of a car horn and looked up. James screeched to a halt in front of him.

'Man, you are never going to believe what happened last night,' said James.

'Try me,' said Roussel, manfully trying to stifle the smile. He wondered what would happen if he said it straight out.

'Well James, let me guess, there was a fire fight last night in Grattan Hill. Eight people were killed and the roof of the house was blown off with a grenade.'

He looked back at James. What he had mistaken for brevity was in fact a restrained and worried concentration.

'Sorry, not trying to be flippant, what did happen last night?'

'It's funny,' said James almost to himself, as they headed off at high speed. 'We had a meeting about this only a couple of days ago.'

Roussel nodded to show he was listening and let him keep talking.

'My boss reckoned it was only a matter of time.'

James looked at Roussel.

'There's a turf war going on, you see. Two rival gangs, isn't there always, vying for control. Now don't get me wrong, there has been trouble in the past. The odd shooting here, a beating there, a stabbing here, but this is serious escalation.'

They pulled up outside number thirty, or at least as close as they could get with the police cordon. They both got out and stood back. Roussel had been present at the aftermath of a couple of gas explosions back home when he was still in uniform: the effect wasn't dissimilar. He felt the tingle of shock run through his body as he realised how lucky they had been. There wasn't much of the house left.

'Fuck, it really is like a war zone,' stated James, echoing Roussel's thoughts.

A uniformed officer was standing at the front of what was left. James flashed his badge and the officer parted the tape and allowed them admittance. He stared hard at Roussel as he went past.

Roussel looked down at himself. Shit, he was still filthy from the night before; he hadn't had time to change his clothes. It was only a matter of time before a seriously distracted James would notice. Thinking fast, he feigned tripping over his own feet and fell headlong into the dust and debris, rolling a couple of times for good measure.

'Jesus, Charles, watch where you're going,' said James. 'Look at the state of you.'

Roussel got up carefully.

'Sorry,' he muttered.

They were standing in what was left of the sitting room.

'So, what caused the explosion?' asked Roussel, making a show of dusting himself off.

'A small explosive charge, most probably a grenade,' said James.

Roussel raised his eyebrows.

'I know,' said James. 'Hard to believe, isn't it?'

'So, do we know who they are?' asked Roussel, getting himself onto firmer ground; information that could be useful.

'Yes we do and that's what's worrying us,' said James. 'On the way here I was telling you about the feud. Well that dispute is between two rival gangs; one based in the north and one based to the south. This is North Cork we're in now, but virtually every one of the dead here are members of the North Cork gang; certainly the ones we have been able to identify anyway.'

'So, basically, they were killed on their own patch,' said Roussel.

'That's what it's beginning to look like,' said James. 'I don't have to tell you how territorial these guys are. This is serious shit. This is serious escalation. The guy who runs this side of town; he's not going to take this lying down.'

'What's his name?' asked Roussel.

'Very interested all of a sudden, aren't you,' said James, with the merest hint of suspicion.

'Only because it's connected, or seemingly connected to the case I'm working on,' Roussel fired back straight away.

'True,' said James grudgingly. 'Anyway, the guys name is Eoin Morrison, but everyone calls him Black Swan.'

'So, you think my man was mixed up in a drug feud?'

'Certainly looking the most feasible explanation at the moment,' said James.

'And who are their rivals?' asked Roussel.

'South Cork is controlled by a man called *the Bullock*,' said James.

He smiled at Roussel's expression.

'I know it sounds funny,' he said soberly, 'but the guy is the complete opposite of amusing. In fact, you can see how this row is escalating. These guys have very similar personalities. They don't back down, they don't take rejection well and they hate being number two.'

Something caught James attention.

'Excuse me for a second,' he said, touching Roussel's arm before walking over to a technician in a white coat. As he watched James, engrossed in conversation, Roussel mentally digested the information he had gleaned.

The guys who had surrounded the house were members of a drug gang controlled by the North Cork overlord. He shook his head; none of it made any sense.

James came back to him.

'Yep, confirmed, definitely a grenade. Do you know what?' he asked. 'I thought I'd seen it all, but a grenade in a quiet suburban street; beggars belief really, doesn't it?'

The journey back was accomplished in complete silence. If it was making James uncomfortable, he sure as hell wasn't showing it.

'Here you go, Charles, here's your stop,' said James. 'Do you want to catch a bite later? I know it's only lunchtime, but I can round up some of the local gang and have a session later tonight if you want? A few beers, bit of a sing song?'

Roussel flashed him a grimace of apology.

'Think the jet lag is catching up with me,' he said. 'Would you mind if we took a rain check?'

'Not at all,' replied James.

He handed Roussel a business card.

'If you sleep in, as I suspect you will, just give me a shout. If I'm not busy, I'll come and collect you.'

'Cheers,' said Roussel.

'Sleep tight,' yelled James, as he drove away.

#

'You've been holding out on us,' said Roussel. 'I told you I wanted honesty; no secrets.'

'Oh, I've plenty of secrets, believe me,' I said, with no trace of humour. 'Just nothing that is relevant to this.'

'Apparently, all those guys who died last night are members of the same gang; an organised criminal empire that controls the north side.'

He consulted his notebook.

'The gang is controlled by a guy called Eoin Morrison.'

I shook my head.

'Sorry, the name means nothing.'

'Everyone knows him as Black Swan,' added Roussel.

I blinked and he snapped his fingers.

'I knew it,' he said. 'You're holding out on us.'

'It's not what you think,' I said. 'Let me explain.'

I extracted my iPhone and showed them the gruesome picture.

Roussel blinked in surprise.

'That's victim number one, our man....'

'Scott Mitchell,' I finished. 'The very man we've been discussing. A couple of days ago, I decided to do some snooping down in the red light district. I got lucky; somebody recognised him and told me he worked for a guy called Black Swan.'

'And you were going to tell us this when?' asked Foster.

'I completely forgot about it,' I said genuinely. 'Speaking of disclosure though, I have been pondering this for the last couple of hours. I think it's time both of you were educated. This, gentlemen, is what we are dealing with.'

I extracted the white ring binder from the hold-all I had been carrying around. Foster gasped as he read the name on the front cover.

'Who wants to go first?' I asked.

CHAPTER 34 – REGRET

19th May 2011 – Nine days after the Storm.

The man who insists upon seeing with perfect clearness before he decides, never decides. Accept life and you must accept regret. – Henri Frederic Amiel.

I pulled the hood as far over my head as I could. I looked like a teenage hoodlum, but I didn't care. Not that anybody would recognise me, but I wanted to be anonymous for a while. I didn't want to feel known; didn't want to feel judged.

I inhaled the fresh, clean air.

I was getting reacquainted with the sky. I didn't feel hemmed in the way I did in big cities; didn't feel the buildings closing in around me like a prison. I was getting used to the changing landscape, where every second shop-front was a pub, and everyone had a smile on their face and a joke on their lips.

I'd left the two boys with their homework. I knew that folder virtually off by heart at this stage. I'd read it so many times, not really out of interest, but more through a healthy sense of self preservation. At least I knew now what a protocol was. I'd even looked it up in a medical journal. The plain and simple statement had indicated that it was *the type, quantity, method and length of time of taking the drugs required for any treatment cycle.*

That's why I'd got out of the flat. I knew there would be questions; I just needed to empty my brain for an hour or so. I looked at my watch. It was coming up for one pm, and I was getting the first stirrings of hunger.

Suddenly, my footsteps started echoing off the pavement in a strange way. I looked down. It was the reverberation of my shoes on the metal hatch that covered the entrance to a beer cellar. I stepped back and peered at the name of the place; John G Hartigan and Son. It looked as nice an establishment as any to get a full belly.

The first thing I'd remembered about Irish pubs was how dim and dingy they were, compared to their modern American counterparts. In the US, you had a myriad of TV screens in the bars, each playing a different channel; a practice I had to confess, I found intensely annoying. You didn't go into a bar so people could shout at you; it was supposed to be a relaxed and peaceful area. That's why there was something about the ambience of an Irish pub that you just couldn't beat. Some of them had been there for literally hundreds of years. When you sat at the bar, the building seemed to settle around you like a warm and friendly embrace. They were there for centuries for a very good reason.

I parked my rear on a stool, and caught the barman's eye.

'Be with you now,' he shouted; an Irish euphemism for *you'll have to wait a second.*

The subtle nuances were all coming back to me. I adjusted myself on the stool and pulled the hood off, safe in the relative anonymity. I let my gaze wander slowly around the interior, drinking in the atmosphere.

Even though the smoking ban had been in force in Ireland for a couple of years, the ravages of nicotine could still clearly be seen on the fabric of the building. Most pubs like these, true traditional pubs, had shunned the home improvement boom of the Celtic Tiger era. People came to pubs for their character, not the paisley print wallpaper and velvet throw cushions.

'What can I get you, squire?' asked the barman, interrupting my thought patterns.

I glanced at the bar menu. It was strangely reassuring to see that some things hadn't changed in decades. It was about as far from Tapas and Sushi as it was possible to get.

'Pint of Murphy's and a toasted ham and cheese sandwich, please,' I said.

'Home for good?' he asked, as he worked.

It was half statement and half question.

I didn't even bother quizzing him on how he knew I was home from the US; at this stage, I was beginning to settle back in. Maybe I really was home this time?

'We'll see,' I said.

The sandwich, when it came, was just like I remembered. The pint, when it came, was just like I remembered too. I drank it slowly, savouring the bitter sweet bite as the alcohol hit the spot. I slid the newspaper across the bar and started reading the headlines.

I was adrift in a sea of relaxation, when I felt a waft of air and then a presence beside me. Definitely female, my subconscious told me, communicating a vague hint of an understated perfume.

'Hello Thomas,' she said softly.

She didn't even have to say my name; the initial word was all it took. For the first time in a long while, I was transfixed; like a rabbit caught in the proverbial headlights. A physical shock went through me. I turned my head slowly and dragged my gaze up to her face.

I wouldn't have immediately recognised her; fashions obviously change, and her hair was subtly styled and a different colour. But weirdly, I could see a ghostly shadow of the girl that I'd known all those years ago; a vague outline, superimposed upon the statuesque and elegant woman standing next to me.

She looked at my face, and the first vestiges of doubt flitted behind her eyes.

'It is Thomas, isn't it?' she asked again, this time with a slight hesitation.

I nodded, not trusting myself to speak just yet, contenting myself instead with another sip of stout.

'Would you like to get a table?' I asked finally, cursing inwardly as my voice came out in a schoolboy squeak. 'Maybe we can catch-up for a few minutes.'

She smiled at the shrill inflection. At least she was smiling. She looked at her watch, seemingly in two minds.

'I'm meeting someone,' she said, 'but okay, I can spare half an hour.'

There was a measured pause.

'It would be nice to catch up,' she added, as an afterthought.

I ordered her a drink as she settled into the corner table. I carried my half empty pint and placed the glass of cider in front of her. She smiled again, this time in genuine amusement.

'I stopped drinking cider about twenty years ago,' she said.

I coloured and made to get up, but she put a hand on my arm.

'No, it's okay, I'll have a few sips,' she said.

I scanned her face, seeing if she had felt the same shock that I had; probably just static electricity.

'So, how long has it been?' she asked.

'Twenty three years, twenty four maybe,' I answered.

She put her hand on my arm again.

'Thomas, just before you go on,' she said kindly, 'can I just say something.'

I nodded, unable to speak.

'I forgave you long ago,' she said.

My throat felt constricted and I couldn't say anything.

'Yes, I had my moments early on, but make no mistake,' she said. 'I didn't sit in a rocking chair facing the Atlantic, staring out of the window and pining for your return.'

'I wouldn't have been so presumptuous,' I managed to say.

'Just to put you at your ease,' she answered. 'On the whole, the last twenty four years of my life have been blessed.'

'You're certainly looking good,' I said, meaning it.

'Thanks,' she replied and then sat back, taking a sip of cider. 'Marriage seemingly agrees with me.'

The two gold bands had been the first thing I'd noticed, but her mention of matrimony drew my attention to her left hand. She noticed me staring and moved the fingers self-consciously, causing the engagement ring to twinkle; it was one hell of a rock.

'He's a lucky man,' I said.

'Yes he is,' she said, agreeing with me. 'And I'm a lucky girl.'

We lapsed into a semi-awkward silence for a couple of minutes, sipping our drinks, while we racked our brains for something else to say.

'Did you stay around the Cork area?' I asked eventually.

'You wouldn't believe it, especially in this day and age,' she said, 'but I've never been any further than Dublin city since you left.'

I was about to ask whether she had any regrets, and then realised the possible connotations of that question if it came from me. I kept my mouth shut; partly because I didn't want to know the answer.

'What about you?' she asked. 'Did you make that fortune?'

'I'm fairly wealthy, yes,' I answered. 'In American terms, I would be nicely off.'

At that particular moment, I had just shy of twelve point six million dollars on deposit, in four numbered accounts.

'You've seen a lot of life,' she said.

It was a statement.

'I've seen my share,' I acknowledged.

'It shows in your face,' she said.

The slightly awkward pause again.

'I always saw you as the boy with too much ambition,' she said suddenly. 'I would categorise you now as the man with too much....'

She searched for a word and found three.

'....world weary resignation,' she finished.

'I'm not unhappy,' I said defensively.

'And therein lies the problem, I think?' she ventured. 'Oh Thomas, don't look so serious, it would never have worked out between us. We were two utterly different people; a star and a planet, in different orbits, in totally different solar systems.'

'Funny,' I said. 'I always thought we were well suited to each other.'

'I'll let you in on a little secret,' she said. 'Even though I begged you to take me with you, I didn't really want to go. America sounded so cool, so exciting, but when I thought about it, everything I needed was here. When I thought about it some more, you were no longer one of the things I needed.'

'That's a bit harsh,' I said to her.

'Is it?' she asked. 'How many times did you think about me when you were over there? How many times did you try and contact me in the last twenty four years?'

She looked at me; my silence was answer enough.

'Sometimes a teenage vision of love is exactly that; a vision, a dream. You've seen life,' she said. 'When does the dream ever equal the reality?'

I sensed a hint of bitterness in her words, but if I looked inside myself, I could see that what she said was true. I hadn't really given her a backwards glance. A bit of teenage angst and then; bang, gone. Pastures new, here we come. She nodded, as she saw my expression changing.

'It's been good to see you Thomas, it really has,' she said, patting my hand. 'It's allowed me to square some things away in my own head.'

'Glad I could help,' I said, a trifle sarcastically.

'Oh Thomas, look at you,' she exclaimed.

She glanced at her watch.

'I am going off to meet my husband in about seven minutes,' she added. 'Even the thought of it is brightening my mood. If you were a doctor and you were measuring my pulse, I bet you would find it increasing.'

She looked at me with a strange smile.

'Do you not know what I'm talking about?' she asked.

My problem was that I knew exactly what she was talking about; the mood lifting, the pulse quickening, the emotions building to the euphoria. That's how I felt when I killed. I smiled back at her.

'You'd better go,' I said. 'You don't want to be late for Mr Right.'

'Don't be nasty, Thomas,' she said.

'I wasn't,' I protested.

And then suddenly the thought came to me.

'Do you remember my confirmation name?' I asked, straight out.

She looked at me and blinked.

'Where did that question come from?'

'Just popped into my head,' I lied.

'You know I don't,' she said with certainty. 'You never told me; refused to in fact.'

She got up and struggled into her coat. I stood up too.

'It's Mary,' I said softly.

'What is?' she asked.

'My confirmation name.'

She glanced at me, and I noticed her eyes were a little misty. I didn't say anything; I didn't have to. There was an awkward moment as I went to kiss her on the cheek at the same moment she went to kiss me, and we gently clashed heads. She dropped her eyes and turned away.

At the doorway, she glanced around quickly and waved; I could tell it was goodbye. The primary emotion that I could ascertain from her was relief; or maybe it was release.

As I sipped at my pint, something she'd said was nagging at the back of my mind. There was something about the feeling she'd described. Something had made me feel like that in the recent past. It had not been killing, and it had not been her. I drained the remainder of my drink, nodded my thanks to the barman and walked onto the street, eyes scanning the road.

'Taxi,' I shouted.

A car swerved over and the front door flew open.

'Yes mate?' he asked.

'Hospital please,' I said.

I told myself on the way up the stairs that it was a fool's errand. She wouldn't be there. But all the same, when I strolled in to find the bed empty and cordoned off with police tape, I couldn't help feeling a tiny bit diminished. A large, stern looking woman in an ill-fitting uniform approached me.

'Can I help you?' she asked suspiciously.

I had to act quickly; I needed to maximise my information advantage.

'I'm hoping you can,' I said, keeping my voice low like a conspirator. 'I'm Charles Foster from the Cork Examiner.'

I was thinking on my feet, combining the two names of my new colleagues.

'We got an anonymous tip-off from a staff member, telling us that something *unusual* had happened recently in one of the female wards.'

She relaxed slightly, and I could tell she was dying to disclose what she knew.

'All our sources are strictly confidential,' I said softly.

'Meet me in the break room in about five minutes,' she said, pointing down the corridor.

A few minutes later, when she walked into the room, I was sitting down sipping a coffee. A mug of the black liquid sat opposite me, with a jug of milk and the sugar bowl.

'I didn't know how you liked it,' I said, as if in explanation.

She nodded distractedly. I had a sheet of paper and a pen in front of me; both stolen from the nurse's station on the way down.

'So, very unusual to find a police cordon around a bed,' I prompted. 'Did someone die? Was someone killed here?'

'A *lady of the night* had been brought in,' she said.

I smiled at the old fashioned verbiage.

'She was bruised and slightly battered; cuts and scrapes. Her *friend*....'

She said the word friend with a sneer.

'....He told us that someone had tried to rape her.'

I sighed inwardly with relief; I'd suspected they had from our last interaction, but at least the apes who handled her had bought that much of the story.

'The timeline is all very blurry after that,' said the matron. 'We have been exceptionally busy over the last week, and I've been working double shifts, but I think it happened the following night.'

'What happened?' I asked, hoping to prompt her again.

'It appears that the same man, the one who had originally attacked her, came back to try and finish the job. Anyway this poor girl's *friend*, who's coming back in after a cigarette, sees this man at her bedside, and the next thing, there are bullets flying everywhere.'

I had seen the plywood roughly nailed into place where the windows had been; the double doors at the end of the ward.

'Was the girl hurt?' I asked.

'More shocked than hurt, I think,' she said.

'What happened to the two men?' I asked.

'I don't really know,' she answered. 'They were out through the doors like a hound after a hare. The police took our statements, but they never told us if there had been any further developments, and we have more than enough to be doing without checking on that kind of information.'

She delivered the last line a little defensively.

'What about the girl?' I asked. 'What happened to her after that?'

'The police took her into protective custody,' said the matron flatly.

There was nothing else I could think of that a newspaperman would ask.

'Thank you, you've been very cooperative,' I said.

She hesitated; I knew why. I slid over the copy of the Cork Examiner that I had also liberated from the nurse's station. It was folded in four. As she opened the first fold, I saw her eyes widen slightly as she saw the neatly arranged fan of fifty euro notes. She let the folded page drop back, then rolled it and tucked it under her arm.

'And none of this will come back on me?' she asked.

'No one will ever know, you have my word,' I said.

I nodded pleasantly as she left the room. I sipped the remainder of my coffee, as two giggling nurses crashed through the door. One of them picked up the TV remote and switched it on. I couldn't figure out why, because as the national news blasted into the room, they seemed oblivious to it; caught up as they were in their own conversation. Young people these days seemed to need multiple sensory stimulations.

I drained the last of my coffee and turned to leave, when I heard something that caught my attention. I walked over to the TV. They had one of those *breaking news* tickers across the bottom, so I could read it too, even though the volume was maxed.

'And in local news,' the honey voiced presenter was shouting, 'ADXR, the international drug giant, have announced a joint-venture with G&E Chemicals, a New Jersey-based pharma company. The joint-venture is being established at the IDA campus in Clonakilty. According to IDA sources, the dual investment will bring fifty jobs to the area initially, with more planned in the next eighteen months. A spokesperson for ADXR told us they were delighted to be investing in both Ireland and the local community of Clonakilty. G&E Chemicals have yet to release a statement, but are understood to be similarly delighted to have secured such a large and well known partner.'

What was it that Foster had said? That we needed a concrete link between Storm and Cork? Well, it appeared we now had one.

CHAPTER 35 – ANTICIPATION

19th May 2011 – Nine days after the Storm.

Fear is pain arising from the anticipation of evil. – Aristotle.

Roussel watched with quiet amusement as Dale came to the end of the file. His lips were moving silently as his eyes scanned the pages. He was a faster reader than Roussel by a factor of two at least. He probably needed to be. The DEA would process an awful lot of paperwork.

'Coffee?' asked Roussel.

Dale nodded absently.

Roussel busied himself in the kitchen. He couldn't get over how small things were in Ireland. His own apartment back home was not even an apartment by American standards, but his kitchenette alone was half the size of the flat they had recently rented.

A sharp crack made him jump. He realised that Dale had closed the folder with a bang, making a sound like a thunderclap. He walked back into the living room with two cups of tea. Neither of them were strangers to the iced variety, but both had developed a real liking for proper English tea; the hot stuff, with plenty of milk.

'It's like being in a movie,' said Dale, with his eyes closed. 'I keep thinking I'm going to wake up.'

'I know what you mean,' said Roussel. 'It's all a bit surreal, isn't it?'

'So, what do you make of our boy?' asked Dale, opening his eyes.

'It's a strange one and no mistake,' said Roussel. 'After what I read about him; after what I know he is and what he does, I really wanted to dislike him. But do you know what, try as I might, I just can't.'

'No, me neither,' said Dale. 'But, do you think he's telling the truth?'

'I do,' answered Roussel.

There was a long and companionable pause.

'So, where do *you* fit in to all of this mess?' asked Dale. 'What's your story?'

'Me?' replied Roussel. 'I'm just a local parish CID detective, who just happened to accidentally pick up a brutal double murder.'

'There's more to it than that though, isn't there?' stated Dale quizzically.

'What do you mean?'

'I can't read people,' offered Dale. 'It's something I've never been able to do well. But I can tell when things are not what they seem.'

'I'm not with you,' said Roussel with a bemused expression.

'Let's put it this way,' said Dale. 'You're not the typical rural detective. I'm not saying they are stupid, far from it. But there is an extra dimension to you, and I just can't put my finger on it.'

Roussel blinked in shock. Dale was full of surprises. He was certainly more intuitive than Roussel had given him credit for.

'I'm a qualified lawyer,' stated Roussel suddenly.

This time it was Dale's turn to blink in surprise.

'Really?' he asked. 'And you gave that up to become a policeman, why?'

'I missed home,' said Roussel truthfully. 'I was in a big corporate firm, full of Yankee WASP's; no offence.'

He directed this at Dale quickly.

'None taken,' said Dale.

'It took me a while to realise none of those guys actually cared about the law. For them, it was purely a game for winning and losing; high-stakes poker, with other people's lives and money.'

He paused reflectively, before continuing.

'I was asked to review a case. It was one of those David vs. Goliath jobs. Guess who we were representing?' he asked sourly.

Foster could guess; he knew the type of law firm.

'Some multi-national company leeching God knows what chemicals and toxins into the ground water; potentially causing all sorts of birth defects and cancers. On top of that, I was the only southerner in the firm. I just reached a tipping point. My parents raised me with morals. I wanted to be able to sleep at night.'

He laughed a short, barking laugh.

'Of course, now I lie awake for other reasons,' he said.

He shrugged, before becoming inquisitor himself, firing the initial question back at Dale.

'What about you?' he asked. 'What's your own path to this point in time?'

'Pretty straightforward,' said Dale. 'This is my first and only job. I didn't have any set direction in mind. I just wanted to pick a career where I could make a difference. Turns out, I'm actually pretty damn good at what I do.'

'Do you have any regrets?' asked Roussel.

'Oh, I've got plenty of those,' said Dale. 'But strangely enough, coming on this trip is not one of them.'

'Married, partner, fiancé?' asked Roussel.

Dale snorted.

'What do you think?' he answered in return. 'The only thing I'm married to is my job, I'm afraid. What a sad stupid cliché that is. The only girls I meet are suspects. What about you?'

Dale returned the question.

'I had a long-term girlfriend,' said Roussel. 'Turns out she was more in love with my prospects than she was with me, and as you say, the only girls I meet now have criminal records.'

Before either of them could ask another question, they heard the front door bang. A large plastic bag full of delicious smells was deposited on the table in front of them.

'Chinese take-away,' said Street, placing a six-pack of Heineken next to it.

'Gentlemen,' he said. 'I think we have a lead.'

#

For a good ten minutes or so, all you could hear was the contented sound of jaws working. I had forgotten how hungry I was, and thought the guys might benefit from a takeaway; seemed I was right. I waited until the rice was depleted and the main dishes started congealing; a sure sign that everybody had eaten their fill. I flicked the caps off the second round of drinks with the bottle opener, and indicated the folder.

'So, what do you make of it?' I asked.

'Well, it certainly clears up the CIA involvement, anyway,' said Roussel.

We all laughed.

'What do *you* think?' I asked Dale specifically.

I was interested in his DEA perspective.

'Overall, a very interesting story,' he said. 'And to be honest, like all the best discoveries, it seems its primary purpose was not what it was originally developed for.'

'So, a bit like Viagra,' said Roussel, interceding. 'That was never expected to have those unfortunate side-effects.'

'Or fortunate, depending on your point of view,' said Dale.

There was a brief chuckle all round.

'Does it give you any more insight into Storm?' I asked.

'I can see why it would be important to someone like the Mancini's. If we use a modern example, we only have to look at the rise of ecstasy. The trend for its usage came about from a user base of almost zero. It was a real fluke; party people looking for love, but look how many billions are now spent worldwide on that one drug.'

He corrected himself.

'Or should I say that one range of drugs. But imagine controlling the supply? Imagine being the sole manufacturer? From reading this, the process of synthesis does not seem straightforward. You would need a lot of equipment and hence a lot of money. Now, I know that drugs are big business and there is a lot of investment on the illegal side, but if you look at what we would call the *problem drugs* currently, the initial outlay is still pretty low all things considered, and you can't control the supply.'

'I don't follow you,' I said, shaking my head.

I could see that Roussel felt the same way.

'Heroin is derived from opium, which in turn is derived from poppies. You can't stop me growing poppies, especially somewhere like Afghanistan. And then you have South America; the coca plant. Especially in the rainforest, there is no way you can control it, you would have to find it first. Marijuana; literally every college dorm room is growing that stuff. But this; this is different, this is big pharma.'

'So, if you need that much investment, how did that guy Nigel manage to get it working all those years ago?'

'Reading between the lines,' said Dale. 'We are talking about wartime. We are talking about the development of something that could have changed the course of history. I'm guessing money was no object. He would have had the best that money could buy at the time.'

'Interesting you should say that,' I said. 'I saw an article on the local news about an hour ago. ADXR are setting up a new plant about a hundred miles from here, in a place called Clonakilty.'

'Can't get much bigger pharma than that,' agreed Dale.

'Well, here's the thing,' I said. 'Apparently, it's a joint-venture between ADXR and a company called G&E Chemicals.'

'Never heard of them,' said Dale.

'Me neither,' responded Roussel.

'I only heard about them recently,' I said. 'It was about a month and a half ago; I overheard a conversation.'

'Go on,' said Dale.

'Like to hazard a guess what G&E stands for?' I asked instead.

They thought about it for a couple of minutes.

'General and every day,' said Roussel.

I shook my head and cocked an eyebrow at Dale.

'Global and effective,' he ventured.

We all laughed, and then it eventually faltered and tailed off.

'Guido and Ernesto,' I said, into the silence.

'I knew it,' said Dale, thumping the table in triumph. 'Didn't I tell you?'

'You certainly did,' I replied, 'but it doesn't really change anything.'

'I know,' said Dale, 'but it makes me feel better, and it gives us something to target. No, in fact, more than that, it gives us *somewhere* to target.'

'Let's not move ahead of ourselves,' I said. 'There are still a few loose ends around here that I'd like to clear up. There's a girl, the one who gave me the inside information on Scott Mitchell. I put her in harm's way and I sort of feel responsible. I think I've deflected suspicion away from her, but I'd like to be sure.'

I looked at Roussel.

'Now, apparently she was taken into custody last night.'

'Why are you looking at me?' he asked.

I could see the thought wheels turning in his head.

'Well I can hardly walk in, can I?' I retorted.

'Well I can *barely* walk in,' protested Roussel. 'I'm only a guest.'

'There's always a way,' I said. 'All you have to do is show a little bit of balls.'

'Are you calling me chicken?' asked Roussel.

'I don't know,' I said. 'Are you?'

Roussel looked at me, and then his shoulders slumped in resignation and a smile spread slowly over his face.

'I'm only doing this because there is a girl involved,' he said. 'I suppose you have a plan.'

'As a matter of fact I do,' I said.

#

'Thanks for picking me up,' said Roussel.

'No problem,' said James. 'I thought you'd be well into the land of nod by now.'

'Couldn't sleep,' said Roussel. 'You know the way; when you've gone past that point of tiredness.'

'Oh, I know it well,' stated James. 'Anyway, what are you doing over here, did you get lost?'

'You could say that,' Roussel lied seamlessly.

If only James knew the truth.

They journeyed the rest of the way in silence.

'So, anything in particular you need to do?' asked James.

'Yeah, I need to check something on the web a bit later. And I'd like to talk to my captain in a few minutes. But I was wondering before that, is there any way you could give me a tour of the station?'

'Sure,' said James.

He stopped to consider something.

'Any particular reason?' he asked curiously.

'Just to see what the differences are, really,' said Roussel nonchalantly. 'You know; between the US and Ireland. Oh, and I'd like to meet a few more of the guys if I could,' he added, as an afterthought.

'Okay, sure,' said James. 'Let me just dump this stuff on my desk, and I'll be back down to you in a minute.'

Roussel waited in reception, his own anxiety growing by the second. He hadn't been particularly convinced by Street's plan, and the more he thought about it, the more flimsy it became. And James had been a little odd too. Roussel didn't blame him.

'Hey James, pick me up, drive me across the city and give me a tour of the station.'

It wasn't exactly standard behaviour.

Before he could think about it anymore, he was rejoined by James.

'So, what do you want to see first?' asked James.

'I don't know, you tell me,' said Roussel.

'Ok, let's start at the top, so.'

They spent the next ten minutes visiting the boardroom, CID and Drug Squad offices, Uniform Patrol Public office, and all the while, Roussel was sweating buckets, doing his best to portray an air of nonchalance. He thought his torture would never end, when they finally arrived back in reception again.

'And last but not least, the holding cells,' said James.

Roussel relaxed slightly; at last, something to do. He was a man of action. As they descended the steps, his anxiety dissolved, as it always did, to be replaced with a steely determination. He kept his hearing half tuned to James, as they continued their descent. He made *I'm listening* noises, as he pulled the phone from his jacket.

He selected the pre-typed text message and hit send.

There was an officer sitting at a desk at the end of the stairwell. Roussel counted four cells in total.

'This is Sergeant Keane,' said James. 'He's our duty officer.'

'So, what do you do down here?' asked Roussel.

'Oh, you know, the usual,' said Sergeant Keane. 'We check on them regularly; every fifteen minutes or so. We also do suicide watch if we're told they are especially high risk, or if we believe that they are of a certain disposition. We also process them as they come in, that kind of thing.'

'And how long would a typical shift be?' asked Roussel.

'Generally we would do eight hour shifts,' said Sergeant Keane.

'And what type of people would you have in the cells; does it vary by day or time of day?'

'Oh, all kinds,' said Keane. 'Drunks, addicts, students, you name it.'

Roussel could see that James was looking at him a little strangely. He hadn't asked a single question on the whole tour, and now here he was, babbling like a gossip girl. The truth was; he was waiting for James's phone to ring. He was also trying to build up a rapport with the duty officer. It was part of the plan.

As if on cue, James's phone blasted out a drum and base ringtone.

'Murray,' he answered briskly.

He listened for a few seconds, his face registering surprise.

'How did you get this number?' he asked.

He held up two fingers, and gestured up the stairs; part one of the plan was working. Roussel acknowledged the gesture with a smile.

'So, who have you got in at the moment?' he asked the sergeant, feigning interest as James took the stairs two at a time.

Sergeant Keane consulted the clipboards that were hanging on hooks behind his desk. As he took them down one by one, Roussel memorised the order. He was hoping the man had a neat and tidy mind.

Sergeant Keane studied each one in turn.

'Drunk; came in last night.'

He discarded the board.

'Addict; found strung out early morning. Number two is empty, and number one has a young woman who was attacked in hospital. She was brought here for her own protection.'

He checked his watch and nodded to himself.

'I've got to do a quarter hour check, back in a sec.'

Roussel's heart was hammering in his chest. It was all going to hinge on the timing. He was about to make his move, when he realised that Sergeant Keane was moving to the far end of the cells. By his reckoning, number four. He waited as the officer went through his practiced routine, cell by cell. The sergeant pulled the slide back on each door and checked the four corners of each cell. The exception was the second to last one; looked like Roussel had been correct on the order. He made his move as the officer completed the last door.

He turned and bumped into Roussel, who had ventured into the cell area.

'Can I see inside one?' Roussel asked brightly.

'Sure,' said the officer. 'We'll take number two, as it's empty.'

He jangled the keys as he turned away; searching for the one he wanted. Roussel realised he only had a second or two. He removed the note from his pocket, and eased the hatch open on cell number one, praying it would be noiseless. There was a slight grating sound as it moved a tiny bit, and he held his breath. Throwing caution to the wind, he slid the note through the gap, and closed it as quietly and silently as he could.

He had his hands in his pockets before Sergeant Keane turned back around. He smiled brightly at the duty officer, who looked like he was about to say something and then seemed to come to a decision to remain silent. He shook his head, as if to disabuse himself of some notion.

'After you,' he said as Roussel entered the empty cell.

Roussel wondered whether the girl would react as required. Only time would tell.

They heard the clatter of footsteps on the stairs, as they returned to the sergeant's desk.

'Well, that was just plain weird,' said James.

'What was?' asked Roussel.

'Some guy from the DEA, standing in reception, bold as brass; said he'd got my number from an international task force report.'

'Sounds like a cock and bull story to me,' said Roussel.

'Oh, his credentials were genuine enough,' said James.

'What did he have to say?' asked Roussel.

'Well that's just it,' answered James. 'He started talking about some rumours they'd heard; something big due to hit the streets. He said he couldn't give me any specifics, but he said Ireland would be one of the first geographies affected.'

'Sounds a little far-fetched,' said Roussel.

'Ordinarily, I would agree,' said James, surprising him. 'But in the last month or so, we've been getting some serious vibes from the Street. Dealers and junkies alike have been getting really excited; drooling over the prospect almost.'

'Really,' responded Roussel. 'So what do you think it is?'

'Well this fellow....'

James squinted at the card in his hand.

'Foster. He seems to think it is something new. But even a new drug can be a variant of an existing one. Just look at the impact caused by crack cocaine. Either way, we're not taking it lightly.'

He turned back towards the cells.

'Thanks Sergeant,' he shouted, before directing Roussel back up the stairs and into reception.

'Do you still need access to the web?'

'No, I'm going to leave it,' said Roussel. 'The tiredness is really beginning to hit me now,' he said truthfully.

'Do you want a lift home?'

'No I think I'll walk, if that's okay?'

'Yeah, no problem,' replied James.

He accompanied Roussel through the main doors and out onto the street. They shook hands.

'See you tomorrow,' said James.

He glanced up at the sky, and noticed the fast moving clouds. They were dark, grey and forbidding and they dominated the distant horizon.

'Looks like a storm is coming,' he stated softly.

CHAPTER 36 – DEFICIENT

19th May 2011 – Nine days after the Storm.

Three things cannot be long hidden: the sun, the moon, and the truth. – Buddha.

Guido settled back into the sumptuous brown leather. His fingernails bit deep into the hide of the arms like a death grip, but if you were scared of flying, it was much better to do it in style.

The Learjet had been one of their more extravagant gifts to themselves, but every time he was thirty thousand feet up and, his body was rigid with tension and terror, he never regretted the purchase.

He opened his eyes and saw Antonio coming towards him with a fresh drink. He smiled at the vision. Of all their staff, Antonio loathed the Learjet the most. Because of his size, he was almost permanently bent double, a huge disadvantage for a manservant, but to his credit, he never grumbled or complained.

Guido glanced across at Ernesto. As in most things, he was the antithesis of his brother. Ernesto's face betrayed none of the tension or anxiety that Guido was experiencing. His body was stretched out serenely on the tan leather recliner as he snored softly, oblivious to his companion's discomfort.

'Your drink, Mr Mancini,' said Antonio formally.

'Thank you, Antonio,' said Guido, as the ice cubes rattled against the crystal. 'That will be all. Go and sit yourself down, give your neck a rest.'

Antonio flashed him a smile of gratitude. Guido pulled his chair upright and opened his attaché case. He was flicking through the papers contained within it, when Ernesto yawned and stretched.

'Have I been out for long?' he mumbled.

'About six hours,' said Guido.

'Did I miss anything?' he asked.

'A couple of bourbons and five hours of sheer terror,' said Guido drily. Ernesto laughed.

'It is the *only* thing you're afraid of,' he stated apologetically.

'I suppose everybody has to have a room 101,' acknowledged Guido.

'So, what exactly are we doing over here anyway?' asked Ernesto.

'I want to check on progress,' said Guido. 'I want to make sure that David and Ben are holding up their end of the bargain. We have invested a lot of our valuable time and finances into this venture, so now we need to reassure ourselves that the investment is being repaid properly.'

Ernesto pursed his lips and nodded. He was just about to call Antonio, when Guido held up his hand.

'Drink?' he inquired questioningly.

Ernesto inclined his head.

'Here, have mine,' said Guido. 'Poor Antonio is having a rest and I've had two already.'

'Cheers,' said Ernesto.

They sat in companionable silence as the sunlight streamed through the small porthole windows of the Learjet's cabin.

'I suspect it won't be quite this sunny when we land,' said Ernesto.

'I expect you're right,' replied Guido.

There was another longer silence this time. All you could hear was the drone of the engines.

'One other thing did occur to me,' said Ernesto, his voice almost shockingly loud in the accumulated silence.

Guido raised his eyebrows enquiringly.

'Well, we are fairly well known; we're pretty famous, or should I say infamous,' he said, thinking about it. 'How are we going to get into the country without causing a stir?'

'Our CIA colleague has been most helpful in that regard,' answered Guido.

He pulled out two US passports and handed one across.

'Meet Ernesto Borza,' he said, 'an Italian American furniture maker investigating investment opportunities in Ireland.'

'And who is my travelling companion?' asked Ernesto.

'Guido Nutini,' said Guido. 'I am your friend and business partner. One of the trips we have arranged is a visit to the local IDA office, and a number of other IDA sponsored events. Of particular interest are the inspections of local businesses made good. Don't worry, there won't be a problem.'

'So, what's the story when we land?' asked Ernesto.

'We arrive into Cork Airport,' said Guido. 'Clear customs and then straight into a waiting Limo that will take us to the Perryville Guest house.'

'Only a guest house?' asked Ernesto.

'This one is for the more discerning traveller,' said Guido. 'You'll see for yourself. Anyway, the accommodation is in a town called Kinsale. It's halfway to where we want to go apparently; all the rich Americans stay there when they're on holiday. Seeing as we fall into one of those categories, and can easily fake the other, I thought, why not?'

They heard a noise from the cabin, and the next thing, Antonio was at their table.

'Landing in fifteen minutes,' he said. 'Fasten seatbelts please.'

As he spoke, the light streaming into the cabin was abruptly cut off as the dense grey mass enveloped the small aircraft. They could feel the downward motion as the pilot shed altitude. Both Guido and Ernesto blinked as the plane suddenly emerged from the cloud cover.

Fourteen minutes later, Ernesto noted with interest that Guido had failed to register their transition from air to land because he was so petrified. Their pilot was especially skilled; money was a great enabler.

Guido was right though, they sailed through customs. They had one sticky moment on the way out. They initially failed to recognise their new surnames being held up on cards in the arrivals hall. Once that faux pas had been overcome, they were escorted in silence to the pickup zone, and both jumped thankfully into the back of the black limo.

The journey to the guest house was quiet and uneventful. They both sat back and closed their eyes. In doing so, each was oblivious to the fact that with every mile they travelled, the vista was changing. They were literally going back in time.

Half an hour into the journey, Ernesto opened his eyes. He watched, transfixed, as the pretty whitewashed cottages alternated with the not so pretty derelict ruins. Living history flashed past on either side of the limo. He nudged Guido awake and started pointing out some of the sights.

'Do you ever wonder where we'd be, if our father had stayed in Italy?' asked Ernesto.

'You know me,' said Guido. 'I don't like looking back. We move forward or we die.'

'Humour me,' said Ernesto. 'Do you think we would be as successful as we are now?'

'People like you and I will always be successful,' answered Guido. 'Cream inevitably rises to the top.'

'Maybe we should go back to Italy after this trip,' said Ernesto. 'Have a little visit.'

'And maybe we shouldn't,' said Guido. 'Papa was never sentimental. Always move forward boys. If a shark stops moving they die. Never stop.'

'Yeah, good advice when you think about it,' Ernesto acknowledged, a little sadly.

'You can torture yourself with thoughts like these,' said Guido. 'Just be content that you haven't had to scratch a living from a few meagre acres, waiting for God and the weather to do their worst.'

'Sometimes I do wish that there were a little more honesty to our endeavours,' said Ernesto thoughtfully.

'We worked damn hard to get where we are,' stated Guido.

'I'm not disputing our work ethic,' said Ernesto, 'but you can still work really hard at something that is amoral and illegal; we are living proof of that. No, sometimes I figure it would have been nice to produce something with sincerity and integrity.'

He pointed to a field where two guys were battling with both the livestock and the weather.

'I bet they don't have trouble sleeping at night,' he said.

Guido looked at him strangely for a second, and decided to let the comment go. It was probably just the strain of being away from home and visiting somewhere new. They rarely travelled; both of them were real home birds.

They nodded in appreciation as the limo swept up to the main entrance of their guesthouse. But guesthouse was just a meaningless moniker really. It was a magnificent building, steeped in centuries old grandeur.

'It's like an old southern mansion,' said Ernesto and they were both silent for a second, each knowing who the other was thinking about.

Somehow, Antonio had managed to get ahead of them with all their bags, and had pre-booked them in. He had also fully unpacked each of their suitcases, and personalised each room to that brother's individual taste. He really was irreplaceable.

As Ernesto changed for dinner, he silently acknowledged Guido's argument. He rarely told him to his face, but his brother was right in most things. It was always better not to look back.

They gave Antonio the night off, with strict instructions to use the Limo for his own ends. He was rarely allowed off duty, but boy, did he know how to enjoy himself when he was. Ernesto chuckled; Alka-Seltzer would probably be required in large quantities in the morning.

The brothers met in the bar. Antonio had specified their pre-dinner routine to the staff in the guesthouse, all of whom had been more than accommodating. Along with the two scotches, a chequer board lay open on a long low table between two leather wingbacks; home from home.

They got so lost in their game that they didn't notice the figure standing adjacent to their table, watching patiently with a sardonic smile. It was not until the roaring flames of the open wood fire cast a flickering shadow across their game board, that they both looked up in unison; like twins.

The brothers collectively drew in a breath, but Guido recovered first.

'What the fuck are you doing here?' he asked.

'Having a little holiday, same as you, I'd wager,' said the stranger. 'Mind if I pull up a chair?'

The stranger didn't wait for a reply, but dragged another chair over and watched as Ernesto and Guido continued to play. The stranger said no more; the brother's games were sacrosanct and the stranger obviously knew enough about them to know that. They would remain mute until one was victor and one was vanquished. The stranger's mouth creased at the corners again as Ernesto's solitary piece was forced into a corner by Guido's three Kings. Only when Ernesto acknowledged defeat by throwing his remaining counter into Guido's lap, did the two brothers turn to the interloper.

'Making sure we got here?' asked Guido, raising an eyebrow.

'In a manner of speaking,' said the stranger.

'You'll get your money,' said Guido.

'Oh, I have no doubt about that,' said the stranger. 'But there has been a, how should I say it, complication.'

Ernesto narrowed his eyes warningly.

'Complication how?' he growled.

'Let me put it this way,' said the stranger. 'Max was holding out on you.'

Ernesto relaxed.

'We know that, you idiot,' he said with a smile.

'It was you who put us onto him, remember?' added Guido sarcastically. 'We've already taken measures to limit his efficacy.'

'So I heard,' said the stranger. 'Pity; I liked Max, most of the time. The problem is though; it wasn't just the folder he was holding out on you with.'

This time it was Guido's turn to narrow his eyes.

'Go on,' he demanded dangerously.

'Well, between the jigs and the reels,' said the stranger, 'I neglected to furnish you, and therefore Max, with the complete file. There is a key section of the protocol missing.'

'What do you mean, missing?' asked Ernesto.

'Missing,' said the stranger in exasperation. 'Not there, intentionally left out, removed. Now either Max wasn't as good at his job as you thought he was, or he was very good at his job and that's why he was trying to pull a double sting with me. He obviously didn't realise that I supplied the file to you guys in the first place. Either way, it puts you in an awkward position. Anything you manufacture without this missing section will be worthless garbage.'

'How do we know you're telling the truth?' asked Guido.

'Why would I lie?' asked the stranger in return. 'You've already made me very rich. I could have disappeared once the wire transfers complete and you would never have seen me again. However, you guys took me by surprise. To be honest, you were my best bet as clients, but I was fifty-fifty as to whether you would go through with it. I thought I'd have a decent interval to come back to you with the missing section, but I'm grudgingly impressed with how quickly you've got things up and running.'

'So it is about money,' said Ernesto.

'It's about more money,' corrected the stranger. 'Isn't it always?'

'So, you're trying to shake us down?' asked Guido.

'I would prefer to look at it more as sealing the deal,' said the stranger.

'And what if we don't?' asked Ernesto.

'Have you not been listening to me?' asked the stranger slowly. 'Your end product will be even more useless on the street than a mountain of breath mints.'

'We've already put a lot of money into this,' said Guido, dangerously softly.

'And none of that investment will be affected,' said the stranger hastily. 'That is why I have come back to you now, so the production process can be modified without any additional expense.'

Guido grunted.

'So, how much are we talking?' he asked.

'Ten percent of your initial investment and ten percent of anything you make on top of that.'

Ernesto started laughing, but Guido put up his hand.

'You want ten percent of our company,' he said slowly and succinctly.

The stranger nodded.

'Let me get this crystal clear, just so there's no ambiguity; you want ten percent of our company,' Guido repeated.

'The way I look at it is this,' said the stranger pleasantly. 'I don't want part of your company, but I do want the monetary equivalent of ten percent in wire transfers, on top of the initial investment. That way, you get ninety percent of something massive, or one hundred percent of nothing.'

They both looked at the stranger for a very long time.

'You're playing a dangerous game,' said Guido eventually, 'but you've got balls and I like that.'

'If we say yes, how soon do we get the missing section?' asked Ernesto.

'We can shake on it now,' said the stranger.

He threw a manila envelope onto the chequer board, sending the counters skating across the polished oak floor like hockey pucks.

Guido looked at the envelope and then flicked his head at the stranger.

'Leave us,' he said.

'As you wish,' said the stranger. 'I'll be in the lounge, waiting to celebrate.'

'So, what do you think?' asked Ernesto, after the stranger had sidled out.

'I think we are bent over the proverbial barrel,' replied Guido.

Ernesto could hear the flint in his voice.

'If I pay for something, I don't expect this death by a thousand cuts. If someone wants to make a deal with me, reach a realistic valuation and stick to it. I hate greedy people who come back for more.'

The irony of his statement was completely lost on both brothers.

'Are there any other alternatives?' asked Ernesto.

'There are always alternatives,' smiled Guido grimly. 'We put a hold on the wire transfers until we are positive we have the full confirmed Protocol. The most important thing now is to get the lines up and running. We shake on this now, and worry about the logistics later.'

Both brothers knew what *worry about the logistics later* meant.

'He doesn't get his money till we are totally happy.'

'What if he has a problem with that?'

'He won't; he is driven by greed, a very predictable animal. Anyway, who said we were going to tell him?'

They clashed their glasses together and laughed, then stood up and embraced briefly.

The perfect storm inched ever closer.

CHAPTER 37 – RESOLUTION

20th May 2011 – Ten days after the Storm.

Always bear in mind that your own resolution to succeed is always more important than any one thing. – Abraham Lincoln.

Roussel leant against the wall and watched the tide of humanity pass him by. For some reason, he couldn't stop smiling. It was always the same when he pulled off something extra dangerous or exciting. It made him feel a little bit more alive. When he thought about everything that had happened to him since he'd arrived in Ireland, it was almost like he was starring in his very own action movie. Move over James Bond; the name's Roussel, Charles Roussel.

He'd been attacked, knocked out, shot at, kidnapped and participated in a fire fight using live rounds. He'd then been blown up by a grenade, while possibly also shooting and killing multiple assailants; so why did it feel so good?

As soon as he'd exited the building, he'd walked straight into a newsagent and bought himself a packet of cigarettes and a box of matches. It was the first time in a long time that he'd purchased his own, rather than bumming them off someone else. He lit one up, revelling in the nicotine hit. It was funny, but it was just like he'd told Guilbeau. Occasionally, there was that rare moment when he just wanted a cigarette. He didn't need it, he certainly didn't crave it; he just wanted it.

'I wouldn't have figured you for a smoker,' said a voice beside him.

He turned to his right, where Dale was leaning against the wall. It looked like Dale had been affected the same way. They grinned at each other stupidly.

'Well, that was exciting,' said Roussel. 'Cigarette?'

He held out the packet.

Dale thought about it for a second.

'Don't mind if I do,' he answered.

Dale waited for the loud flare as the match ignited, and inhaled the smoke deep into his lungs. But it was strange, this cigarette felt different from all the others he'd secretly smoked. Like Roussel, it was something he wanted to do, a reward to himself. It was not something he needed to do; there was a subtle difference.

They stood there, smoking in companionable silence.

'So what was all that about, do you think?' asked Dale eventually.

'That is the funniest thing; I was just about to ask you the same question.'

'Well, you've got to admit, it is very odd. Asking us to virtually break into a police station, and then just slip a note under the cell door of a girl who may or may not be the one he told us about.'

'There was nothing offhand about it,' said Roussel grimly. 'And make no mistake; she's the correct one all right.'

'How do you know?' asked Dale.

Roussel glared at him.

'I'm a detective,' he said. 'That's what I do.'

'Bizarre behaviour anyway,' said Dale, choosing to ignore the inference.

'Oh, I'm not so sure about that,' said Roussel thoughtfully.

'What do you mean?' asked Dale.

'Well, she's not a girlfriend for a start,' said Roussel.

'How do you know that?' asked Dale.

'Oh, come on,' said Roussel. 'He's only been in the country a week; less than that in fact. He's a middle aged mob enforcer, with his best years behind him, hiding from a death squad. She's a young and completely unconnected prostitute.'

'So, what are you thinking?' asked Dale.

'The one issue I'm having big problems with,' said Roussel. 'Maybe it's because I'm closer to it, but Scott Mitchell, victim number one in my double homicide, the man that Street freely admits to shooting. He is the fly in the ointment for me. I spent a lot of hours agonising over who he was, and what he was. Not only does he not fit into our puzzle, he's a piece of a completely different puzzle, out there on his own, where we don't have any of the other pieces.'

'So, how does the girl fit into that?' asked Dale.

'According to my man James,' said Roussel, 'Black Swan would be about the same age as Street. Now I don't know if you've noticed it or not, but this place feels very parochial to me. I'm convinced there's a link between those two, Black Swan and Street, and what's more, I think Street is convinced of it too.'

'Do you think he knows Black Swan?' Dale asked curiously.

'I don't think he does,' said Roussel. 'Certainly not in his current guise anyway; I don't get that impression from him.'

'Yeah, I know what you mean,' said Dale. 'For a criminal, he is oddly honest.'

'But back to the girl,' said Roussel. 'I don't think it is all bullshit. I do think there is some genuine concern there for her well-being, but I also think he's using it as an opportunity.'

'An opportunity for what?' asked Dale.

'An opportunity to lure Black Swan out into the open,' answered Roussel.

He blew out a stream of smoke and regarded his companion closely.

'Make no mistake,' he said. 'We need to be very careful that we don't get side tracked on this one. I don't think this is your normal drugs based feud. I think this aspect of the case has always been personal.'

'So extra vigilant,' said Dale.

'Extra vigilant,' echoed Roussel.

Almost in unison, they threw their butts to the floor and carefully ground them out. They watched the ebb and flow of rush-hour Cork on the busy street, each lost in their own subconscious worlds.

For Roussel, his thoughts brought him back to the gentle swish of the tree branches, as he stood alone in the small and carefully tended graveyard, pondering what might have been.

For Dale, his thoughts brought him back to field upon field of tall Midwestern corn. The image was so vivid that he could feel the ears of wheat smacking off his hands, and the sun on one side of his face. It occurred to him that coming away to a different country had made him realise where home actually was. He needed to go and visit with his family very soon.

The sound of a horn jerked them both out their thoughts.

'Are we getting in ladies, or just standing around?' asked Street.

#

The two guys bundled into the back. I kept one eye on them and one eye on the wing mirrors as I carefully manoeuvred the car into the rush-hour traffic. I acknowledged the taxi horn blast with a finger; cheeky bastard.

'Jesus, you guys were miles away,' I said. 'What were you dreaming about?'

'Nothing,' said Roussel.

'Actually, I was wondering if I could get access to the Internet somewhere?' asked Dale.

'I thought you were off the grid,' I said.

'I am,' he answered. 'But my partner said he'd keep me updated. I haven't heard from him, so I'm thinking there might be something in e-mail.'

'Okay, but I don't trust information technology,' I said. 'I don't trust anything I can't control. So we'll go somewhere generic, virtually untraceable. It'll give me a little peace of mind.'

I circled back around, and eventually found what I was looking for. We pulled up twenty yards ahead; the only place we could park. I stuffed a coin into the meter; last thing I needed was a parking ticket.

It was a typical Irish Internet cafe. There were a few scrappy and beaten up PC's, and an Asian guy behind the counter selling discount phone-cards to any destination in the world.

There were plenty of PC's free. The place was empty, but we clustered around one in the corner to give us a little bit of privacy. Dale sat down; he obviously knew his way around a computer. After a couple of minutes of furious typing, he shook his head.

'Nothing except a bit of spam,' he said with a tinge of disappointment.

The word *spam* triggered something deep inside my brain. A vision flashed across my subconscious.

'Can you get G-mail on that thing?' I asked suddenly. 'Can you pull up the login page?'

'Sure,' he said, as the page slipped into view. 'What's the username?'

'Don't laugh,' I said, 'but its *werunthistown*, all one word.'

I could see Dale smiling as he typed it.

'I would never have guessed that,' said Roussel.

'That's the whole point, isn't it?' I said. 'Anyway, I'm sure they've changed the password at this stage, but it's worth a try.'

'What's the password?' asked Dale.

'Francesco,' I said.

'Their father's name,' I added, in answer to their unspoken question.

Dale typed it in and hit enter; no dice.

'Try it again,' I said. 'Maybe you typed it wrong the first time.'

Dale tried it again; no, fuck it.

I put my chin in my hand, and thought for a couple of minutes. I thought about Francesco Mancini. I'd never met him, but what did I know about him? There was only one thing really.

'Okay, try this one more time,' I said. 'Try *francesco68*, the digits not the words.'

'I'm in,' cried Dale incredulously.

'The year their father died,' I said, by way of explanation. 'They used to tell me all the time.'

'So, what are we looking for?' asked Dale. 'There is an awful lot of spam in here.'

I smiled. The word *spam* had triggered the memory; Antonio wrestling with the spam filter on the brother's laptop.

'They only use this for Internet related activities, so don't get your hopes up.'

I directed this to Dale, who was browsing intently through the inbox.

'None of their business dealings are online. They just use it for shopping.'

Roussel laughed and we all joined in. The idea of two crime bosses buying books on Amazon, and ordering pizza from Domino's, was actually pretty amusing.

'Well now,' said Dale. 'Here are two very interesting things.'

He double clicked on the first attachment; an invoice for Avgas. He used the mouse to scroll down and highlight the quantity delivered.

'Do they have a private plane?' Dale asked.

'They do,' I replied. 'A Learjet, why?'

'Well it looks like they very recently fuelled it up. And check out this one; it's even more interesting,' he said, double-clicking the second attachment.

I read the top line.

Perryville Guesthouse, Kinsale, County Cork.

'Dear Mr Nutini,' read Dale. 'Please find attached confirmation of your booking of the nineteenth May through to twenty fifth of May 2011. Number of rooms: three, non smoking, occupants names Ernesto Borza, Guido Nutini and Antonio Pizoni. All additional requests acknowledged and actioned as requested. We look forward to welcoming you to Perryville Guesthouse and we hope you enjoy your stay.'

'I don't know about you, gentlemen,' I said, 'but maybe it's time we took a little bit of a road trip.'

#

Back at the apartment, we mobilised for the journey. We looked at the coffee table with a holdall full of guns and a black dustbin bag stuffed with a few clothes and toiletries.

'Jesus, it's like a scene from reservoir dogs,' I said.

'What should I do about James?' asked Roussel. 'He is my liaison, and given he is a member of the drug squad, he could be useful.'

I nodded thoughtfully.

'Give him a ring and tell him you're off to do a bit of sight-seeing.'

Roussel's eyebrows crawled up his face.

'Jesus man,' I said. 'Do I have to do all the thinking around here? Use your imagination. You're American; Americans like sightseeing, he'll buy it.'

Roussel pulled out the card and rang James. The conversation was short.

'You're right,' he said. 'It didn't faze him in the slightest.'

'Told you,' I stated emphatically. 'It's a huge thing, especially down here in the south. All Americans do it, even the ones who only come over for business. They always spend a day or so sightseeing. It's just the done-thing.'

'Before we go,' said Dale. 'Seeing as there were no e-mails, I need to check in with my partner; see if there have been any developments.'

Dale sat at the kitchen table and dialled the number. He put it on speaker, but gestured for us to be quiet. There were clicks and pauses as the connection was made and then the unmistakable long ring of an American phone system.

The call was answered on the third ring, one single word.

'Dodds!'

'Hey Dodds, it's me, Dale,' said Dale.

'Dale, Jesus Christ, where have you been?' asked Dodds, his voice changing. 'Hold on a second, I'm just transferring you somewhere more confidential.'

He was almost whispering.

Two or three more clicks and then the hold music.

'Dale?'

The single word echoed into the room.

'Agent Fox,' said Dale, the surprise evident on his face.

He held up a finger to his lips, a signal to us to reinforce his earlier entreaty for quiet.

'Are you alone?' asked Ray.

'Yes Sir,' said Dale.

'Good.'

They heard the sound of a door being forcefully closed.

'Dale, I'm here too,' added Dodds.

'Well, firstly it seems I owe you an apology,' said Ray slowly.

Dale blinked in surprise.

'How so?' he asked, more of a knee-jerk reaction than an actual question.

'We got a call from the director of the CIA.'

Roussel looked at me in surprise; I'm sure I must have looked equally astonished to him.

'Did you just say the director of the CIA?' asked Dale, qualifying.

'The one and only,' said Ray. 'But before we get into any of that, the first thing we need to tell you is that you are in serious danger. According to the director, you need to be *very* careful. You are straying into the middle of some serious shit and your life is potentially in jeopardy.'

'Me specifically?' asked Dale.

'You specifically,' said Ray. 'Now he wouldn't say who the danger would be coming from, but we think it's this guy Thomas, a.k.a. *the Street.*'

I smiled.

'Okay, I'll bear that in mind,' said Dale, looking at my expression and trying not to laugh. 'So, what can you tell me?'

'Well for a start, Storm is a CIA sanctioned project. We weren't told why it was originally developed; we were just told that if you wanted to design the perfect drug, you couldn't get any closer to it than this.'

'So, definitely officially CIA sanctioned?' stated Dale.

'Absolutely,' responded Ray. 'But this is where the complication seems to arise.'

'I love the word complication,' said Dale.

Ray laughed.

'I know exactly what you mean. Apparently Storm, this project, this drug, was extremely confidential. There were only four copies of the protocol folder.'

'The CIA Director himself was the keeper of one of them, I'm guessing,' stated Dale thoughtfully. 'So that leaves three others. Do we know who the custodians are?'

'No we don't. I was told that the knowledge of who held which copy was well beyond my pay scale,' replied Ray. 'From which I can only deduce that the people are extremely well known, or extremely senior, or a little bit of both.'

'Or he just didn't want to tell you,' said Dale.

'That too,' agreed Ray.

'So, what's the significance of this small group of people?' asked Dale.

'Well, apparently, one of the three individuals has gone rogue. Not only that, but two copies of the Storm protocol folders are missing. Now, the director thinks the reason two files were taken was so that they could be compared. Apparently, with a lot of these protocol files, they leave key documents out of each one, so you need the complete set for the information to be one hundred percent accurate. Like a kind of failsafe mechanism, if you will.'

'Makes sense,' said Dale.

'Unfortunately, that wasn't the case here,' said Ray sadly. 'Both folders are complete. Not only that, but the rogue agent knows exactly how much the information is worth on the open market.'

'And that brings us onto the next interesting fact,' said Dodds, taking up the story. 'Apparently the Mancini's are in the frame as the most likely customers for this information.'

Dale smiled again. Three out of three wasn't bad at all.

'So, what now?' asked Dale.

'Keep your head down and try and stay out of trouble,' replied Ray. 'Just remember, Dale. Until we get some more information, there is nothing you can do. You are completely unofficial with absolutely no jurisdiction in that country.'

'Understood, boss,' said Dale.

'Take care of yourself, Dale,' said Ray.

'Yeah and try and stay out of trouble, partner,' said Dodds.

Dale heard the single uninterrupted tone indicating they had hung up. He turned the speaker off and spun around to face his colleagues.

'So, what do we make of that, boys?' asked Dale.

'Looks like we're going to Kinsale,' said Roussel with a grin. 'Maybe I wasn't telling James a lie. Looks like I may be sightseeing after all.'

CHAPTER 38 – RETRIBUTION

20th May 2011 – Ten days after the Storm.

To be left alone, and face to face with my own crime, had been just retribution. – Henry Wadsworth Longfellow.

He sat alone in the dark. He did all his best thinking when the inky blackness overwhelmed him. You could think whatever you wanted to, especially if you were in the places where the light could not penetrate.

For instance, you could think happy thoughts; self delusional imaginings of the utopian ideal of a family, where everyone smiled and laughed and loved each other. You could block out the reality; the painted on smiles, the lies and half truths. You could drown out the screams, the rants, and the thuds of inanimate objects hitting walls.

He sat at his desk in his study, and drank in the dark.

All the rooms in the house had blackout curtains. It had been one of the stipulations he had placed on the builders during the refurbishment.

He held a pen in the air in front of his face and twirled it between his fingers. He could see it turning, and yet he knew he couldn't. One of the many wonders of the brain; some would call it visualisation, whereas some would call it self-delusion. Even though he knew he couldn't see the pen, his brain was telling him that he could. No, it was cleverer than that; it was showing him that he could, if he really believed it was there.

So where did dreams end and reality begin? Eoin had always had a problem differentiating the two.

Eoin had never visited his parent's grave. He'd paid for the bare minimum; he didn't even go along to any of the services in person. He knew how it looked to friends and family, but he didn't care. His parents had betrayed him. There was no going back for him, even in death. He had crossed the Rubicon, gone over that invisible line in the sand. How he wished to God he'd never got up that night.

He'd grown up knowing he was special. He didn't see his parents a lot, but when he did see them, they always told him what a clever, handsome and superior boy he was. There were never any harsh words; they didn't spend enough time with him for that, but they bought him everything he wanted. They bought him toys, they bought him games, they sent him to the best private schools; they even bought him friends. But as an only child, with no frame of reference, he mistook their financial generosity for love, and the vicious circle became ever more vicious.

The more he asked for, the more he got, and consequently, the more he believed he was loved. He was their best boy, their good boy, their only boy. It was that part he loved the most. He was the only one, part of the trinity; mother, father, son, a symbiotic unit.

He twirled the pen in his hand, and saw it move in his mind's eye, as clearly as he remembered the words that had been exchanged that night, like barbed weapons.

Back in those days, he would sneak out of his room at night and lie face down on the landing. If he was quiet and he strained his eyes, he could see the television.

That particular night, he hadn't heard the light girlish laughter of his mother, or the heavy, almost false laugh of his father. Instead, he'd felt something else, a dense cloud of tension, hanging in the air like fog. He should have gone back to bed at that moment; he should have turned and slipped noiselessly back up the stairs. His life would not have been so drastically and dramatically changed, if he had just turned and clicked the door closed on his bedroom.

'Where the fuck have you been?'

It was his mother's voice, but it sounded different, slurred. He hadn't known why then, but he knew now; she'd been drinking heavily. She did a lot of that, especially in later years.

'Can we do this some other time, I'm tired.'

This time, it was his father's deep and gruff voice.

'No, we fucking cannot.'

His mother's reply; there was a crash and a tinkling sound.

'That was clever.'

His father speaking again.

'And you'd know all about clever, wouldn't you? Mr fucking big shot. Well just tell me one thing. Just tell me why her?'

His mother's voice had cracked at the end.

'Because I love her,' his father had said simply.

Eoin had heard a scoffing sound.

'Love! Don't give me that crap. You don't know the meaning of the word. The only person you love is that twisted image you have of yourself; the big important man about town.'

Eoin had crawled on his belly as far forward as he could go. If he hadn't seen the shrug, he would have assumed his father had shrugged anyway. It was what he did when he had nothing to say.

'You sicken me,' she'd said. 'What about me? What about our son?'

Eoin had seen her hand come into view, as she'd flung it in the direction of the stairs.

'That loveless fruit of a loveless marriage is not my son. He's your son.'

Eoin had swallowed the cry that he'd wanted to scream. He'd wanted to fly down the stairs to confront the stranger who'd kidnapped his father. He'd wanted to beg, to entreat, to plead. Why was he talking that way?

Even though he could not see her face, Eoin could visualise his mother's eyebrows narrowing, as they always did when she was annoyed.

'You cannot deny him,' she'd said, dangerously softly.

'No, I can't deny him and I never would,' his father had acknowledged. 'But I don't love him, and that's because of you. I don't love you and it's poisoned my feelings toward our son. So I'm leaving both of you; more for your sakes than mine. We'll all be better off out of this prison we call a family.'

'You can't leave me. Without me you're nothing,' his mother had shouted. 'My parent's money made you, and with their power and influence, they can break you too.'

She'd snarled the last bit like a tiger.

'Maybe so,' his father had said resignedly, 'but I'll take my chances. You can keep the house. I have no need of it. I can't live like this anymore. I'm going to live with people I truly love.'

Eoin hadn't picked up on the subtle nuance, but even as sozzled as she was, his mother had leapt on it like that self same tiger.

'What do you mean by people?' she'd asked, dangerously quietly.

He'd seen his father sit down heavily. Eoin could see his face muscles working overtime, as he'd tried to think of an excuse, a diversion. It was then that he'd looked up; he'd seen Eoin lying on the landing and their eyes had locked. Eoin had seen the pain and suffering and regret in almost equal measure.

'You have a half brother,' his father had said.

The fracture of the cosy image that Eoin had built of his world had started from that second, and it was still getting larger.

A discreet knock on the door brought him forward thirty years. Had it been that long? Three quarters of his life looking for vengeance. He'd forgotten how to love and now rage was driving him on. No, that was wrong; it was the revenge itself that drove him now. He needed closure, and in his mind, it was the only way he would get it.

He clicked the switch on the bankers' lamp that was situated on the desk in front of him, and blinked as the room was instantly enveloped in a soft golden glow.

'Come,' he said softly.

The door opened and Dave Keegan walked in. As he sat at the desk and settled into the chair, Black Swan could see that he was twitchy. That was never a good sign with Dave. Black Swan rolled the biro between his fingers from the index to the pinkie and back again. Dave watched, mesmerised, as the pen traversed backwards and forwards like a metronome.

'So?' asked Black Swan.

Dave kept silent; he knew what was coming. It was always best to let Black Swan get it off his chest.

'I'm presuming it isn't good,' said Black Swan. 'I can read you like a book, Dave. You're transparent.'

Dave looked up and then wished he hadn't. There was an unmistakable and unspoken question on Black Swan's face.

'We were unable to neutralise the target,' Dave mumbled.

Black Swan nodded, almost to himself.

'I saw the papers; we made quite a mess of the house at least. How many did we send? Two?'

Dave swallowed hard.

'Nine,' he said.

'Nine,' said Black Swan softly.

The pen he'd been twirling between his fingers suddenly snapped.

'Nine!' he screamed.

He got up from behind his desk and walked around. He bent down until his mouth was just inches from Dave's ear. Dave closed his eyes and braced himself for the hairdryer.

'Nine!' screamed Black Swan again. 'You're telling me we sent nine heavily armed men to kill one person and they failed.'

'He had help,' said Dave quietly.

'What do you mean, he had help?' asked Black Swan. 'Unless it was a team of navy seals, of course,' he added sarcastically.

He paused, as another idea formed.

'Anyway, how could he have a team, he doesn't know anybody here; he's been gone too long,' he finished.

'Well he's certainly found some allies now,' said Dave. 'At least according to our eyewitness he has. And they were not afraid to defend themselves.'

'So just how many of this goon squad survived?' asked Black Swan.

'Just one,' said Dave.

'Just one, Christ almighty, how did they kill eight people. How many *friends* are we talking about here?' asked Black Swan thickly.

He returned to his place, and sat down heavily.

'The eyewitness reckons three, maybe four in the house.'

'All armed?' asked Black Swan.

'Seems like it,' said Dave.

'Where did he get the guns?' asked Black Swan, almost to himself.

Dave knew he was out of the woods, blame wise.

'He must have some contacts here,' replied Dave. 'Either that, or he made some contacts after he landed.'

'We need some more intelligence and we need it yesterday,' said Black Swan. 'We knew he was a mob enforcer, but he must be more connected than we first thought.'

'Well, he did work for the Mancini's,' said Dave.

Black Swan's face hardened.

'So the mistake appears to be mine,' he stated remorselessly. 'I underestimated him; I assumed he was just some low life bar room thug.'

He stopped to compose himself for a few moments.

'Dave, I want to know everything there is to know about this ghost. I want to know where he lived over there. I want to know how far up in their organisation he was. But most of all, I want to know who his new friends are, and where he's getting his weapons.'

'That could be a fairly tall order, boss,' said Dave. 'Look how tough it's been to get any information on him over the past twenty years.'

'We found him though, didn't we?' said Black Swan. 'I'm just sorry our original plan didn't work. But time is on my side. I found him once, I'll find him again.'

He paused to consider his next sentence.

'So, does this eyewitness have anything more to add do you think?' asked Black Swan, changing tack.

'Nothing that he hasn't already told me,' said Dave.

'I want to talk to him,' said Black Swan. 'Where is he?'

'Safe,' replied Dave.

'Let's go,' said Black Swan.

#

They drove in silence, the only sound the thrum of the tyres on the newly resurfaced road. Dave also fancied he could hear the intensity of Black Swan's thoughts. His employer could be a focused and scary guy.

'Can I ask you a question, boss?' Dave ventured into the silence.

Black Swan looked up.

'Sure.'

'Who is this guy?' asked Dave. 'What is this guy?'

Black Swan said nothing.

Dave carried on blithely, the words tripping over each other as he hurried to get them out.

'One of the things I like about you, boss, is that you are so rational,' said Dave. 'You consider problems and think things through. When you act, you generally act decisively, after weighing up the pros and the cons. But this....'

Dave searched for the word.

'....quest. This revenge mission just does not make any sense to me. There's no rhyme or reason to it. It's just so out of character for you.'

Black Swan smiled.

'I don't know how many times I've asked myself that very same question, and told myself those self same facts,' he said.

He sat back and pondered the question for a while.

'Do you know what, Dave,' he said, 'and this is no idle boast, I can guarantee it. If I'd put half the amount of energy into my business as I've channelled into this *revenge mission* as you call it, then *the Bullock* would be history, and I would already be controlling large parts of the Dublin trade.'

'So why?' asked Dave.

'I suppose it's a bit like the white powder we peddle,' answered Black Swan. 'A junkie doesn't question why he's addicted; he just chases the object of his addiction. Since I was ten, there has been this huge unanswered question in my life. It's got to the stage now where it doesn't matter what the answer is, as long as there is an answer.'

Dave could almost see the hurt in Black Swan's eyes, as he remembered.

'This unanswered question; it basically destroyed my childish vision of the perfect family. And to cap it all, it turned out I was the only one who believed it anyway, which makes it worse; living someone else's pretence.'

'So, why does it matter so much?' asked Dave.

Black Swan shot him a sharp look. Dave knew he was on dangerous ground, but he just wanted to know at this stage.

'Your parents are dead, right?' he asked.

Black Swan nodded.

'So, this is revenge for them then?'

'It's more complicated than that,' said Black Swan. 'Some of this is retribution for what I could have been and should have had. To be brutally honest with you Dave, I have no feelings at all. You know that; you've seen it. People talk about love and hate, I see none of that; it's invisible to me. If someone owes me money, I'll have them roughed up; if they persist, I'll have them killed. Sometimes, I'll slip on my leather gloves and hurt people myself. Not because I like doing it or love doing it, but because it is expedient. It is an expected response to certain stimuli that will get me results in business. It's exactly the same as this revenge or whatever you want to call it now. I just need closure. That's all it is at this stage. I know practically nothing about this guy; I just hate what he stands for. It's a promise I made to my ten year old self, and I'm going to keep it.'

Dave glanced at his boss in the rear view mirror.

'We'll find him, don't worry,' he said softly.

'I know you will,' said Black Swan.

Five minutes later, they pulled up outside a rundown Georgian terraced house. At first glance, it looked like any normal crumbling collection of student bedsits. In fact, everything had been engineered to give that impression.

The two men ignored the steps up to the faded, but still impressive eighteenth century facade. Instead, they opened the gate in the front railings, and trotted down the modern fire escape into the tiny basement level courtyard.

The door was set into a wall, the same one that supported the main staircase up to the ground floor. A battered old post box was hung at eye level next to it.

Dave took out a key and opened the post box. Inside was a gleaming metal keypad. He entered a pin number and the door opened inwards with a click. They stepped across the threshold into a dimly lit corridor, and walked to the first door on the left. Dave opened it and went straight in. The glare of the overhead lights was blinding, especially after the relative murk of the passageway.

The room was equipped in a way that would put most private clinics to shame. There were two large hospital beds against one wall, one of which was very much occupied.

The large austere male nurse turned around as the two men entered.

'Leave us,' said Dave brusquely.

The field hospital, as he called it, had been his idea. Black Swan had been hugely supportive. It kept any of their men who were injured out of custody, and they could be convalesced and put back onto the street as soon as was reasonably possible.

The occupant was hooked up to various machines. They could see a self administering morphine dispenser, but the man's forehead was still creased in pain. He stiffened when he saw Black Swan and Dave. They heard his breathing quicken, and the gasps were loudly amplified by the full face oxygen mask he was currently wearing.

Dave removed the mask, prompting a flash of fear in the man's eyes, as his airway became restricted; his chest rising and falling in a shallow and laboured fashion. Dave quickly slipped the nose tube over the man's head, and then waited until his breathing had returned to a semblance of normality.

Black Swan pulled up a chair and sat beside the bed, like a concerned relative.

'So, what's your name?' he asked softly.

'Adrian,' the man gasped.

'So Adrian,' said Black Swan. 'I hear you guys got yourselves into a spot of bother.'

Adrian coughed; one of those full bodied coughs that may have been agony or laughter, it was hard to tell.

'You can say that again,' he whispered, his eyes pain filled and bloodshot.

'Tell me everything you remember,' said Black Swan soothingly, sitting back.

'Well, Decco collected us all from the pub car park in the van like he always does. He said it was going to be easy. He said it was going to be like a turkey shoot.'

Adrian coughed again; tiny blood drops could be seen forming on the crisp white sheets. Black Swan waited patiently for him to continue.

'When we got to the house, Decco sent four guys round the back. I was one of them. As we got into position behind the house, I heard Decco shouting a name, Thomas I think it was. There were several volleys of gunfire. We waited and got ready to hit them from behind, but as we were approaching the back door, it literally disintegrated in front of us.'

He coughed again.

'It was like that scene from the start of *Saving Private Ryan*. I'd never really heard a bullet in flight before. I was always the one launching them. It was chaos; screams, shouts, bullets flying everywhere. And then I was hit; two in the leg and one in the chest.'

He coughed for a third time, as if trying to emphasise the injury.

'At that stage, we had three down. They looked pretty dead and I wasn't sticking around to check. I managed to scramble out of the yard. Next thing I hear a scream and then boom; knocked me clean off my feet. I didn't even look back. I rang Dave and here I am.'

'Anything else you can remember?' asked Black Swan.

Adrian shook his head. He looked drained and tired.

Black Swan got up. He gently removed the oxygen tube from Adrian's nose. Adrian smiled at him gratefully, and this time, when the laboured breathing returned, he wasn't scared. Adrian noticed distractedly that Black Swan was wearing a black leather glove. He didn't see the small, hospital issue pillow until it was too late; until Black Swan caught it from Dave, and jammed it down over Adrian's face. He scrabbled weakly, his hands plucking ineffectually at Black Swan's arms, his legs kicking feebly under the tightly tucked hospital sheets. His movements became progressively less frantic, until finally they ceased altogether.

Black Swan looked at Dave impassively.

'He's in a better place now. I hear hell is pleasant at this time of year.'

The nurse returned and regarded the stiffening corpse impassively. He pulled the sheet over Adrian's head, and then busied himself disconnecting the tubes and wires.

As Black Swan and Dave watched, the man seemed to pause and then it was like one of those comedies where the light bulb comes on over the main characters head. He walked, or more accurately, jogged out of the room and returned a minute later. He whispered to Dave as he handed over the plain white envelope.

Dave dismissed him with a wave of his hand. He extracted the contents and quickly shuffled through the documents contained within. He briefly paused and Eoin could see his lips moving. He was shaking; Eoin hoped it was with excitement.

Dave wordlessly handed over the contents of the envelope.

Black Swan browsed through the photographs, as the hate rose from them and took physical form. Thomas Eugene O'Neill. There must have been twenty pictures; shots from long and short range and from all angles. There was also a brief handwritten note.

I managed to place a GPS tracker on subject, as well as an electronic surveillance device for listening. He has already destroyed the listening device and will discover the tracker eventually but it could be useful for the time being; gives me a slight advantage. He is currently on the way to Kinsale. Use this knowledge and act on it wisely.

'This is great news,' said Dave with a smile, punching his boss lightly on the arm.

'Is it?' asked Eoin.

'What do you mean?'

'I know why I want him,' said Eoin. 'But I don't like competition.'

CHAPTER 39 – REMEMBRANCE

21st May 2011 – Eleven days after the Storm.

The remembrance of a beloved mother becomes a shadow to all our actions; it precedes or follows them. – Anon.

'It's funny,' said Dale, as the green fields flashed past the windows, 'but even though I've been trained vigorously in the use of firearms. Even though I practice regularly, and I'm a very good shot. Even though I do all these things, and know that the sole purpose of a gun is to kill.'

He paused and then sighed.

'Even though I am well aware of all those facts and accept them, I still never thought I would ever kill another man with a gun.'

'You may not have,' said Roussel. 'There were a lot of bullets flying and only three targets went down.'

'Yeah, I suppose, but the law of averages would suggest that I killed at least one of them,' said Dale.

He paused again, this time for a little longer.

'Did you ever kill someone?' he asked Roussel eventually.

Roussel looked at him sourly.

'Before yesterday I mean,' Dale clarified hurriedly.

Roussel paused for a few seconds.

'Back on the beat, when I was a new recruit in the Sheriff's Department,' said Roussel. 'I was called to a disturbance outside a nightclub, or rather we were; my partner and me. The bouncers had already ejected the guy; he was drunk and disorderly. He'd been systematically harassing all of the single ladies at the bar; getting real mouthy and suggestive with them. So the owners called us in. When my partner and I got there, he was screaming and shouting and kicking the door, demanding to be let back in. The bouncers were standing off; they'd had enough. We told him to calm down. He shouted *I'll show you fucking calm.* He bent down; the next thing, he'd got a gun in his hand.'

'What did you do?' asked Dale.

'The first shot went between me and my partner; took the window out of the patrol car. The second shot hit my partner in the thigh. Scumbag didn't get time for another one. We'd been taught to aim for the big sections of the body. The bullet mushroomed and blew his heart clean out through the back of his torso. There was a full investigation, as there has to be with every firearms discharge on-the-job. There was never any question it was anything other than a justifiable homicide.'

'Did you ever question yourself though?' asked Dale.

'Brian and me were partners for a long time before I joined CID,' said Roussel. 'We're still good friends; play a lot of racquet ball, when we can find the time. Every time I see that scar on his thigh, where they had to rebuild his shattered femur, I give thanks to the Lord that I had the guts to pull the trigger that night.'

Dale turned to me.

'So, do you ever get used to killing?' he asked.

'Now there's an interesting question,' I replied. 'Do you ever get used to killing? I can only give you my perspective, but I suppose it's like everything. The first one is always the hardest; then it just gets easier. I wouldn't say you ever fully get used to it, I would say you more get desensitised to it; desensitised to death that is.'

'So, could you pull your gun now and shoot both of us dead?' asked Roussel.

'Absolutely not,' I said.

'Why not?' he asked.

I laughed.

'Well for a start, I was hoping you'd noticed that I wasn't just some crazed killer,' I answered, slightly affronted. 'But for me at least, I always needed a justification. Guido and Ernesto knew that, and in some ways I think they were happy with it too.'

'So, are you claiming some morality behind your killings?' asked Dale interestedly.

I thought about it.

'Morality might be the wrong word,' I said. 'Obviously, taking a life is wrong; certainly, if you follow the Ten Commandments, it's a mortal sin. But I would always look deeper that.'

'Give me an example?' asked Roussel.

'If I was asked to retire an individual,' I said, 'I would look at his track record and see what he'd done. With most of the business arrangements I engaged in, the targets were killers, pushers, enforcers. So I would justify to myself that I was saving innocent people from death, by killing.'

'It's a bit of a tenuous link, don't you think?' asked Roussel.

'It's a self-justification that has evolved over time,' I said. 'I can live with it.'

'How did you get into that particular game anyway?' asked Dale. 'Not what you would expect from a lonely Irish Immigrant barely out of his teens.'

'It's surprising what people adapt to when they have to,' I said. 'When I left Ireland, I was a big thick naive Mick. My American streets weren't paved with gold, as I'd been led to believe, they were paved with shit. So there I was, scratching a living working two or three jobs, when this Colombian gang surround me. I was dragged into an alley in Brooklyn on the way home one night. They worked me over nicely; left me for dead, or at least that's what I thought at the time. Two kindly gentlemen happened to find me; father figures and Catholic like myself.'

I laughed.

'They helped me back on my feet, paid my hospital bills and then put a gun in my hand, and told me where the gang normally hung out. I was just going to fire a few shots over their heads; frighten them a little, as I told them who I was, and why I was there, naïvely not realising they'd be packing heat. I had to kill them all. It's a dog eat dog world, and since then I've had a ten course barbecue.'

'The story the CIA man told us,' acknowledged Dale.

I nodded.

'Of course, the Mancini's had me from there. Illegal alien, legal alien; what's the difference, when you are facing time on multiple murder charges? But that day in the pharmacy everything changed. To use that dog analogy again, every dog has its day.'

'So, can you teach an old dog some new tricks?' asked Dale with a smile.

'Let's hope so,' I said.

'How do you feel about the Mancini's now?' asked Roussel.

'Well it's funny. Maybe I've just got too jaded and cynical, but I don't blame them and I don't hate them. Getting rid of me is really just an expedient business proposition for them. They would regard it just the same as if they were changing their accountant. To be honest, yeah, they may be vain narcissistic old men, with huge egos and as mean as stray dogs, but they were like fathers to me when I needed it the most.'

'So, have you given any more thoughts to the other issue we have?' asked Roussel.

I looked at him with a puzzled expression.

'Who do you think this guy Black Swan might be? Why does he have such a hard-on for you?'

'I have given it a lot of thought,' I said, 'but I'd appreciate hearing what you guys think?'

'Well, as you said yourself,' said Roussel. 'For the Mancini's, this is business; maybe a little bit of regret, but mainly business. But for Black Swan this is personal. In some way or other, in some other life, you have seriously pissed him off.'

'Do you know what?' I said. 'I've been looking at it in the same way, and I came to the exact same conclusion. But for the life of me, I cannot think of who he might be, or what it could be that I've supposedly done to him. Our paths can't have crossed for at least twenty to twenty five years. I've had nothing to do with Ireland during that time. I've racked my brains, and I just cannot remember a single possible matching scenario, either person or place.'

'What about historic grudges; against your family maybe?' queried Roussel.

'No, I don't buy that,' I said. 'We had a very simple and happy life.'

'What about your parents?' asked Roussel.

'Mum was universally liked,' I said. 'If she'd had enemies, they would have liked her too.'

'What about your Dad?'

'He died when I was fairly young,' I said. 'I don't remember him around much. He was gone most of the week, and a lot of the weekends too. Even most Christmases, he was only there sporadically.'

'Well, this might be something or it might be nothing,' said Dale suddenly, 'but your dad's name was....'

He consulted his notepad.

'....Richard, right?'

I nodded.

'Well, in the register of marriages, births and deaths, they have no record of him at all.'

I was stunned for a second.

'Isn't there a possibility that they just couldn't find the documents?' I asked.

'It's possible,' said Dale. 'Although I think it's highly unlikely. After all, they went to the trouble of trying to cross reference the records for your mother and your father. If they'd found anything, they would have definitely attached them.'

'They must be somewhere else,' I said flatly.

Dale held up his hand.

'Well, I do have a reason for mentioning it. You know how fond I am of tenuous and circumstantial information. And when you think about it, there is something very odd about Scott Mitchell and his attempt to pass himself off as Alan Murphy, your long lost boy. Whoever is behind this scheme is targeting something very specific here; the relationship between a father and a son. Tie that back in with the lack of information about your father. It's just too much of a coincidence not to warrant a follow-up.'

'Are you saying there's something dodgy about my father,' I said with affront.

'I'm not saying anything of the sort,' said Dale. 'I'm just saying it warrants further investigation.'

'Do you have a family lawyer?' asked Roussel suddenly.

We both looked at him blankly.

'A solicitor, you mean?' I asked. 'Looks after legal affairs?'

He nodded.

'When my parents passed away, they left an awful lot of documentation behind them. I asked the lawyers to hold onto it all for me for a small fee. Couldn't bear to go through it all at the time,' he said, a little sadly.

I snapped my fingers.

'Damn it Roussel, you're right,' I said. 'There was a box of papers that the solicitors wanted to send me at the time my mother died. Like you said, I couldn't face it then, it was just too raw. I have no recollection of what I told them to do with it all.'

'They might still have it?' inquired Roussel softly.

'Carpe Diem,' I said softly.

'What?' they both said together.

'Seize the day,' I added. 'You believe this could shed more light on my father, which incidentally I don't. But you are both experienced investigators, so I can't ignore it. We are only about fifteen minutes away from their offices. What's a little detour, to sort this out once and for all?'

I pulled over to the side of the road, and scrolled through my phone, until I came to the number I wanted. I always kept my phone contacts completely up-to-date. It had saved my life more than once.

Just over ten minutes later, we were heading back into town. I had managed to secure half an hour with one of the managing partners.

'You guys stay here,' I said, as I parked up across the street. 'Don't do anything stupid.'

I walked into reception and gave the receptionist my biggest smile.

'Thomas O'Neill to see John Maguire,' I said brightly.

'Certainly, Mr O'Neill,' she said to me. 'Come this way.'

She led me down the corridor into a large, generously equipped boardroom. A dusty storage box sat on the table with the lid removed, and some of the files had already been spread over the large expanse of mahogany.

'Mr Maguire will be with you shortly,' she stated. 'Would you like a tea or coffee in the meantime?'

'Just some water if that's okay,' I answered. 'Many thanks.'

I started shifting aimlessly through the files.

'It's still the best way to read documents I think,' said a voice behind me. 'Words written down on a sheet of paper, just like God intended.'

I turned around to get a good look at John Maguire. He must have been in his late sixties. He was probably only working now because his name was above the door; Molloy and Maguire solicitors. He had a pleasant roundish face and a beaming smile, but with that unfortunate affliction that some men get as they grow older; the legion of grey hair circling the scalp with nothing on top.

He shook my hand warmly.

'I'm with you,' I said. 'I can't read anything on a computer screen. I have to print it out.'

He nodded with understanding, and then stared at me questioningly.

'I'm looking for some documents pertaining to my father,' I said, rather formally.

'Which documents would those be?' he asked politely.

I thought about it for a minute or so.

'I'll know them when I see them,' I said.

'As you wish,' he said. 'I'll unpack, you can sort.'

First thing out of the pile was my mother's death certificate. I'd seen a lot of death, and it hadn't affected me in the slightest, but this particular document brought a lump to my throat. I knew why of course; still a lot of unfinished business.

There were numerous other documents, relating to the original purchase of my current house, and the sale of the old house on Merchants Quay, but strangely enough, on both documents, my mother was named as the sole owner. I scratched my head.

Then out of the blue, I pulled another document out of the pile; my mother's birth certificate. I gave it a cursory glance over and then put it to one side. I was about to pick up the next document, when something made me go back.

'This is odd,' I said to the aged solicitor. 'Check out my mother's maiden name?'

I pointed to the area on the document.

'Maiden name?' he responded, looking at me with a puzzled expression. 'Your mother was never married.'

If he had shot me, I wouldn't have been more surprised.

'What do you mean, she wasn't married?' I asked, almost in a whisper.

'I'm not sure I can put it any plainer, young man,' he said. 'She wasn't married. There is no marriage certificate, no mention of a husband, no joint accounts, nothing.'

I scrabbled around on the desk. He looked at me in alarm, as documents started to go flying. At last I came up with the document I needed, holding it aloft like a trophy.

'My birth certificate,' I said.

I almost ripped the document, I was so eager to unfold it. I read the single word, beautifully scripted in fountain pen. And then, as the full impact of the word sank in, I flopped down onto one of the chairs. He plucked the document from my nerveless fingers, his lips echoing the word that was repeating over and over in my own head; *unknown*.

'How can that be?' I asked finally, in a choked whisper.

He pulled up a chair and sat down facing me.

'You've got to remember,' he said kindly. 'Ireland was a different place back then. In some ways you're lucky that you and your mum were able to stay together. In most cases, children born out of wedlock were forcibly removed and put into care homes.'

Both he and I instinctively shuddered at the thought.

'But hold on a second,' I said triumphantly. 'I have a copy of my birth certificate which states that my father is Richard O'Neill.'

He shook his head a little sadly.

'Back then, when the mothers were getting copies of the certificate,' he said. 'They would ask for the *father's* name to be filled in.'

I didn't like the way he accentuated the word father.

'Sometimes, all they had to do was ask, other times a small quantity of money would change hands.'

I shook my head in disbelief.

'But I met him, I knew him,' I said.

'Did you really?' he asked. 'In those days it wasn't unheard of for cousins of the mother to play the part, or even brothers.'

'So the man I knew as my father could have been my uncle or my second cousin?' I asked.

'He could,' he answered. 'I'm sorry, young man.'

He patted my shoulder.

'I thought you knew; that you were seeking information on your father to track him down. I didn't see it as unusual. I thought you were on a quest to find him, and were looking for some specific information.'

'Yeah, that's pretty ironic isn't it,' I said, a little sourly. 'I come searching for my father, and find out I really do need to be searching for my father.'

I stood up abruptly.

'Thank you, Mr Maguire, for taking the time to see me at such short notice.'

He shook my hand and looked at me with concern.

'Are you sure you're okay?' he asked.

'I'll be fine,' I said. 'Thanks again.'

'Take care of yourself, Thomas,' he said.

I walked back into reception and asked the receptionist if I could use the restroom. She pointed at a different door on the other side of the corridor and handed me the key.

I sat down in one of the cubicles with my head in my hands and did something I had not done for almost thirty years; I cried.

When I exited the front door of the building some five minutes later, the outpouring of emotions had hardened my resolve like steel in a forge. Someone had made this personal. Now it was personal for me too; bad move on their part.

CHAPTER 40 – IMPERFECT

21st May 2011 – Eleven days after the Storm.

There is always a 'but' in this imperfect world. — Anne Bronte.

The steering wheel danced and twitched in his hands as the large, low-profile tyres continually fed back to him what the car wanted to do.

At this stage of his life, Ben could afford pretty much any car he wanted and he had test-driven most, but the Mazda was still his favourite. Full four seat practicalities, allied to a free revving rotary engine. Couple that with an almost ideal forty nine to fifty one percent weight distribution, rear-wheel drive and perfect temperament. It was the easiest car to push to the limit that he had ever driven, and no matter how much punishment he dished out, it would absolutely never fight him back. It didn't have a lot of torque, but if you kept the revs high, and your foot planted, you could have a serious amount of fun.

Ben always went to work early; partly because he was a hard worker, but mostly because it was the best time for driving fast, especially in the wilds of West Cork. In the light of the early morning dawn, when the conditions were just right, you could see for miles. He could throw the car into the corners, secure in the knowledge that there was nothing coming towards him; nothing to spoil his enjoyment of just pure driving.

He glanced up; the way ahead was clear as far as he could see. As the corner approached, he turned in tight and kept his right foot firmly to the floor. He carried the speed into the apex, and felt the back starting to breakaway as it always did. He fed in just enough opposite lock to power slide through, before straightening up with a double shimmy. In no time at all, the next corner was upon him, and as he slid through corner after corner, the exhaust note growled back at him, echoed and amplified by the close cropped hedgerows.

'It just doesn't get any better than this,' he whispered to himself.

He shot through the entrance to the estate. Hand-braking the Mazda into the car park, he showered the front of the building with gravel and small stones. He put his hand on the bonnet as he got out, and nodded in satisfaction.

It was scorching, red hot, a sure sign that man and machine had been moving and performing in perfect harmony.

'Morning, Mr Collins,' said Bill, as Ben walked through reception.

Bill was one of the team of security guards that they'd employed, as the facility had started to take shape. Unlike most other security firms, this one was a spin off from David's core business, and had a number of unique advantages over other firms. Not only did Bill have access to weapons, but he was well trained in their use, and application, and not afraid to employ them should the need arise. The facility was in very safe hands indeed.

As Ben sat at his desk, the smile slowly faded from his face. He had to now try and find the words to tell David that there was a little bit of a hiccup. It was nothing they couldn't handle; Guido and Ernesto were their business partners after all, but he knew David's initial reaction would not be positive, even though it had been the Mancini's who had informed Ben of the issue.

Ben had been through the calculations in his head the previous night; he believed in having all the ammunition he needed up front, so he worked them through again on the pad in front of him, realising his initial estimations were spot on. There would be no material disadvantage from a monetary point of view, which would be a relief in itself to David. The only problem was time, and this was the commodity that was most precious to his boss.

David was getting increasingly anxious. He had moved his base of operations away from the city and out to the country. Even though David loved his Clonakilty bolt hole, he felt removed from the action in the city and felt more exposed to exploitation and danger. It was taking much longer than they'd originally planned to get the factory up and running and David had pumped a lot of his own money into it as well. Ben knew that David did not get nervous, and he also knew that at the moment David was extremely nervous. He was a hands-on business man. He had to be able to touch his business, so he was finding the distance very stressful.

Ben looked up and caught sight of the framed certificate on the wall opposite; *Harvard school of business*. He was a long way from the Ivy League now.

It was prophetic that his tutor at Harvard had told him once that he would make money at anything he did, regardless of whether it was legal or illegal. Ben had no qualms and no preference either way, it was just he'd found the *illegal* route to be a little bit more profitable and a little bit quicker.

Where his exceptional intelligence came into play, was making sure that his name and his actions could never be linked to any of their illegal activities. He was more than happy for David to take the limelight, but it took a huge amount of energy and concentration to keep his own name purged from the records. He didn't really care about what his boss did, and whether it was against the law. He didn't give a second thought to the consequences of David's decisions or his actions, as long as they could not be linked back to him. In that respect he was no different from most corporate managers; corporate responsibility was not a word in his vocabulary.

Yes, his boss used euphemisms sometimes, and Ben pretended he didn't know what they meant; more for David's sake than his own. He was not stupid; he knew what the company did and how it made its money, but as far as he was concerned, his conscience was clear. If circumstances ever conspired against him, he could use the age-old defence; one that had not been modified or changed in generations. *I was only following orders.*

A shadow darkened his door, and a minute later, a cappuccino was placed on the desk in front of him. He could see the steam rising through the drinking aperture on the safety-lid. For a second, he smiled. David was nothing if not a creature of habit. Ben looked at his watch; always the same drink and always the same time. He wordlessly grabbed his coffee, got out of his chair and the practiced routine began once more. He followed David the twenty yards or so down the corridor to the corner office.

David made himself comfortable as he always did, and leant back in his leather recliner with his hands crossed behind his head.

'Thanks for the new girl by the way,' said David. 'Gave her a test drive last night, if you know what I mean.'

They both laughed in a coarse and earthly fashion for a minute or so.

No, you didn't, Ben thought silently to himself.

Both of them knew that David rarely touched the girls. They gladly agreed to share his bed, because they knew he was not looking for sex, and it was a welcome reprieve from the harshness of the street. Neither David nor Ben would have vocalised the thought, but for vastly differing reasons.

'First off,' said David with a beaming smile. 'What do you know about this?'

He held up a copy of the Cork Examiner; the stark headline shrieked against the backdrop of a full size picture of a half demolished building.

Eight dead as drug war escalates.

'They all belong to Black Swan,' David said with a huge grin, as he passed the paper over.

He watched impassively as Ben read the story, his lips moving silently.

'Sorry to disappoint you, boss, but it wasn't anything to do with us.'

'If not us, then who else?' asked David with a puzzled expression. 'This is bad karma, Ben. Apart from me and Black Swan, there is no one else who has that type of firepower. They took down eight guys, for fucks sake!'

'It definitely wasn't us,' said Ben soberly. 'Unless someone else is trying to muscle in on our territory; one of the Dublin gangs maybe?'

'We would have heard at least a vague murmuring of a rumour, if that was the case,' said David. 'Wouldn't we?'

'An internal feud then? Maybe someone got fed up with their lowly position in the hierarchy.'

David's face cleared.

'Ben, I think you might just have put your finger on it. There's very little loyalty among these guys.'

'You really think so?' asked Ben. 'Something doesn't smell quite right to me.'

'Let's be extra vigilant,' said David. 'I don't mind fighting a war on a single front; I don't want to have to start fighting a war on two fronts, especially when I'm stuck down here and effectively blind.'

'I'll get the word out,' acknowledged Ben.

'Still, it does make me a little nervous,' said David. 'I feel very exposed in this neck of the woods. Anything could be happening in that city. Our guys wouldn't exactly be the most loyal.'

'I think you'd be surprised at our guys,' stated Ben. 'Loyalty has its price, just like everything else and we pay top dollar.'

'Even so,' said David. 'I'm getting a bit jittery. We need to get this plant up and running, and we need to do it real soon.'

Ben hesitated and David saw the hesitation. Ben hadn't expected to have to confront the issue so quickly.

'Spit it out, man,' demanded David. 'I can see you've got something on your mind.'

'The Mancini's rang me last night,' said Ben. 'There's been a slight hitch.'

'What do you mean by a slight hitch?' asked David. 'How slight?'

'Apparently the protocol we are working to is incomplete. We need to stop all construction on the lines until we can verify the revised protocol in full, and ensure that the currently constructed production processes need no further modification.'

'So, more fucking delays,' stated David, holding his head in his hands.

'They've promised to bring the complete extended protocol with them tomorrow, when they finally come to meet us,' said Ben.

'Yeah, was going to ask you about that?' said David, changing tack. 'Is there anything that we need to be aware of prior to the meeting? What do we actually know about the Mancini's? Other than what we can read in the papers, of course,' he added.

'Information on them is quite difficult to come by,' replied Ben.

He looked at David's expression and held up his hands in mock surrender.

'Hey, I'm not giving you an excuse,' said Ben. 'I had to go to hell and back to get this information. And I had to be doubly careful they didn't find out I was prying; apparently they are fiercely protective of any information pertaining to their personal lives and reputations.'

'As are we all,' acknowledged David. 'Sorry, didn't mean to stop you, go on.'

'Ernesto and Guido Mancini,' began Ben. 'They were born in Little Italy to one Francesco Mancini and his wife Maria. Francesco had gone over to America from Napoli in the twenties, with a tiny bit of money, and some very big ideas. He was not a big physical man by all accounts, but he had an aura about him, a presence. He was able to rally people around him and create strength in numbers.'

'So, the father was the driving force,' said David.

Ben could see where his thoughts were going.

'Yes and no,' said Ben. 'Francesco worked hard, very hard, and galvanised the Italian immigrant population around him. He brought a work ethic and a sense of worth to the community. But this is where he was different from his sons. He was ruthless, yes, he bent the law, yes, but Guido and Ernesto took it to a whole different level. It was a large semi-illegal empire when they inherited it, but they built it into a criminal corporation.'

'Don't get me wrong,' continued Ben. 'Francesco was no angel. By the time he died in 1968, he had amassed a nice modest fortune and a substantial business empire; mostly property and small businesses, a mixture of legal and slightly shady activity. Guido and Ernesto took over when they were young; very young.'

'What age were they?' asked David.

Ben thought about it for a second.

'About the same age as you and John were,' he said quietly.

'So, they took over in 68,' prompted David.

'Yep, and they didn't have it easy,' said Ben. 'Just prior to Francesco's death, there was already a simmering feud; one which he had managed to quell by sheer force of personality, but the alliance was uneasy to say the least. When he died, there were initial rumblings that the Mancini brothers would not be recognised as his true successors. There were two particular men in the area who were extremely vocal. Their names were Giuseppe Mizzoni and Gianfranco Forlani. Within a week of Francesco's funeral, both men had disappeared and there was no more talk of the brothers not being the rightful airs to the empire.'

'So, they showed their ruthless streak early on?' asked David.

'They had to,' said Ben. 'Little Italy in the seventies was not for the faint hearted.'

'So, it was the two brothers who built up the business,' stated David.

'I think they were a product of their time, much as Francesco was a product of his,' said Ben. 'Francesco was extremely wealthy by the standards applied to people of the day, but he hadn't the same opportunities that Guido and Ernesto were presented with. The late sixties/early seventies, especially in America, and especially along the East Coast, was a real purple period when it came to the drugs trade. It gave Guido and Ernesto the opportunity to get in at the ground floor. It was an opportunity they grasped with both hands. Before long, they'd expanded their reach across the whole of the eastern United States.

The West Coast was a much harder nut to crack, and to this day, they wouldn't have as much penetration there as they would like. But they were one of the first to apply true supply-chain logic to the drugs trade, and hence they are now worth conservatively multiple billions of dollars.'

'As you were reading that; as you were telling me that, I was getting goose bumps. The hairs on the back of my neck were standing up,' said David.

'Yeah, some pretty scary parallels,' said Ben.

'Not only that,' said David. 'But you said it yourself. They were there at the start in the sixties and early seventies. They were able to translate that head start into a huge business success. I would see the current opportunity that we have in the same light. We are on the cusp of a new era, and I am in at the ground floor. I would even go so far as to say that we are in the driving seat.'

'So you think the market is big enough for a new drug?' asked Ben.

'Just look what happened with ecstasy in the nineties,' said David. 'The key to this is going to be the marketing; to take a leaf out of Apples book.'

'I don't follow,' said Ben.

'Tell people what they want, before they actually want it. Who ever heard of an iPod in the sixties?'

Good point,' responded Ben.

'If this drug is as good as they say, then demand is going to be astronomical. If you control the supply....'

Ben looked at David levelly.

'You've invested a lot of money in this. Pulled a lot of strings and called in a lot of favours. If this doesn't work....'

He left the rest of the sentence unsaid.

'You have to speculate to accumulate,' replied David, 'and I have a good feeling about this as an investment.'

'We'll see,' said Ben.

'Don't be so pessimistic,' said David, clapping him on the back. 'You money men are all the same. The glass is always half empty with you. Now fuck off out of my office, I've got a few calls to make.'

Ben was deep in thought as he strolled back to his own office. He'd been struck by the similarities between the two sets of brothers, as he was relating the history to David.

He had an uneasy feeling that David had known much of the information before. It wasn't like him to risk so much on an uncertainty. Maybe he'd got caught up in the romance of the story. Maybe the parallels with his own background were too stark for him to see the wood for the trees. He felt David was adding two and two and making seventeen.

Only time would tell.

CHAPTER 41 – AGGRESSION

21st May 2011 – Eleven days after the Storm.

War consisteth not in battle only, or the act of fighting; but in a tract of time, wherein the will to contend by battle is sufficiently known. – Thomas Hobbes.

Street climbed wordlessly back into the car. He started it up, and screeched out of the parking space with barely a backward glance. Neither Roussel nor Foster was stupid enough to ask him how it had gone. They both recognised a situation when somebody just didn't want to talk; they were both investigators after all.

As the car travelled on towards their destination, the atmosphere within the car was tense and strained. It was unusual and a little bit unsettling for Roussel and Foster to see their newfound colleague so upset. In a short period of time, he had become more than a colleague and it was difficult for them to see him in such obvious and emotional distress. They also knew how pragmatic he was; it was only a matter of time before that emotion was channelled into action.

#

I was trying to seize on something, anything really. There had to be some definable characteristic, an identifiable personal trait. I didn't start off without a dad. Early on, there was definitely a man physically in the house, at least some of the time, calling himself my father.

I didn't know if it was worse to have never experienced it, but to be told in your mid forties that the man you'd worshipped, the stylised ideal you'd held aloft for so long, was possibly an imposter, a pretender to the crown; that was hard. That was tough to take.

The words of the solicitor, John Maguire, had cut deep.

'But your mother was never married.'

Like all words of truth, the minute I'd heard them, I'd felt released. I was now free from all doubt; the half remembered rows and the childhood insecurities.

As the tyres ate up the miles, and my two new companions sat silently and respectfully in the back, I tried to conjure him up from the depths of my memory; the mystery man, my father.

Everywhere were snippets; brief memories here, shallow memories there. And then, as I remembered the key points in my early life; birthdays, Christmas, first time to ride a bike, I could see my mother in perfect clarity, smiling, clapping, laughing, but with a shadow behind her eyes. I could also see an occasional ghost standing beside her, blurry and indistinct.

'I don't remember much about my dad,' I said at last, out loud. 'And it looks like there was a good reason for that.'

I glanced in the rear view mirror. They were listening intently.

'The thing that upset me the most when I heard it first,' I said. 'Not the fact that he wasn't married to my mother. I could have easily dealt with that. Living out of wedlock, so what? It was the fact that it might have been a relative playing a role. And the thing that hurts the most?'

I could feel my voice choking.

'My mother was probably complicit in the whole thing.'

'Don't judge her too harshly,' replied Foster.

'And what exactly would you know about it?' I spat disdainfully.

'More than you know,' said Foster, a little sadly.

'Try me,' I said.

'I was born at the height of the Disco boom,' he replied.

Roussel and I smiled, despite ourselves.

'I was the product of a liaison between two lawyers; I think a small quantity of cocaine may have been involved too. I was lucky; she carried me to full-term, others of my generation were not so lucky. By all accounts, it was something to do with a devout Catholic mother and an inheritance in jeopardy. Whatever the reason, the ending was never in doubt. I was left in a small Catholic orphanage in Queens.'

'So, what about your parents?' asked Roussel. 'Where do they come in?'

'My parents....'

Dale accentuated the word *parents*.

'....were from the Mid West. They married young and went to New York to make their fortune. Initially, they were all about the work. They couldn't have kids; my mother was born with key parts of her plumbing missing. Neither of them thought it would be a problem in their youth. When they got to thirty, they realised how wrong they were. They moved back to the family farmstead near Dayton, Ohio. When they left New York, they didn't leave empty handed. They had managed to acquire a piece of it; me.'

'When did you find out?' asked Roussel interestedly.

Dale turned to him.

'I've always known,' he said. 'My parents never kept anything from me, and it's funny; maybe it's the way I'm made. Maybe I see things differently from other people, maybe it's purely because I am adopted, but I never once thought about tracing my birth parents.'

He said the word *parents* disdainfully this time.

'As far as I am concerned, my real parents live on a small farm in rural Ohio. They are the ones who comforted me when I fell down or failed. They are the ones who taught me right from wrong. They are the people who gave me the strength of character to be who I am. And it was them who raised me right, and released me into the world, which in turn gave me the inner strength to make my own mistakes.'

He glanced up at the mirror, so that he could catch my gaze, and when he caught it, he held it.

'So, actually, I do know a lot about it,' he said. 'And the one thing I'll share with you is this. For every selfish career woman; for every couple not ready for that kind of commitment or responsibility, there is a corresponding young woman or couple, desperate to have a child at any price. So don't judge your mother too harshly. Who knows the pressure she was under?'

I finally broke his gaze and looked away, slightly ashamed of my outburst. I hadn't had a bad life, certainly not a bad childhood. Maybe what Dale said was true; maybe I had finally laid that first ghost to rest.

'Sorry about that,' I mumbled.

Dale shook his head.

'Don't worry about it,' he said. 'You weren't to know. But don't be so quick to judge in future.'

I nodded to acknowledge what he'd said.

'So, does this tell us anything new about the situation with Black Swan?' asked Roussel.

I was about to answer when Dale piped up.

'I think it's even more likely now,' he said. 'It definitely has something to do with you and your father. One or the other, or both of you, but like I said before, this is personal. You are personal to him, and if you can't think of a reason why, then it has to be down to your father. Maybe it's as simple as that old saying *the sins of the father.*'

We chewed on that for the rest of the journey, in a slightly stilted, but still companionable silence.

As we got nearer to the coast, the scenery started changing, and I could feel our collective spirits lifting.

The sea in Ireland was not the glorious azure blue of the Pacific Islands, or the deep emerald green of the Adriatic or Mediterranean. It was a typical dull and soft Irish day; a fine, almost invisible spray that doesn't seem to be wet.

As we descended the hill into Kinsale, the grey clouds seemed to swoop down to meet the grey sea on the far horizon, and it was difficult to decide where one finished and the other began.

I had been to Kinsale once as a boy. I hadn't remembered it being so picturesque. Things like the view don't affect you when you are that young. Looking at the picture postcard houses and beautifully manicured streets and shop fronts, it seemed an unlikely birthplace for a new illegal addiction.

'Strangely enough, this feels a bit like the East Coast of the US,' said Dale. 'There's a real Boston feel about it, especially around the harbour.'

'Yeah it was originally a fishing port,' I said. 'But certainly, in the last thirty to forty years, it's become much more synonymous with food and sailing and expensive holiday homes; very much the lifestyles of the rich and famous.'

We circled the harbour slowly, until I found what I was looking for; a basic pay-and-display car park. I manoeuvred into a space, careful to centre it between the white lines; something my mother had drilled into me when she'd taught me how to drive. I ignored the looks from the other two, as I continued to move in and out, straightening the car until I was happy.

'Don't say a word,' I said, prompting them to smile with amusement and raise their hands in a gesture of supplication.

'Stay here,' I continued, as I hopped out. 'Don't touch anything. I'll be back in a minute.'

The last thing I needed was to get clamped, and in these little picturesque villages, they took their car parking very seriously. It was a huge revenue stream for them.

As I pumped my small change into the ticket machine, I failed to register the two cars; large black saloons, each one containing four large and forbidding looking gentlemen, dressed mainly in black.

I hit the green button to print my ticket. The sun was starting to break through the clouds, penetrating the gloom like golden rods of light. As I passed slowly back behind the two parallel parked BMW's, all eight doors opened simultaneously. There was something about the symmetry of the action. The choreography of the movement rang faint alarm bells at the back of my head.

I was almost level with my own car, when I saw Roussel turn around in the back and his eyes widened in horror. The unease I'd felt seconds earlier hardened into grim resolve. At last I had something to channel my anger and frustration into. I took a deep breath, in through the nose and out through the mouth. I felt my muscles bunch and harden.

I whirled just in time; as the baseball bat was at the top of its down stroke. I caught it just before it started on its return trajectory, and viciously twisted it out of my attackers grasp. I reversed my grip and then jammed the metal end of it straight back into my assailants face as hard as I could. I felt bones crack and he went down with a scream of agony. I reversed the bat again, using it as a staff this time to deflect an attack from the right. The iron bar splintered the bat in two under the force of the impact, but before he could react, I grabbed his wrist, spun inside and threw him straight over my shoulder. He landed with an almighty crack on his back and I followed up, dropping a knee straight into his exposed groin. He curled into an agonised ball, like a spider does when you touch it. He wasn't getting up again anytime soon.

I relieved him of the bar, using it to quickly parry another blow from a bat. Grabbing the arm holding the weapon, I jabbed the bar into my assailant's stomach, causing him to double up. As he bent over involuntarily, I caught him on the way down, my knee rising savagely into the middle of his face. He was out cold before he hit the deck.

At this stage Roussel and Dale were out of the car, standing slightly back from the action, but watchful and ready. I grabbed the weapon from the attacker's nerveless fingers and threw it across to Roussel. That was more like it; we were beginning to even up the odds.

The five remaining assailants stood back. I could sense a pervading air of uncertainty begin to infiltrate their ranks, until one of their number stepped forward. He held a pickaxe handle, and as I watched, he theatrically twirled it around his head and from side to side. His action seemed to rejuvenate his gang, who closed in menacingly.

My eyes never left his. I clung grimly to the small iron bar; I was beginning to really like it as a weapon.

When he attacked, I had thought I was ready for it. Every nerve and sinew was tensed for the thrust, certain that I could read his intentions. However, my reflexes fired just a fraction too slow; he was a much younger man and had trained himself well.

The handle came down in a blur of speed. If it had connected, it would have caved my head like a melon. As it was, I felt the sting on my upper arm, as it glanced off. Roussel had been watching proceedings warily, holding the bat like a baseball player. He was a younger man than I, and had reacted instinctively to the down thrust from my opponent. The attacker wasn't expecting a counter attack, and had left himself wide open. The Bat whirled savagely in a wicked arc, to catch him cleanly on the side of the temple. The force of the blow literally lifted him off his feet. He clattered unconscious to the floor in front of Foster, who relieved him of the stout pickaxe handle. The odds were seriously beginning to even up now.

I guessed that the remainder of the group were now leaderless and rudderless. They were exchanging uncertain glances between them; a sort of collective paralysis. I knew one of them would make a move, but I had a feeling that it wouldn't be coordinated. I was wrong.

The attack, when it came, was simple and direct. Two of them came straight for me. They were holding short clubs or coshes. I managed to parry one, but the other blow glanced off the side of my head. It still connected fairly heftily, and my vision blurred for a second. I felt myself going down and they followed up their advantage; I felt the boots thudding viciously into my side. I blinked the tears out of my eyes, and curled into a foetal position to try and protect myself as best I could.

As my vision cleared, I saw Dale divert an attack and then follow up with a swinging kick to the groin. It was simple, but effective. The next thing I heard a crack, and one of my assailants fell over me. He was out cold.

'Street, watch out!' yelled Dale.

I jerked my head backwards to evade the steel toed construction boot. As it whistled past in midair, I caught it and even though I was still prone on the ground, I swung my right leg around through the back of his calf; the one he was still standing on. He hit the deck with a crash and I heard the whoosh as the air was compressed out of his body. Dale followed up with the pick axe handle, as though he was swinging a golf club, catching him squarely in the groin; seemed it was his speciality. Either way, the attacker wouldn't be getting up for a while. I sprang to my feet with Dale beside me and we turned to Roussel.

His attacker had dropped his weapon; both men were of a size, and seemed to be fairly well matched. They were grappling for grip, but as we watched, Roussel managed to get a chokehold; probably a legacy of his uniform days. He tightened his arm around his assailants airway until the scrabbles got weaker and the kicks got lighter, and he eventually slumped in Roussel's arms.

I could feel the bruises beginning to form; my body was already stiffening as Roussel opened his arms and let his opponent drop to the floor.

I grabbed the guy Roussel had taken out earlier; the one I believed was the leader. I popped the boot on the rental car. Roussel guessed my intention and the two of us transpired to stuff the unwieldy and awkward body into the back, cramming the uncooperative limbs in any old way.

Once he was in, I did a cursory sweep of the boot around him. The holdall and its precious contents were under the front seat, so I didn't have to worry about that, but I threw out the Jack and the tire iron. I didn't want him getting access to any potential weapons.

I slid into the driver's seat, feeling stiffer with every stride. The rear doors closed together as my two colleagues got back in again.

'Everyone okay?' I asked.

Like me, they were grinning like idiots. There was nothing like a bit of combat to get the blood circulating.

'Couple of cuts, couple of bruises, nothing that won't heal,' said Roussel.

'Same here,' said Dale.

'There's been a change of plan,' I said, slipping the car into reverse, and burying the throttle.

As we shot backwards out of the space, I braked, engaged drive, hauled on the steering and gave it everything she had. I turned to the others.

'I think it's time we got some answers.'

CHAPTER 42 – AVARICE

21st May 2011 – Eleven days after the Storm.

The avarice of mankind is insatiable. – Aristotle.

Black Swan sat at his desk. It was probably the location where he spent most of his time when he was in the house. The study was his favourite room. He had never been afraid of hard work; in fact, the engagement of his brain had always been his antidote to the problems in his personal life. Sometimes, he would raise his head from his books, only to realise it was three o'clock in the morning. He got lost in facts and figures; they were his friends.

All you could hear at that particular moment was the feverish scratching of pencil on paper. Black Swan hated pens. They were permanent. If you made a mistake with a pen, it was glaringly obvious for all to see. A mistake with a pencil was different. It could be discreetly and easily eliminated; like a lot of his competition.

As usual, the blackout curtains were down, but the warm glow from the green banker's lamp illuminated the pad full of figures that he was working on. Eoin always did his maths by hand. He didn't even own a calculator. Yes, he would verify the figures in his spreadsheets later on, but the majority of the calculation was done by him. He was the solitary architect of his business success. He didn't rely on machines to do it for him.

The young Eoin had always loved maths. It was governed by absolute rules; there was no ambiguity. It was not open to interpretation, it was either right or it was wrong. It really was that simple. If only life mirrored it.

His cell phone rang, which was unusual in itself. Very few people had his phone number. He picked it up, noticing with interest the *unknown number* flashing. It was even more unusual for him not to know who was calling him.

Ordinarily, he would terminate the call immediately, but this time, on impulse, he answered it.

'Hello,' he said softly.

'Is that Eoin Morrison? Or should I call you *Black Swan* like everyone else does?'

It was a self assured and confident voice.

'Who is this?' asked Eoin in irritation.

'It's not *who* you need to worry about, rather you need to ask yourself why?'

Black Swan hated riddles and games, but he also had the feeling that this was neither. He was intrigued to see where it would go, so he suppressed his rising annoyance.

'Ok, I'll bite,' said Eoin. 'What can I do for you?'

'I think we can help each other out,' said the stranger. 'Do you know the Eastern Tandoori in town?'

'The one at the end of Patrick Street?' asked Eoin.

'If you say so,' said the stranger. 'Anyway, meet me there tonight at seven o'clock. Bring your cheque-book and an open mind. I don't like paying for dinner, and I have some information I think you may be very interested in. Oh, and come alone.'

'Ain't gonna happen,' said Eoin.

'Well then, just make sure I can't see the watchers,' said the stranger. 'If I see them, I'm gone.'

Eoin smiled.

'If they see you, you're gone,' he responded, to the empty line.

#

Eoin liked to be unfashionably early for any appointment. As he sat in the booth, he could see why the Eastern Tandoori had been chosen. Most of the tables were set for two, and they were all situated for maximum privacy. He hated those restaurants where the tables for two were all in a single line, and you could hear the conversations either side of you more clearly than those of your companion.

The inside of the restaurant was dark and gloomy, almost oppressive, but again the ideal interior for discretion. Eoin sipped his iced tap water, smiling at the laminated simplicity of the menu. Most of the establishments that he normally frequented would not have had a plethora of helpful colour photographs for the un-initiated. That was normally reserved for Spanish seaside holidays. An indication on how multi-cultural Cork had become, maybe?

Eoin was still chuckling, when he realised the bench in front of him was no longer empty.

'Your people are good,' acknowledged the stranger. 'I couldn't spot a single one of them as I made my way in.'

'You were hardly expecting carnations were you?' answered Eoin sarcastically. 'All my guys are ex-special forces; hardened professionals. A lot of people in my line of business tend to use just hired muscle. I prefer to pay a bit extra. It always pays off in the long run.'

'What makes you think I'm interested in what your profession is?' stated the stranger.

'Let's not play stupid and childish games,' said Eoin. 'We both know that you are well aware of what it is that I do, otherwise you wouldn't be sitting across the table from me. I can also tell you that the only reason you're still alive and sitting across the table from me, is because I'm intrigued by what it is that you want; no other reason.'

The stranger raised an eyebrow.

'Are you always so direct? I must say it is nice and refreshing to immediately know where you stand. It seems we understand each other, Mr Morrison? May I call you Eoin, or should I call you Black Swan.'

'What's in a name,' he said. 'You can call me Eoin for now.'

They were interrupted by the fast talking and almost unintelligible waiter. They delayed any further conversation until their orders had been taken, and the garish menu's had been cleared away. Both were secretly amused that they had chosen exactly the same starters and main courses, each wondering if the other were playing mind games.

'Can I be frank, Eoin?' asked the stranger.

'Knock yourself out,' said Black Swan.

'Essentially, I have some information for you. It's not a normal information exchange, because it is not normal information, even given the boundaries you would usually attach to the word normal. It is going to require you to suspend your disbelief and take a huge amount on trust.'

Black Swan sat back and regarded the stranger carefully, but did not interrupt.

'It will also require you to make a couple of large leaps of faith. There is little proof, evidence or corroboration of this information and you need to accept that up front.'

Black Swan arched an eyebrow, but still said nothing.

'However, if you choose to accept that hypothesis, I can share with you the reasons why you should be interested.'

'Can you be more specific?' asked Eoin sarcastically.

'All in good time,' said the stranger, ignoring the comment. 'Oh yes, and by the way, I forgot the most important thing. This *could*, and I stress the word advisedly. This *could* allow you to make the jump from half control to full control of the drugs market in Cork. Hell, it could make you the biggest player in the country. You should think about that for a second, before we go on.'

Black Swan was about to respond, when the starters arrived. By mutual consent, they picked up their knives and forks and dispatched their Onion Bhajis with practised ease. Only when both sets of cutlery were neatly brought together at the bottom of their plates, did the discourse continue.

'So let me get this straight,' said Eoin slowly. 'You want me to suspend my disbelief in something that I may or may not believe.'

The stranger nodded.

'And you can provide me with no corroboration, no evidence, nothing substantive to prove that this information is worthy of anything other than contempt.'

'That's about the size of it,' replied the stranger. 'Maybe there is one thing that will persuade you, but there is also a huge amount of trust involved.'

'I was just checking,' said Eoin.

He glanced at the stranger across the gloom.

'Making sure I hadn't missed something fundamental,' he added sarcastically.

The sarcasm seemed lost on his companion. He was just about to ask another question, when the main courses arrived. Eoin was glad in a way; it gave him time to think.

As he watched his dinner companion slowly dispatch a Chicken Tikka Masala, he tried to work the angle, but his brain just couldn't do it. This person was either totally genuine or a complete and utter bluffer, and aside from assassination, he couldn't think of any other reason for someone to use subterfuge to get close to him. Even though he knew Dave and his team were close, he still shivered involuntarily. He had never considered assassination before, but he knew it was a real possibility.

He shook his head; no, somehow this person did not give off the right signals. Eoin was a good judge of character, he could dispassionately analyse. His dinner companion was ruthless, ambitious, maybe even a killer, but they were not there tonight to kill him, he was sure of that.

It was a natural assumption though. If the stranger felt the same way as David did about Eoin, it was the perfect scenario; a dimly lit, sparsely populated restaurant with easy escape routes. Eoin didn't know anyone else who would make the investment in time and effort. Someone who knew his organisation; who he was, where he could be found, how he could be contacted?

'I know what you're thinking,' said the stranger, echoing his thoughts. 'So don't be so naive. If I wanted you dead, you wouldn't be sitting here now. I'm not stupid; I know what goes on in this town. I know where it happens and I know who the main players are. As one of those *main players*, I'm giving you a rare opportunity. If you don't want it, don't waste my time.'

'Are you threatening me?' asked Eoin.

'Merely stating a fact,' said the stranger. 'Maybe this will help you decide.'

He threw a fat brown envelope across the table. He clicked his fingers and the ever attentive waiter was at his side in seconds.

'Bring me a coffee and a cognac. I'm in the mood for a comfortable wait,' he said, glancing at Black Swan with a smile.

At first Black Swan had thought it was money. This idiot obviously doesn't know me at all, he'd thought to himself. He was surprised therefore to extract a carefully bundled and annotated document.

An hour later, Black Swan sat back in his chair. He had read the file from cover to cover, not once but twice and had then re-read certain paragraphs for a third time. He waved unseeingly for attention, and before the waiter had even got to the table, he motioned towards the mug and glass that sat in front of the stranger and mouthed *same again*. The waiter nodded his understanding, even though Black Swan wasn't even looking at him.

As the cognac was placed in front of him, Black Swan took a sip, relishing the impact of the fiery liquid.

'That's quite a story,' he said, tapping the letter sized pages. It was the first thing he'd noticed. Little details always nagged at him. The document; the whole folder in fact, had been printed in America.

'It's no story,' responded the stranger.

'Come on,' answered Black Swan. 'It's very well-written I'll grant you that, but I'd recognise a story anywhere.'

The stranger smiled.

'I was like you; I was unbelievably sceptical. That was, until I saw a demonstration of it in the flesh.'

Eoin's eyes narrowed.

'You've seen it in action.'

'Whatever reason you think I'm here,' said the stranger. 'You need to purge it from your mind right now. The reason I am here is because Ireland is struggling economically. The reason I am here is because they have one of the best state agencies in the world for attracting foreign direct inward investment. They are desperate to create jobs and they have more pharma companies per head of population than any other country on earth. In other words, ideal breeding conditions for a drug like this.'

He indicated the folder.

'A breeding ground where the manufacturing can be camouflaged as a legitimate operation, and where the choice of supply chain is huge. I think they call it hiding in plain sight. Make no mistake; the efficacy of this product cannot be questioned. This drug works and it will be huge.'

'Why are you talking to me?' asked Eoin.

'Have you heard of the Mancini's?'

The change in the conversation took Eoin by surprise.

'Hasn't everyone? If it's illegal in America, they're involved in it.'

The stranger inclined his head.

'You are correct. So, would it surprise you to discover that they were setting up the same type of operation as I have just described, right under your very nose?

The stranger paused.

'Ask yourself this? You are independently wealthy, you already have the supply lines and the distribution network setup, and you know this part of the country intimately, so why did they not approach you about a joint venture? Think about it; there are not that many others out there who would be willing to invest in such a scheme.'

Black Swan laughed.

'You've got that right,' he said.

The stranger changed tack.

'Well, I can only think of one other, and he's certainly very interested.'

'How interested?' asked Black Swan, his eyes narrowing.

'Now that would be telling, wouldn't it? Suffice to say that negotiations have reached an advanced level.'

'So, let's just say hypothetically that I *was* interested in muscling into this little scheme,' said Black Swan. 'And I'm not saying I am,' he added hastily.

No point in divulging his cards; he always tried to maintain the upper hand in any negotiations.

'What sort of up-front investment figure are we talking about?'

'You tell me, you've read the file,' said the stranger. 'What do you think something like that would be worth?'

'One million,' said Eoin, sitting back.

The stranger gave a small chuckle.

'You're not taking this very seriously are you?'

'It's tough to estimate based on this ethereal material you've given me,' said Eoin, tapping the file. 'That was an opening guess. Let's say double that to two million.'

The stranger faced him, and stared at him.

'Not even close,' he stated implacably.

'Ah, come on, give me a break, I'm thinking on my feet here,' said Eoin.

'This is a business investment opportunity to completely control the drugs trade in this country,' responded the stranger impassively. 'We're not talking about small change here.'

'Five million,' said Eoin.

The stranger paused.

'Certainly much warmer,' he said, 'but you're still south of the real figure.'

'Okay, seven million,' said Eoin. 'That's about all I would put in as an initial investment.'

The stranger looked at him for a minute or so.

'That's about what I calculate has gone in so far.'

'So, who are we talking about?' asked Eoin, although he feared he already knew the answer.

'I didn't figure you for a stupid man,' said the stranger. 'I think you know exactly who I'm talking about.'

'If they're already dealing with who I think they're dealing with,' said Eoin. 'They will need to be very careful. How can I put this tactfully? He's not a nice person to conduct business with.'

'Don't worry about David,' said the stranger, confirming Eoin's worst fears. 'The Mancini's believe they can easily handle him.'

'So, how can I guarantee a piece of this action?' Eoin asked.

'You can't,' said the stranger. 'The Lord giveth and the Lord taketh away, or at least the Mancini's do.'

'So, what's in it for you? Why are you telling me all of this?'

'Let's just say that in a previous life, I did not see eye to eye with Guido and Ernesto Mancini, and I always try to help destabilise any of their business ventures.'

'What makes you think I'll help you?' asked Eoin.

'Nothing,' said the stranger. 'I'm merely alerting you to the fact that your closest rival has a massive advantage over you. How you choose to handle that information is your business.'

I need to warn you up front,' said Eoin, dabbing his lips with a napkin. 'I don't take rejection well.'

'I don't care what you do or don't do,' said the stranger calmly. 'As I said, use the information as you will.'

'You're a cool customer, aren't you?' stated Eoin.

'I can afford to be,' said the stranger.

He didn't elaborate any further.

'I'll be in touch,' he said, getting up from the table. 'Oh, and by the way, I lied before about your men. I picked out every one of them. So don't even bother thinking about getting me followed. If I have to lose one of them, it will just piss me off and you don't want that.'

Black Swan took a deep breath and closed his eyes. He took another deeper breath and counted to ten slowly. He knew a lot was at stake. He also knew that one way or another, he was getting a piece of it. The stranger was right, he had the information and now he was going to use it.

He opened his laptop and booted it up. He opened the GPS tracking program and saw the dot, as it tracked away from the Eastern Tandoori and moved slowly up the length of Patrick Street. There was more than one way to follow someone. He started laughing and found he couldn't stop, prompting startled and bemused glances from the waiters and other diners.

CHAPTER 43 – DIALOGUE

21st May 2011 – Eleven days after the Storm.

Be content to act, and leave the talking to others. – Baltasar Gracian.

I didn't ordinarily do torture. Not through any moral or religious obligation, but over the years, I'd found it to be messy and counter-productive, and aside from that, I had never yet managed to get anything useful from it.

In my line of work, it was better to kill them quickly, cleanly and be done with it; minimum mess with minimum fuss. This time was different though; this time I was going to get some answers.

Was it torture? Maybe torture would be too strong a word. Direct and forceful interrogation; I would be direct and forceful. This bastard was going to talk.

We had driven a short way out of town, until I'd seen what I wanted; a derelict and abandoned farm with a barn.

We left him locked in the boot while we scouted around the small farmyard. In the barn, there were two loose boxes that had originally been used for horses; perfect for what I needed.

I popped the boot, anticipating what he was going to do. It was just too quiet and we had been driving for too long. As the lid sprung open on its hinges, he dived out, only to meet the butt of the gun coming down. He was consistent if nothing else, and slipped to the ground in a crumpled heap.

We dragged him into the barn, and using the four tow ropes we had purchased on the way, we secured his ankles and his wrists to the two upright posts that stood either side of the entrance to one of the loose boxes. I took a step back and regarded my handiwork.

'He looks like that Da Vinci image you always see,' said Roussel. 'The one with the arms and legs straddled; can't for the life of me remember what it's called.'

'I know the one you mean,' I acknowledged.

'Vitruvian Man,' said Dale softly.

305

Trust him to know.

I picked up the old metal bucket that I'd spotted standing in the corner and walked outside. Like in most farms, there was a rainwater butt to collect run-off from the roof. I slid the lid off and immersed the bucket in the icy water. I carried the full container back into the shed, slopping the liquid messily on the ground as I walked.

I lifted it awkwardly and threw it full force into the face of the slumped figure. He twitched as though I'd electrocuted him, and I smacked him on the cheeks a couple of times until his head lolled upright and his eyes opened.

'Time to wake up,' I said, slapping him twice more for good measure.

You could see the marks of the individual fingers on his cheek.

As consciousness returned, so too did awareness. I saw the realisation and understanding flit like shadows across his face. He took in the whitewashed stone walls and the bleak exterior landscape. He briefly thrashed about against his restraints, as if he were testing them for strength, and then almost immediately gave up. There was something fatalistic about his demeanour. He knew he wasn't going anywhere, except maybe to hell.

'So, let's get the pleasantries out of the way first,' I said. 'This....'

I indicated Roussel.

'....is Charles Roussel, a detective with the Louisiana CID. He wants some answers.'

I punched the captive suddenly and without warning, straight to the stomach. He doubled up, or at least as far as his restraints would allow, almost retching as the air was expelled forcibly from his lungs. We waited for his laboured breathing to return to normal.

'This....'

I indicated Dale.

'....is Special Agent Dale Foster of the DEA. He too would like some answers, and me....'

'I know who you are,' he responded hoarsely, bracing himself for another impact.

'I am Thomas O'Neill,' I said, ignoring him. 'I also want answers, and that's where you come in.'

At first I thought he was about to beg. His head was down as if in prayer, but then I heard the tell-tale sound of phlegm being hawked. The gobbet of spit landed neatly on the toe of my boot. He had spirit, I'd give him that.

'That was nice,' I stated, wiping the tip of my foot with the other.

This time the ball of spit hit me full in the face. I made a big deal of cleaning it off, taking the time to theatrically remove it with my handkerchief.

'That wasn't very nice at all, was it?' I asked. 'Your parents obviously didn't educate you in the social niceties.'

I stood up close and then swung my elbow into the side of his face. It was not a powerful blow; it was not meant to break or crack anything, it was more a statement of intent.

He shook his head dazedly, and worked his lower jaw a couple of times. I'm sure he would have rubbed it, if his hands were free.

'So, where was I?' I said slowly. 'Oh yes, answers; who sent you?'

'No one,' he replied.

'How did you know where to find me?' I asked.

'We picked you at random,' he said.

I nodded and rubbed my chin.

'Hmm, interesting,' I said.

I motioned at the holdall and then Roussel. He looked at me blankly.

'The bag, bring it over,' I responded, exasperatedly.

Roussel moved surprisingly quickly for a big man, and as he handed the holdall over, I saw the captive's eyes widen slightly.

'Yes, it's a gun,' I said, as I extracted it from the bag.

I saw his eyes widen still further.

'And a silencer,' I added pleasantly, as I screwed the shiny silver cylinder onto the end.

'So, this is how it's going to play out now,' I said, waving the gun gently in the air. 'I'm going to ask the same questions again, and this time you're going to give me the answer I want, do you understand?'

He nodded, but to his credit I couldn't see a trace of fear; bravado yes, but not fear. Not yet anyway.

'Who sent you?' I asked.

He looked at me malevolently.

'I have no master,' he said.

There was an unmistakable *phut* sound from the muzzle of the silencer, and a splinter came off the right-hand post, just above his ankle. I saw him jump slightly, but he recovered quickly.

'You missed,' he stated flatly.

'How did you know where to find me?' I asked.

'We picked you at random, I told you that already,' he answered sullenly.

This time, the *phut* was accompanied by a thud, as the bullet embedded in the left-hand post, this time to the left of his knee.

'You're not a very good shot, are you?' he said.

'Who sent you?' I asked a third time.

'I don't work for anyone except myself,' he said.

The third time, the *phut* sound and his scream of agony almost coincided. I waited for the cries and profanities to abate.

'It's only a flesh wound,' I said. 'Straight through the fat and muscle in the top of the leg; you'll live. Who sent you?'

I placed the barrel of the silencer under his chin to lift his head, forcing him to look at me. I could see the pain but also still too much bravado.

'Who sent you?' I repeated, shouting this time.

He spat in my face with real venom. There was another *phut*; another almost parallel scream of agony.

'It's just the fleshy part of the thigh,' I said, over his howling. 'The other one this time though. Hopefully I've missed all the major veins and arteries; only time will tell. The problem for you, given your current predicament, is that you're going to find it increasingly difficult to stand up, which will put additional strain onto your wrists, and you'll then get into a vicious circle of pain prompting more pain. All you have to do is tell me who sent you, and I'll stop the pain.'

'Fuck you,' he said.

His eyes followed the muzzle of the silencer up to his shoulder. He started shaking his head.

'No!' he cried; too late.

There was another scream, another stream of profanities, but this time, they started turning to entreaties. I could see the cycle of pain starting to take effect; he was finding it difficult to stand. The bullet wounds weren't bleeding that heavily, but because I'd shot him through muscle, it was diminishing his ability to use his legs. This was forcing him to hang from his wrist restraints, which was now causing pain in his shoulder.

'You know how to stop it,' I said, tapping the muzzle thoughtfully against the side of my cheek. 'Just say the word.'

'Thomas.'

My name was spoken behind me. I turned.

Both Dale and Roussel were looking at me. I knew what they were thinking, and when Dale opened his mouth to speak again, I knew what he was going to say.

'Don't even think about it,' I said implacably. 'I told you this was personal for me. I also told you that I was going to handle some of these things my way, so back off.'

'We don't have to like it,' responded Roussel defiantly.

'I don't care whether you like it or not,' I said flatly. 'If you don't want to watch, then fuck off, but leave me to get my answers my way.'

I stared them down. Neither of them said anything further, but neither of them moved either; there were answers aplenty in that one action.

I could see my captive was getting tired. The wounds were taking more of a toll on him than I'd thought they would. Torture definitely wasn't my thing, so I didn't know how to judge these types of injuries. I needed to get answers fast. I placed the muzzle against his other shoulder.

'Tell me what I want to know, or this one is gone as well,' I said menacingly.

He looked at the gun, and then at me, and I saw what I'd been looking for; complete and utter supplication and surrender.

'Who sent you?' I asked.

'Dave Keegan,' he answered immediately, and without hesitation.

It wasn't the answer I had been expecting. I must have blinked in surprise, because he smiled a little through the pain.

'And just who the fuck is Dave Keegan?' I asked.

'He's the head of security for Black Swan,' he answered.

My face cleared; now I was beginning to understand.

'How did you know who I was? How did you manage to target me?' I asked.

I glanced around at Roussel and Dale as I asked the question. They were sitting as far forward as they could; listening intently to every word.

'We were all brought in for a briefing last night,' said the captive. 'Photographs of you were circulated among the group. They were definitely recent photographs, because you happen to be wearing the same clothes you are now. We were told you would be in Kinsale. Apparently they got the photographs and a note anonymously and then to top that, some girl came forward; gave them fresh information about where you would be, which corroborated the note. They requested that we stake out the likely main areas, with spotters covering all the major routes. Their job was to communicate back to the main group in the car park. It was a complete stroke of luck that you literally delivered yourself to us.'

'Were you told to watch for anybody else?' asked Dale suddenly.

The captive glanced up as though he hadn't seen Dale or Roussel before.

'Only him,' he said jabbing his head at me, and then wincing at the pain in his shoulder.

'Were you told anything else?' I asked.

'We were told to bring you in alive if possible, but dead or badly beaten would also have been just as good.'

'So what do these guys want with me? What did you say their names were again; Dave Keegan and Black Swan?' I asked.

'Don't think it's anything to do with Dave,' said the prisoner, offering his opinion for the first time. 'It's his boss who has the hard on for you. Dave is just doing his masters bidding.'

'Do you know why?' asked Roussel.

'No idea,' said the prisoner.

He turned back to me.

'But you must have seriously pissed him off in another life.'

I shrugged the comment off.

'There, that wasn't so hard was it?' I said.

I bent down and pulled up my left trouser leg, extracting the knife I always kept in the ankle holster. The captive watched with trepidation and horror, his eyes following the blade as it travelled almost in slow motion.

Roussel and Dale watched in morbid fascination as I suddenly moved; cutting loose his bonds with four brisk, clean slices. With nothing there to support him any longer, he pitched forward. I caught him cleanly and gently lowered him to the floor.

As he moaned and shifted around on the ground, I went to the car and extracted three or four cheap, clean T-shirts from our stash. I walked back and dumped them on the ground next to his prone body. I refilled the bucket with water and I uncoiled the remainder of the tow ropes and set them beside him. I also extracted his phone from his inside pocket, and placed it on his uninjured side within easy reach of his good hand.

As I turned to leave, I accidentally caught his leg a glancing blow with my foot, causing him to wince in pain.

'Sorry,' I mumbled.

I bent down, re-holstered my knife and then walked back to the car. I waited in silence for Dale and Roussel to join me. I could see the two of them in my rear view mirror. They were heatedly debating something. I couldn't hear what they were saying, but I had a fair idea what it was about.

Eventually, they seemed to come to a decision. As they got in, they slammed the doors so hard behind them, that the car rocked on its suspension.

'What the fuck was all that about? Do you not think that was slightly over the top?' Roussel asked, his voice dripping with sarcasm. 'You could have got the answers you wanted without half killing him. Or was that for our benefit; to prove what a big man you are?'

'I didn't kill him, did I?' I protested. 'And no, I'm not trying to prove what a big man I am; I don't need to, especially to either of you.'

The steel was evident in my voice.

'I needed answers, he could give them to me, he gave them to me; job done, simple as that.'

'You could have made us accessories to murder,' protested Dale.

'Could have, but didn't,' I said. 'I had no intention of killing him. I've left him with water, material for bandages, rope for tourniquets, and a phone to call his friends. If he dies, it's not on my conscience.'

'Jesus, you can be a cold hearted bastard sometimes,' said Roussel.

I laughed humourlessly.

'You're only learning that now,' I said. 'I kill people for a living, remember?'

'So, was all that violence worth it?' asked Dale.

'Then or now,' I asked, but it was a rhetorical question and he looked at me with a puzzled expression.

'Well, point number one, I resent the implication of *all that violence*,' I said sharply. 'I shot him through muscle and fat. The only lasting effects he'll have will be the scars; something to boast about to his future girlfriends. And point number two? Yes, in answer to your actual question, I do think it was worth it, because before, we were guessing at the relevance. Now we know for certain.'

'What do we know though?' asked Dale.

I could see he wasn't convinced.

'Well, we definitely know that Scott Mitchell is connected to Black Swan and we now definitely know that Black Swan has a thing about me.'

'Richard O'Neill is the key to it all,' said Dale. 'We need to find out more about Richard O'Neill.'

'Well, I told you what the solicitor said,' I answered. 'He was playing a part; probably just a pseudonym.'

'Maybe, but the solicitor also said that he was probably a relative of your mother, and that is the key here, I think. Identify him and we potentially have some real answers. Does she have any living cousins, brothers, sisters?'

I shook my head.

'All her siblings are dead.'

'In fairness, she never told you about your father. She could have kept other things from you,' said Dale gently.

I could feel my anger rising, but before it reached the point of no return, the reasonable side of my brain, the logical part, took over and I acknowledged silently that Dale could well be right.

'So, I could have relatives still around that I don't know about?' I stated flatly, as if acknowledging it to myself for the first time, which in a sense I was.

'Yes you could.'

'So, how do we make headway on that?' I asked, as I fired the car into life.

Dale and Roussel looked at each other. They simultaneously removed their phones and dialled, smiling at each other as they did so.

'Hey Dodds, it's me,' said Dale. 'Do you have a pen handy? I need you to check some details for me.'

'Hey James, it's me,' said Roussel. 'What? Yeah, Kinsale is lovely. But a few things came up while I was here. Can you do me a big favour? I need to trace down a couple of leads.'

I smiled and engaged drive, accelerating smoothly back onto the road to Kinsale.

CHAPTER 44 – REJECTION

22nd May 2011 – Twelve days after the Storm.

Reject your sense of injury and the injury itself disappears. – Marcus Aurelius.

Black Swan hated waiting. He never had to wait for anything; he was always the one in control. He was the director, constantly giving the orders and deciding on the strategy. Other people had to defer to him. That was the way it was.

He smiled broadly as the next song came on the radio.

'Huey Lewis and the news, folks with – I want a new drug.'

How ironic. He didn't need a new drug; he had his old one, and he was well and truly addicted. The only drug he'd ever craved was power. But craving it and attaining it were two different things. Society would judge him differently if they knew the truth about his rise to the top; or maybe they wouldn't. He was a drug dealer after all, whichever way you sliced it.

He remembered his initial interview with *Bull* McCabe.

'I like you,' Bull had said. 'There is something thoroughly engaging and honourable about you. But there's something scary about you too. There's a rod of iron running through you boy. Don't ever lose that, not for anybody.'

He thought about David McCabe, his nemesis. It was probably just as well that things had turned out the way they had. They were too alike.

Still, he couldn't help wondering what would have happened if they had united instead of splintering apart. Strangely, he didn't think either of them would have been quite so successful.

As he knew well, nothing motivated like rage. Nothing got you out of bed in the morning like a good healthy dollop of hate.

It was truly ironic really. The reason David hated Eoin was utterly and entirely without premise. The truth was; Bull McCabe had intentionally stepped down in favour of Black Swan. He had been getting older and slower, and had early on recognised the steel that ran through Eoin, like letters through a stick of rock. The Bull had felt he could temper and forge the steel from afar, in his own image.

The twins had been too young to take over; they hadn't fully realised what would be expected of them in the family business. The Bull had not known which way they would go; it would have been tough initially, finding out exactly what misery and suffering had to be perpetuated, just so that you could live in luxury. It took an unusual kind of person to overlook the despair and misfortune that other people were required to endure.

Because of that, Eoin had been the one initially tasked with growth and development, making sure the boys had something worthy of their inheritance, should they choose in the future to accept it.

Bull had taken discrete steps to keep hidden, but he had always been in the background, watching, directing and approving.

The sheer irony of it all was that in the end, the Bull had been the architect of his own demise. After years as a widower, he'd started an illicit affair with a married woman. Her husband had been an accountant, as meek and mild as they came, but when he'd found out about the affair, something inside him had snapped.

He'd bought a gun, illegally of course, and in a delicious irony, had acquired it through an associate of the Bull himself. He hadn't cared who Bull was. In truth, he'd had no idea *what* Bull was, nor would it have made a difference if he had.

Like all cuckolded husbands, he'd wanted revenge. From the testosterone fuelled depths of his bitterness and failure, the rage and hate had festered and heightened. He'd followed the Bull home one day after an assignation with his wife. He'd then sat outside, day after day, watching and waiting while the rage got stronger. One day, the inevitable happened; he'd snapped and trailed Bull to his favourite pub. He'd waited outside for an hour, allowing the resentment and hostility to build unabated, until he'd reached the point of no return. He'd calmly walked in and emptied the entire clip into an astonished and helpless Bull, in front of an incredulous and horrified clientele.

The police never found out about the affair or the accountant assassin. The investigating officers were told to keep it short and sweet and to make no waves. Eoin had paid a lot of money to keep it quiet, and had then paid a lot more money to commission his own discrete investigation.

There was obviously no way he was letting the police know the real story; it suited him at the time to let the police think it was a drug feud, little realising, although he should have done, that the spotlight would eventually alight upon him.

The accountant had become overwhelmed with guilt, so one week after the killing, when his maudlin and depressed wife was out shopping, he'd run a pipe from the exhaust through the window of his car. As it had idled in his garage, he'd simply opted out of life and gone into a deep and never ending sleep.

The police had put it down to pressures of work. The company that the accountant had worked for had been going through very hard times, so it had not been seen as an unusual or out of character act. In another strange and bizarre twist of fate, he'd been buried in the same Clonakilty graveyard as the Bull, only two plots away.

When Eoin had joined the company, the twins had initially loved him. They were not too distant from Eoin in years, and had very similar tastes and very similar personalities. Love did not figure large on any of their agendas.

David had regarded Eoin's accession to the McCabe throne with deep suspicion. Whenever David asked his father what had happened, the Bull refused to be drawn on it.

'It's none of your business boy; at least not yet, it's not.'

The Bull was a proud man. David wrongly interpreted his silence as a refusal to acknowledge his failure to hold onto his own company; a stubborn denial of the loss of his empire to a suave and ruthless interloper.

The truth was; Eoin had been targeted with building and expanding the business, specifically for the twins to someday inherit. Unfortunately the accountant, along with his own short sightedness and stupidity, had scuppered Bull's plans.

The first part of the exercise had been executed flawlessly. All of the company incorporation documents had been signed over to Eoin as per their gentleman's agreement. Bull had insisted that the only way it would work was if Eoin had absolute authority.

However, all of the documents pertaining to the second phase, the inheritance rights of John and David, had still been in the middle of being drafted, when Bull had died in a hail of bullets. So when the will had been read, it came as a complete shock and surprise for the twins to discover that the true and rightful heir to their company was Eoin Morrison.

David had continually refused to believe that Eoin had not had anything to do with his father's death and when John had died, the gulf between them became insurmountable. It still made Eoin sad, especially when he knew the police had the same subtly different version of their feud; one that was just plain wrong.

But Eoin did not hate David McCabe.

The same could not be said in reverse.

David despised Eoin Morrison.

Who was Eoin to judge though? Eoin hated Thomas O'Neill with the same ruthless and passionate intensity. Did the chain end there, or was the circle of hate as strong as ever?

Black Swan shivered. He was only wearing slacks and a shirt, and the problem with most of the old Georgian houses was that they tended to retain the cold and block out the heat, the reverse of what was required. The insulation he had installed was ineffectual against the massive heat sink of the large stone walls.

Even though the house had been rebuilt with a sophisticated under floor heating system, Eoin preferred the honesty and integrity of a real open fire. He ambled over to the fireplace, and from the ornate brass bucket that was set to one side of the large slate hearth, he started picking out one of the free local papers.

He ripped out the pages and balled them to create kindling. He was just about to ball his fifth sheet, when something caught his eye. He smoothed out the page and read the information slowly. He took it back to his desk, oblivious now to the cold, and placed it centrally on the large leather bound blotter. Pieces of the puzzle started flying in from left and right, like well rehearsed stagehands in a theatre production.

The first thing that had struck him upon finishing the Storm dossier had been the sheer scale of operation that would be required to house such an undertaking. This could not be hidden in attics and garden sheds. His keen intelligence had identified the intrinsic scale of the production process. That information had obviously stayed in his subconscious, and his brain had been picking at it like a sore. When he saw the article about the new pharmaceutical investment in Clonakilty, the dots had immediately connected themselves, especially as he already suspected who one of the main investors was.

He pulled his laptop from his desk drawer and flipped it open. A rudimentary web search on ADXR returned millions of hits. He would have expected nothing less. ADXR were a publicly traded company. All of their information was in the public domain, especially if you knew where to look.

One of Eoin's hobbies was the stock market. When you had millions of Euro in the bank, you could afford to indulge yourself. Eoin clicked open his company search program. Pretty soon, he had a listing of the ADXR board, all of their curriculum vitae's, and copies of their last three quarterly financial statements. It was not new information to him. He always did an in-depth analysis of any potential investment and coincidentally, ADXR were one of the stocks he held in quite large numbers.

He smiled.

The other company mentioned in the news release; they were something different again. There were only a couple of dozen hits related to G&E Chemicals themselves, most of which were cached copies of the same media statement, just located on differing news media websites. This company was definitely worthy of investigation.

Eoin had long ago recognised the power of networking. His softly spoken manner and fearsome reputation combined to ensure he was never ignored when he wanted something, and his network extended to every sphere of local and central government. He also made sure his information sources were well looked after.

He flicked through the Rolodex on his desk. Even though he had all his numbers in his smart phone, he didn't have one hundred percent confidence in them. Some things he just wouldn't trust to technology. He dialled the number.

'Hey Graham, its Eoin,' he said as the phone was answered. 'Eoin Morrison. I need you to do me a favour and I need the information very quickly, do you understand?'

He smiled.

'Good, now listen carefully....'

Ten minutes later, the phone on his desk rang, startling him out of his semi-slumber.

'Morrison,' he said.

He listened closely and waited for the pregnant pause to indicate the information had been delivered. He hung up without saying anything. There was nothing that needed to be said. He made a mental note. Graham would be a grand richer by the end of the day.

Eoin pulled his writing pad towards him and scribbled down everything the caller had told him. Eoin's short-term memory was almost flawless, and for anything up to a page, he could recall it letter for letter.

Only when he had finished writing it all down, did he start trying to analyse and understand what it was that he had been told.

He looked at the list of companies that his contact had given him. It never ceased to amaze him how governments made it so easy to facilitate the evasion of tax. Granted, you had to be a very good company lawyer, or at the very least have a solid understanding of company law, but once you had that, your tax bill rapidly declined.

Eoin was the latter, self taught and sharp as a steel blade, and even without a degree, there were few in the country who understood company law as well as he did.

He started from the top, from G&E Chemicals, as he knew from experience that it was like playing a game of *pass the parcel*. For every layer you stripped away, the closer you got to the prize. And sure enough, by the time he was down to the last layer of the onion, he was not in the least bit surprised to find out who the company was and who controlled it.

West Cork Bull Investments Ltd, through a convoluted series of holding companies, held a thirty three percent stake in G&E Chemicals. The directors of the company were David McCabe and Ben Collins.

Black Swan dialled the number from memory. His desk mounted speakerphone echoed the ring tone and then as it turned to white noise, he started speaking. He didn't even give the other party the chance to introduce themselves.

'Dave, I'm e-mailing you some details,' he said curtly. 'I want you to put all of our resources on this and let me know as soon as you can if there is anything further you can find out?'

Eoin had been about to hang up, when he heard the entreaty.

'Boss?'

'What is it?' Eoin asked.

'Maybe nothing,' he said. 'But I'm hearing a lot of noise from the Clonakilty area. I know West Cork wouldn't be a major base for us, but just wanted you to be aware. Something is definitely afoot in the reeds down there.'

'Thanks Dave,' said Eoin.

It was all starting to hang together.

He hung up without saying goodbye. He busied himself with the process of typing and documenting, not sitting back until the small bundle of documentation he had created was winging its way across the ether.

He had a feeling somebody was playing games with him. After the cryptic conversation of the last day or so, he had been utterly certain he would find the Bullock somewhere in the paper trail, but knowing it and confirming it were two different things.

He was not sure how he felt about it now. It just made no sense to Eoin. Someone was using him for their own selfish reasons, and Eoin did not like it one little bit.

He also felt seriously conflicted. If the Bullock had thought enough about Storm to invest, then it was adding to his own growing confidence in Storm as a commercial opportunity.

Regardless of how David McCabe felt about him as a person, Eoin trusted his professional judgement implicitly. You didn't get as big as David; grow the business as fast as he had, without having a keen sense of what made money and what didn't. But more galling even than that, was that David had got in ahead of him. If it was the last thing he did, Eoin would make sure the Bullock did not profit a single penny from the investment.

The strident ringing of his mobile made him jump. This time though, when he checked the number, he recognised immediately who it was. He always added them to his phone, and he couldn't help but smile at the *Tandoori stranger* that was flashing back at him from the LCD display.

'Hello Eoin,' said the familiar voice.

'I had a feeling it wouldn't be long before I heard from you again,' said Black Swan.

'So what's your verdict?' asked the stranger.

'Does it matter?' asked Eoin in return. 'I thought you didn't care what I did, one way or the other?'

'Well, it turns out that I do,' said the stranger. 'I'm interested to find out what your answer is?'

'I'm afraid the answer is none of your business,' answered Eoin.

'You gave me the impression that it most definitely was *your* business last night,' said the stranger.

'I don't like playing second fiddle to anyone. I won't play second fiddle to one particular party, and you know exactly who I'm talking about. I also intensely resent being played for an idiot.'

'That's what you think I am doing, is it?' asked the stranger.

'You definitely are,' replied Eoin. 'I do have above average intelligence, so give me some credit.'

'And nothing I can say will convince you to get involved?'

'Who said I'm not going to get involved. It's merely your motivation for providing me with the information that I'm beginning to doubt.'

'I told you my motivation. I'm not playing games here. What makes you think I am?' asked the stranger.

'I refer to the aforementioned above-average intelligence,' said Eoin.

It was then that he realised the call had been terminated. He smiled; he didn't care. If someone wanted to play games with him, he was an exceptionally good player and he didn't like losing.

CHAPTER 45 – HYPOTHESIS

22nd May 2011 – Twelve days after the Storm.

The great tragedy of science: the slaying of a beautiful hypothesis by an ugly fact. – Thomas Henry Huxley.

'I don't know what I'd do without the smart phone at this stage,' said Dale. 'You can get your e-mail and internet, literally at the touch of a button.'

'Yeah, it's great,' echoed Roussel. 'Everything is pretty much instant these days, isn't it?'

He had barely got the words out, when there was an almost simultaneous symphony of e-mail alert tones.

'You go first,' said Dale. 'Given that your contact is local, they're much more likely to have found out something relevant.'

I watched Dale watching Roussel in the rear view mirror, his face a study in concentration. Roussel was shaking his head slightly and frowning. As he glanced up at me, I could tell he was disappointed.

'James had another scan through all their manual files and also took one last trawl through all of their online systems,' he said. 'Unfortunately, he didn't manage to unearth anything new. As far as the records are concerned, Richard O'Neill doesn't exist and never existed; certainly the one that was purported to be married to your mother, anyway. To the extent that he can confirm it, James has not managed to unearth any known surviving relatives on your mother's side of the family. However, the department have a genealogical investigator on a retainer. They have offered to engage them if I think it is sufficiently relevant to the case. I told them that I thought it was.'

'That's positive then, isn't it?' I stated hopefully.

Roussel smiled grimly.

'The investigators are not quick, according to James. Most of the relevant records, especially in Ireland, are manual and generally geographically disparate; nothing really useable there.'

He sighed.

'It was a long shot,' I said. 'Don't worry about it.'

I turned to Foster.

'So that leaves you, Dale. Did you get anything interesting?'

Foster was so engrossed in what he was reading, that he didn't hear the question.

'What about you, Dale?' I asked again, this time a little louder.

He looked up in surprise.

'Did you get anything?'

His expression clouded a little.

'I got something,' he said distractedly, as he tried to focus on the information.

'So what did you get?' I asked, my excitement slowly starting to build.

'Come on man, spit it out,' said Roussel eagerly.

'Not so fast,' he said. 'Let me go through this methodically. I think it will make a lot more sense to everybody if I understand it myself first. I'm not saying any of this information is relevant to our search, but at least it's another potential avenue to explore.'

He composed himself and scrolled back to the start of the e-mail.

'So you remember my partner and my boss had a conversation with the director of the CIA? Well....'

He paused for effect.

'....because of the importance the CIA has attached to this investigation, they've given my partner access to the restricted federal databases; the ones that were previously off-line to both me and Roussel.'

He looked up at me then, with a smile on his face.

'Apparently, in your early days, they were none too sure about your political leanings. They knew the Mancini's were apolitical, but this was the early nineties and Northern Ireland was heading towards the first IRA ceasefire. All federal agencies had been put on heightened alert for any suspected Irish republican involvement or activity.'

'So what does all that mean exactly?' I asked. 'I have a file in Langley?'

'It means that both you and your background were subjected to a much more rigorous security check than they might otherwise have been, purely because you were Irish. There's a catalogue of all your suspected crimes, as there is in the regular FBI database. The information is much more detailed however, and you'll be pleased to learn that you were deemed neutral in respect to possible republican terrorist activity or involvement.'

'Good to know,' I said with a grin.

'They also focused on any major ties you had or would have had with folks back in Ireland. For you, that was limited to just two people.'

I hazarded a guess.

'My mum and Kathleen Murphy.'

Dale nodded.

'They zeroed in on Kathleen first,' he said. 'I think primarily because she was a contemporary of yours. You met when you were both very young, so more likely to be jointly radical and revolutionary. She was around the same age as you, and from the same generation, so much more likely to have and hold the same political ideals. But she was very quickly disregarded.'

'How so?' I asked.

'She seems to have got married very quickly after you left for America,' said Dale. 'About six months to be precise.'

Funny that she never mentioned the timeframe to me, I thought. And then I realised she had been hinting at it, especially towards the end of our conversation.

'She had two kids in very quick succession, too.'

The first sentence had thrown me slightly, but this one really hit me with a jolt. She'd definitely never mentioned that. I didn't know why it bothered me so much, but it did.

'Two boys; both of them would be in their twenties by now. Her husband is a schoolteacher, maths if you're interested, plays Gaelic football, fanatical GAA supporter.'

The way he pronounced GAA sounded funny, maybe because he wasn't Irish; he was reading the text straight from the screen without any context.

'They were deemed to be very patriotic, but not republican; certainly not in the standard security risk interpretation of republican that is.'

I nodded.

'So that leaves my mother,' I said.

'So that leaves your mother,' echoed Dale. 'You'll know most of this already, but bear with me. It gets better.'

He read steadily down the page.

'She was born in Cork City, the oldest of five children.'

I looked at him with a puzzled expression.

'Don't you mean four?' I said.

'The eldest of five,' he repeated. 'There were two girls and two boys, plus your mother of course.'

'One girl and two boys,' I said, getting annoyed.

'James O'Neill, the eldest boy,' continued Dale, 'died as a result of injuries sustained in a dockyard accident when your mother was about twenty two.'

I nodded.

'Yep, I remember that story well,' I said.

'John, the youngest boy, died about ten years ago. He was a heavy smoker, who finally succumbed to lung cancer after years of battling with emphysema.'

'I sent a mass card,' I said, and then noticed both their expressions. 'I was busy. Give me a break, I barely knew the guy.'

I paused, affronted.

'Go on,' I said eventually.

'Catherine died about five years ago. She'd permanently moved to Australia in the Sixties, around the time her brother died. She'd already married her late husband in Ireland, and they'd gone off to make a new life for themselves.'

'A lot of people did in the Sixties,' I responded. 'I sent a mass card for that funeral too.'

I said it as though I had to justify myself. I ignored their expressions.

'Which just leaves Joan unaccounted for,' said Dale.

'Who the hell is Joan?' I asked.

'Joan is your aunt. The one that is currently alive and well and living in Rosscarbery,' said Dale.

#

'Do you think this is a good idea?' asked Roussel.

I'd spun the car savagely around, and was busy setting the Sat Nav for Rosscarbery.

'I haven't gone soft in the head, if that's what you mean,' I said, concentrating on the road. 'But this could give us some answers.'

'And it might not,' said Roussel. 'They may have been estranged; they may not have been in contact for years.'

'I'm aware of that,' I said. 'But at this stage, aside from everything else, I just have to know.'

Roussel shrugged. There was nothing more he could say.

'The one thing we do have in our favour, or we should have if we're lucky, is that she never married,' stated Dale. 'So unless she changed her surname for other reasons, she should be easy enough to find.'

'What other reasons?' I asked.

'I don't know,' snapped Dale. 'It's your country, you tell me. Seems a lot of strange things happened in the past when it came to families. I'm just trying to be upbeat about it.'

'You're right, there is only one,' interrupted Roussel.

He'd looked her up in the online phone book as Dale and I had been talking. He extended his phone forward and I typed the address with one eye on the Sat Nav, while trying to keep the other eye on the road in front. It was a hairy few minutes.

As it recalibrated the journey; one which would lead us straight to the Aunt that I never knew existed, it prompted a new train of thought. If I was not aware of her, did she know anything about me? Roussel had raised a valid point; they could have been estranged for years, in which case I would be a stranger. At least it would put us on an equal footing. We would be equitable; both equally lost.

'So was she the older or younger of my mother's sisters?' I asked Dale, more for something to say than through genuine interest.

The answer surprised me.

'She was the youngest of all the children, not just the girls,' he said, 'and quite considerably younger than the others. In fact she is not that much older than you. Ten, maybe fifteen years max.'

We journeyed the rest of the way in silence. I knew what they were thinking and I didn't blame them. I wasn't being entirely dishonest with them. I truly did believe that following this lead could possibly assist in our investigations, but there was that very small part of me, the tiny frightened boy with no family, that was desperate to seize on any connection, no matter how tenuous.

As we neared our destination, I was glad that the Hertz rep had persuaded me to part with the extra cash for the Sat Nav. Like a lot of small provincial towns, Rosscarbery was the name for the town-land as well as the town itself. We traversed the main street, such as it was, and were directed out through the other side. We turned right down a typical country lane and were brought to a stop outside a plain whitewashed bungalow. It was set back a bit from the road, probably on at least an acre. The gates across the driveway were closed, so we couldn't pull in. I told the other two to wait.

As I approached the path to the front door of the house, I noticed a woman working in the garden. She was humming softly and tunefully. A small Jack Russell terrier was running around the lawn and into the flower beds. Every minute or so he would dash back to her, prompting a peal of laughter, soft and melodic, like water flowing through a mountain stream, until she threw his ball and sent him on his way again.

I raised the latch on the wrought iron gate and pushed it gently inwards. The rusty hinges protested as it swung towards the house. She stood up, as I eased myself through the small opening. The sun was well and truly out and she had to hood her eyes with her hand to shield them from the glare. She moved onto the path as I approached.

Suddenly, the sun disappeared behind the fast moving clouds. She saw my face clearly for the first time, and her hand flew to her mouth and her face drained of colour.

'I knew this day would come,' she said, in the same soft melodic tone.

It reminded me very much of my mother. I looked at her with a puzzled expression.

'You're Mary's boy,' she said.

It was not a question.

She turned and wordlessly headed for the open front door. She turned in the doorway. I stood stock still as she beckoned me impatiently inside. I turned to my companions.

'Stay there,' I mouthed, and then headed down the path to join her.

In the hallway, I heard the unmistakeable clinking of someone busy in the kitchen.

'Head into the sitting room, Thomas,' she shouted, anticipating my indecision. 'It's the first door on your left.'

She knew my name. It was a start at least.

I opened the door into a typical rural front room. They were generally only used for special occasions; birthdays, religious holidays and of course Christmas. The kitchen was the living beating heart of most Irish country houses.

Instead of sitting, I gravitated to the sideboard, where there were a large collection of photographs on display. They were mostly old and black-and-white. Of the ones I recognised, it was generally the locations; very few of the people. There was one photo which appeared to take pride of place, right in the heart of the shelving unit. It was the largest and it was the centrepiece, a group photograph. I recognised my mother, she must have been about twenty, and yes there were two guys and two other girls in the frame; all smiling and laughing.

I continued browsing and then; wham; I was stopped in my tracks. There it was, literally in black and white. Mother, Father, Son. I was amazed in one way; shocked at how closely my mental image matched the reality. I'd been carrying it for decades, but there was nothing about this photograph that surprised me.

A noise behind me brought me back. I heard a rattle as the tray was put down on the small occasional table. I turned around.

'They were a handsome couple, weren't they?' she said simply. 'I'll let you get your own tea if you don't mind. I don't know how you like it.'

The cups were delicate bone china with matching saucers. They displayed an intricate Chinese design in blue; no teabags whacked into mugs here. I sat in the armchair opposite her and we sipped politely for a couple of minutes, until I could take it no longer.

'How did you know who I was?' I asked.

'You've had that same facial expression, almost since the day you were born,' she said. 'I always used to describe it as relentless determination. Also there's the shape of your head. The features haven't really changed; you've always had a nice face. Deep down, I always felt you would grow up to be a decent man.'

I smiled at the earnestness of her statement.

'I'm not sure I'd agree with you on all of that,' I said. 'I would especially quibble with the part about me being a decent man.'

'Bad deeds don't necessarily equal a bad person,' she said enigmatically.

'What else was it you said?' I asked, becoming uncomfortable. 'I knew this day would come.'

'When you finally came to find me,' she finished. 'I knew you'd find out the truth eventually. I told Mary that. I begged her, but she didn't listen. She refused to listen actually, she was blinded; they both were.'

'Her and my father, you mean?'

'Is that what he was?'

She laughed abruptly.

'So, is that why you've come? To try and find out the truth?'

'I found out the truth in a solicitor's office about twenty four hours ago,' I said grimly. 'I don't necessarily need the truth, what I need is the truth explained.'

We digested that sentence for a while, with our cups occasionally chiming a crisp clean note, like a tuning fork, on the edge of our saucers as we sipped.

'You're my aunt,' I blurted out suddenly.

'I am,' she said, 'but I'd prefer it if you called me plain old Joan.'

I smiled.

'Sure.'

I paused before rushing headlong in.

'So why did I know nothing about you, Joan?' I asked.

'Are you sure you want to know?'

'I've never been surer,' I said.

'All families have secrets,' she said.

I didn't say anything.

'Mary and me were inseparable when I was growing up,' she said. 'In truth she was probably more a mother to me than our mother was. Even though she was the eldest, we always had a strange bond; one that transcended age or generational differences. Where the others left home, she stayed. She got a job and looked after the parents and me.'

'Then what?' I asked.

'Everything was going okay for us. We weren't rich, but we were happy. James's death was a setback; none of us were expecting that. I think that's why Catherine left for Australia. They were all running away, but not your mother. You probably know that better than me. She was rock solid; a foundation for the rest of us to cling to. And then in the blink of an eye, everything changed. She met him.'

'My father?' I asked again.

She nodded.

'According to both of them, it was love at first sight. It was initially a one night stand; they literally bumped into each other in the street. They promised each other, or rather he made her promise him, that it would be the only time they would ever see each other. And that was it for both of them, or so they thought. You were born almost exactly nine months later.'

'So, she was a single mother?' I asked. 'It must have been tough in those days.'

'It was,' she said flatly. 'But even then, it wasn't too late. Things could have gone back to the way they were before; in fact it was almost better. Our parents had accepted the situation with minimum fuss, and absolutely doted on you. I thought you were the most exquisite baby I had ever seen.'

I smiled at the description.

'But about two years after you were born, they bumped into each other again, completely by chance, and this time neither of them was prepared to say no to themselves or to each other.'

'So what happened?'

'She sat us down, my parents and me, and told us she was leaving, taking you with her. The way we interpreted it, and rightly so in our eyes, she was to become a kept woman. He bought them a big house on Merchants Quay that he registered in her name. The only proviso, and it seemed a big one to us at the time, was that she always be available. No, in fact, that both she *and* their child should always be available, to play happy families whenever he wanted.'

I could see the sadness cloud her expression.

'Harsh words were exchanged between your mother and me. I said some things that I could never really take back. I loved your Mum, more than anyone I've ever loved; like I said, she was closer to me than our own mother. They say the line between love and hate is very thin; well I guess it is. She never spoke to me again; in point of fact, I never saw her again after that.'

'This guy, was he like a playboy or something?'

'If I could spit, I'd do it right now on the ground,' she said. 'I know he was your father, but he was a weak, vain and selfish excuse for a man. Believed himself in love, when the only thing he was in love with was the idea of being in love; oh, and himself, of course.'

'I remember him being around,' I responded, almost defensively.

I'd also noticed the tense she had used to describe him. Did she mean anything by that?

She looked at me kindly.

'Oh, he was the model husband and father early on,' she said. 'The problem was; he was eventually found out by his wife.'

'He was married?' I exclaimed, although I wasn't really surprised.

Joan had been leading up to it in a roundabout kind of way.

'They say hell hath no fury like a woman scorned, and boy did she unleash the fury big time. He'd left her you see, to be with his love.'

The sarcasm was literally dripping off the word *love*.

'He lasted about a week. His in-laws cut him off, the majority of the money was provided from her family fortune and he discovered that financial security was more important to him than you and your mother. The only thing his wife's family didn't find out about was the house he'd bought for Mary and you; maybe because it was in your mum's name. When he died, she was able to sell it. She managed to live off the proceeds, almost to the day that she too passed away.'

'Were you there?' I asked. 'At the funeral?'

She turned to me and I saw the tears welling up in her eyes; more than I had managed when I had first heard of my mum's passing.

'It was the least I could do,' she said.

She looked at me and guessed my thoughts.

'At least one member of her family was there at the end. It was a good send off; she had a lot of good friends and there was a lot of goodwill.'

'We didn't have a bad life,' I acknowledged.

'No you didn't,' she said.

'So, do you know who he was?' I asked, reverting to the same tense that she had used. The word *died* was pretty final when referring to a person.

She looked at me then; those cool grey eyes in the tanned and pleasant face that reminded me so much of my mother, only less tense and more relaxed.

'I'll never forget that name till the day I die,' she said. 'Michael Morrison.'

CHAPTER 46 – CLANDESTINE

22nd May 2011 – Twelve days after the Storm.

If we could read the secret history of our enemies we should find in each man's life sorrow and suffering enough to disarm all hostility. – Henry Wadsworth Longfellow.

'Hey Boss!'

Dodds nudged Ray and continued whispering.

'I knew it was called the Pentagon, but I didn't realise it was in the actual shape of a pentagon. Does that sound stupid?'

'It does a bit,' whispered Ray, trying not to laugh.

They were in a taxi in Washington DC, heading out of the airport complex. Both of them had been summoned to see the director, a journey that would take them directly to the middle of the spider's web.

'Why are we whispering?' asked Dodds finally.

'I don't know,' said Ray in a normal voice. 'Probably makes fuck all difference. Most of these taxi drivers barely speak English, certainly in New York anyway; not sure about DC.'

As he finished what he was saying, they caught their first glimpse of the massive building up close. Ray had seen it before, in television programmes and on the news. There had been a lot of coverage over the years, especially around the nine eleven attacks, but when you saw it in the flesh for the first time, you realised just how big it really was. The taxi driver dropped them as close as he could to their designated entrance. They both smiled at his garbled and barely comprehensible effort to tell them the fare. It looked like they were not wide of the mark where DC taxi drivers were concerned.

Even though they were both federal employees, Ray was amazed and more than a little bit heartened by how forensically his identification was studied. There was certainly no complacency on show that he could see; nine eleven had taught all the agencies a valuable security lesson.

They were escorted into one of the main lobbies, all gleaming marble, chrome and stainless steel. They were asked to wait, and the seconds quickly became minutes.

Ray was just about to refill his paper cup for a third time at the mirrored metal water cooler, when an impassive looking man in his early twenties approached, wearing a dark suit and Ray Ban Aviator sunglasses. Ray and Dodds looked away from each other; they wouldn't have been able to keep a straight face otherwise.

'Gentlemen,' he said formally, 'if you'd like to follow me please.'

The trio walked over to the phalanx of elevators. There were no buttons, just security proximity readers. The unsmiling young man flicked his badge over the black square of plastic and the doors glided open.

Inside the lift, he hit the button for the top floor; the fifth floor no less. It may have been a huge building, but it was not a tall one. Ray felt no sensation of movement, but within seconds the light for the fifth floor illuminated with a ping. Before the automaton could badge them out, Ray flicked his DEA badge across the card reader. It beeped, but the red light in the centre of the pad stayed stubbornly red.

'Just checking,' said Ray with a smile.

'Please don't do that again,' stated the young man brusquely.

Even though Ray outranked him by a considerable number of grades, it was definitely a dressing down. They had a real bigwig about themselves, these CIA types.

They exited the lift in silence and were escorted for what seemed like a mile along the featureless corridor. Everyone they met seemed to be equally as unfriendly and unsmiling as their host.

They were eventually escorted into a small and spartan ante room. It was like a doctor or dentist's waiting area, only without the tattered and outdated magazines. Dodds and Ray sat down on the hard plastic chairs. Their escort nodded briefly before turning on his heel and briskly walking out. Ray wouldn't have been surprised to have heard the sound of a key turning in the lock.

'Well, he was a bundle of laughs, wasn't he?' said Dodds.

Ray smiled.

'Paranoid delusions are us, with a little bit of arsehole thrown in.'

They both laughed.

'And he's definitely seen *the men in black* too.'

They laughed until their sides ached. They both knew what it was; release of tension. Eventually, they calmed down; sitting and fidgeting inside that small room for what seemed like an eternity, but in truth was probably no more than twenty minutes.

The door to the main office suddenly burst open, causing Ray and Dodds to jump. A man seemed to suddenly materialise in the middle of the room. Maybe it was because of his size; he dwarfed both Ray and Dodds, neither of whom were small men. It might also have been because of his presence. There was an aura around him that Ray recognised immediately. It was the essence of power.

He looked from one of them to the other and raised his eyebrows.

'Agent Fox?' he asked.

'I'm Ray Fox,' said Ray.

The lines on his face cleared.

'CIA Director Nicholson,' he said. 'Winston Nicholson'

His handshake was as large and overwhelming as he was. Ray could almost feel the bones splintering in his hand, as his arm was pumped enthusiastically.

'And you must be Agent Dodds,' he said, subjecting Dodds to the same treatment.

He motioned them towards his office and stepped aside to allow them in first. There were two chairs set up facing an enormous desk, but instead, he motioned them to the far corner, where two leather couches faced each other across a large square coffee table. Whether by accident or design, they ended up facing each other like adversaries, Winston on one side with Ray and Dodds on the other.

'Coffee or something stronger?' asked Winston.

Both Ray and Dodds attention had been immediately drawn to the large drinks cabinet in the corner. Rank very definitely had its privilege still.

'Coffee would be fine,' said Dodds.

'Same here,' replied Ray.

The director pushed a button on an intercom beside him.

'Three coffees when you're ready,' he said brightly.

He turned back to the two guys.

'Glad you could make it over,' he said.

'Did we have a choice?' asked Ray, echoing what Dodds was thinking.

'Probably not,' acknowledged the director. 'But I'd like to think that the natural curiosity inherent in all investigators would have brought you here, even if I hadn't told you that you had no alternative.'

Ray inclined his head.

'Touché,' he said.

Ray and Dodds glanced down at the table, both noticing that there were two forms facing them with pens placed diagonally across the pages.

'What are these?' asked Ray.

'Non-disclosure agreements,' said the director.

'But we've already signed those as part of our federal induction.'

'Not these you haven't,' said the director. 'I would read them very carefully before you sign them.'

He was more than halfway through his coffee by the time Ray and Dodds finished reading the documents; the beverage had been delivered by an extremely attractive secretary, of which both men were oblivious.

They looked at each other. Dodds whistled softly under his breath, a high then a low note.

'You got that right,' said Ray.

'So, what happens if we don't sign?' asked Dodds interestedly.

'You don't have a choice,' said the director. 'Not if you want to find out the information that you require.'

'Just asking,' said Dodds, before both he and Ray dashed off their signatures.

'Okay,' said the director. 'Now that's out of the way, let's get down to business. I've already briefed you on Storm, so I'm not going to go over old ground. You know it's a drug, you know its efficacy; in fact you know all that would potentially happen if it was ever to hit the streets....'

He paused.

'....or do you?' he finished.

Ray put his head on one side.

'I don't follow you,' he said.

The director smiled.

'Not many people do,' he said. 'Okay, let's take it back to square one.'

He paused again to marshal his thoughts.

'This drug was originally developed by an English biochemist, who became obsessed with communism. He became so obsessed with the socialist notion of equality that he designed a drug to create it, or at least that was his original intention. Like most drugs, or like a lot of drugs, let's not generalise; like a lot of drugs, the sense of euphoria it gave to its takers was merely a side effect, not the expected result.'

He paused again.

'And now you need to bear with me,' he said. 'I'm going to tell you two seemingly unconnected pieces of information. The thrust of the conversation will become clear, I promise.'

Ray and Dodds both nodded.

'The Storm project or the Storm Protocol as it became, was formally inducted almost exactly two years ago,' said the director. 'Up until that point, it had been a dream for two ambitious young employees. Or to put it another way, one ambitious young employee and one disenchanted lab technician.'

'This agent had discovered the dusty old file, and had seen the potential benefits. He had spent a further five years with the aforementioned laboratory technician, honing and improving the compound. Up until that point, no resources had been committed to it and it was only really available in tablet form. Tragically, the lab technician who worked on the project was killed in the Pentagon car park, the night the protocol was first presented to me.'

'Did you think they were connected?' asked Ray.

'At the time, no,' answered the director. 'This is the biggest low rise office block in the world. There are almost twenty nine thousand people working here. It's not unusual, unfortunately, in a population of that size, to lose people to accidents and murder.'

'But you think they're connected now?' stated Dodds.

'I think they're connected now,' echoed the director. 'I have no doubt in fact. Especially after all that has happened over the last few weeks. Anyway, back to the story.'

He poured himself a glass of water.

'With the establishment of the officially sanctioned project, came the development and refinement of the protocol. Thanks to that investment, we've now been able to synthesise the substance in both liquid and gaseous form. So we now have our nirvana. We have a biological weapon that enables us to disarm enemies and opponents in a safe and bloodless fashion. No collateral damage; the ultimate scenario.'

Ray raised his eyebrows and made an *hmmm* sound.

'You don't approve,' said the director sharply.

'Not my place to approve or disapprove,' said Ray. 'It just seems that as a country, and specifically as federal law enforcement bodies, we keep on making the same mistakes.'

The director ignored the subtle rebuke.

'Which leads me neatly on to the other seemingly unconnected piece of information,' he said, clearing his throat and then draining the rest of his water. 'The early days of the war in Iraq and the fight against terror in Afghanistan were different from the first Gulf War.'

The change of subject made both Ray and Dodds blink.

'Yes, they were still fought under the same conditions, under the same glare of the media spotlight, but no matter how our armed forces tried to spin it, the opposition in Iraq and Afghanistan were tougher and more resilient, and the allied forces were sustaining casualties.'

'As a nation, we didn't hear that, certainly not initially,' said Dodds. 'Some of the reporting is starting to get more critical, but still pretty low key.'

'The actual fatalities are fairly low for such an aggressive and sustained campaign,' agreed the director. 'The hidden issue is with the injuries. Our troops are returning with missing arms, missing legs. Thousands and thousands are coming back; literally tens of thousands of amputees. In a way, it is more shocking and brutal than the fatalities, especially for the amputees themselves, and their families of course. It is the hidden story of this campaign, gentlemen.'

He tapped himself on the chest vigorously.

'So, we talked to the armed forces.'

'We meaning the CIA?' asked Dodds.

The director nodded.

'We started doing some statistical analysis. We took a look at every fatality and every injury. Where did they happen? How did they happen? Why did they happen? At the end of that analysis, we reached a disturbing conclusion. A disproportionately large number of our troops had been killed or maimed while trying to clear heavily fortified, static enemy positions.'

'So what's this got to do with Storm?' asked Dodds.

'All will become clear,' said the director. 'Bear with me for a couple more minutes.'

'That's good,' said Dodds, 'because I'm not seeing the connection yet.'

Ray glanced across and shot him a look of warning. Dodds shrugged. The director seemed oblivious to both actions.

'Does anyone remember *MASH*?' asked the director suddenly.

'The Korean war comedy,' said Dodds. 'That was a great show. Still holds the record for audience figures I think?'

The director nodded.

'One of the strangest things to flourish in wartime is the advancement of medical techniques and technology,' he continued. 'Yes, MASH was a comedy, but the reality was Korea, Vietnam, Iraq, Afghanistan, all those conflicts have seen huge advances in the appliance of medicine. Army doctors and medics have pushed the envelope further than most, mainly because they have to.'

He paused to further assemble his thoughts.

'Do you remember a film called *Jacob's ladder*?' he asked.

'The one with Tim Robbins,' answered Ray. 'He was a Vietnam veteran I think, suffering all sorts of hallucinations.'

'That's the one,' said the director. 'So would it surprise you to know that war is also a fertile breeding ground for drug research?'

Both Dodds and Ray went to speak at once, but the director held up his hand.

'Just hear me out for a second,' he said, 'then you can comment.'

They both sat back reluctantly, if not actually relaxing.

'In the last three months, the prorated percentage of fatalities and serious injuries, including amputation, has been reduced by forty eight percent.'

'That's only because we are pulling all the troops out,' protested Dodds.

The director shook his head.

'No, I'm talking about prorated. These figures are worked out based on the number of fatalities and injuries as a percentage of the troops deployed at that particular time.'

'Less dangerous missions?' ventured Ray.

'Far from it,' said the director. 'With fewer troops on the ground, it is possibly more dangerous now than it ever was.'

'So this has something to do with Storm,' said Dodds.

'This has everything to do with Storm,' responded the director. 'Forget everything I've already told you about this drug. Yes, it's almost instantly addictive, it does create almost one hundred percent compliance with any subject that takes it, and it does introduce almost unimaginable highs, but there is another far more sinister side effect that you won't find in any of the protocol folders apart from mine. It is the reason, in fact, why you had to sign a new nondisclosure agreement.'

'Now you're starting to scare me a little,' said Ray.

'You have every right to be scared,' said the director. 'When this drug breaches a specific concentration level in the body, the taker loses all self control. The drug itself and the acquisition of more becomes the only focus. Subjects who have entered this state will do anything, and I mean anything. The effects are not reversible and pretty much fatal.'

'So it kills you?' asked Dodds.

'Not the drug itself,' said the director. 'But the things you will do under its control. Let me be very clear. When I say you lose self control, you literally become a machine; one which has only one purpose. Pain and suffering do not exist.'

'And you know all this because you've been testing it,' stated Ray dispassionately.

'We knew about this unique side-effect before,' said the director. 'Why do you think we developed it? Ostensibly, Storm was created as a weapon to control minds. If we could do this, we could prevent bloodshed and protect our troops and soldiers in combat situations. That was its original purpose. But we took it a stage further. We've developed it as a weapon of destruction. We've honed it into a gas; colourless, odourless and tasteless. Our troops on the ground have been firing smoke canisters into enemy compounds, outwardly to provide cover for our attacks, but the smoke canisters contain concentrated levels of Storm. Once the canisters are in you sit back and wait.'

'Why wait?' asked Dodds.

'Depending on body type, height, size, mass, the effects kick in around the seven hour mark. Our troops sit back until all of the gunfire and bloodcurdling screams have died down, then they carefully enter the compound. After a dose of Storm, normally all they need to clean up an enemy compound is a hose for all the blood and entrails.'

'So why not just stick to the original usage? Why not stick to the bloodless scenario?' asked Ray. 'It makes a lot more sense to me.'

'Because the effects wear off very quickly, and we are then left with large groups of potentially dangerous opponents, which we have to feed, clothe, house and guard.'

'So this is all about economics?' said Ray incredulously.

'Isn't it always,' said the director. 'It also saves us a fortune in munitions, as they end up slaughtering each other. We only need to retain our guns for personal protection.'

Everyone collectively shivered, even the director.

'So, this makes killers out of people?' asked Dodds.

'As I said earlier, it removes all self-control and all inhibitions. Once you've taken this in sufficient quantities, you're no longer human. You become a creature with the twin aims of eliminating your opposition, your competition if you will, and acquiring more of the drug.'

'So to use your movie theme, it would be *night of the living dead?*' stated Ray.

He wasn't smiling and neither was the director.

'A very good analogy, Agent Fox,' he said. 'But I would go further. If this drug gets into widespread circulation, there will be hundreds, thousands, maybe tens of thousands of deaths. These creatures will kill anything they regard as competition, and they absolutely positively will not stop until they get what they want. In fact, imagine a zombie and the terminator combined.'

Dodds shook his head.

'This is too fantastical,' he said. 'Things like this only happen in the movies. A drug that creates zombies! Pull the other one.'

'Unfortunately Agent Dodds,' said the director. 'Not only is it true, but it leaves us with a unique problem, one I believe that one of your agents can help us with.'

'You're talking about Dale now right?' said Ray.

'Agent Foster, yes,' replied the director. 'I know he's over there without jurisdiction, but you seem positive you can trust him. We need to make sure that whatever he does, he gets those files back. I have an agent there at the moment,' said the director, 'but I'm going to need Agent Fosters help.'

'Why do you need Dale's help, if you have an agent over there?' asked Ray.

'The scale of the operation we are trying to break down is very large,' said the director. 'Not only does Agent Foster have invaluable domain knowledge in the area of narcotics, but I have it on good authority that he has hooked up with a team who seem more than capable of looking after themselves.'

Dodds and Ray looked at each other in surprise.

'Gentlemen,' said the director, not allowing them any pause for further thought. 'At the end of the day we need his help. If this stuff gets out onto the open market, God help us all.'

CHAPTER 47 – CONSPIRACY

10th April 2011 – One month before the Storm.

A conspiracy is nothing but a secret agreement of a number of men for the pursuance of policies which they dare not admit in public. – Mark Twain.

As a child he had always loved order. They say that you rebel against the background you were brought up in, but he'd been the opposite. His parents had been very traditional. His house had been orderly and logical and he'd relished it. It had not been a warm happy house, but it hadn't been cold and unhappy either. Somewhere in between would have been fair; they were an average family.

He supposed his love of the alphabet stemmed from this upbringing. The letters represented order; grammar gave him a defined set of rules within which he could work and never deviate. He excelled in English at school and it came as no surprise to anyone when he enrolled at Sandhurst Officer College. His father had been a career soldier, and the army represented everything he loved; a set of regulations outside of which he could not step and wouldn't want to anyway. He was the opposite of spontaneous. His friends would have described him as solid and dependable, but a bit boring too; Major Ian Reid, the perfect officer.

He quickly rose through the ranks, and it was with a sense of pride that he became the head of media relations for his regiment. He dealt with all aspects of communication, but his favourite was always the written word. He would delegate the others; retaining veto on all of the DVD's, websites and TV news segments, but always reserving the written parts for himself. There was no one in the team who could write speeches and condolence letters better than him.

He never meant any of it of course. Words for him were tools to fix any situation; a means to an end. A soldier standing on a landmine was messy and unfortunate. Major Reid could use words to clear up the mess, to make everything sensible and ordered and clean again.

He signed the letter he was working on with a flourish, and placed it into the labelled envelope. She had looked so sad at the funeral, the mother. Her son had been the sole victim of an attack on a Taliban fortified position, but when the colonel had got up and delivered the eulogy, she had seemed soothed and comforted by it. From where he was sitting, Major Reid could have sworn it gave her a sense of hope. He was proud of his work, and even though he didn't normally do so, he decided this time to mail her a copy. Hopefully, she could revisit it and gain additional comfort from it.

He dropped it into the out tray and headed off to the mess for dinner.

He never gave it a second thought.

#

Roughly a week later, he watched the barman switch to another channel and felt the slight impact as his colleagues all slapped him on the back and congratulated him.

'You looked good sir,' said Robinson. 'No offence, but you are the best we've got at speaking at length, but yet saying absolutely nothing at the same time.'

'None taken,' he replied. 'It is a special skill. With words you can spin anything. Maybe I should go into politics?'

'The army's loss if you do,' said Campbell. 'You'll have another pint before you go?'

'No, early night for me I'm afraid,' he responded. 'There was another ambush last night apparently; two casualties and one fatality. Have to get something written for the CO before they arrive back at base.'

He threw a fifty onto the bar to ensure a good time would be had by all except him.

'Well done guys,' he said, before making his excuses.

He nodded to the MP's on the way back to his small maisonette. Another perk of army life; you didn't have to look for accommodation. It was small and basic but that's all he'd ever needed.

He went to unlock the door, and realised he'd left it unlocked; good job there was plenty of security. He locked it behind him and switched on the hall table light and the first thing he noticed was a shapely pair of legs extending from one of his leather wingbacks in the sitting room. He walked in and confronted the intruder; an elegant looking woman in her late forties.

'Did you write this crap?'

She was waving a piece of paper at him. It was both a question and an accusation rolled into one.

He ignored her.

'How did you get in here?' he asked, with all the authority he could muster, already knowing the answer.

'The front door was open,' she said stiffly.

'You'll have to leave, I can't talk to a civilian about army matters,' he said sternly, taking a step toward her.

The bang made them both jump. He felt the bullet impact into the wall to his right; saw the plaster disintegrate and the small whiff of smoke from the old service revolver she was holding.

'That should bring them running,' she said with satisfaction.

She gestured to him that he should sit in the other chair; the one opposite her.

'Sean gave me this; insisted I keep it under my pillow. *Shoot them in the guts, Mum* he told me. It's the biggest target apparently.'

She paused for a couple of seconds.

'But you have no idea who I'm talking about, do you?'

He ignored the question.

'The MP's will be here in a matter of minutes,' he stated.

'Let them come,' she answered.

'What do you want?' he asked.

'I want to know who wrote this garbage?' she said, throwing an envelope at him. 'When I asked at the gate they said you were the *media* liaison. They even gave me directions to your house. Very helpful they were. I obviously don't look dangerous.'

He glanced at the envelope and recognised the backward sloping capital letters immediately.

'I did,' he said haughtily.

'Sergeant Kelly was like a brother to his unit; bonds of brotherhood that even in death could not be broken.' she said, quoting directly from the letter.

She looked up, and this time there were tears in her eyes.

'He didn't like being a sergeant,' she continued. 'He disliked the petty jealousies; found it hard being in charge. He couldn't get used to the sniping at him and name calling behind his back. But you were right in one thing, Major.'

She accentuated the word *major* slowly and a little sadly.

'He would have done anything for those guys; he would probably have put them ahead of me, in fact.'

'That's the army, Ma'am,' he said. 'That kind of camaraderie is hard to fathom or break unless you've lived it.'

She laughed without humour.

'He was an only child, you see; an accident. I told him that once; that he was an accident. I was really pissed off with him and wanted to hurt him. I think I managed it.'

She paused again.

'But being an only child of course, he had no brothers and sisters. The army gave him an instant family; he craved their approval. I think they secretly laughed at him a little behind his back. They thought he was a little weird; a little too needy for an NCO, but he was winning them over, or so he thought.'

'Why are you telling me this?' he asked uncomfortably.

She waved the letter at him.

'Because this boy died perfectly,' she said. 'This boy is ascending straight to the angels. But my boy wasn't an angel. He was raw and flawed and honest, and because of that he wrote me a lot of letters. They were full of rage and pain and terror and love, but never perfection.'

She indicated the letter again.

'I don't recognise the person on this page; it sure as hell is not my son.'

'I was only saying what I thought you would want to hear,' he said defensively.

'But you didn't know him; how could you? You didn't even know what his name was, how could you know what he was like?'

She stopped and the tears came afresh, but the revolver was unwavering.

'I pushed him into the army,' she continued. 'I couldn't stand having him at home. He was getting bigger and stronger and harder to manage. He did not do well at school; he was always more physical than cerebral. He was getting into rages, mostly directed against me.'

She saw his face and corrected herself slightly.

'He was never directly violent towards me you understand, but would smash chairs and throw plates. He hated the fact that he had no father and he blamed me for it. In truth, I didn't know who his father was, but he never believed me.'

'I don't see what this has to do with me?' Major Reid asked, genuinely puzzled.

'I'll tell you what it has to do with you,' she said. 'I was doing okay or so I thought. The funeral was hell; I hate all that pompous bullshit and so did Sean, but you have to put up and shut up for Queen and country. The speech was particularly irksome; that arsehole of a CO hadn't a clue who he was talking about, but I got through it, and got a flag for my trouble.'

She looked up at him then, her eyes narrowing through the tears.

'And then you send me this same bullshit all over again. All you have given me with this crap is empty platitudes; what am I supposed to do with those?'

'It's a bit of a deviation from protocol,' he said stiffly. 'But I thought you might appreciate it as a token to remember him by.'

She laughed humourlessly.

'And there lies the problem I'm afraid. With all your fancy words, you can't give me what I want.'

'What the fuck do you want from me?' he asked sharply, before he could stop himself.

He was getting genuinely frustrated.

'Now we're getting somewhere,' she said. 'A bit of feeling; a little bit of emotion bubbling to the surface.'

'I don't make the rules,' he said defensively.

'No, but you carry them out with ruthless efficiency, I bet,' she said. 'At the end of the day Major, not a single person has been able to tell me what I want to know.'

'Ok I'll bite,' he responded stiffly. 'What do you want to know?'

'Well for a start, how did he really die would be nice. Taliban fortified position does nothing for me as a mother. Was he alone? Did he die immediately? Was he frightened? Was it instant? Did he suffer? You see, his letters to me outlined a disturbing portrait. He talked of creating monsters and watching them rip each other to shreds as squads of soldiers watched and cheered. He talked of wholesale slaughter; rivers of blood running through the towns and villages. He talked of special suits and masks. And pointedly, his last letter to me told of a malfunction with some equipment, and how he would have to lend his own to one of his men. He was too petrified to bring it to the attention of his commanding officer, but also terrified of the consequences of not wearing the proper equipment.'

Major Reid shook his head.

'I can't answer any of those questions,' he said.

'Can't or won't,' she retorted sharply.

'I just don't know the circumstances in this case,' he said apologetically. 'I just can't remember it. I get so many of these to comment on, that I just put in the normal phrases that I think people will want to hear.'

'Thank you Major,' she replied, getting genuinely emotional. 'At last I have a true statement from the army.'

She took a moment to compose herself.

'The problem with you people is that boys like Sean are commodities; the same way as tanks and planes are. If you lose one, you replace it with another, but let me tell you; he was not a commodity. He was a lonely frightened boy, whose last days on earth seem to have been lived in a perpetual state of terror.'

She looked at him again, her face twisted into a mask of sadness.

'Do you know the worst thing about it Major; the thing that has tortured me more than anything over the last month? My last words to my son were said in anger. I never got a chance to take them back.'

The front door splintered inward, and they both jumped a second time. Before they had a chance to register what was happening, three marines had leapt into the room; Major Reid could see the infra red laser sights from their rifles illuminating key parts of her body.

'I'll sort this out,' he said gently to her. 'And if it's any consolation, I really am very sorry.'

He made to turn to the Marines.

'I'm sorry too, Major,' she said softly. 'Do you know what? I used to think I couldn't live with him; that I would have been better off if he hadn't been born. It's taken this to realize that I can't live without him.'

With that she raised the weapon towards him.

'Goodbye Major,' she said. 'Please find out what happened to my baby. Let at least one of us rest in peace?'

She pulled the trigger once again and the brutality of the bang made him wince, until he realised the shot had whistled harmlessly wide.

'Gun!' shouted one of the marines.

'No!' shouted Major Reid, as he heard three further shots ring out.

He felt a fine spray on his face; he could taste the iron and salt from the blood.

#

It was exactly one month since the shooting. It had been an up and down journey; in a way he felt totally to blame. It was his careless words that had triggered the series of events of that evening; events that ultimately led to someone's death. Nothing that anyone had said to him since could change that.

But with acknowledgement of accountability comes freedom to change. Nobody had been prepared to discuss Sergeant Kelly's death. The more he dug, the more he found inconsistencies and untruths. He was determined to get to the bottom of what had happened on that fateful day on a lonely and isolated Afghan hillside.

He still loved writing, but he tempered the power of the pen with a wiser head. He had realized that in his position he had a responsibility; a duty to fulfil to both his living and fallen comrades. Today was a case in point. He shaded his eyes and scanned the topmost sections of the stark Sandstone monument. He could just make out the freshly etched letters after the name – Sergeant Sean Kelly MC; Military Cross. It was the least he could do, maybe driven more by guilt than anything else, but a start nonetheless on his road to re-humanization.

He thought Sergeant Kelly's mother would approve; he hoped so anyway. He was making real progress at last; he had persuaded someone to talk to him off the record. Something was emerging about a shadow operation that was being run out of the US 101st Airborne Division based in Iraq, but carried out by British troops from One Rifles in Helmand province.

He saw a glint of metal from a hillock on the far side of the monument; odd. As he shaded his eyes to catch a better glimpse, a third one appeared in the centre of his forehead. He teetered backwards and fell with a thud, dead before the sound of his fall echoed off the bleak sandstone walls.

CHAPTER 48 – EXPOSURE

22nd May 2011 – Twelve days after the Storm.

Constant exposure to dangers will breed contempt for them. – Lucius Annaeus Seneca.

He held a photograph in one hand and a mirror in the other. He was working himself up to the moment; the unveiling of the enemy. His initial glance at the surveillance intelligence they'd received had burned into his retinas, like the feeling you getting looking directly at the sun. He hadn't been able to pluck up the courage to have a second look, so he'd handed the envelope full of photographs back to Dave to enable him to brief the intercept teams.

When he'd come home from work that same evening, he'd found the bundle sitting on his desk like an unwelcome guest, silently highlighting and accentuating his cowardice.

As he'd busied himself in the kitchen, preparing his evening meal, he'd felt its malevolent presence, calling to him and repulsing him in equal measure. Now, here he was, stuck in a quandary, unable to take his eyes off the mirror.

It had been a stupid idea; comparison.

What was he trying to prove?

He studied his own reflection dispassionately. He wore his black hair long, swept proudly back from his high forehead. There was no parting, and a lot of hair cream was required to sculpt it into position. His face was tanned and surprisingly unlined for someone with as chequered and stressful a career choice. His lips were full, with an almost perfect cupids bow shape, and his chin was strong and resolute; a face with hidden depths, a face with character.

He quickly flicked his eyes from the mirror to the photograph and back. He saw nothing except a blur of grey. He would just have to suck it up.

Eventually, he just flicked his eyes across to the photo and anchored them there. Once he'd focused on the image, as he'd known would happen, he found it impossible to tear his eyes away from it.

He noticed with grim fascination the tight, buzz-cut armed forces hairstyle, in stark contrast to his own luxuriant mane. The image had pale smooth skin with no wrinkles or worry lines, but the lips were full, with the same distinctive shape, and his eyes were identical. Not in colour, as Eoin's were grey and the image had eyes of a piercing blue, but they both burned with the same intensity of purpose.

It wasn't any of the physical characteristics that surprised Eoin, though. The photograph he was looking at on the surface was essentially of a fit looking man in his mid forties, nothing more. No, the thing that surprised Eoin, shocked him even, was the overall feeling he got when he studied the photograph. There was an all pervading sense of purpose about the person, a supreme self confidence. They were comfortable in their own skin, but also exuded an aura that they were an individual not to be trifled with.

He could almost smell a whiff of aggression, a tincture of menace. The face was different, but he saw that self same attitude every day. It faced him in the mirror when he shaved.

'Hello Brother.'

He startled himself when he realised he'd said the words aloud; trying them on for size.

Half of the reason why he hadn't wanted to look at the photographs was because he hadn't wanted any visual memories. He just wanted to wipe that part of his life clean. But having now seen his brother in the flesh so to speak, he was surprised and a little pleased to note that putting an identity to his hate had not changed the underlying emotion. He really was as heartless and ruthless as he believed. In a strange way he felt vindicated. He looked back to the mirror again and a serene smile pushed up the corners of his mouth.

He put down the mirror and flicked a switch on the side of his desk, plunging the room into darkness. He still had the imprint of the image burned into his memory, and he drank it in, relishing the final moments of his three long decades of torment.

After years of resentment and bitterness, he could finally release his father from the mental chains he'd been consigned to for the last thirty years. His family would be re-habilitated; the happy memories would be dredged from the depths and remanufactured to plaster over the void.

He reached across the desk, his hand falling straight to the object he was looking for. He caressed it for a few moments, marvelling at the sleekness of the design and the cool smoothness of the marble, wonderfully at odds with its primary purpose.

He spun the wheel quickly with his thumb. He could see the miniature sparks as they jumped toward the flammable liquid, impatient for conflagration. And then, the delicious moment when spark and liquid combined, the whoosh as ignition became fire.

Like all his lighters, it was set for the largest flame, and it danced and flickered like a beacon in the darkness. His breathing made it shudder rhythmically, in tune with the rise and fall of his chest.

Eoin studied the photograph in the flickering artificial twilight. Exposure: the amount of light that was allowed to fall on a photographic image. It was how the picture had been created, the process by which it had come into being and had then, as a finished product, found its way into his possession.

But it had also exposed his feelings, given him the emotional tools he needed to cast off the legacy of the past and move into the unknown territory of a future, potentially without rage or hate.

The thought filled him with uncertainty. Was that a good thing? He didn't know, maybe he needed a new focus point; only time would tell. But for the here and now it was definitely what he needed; to reclaim the past and to reclaim his family.

He moved the picture close to the flickering glow. He turned it onto one side, so that the corner was pointing down at an angle, and moved it toward the tip of the flame where the heat was starting to dissipate; the point where the orange of fire became the white of smoke.

He could see that self same smoke starting to blacken and obscure the image, and then, all of a sudden, the fire took hold of the picture. Large areas of the paper started to tear open and crackle. There was a pungent whiff in the air, as the chemicals were released from their slumber, reacting with the heat and flame.

He dropped the burning pile into the large crystal ashtray on his desk, the circular one. As he watched, the picture warped and constricted until the paper had been converted into nothing more than a pile of smouldering ash.

'Goodbye, Brother,' he said softly, before extinguishing the lighter and switching the lights back on.

He blinked at the sudden intense assault on his eyes. He waited until the white spots dissipated.

He went to pull the ashtray forward. It bogged down on the leather and then jerked toward him, leaving a trail of ash in its wake across the blotter. He smiled; his cleaner was always complaining that she had nothing to do, so at least she could earn a little bit of her money this week.

He pulled the waste paper basket out from under his feet, and tipped the contents of the ashtray into it in one clean fluid motion. Finally, after thirty years, he could say goodbye to the past and say hello to the future.

His fingers trembled with excitement as he fumbled the keys out of his pocket, dropping them with a clatter on the floor in his haste to extract them. He stooped awkwardly while he picked them up. He flicked through the keys until he came to the one he wanted; cut specifically for a single purpose all those years ago.

To his right hand side, above the three drawers, was a thin strip of wood veneer with a keyhole set into it. It looked too thin to be a drawer and people confused it with the blanking plate for the locking mechanism, which had been the original intention.

He turned the key a full-turn and then a quarter more. Using the body of the key, he pulled out the hidden drawer until it protruded about an inch and a half.

He removed the key and placed it back on his desk. He'd been waiting for this moment for so long, he wanted to savour it for a while. He closed his eyes for what seemed like an eternity, and then opened them again as he realised it looked like he was praying.

In a sense he was.

He reached down to pull open the drawer, noticing with a detached disinterest that his hand was shaking almost uncontrollably. It slid soundlessly out, revealing a sea of green baize. Fixed to the front of the baize was a black leather tab. He used this to lift the lid, which exposed the hidden compartment underneath. Nestling within this padded environment was a picture frame.

This was no ordinary frame, however. The rear had been manufactured from the finest bog oak. Fastened to this had been a skin of pure platinum, so thick in places that the jeweller had jokingly recommended that he double his house contents insurance.

He lifted it reverently and turned it over slowly in his hands, careful not to cause smudge or burnish marks. The compartment had done its job. It was as clean and dust free as the day it had been interred all those years ago.

He turned it over, pulled out the awkward looking leg on which it stood, and set it down in the middle of the blotter. There was a blank area of his desk that had always looked slightly incongruous. He slid the picture back into this opening, making sure to centre it and line it up perfectly.

Mother, father, son; an excursion to Cobh one summers evening. The sun was shining, all of them were smiling and he was in the middle, at the centre of the family where he had always belonged.

Home at last.

He didn't know how long he stared at the picture, but the next thing he remembered was the whir of the lift motor outside. Dave was back. Eoin waited in silence, purging his mind of distracting personal emotions; now it was time to focus.

There was a discreet knock on the door. Black Swan didn't answer; he rarely did, and after a polite interval the door swung open and Dave walked in. He was grim faced but Eoin smiled inwardly. Dave was always grim faced, even if he was happy.

'So, what did you find out for me?' asked Eoin.

'Well, number one,' said Dave, 'it's definitely McCabe and Collins. I heard through one contact that David has moved to Clonakilty permanently.'

'Into the holiday home?' asked Eoin.

'So it would seem,' said Dave. 'They are in the IDA technology campus; about five minutes drive from McCabe's place. The manufacturing facility they have acquired down there is pretty large. I managed to get some surveillance footage from the same contact.'

He threw another brown envelope onto the desk in front of Eoin, who smiled wryly at the irony of the action. He slipped the photographs out and studied them one by one. It was a typical IDA industrial unit, stoutly built with steel cladding and a flat steel roof. Adaptable to a number of uses, and yes, given the perspective in the picture, it was very big indeed.

'You've got to admit, it is pretty brilliant,' said Dave.

'What is?' asked Eoin.

'Well, think about it,' answered Dave. 'Just look at how big Pablo Escobar got in Colombia. That was no accident. The reason he managed to grow so big, so fast, was that he was ruthless, plain and simple. He controlled pretty much all the supply. If you control it all, the rewards are enormous.'

'To be honest, even though it is McCabe, I have to grudgingly admit it is a masterstroke,' said Eoin. 'Especially when you think we are coming into a recession. Any hint of an investment, any hint of job creation is going to be welcomed with open arms. Liquidity checks, financial checks, background checks, they are all going to be that little bit less stringent and thorough than they were before.'

Dave laughed.

'Not only that,' he said, still chuckling, 'but they will probably get financial assistance from the state too.'

'So, how do I stop them?' asked Eoin. 'I don't particularly care about his partners; McCabe is the one I want. I don't care what it takes, but David is not getting a red cent out of this venture, if it kills both him and me in the process.'

'It may well do that,' replied Dave dryly. 'We've got two avenues we can go down, as far as I can see. The first is the legal route; take all the information we have and give it to Ryan and his boys in the drug squad; anonymously of course.'

Eoin shook his head.

'Apart from the fact that I probably need to be further away from those guys than McCabe does, they'd just fuck it up. What's the other alternative?'

'Well, I've already got the place staked out,' said Dave. 'So we watch and we wait and we see what happens. To be honest, I think it's a great opportunity. At some stage, pretty much all of McCabe's organisation is going to be in that one building. If we can assemble a large enough force, I think we can do some serious damage.'

'So what are we waiting for? Get a team together.'

Eoin paused, as though the words he'd spoken had jogged something deep inside his memory.

'Which reminds me,' he said. 'Where is he?'

He looked pointedly at Dave. He noticed the downward glance and the shuffling of feet and the slight reddening of the complexion.

'Yeah, about that....' said Dave.

The long agonised scream of anguish could be heard over a mile away, as the photograph was turned face down onto the desk.

CHAPTER 49 – EXPECTATION

22nd May 2011 – Twelve days after the Storm.

Life is so constructed, that the event does not, cannot, will not, match the expectation. –
Charlotte Bronte.

When Tony dropped him off, he was looking forward to relaxing in his favourite chair, the one that looked out over the sea. He would shake off his shoes and catch up on the evening paper, maybe even have a beer or two. But as his key turned in the lock and the door swung open, he encountered something in his house that he hadn't experienced in a very long time; cooking smells.

He dropped his laptop and the paper beside his favourite spot on the sofa and followed the trail. It took him through the double doors and into the dining room where he noted with interest the table set for two, the lit candles flickering in his back draft as he continued on his way.

David carried on through the dining room, and as he neared the kitchen, he heard a soft singing. He stopped in the doorway, realising that she hadn't noticed he was there. He leant against the door jamb and studied her with interest.

He had been so preoccupied over the last two days that he had barely noticed her presence, despite the empty boasts to Ben that very same morning.

Her white blonde hair was tied back in a simple ponytail. She wore no trace of make-up; no trace of the war paint, the disguise she required to do what she did. She was wearing a pair of figure hugging jeans and an oversized shirt; David recognised it as one of his own, a Ralph Lauren that was well past its best. He noted how much better it looked on her, surprised that he'd noticed at all. She wore no shoes or socks and he was struck by how shapely and exquisite her feet were, compared to his size eleven boats.

She continued to work in that completely unselfconscious way that people do when they think they're alone. She was so relaxed and so peaceful that he felt strangely dirty; like a voyeur.

He coughed loudly and involuntarily, startling both of them. She turned to fix him with a direct and unwavering stare. All he could hear was the sizzling of the stir fry and the hammering of his own heart as it beat fiercely inside his rib cage. He couldn't look at her and he felt her eyes probing the space between them, desperately trying to make eye contact until he relented and their fields of vision combined and locked.

She held his gaze gently, almost caressing it with hers. He felt the emotion welling up and had to choke it back. He could feel his guard dropping and he couldn't afford to let it slip.

Or could he?

He had to play a part for so much of the time, to act in the way that people expected of him, that he found it very difficult to relax. But he met her challenge head on, and in his own kitchen, he found David McCabe, the lonely orphan boy, seeping slowly back, eliminating the Bullock minute by minute.

'I didn't know what was....expected,' she finished awkwardly, pointing at the dinner and then gesturing toward the dining room.

'I'm sorry?' asked David.

He hadn't really been listening.

'Being brought to this house,' she replied. 'I didn't know what was expected of me.'

David tried on his loud manly laugh and it was then he realised how patronising and chauvinistic it sounded.

'You don't have to do the cooking,' he said. 'We have staff to bring us food.'

He watched her face collapse slightly. He was not used to saying and doing the right thing.

'Unless of course you want to,' he finished hurriedly, tailing off.

'It smells delicious,' he added hopefully.

'Are you hungry then?' she asked.

He smiled and then started laughing, he didn't know why; maybe a release of tension. She joined in and he was astonished to realise that her laugh was genuine.

'Do you know what?' he said, relaxing with every second. 'I'm bloody starving.'

He busied himself in the kitchen, finding with embarrassment that he knew where very little of his own belongings actually were. By the time she had boiled and decanted the noodles onto two plates, he had only just managed to find the condiments and napkins. He put out two Italian beers, popping the tops with a hiss of exploding gas. He placed two glasses of water at each setting and a large wooden chopping board for the wok.

He sat down at the far side and watched as she dropped the pan onto the makeshift mat, the contents still spitting and sizzling wildly. She proceeded to start serving and he saw with some amusement the portion size she gave herself. She looked at him and noted his eyebrow curling upward questioningly.

'I don't always eat this well,' she answered simply.

There was nothing he could say to that.

'Also, it's a pleasure to cook with such simple and wholesome ingredients,' she added.

He blinked; he wasn't used to a woman being so forthright and straightforward. Who was he kidding; he wasn't used to a woman full stop.

'Excuse me,' she said, as he helped himself.

She was back in a couple of seconds. She offered him the packet; chopsticks, another thing he didn't realise he had.

'No thanks,' he replied, shaking his head.

There was a sudden crack as she broke the implements apart, and then she tucked in with gusto, noticing his eyebrow rising again as she did so.

'Backpacked around Asia after I got my degree,' she said. 'Now I can't eat Asian food any other way.'

He stopped chewing.

'Don't be too surprised,' she said, 'there's more of us than you think. We're not all uneducated crack addicts.'

He pondered the word *us* before taking the plunge.

'So how did....'

'....so how did a nice girl like me end up in a place like this?' she completed, smiling.

He looked down in embarrassment; he didn't know why.

'Like a lot of people do, I expect,' she said. 'I needed the money.'

He looked at her then with an unbroken stare, feeling the first faint stirrings of pity. She mistook his pity for distaste and felt an unreasonable need to justify herself.

'I'm not a streetwalker.'

She paused.

'Not that those poor girls have anything to be ashamed of,' she followed up quickly. 'I was just in a better and luckier position financially when I started.'

'So a high-class hooker,' said David, wincing as she looked up sharply.

'Escort?' he ventured.

She nodded.

'Better,' she said, smiling at his discomfort. 'Not so sure about the *high-class* bit, but initially I started doing escort work, accompanying wealthy businessmen to functions and balls. If they wanted to take it further, then it was an optional extra that could be negotiated. I built up a very good and very loyal clientele. It got to the stage where I only needed to work one day a week, maybe two days max. And then, I got lazy and complacent and I was raped.'

David's head jerked back up in surprise.

'Oh it happens all right,' she continued, chewing thoughtfully. 'Even though I was an escort, everything I did with my dates was consensual. They fully understood that. I was in charge.'

She must have mistaken his expression for judgement because her face hardened.

'I make no apologies for what I do,' she said, fixing David with a firm and direct stare. 'This particular client wanted me to do something that I just didn't want to do, so he decided to force me. As far as he was concerned, he was paying for sex and he was going to take it how he wanted it. My feelings didn't come into it at all for him.'

'What did you do after that?' asked David, his voice barely above a whisper.

'From that day on, I swore I would never be put in that position again.'

'What's your name?' David asked.

She seemed flustered by the sudden change in tack.

'Sam,' she answered.

'Well, Sam,' said David, and he could feel the intense and suppressed rage in his voice. 'You have my word. I guarantee that you will never be put in that position again, and if anything happens to you, I will hunt them down and kill them myself.'

She smiled at the almost juvenile earnestness of his statement, and then noticed the look in his eye.

'You're serious aren't you?' she said.

He nodded and she noticed a single tear tracking down his cheek.

'You're not the arsehole they said you were,' she said.

'You must have me on a good day,' he answered, blinking another tear away and wiping his face on the napkin. 'So, what did you expect?'

'Not you anyway,' she said, a little playfully.

'Should I take that as a compliment?' asked David.

'It was meant as one,' she said.

'So, is that how you came to work for us?' asked David.

'I approached one of your guys,' she said. 'I crossed his palm with silver, and he made sure the ex client who raped me had an extra long stay in hospital. I especially wanted him to know that the beating had come courtesy of me.'

David smiled; he really liked her.

'We worked out a system then, him and me. He organises a guy to run security for all my liaisons. That person stops the tricks on the way in and makes it very clear what will happen to them if they try something that I don't like. He then stops them again on the way out and calls me to make sure they didn't. I give your organisation a percentage of my take; larger than I'd like to, but it keeps me safe and that's my priority.'

'Ben organised that for you,' said David.

It was a statement not a question.

'Normally the girls have no choice whether they come here, according to Ben. He gave me the option, and I have to say I was curious.'

'So, what do they say about me?' asked David interestedly.

'You really want to know?' Sam asked.

David swallowed hard and nodded.

'I'm paraphrasing here,' she said, 'but unfeeling, unthinking wanker with a God complex. Will do anything for money and doesn't care about any other living thing.'

'Don't sugar-coat it then, I can take it,' said David wryly.

'You asked,' she said defensively.

He smiled disarmingly.

He was a strange one, she thought. Not your typical gangster.

'So what's your story?' she asked. 'How did you become such a cold hearted bastard?'

'Be careful,' David warned, half heartedly.

'I'm a good judge of character,' she said. 'You won't hurt me.'

David inclined his head.

'Touché,' he said. 'But in answer to your question, I don't really think I have a story.'

She smiled.

'Everyone has a story.'

He thought about it for a few minutes, looking for a place to start.

'I loved my dad,' he stated simply. 'He owned a very successful suite of bookmakers and gambling businesses. Turned out he was also one of the most successful drug dealers in the country.'

'And how did that make you feel when you found out?'

'To be honest, I'd always kind of suspected there was some illegality there. We were pretty rich; not the kind of rich you get as a standard taxpayer. I think John was more shocked than me initially, put it that way.'

'John?' she asked.

'My twin brother,' he said. 'He died in a violent altercation just after Dad passed away. The problem with John was he had a temper and an ego to match, a lethal combination, especially in your late teens.'

He stopped, aghast at himself. He had never spoken about John to anyone in such disparaging terms before.

'What about your mother?' asked Sam.

'She died when I was very young,' said David. 'My dad brought me up.'

'It shows,' she said simply.

There was nothing he could think of to say in response.

'Is that why you hate me?' he asked eventually.

'I don't hate you,' she said softly. 'I don't even dislike you. I'm a realist, David.'

She used his name for the first time. He liked it.

'If you didn't do what you do, somebody else would. It's a dog eat dog world out there. Perfection is a dream, equality is a dream. Mankind is essentially animalistic; survival of the fittest.'

'That's certainly an interesting way of looking at life,' said David.

'It's a pragmatic way of looking at it,' she said.

She picked up her beer and took a swig.

'I choose my way of life. I'm lucky, nobody forced me into it, but if you look at what I do in the cold light of day, am I any different from you? What I do is illegal, morally reprehensible to the sheltered middle class majority and really quite lucrative. I'm not going to judge you by any standards other than my own.'

She clashed her beer bottle with his.

'So whether you like it or not, David, we are two of a kind.'

They finished the rest of the meal in a companionable silence. When David got up to clear the plates away, Sam got up to help him. As she loaded the dishwasher and cleared away the condiments, he was frozen briefly in amazement and wonder at the sheer domesticity of the evening; it was a very surreal feeling.

He walked on through into the lounge and sat on the sofa in his favourite corner. As he picked up the paper, she ventured in.

'Do you mind if I turn the TV on?' she asked.

'Knock yourself out,' he said, not unkindly.

As he shook the paper open, the TV blared, and he felt the pressure on the sofa as she sat next to him. It was an odd, almost alien sensation. She swung her legs up onto the couch and leaned back against him, snuggling in. He spent the next hour trying to concentrate on the content of the evening paper and trying not to move, while the TV blasted the latest soaps. Ordinarily, it would send him into a rage if he didn't get precisely what he wanted. He couldn't understand why it hadn't, which was even more confusing.

Eventually, his body could take no more of it. His muscles started cramping, he was dog tired anyway. He tapped her gently on the arm, causing her to jump. She was engrossed in whatever rubbish was playing on the large plasma screen.

'I'm absolutely bushed,' he said. 'I'm going to call it a night, if that's okay?'

She moved away slightly to allow him up. He smiled as she slid completely into the corner; his place. He couldn't understand it, but his heart was hammering in his chest as he moved out into the hall; like he was scared or nervous. Either that or he was having a heart attack.

He walked down the corridor to the master bedroom. The first thing he did was to open the double doors to let in the sound of the sea. He had done it every night that he was in the house, as far back as he could remember. He then moved into his en-suite to shave and brush his teeth.

When he came out again, Sam was sitting on the bed. She had removed the jeans and unbuttoned the shirt. He could see glimpses of flesh where it sagged open. He found it very erotic. He sat on the bed next to her, wearing only his boxer shorts, but made no move towards her.

'You don't have to, you know,' he mumbled under his breath.

She reached out her hand and gently lifted his chin, turning his head to make him look at her.

'I know,' she said.

'I'm not very good with girls,' he said, feeling his cheeks flush. 'I never really was. I just can't relax.'

'Don't worry about that,' she said, leaning behind her and flicking the switch. The lights went out, and all he could hear was the lapping of the waves and the soft inhale and exhale of her breathing, as he sensed her face approaching his.

'That's my speciality,' she whispered.

#

Much later, he found himself sitting on the shore. As his fingers trailed through the damp sand, he felt strange; like the world had shifted on its axis. His world certainly had. He couldn't help smiling. He looked back towards the bedroom. He couldn't see her in the dark, but he knew she was there. Did good things happen to bad people? It looked like he was living proof of that.

He pulled out his phone and dialled the number. It rang so many times it went to number unobtainable. He had to hit the redial button two or three times before it was picked up.

'Hello,' said a voice sleepily. 'Who is this?'

'Who the fuck do you think it is?' asked David, smiling broadly. 'Who else is going to be ringing you at three forty five in the morning?'

'Jesus boss, come on, have a heart.'

'What else would you be doing?' asked David.

'Sleeping,' Ben ventured.

'It's completely overrated,' said David. 'Anyway, just wanted to touch base with you; make sure everything is lined up for tomorrow.'

'And you rang me at three forty five in the morning to ask me that?' stated Ben stiffly.

'Careful,' responded David.

'Sorry boss,' replied Ben in a more conciliatory voice. 'Yes, I spoke to Antonio yesterday evening. The brothers will be here at five pm with all the necessary paperwork. I've drawn up contracts which their lawyers and ours have mutually agreed upon. Once we have the remainder of the protocol, there should be nothing more to stop us.'

'Excellent,' said David brightly.

'Is everything okay boss?' asked Ben hesitantly. 'You don't seem yourself?'

David pondered that question. Ben was right; he wasn't himself, he was better than himself. He felt faster, stronger, more alert and more intelligent; he felt invincible.

'Never better,' he added. 'See you tomorrow.'

He hung up on Ben and turned back to the sea. He could feel it ebbing and flowing; could hear the small breakers rolling onto the sand at his feet with a crump.

He picked up some large flat stones and started skimming them out across the waves. He could hear them flicking across the surface.

His smile got broader.

CHAPTER 50 – REFLECTION

22nd May 2011 – Twelve days after the Storm.

It is a most mortifying reflection for a man to consider what he has done, compared to what he might have done. – Samuel Johnson.

There were a lot of advantages to a normal job, he knew that. You got to sit at the same desk with the same chair and the same nine to five habit. He'd gotten used to it, the dulling of his senses by the humdrum of boring routine, but at the same time, there was nothing that could come close to the thrill of fieldwork.

He'd been surprised when the recruiter had approached him all those years ago, but with the benefit of hindsight, he couldn't now see why. He'd been studying politics and modern history at Yale, and was on target to be in the top ten for his year. In addition to his cerebral skills, he'd been incredibly athletic. A competition swimmer when he was younger, he could swim the hundred metre freestyle in under a minute.

In college, he'd switched his allegiance to marathon and was a regular competitor. Of course, the other thing he'd had in spades, and probably the one thing that had singled him out to the recruiter above all others, was his burning ambition to succeed.

So, on the face of it, looking back, he was a no brainer. He'd possessed the holy trinity; brains, physical fitness and an all consuming intensity of purpose.

He smiled; he still did, too.

Until the recruiter had spoken the word, he would never have considered it as a profession, but when he'd heard those three letters in that particular order, C – I – A, it had resonated through his being, conjuring up a whole vista of intrigue and opportunity.

There'd been a romantic element to it as well, if he was honest. It was every boy's fantasy to be a spy, to live like James Bond. The reality hadn't quite matched the dream, but sometimes it came fairly close.

So it was pretty much the perfect job, and at first that had been enough. But as he got older, the finer things in life started to matter, and the money he earned became a very big issue. The more programs he became involved in, the more he realised that governments and countries essentially existed on varying combinations of greedy politicians and political kickbacks. These uneasy alliances were propped up by enormous and complicated systems of bribery and corruption.

Fraud on the scale he saw did not come cheap. He watched massive sums of money change hands, and then collected his paltry pay cheque at the end of each month.

Storm had been a big eye-opener for him.

Coincidentally, a few months earlier, he'd been alone in his modest apartment, daydreaming of ways to make money.

Imagine creating the perfect drug....

This had been one of the scenarios he'd played around with in his head. He'd thought of everything; manufacturing, distribution, potential ways to keep it hidden, and then, when he first saw Storm leap out at him from that file, it had all come flooding back.

It was as though someone had smacked him across the face with the back of their hand, and the ideas and the schemes had literally slammed back into his brain.

There were downsides to his plan of course. He'd have to swap his real-life for an alternate reality. Physically, it would be no problem. He'd spent a lifetime staying hidden; a twilight warrior operating only from the shadows. No, it was the logical changes that had the potential to be tough. He would have to sever all contact with family and friends. Wham; he would be gone, never again able to see or contact them again.

He smiled broadly to himself. Some men would see it as a god-given miracle of opportunity. To cast off their humdrum lives and become someone else. The ultimate Walter Mitty fantasy and of course the money would help; it was nothing without the money.

The thought of the end-game payout focused him back to the job in hand. He hadn't been paid yet, so he needed to stop daydreaming.

He sat alone on a dry stone wall. It transected a grass hillock, and was set high up across the road from the industrial estate. He raised his infrared binoculars and scanned the perimeter. He had been very impressed with the way the construction and fit out of the facility had been approached. From the assembly and build of the production lines, to the security, to the sheer speed of fabrication, the whole thing was very impressive; the Mancini's had selected their local partner well.

He'd done a bit of digging into David McCabe and had initially been very sceptical. David had seemed at face value to be your typical drug dealing hothead. The first hint of deviation from the norm had been Ben Collins. The Harvard Alumni ran the McCabe Empire on solid management foundations.

The other thing to impress him about the young David had been his decision making. There was no procrastination, he always weighed up the options quickly and then, bang, decision made. He was also prepared to put his own money where his mouth was; always an admirable quality.

He placed the binoculars next to him on the wall and extracted his phone. He'd picked this spot to make the call because it had cell phone coverage, but there were very few towers around compared to an urban landscape. It would make it much more difficult for them to pinpoint his exact position. He knew they would locate him, he had no doubt of it, but his remoteness held another advantage. He would merely crush the device and buy another, and be gone like a ghost before the search teams could even mobilise.

He sat for a moment, breathing slowly and deeply. He knew he would have limited time and wanted to enjoy every second of it. He rehearsed what he was going to say in his head, over and over again, until he was satisfied, and then dialled the digits from memory. It was not the kind of contact number that you wrote down.

As he listened to the clicks and onward connections, he smiled grimly. He knew the call would be routing through at least one listening station, Cheltenham in the UK. When it got to the US, all calls, regardless of carrier, were passed to the NSA for screening and correlation. They say an eavesdropper never hears good things about themselves or others. He hoped any audio interloper would enjoy this particular conversation.

He felt a momentary flash of panic as he heard the familiar barked response.

'Nicholson!'

He quickly recovered his composure.

'Hello Winston,' he said.

He heard the sharp intake of breath. He'd expected no less, smiling happily to himself.

'You....' stuttered the director. 'You've a nerve ringing me.'

'I like to think that's why you employed me in the first place,' he said, 'because of my nerve.'

'We will trace you,' said the director, matter of factly.

He nodded.

'I know you will,' he said, 'but it's not like you don't know where I am. Being able to trace this phone will give you no material advantage what so ever.'

'How can you be so sure?' asked the director.

The stranger looked around at the miles of rolling deserted fields and hills.

'Let's just say I have an instinct for these things,' he said.

'So what do I owe the pleasure of this call?' asked the director. 'You haven't just called to gloat have you? I didn't think you were that pathetic?'

'You know me. I just can't help myself sometimes.'

'So that's genuinely why are you ringing?' asked the director soberly. 'You may be a shallow arsehole, but you'd normally have a more serious purpose for your communication than mere gloating.'

'If you want the honest truth, I'm giving you an opportunity,' he said.

'An opportunity for what?' asked the director.

'To ask questions,' said the stranger.

'Like what?' asked the director.

The stranger got a little tetchy for the first time.

'I don't know,' he snapped. 'You're the director of the CIA. I'm sure you can think of something intelligent to ask.'

There was a long pause on the other end of the line.

'I know it shows a singular lack of imagination,' said the director. 'But I've been through this conversation over and over again in my head, and the only thing I can come up with is *why*?'

'Not a lack of imagination at all. In fact a very good question,' said the stranger, his lips creasing at the corners.

He'd hit a nerve with that one.

'There's a number of reasons really, the most important one being that I could.'

The director snorted with derision.

'You'll have to do better than that.'

'Okay,' said the stranger. 'Try this one. I had a product, I had an idea to exploit that product, I had the means to get access to that product, and I had the opportunity. The rest, as they say, is history.'

'Bullshit,' stated the director forcefully. 'Give me a proper reason. All you've given me is a fucking mission statement.'

'Okay,' said the stranger, losing his temper. 'If you want a reason, I'll give you a reason. I was sick of watching everybody else benefit. I was sick of seeing all of that money change hands; all of that corruption and all of that illegality, and nobody seeming to care. Then worst of all, after seeing all those grubby little deals being done behind the scenes, to have to take that insult of a paycheque at the end of every month.'

The director scoffed.

'So, you're trying to occupy the moral high ground.'

'I think I can safely say I'm on higher ground than you at the moment,' said the stranger. 'You're the director of the CIA, for fuck's sake. Double dealing, country destabilisation, overthrowing one despotic dictator for another; who are you to lecture me on morality?'

'Well, seeing as we're on the subject of morality,' said the director. 'How exactly do you square away the efficacy of this drug with your plans for it? If this gets onto the open market, there could literally be thousands of deaths. You know what it does? You know exactly what outcome number two is. Do you want that on your conscience?'

'People die every day,' responded the stranger. 'Some of them are drug addicts. Nobody is forcing them to take this stuff; my conscience is clear.'

'So you're fully aware of what this drug can do and yet you're completely prepared to sell it to the highest bidder?'

'Absolutely,' said the stranger, 'and let's be very clear about this. Your argument has absolutely nothing to do with morality and everything to do with the fact that Storm was a project sanctioned by you; a fact that is spelt out in all four protocol folders. If this gets out, your career is sinking faster than the Titanic.'

'There is that aspect of it, granted,' said the director. 'But I'm not a monster either and I don't want all those deaths on my conscience.'

'And that's the difference between you and me,' acknowledged the stranger. 'I have no qualms about having your resignation or sacking on my conscience. In fact, if I'm honest, it's a little bit of a fringe benefit for me.'

'You bastard,' said Winston with feeling.

'That's better,' replied the stranger. 'Now we're getting somewhere.'

'We will find you,' said the director again.

'Oh, I don't think you will,' said the stranger. 'I think you trained me far too well for that.'

The stranger looked at his watch. It was coming up on the time where the triangulation would be complete and his position would be compromised. He enjoyed this bit; the thrill of pushing the envelope just that little bit further.

'So I guess this is goodbye,' continued the stranger.

'I guess it is,' said the director ironically. 'I can't say I'm sorry about that.'

'I wish I could be there to witness your humiliation,' said the stranger. 'I'll just have to content myself with the mental images.'

He had exceptional hearing, so he heard the sound of a door opening in the background.

'We've got him,' someone whispered.

He looked at his watch and nodded to himself; bang on time.

'Goodbye Winston,' he said. 'See you in hell maybe?'

He hung up and powered off the phone, took off the back cover and extracted the battery. He threw it as far away as he possibly could. Once that was taken care of, he removed the SIM card and placed it on a flat rock; one that sat proud of the dry stone wall he was leaning against. He picked up another bigger rock and ground the SIM into dust. He then placed the phone on the same anvil rock and smashed it into tiny pieces.

He slipped the infrared binoculars into his backpack and set off across the hills. He'd bought a portable GPS unit when he'd landed in Ireland and he would quite literally have been lost without it. Even as it was, with the sun setting behind him and the footing uneven and treacherous in places, he had to be careful on the two mile hike back to his car.

As he walked, he reflected on the conversation. It had been nice, but he hadn't got as much pleasure out of it as he'd thought he would. He'd always disliked the director, but he obviously didn't hate him, certainly not as much as he'd thought. He just felt a quiet satisfaction, mingled with a tinge of sympathy. It was good to get one over on Winston Nicholson, especially as there wasn't a damn thing Winston could do about it. The money that would be lodged in the numbered Swiss account would be all the more pleasurable for it.

He cursed loudly as his foot slipped on a wet rock, but then silently admonished himself; a slightly turned ankle was a small sacrifice for the return he would get from this mission.

Eventually, just as he thought he would have to revert to the night vision glasses for walking, the outline of the small village emerged from the gloom. He tracked along the main street till he came to the pub. Sure enough, his car was still there, along with a significant number of others; it certainly would have aroused no suspicion. He threw his back pack into the boot and removed a small package from the glove compartment. It was another ready to go phone, nestling in there with three others.

He powered it up.

He was secure in the knowledge that he was outside the triangle they had used to locate him from his last co-ordinates. Even though he had destroyed the old phone, if he'd powered the new one straight away, they would have seen it immediately. He fully reclined the seat and dialled another number from memory. It was answered on the second ring.

'Yes!'

A one word response, curt and to the point.

'Hello, Antonio, it's me.'

'What do you want?' he asked sharply.

Antonio's opinions on acquaintances of the Mancini's tended to reflect Guido and Ernesto's own reactions to those self same acquaintances. Consequently, Antonio did not think much of the stranger.

'I'd like to speak to Guido please?' stated the stranger.

'And what if he doesn't want to speak to you?' asked Antonio.

'He will,' said the stranger, 'so I would advise you to give him the option, not make the choice for him.'

He heard a couple of guttural curses in Italian and then the sound of footsteps and whispering.

'It's a dangerous game you're playing with me,' said a voice.

It was Guido, and he wasn't happy.

'Just want to make sure my money is all ready,' said the stranger.

'You'll get your money. As soon as we've verified the protocol is complete, the transfer will be made.'

'And when will that be?' asked the stranger.

'Probably tomorrow,' said Guido.

'So can I be there?' asked the stranger. 'I'd like to witness the contracts and signatures. It would be a fitting end to my involvement.'

'Have you been spying on us?' asked Guido incredulously.

'Number one, I think you're forgetting my background,' said the stranger, 'and number two, in the CIA we don't look upon it as spying. I'm merely keeping my best interests at heart and looking out for my investment, as you would too.'

'Five pm,' said Guido curtly. 'You obviously know where.'

The stranger smiled. Another hang-up, but it wasn't about making friends and influencing people. Good job really.

His payday inched ever closer.

CHAPTER 51 – CLARIFICATION

23rd May 2011 – Thirteen days after the Storm.

Clarity is the counterbalance of profound thoughts. – Luc de Clapiers.

I lay there staring up at the ceiling. It was one of those polytex ceilings; not smooth, but rough and knobbly, the kind that decorators curse. It looked like the surface of the moon, photographed from a long way away. I had been staring at it for a long time.

The light from the dawn was streaming through the dagger shaped gap in the full length curtains, casting weird shadows on the far wall. As I lay there, I started to create images in my mind, ostensibly playing a mental game to while away the time; connecting the raised areas of the ceiling together to form pictures. Like a bizarre form of join the dots.

All the while, my mind was in turmoil.

I'd always had a father; I knew that, but now I really did know who he was. Every time I tried to focus on a particular fact or statement, it fractured into a million tiny fragments, each screaming for priority. I just could not focus on anything. I'd wanted answers, now I had them. Now I had to learn to live with the consequences of that information.

I had a half brother who was trying to kill me. In a country like Ireland, where family was sacrosanct, I found that one fact, above all others, hard to assimilate and reconcile. It prompted a myriad of other questions that I also didn't want to face.

My mother must have known of my half brothers existence, and yet she had let me lead my life in blissful ignorance, why? And what had I personally done to cause such offense to someone I didn't even know?

It was the ultimate irony really. In my line of work, there were people who really should have wanted me dead that just didn't, and yet here was a direct relation, literally a blood brother, who wanted me killed. It just didn't compute.

Eventually I could stand it no longer; the voices were driving me mad. I threw off the covers, and threw on a T-shirt and trousers.

In just my bare feet, I padded down into the reception area. The night porter was dozing fitfully, but like all seasoned hospitality workers, he jerked awake and slipped seamlessly into urbane professionalism. He looked at his watch and smiled.

'You're up and about very early this morning,' he said, adding, 'sir.'

'Couldn't sleep,' I said simply. 'Anywhere I can get a cup of coffee at this time in the morning?'

'Sit yourself down over there,' he said, indicating the lounge area, 'and I'll be back in a moment.'

He hopped up and disappeared through a door marked *private*. True to his word, he was back a couple of minutes later with a tray. There were two mugs of steaming liquid, a sugar bowl, a milk jug and a plate of digestive biscuits.

Yes, it was instant, but as I added the milk and the sugar, I didn't care. It was delicious and just what I needed. We toasted each other silently, and then I fished in my pocket for some loose change.

'What do I owe you?' I asked.

'It's on the house, sir,' he replied. 'It's only instant after all. Not really in keeping with our gastronomic surroundings.'

He indicated the lobby area of the small boutique hotel we had booked into last night. My iPhone trip advisor search had called it a food lover's paradise.

'I'm going to head back upstairs if that's okay?' I said.

'You're the customer, you don't need my approval,' he said, winking. 'Take care of yourself, sir.'

The advice echoed in my head as I walked carefully back up the stairs, step-by-step. It was good advice; a creed that I'd lived my life by. Taking care of myself was a professional necessity, but now I'd learnt that it wasn't just about me anymore. There was another that shared my bloodline; another delicately joined by the twisting invisible strands of DNA. It was all very confusing.

Back in the room, I fluffed up the pillows behind me and sat upright on the bed. As I took another sip of the coffee, I realised that I wasn't alone in consciousness any more.

'You had a bad night,' Dale stated simply.

He pulled himself upright and rubbed his hands backwards and forwards over his skull vigorously.

'I had many a similar sleepless night,' continued Dale. 'Wondering about what could have been and what might have been. At the end of the day, Street, you and I are the same. We deal in absolutes, we deal in reality, we deal in positives and negatives, not ifs, buts and maybes. My family are my family. If my birth parents decided to come and find me, I'd deal with it there and then and move on. You can't go back.'

'Easy for you to say,' I said.

'Easy and true,' he said with a smile. 'You need to focus on the here and now. We know Black Swan is your brother, we know he wants to kill you, so now we just need to figure out why?'

Dale had hardly finished the words when the phone next to his bed rang loudly. Roussel jerked awake and wiped the sleep from his eyes as Dale listened. Wordlessly he beckoned me and Roussel closer. He flicked the phone into speaker mode and set it down on the bed between the three of us.

'Okay, you're on speaker,' said Dale.

'This is Special Agent Ray Fox of the DEA,' squawked the phone. 'I have with me Special Agent Dodds, also of the DEA.'

There was an acknowledging grunt in the background.

'I run the field office that Dale is attached to, and that's how I managed to get mixed up in all this mess,' he continued ruefully.

'Now Dale,' he said. 'I know you've managed to acquire some....'

He searched for a word.

'....colleagues. Can I ask them to introduce themselves, so at least I know who and what we're dealing with here?'

Dale winked at me. Roussel saw the wink and indicated himself. I nodded my understanding.

'Detective Charles Roussel, badge number 6566, St James Parish CID,' he answered.

'And exactly whereabouts would that be, Detective Roussel?' asked Ray.

'Louisiana,' said Roussel.

'Louisiana,' repeated Ray slowly.

We could all hear the puzzlement in his voice.

'Thomas Eugene O'Neill,' I said. 'Private Citizen.'

This time, there was a strangled cough.

'*The* Thomas Eugene O'Neill,' said another voice, obviously Agent Dodds. 'The same man who is wanted in the state of New York for extortion, protection, prostitution, drugs, and multiple assassinations and murders.'

'None of it proven,' I answered, 'but yes, one and the same.'

'We can go into all of that later,' suggested Dale into the deafening silence on the other end of the phone. 'The most important thing at the moment is that I would trust both of these guys with my life, and in point of fact have done so on more than one occasion in the last forty eight hours. Anything you can tell me, you can tell them.'

We heard the sound of a hand being placed over a microphone and some forceful whispering.

'Okay,' said Ray eventually. 'I'm going to take that at face value. But if any of this makes it into the public domain, I can't guarantee your lives let alone your jobs, do I make myself clear?'

'Perfectly,' said Dale.

'As a bell,' added Roussel.

'No argument from me,' I replied.

'Okay, first thing to let you in on is that myself and Dodds are in Virginia; Langley to be precise.'

We all looked at each other. We didn't need to vocalise our question, we all knew exactly what those two words meant.

'We are currently speaking to you from a secure line in the CIA director's private meeting room.'

This time, none of us could hide our surprise.

'The director is fully aware that we are speaking to you. Unfortunately, he can't be here himself. He had an important engagement that he had to take care of otherwise he would have related these facts to you himself.'

There was a temporary silence as this was digested.

'The other thing I will say before we start,' continued Ray, 'is that myself and Dodds had to sign an additional NDA on top of our standard federal government one, so it goes without saying that this information is highly classified.'

'Understood,' said Dale.

'Okay, straight to it,' said Ray. 'I'm presuming you all know about Storm. I'm not going to rehash old information if I don't have to.'

'We have a copy of the Protocol folder,' said Dale helpfully.

'Okay, so you know about as much as we did up until about seven hours ago.'

There was a longish pause.

'What you don't know,' stated Ray, 'is that in Iraq and Afghanistan they have been running trials using Storm against the Taliban and Iraqi insurgents.'

'Using Storm how?' asked Dale. 'Making addicts of the population?'

He was genuinely puzzled, as we all were, and then his face cleared.

'Of course,' he said. 'We've been focussing on its potential modern use as a recreational narcotic, but we have to remember, Storm was originally developed to create compliance in a populace. They're tapping into that, and using it for its original intention.'

'Yes and no,' said Ray. 'Yes, as you say, it was first developed as a biological weapon. You've read the file, same as us. It was originally envisaged that it would be possible to enslave a population, albeit temporarily. This is what drew the CIA to the drug in the first place. But there is a much more sinister twist in the tail.'

His voice became grave and serious.

'It has a use case that was not in your Protocol folder.'

'Go on,' prompted Dale. 'We're listening.'

'When you attain a certain quantity of this drug in your bloodstream, it does not make you compliant, it turns you into a mindless killing machine whose only thought is to acquire more of the drug, and who regards every other human being as competition to be eliminated. Once you attain this mindless state there is no going back; you will remain that way until you die, which will be very soon after.'

There was a stunned silence this time.

'That sounds a little far-fetched,' I said. 'That's pretty strong language isn't it; mindless killing machines?'

'That's what we said, Thomas,' replied Ray.

Both of us were startled as to how my name sounded coming from his mouth.

'But the director was adamant. This drug is very much a double-edged sword. If it gets out there into wider distribution, it will cause havoc among the drug taking population, but if people start taking it in the wrong quantities, which inevitably they will....'

He left the rest of the sentence unfinished. He didn't need to spell it out.

Dale suddenly snapped his fingers.

'So there were always two purposes to it.' he said. 'An overt one and a covert one; think about it.'

'What do you mean?' I asked.

'The director sanctioned this drug in spite of knowing what the side effects were for the simple reason that the intent was to develop a drug with two purposes. The first purpose, the overt purpose, was as an effective and harmless biological weapon.'

'Still a weapon though,' I said.

Dale agreed.

'Yes, you could argue a lot of things against it. Contravenes peoples human rights, takes away freedom of choice, but in a legitimate conflict situation, you can see something like Storm being used in preference to traditional weapons; something that makes people compliant for a finite period of time till you have them disarmed and locked up as required.'

'I can see the value in that,' I said.

'But the second use, the covert and possibly primary use, certainly the one they would have been testing in Afghanistan and Iraq, does ostensibly the same thing, only this time there is no need for messy and expensive prisoners. But imagine the public outcry about a drug developed specifically to turn a whole populous into mindless zombies. The political and international outcry would be enormous; governments would literally fall.'

'Well the CIA director described it in a slightly different way,' interjected Ray, 'and from a slightly different perspective, but yeah the upshot is pretty much the same, whichever way you cut it. He needs to get those folders back and eliminate any trace that they ever existed.'

'We'd love to help, boss, really we would,' said Dale. 'The thought of this drug getting onto the open market, even without knowing all of these nasty side-effects, was enough for us to want to try and stop it, but we are making headway very slowly. Roussel is the only one with jurisdiction, but even that is very limited and his influence only goes so far; they have other priorities in the drug squad.'

'Believe me, that's the least of your worries,' said Ray. 'Jurisdiction simply does not come into it. I'm going to state this as simply and as bluntly as I can. You will be contacted shortly by a CIA operative who will identify himself as Agent B. He has some details to share with you, including who is involved and where they are located. I hate doing this to you Dale, but you are the only man I have down there.'

Ray corrected himself.

'No, in fact you are the only *men* I have down there. I'll leave it up to you. I can't order you to do it, but I think each of you have a conscience, even the contract killer.'

I ignored the implicit statement in his last remark.

'When is this guy going to contact us?' I asked.

'That's where the director is at the moment,' said Ray. 'He's talking to his agent on the ground, giving him a full briefing about you, Dale. The agent seems to know about your friends already.'

I looked at the other two. There didn't seem to be much more to say to that.

'Okay boss,' said Dale. 'Talk to you later.'

'Good luck,' responded Ray.

He paused.

'Good luck to all of you.'

The line went dead.

'So what do you make of that?' asked Roussel into the silence.

'Be a nice change to work on the right side of the law,' I said with a smile.

Before Roussel had a chance to answer, Dale's phone went off again. He switched it to Speaker mode before he hit the green button.

'Yes,' he said.

'Dale Foster?' asked a voice.

'That's me,' answered Dale. 'Agent B?'

There was a pause.

'Okay, here's the deal. Meet me in the Armada Bar at one pm sharp. Sit at the bar in a line of three, with a Guinness in front of each one of you.'

'What if there's no room at the bar?' asked Dale.

'Use your imagination,' said the voice grimly. 'See you in two hours.'

CHAPTER 52 – REVELATION

23rd May 2011 – Thirteen days after the Storm.

The revelation of thought takes men out of servitude and into freedom. – Ralph Waldo Emerson.

I sat looking at my pint. As the dark liquid settled, I turned the glass slowly on the beer mat, using my fingers to clear the condensation from the outside. I smiled as my two companions copied what I was doing. They must have thought it was part of the Guinness drinking ritual. Three cheers for cultural differences.

'Slainte,' I said, picking up my glass suddenly and drinking deep.

'Cheers,' responded Roussel.

'Good health,' replied Dale.

All you could hear were multiple swallows.

'It's like a game of chess, isn't it,' said Roussel, into the companionable aftermath.

'So why do I feel like I'm the one being setup for check mate?' I asked. They both laughed.

'All the pieces are starting to come together though,' said Dale.

'And maybe I can add the missing piece to that,' said a voice behind us. We whirled around and then stopped.

'Not who you were expecting, am I?' he asked, smiling, before turning his attention to the barman. 'Pint of Guinness please, when you're ready.'

He indicated a free table in the corner.

'Come on,' he said. 'Let's head over there. I know you have a lot of questions.'

We did as he asked, and moved across to the empty section he'd pointed out. He waited until we had all stopped shuffling and fidgeting our way in, and we in turn waited until the young lounge girl had delivered his pint to the table, gleefully pocketing the almost fifty percent tip he offered her.

369

'You're not the agent we hooked up with in Street's house,' stated Roussel.

'No I am not,' he acknowledged.

He held up his hand as we all started talking at once.

'Let me give you a bit of background first,' he said. 'If that doesn't answer all your questions, then I'll gladly field any that you have after my explanation. Fair?'

I picked up my pint and took another sip.

'Go ahead,' I prompted. 'We're all ears.'

The others nodded their affirmation.

'Allow me to introduce myself,' he said formally. 'My name is Agent David Bruce. I was recruited directly into the CIA from college; UNC if you're interested. I spent five long and happy years in the field, but was invalided out of active fieldwork.'

We exchanged a quick glance, the three of us. I had noticed a slight limp as he'd brought us across to the table and the others had obviously noticed the same thing. He interpreted the shared glance correctly.

'I was shot in the foot,' he said, 'and before you even think of making a joke, believe me I've heard them all before.'

He waited until we had all assumed serious expressions again.

'Anyway, after I recovered, I wasn't even sure that I wanted to stay in the CIA. I was completely undecided and at a loose end, so one day, my boss took me aside. He knew I was a good agent and wanted to retain me. There was an opening in Langley he'd heard about that was right up my street.'

'He managed to tempt you to stay then?' stated Roussel.

'That he did,' said Agent Bruce. 'Information Technology was one of my passions and he knew that.'

'So it was a computer project?' I ventured.

'In a manner of speaking,' said Agent Bruce. 'Basically the CIA information department were a huge way down the road with computerisation; so far in fact, that they had started looking at their older paper files. There were approximately twenty rooms, stacked floor to ceiling with yellowing folders and documents, some of them dating back even before the Second World War. My job was firstly to recruit a small team of like-minded agents to help me. Then we had the onerous task of going through those paper files, indexing and archiving anything relevant until everything was done.'

'And that's how you found Storm.' stated Dale.

'And that's how I found Storm,' repeated Agent Bruce. 'I distinctly remember the day. My foot had been playing up; it was very rainy and wet outside and the damp seems to adversely affect it. I had propped it up on a stool in my office. One of my colleagues came in and handed me an innocuous dusty looking file. We used to batch them together every morning and give ourselves a quota to get through during the day. It was the last left in his pile, but it was quite late in the evening and he was running late. He wanted to get off to see his girlfriend, so I said, yep, no problem, go-ahead, I'll take a look. In that one action, gentleman, I literally changed the course of my life.'

'So, how soon did you recognise its potential?' asked Dale.

'It was pretty much instant,' replied Agent Bruce. 'Believe it or not, I'd majored in Pharmacology at UNC. The North Carolina colleges specialise in medicine. I knew the CIA was also keeping tabs on certain chemical formulas and I liked to keep my hand in and stay current with modern developments. When I saw the main pivotal research was around acetylcholine, my interest was immediately piqued. I also knew how significant some of the derivates were from that family of compounds. We're all aware of Rohypnol for instance, but reading on through the file, I knew that with modern methods, there was a chance we could eliminate the fatal flaw.'

'So it was never intended to be a double-edged sword?' asked Dale.

'That's where it gets a bit complicated,' said Agent Bruce. 'I knew I had something on my hands worth developing, but I couldn't do it full-time because of the role I was in. Also, I felt that it was only my pharmacological background that had enabled me to see through a lot of the jargon in the original file. If I'd presented it *as is* to any senior official, I'd have been laughed at. Now, I'm sure it wouldn't shock you to learn that there is a rather large lab complex in the basement of the Langley building. I knew a couple of the guys down there. I was always bugging them to get a loan of their latest industry periodicals. A few of them knew my background; one particularly, James White, I got to know very well.'

'How did you know you could trust him?' asked Roussel.

'At the time I didn't,' said Agent Bruce. 'I took a gamble. He read the file through and had the same concerns as me, but we both believed that with more modern methods of synthesis and isolation, we'd be able to eliminate the flaw. We worked in secret for almost two years, both of us working between fourteen and sixteen hour days; synthesising, isolating and re-testing in an endless cycle.'

'So what happened?' asked Dale.

'You know what happened,' said Agent Bruce.

'We know what the outcome was,' argued Dale, 'but we don't know what actually happened.'

Agent Bruce glanced at him.

'We sat down together, James and me, and took stock of the situation. We sat there despondently, slowly convincing ourselves that our two years of hard work had been wasted. But an offhand remark he made triggered something in my head. Rather than try to eliminate the fatal flaw, I saw it as an additional bargaining tool; a double selling point for the product. So we tried a different approach. This time, we endeavoured to hone, enhance and control it. Identify the concentration limit required, identify the time limit; in other words, make the flaw work in our favour.'

'And did it work?' asked Roussel.

'And then some,' agreed Agent Bruce vehemently. 'In the course of his work, James experimented a lot with laboratory animals. Over the years he'd constructed a maze for lab rats, to ease diagnosis of stimulus and response conditions. He didn't like it, but we took that maze as the basis for the labyrinth we constructed for our first test with the director.'

'The one that's detailed in the Protocol folder,' I said.

'One and the same,' he replied.

'James is the lab technician that was killed?' ventured Roussel hesitantly.

'How did you know about that?' he asked suspiciously.

'The CIA director,' confirmed Roussel.

'Of course,' agreed Agent Bruce. 'It was actually that very same night; a very sad business.'

'Do you have any theories?' I asked.

Agent Bruce scoffed and then laughed sourly.

'I don't need theories, Mr O'Neill,' he said. 'I know exactly who did it.'

'So, what did you do about it?' I asked.

'Nothing I could do,' said Agent Bruce flatly. 'By that stage, the project had been formally acquired by the deputy director. I was excluded, pushed to the sides. It was no longer *my* project, so I stuck with it and bided my time. I was afraid somebody was going to take the credit for all my hard work, or worse, try to eliminate me as well. I had to keep my wits about me for sure.'

'So, it never occurred to you that someone would exploit the hallucinogenic effects of the drug?' I asked.

'It honestly never occurred to any of us,' he said. 'We often laughed about it; that it seemed like the perfect drug on the surface, and how appearances could be deceptive, but I never in a million years thought someone would seize on that aspect and then try and exploit it for monetary gain. And apart from that, all our tests to that point had been on animals. We only had the original file to describe the effects it had on human subjects.'

'But it's been tested on humans since.' said Dale.

It wasn't a question.

'It absolutely has,' said Agent Bruce. 'It's now more or less perfect for what they want. The problem is that in the trials they are conducting, mistakes are starting to creep in.'

'It's inevitable really, they're in a war zone,' said Roussel. 'Not the place for steady and rational thoughts and deeds.'

Agent Bruce nodded.

'But given the issues we've seen with those trials, bearing in mind we are talking about a targeted military demographic, if this gets onto the open market, the ensuing outcome will be nothing short of catastrophic.'

'So, how come you're over here and intimately involved, if you were sidelined on the project?' asked Roussel.

'The director needed someone up to speed quickly,' said Agent Bruce. 'He knew I'd never really gone away. I was always hovering in the background, keeping an eye on it. Much as I found what they were doing with it distasteful and barely ethical, I still had a stake in it. So, when he came to me and told me he needed my help, I jumped at the chance.'

'You know who the rogue agent is?'

'Oh I know who it is all right,' he said. 'I'm just not going to share that information with you; not something you need to know.'

'So, why are you here?' I asked. 'What is it that we do need to know? What do you need from us?'

'Well, I'd be surprised if you haven't already pieced together a lot of this,' he said. 'But I'll lay it all out for you anyway. The rogue agent has a copy of the Protocol folder. The rogue agent knows that the fatal flaw exists, as does everybody within the CIA who was there for that fateful demonstration, even though it is only listed in one copy of the document. In the director's version of the file, it is listed as outcome number two, but I think *fatal flaw* describes it much better, don't you?'

We all nodded.

'The rogue agent passed the file to the Mancini's but obviously did not share the fatal flaw with them. In fairness to the brothers, I think even they would draw the line at their customer base ripping each other to shreds.'

'So, they think they actually do have the perfect drug,' I said. 'And nothing they have been told since then has disabused them of that notion. The compliance piece won't bother them; in fact it would make it more appealing for them. Knowing them like I do, they will act quickly to exploit their competitive advantage.'

'The Mancini's have hooked up with a local drug dealer, a man called David McCabe who goes by the nickname of *the Bullock*.'

'We're familiar with David already,' said Roussel.

'And this is where I may have been a little bit clever, if I say so myself. I met with Black Swan, the other major dealer and told him the whole sorry tale.'

He chuckled to himself and then saw our faces.

'You know him?' he asked, his eyes narrowing dangerously.

'Only by reputation,' I said quickly.

'Yeah, he was none too pleased when I told him, but it was a worthwhile exercise. I'm fairly sure he will have located the factory by now too. He didn't confirm it in so many words, but I have a feeling that he might yet cause some trouble for young David and his new partners.'

'Be careful with Black Swan,' I cautioned. 'He's not a man to be trifled with.'

'I can look after myself,' he said.

'So David McCabe is the Mancini's local contact?' prompted Dale.

'He is, but they needed something more. Guido Mancini knows one of the top board members in ADXR personally. The man is an idiot and easily led; a typical high ranking executive who perceives himself a lord of the universe. It was simple for a man like Guido, a master manipulator, to plant the seed of the idea. A joint venture was formed between ADXR and one of the Mancini companies, G&E Chemicals, ostensibly to produce an Alzheimer's cure. It is truly brilliant really, as the compound elements are very similar. McCabe and his business associate Ben Collins have even managed to get backing from the Irish Industrial Development Authority.'

'So, the Irish Government have put money into this?' asked Dale incredulously.

'They have indeed. But here is where I need your help. The plant is in Clonakilty on the IDA campus. The Mancini's are meeting McCabe there in person for the first time tonight, and the rogue agent will be there too. It is the perfect opportunity to snatch the folders back.'

'Are we involving local law enforcement?' asked Roussel.

'We can't,' said Agent Bruce. 'There's too much of a chance that the folders would fall into Irish Government hands. We cannot afford leaks of any kind.'

'So, why do you need us?' I asked.

'Sheer weight of numbers, and certain professional abilities,' he said. 'Believe me, if I could do this myself I would, but I can't. And let's be clear; we will be heavily outnumbered, they will be ruthless and they will be armed. From what I've been told, you guys are all handy with a gun and bring other skills to bear.'

He didn't elaborate on what he thought those skills might be.

'So, are you with me?'

We glanced at each other. Dale had been right; all of the pieces really had come together. I held up my pint.

'Let's do it,' I said.

Roussel and Dale held up their drinks.

'Agreed,' they echoed.

Agent Bruce smiled.

'Welcome to the team,' he said.

We all drained our glasses.

'Tonight is going to be pretty hectic,' he said. 'There's a lot of planning we still need to do. All the detail stuff needs to be worked out. That's where this is going to succeed or fail.'

We jointly agreed.

Leaving Agent Bruce to settle his tab, we milled about on the pavement outside, waiting for him to join us.

'What do you think?' asked Dale.

'I think he's absolutely genuine,' I said. 'He really meant it when he said he would rather do it by himself. And he's right; these drug dealing lads would have plenty of firepower. They may not necessarily be the best marksmen in the world, but they love their guns.'

I was about to continue when the door opened and he limped slowly out.

'There's a storm coming,' he said. 'My foot always gets worse when it's about to rain.'

We all realised the significance of what he'd said about ten seconds later. He smiled and nodded.

'I know, spooky isn't it?'

No one said anything more; we didn't have to.

'I'll be over to your hotel in an hour; we can rendezvous there.'

I didn't ask him how he knew where we were staying.

He stepped out across the street and we turned to walk back to our hotel. We had not gone more than twenty five yards when I saw a man seemingly asleep behind the wheel of his car. As we drew level, he miraculously woke up. Milliseconds later, the engine fired into life, as he gunned it out of the space towards the pub we had just vacated.

Agent Bruce had just breached the midline of the road on his slow traverse towards the other side. The car was showing no signs of stopping; in fact it was accelerating all the time. I tried to shout a warning to Agent Bruce, but it was too late. Mercifully, he didn't see the car. The unknown assailant planted his foot on the throttle. I winced as I felt the bang and scrape as Agent Bruce thudded across the roof of the car. I watched in horror as he landed in a heap of implausibly twisted limbs; like a marionette with all the strings severed.

I knew instinctively that he was dead.

CHAPTER 53 – CONGREGATION

23rd May 2011 – Thirteen days after the Storm.

I have hated the congregation of evil doers; and will not sit with the wicked. – Psalm 26:5.

I started sprinting after the speeding vehicle. The twenty year reflex kicked in as I reached for the gun, my scrabbling fingers finding nothing but damp cotton. Old habits die hard.

I heard the sound of tearing and rending metal as the car smashed into a line of parked cars, before it screeched around the corner and accelerated away. I had to stop and put my hands on my hips to catch my breath. I hadn't realised until then how unfit I was, and had to recover for a couple of minutes before I could jog slowly back.

A crowd had started to gather and with it came the whispered questions. Who was he? Who saw what? How did it happen?

Dale was working furiously on Agent Bruce. I caught his eye. He was obviously experienced in CPR, and he shook his head imperceptibly. As far as he was concerned, Agent Bruce was gone, but once he'd started the CPR, he couldn't stop; not until the patient was pronounced by a doctor or a paramedic. We watched as the crowd built, the whispers of the onlookers drowning out Dale's chanted numbers.

'One one thousand, two one thousand,' he muttered under his breath, as he tried to affect a miracle.

Eventually, we heard the wail of a siren in the distance. The streets were very narrow, and the paramedics reached us on foot long before the ambulance did. They skidded to a halt beside us. One counted down with Dale, deliberately coordinating the moment he took over the compressions so as not to break the rhythm. The other readied the defibrillator.

They worked feverishly for another fifteen minutes, shocking him three or four times in the process. He was pronounced dead precisely twenty minutes after they first arrived.

At that stage, the three of us had been asked to wait. We were to be questioned by a member of the Gardai. A number of witnesses had come forward from the pub and had pointed us out as Agent Bruce's last companions.

'So, what do we do now?' I asked quietly.

'We answer their questions, we answer them truthfully, and we'll be sent on our way,' said Roussel.

'Are you sure about that?' I asked.

'Absolutely,' said Roussel. 'We have to tell the truth, especially because of my situation. I have the most to lose here. If James finds out about this and I wasn't the one to tell him, who knows what could happen?'

'Just remember what's at stake here,' I said. 'You'd better be right.'

'I'm right,' he said. 'I don't like it, but I'm right.'

Eventually, a young Garda came over to take our statements. The ambulance had long since left and the crowd had all but dispersed.

'So, which one of you gentlemen wants to go first?' he asked with a smile.

Dale and I both looked at Roussel.

'Hi there,' said Roussel, extracting his ID from his pocket. 'Detective Charles Roussel; over here following up some leads from a case I'm working on back home in Louisiana.'

'Would that be in Kinsale?' asked the Garda, showing a remarkable lack of surprise. 'Those leads that you're chasing, that is?'

'No, Cork City,' answered Roussel.

'Do you mind me asking what you're doing here, then?' asked the Garda. The smile was slightly more fixed and wooden.

'Just taking a few days off with a couple of friends,' said Roussel.

'Can you tell me who your liaison is?' asked the Garda.

'Yeah, no problem,' said Roussel. 'It's Detective James Murray of the Cork drug squad.'

'Just a second,' said the Garda, and walked off.

We heard the static as his radio bristled. He then extracted his phone. We heard the digital tones of the dialled number and then the brief conversation that followed. We all strained our hearing, but we couldn't tell who he was talking to and all his answers were fairly monosyllabic. The discourse was brief and he returned with a very different look on his face.

'Detective Murray would very much like you all to wait at the station for him.'

The way he said it left us in no doubt that our options were limited.

Dale was the first to put the theory to the test.

'So, do we have a choice?' he asked.

'It would be in your beneficial interest, sir, to accompany me.'

'Is that a no, then?' asked Dale.

'Please follow me.'

Dale shrugged and we followed the young officer in single file back to the Garda Station in Church Square. He escorted us to the main interview room. In fairness to him, he made us all a cup of tea while we waited, after taking note of our names.

It was funny, but given my background, it was odd to think that this was the first time I had been in a police interview room. I knew Roussel and Dale would be veterans, but I was sure their experiences were always from the other side of the desk.

We waited another forty minutes, none of us in much of a mood for talking. We were all reaching the point where we were starting to slip into boredom induced naps, when the door suddenly flew open.

The garda who'd escorted us to the station entered the room first. Then another gentleman, this time in plain clothes, came in behind him; obviously Detective James Murray.

The young officer pressed the record button on the voice recorder; the one that we had all failed to spot before.

'Garda Pat Spillane and Detective James Murray have just entered the room. For the tape, already present are Detective Charles Roussel, Dale Foster and John O'Reilly.'

He looked at his watch.

'Interview started at four forty six.'

We had already decided it would be best not to use my real name.

Roussel started the ball rolling.

'So, is this an interview?' he asked.

Detective Murray looked up with a measured stare, his eyes narrowing.

'I'll tell you something Charlie,' he said. 'I don't know what the hell is going on, but I promise you something. We are not leaving this room till I get some answers.'

We were sitting in a line opposite Detective Murray, and I noticed that Dale was keeping his head down. I also knew why.

'You guys are going to an awful lot of bother for an accident,' I said, slipping back into what I hoped was my natural brogue.

'And who the hell are you?' he asked.

'Just a friend,' I said. 'I got talking to the boys in a pub. We seemed to share the same kind of interests.'

'You lived in America.'

It was a statement, not a question.

'I did,' I acknowledged, 'along with half the other guys of my generation. I didn't realise it was a crime until now.'

'When did you get back here?' he asked, not taking the bait.

'About a year ago,' I said.

'Anyone who can verify that?' he asked.

I looked him straight in the eye.

'About half of Cork,' I lied with bravado.

'Who was this guy?' Roussel asked. 'The one who died, I mean.'

'You tell me, you were with him,' he said.

'We met him,' I corrected, 'we weren't with him. He heard Charles's American accent; he was American himself, so asked if he could join us. We said, yeah, no problem, had a little chat, I gave him a few tips on places to visit and then we left. Two minutes later, bang, he's dead by the roadside.'

'Did you know his name?' asked Detective Murray.

'We didn't,' I answered, this time untruthfully.

It could have caused us complications.

'He didn't even tell you his name,' said Detective Murray incredulously.

'Look, we had a pint with him. We chatted to him for twenty minutes. He left, we left. He walked with a limp, and then he was hit by a car. What more can I say.'

Detective Murray regarded me impassively for a few minutes.

'He had no ID on him, you see. Nothing in his wallet, no driving licence, no passport, no travel documents, nothing. That in itself, let me tell you, is very rare.'

'But it does happen,' said Dale, looking up.

I watched Detective Murray's face as it went through the various stages; surprise, shock, incredulity and then anger.

'You!' he exclaimed. 'What the hell are you doing here?'

Dale froze and it fell to Roussel to answer.

'We met outside the police station,' said Roussel. 'The afternoon after you gave me that tour, remember? As two Americans in a strange country, and fellow law enforcement professionals to boot, we decided to hook up and do some sightseeing together.'

I secretly applauded Roussel. It was thin, mighty thin, but it was plausible, just. Detective Murray was having none of it.

'And you expect me to believe that?' he asked, laughing bitterly.

'I don't expect you to do anything,' said Roussel. 'That's the truth, end of story.'

'I don't think so Charlie boy,' responded James. 'I have an instinct for these things. You guys are up to something and you are also hiding something, two traits that I just cannot stand.'

'At the end of the day,' said Roussel without pausing, 'there is no case to answer here. You know as well as I do that there are five or ten witnesses who can put us on the other side of the road when that guy was hit. It was a hit-and-run for god's sake. I don't know what you want from us? So either charge us or let us go.'

Roussel finished the sentence in exasperation and stared at Detective Murray defiantly.

'I like you James,' he said, 'but at the end of the day this is about the law. We're not doing anything wrong, we didn't do anything wrong. We casually hooked up with a guy for a pint; he ends up dead, a hit-and-run. I'm sorry about that, but that's as far as it goes.'

Detective Murray regarded Roussel balefully for a few moments.

'I work in the drug squad as you well know,' he said. 'Because of that, I'm used to dealing with people who are dishonest. There is no one more underhand and untruthful than a junkie looking for his next fix, so I have an instinct for when something smells bad. There is a stink coming off this situation like you wouldn't believe, and I'm going to promise you now that I will find out what you're up to. But you're right, at the moment I can't charge you with anything, much as I'd like to.'

He nodded to the young garda, who leaned across and hit the button on the voice recorder.

'Interview suspended at five o'clock precisely.'

'So that's it, we're free to go?' asked Roussel.

'You're free to go, Charlie,' said James. 'But let me tell you this.'

He looked at each of us in turn as he spoke.

'If I find out that any of you are mixed up in anything that you shouldn't be, then I will have the book thrown at you, do you understand? In fact, I won't have it thrown; I'll take the greatest of pleasure in throwing it myself.'

We all nodded meekly.

'Now get out of my sight.'

We didn't need asking twice. We leapt up from our chairs and virtually ran out of the office, walking briskly and not stopping until we were in the relative safety of Church Square.

I scowled at Roussel.

'This is entirely your fault,' I stated with venom. 'I told you that we shouldn't have gone to the police.'

'On the contrary,' said Roussel with a broad smile. 'It's had precisely the effect I hoped it would.'

Dale and I looked at him in puzzlement.

'I knew James would not be happy, especially when he found out about Dale. I got to know him pretty well over the last few days. He's a very good police officer and he's not going to let this go. I think that will work in our favour.'

'What you mean?' I asked.

'Well, he is more convinced than ever that something is amiss. I don't think there is any harm in having someone like James on our side, even if all he is going to do is re-examine some of the facts.'

I shrugged.

'I'll take your word for it,' I said. 'Law enforcement is a sweet mystery to me. But one thing I do know; we need to plan tonight very carefully. Let's head back to the hotel. I have a feeling that it's all coming to a head.'

#

'So what do you make of that, Garda Spillane?' asked James.
'I don't think they're on the level, sir,' said the garda.
'Damn right they're not,' said James.
He tapped the end of his pen thoughtfully on the desk in front of him.
'All we need to do now is try and find out what it is they're involved in.'
'Already on it, sir,' said Garda Spillane.
'What do you mean?' asked James.
'One of my buddies is heading out; he's off shift. I've asked him to keep tabs on our friends. My shift is over in about ten minutes. I'll get changed into civvies and relieve him.'
James smiled broadly.
'I like your style Garda Spillane. You'll go far.'
'You can call me Pat, sir,' said Garda Spillane.

#

As he changed into his suit, Ernesto could not shake off the uneasy feeling that had been brewing since the morning. Neither of the brothers was what you would call emotional, but Ernesto certainly put more store in his feelings than Guido did.

He'd had the dream again. He was a successful farmer and everywhere he turned there were acres of wheat and corn stretching as far as the eye could see. It was such a bountiful harvest, shiny and gold, that he felt like a modern day Midas. And then, his self-satisfied smile turned to horror as he realised his bounty was not golden, it was ablaze. The flames were literally rushing towards him. He could hear the roar as they consumed everything in their path. The fiery wall of death reared up in front of him, and just before it hit, he screamed and woke up.

He didn't know what it meant, he never did, but he just knew the portents were not good.

He went to find Guido, noting with annoyance that he wasn't in his room. He went to find Antonio instead, who was patiently ironing shirts.

'Do you know where my brother is?' he asked.

'I believe he's gone downstairs to wait for you,' said Antonio. 'I will be down in a few minutes when I have everything packed and the bill settled.'

'Thanks Antonio,' said Ernesto.

381

When he entered the bar, Guido was sitting waiting for him, as was a glass of the finest cognac. Ernesto sat down, overwhelmed with a sense of love for his brother. By the time he had raised his glass to his lips, all feelings of misgiving had left his body.

'To us,' said Guido. 'Salute!'

'Salute!' said Ernesto.

Their glasses clashed together as they toasted another successful partnership. In the fireplace behind them, the flames buzzed and flattened as the gathering wind blew an occasional gust down the chimney.

CHAPTER 54 – DESTINATION

23rd May 2011 – Thirteen days after the Storm.

By prevailing over all obstacles and distractions, one may unfailingly arrive at his chosen goal or destination. – Christopher Columbus.

We all stood clustered around the battered old holdall.

'Do you think we'll need it?' asked Dale.

'I think it's going to be absolutely essential equipment, unfortunately,' I said. 'The one thing we do have in our favour is the element of surprise, or at least I hope we do, but we need to make sure we exploit that above all else.'

'Where are we going then?' asked Roussel.

'Well, Agent Bruce confirmed our initial suspicions about the ADXR and G&E Chemicals tie up, may God have mercy on his soul. We'd pretty much worked that one out already, but it looks like David McCabe and the Mancini's are planning to produce high volumes of this stuff from a facility in Clonakilty.'

'And then what? Stockpile it?'

'If you've seen the west coast of Cork,' I said, 'then you'd understand what we're up against. There are so many inlets along the coastline that it would be absolutely impossible to patrol it all. There are literally thousands of coves, beaches and natural harbours; a myriad of places to load any type of merchandise onto boats, and get it out of the country and into circulation with zero chance of discovery.'

I fetched the large-scale ordnance survey map we'd bought on the way back to the hotel, put the holdall on the floor, and spread the large paper sheet fully out across the table. I took out my phone and typed in *ADXR Clonakilty*. I went to Google maps and it helpfully highlighted the actual unit within the industrial park.

I panned out to get an idea of where it was in relation to the town, and then set the phone down next to the corresponding location on the map.

'So,' I said. 'It looks like we go through the town and out the other side to this roundabout.'

I pointed to the spot, took a black marker, drew a little circle around the roundabout, and then drew a larger circle on another part of the chart that was not relevant to our journey or plan. I then joined the two with a straight line. Keeping my eye on the phone, I transposed a small sketch of the unit into the larger circle, mainly to highlight its orientation in regard to the map.

'Okay,' I said. 'It looks like there is nothing around it but fields, which is good. It helps contribute to the element of surprise. I'd say, given the organisation we're dealing with, security will be fairly tight, so that could be a problem. The ideal scenario would obviously be multiple entry points. The front entrance is likely to be heavily guarded, probably augmented by a camera system, so our best bet is going to be doors at the extremities of the building. Now, I don't know what it's like over here, but in the United States, there are regulations about certain size buildings having a certain number of fire doors. I think they will be the key to us gaining entry.'

Roussel chimed in.

'You both heard what Agent Bruce said as well; about Black Swan and some of his crew possibly trying to muscle in on the action.'

'If so, it's going to get very busy around there,' I acknowledged, 'so we need to be very careful.'

'How are we going to communicate?' asked Dale.

'Good point,' I said. 'Do we all have each other's numbers?'

We diligently swapped numbers and then we all made sure we had our hands-free kits with us and that they still worked. As we left the hotel with the holdall and the rest of our meagre belongings, I had a strong feeling that we would not be back.

#

Dave was in his element, as he always was when he had things to do. He was a man of action like his boss; he couldn't stand the long periods of nothing. Chauffeuring, chaperoning, guarding and protecting; all of it quite stressful, but there was minimal action in it. He smiled; the action, when it came, more than made up for the large chunks of boredom.

Dave was meticulous when it came to planning. It was why the failures of recent days had irked him, but realistically it was all part of the process. You couldn't account for the quality of your opposition; you just had to plan around it as best you could.

He studied the surveillance photographs that had been supplied to him. He had a guy watching the place now, an old friend from the army who knew what Dave was looking for when it came to buildings. He spread the pictures on the table in front of him, and made neat notes in small capital letters.

The building had one main entrance which would be heavily guarded, but it had a further six sets of emergency exits. There were two sets on each side of the building and two sets at the back. His plan was simple; they would overpower any external security, disable the alarm system, lever open the fire doors and assume control.

He made some final annotations to his large-scale map and then packed the map, his notes and the photographs into a folder.

He went to find his boss, knowing exactly where he would be. He knocked on the door and entered like he always did. This time though, Eoin did not turn on his desk light. Dave had to navigate to the chair by the meagre light filtering in from the half open door. He couldn't see Eoin clearly, but in truth he didn't need to. He knew he would be reclined all the way back, eyes closed, his face a picture of serenity.

'Are you sure you want to do this boss?' asked Dave, into the silence.

'The more I think about it, the more convinced I am,' he said.

'Why do you hate McCabe so much?' asked Dave.

'That's just it,' said Eoin, his eyes snapping open and his chair tilting upright. 'I don't. He's the one with all the rage in his heart, not me. I'm just protecting my interests. It's a fine line.'

'What do you mean by a fine line?' asked Dave.

'Think of it in boxing terms,' said Eoin. 'I'm like a very defensive boxer. I don't really want to hurt him, but by the same token, I'm not prepared to be beaten senseless. Do you understand what I mean?'

Dave nodded.

'So, why go after this place then?'

'Very simple,' said Eoin. 'It's all about the balance of power. At the moment I have it. If he gets this plant up and running, and starts selling this stuff in the quantities he thinks he can, then all the power shifts to him.'

'Makes sense,' responded Dave uncertainly.

'You don't sound convinced,' said Eoin.

'It just seems like a very drastic step,' stated Dave.

'Are you afraid?' asked Eoin.

'Aren't you?' countered Dave.

'Strangely enough, I'm not. Maybe I have an overinflated sense of my own mortality, but today is not the day I'm going to die.'

By this stage they had walked the long corridor between the house and the mews garage. As they got into the Mercedes, Eoin spoke with surprise.

'We're not taking this to Clonakilty, are we?'

'No, I thought it might be a bit conspicuous,' said Dave with a smile, 'especially the personalised number plate. No, we're heading over to the industrial unit to liaise with the guys. We'll be driving down to Clonakilty in a fleet of old Ford transits.'

Eoin waited until the car was running and they were both safely seated inside.

'So, Dave,' said Eoin, as they pulled out of the garage and onto the main road. 'Do you mind if I ask *you* a question for a change?'

'Go ahead, boss,' replied Dave.

'Why have you stuck with me over the last few years?'

Dave considered the question for a few minutes.

'Well, the pay is good, the hours are good and there are a lot of fringe benefits. To a large extent I'm my own boss, too.'

Eoin looked at him sideways.

'Oh, I know you're the boss,' said Dave hastily. 'But you don't constantly tell me how to do my job. You're not micro managing me; I hate that shit. You don't tell me how to guard you, chauffeur you or protect you. I make all those decisions. So I suppose that's pretty cool in a way too; trust and respect.'

'Would that be two-way?' asked Eoin.

Dave glanced at him in the mirror.

'Would I trust and respect you? Absolutely, trust and respect have to be mutual; they have to be two-way, otherwise it just doesn't work.'

'Do you like me then?' asked Eoin quietly.

Dave was taken aback.

'You don't, do you?' stated Eoin flatly.

Dave sighed.

'It's not as simple as that.'

'We have a working relationship,' said Eoin hopefully.

'Exactly,' said Dave. 'We have a working relationship, which tends to complicate things. If you put respect and trust to one side, the question becomes would I go for a pint with you? I would, but I'd feel obliged to, whereas with one of my mates, I'd go because I wanted to. It's not that I don't like you boss, it's just that our working relationship makes it impossible to be mates; I suppose that's what I'm saying.'

'I don't really have any mates,' said Eoin.

Dave looked at him again.

'I think that's more a personal choice than anything else though, isn't it?'

'I suppose it is.'

He was still in a world of his own when they pulled up outside the industrial unit.

He followed Dave into the building; he rarely got involved in operational logistics. He felt a twinge of anticipation as he saw all the guns laid out on a side table. The hubbub of conversation ceased as they walked in. There were about a dozen guys standing around chatting, and they parted reverentially to allow Dave and Black Swan access to the central area.

Eoin stood back a little to give Dave some room to spread his maps and diagrams across the table. The men gathered around and Black Swan could see that Dave had split them into sections; four in total with a leader for each team.

'Okay, this is the way we're going to play it,' said Dave.

He indicated a large, dark haired man with a thick angular face. He was wearing a sleeveless T-shirt and his upper arms and chest area were covered with tattoos.

'Pavel?' asked Dave. 'Ready?'

The man nodded.

'Your team are going in first. You're going to be responsible for securing the perimeter and then neutralising the alarm system. You will be the advance guard. Take what you need, and head out in the first van, the red one.'

Dave indicated the table laden with guns.

Pavel nodded curtly. His team grabbed their weapons and walked away.

'Okay, listen up the rest of you. Deano....'

Dave, indicated a large, thickset, blond haired guy with a beard and a misshapen boxer's nose.

'You're team two.'

Dave paused as the walkie-talkie buzzed beside him.

'We're rolling, boss,' came the message, in heavily accented English.

'Roger that Pavel,' said Dave. 'Okay Deano, your team are taking the rear. Grab what you need and make sure you also take a couple of those jemmy bars. The alarm should be neutralised by then, but you still have to get those fire doors open. Johnno....'

Dave directed this to a small, barrel-chested, bald-headed guy.

'You're team three. You're heading for the left side of the building.'

David indicated the doors he was talking about on the surveillance photos.

'Take what you need; again, make sure you take the crowbars.'

'No problems, chief.'

'Brian....'

Dave pointed to the last man.

'You're the team going in from the right. Assemble your weapons, pry bars and wait for the signal.'

'Got it boss.'

Dave picked up the walkie-talkie again.

'Team two,' he said.

'Roger,' came the crackling reply, 'we're rolling.'

'Recce your area,' said Dave. 'Don't start moving in until I say so.'

'Roger that.'

'Team three?'

'Go ahead boss.'

'Get yourselves in position, but do not move in until I give the word.'

'Roger.'

'Team four,' shouted Dave across at the guys.

Brian looked round.

'Do not move in until I say so, do you understand?'

'Yes boss.'

Team four left and they heard the sound of the van starting up. Dave walked over to the warehouse door and hit a switch. The shutter started grinding up into the roof.

'Back in a minute, boss,' he shouted.

Black Swan heard the car start and then the Mercedes shot through the doors and screeched to a halt.

'Don't want to lose it now, do we,' said Dave with a smile.

Black Swan stood admiring the table. The weapons were laid out like tempting treats in a shop window. Dave selected an automatic pistol and three ammunition clips. He loaded one and pocketed the others, then noticed that Black Swan was watching him curiously.

'Can I have one?' asked Black Swan, almost shyly.

Dave didn't know what to say.

'Well, they are all yours, I suppose,' he said. 'Have you shot a gun before?'

Black Swan picked up a similar automatic pistol and clip. He slammed the clip home and made sure the safety was off. He chambered a round and then turned to the rear wall where there was an old Pirelli calendar hanging on a bent nail. He aimed almost casually.

The bang was deafening in the confined space, and Dave jumped; he hadn't been expecting it. He recovered his composure and walked over to the calendar. He was sure the model had been an attractive girl, but it was impossible to tell now. The area where her face should have been was obliterated.

'Where did you learn to shoot like that?' asked Dave breathlessly.

'Years ago, the Bull made me do a week's shooting in the Czech Republic; mainly handguns, one of those fake Stag weekends. It seems I was a natural.'

'Do you know what boss?' said Dave, smiling. 'You really are full of surprises.'

#

I sat on a dry stone wall next to Roussel and Dale, unaware that almost the exact spot had been occupied only the previous evening. We'd acquired some binoculars from a fishing tackle shop, but we had no night vision. Once the darkness closed in, we would have to get close. Still it was May; we were heading towards the longest day with a vengeance. It was a calm clear night. I smiled as I remembered that night back in Louisiana; it seemed like a lifetime ago. A storm was on the rise tonight too, it was just not of God's making this time.

'So what do we do now?' asked Roussel.

'Now we wait,' I said, focussing my glasses on the large grey building ahead of us. "Now we wait.'

CHAPTER 55 – ACCEPTANCE

23rd May 2011 – Thirteen days after the Storm.

Generally speaking, the way of the warrior is resolute acceptance of death. – Miyamoto Musashi.

The consultant emerged from the doorway of his consulting room. He was wearing a shiny grey suit, last fashionable about twenty years ago. David was strangely reassured; surely someone as badly dressed as this could only be the bearer of good news.

The consultant's face was inscrutable as he searched the waiting room, before a tiny glimmer of recognition lit up his features. He looked like a caricature of the puppet Punch, with his large beaked nose and full fleshy lips. The image was completed by the wisps of blonde hair, which were receding badly on the top and at the temples.

'Mr. McCabe!' he called sharply.

A glimmer of relief showed as David stood up; another exorbitant fee banked. He nodded curtly as David moved inside.

The consultant walked around to the other side of his large mahogany desk as David settled himself into the small uncomfortable G-plan cast off; obviously a plan to keep consultations to a minimum time. They sat in silence as the consultant read silently through the file. He made the odd grunt as he read, peering over the top of his glasses, an action that made David silently question why he was wearing them. After about five minutes of reading, his lips stopped moving and he closed the file with a slap, making David jump.

'Mr. McCabe,' he said. 'The cancer is end stage. There is absolutely nothing we can do. You're dying. Go home and someone will be in touch about respite care.'

He got up, staring at David in irritation, as if wondering why he was still there. He pointed at the door, indicating that the consultation was over. As David stumbled out into the waiting room, bewildered, his mind in turmoil, he heard the consultant utter one last word.

'Next!'

David got into his car and dried his tears on his sleeve. The enormity of what he had just been told would not sink in. He lay back in the seat and closed his eyes. He stroked his chin, feeling the day's worth of stubble. It felt good; at least there was still testosterone in his system. The cancer had not robbed him of his manhood. It was starting to feel that way. It had not robbed him of the last shreds of his humanity either. That's why he couldn't focus on anything.

His brain refused to accept the information it was being asked to process and he slipped into a fitful sleep.

His body started twitching as he dreamed. He saw the street corners in his subconscious; the ones that his drug runners stood on to sell their wares. He patted the pockets of his own hand-tailored leather jacket. They were bulging with the little plastic bags full of white powder. The kids sidled up to him with money at the ready, some of them as young as twelve years old. He didn't care. He wasn't their fucking guardian. He was just fulfilling a demand; he didn't make the rules, he just lived by them. And no bad life it was either.

In his dream, the kids surrounded him, jostling him. They were fighting each other; trying to outdo all the others as they pushed their money toward him like autograph hunters at a boy band concert. They all wore the same uniform; Addidas three stripe track suits with the hoods up. David was annoyed because he could not see their faces, so he told them to pull their hoods down or they'd get no gear. The hoods all came down and he stifled a scream; they had no eyes, just dark bottomless pits of despair.

He woke, bathed in sweat, silently screaming. As he slowly recovered, he knew with utter conviction that he would continue to have that same dream; every time a little bit more vivid. Maybe the clarity would be defined by his mortality; the clearer the dream, the nearer the end.

He'd never previously thought about what he was doing in terms of morality, but the past day or so had made him wake up. For him, it had all been about the here and now. Money equals power, power equals prestige and respect. Fuck spirituality.

He got out of the car, oblivious to the sweat soaking through his immaculately tailored clothes. Sartorial elegance was not currently high on his list of priorities.

The clinic was on the south side of Cork. He had driven himself over to give Tony a break and instead of going straight home, he started walking through his domain, his kingdom, the poorer parts of the south city. He visited the actual reality; the street corners of his dream, and looked at them through different eyes. He saw poverty and deprivation, he saw emptiness and desolation. He saw the flotsam and jetsam of society, rejects cast aside and cultivated by demonic agents of capitalism. He saw pale imitations of his younger self; callow youths obsessed only with material wealth, pedalling junk to anyone with the money. Is this what he wanted to do with the remainder of his life; trade off the misery of others? Did he have a chance to repent, especially when his mortality was defined in weeks rather than years?

He didn't know why, but as he headed back to the car, he felt his feet stray across the threshold of the old church; the first time he had entered one since his communion. The feelings were strangely familiar and somehow comforting because of it. He had a sense of foreboding; fear and trepidation of the known and the unknown. He dragged himself toward the confessional booths and ducked inside the nearest one. It had a sign similar to the one you see at supermarkets when the checkout lane is open, which made him smile weakly.

As the curtain dropped behind him, he was assaulted by the unmistakable smell of alcohol and cigarettes; the twin vices, it seemed, of any aged priest. Not that David blamed them; with a vow of celibacy, there was fuck all else for them to do. The hatch was slammed back, and the priest waited for the opening words.

'Forgive me father, for I have sinned,' David stated softly. 'It is fifteen years since my last confession.'

'Go on, my son,' the priest prompted.

So David did. He told him the whole story of his life and in the telling realized that forgiveness was beyond the bounds of the time that he had left. As David finished his tale, he pondered the forces that had driven his feet through the door, as the priest sat in silence, his nasal breathing the only indication that someone else was there.

'Nobody is beyond redemption,' he said eventually. 'But before God can forgive someone, they need to forgive themselves.'

He paused for a minute.

'I fear this is where you will find the most resistance. Say five *Hail Mary's* and twenty decades of the rosary.'

'Thank you, father,' David replied.

He'd never given much thought to confession before. It was just an instinctive church thing, like making the sign of the cross. It was only when he needed it now, that he realized how powerful it was. On paper, it seemed to be the most unfair system in the world. You got to unburden yourself to a complete stranger; transferring the enormous weight of your guilt to someone else, and while maybe not relieving you completely, it certainly made that burden feel much lighter. As David lifted the heavy velvet curtain, a shaft of sunlight invaded the booth and he felt a lightness of being that he had not felt in months.

It was then that he heard a new sound. The priest was crying; very softly, but crying nonetheless. David wanted to go back and apologise but he couldn't. He didn't blame the priest; it wasn't much of an epitaph on a life really.

When he got back to the house, he dropped the keys of the car back to Tony. He asked him to head off and collect Ben and then come back to pick him up for his date with destiny.

Ordinarily, he would have been unable to think of anything else, but at that moment, the knowledge of the impending journey was merely a slight disturbance deep in his subconscious. It was like the itch of a mosquito bite while you're reading; a vague irritation which you more or less ignore. No, he had more important things that he needed to resolve before he left. He sat in the armchair and as the leather creaked under his backside, he smiled for probably the first time that afternoon. Sam looked up from the book she was reading and noticed that he was watching her.

'What?' she asked, self consciously.

'Just admiring the view,' he said.

She laughed.

'I don't know about that,' she said, and went back to her book.

David strained his eyes to see if he could discern the title of the book she was reading. She had squealed with delight when she'd discovered the library. David's Dad had developed a huge passion for books during his lifetime, and had created a large library to house his collection.

There was very little furniture in the room. Two easy chairs facing the fireplace, with every other wall lined floor-to-ceiling with glass fronted bookcases. Sam had run from cabinet to cabinet, chattering excitedly to herself.

'What is it about books that you love?' he asked her now.

He maintained his father's collection lovingly, but he'd never understood the obsession.

'They're like friends,' she said, looking up. 'If you have a book, you are never alone. They're a barometer of emotions. If you're feeling sad, you can read a favourite chapter and your mood lifts.'

'Doesn't that get boring?' asked David.

'Are memories boring?' asked Sam. 'It's the same thing really, isn't it?'

David thought about his own turbulent maelstrom of memories.

'Yeah, you're right,' he conceded. 'Mine are certainly never boring.'

At last his vision focused properly and he managed to read the title of the book.

'Aldous Huxley,' he repeated. 'Brave New World; what's that all about?'

'It's about a utopian society where children are no longer brought up in families, they're fertilised and grown in bottles. Where drugs are legal and encouraged and pretty much everything is done in the pursuit of pleasure.'

David thought about it for a couple of minutes.

'That sounds pretty horrible actually,' he said seriously, thinking about his dream.

'The pursuit of pleasure for the sake of pleasure,' agreed Sam. 'I see it in the faces of my own clients; morally corrupt and bereft.'

'Isn't that what I'm trying to accomplish?' asked David quietly.

'Maybe so,' said Sam. 'But by the same token, some people just can't do real life. They need to have their senses dulled.'

'I don't want to live like that anymore,' said David suddenly.

Sam blinked.

'If I asked you to stay with me, would you do it?' asked David.

'What's the catch?' asked Sam.

'No catch,' said David. 'It's just with you I feel human, and I want to keep feeling human.'

'You know that Ben is paying me for this,' she blurted out suddenly.

The guilt had been eating away at her. She wanted their conversations to be rooted in foundations of honesty. She felt at home with David; an emotion she had not expected.

'I don't care,' said David. 'I'll pay you double what he's paying if you'll stay; triple or quadruple even.'

'It doesn't work like that, David,' she said gently. 'You can't buy everything you want, no matter how much money you have'

She looked over at him. He looked crestfallen and defeated.

'But yes, I will stay,' she continued, 'on one condition. I don't want payment, all I want is bed and board and we'll see how it goes.'

There was a loud single knock on the front door.

'That'll be Ben,' she said.

'Will you still be here when I get back?' he asked, making no move to get up.

She got up and placed the book deliberately to one side. He waited expectantly as she crossed the divide between them. She bent down and kissed him on the cheek.

'You're not a bad person David,' she said. 'Even though everyone has told you that and you've tried to convince yourself. Just remember that. Try and reach back and grab onto the person you used to be. So go and do your deal. We can talk about things when you get back.'

He smiled, and this time it extended to his eyes. She could see a renewed sparkle in them as he walked backwards slowly and then turned and virtually skipped through the door.

A shadow passed across her face, and she shivered; like someone had just run roughshod over her grave. She went back to her chair and settled down with the book, but she couldn't shake the feeling, no matter how deeply she tried to bury herself in the words. Eventually, after about half an hour she gave up and went into the sitting room.

She snuggled into the corner of the couch, David's corner, and switched on the large screen. As she watched the flickering images, she tried to use them to blot out the sinking feeling in her stomach.

#

David stopped at the end of the corridor. Even though he was out of earshot, he stifled the sobs, crying silently for a minute or so. Then he quickly walked to the bathroom, doused some water on his face and forced a smile to rearrange his features. He opened the door and replaced the mask. The Bullock was back; for this evening anyway.

He motioned Tony to get back behind the wheel and slid into the rear, next to his right hand man.

'You look pleased with yourself, but in a slightly depressed kind of way.' said Ben, half statement and half question.

'Let's just call it a matter of life and death and leave it at that,' said David mysteriously.

Ben looked at him strangely, but he didn't seem to be joking.

'Leave it Ben,' added David. 'Maybe I'll tell you over a glass of whiskey someday. At the moment we have other things to concentrate on.'

'True,' said Ben.

They journeyed the rest of the way in silence; one of them thinking about the implications of success and the other thinking about the implications of failure. Ben looked at his watch. They were about five minutes early. David made no move to get out, so neither did Ben.

'We'll wait for them in the car,' said David. 'We can all go in together then.'

They sat in silence for another minute or so.

'Do you have everything you need? You brought it all with you?'

Ben placed his briefcase on his knees and patted it in a self satisfied way.

'I always carry it with me, all of it. I don't trust the safe to something this valuable.'

David glanced across and then lapsed into silence again.

'Someone's coming,' interrupted Tony suddenly.

They all watched as a large black limousine pulled into the business park, slowly negotiating the roundabout before pulling up outside the building. David looked at his watch. It was five pm exactly, an impressive display of timekeeping. They watched for two or three minutes. There was no movement of any kind from the dark Mercedes.

'Looks like we'll have to make the first move,' said David. 'Tony, would you do the honours?'

Tony grunted and got out of the car. He proceeded to Ben's side and opened his door first. As Ben slid out, Tony stepped around the back and repeated the procedure on the other side.

Ben waited at the front of the car, briefcase in hand, as David joined him. They walked over to the waiting car, both of them feeling a tiny bit foolish and more than a little exposed.

They waited, each holding their breath as the tension built.

Suddenly, the passenger door flew open, causing them to both jump slightly and then exchange mildly uncomfortable glances. As they watched, an enormous man got out and regarded them inscrutably for a few seconds.

'Antonio?' ventured Ben hesitantly.

The big man nodded. He moved to the back and opened the door. He bent down and they heard low voices. Then two men stepped out in quick succession and turned to face them.

Ben and David approached the two older men slowly, heeding the warning in Antonio's eyes. To David, they looked like ordinary pensioners. He didn't have a point of reference really, as his father had been pretty young when he'd died, but he had been expecting them to have more of a presence. Granted, with their sharp suits, piercing eyes and slicked back hair, they did look like the archetypal mobsters, but even so, he'd been expecting Al Pacino.

'David McCabe?' asked one, and David immediately revised his opinion. This was a voice used to command; used to getting its own way.

'Mr Mancini,' acknowledged David, walking forward and taking a surprisingly firm handshake.

'Guido, please,' said the man, in a harsh New York brogue. 'And this is my brother, Ernesto.'

'Pleased to meet you both,' said David, shaking the other hand.

He indicated Ben.

'You both know my associate, Ben Collins; well, you've spoken on the phone at least.'

They nodded and more handshakes took place.

'Well,' said David, 'shall we go in?'

He indicated the main entrance and they were about to go through, when a car came screaming into the estate. David noticed the small Hertz sticker on the rear window as it braked to a halt in a shower of small stones.

'Who's this joker?' asked David, as Bill came rushing over.

Ben could see the security guard instinctively reaching under his jacket for his weapon and motioned him surreptitiously to hold off for a second.

The stranger walked up to the group of men, laughing quietly to himself.

'What's this?' he asked. 'Guido, did you not tell your hosts that I was coming?'

#

I kept the glasses trained on the entrance. When the BMW arrived and the three men got out, I passed the glasses to Dale and then Roussel.

'That must be David McCabe and Ben Collins,' said Roussel.

'A reasonable guess,' I said.

'Hang on,' said Roussel. 'What's this?'

We saw a large limousine sweep around the roundabout and into the car park. I clicked my fingers impatiently at Roussel, who reluctantly handed the glasses back.

As I focussed, I felt the familiar flip in my stomach; Antonio, Guido and Ernesto. They had been my friends and colleagues, and dare I say it, family for many years. I still felt the conflicting emotions.

'Is it the Mancini's?' asked Dale excitedly.

I nodded slowly. Then I saw another car scream into the car park.

'Who's that?' asked Roussel.

As he got out of the car, he looked around him. The last time I had seen those eyes had been on the other side of the window ledge in my mother's house, framed in plaster dust.

'This is starting to get interesting,' I murmured. 'Our double dealing CIA friend is back; the one from my mum's house. He must be the mole.'

'Are you sure?' asked Roussel.

I nodded absently without replying. I had seen a flash of movement across the fields. I swung the glasses over and saw four men crouching behind a stone wall. They were talking quietly, and as they moved I saw the glint of sun on blue steel.

'Looks like things are really starting to heat up now,' I said.

I tapped the holdall beside me.

'Good job we have some means of cooling things down.'

CHAPTER 56 – CONFRONTATION

23rd May 2011 – Thirteen days after the Storm.

Confront them with annihilation, and they will then survive; plunge them into a deadly situation, and they will then live. When people fall into danger, they are then able to strive for victory. – Sun Tzu.

Bill watched the *executives* entering the building with a mixture of amusement and contempt. Who were they kidding? He knew what they did, despite the elaborate subterfuge.

He was similar to someone who worked in a brewery or a cigarette factory. You didn't have to like smoking or drinking to work there, but it paid the bills and he had to admit; this job really did pay very well.

He thought of his daughter, struggling to forge a normal life with cystic fibrosis. When he thought of her, his qualms were easy to dismiss.

Ben had told him that they had special guests coming this evening, so he'd stepped up the security accordingly. Normally, there were only two, this evening there were seven. He'd also rostered himself on to manage and coordinate.

Bill let a polite interval elapse before he followed his employers and their guests back through the front entrance.

'Hey chief,' said Vinnie, the guard behind the desk.

Another ex soldier, he was almost impossibly cheerful, almost all of the time.

'Hey Vinnie,' said Bill. 'Can you tell me what zones are alarmed at the moment?'

Vinnie checked the panel behind his head, squinting over the top of his reading glasses.

'All zones alarmed except the upstairs offices and the reception area,' said Vinnie.

'Okay, switch off the zones on the main production floor,' said Bill, 'but keep all the external access points alarmed.'

'You got it, chief,' replied Vinnie.

'You going out for a fag?' asked Bill, extracting his pack and his lighter.

'It's awfully tempting, chief,' he said, 'but I've been off them since Good Friday. I really want to give it a go this time.'

'Wish I had your willpower,' said Bill with a smile.

'So do I,' said Vinnie, with an answering smile.

Bill walked back the way he had come in, out through the reception doors, and felt the cool West of Ireland breeze fresh on his face. They were near the sea and he could feel the salt hanging in the atmosphere. He inhaled deeply, a large lungful of the fresh life-sustaining elixir. He put a cigarette in his mouth, thinking how ironic it was that he was just about to deliberately pollute the pure clean air of his last breath.

He cupped his hand around the lighter and pressed the switch, but the wind blew the flame out immediately. He swivelled until he felt the wind on his back and then clicked the switch again. As he did so, he saw a flicker of movement.

It took him a couple of milliseconds to register the gun that the crouching intruder was holding out in front of him. A couple of milliseconds more and he had identified the fact that there was a silencer screwed into the barrel.

He saw the muzzle flash and felt the small stones kicked up against his legs, as the bullet impacted between his feet. The cigarette dropped from his lips and the lighter dropped from his hands as he dived sideways, reaching under his jacket as he did so.

In his mind, he was immediately transported back to the Lebanon and some Arab terrorist was trying to kill him. He fell heavily and winded himself, partly because of his age and partly because his hand was inside his jacket, probing for the gun.

Even though he was almost breathless, he kept rolling. He knew it was his only chance to evade the bullets. His hand closed around the butt of the weapon and still he kept rolling. He could hear the sound of the silencer in a measured beat, the whistle and whine of the bullets as the words of his training ground instructor came back to him.

'Always a moving target son,' he'd shouted at the top of his voice. 'You always need to be a moving target!'

The sound of silencer and bullets ceased and he heard the unmistakable sound of a clip being loaded. He took a chance and stopped rolling, turning onto his back. His own weapon cleared his jacket and he aimed and fired almost simultaneously, just as his assailant's barrel came up. The report from his weapon drowned out the small *phut* of the silenced round. He felt a stinging pain in his shoulder, but at the same time he heard a cry of agony. He rolled again and the pain in his shoulder intensified.

He tried to ignore it, instead focusing all his energy on staying alive. As he turned onto his back again, he held the gun in front of him. Cautiously, he inched his head up off the ground to look ahead and saw his assailant sprawled between clumps of rough grass and heather.

Bill levered himself up with difficulty and walked slowly towards the shooter. His army training had always instilled in him the need to go for the big targets. By a combination of luck and design, he had hit the man squarely in the chest. By the look of it, his heart was gone. The stranger's eyes had rolled up into his head and he was scrabbling weakly at the ground.

'You shot me, you bastard!' shouted Bill.

It was all he could think of to say.

Suddenly his legs buckled. At the same instant, he felt a terrible pain in his chest as he sank to his knees. He looked down in surprise to register the fact that his crisp white shirt was turning red with blood. The shock of the discovery seemed to drain the strength from his body and the gun slipped from his powerless fingers. His vision started to cloud. He lifted his head with difficulty and saw the outline of a man framed against the sun.

'So did I,' said a voice in heavily accented English.

By the time Pavel heard the silenced report of his second shot echo off the hills behind him, the impact of the actual bullet had knocked Bill backwards in a messy twisted heap of limbs. Pavel walked up and spat on the blood soaked body and then savagely kicked it. He hadn't been expecting to encounter any resistance, let alone lose a member of his team.

His earpiece barked into life. He transmitted his reply. Two of the targets had been neutralised, but were alive. Bill had also been neutralised, but he had not been so lucky.

Pavel was not happy. As he walked into the main reception, he was not in the mood for chit chat. Vinnie looked up, not yet registering anything except surprise.

'Hey,' he shouted. 'You can't....'

He hit the desk with a loud thud. Two shots to the head; Pavel couldn't be bothered messing around trying to disarm people any more. Vinnie was stone dead, even before his head slammed into the front desk.

Pavel walked around the desk, grabbed the prone guard by the collar and dragged him to the floor behind the counter where he wouldn't be casually spotted. Turning his attention to the Alarm panel, he opened the front cover and studied it implacably for about a minute. He seemed to come to a decision. He took a spare clip from his inside pocket and reloaded. Whipping the gun up suddenly, he emptied the entire magazine into the panel, which duly exploded in an electrical cacophony of hisses and crackles. He closed the front cover to hide the devastation.

He hit the transmit button on his headset again.

'Team one in position, all objectives achieved,' he said.

Black Swan and Dave heard it from their place of concealment.

'Roger that,' said Dave. 'Teams two, three and four, I want you to standby for further orders.'

Eoin grabbed Dave's shoulder.

'I want all the major players taken alive and unharmed,' he said. 'I repeat; David McCabe, Ben Collins, Guido and Ernesto Mancini and the rest of their colleagues must remain unharmed. Other collateral damage is permitted; I won't cry about the security personnel, but the main players must be unharmed, do you understand?'

Dave nodded.

'Unharmed,' said Eoin again, to emphasise his point.

'Okay, Teams two, three and four, you are a go. Secure the perimeter and then secure the building. No injuries other than to security staff. I repeat, no injuries other than to hired security.'

'Roger,' Dave heard three times, from three slightly different voices.

The table was set and the pieces were now moving.

#

There was an awkward silence as they clustered around David McCabe's conference-room table.

'Who is this arsehole?' asked David eventually.

'Let's just say that I am the provider of all your future bounty,' said the stranger grandly.

'What he means to say,' said Guido disdainfully, 'is that he is a double agent, the man who provided us with the opportunity to acquire Storm.'

'Hey, don't knock it,' said the stranger. 'You need people like me.'

'I agree, you have your uses,' acknowledged Ernesto sourly. 'But a man without honour is not a man.'

'Fuck you,' said the stranger.

He felt Antonio bristle and Ernesto put a warning hand on his arm.

'That's right, keep your pet monkey at bay,' sneered the stranger.

Antonio sat back and smiled. The smile told the stranger that if the opportunity ever presented itself, Antonio would not hesitate.

'You need to be very careful Mr....' responded Guido.

'No names,' said the stranger sharply, with the first hint of anxiety.

'Whatever,' said Guido, 'but let me just say Mr No-name, that you seem to have hurt his feelings, and Antonio has a very long memory.'

The stranger shrugged dismissively.

'I'll take my chances.'

Ben had been watching the proceedings carefully, waiting patiently for an opening. He took the opportunity and cleared his throat politely.

'Ever the diplomat, eh Mr Collins?' said the stranger. 'Let me guess. You want the missing piece of the puzzle, would I be right?'

Ben ignored the stranger.

'Do you have the addendum?' he asked Guido formally.

Guido snapped his fingers and Antonio placed a small attaché case on the desk in front of them. They all heard the familiar double-click as the latches were released and the lid was opened. Antonio extracted a twenty page document held together with a large paper clip. Ben and David exchanged a look of relief.

In turn, Ben slid a much larger document across the table.

'Final contract for review,' he said.

Guido clicked his fingers for Antonio to pick it up.

'Our lawyers will look it over,' he said disdainfully.

'I expected nothing less,' said Ben, trying to stifle a smile.

'Can we see the production lines?' asked Ernesto, trying to suppress his eagerness.

He was the more operational of the brothers; the one who understood project planning and logistics, and who loved seeing the end product of both.

'Certainly,' said David.

He cocked an eyebrow at his colleague.

'Ben?' he asked enquiringly.

'Follow me,' said Ben.

He led the way, with the Mancini's tagging directly behind. Antonio and the stranger brought up the rear, with David joined onto the end of the motley caravan.

Ben led them down the stairs and through reception. He flashed his badge at the proximity reader and entered his pin, and proceeded to hold the door open as the others filtered through.

This was Ben's first mistake in almost six months of meticulous planning. In his haste and eagerness to please, he had completely missed the lack of security guard in reception.

It would come back to haunt him.

He walked over to the main lighting panel. Even though it was dark, he knew exactly where it was. He flicked all of the switches up and everyone blinked in the sudden harsh artificial light.

'What was that?' asked Ernesto suddenly.

'What was what?' asked Ben, as he walked back to the main party.

'I thought I heard a noise,' he said.

'Must be just the wind outside,' said Ben.

That particular second, a hundred yards away, one of the wires in the ravaged alarm panel gave up its desperate fight. The tensile strength of the individual strand, all that was left of the original siren wire, was not enough to overcome the natural inclination of the burnished copper to pull away from the panel.

The second the strand gave way, the wire popped and the building erupted in a cacophony of sound. The sirens were so loud they hurt. The occupants had to shield their ears. David was livid, but as he glanced over at Ben he saw his friend's jaw drop in astonishment. David followed the direction that Ben was looking and his expression hardened. Two security guards were walking towards them in handcuffs, being alternately dragged and pushed by four men armed with pistols.

They heard a noise on the other side of the building. This time a larger gang approached; eight members all told, each carrying a pistol and pushing one more handcuffed security officer. Then they heard another bang from behind them, and the alarm klaxon ceased.

Antonio's hand flew under his jacket.

'I wouldn't do that if I were you.'

The clipped eastern European request came from behind them.

Antonio froze and looked around. Four guys with pistols emerged from the very passageway that the group had transited with Ben just moments earlier. Antonio was brave but he was not foolhardy. His hand dropped.

'Into a line please with your hands outstretched,' instructed Pavel.

All the men in the group complied. Pavel indicated one of his men, who stepped forward to do a thorough pat down on each individual in turn. He found two weapons. Antonio unsurprisingly had one. The look he gave his disarmer was implacable. Suffice to say, the gentleman in question was glad there were four or five guns trained on Antonio at the time. The other weapon belonged to the CIA operative, who was more than happy to surrender it.

'I don't like the damn things anyway,' he responded, as the weapon was handed over. 'I was always more in danger of shooting myself than anyone else.'

He chuckled, but no one else thought it was funny.

Pavel thumbed the transmit button again, as the captives regarded him dolefully.

'Targets acquired,' he said.

'Casualties?'

The response was static filled.

'Two guards dead, one of my team also, no other injuries to report.'

'Okay, we're coming in,' said the same static voice.

'Keep your hands up,' intoned Pavel brusquely, as Guido started to lower his arms.

'It's okay,' said a voice behind Pavel. 'Everyone can put them down now.'

As the two guys came into view, there was a sharp intake of breath from Ben. David's face seemed to collapse in upon itself until he was almost unrecognisable.

'Hello David,' said Black Swan softly.

He was strangely subdued and there was not a hint of triumphalism about his attitude or demeanour.

'What the hell are you doing here?' asked David.

It sounded like he was chewing his way through a mouthful of broken glass.

'Seems your operation may not have been as clandestine or discrete as you may have first thought,' answered Black Swan.

'There are no leaks in my organisation,' stated David.

'I think you might be right about that,' said Black Swan.

He indicated the CIA operative.

'But it appears our friend here may not have had the same level of secrecy surrounding his own affairs.'

The stranger inclined his head in acknowledgement.

'Guilty, I'm afraid,' he nodded sadly. 'I thought I'd managed to neutralise the threat, but obviously not. Pity about Agent Bruce; he was a nice if misguided man. He really should not have tried to get between me and my fortune.'

He turned to Black Swan.

'It was you, wasn't it?'

Black Swan nodded.

'Do you mind me asking how he gave the game away?'

'He pretty much told me the whole story. He named no names of course, although there were some thinly veiled hints, but the rest of it was stone cold truth. He was deliberately trying to get me involved. I don't like being played, but the rewards in this case outweighed the annoyance.'

'I should have offered him an in,' said the stranger. 'I was being too greedy I think. As my dad used to say, fifty percent of something is better than one hundred percent of nothing.'

The stranger paused.

'How did he die?'

'When we met that first night in the restaurant, I managed to get a tracking device on him,' said Black Swan. 'I had someone follow him. When I felt he was no longer useful, I ordered him gone; they ran him down in a car.'

The Mancini's snorted in disgust, which the stranger chose to ignore.

'So, what happens now?' asked David, focussing his attention directly on Black Swan. 'Going to finally finish the job you started? Eliminate the entire McCabe family from the face of the earth?'

'That depends on certain things,' said Black Swan.

'Actually that's almost right,' said a voice behind Pavel. 'But I have a few questions that I really need some answers to first.'

CHAPTER 57 – ARMISTICE

23rd May 2011 – Thirteen days after the Storm.

Peace is an armistice in a war that is continuously going on. – Thucydides.

I walked out of the tunnel and into the harsh artificial light, keeping the gun extended ahead like a warning beacon. As I approached the point where Pavel was standing, all eyes were on me and I heard a deep intake of breath from both Guido and Ernesto. I felt the familiar twist, deep in the heart of my stomach; I would have to deal with that emotion as best I could. A number of the weapons started to swivel my way, as did one or two bursts of contemptuous laughter. I cleared my throat.

'Before anyone gets hurt, we all need to relax a little bit, I think,' I said.

I raised my voice slightly, so they could all hear the next words.

'Mr Roussel, Mr Foster, would both of you mind illustrating to these gentleman why compliance would be a good idea.'

There were two short bursts of shatteringly loud machine gun fire. Most of the occupants of the room ducked instinctively, as the debris showered down on them in fragments of ceiling tiles and plaster dust. Dale and Roussel emerged from the shadows on either side, weapons poised and ready.

'And let's bear in mind one vital fact,' I continued. 'These guys care for nobody but me, so you gentlemen need to make sure there are no itchy trigger fingers out there. In fact....'

I continued on in a chatty, upbeat tone.

'Let's all put our guns on the ground in front of us; we'll all feel much more comfortable after that.'

I held up my own weapon to show them, and then placed it gently on the ground at my feet. Dale and Roussel gestured with the muzzles of their machine guns; the meaning was clear. You could hear the multiple metallic clunks of cold steel being placed carefully on the painted concrete floor.

'That's better,' I said, when they'd all finished.

'What about them?' asked Pavel inscrutably, gesturing at Roussel and Foster.

'What about them?' I asked. 'I think they'll stay exactly where they are, if only to keep the rest of you honest. I'm sure there are a number of heroic hot heads amongst you. I feel it is only right to try and stop anyone doing something stupid.'

I let my eyes wander around the interior of the featureless warehouse. I ignored all the hired hands, the faceless ones, but as I continued to look around, I felt eight pairs of eyes boring into me. I met the gaze of the first; Antonio, my former colleague and friend. There was no antipathy in his stare, no challenge, no outrage, he just shook his head and then smiled sadly; like a headmaster admonishing a repeatedly offending pupil.

I ignored my friend the CIA mole; from his expression, I could tell he was not best pleased to see me. It was nice to see the smug superiority wiped from his face.

The next brace of eyes told a very different story altogether. They burned with a special kind of hatred; the kind reserved for embarrassing and irrepressible mistakes.

'I don't know why you guys are so upset,' I said dryly. 'I'm the one you tried to kill.'

'You broke the code,' said Ernesto coldly.

'I think you'll find that I didn't,' I replied. 'I was merely defending myself. Give me some credit. If I had gone back to you with the folder as planned, I wouldn't be standing here now, would I?'

Neither of them replied.

'Exactly,' I said. 'That's all the answer I need.'

I looked at my CIA friend.

'And besides,' I said, indicating the agent. 'Our friend here had left a helpful post-it note on the folder, outlining who he was going to pass it on to. I didn't know what it was that I had exactly, but from the note, I knew he was giving it to you guys. I knew that you wanted it badly as I'd seen the desire etched on your faces, so I figured it would probably be a good bargaining tool.'

Guido smiled; almost a sickly smile.

'Look, errors were made on both sides,' he said, maybe a little too hastily. 'We've come to realise that we made a big mistake trying to forcibly retire you. Can you not do the same for us? Acknowledge that what you did was wrong too, and then we can all get back to the way it used to be.'

I thought about it for a second.

'You know what, Guido,' I stated, 'you're right.'

He blanched at my use of his given name; the first time I had done so in over twenty years.

'I did make a mistake, a big one. I should have got out of this game about fifteen years ago, when I still had the chance of a semi-normal life.'

Ernesto's eyes narrowed.

'But that's just it, Street,' he said. 'You just don't get it, do you? You're not normal, any more than we are. You're not capable of walking away; this is what you do and who you are.'

'I don't think so,' I said implacably. 'Watch me.'

'Good luck,' Ernesto said.

His face was unreadable.

I turned to the next two gentlemen. They were obviously together; their physical proximity and shared responses gave it away.

'And who might you two be?' I asked.

'David McCabe,' said one, indicating himself, 'and Ben Collins,' he continued, indicating his companion.

There was not a shred of fear in his response.

'So you're the local brains behind this operation,' I said, gesturing around the large room that we were all standing in.

David smiled without a trace of humour.

'Who are you?' he asked.

'He's my brother,' said a soft voice into the silence.

All eyes swivelled towards the speaker, their expressions ranging from mildly surprised to complete astonishment. Of the eight men who mattered in that room, I now at least knew which one of them was my half brother.

Black Swan, the man trying to kill his own flesh and blood.

I studied him and he studied me right back. There was nothing remotely similar from a brief outward glance that would tie us together as brothers. We neither looked alike nor sounded alike. I continued to stare at him with a morbid fascination. There was the sound of bitter laughter. I flicked a glance to see who was speaking; David McCabe.

'What kind of stunt are you trying to pull here?' he asked between chuckles. 'You don't have a brother. What do you take me for?'

I ignored the outburst. I had eyes only for one man.

'Why?' I asked him directly.

He in turn was focused entirely on me.

'Why what?' he asked.

He was giving nothing away.

'Why did you go to all of that trouble; all of that elaborate subterfuge? Why that stupid sting operation you tried to pull with that small time dealer, Scott Mitchell? Trying to pass him off as my son?'

I had an unreasonable urge to show him how much I knew about his little scheme.

'But the main question, especially as I seem to be all the family you have, is why?'

'Don't you dare use that word!' he said.

He was truly affronted.

'You are not family.'

'I think you'll find brothers normally are!' I responded dryly.

He ignored my response and his voice rose slightly in cadence and shrillness.

'You ruined my life,' he stated simply.

I blinked.

'I didn't even know who you were until two weeks ago,' I said. 'How could I possibly have ruined your life?'

'You stole my father,' he said slowly. 'You and that bitch who called herself your mother.'

I stiffened and bristled.

'Now hold on a second,' I said.

'No, you hold on!' he shouted. 'I've been waiting years for this moment. You're going to stand there and listen to what I've got to say.'

The spittle was flying from the harshly compressed lips.

'Your mother had sex with my father; a married man.'

He almost screamed this bit; as though it was incomprehensible to him.

'Nine months later, she had a bastard, you.'

Here he jabbed a finger in my direction.

'But not content with that corruption, she had to seek him out again and steal him away from his legitimate family.'

There were tears in his eyes now.

'He told me I was the loveless spawn of a loveless marriage. The day he left is the day I died and I've been dead ever since.'

'That's hardly my fault is it?' I said quietly.

'But it is,' he screamed. 'He said he loved you more than me!'

I felt the familiar emotions bubble over.

'My father,' I said, hissing the word *father* and then spitting on the imaginary spot where it landed, 'left me when I was seven years old. Let me tell you something, he was no father to me.'

'That's only because he was blackmailed into it. He'd already made the decision to go and live with the slut and her bastard. So you see, in my eyes, whether you like it or not, you were effectively responsible for the death of my family.'

'So all of that detailed planning with false names and documents?' I asked, still reeling from the onslaught. 'What was all that about?'

'I wanted you to suffer the way I've suffered,' he said. 'I wanted you to feel the same mental anguish I had to go through.'

He paused for breath; the anger and rage was really taking it out of him.

'When we were doing the research on you,' he continued, 'we found out about Kathleen Murphy and your relationship with her. We then had a complete stroke of luck and managed to track you to the house in Louisiana through one of the Irish genealogy websites.'

'Yeah I was going to ask you about that?' asked Roussel suddenly.

'Thomas Eugene O'Neill is not a common name,' replied Black Swan, glancing briefly at him. 'And it is even less common when it surfaces on a sporadic search of deeds to properties in the US. It was easy from there to fake a birth certificate.'

'But why?' I asked again.

'I wanted you to go through what I went through,' said Eoin. 'I wanted you to become a father and then have your child cruelly taken away from you. I wanted you to go through all those positive emotions. Thinking you had found a long lost blood relation, finally a son and heir. Then I wanted to be the one to tell you myself, just before I killed you; that it was all lies and you were going to die sad and alone.'

I looked across at Dale; he was shaking his head. It was as he had predicted, but with a less than subtle and frankly quite disturbing twist.

'So all of that elaborate plotting and scheming was solely for my benefit,' I said incredulously.

'I've dreamt of nothing else for the past thirty years,' he said. 'I can't tell you how much I hated you. And what's especially gratifying for me? Now that I've met you in person, it has not dulled that hatred one iota; in fact, if anything it has amplified it.'

I glanced across at Roussel and Dale. I could tell they were as shocked as I was. The depth and ferocity of the hate was something I had rarely encountered. I looked at his face. I saw the uncontrollable twitching of the muscles, the tensing and relaxing of the jaw, the maniacal glint in the eyes. I was not a coward, but at that particular second, I was seriously afraid. He was almost at the point of no return. I could sense that he was just at that crossroads where his subconscious desire for revenge was about to overrule his sane sense of self preservation.

'How did you find us in Kinsale?' I asked.

'That stupid working girl you were trying to protect; she spilled her guts to me first chance she could get. Didn't think she would betray you that easily did you? Mind you, I did give her a handsome reward.'

His response chilled me, but I didn't get a chance to question him further.

'So this has nothing to do with Storm?' asked Roussel, suddenly breaking the tension.

Black Swan didn't even look at him; his stare was unblinkingly focused on me.

'I didn't even know about it until last week,' he said.

He pointed his finger at me again.

'This is all about him,' he said. 'Always has been, always will be.'

'What happened to....'

I was about to say *my father* before another word escaped.

'....him?' I finished.

'*My* father, you mean?' he asked, using the possessive word deliberately. 'I never forgave him. Even though he tried to talk to me, I never spoke another word to him.'

'Even after he went back?' I asked.

'Especially after he came back.'

He spat the words out.

'After hearing what I'd heard from his own lips and seeing it in his face, I could never forgive him. It remained between us till the end. I never regretted it.'

'So what happens now?'

'Well Mr O'Neill or whatever the fuck your name is. I don't care how long more it takes. I don't care where you go or what you do. I will locate you, I will hunt you down and I will kill you, because it's the only way I can get my father back; it's the only way I can grant him absolution.'

I looked at the rapture on his face as he described my death, and realised he was totally genuine; he meant every word he said.

'And you?' I said, gesturing to the man next to Black Swan; the only one I had not spoken too; the one who had remained silent and immobile throughout the whole story.

'Dave Keegan,' he said. 'I suppose you could call me a soldier of fortune. I was facing a life of boredom and slow self-destruction until the boss here showed me a glimpse of an exciting alternative lifestyle.'

'Ex army I'm guessing,' I said.

'Is it that obvious?' he answered.

'You can normally tell,' I said.

'Yeah, it's taken me years to realise it,' he said. 'But do you know what?'

He looked from Foster to Roussel and back to me and then finally across to his boss.

'I'm a bit of a thrill seeker.'

I felt something hit me hard in the face. I should have been expecting something, but instead I recoiled. He'd used one of the oldest tricks in the book; flicking all the loose change out of his pocket at me. As I staggered back, he stooped, picked up the gun, rolled and fired.

I felt a stinging pain in my leg and fell awkwardly to one side. I heard the whistle of another bullet as it flew over my head. Roussel and Foster recovered from their momentary paralysis. I heard the chatter of the machine guns as they laid down sporadic covering fire. Thankfully I had also fallen directly onto my gun. I scrabbled frantically for the weapon and then managed to skitter around the back of one of the larger disassembled machines.

As soon as I made cover, the short bursts of machine gun fire ceased. Both Roussel and Foster had limited ammunition and I'd told them to conserve it, just before we'd entered the arena.

'Looks like we have a bit of a stand-off,' shouted Black Swan.

My leg was pumping blood and I was starting to feel exceptionally lightheaded. I shrugged myself out of my jacket with difficulty, ripped the sleeves into strips, and then tied the fragments around the top of my thigh as tightly as I could. It seemed to staunch the bleeding somewhat, and the pain stabilised into a dull ache.

'Seems you may be right,' I shouted back.

'I'm sure we can come to some arrangement,' said Black Swan.

I felt two or three more bullets thud into the machine that I was hiding behind.

'I'm sure we can,' I said. 'Give me all of the material relating to Storm and I'll think about letting you all live.'

'You're in no position to bargain,' said Guido. 'I think you'll find that one way or the other we hold all of the aces.'

My brain was trying to ignore all the outside influences and concentrate on the injury, but try as I might to divert myself from the reality, I couldn't see a good outcome.

I feared Guido was indeed correct.

We were outgunned, outnumbered and a long way from home.

CHAPTER 58 – CULMINATION

23rd May 2011 – Thirteen days after the Storm.

Action should culminate in wisdom. – Hindu Scripture.

James had two pet hates. He didn't like being lied to, and he didn't like being taken for a fool. He knew Roussel and Foster were up to something, and he knew it had something to do with the case Roussel was working on. With Foster involved as well, drugs were bound to be part of the equation.

Garda Spillane had been as good as his word. It was difficult to find good hard-working staff, but he'd taken over from his off-duty friend and followed the trio all the way to Clonakilty.

He'd reported back to James twice.

Once, to brief James on what was happening and give him directions on where he should go, whilst also alerting him to the gunfire and the assault he'd seen on the building.

The second contact had been made when the three targets, Foster, Roussel and their Irish friend had headed into the thick of the action.

When he'd received the second call, James was glad he had managed to convince his colleague, Sean Fitzsimons, to come along.

'What do you make of the situation?' asked James, for something to say.

'Well, as you've explained it, we've got a rogue detective from Louisiana, a lone DEA agent with no jurisdiction and an unknown Irish-American quantity, staking out an IDA building in Clonakilty. We've had reports of a number of people entering the premises and then a further report of an unknown group of men taking the same building by force.'

'Do we know what that building houses?' asked James.

'Just checking it now,' replied Sean. 'It's registered to G&E Chemicals, which in turn is partnered with the ADXR Corporation.'

'So, on the surface it seems legitimate,' said James.

'On the surface, yes,' said Sean, 'but ADXR are a pharma giant; does give credence to your DEA drugs tie in.'

'Maybe they are manufacturing controlled substances,' said James. 'Morphine or heroin or something like that would make a tempting target for any gang.'

'It would certainly explain why a group would want to take it by force,' replied Sean.

James closed his eyes briefly, even though he was driving. All the thinking was giving him a headache.

When he opened them again, he glimpsed the sign for Clonakilty. He followed Garda Spillane's verbal directions. As agreed, he pulled off onto the verge, a short way from the campus, where Garda Spillane himself was waiting.

He hopped into the back, before the car had even come to a complete stop.

'Thanks for doing this,' said James, turning around in his seat.

'No problem at all,' said Garda Spillane.

'So, have there been any developments?' asked James.

'Not since the last time I spoke to you,' said Garda Spillane. 'Like I told you before, I followed the guys here. They went up onto that hillock.'

He pointed out an area overlooking the front of the building.

'No sooner were they in position, than a number of other smartly dressed gentlemen arrived in two cars; about six or seven of them. They spoke briefly, before entering the building. Ten minutes later, a sizeable number of men took over the building by force.'

He swallowed hard.

'There was gunfire; at least one man is down I think, but I did what you said and waited until you arrived.'

'Discretion is always the better part of valour,' agreed James. 'Anything else?'

'That's it I'm afraid. Five minutes ago the three of them headed down from their lookout towards the building. I couldn't be certain, but it looked like they were armed.'

'Okay, show me where you think this casualty is,' said James.

They alighted from the vehicle and Garda Spillane led the way.

He brought them close in to the hedgerow and around the left side of the building. They kept low and moved as quietly as they could. It was typical West Cork scrubland; heather and gorse in abundance, with patches of small rocks and coarse green grass.

They had gone no more than fifteen feet, when James saw a splash of colour that did not belong in a West Cork field. As he approached, the outline of a man emerged from the heavy damp undergrowth. James estimated he was in his forties. He was lying on his back.

He wore black trousers and James guessed that at one time his shirt would have been white. He bent over and felt for a pulse; nothing. It was then that he noticed something shiny a couple of yards away. As he walked another body emerged from the heather and gorse. He stopped and checked the pulse on this one too; nothing.

He picked up the object that had attracted him and hefted it in his hand. It was a well balanced 9mm pistol. Like all drug squad officers, he'd done his firearms handling. He expertly unloaded the clip; still plenty of ammo.

He flashed the clip at his partner who guessed his intention and searched the prone body of the guard. There were two more clips stashed in his inside pockets.

'Unusual armament for a security guard, wouldn't you say?' asked James softly.

They crouched down to take stock. James accepted the spare clips from his partner, and loaded the gun.

'Can you shoot?' asked James.

He knew he was a better marksman than Sean, but was unsure about the young garda.

'Only an air rifle, sir, when I was younger,' he said. 'I used to help clear the crows out of the fields. And even then, I missed more than I hit.'

'I'll keep the gun so,' whispered James.

Suddenly, they all flinched and threw themselves to the ground. Two rooks took off in a shriek of beating wings as the unmistakeable stutter of automatic gunfire carved through the silence, echoing off the rolling hills behind them.

'Jesus Christ,' whispered James. 'Is everybody okay?'

He looked left and right to make sure his companions were nodding.

'What the hell is happening here?' asked Sean slowly.

'Here's what we're going to do,' said James decisively. 'Garda Spillane, you head back to the car.'

'Pat,' he whispered with a smile.

'Ok, Pat,' said James, with the glimmerings of a smile himself. 'You head back to the car. There's a police band radio in there. Get reinforcements down here now. If you have to, get patched through to Inspector Ryan in Cork city drug squad. Tell him where we are and what's happening. He'll get something moving for you.'

He turned to his colleague.

'Sean,' he said. 'You and I will head inside.'

He corrected himself.

'You and I will sneak inside, and try and find out what's going on. And preferably without getting each other killed in the process.'

Garda Spillane didn't hang around. They watched his retreating back for a second, while James scanned the outside of the building.

'Let's go in via the front,' he whispered. 'Are you ready?'

Sean nodded.

'This is why I joined I suppose; for all the excitement,' he whispered back.

They smiled wryly at each other before they headed off in single file towards the main entrance. As they traversed the roundabout, they dropped to the floor again as a number of more sustained bursts of gunfire opened up, much louder now, as they were almost at the entrance.

The shooting ceased, and they heard a couple of shouts. They moved inside, with James leading the way. They ducked behind the desk for temporary shelter and located a second victim.

James motioned to Sean silently, indicating that he should search the body. Sean gently rolled him over. It was easy to see what had killed him; there were two large holes in his forehead. Sean raised his eyebrows as he extracted another pistol and a spare clip; weapons, weapons everywhere.

There seemed to be only one way onto the factory floor. As they approached, they could hear shouts and the zing of the occasional bullet.

James gestured to Sean and they both got down, sniper style, and inched their way in. As they cleared the end of the corridor, they saw the man that James knew as John O'Reilly. His face was masked with pain, his back propped against one of the large machines that dotted the production line floor.

#

I closed my eyes in an effort to drag my focus away from the injury. When I opened them again, I saw Roussel's liaison officer, DS Murray, emerge from the gloom of the entrance. Even though I was surprised to see him, the emotion did not appear to be mutual. Give him his credit though, his first thought was for my welfare.

'Are you hurt badly?' he whispered.

'Just a flesh wound,' I said softly, 'but it's bleeding quite a lot.'

'Here, let me,' he said, keeping his voice low.

He undid the makeshift knot, and then pulled it as tight as he possibly could. As he secured it in place, the now effective tourniquet seemed to make a huge positive difference. I immediately felt stronger and more alert. He saw me glancing at his companion, who had shuffled into place on the other side of me.

'DS Sean Fitzpatrick, meet John O'Reilly,' whispered James.

'Thomas O'Neill,' I corrected him, 'a.k.a. *the Street.*'

I watched his eyebrows almost crawl off his forehead.

'I know, I'll discuss it all in detail later over a pint,' I said softly. 'If we live that long, of course?'

'So what's the story?' asked James, demonstrating remarkable self control.

I could almost feel the questions exploding out of his head.

'Well for starters we've got Black Swan and a guy called Dave Keegan,' I whispered.

'They're here?' prompted James excitedly.

'With about ten or twelve other men,' I said.

'Go on,' said James.

'We have David McCabe and a Ben....'

'Collins?' finished DS Fitzpatrick.

'That's the fella,' I whispered. 'He's here too.'

I could hear muttering from within the room, so I tried to lower my voice still further.

'Guido and Ernesto Mancini, Antonio their bodyguard, and another guy that I've met before whose name escapes me,' I said a little mysteriously.

I didn't want to expose the CIA angle yet.

'They make up the gathering.'

'You're full of surprises,' said James.

I could feel the irony dripping off the sentence.

'I'll be quick,' I said, 'because I have a feeling this is all going to kick off very soon. The Mancini's, McCabe and Collins met here in the car park, and then continued their conversation inside.'

I neglected to tell them that they'd also swapped documents of some kind, and both Collins and Antonio had attaché cases with them.

'Black Swan and his men stormed the building. In the ensuing confusion, Roussel, Foster and I managed to take them by surprise.'

'Roussel and Foster are here too?' asked James.

I nodded.

'But that guy Keegan was somehow able to distract me briefly, and then managed to get a shot off.'

'So, it's a bit of a stand-off now then?'

'And they don't know you're here, which might play to our advantage. So, here's what I need you guys to do, and you're going to have to trust me on this,' I whispered urgently to James.

I continued on, holding up my hand to silence his protestations.

'You need to move out into the extreme flanks of the building. DS Fitzpatrick, you go out left, James you go out right.'

I checked that I was still wearing my Bluetooth headset.

'Attract the attention of Roussel and Foster. They will be the only ones with automatic weapons. DS Fitzpatrick, you'll need to show your man your warrant card; they won't shoot first.'

I looked at them to make sure they were listening intently.

'Now this is very important. Make sure you manoeuvre them out through the side doors of the building. The rest of the men are all in the main body of the factory, and as such, don't have direct line of sight to the outer walls. This may work to our advantage, as you should be able to exit unnoticed. Get the guys to send me a text when you're outside and then I can make a run out through the front; the way you came in. In the meantime, as you move into position, I'll put down a bit of covering fire; try and divert the attention away from you. Hopefully they'll start killing each other and save us the trouble.'

The two guys nodded.

'So, you understand what it is you're doing?' I asked, one more time.

They nodded again.

'Ok, off you go, keep to the shadows and good luck.'

They shook hands sombrely with me and then scurried out into the dark recesses along either side of the building. I counted silently to five and then pointed my weapon upwards and fired three rounds in quick succession, deliberately placing all the focus on myself. I was making it up as I went along, but the first part of the plan was in motion; time to start the second phase.

I got to my feet, shuffling around a concrete pillar to peer out into the main body of the production floor, when a movement caught my attention. I managed to silently adjust my position and shift to the side of the pillar, just as Ben Collins and David McCabe went creeping past me on the other side. They kept as silent as they could, and by the look of it, they'd managed to evade detection.

I waited for them to get to the end of the corridor and out through the doors. To my surprise, they turned to the left, instead of heading straight out. I was expecting discretion not valour.

I followed a discreet distance behind, moving surreptitiously into the reception area and saw one of their retreating backs disappearing up the stairwell.

I moved up the steps as quickly and carefully as my leg would allow, reaching the small office at the end of the corridor, just as a beep sounded in my headset. One team had made it out of the building safely. As if on cue, I got a second beep. I put my hand on the door handle and pushed it open.

They were huddled together at a large meeting room table. They looked up in surprise as I hobbled into the room. Their gaze drifted from the weapon I held outstretched in my hand, and then back to the documents they were carefully laying out on the large flat surface.

'Move away from the table,' I said quietly. 'And keep your hands where I can see them.'

They did as they were asked, and surprisingly, the overriding emotion, especially on the face of McCabe, seemed to be one of relief. I kept my eye on them as best I could as I started throwing the documents back into the open attaché case. I clicked it shut and tucked it under my arm.

'It's been nice doing business with you, gentleman,' I said, backing out.

I stopped short of the door as I felt something cold and metallic on the back of my neck; an eerie echo of thirteen days earlier.

'We meet again, Mr O'Neill,' said the voice.

I knew immediately who it was.

'David, Ben, my quarrel is not with you. Get out before I change my mind.'

They didn't need asking twice. They scurried out like rats from the sinking ship.

'Turn around,' he ordered.

I shuffled slowly around, as fast as my leg would let me, until I was facing him. The anger and hatred burned as brightly as ever.

'Okay, so I don't get to gloat the way I wanted to,' he said, 'but at least you'll know who sent you to meet your maker.'

Time seemed to slow down. I could sense his finger building the pressure on the trigger. At about the same time, I could sense his realisation that he had made a basic error; he was standing slightly too close.

I flicked up my left hand to deflect the gun; the bullet impacted into the solid stone masonry of the wall. At the same time, my right arm swung in towards his head, the bottom edge of my hand connecting to a point on his neck an inch or so below the skull. His legs buckled from under him, his eyes rolled into his head, and he fell to the floor.

When he came to, I had moved slightly away from him; the distance he should have been standing.

'I've got no quarrel with you,' I said, as he got up slowly. 'Let's call it quits and you can walk away.'

'I can't call it quits,' he said, rubbing his neck thoughtfully, 'so you need to do it now, or I'll never stop coming for you.'

'Don't push me,' I warned.

'Do it,' he screamed. 'Do it!'

He leapt at me as I'd known he would. I re-adjusted my stance, and the butt of the gun connected with his temple with a dull thud. He dropped to the floor, out cold again.

'I'm sorry,' I whispered, 'but I can't have another pointless death on my conscience.'

I took one last look around the room and then headed back through the doorway. I didn't see the shooter; rather I heard the bullet thud into the frame of the doorway. I pulled back instinctively, as a volley of shots ripped through the cheap plasterboard partition.

There was no way I could shelter in this room, even if I could lock the door, which I couldn't. My eyes scanned the room, coming to a cold and calculating decision. I hobbled towards the window, ignoring the bullets as they flew through the studwork to impact on the far masonry wall. I ducked instinctively as I heard a large crash, then raised my weapon and fired twice. The window exploded outwards in a million fragments.

I lifted my leg awkwardly over the sill, ripping my trousers on the jagged edges of glass. I saw a shadow darkening the doorway and didn't hesitate. As I launched myself out, I tried to land on my good leg, but I hadn't factored in the slope of the roof. I hit with the wounded leg first, which buckled under me, and I spun helplessly towards the edge.

Luckily or unluckily, there were skylights dotted across the surface. I rolled straight into one. The impact on my spine was bone juddering, and forceful enough to knock the wind out of me. I wasted no time; unclipping the Perspex covering as I fought to regain my breath.

Seeing the stack of cardboard boxes underneath the window, I threw the attaché case into the hole and dived headfirst after it through the open skylight, just as a volley of bullets shattered the hinged plastic cover above me. I was exceptionally lucky; the boxes were half empty and took the major force of the impact. I rolled and landed heavily on the concrete; it was becoming a bit of a painful habit. I got up stiffly, rubbed my aching back, and shuffled toward the exit. As I walked, it became apparent that I was not alone, not by a long shot.

I felt their eyes on me first, and the hairs on the back of my neck stood up as I felt their weapons on me too. I hobbled into the open area in the middle of the floor. The open skylight was acting as a weird spotlight on me, as I grabbed onto the edge of the builders skip for support.

I waited for them to form a circle, like the old Wild West and then the one called Pavel moved forward from the shadowy circle to face me.

'You're pretty good,' he said.

His accent was so thick I could barely understand what he was saying.

'But not good enough, I think; time for you to die.'

He was slow and he was arrogant, two things that had always pissed me off. It also gave my subconscious an impossibly long time to register the enormous propane tank at one end of the production floor. I flicked up my weapon and fired a single shot.

'Missed,' he said, with a crooked smile.

'I don't think so,' I replied.

The explosion, when it came, was more of a whoosh. It started as a tiny dot and then the rapidly intensifying fireball seemed to grow and expand, consuming everything in its path. One or two men screamed as the roof seemed to peel off. The flames came roaring towards us, like the fingers of Satan, straight from hell.

I rolled into the skip and pulled the sheet of plywood across my body, milliseconds before the fiery tidal wave hit. I heard the anguished screams cut off abruptly, as the fireball continued its relentless journey. I could feel the heat on the plywood above me, and could feel the flesh of my fingers burning. I had to endure the agony to keep my shield in place.

Then, just as suddenly as it had started, it was gone. I relaxed and my brain must have hit the kill switch, as the next thing I remember was a shouted *here he is* and the plywood was roughly cast aside. Both Roussel and Dale towered over me.

'Is he alive?' asked Dale anxiously, as the paramedics started work.

'Of course I'm bloody alive,' I said sourly, before dissolving into a coughing fit.

The two of them laughed with relief, and it was kind of touching for me to realise how concerned they were.

'Fucking hell, Street,' croaked Dale, who rarely swore. 'You've destroyed any chance we have of getting any of the documentation back.'

I looked around. I could see what he meant. The roof was gone and everywhere was still smouldering.

'Isn't it better this way,' I said. 'Gone up in a puff of smoke?'

'We really needed those documents,' he said a little sadly, 'if only to save our careers.'

'Roll me over to one side,' I said to the paramedic.

'Why; are you hurt?'

'Just fucking do it, will you!' I shouted crossly.

They gently rolled me to one side, and there, lying beneath me, nestled in the builder's rubble, was the battered attaché case.

'I just couldn't help myself,' I said weakly.

I started laughing, and was still laughing when the morphine went in and the pain dulled to a throb and then to nothing.

CHAPTER 59 – ANTICLIMAX

28th May 2011 – Eighteen days after the Storm.

Suspense is worse than disappointment. – Robert Burns.

I walked through the large stone gates with a mixture of trepidation and excitement. I had basically pretended that the funeral hadn't happened; simple as that. There were a lot of conversations that I needed to have with her; topics that a son should have discussed with his mother, all those years ago.

All the communications normally shared were in our case lost in our fractious and tempestuous relationship, not helped by her early onset Alzheimer's. Back then, I'd revelled in the discord and chaos it brought. Now, twenty plus years later, all I felt was a gnawing chasm of guilt, widening year by year.

It was simple really; isn't it always? We had just never completely gelled as mother and son in those later years; never aligned on any of those really important levels. We'd never had one of those eureka moments; one of those shared laughter, I know what the other person is thinking before they do, moments. We were always slightly out of tune, like a grainy TV picture, or a crackly radio station, sometimes crystal clear in our understanding and then suddenly adrift in a shower of static. But at the crux of it all was one simple thing; my stubbornness and single mindedness.

I could always see how hard she was trying, but it was like a game and I couldn't help myself. I think deep down I had convinced myself that if she loved me, really loved me, then she would never give up. So the harder she tried, the more difficult I would become. I would let her get so far; she would think we were making progress, and then, wham, I'd let fly with all the teenage histrionics I could muster. She was dead before I realised what a complete and utter bastard I'd been, our relationship a wasteland of wrong turns and infinite, unfulfilled possibilities.

So here I was, pathetically trying to find redemption; hoping against hope that a headstone could dispense forgiveness, but knowing deep down that it could not.

The realisation that redemption was beyond reach did not make me sad; it made me angry.

'This is not how it was supposed to be,' I screamed silently at the headstone. 'You were supposed to give me contentment and closure in answers, not confusion and turmoil in questions.'

I felt a lump in my throat as I approached the cold granite monument to my squandered opportunities.

And then I stopped.

There were fresh flowers on the grave.

I looked at the carefully manicured mound, and my thoughts anchored back to those spiteful words uttered by Black Swan.

'That slut of a mother,' he'd said.

God forgive me, but I couldn't purge my mind of those hurtful images. My mother with another man, my mother with other kids; the thoughts competed with each other for space.

I wandered aimlessly for a couple of minutes, eventually sinking onto a bench. I hadn't even brought any flowers myself. What the hell was I doing? What was I trying to prove? What was I looking for?

I had to accept there were things about my mother I would probably never know.

I heard the sound of whistling. It was the old crooner classic, *fly me to the moon*; I recognised the refrain. A tall athletic young man was holding a green canvas bag full of gardening tools. I watched open mouthed as he placed the bag next to my mother's plot, and started laying out his tools methodically, like a surgeon in an operating theatre.

He caught my eye. If he was aware of the fact I was staring at him, he didn't give it away, acknowledging my gaze with a slight smile, before turning to his work with a rapt concentration.

I walked slowly towards him, my mind racing, trying to calculate the infinite possibilities. He glanced up again as I approached, his initial greeting turning to puzzlement and indecision as he wilted under the intensity of my examination.

'Can I help you?' he asked hesitantly.

I was just about to answer, when I heard a familiar voice behind me.

'Adam, where are you, I told you to slow down?'

He looked up with a guilty smile, but didn't answer.

'Didn't I ask you to wait for me?' she asked, in a light-heartedly admonishing tone.

She was about to continue, but as I turned, she stopped. My heart was racing, but she looked at me calmly.

'Hello Thomas,' she said slowly. 'We meet again. I thought you were long gone.'

It was not an apology, merely a statement of fact.

'But where are my manners?' she said. 'Let me introduce you to my son, Adam.'

The young man coloured and brushed his hands on his jumper, before taking my hand and shaking it firmly.

'Pleased to meet you,' he said.

'Thomas O'Neill,' I responded dazedly, as if by way of explanation.

'Ah, the New Yorker,' he said, his face clearing.

There was an awkward silence.

'Adam, can you cope on your own for a while?' asked Kathleen. 'I fancy a quick stroll with an old friend.'

'Sure,' he said. 'Take your time, I'll be waiting.'

I offered her my arm which she linked as we headed off on a slow circuit of the cemetery. I said nothing, content for her to speak when she was ready.

'I hope you don't mind?' she asked at last.

'I'm quite touched actually,' I replied.

She looked at me and smiled her famous sardonic smile.

'I didn't do it for you,' she said. 'Mrs O was always very good to me. The funeral was just very....'

She searched for the word.

'....cold. It seemed a shame for her to be laid to rest without someone to look after her.'

I ignored the intentionally barbed words.

'You don't come just for....'

'No, I have other reasons for being here,' she said, without elaborating.

'Well, thank you anyway,' I said.

'You're welcome. I'm surprised to see you here, in fact,' she said. 'Confronting your emotions, asking for forgiveness maybe? Surely that's too messy and irrational for Thomas O'Neill. You prefer the clean break, don't you?'

Same old Kathleen, forthright as ever with no punches pulled. There were very few people who would speak to me like that, even less who I would let do it with impunity.

'Starting an initial dialogue,' I replied honestly. 'We'll see where it goes.'

'So, you're staying?' she asked.

'I'm not sure,' I replied. 'It depends on a couple of things, but if I do leave, it's not because I'm running away. I'm not prepared to do that any longer.'

'I believe you.'

'So, Adam?' I asked, changing the subject. 'Is he your eldest?'

She held my gaze, searching for the motivation behind the question.

'He is my eldest, yes, and no, he's not yours, if that's the question you're asking.'

I felt an immediate stab of release, and then a faint flash of guilt at the feeling of relief.

We'd managed to make our way back to the plot, where Adam was putting the finishing touches to the weeding.

'So, I guess this may not be goodbye,' she said, shaking my hand solemnly as Adam tidied his tools away.

'Oh I think it probably is,' I said.

She smiled; she knew what I meant. I was glad I didn't have to explain it to her. I probably wouldn't have been able to.

'Your leg?' she asked. 'I couldn't help noticing you were limping slightly.'

'A tear in the muscle,' I said truthfully, not elaborating.

'Goodbye Thomas,' she said, winking at me.

I sat on the bench and watched the two of them amble toward the exit. There was an air of easiness about them. Even watching them from behind as they walked away, you could see how comfortable they were with each other; love given and received with no thought of a return on your investment.

I heard the laughter and the jollity in their voices, but it didn't make me feel jealous, just happy and contented for them. From the second I'd found out she had kids, there'd been that nagging feeling at the back of my mind; why hadn't she told me herself?

As soon as I'd met Adam, I knew he wasn't mine and as soon as I'd seen the expression on Kathleen's face, I knew why she hadn't told me. She hadn't wanted to upset me; hadn't wanted me to imagine what might have been.

Maybe I would want to be a father one day, but at that precise moment, I realised that I didn't, and that was okay.

'I need to find a partner first,' I said softly and sardonically under my breath. 'That's generally the way it works, isn't it?'

I leant back and closed my eyes, feeling the heat of the sun on my face. Maybe I was on a fool's errand; talking to the dead indeed. It was the living I needed to be talking to.

Suddenly, I felt the pressure of something hard pressing into the base of my neck. I smiled to myself in genuine amusement. I seemed to have made a lot of enemies in a very short space of time.

'So, Mr O'Neill, we meet again,' said the voice.

My face cleared.

'It's funny,' I said, 'but I had a feeling it would be you. I didn't think you were the type of guy to let something like this go.'

I could feel the gun barrel trembling on my skin as he spoke.

'You cannot begin to understand how much money you have cost me,' he said. 'With the Mancini's both dead in the explosion, there is now no way my wire transfers will be completed. And with the human cost of my endeavours to contend with too, you have effectively ended my life and for what; for a big fat slice of nothing.'

'I wish I could take all the credit,' I responded, 'but I had a lot of help from Charles and Dale.'

'I'll deal with them later,' he said, 'make no mistake about that. But you're the one I really want.'

'For a cold fish, you're getting very emotional.'

He ignored me and I could feel the spittle on the nape of my neck as he talked, viciously throwing the words at the back of my head.

'From the moment I saw Storm, I knew it was the big one,' he said. 'I knew it was my one chance and the Mancini's knew it too. We shared the vision.'

'Did they know about the fatal flaw?' I asked.

'Of course they didn't,' he said indignantly. 'Are you mad? I was trying to sell it to them.'

'And you had no crisis of conscience over that?'

He snorted with derision.

'That's rich, coming from the professional killer,' he answered, 'but no I didn't. If somebody takes a drug, they have to accept the consequences. If it ain't prescribed by a doctor, don't take it, that's my motto. Every time someone smokes a joint, every time somebody drops a tab of ecstasy, they're taking their life in their hands. They might not believe it, but they are.'

'We're talking wholesale slaughter here,' I said.

'All drugs have side effects,' he said. 'This one is just a little more extreme than most.'

'You know they're looking for you don't you?' I responded, changing the subject.

'You forget who you are talking to,' he said.

'Oh I don't think I do, Mr No-name,' I said. 'Or should I call you the deputy director, or maybe Deputy Director Grant, or just Carl maybe?'

'How do you know who I am?' he asked.

I could picture his eyes narrowing.

'It was actually quite easy to piece together,' I said. 'It had to be somebody senior in the organisation; there aren't that many people below the director himself, and would you believe the CIA website provides helpful photographs. There you were in black and white; I would have said colour, but that would have been racist, wouldn't it? Must have been tough though, ditching the family and starting a new life for nothing.'

'You're about to find out how tough,' he said. 'To be honest, my wife and I were not getting on. The kids had grown-up and didn't need me anymore. And I had quite literally millions of reasons to be happy; until you came along, that is.'

'You've a very recognisable face,' I stated helpfully. 'I don't think there are many places you can go.'

'Oh you'd be surprised,' he said. 'Anyway, I've had enough of this chit chat. It's time for you to say goodbye.'

I felt a renewed pressure on the back of my neck.

'Any last requests?' he asked.

'Can I at least go and say goodbye to my Mum?' I asked.

'Don't take me for a fool,' he said. 'How do you think I found you? I've been watching you, waiting. I know what you've been doing for the last few minutes. You're not getting off this bench.'

'The sign of the cross then?'

He started laughing.

'A religious hit man; that must be a first. You ain't getting off this bench,' he said, 'but go on, whatever.'

I closed my eyes and as I made the sign of the cross, I muttered the familiar refrain under my breath.

'In the name of the father, and of the son, and of the Holy Spirit, amen.'

I heard a sharp crack, like a twig breaking, but I felt no pain. The pressure on the back of my neck disappeared as Carl Grant, the erstwhile deputy director of the CIA, collapsed to the ground.

I stood over him; there was a tiny hole with a trickle of blood at his temple. I flicked his head over with the toe of my boot; the same could not be said for the other side. There was a large mess of smashed bone, blood and grey matter.

Silly man; to the end he'd believed he was one step ahead of everybody else. It was no accident that he'd fallen next to a fresh, open grave. I bent down with difficulty and straightened him out as best I could.

I got up awkwardly and rolled him like a log with my foot until he fell into the pit with a muffled thud. I straightened my leg and waited for the throb to return to a dull ache. I felt a slight pressure on my shoulder and I turned around. Two men dressed in overalls materialised beside me, one of them carrying what looked like a large camera case. Incongruously, both were wearing sunglasses, even though it was dull and overcast.

'Thank you, Mr O'Neill,' said the one with the case. 'We'll take it from here.'

He handed me a plain white envelope.

'Just remember, sir,' he continued. 'No deviations; the director wouldn't like that.'

I smiled.

'Perish the thought.'

They set to work. By the time I reached the austere stone gateway, the grave had been fully closed and there was no trace of the two young men, apart from two sets of overalls that lay draped across the front of a nearby wheelbarrow.

EPILOGUE – AFTER THE STORM

30th May 2011 – Twenty days after the Storm.

The little reed, bending to the force of the wind, soon stood upright again when the storm had passed over. – Aesop.

Roussel wound the window down, partly to get some fresh air, but mostly to let the cold onrush blow the cobwebs away.

Roussel and James had parted on good terms. James even admitted in a weak moment, during his third pint of Guinness, that in the same circumstances he would have done the same duplicitous thing himself.

Roussel had fully debriefed both James and his boss, Inspector Ryan, but he'd used a prearranged cover story; the one he, Foster and Street had engineered to conceal the ugly parts of the truth. The Mancini's had been in Ireland to agree a major drug supply deal with both Black Swan and the Bullock. One of the rivals had got wind of the deal being offered to the other, and the resulting fire fight had ensued. No mention had been made of the briefcase which Foster had managed to retain and hide.

To James and Inspector Ryan, the scenario presented to them was both neat and believable. The only fly in the ointment for them was that neither Black Swan nor the Bullock had been found amongst the debris of the explosion. They couldn't be missing presumed dead, so they were just plain missing. Other than that, when the debriefing was over, a good time was had by all, and lots of drink flowed as they jointly celebrated a famous victory over the international drugs trade.

At the airport, Roussel had been genuinely emotional as Dale and Street had packed him off home. They'd formed a bond, the three of them, and he was pretty sure, no, he was certain, that they would stay in touch.

Roussel pulled up across the road from the entrance. Some of the *police line; do not cross* tape was still fluttering in the early evening breeze. As he stared down the long gravelled laneway, he thought about his earlier visit a fortnight ago.

He'd already told the captain that the two cases were solved which had made both of them very happy men.

He made sure nothing was coming from either direction and then floored the accelerator. He flew up the driveway, only slowing down as he got to the curve at the top and the mansion came slowly into view.

He sat there with the engine idling. Street was a lucky man. They had discussed the house, and Street had hinted that maybe Roussel could negotiate a rent or even buy it one day.

One way or the other, the last two weeks had demonstrated to him that he needed to be home. They had also amply shown him where home was and where it was not. He wearily resigned himself to another few years in his crappy apartment, and tried to think of more upbeat topics on the way back to the place that was beginning to have a temporary permanence.

The only parking spot he could find was about as far from his apartment as it was possible to get. He trudged across the parking lot and up the stairs, getting more tired by the second. With what seemed like the last of his strength, he pushed through the screen and tried to open the front door. It swung inward a couple of inches and then jammed on something. It took him a couple of minutes, but he eventually managed to use one end of his stiff leather belt to push the package backwards, so that the door would open.

He picked it up and turned it over, absently throwing his keys on the sideboard. He recognised the big jagged slashes of Tony's capital letters. *SOMEBODY UP THERE LIKES YOU! SEE YOU SOON, TONY AND MARLENE.*

As soon as Roussel opened the package, he knew precisely what it contained. The bundles of documents were identical to the ones he'd seen before, only this time they were the originals. The documentation pack was held together with a large paperclip, the front page of which was a simple dictated note.

To the rightful owner of Augustine Mansion; look after it, you deserve it. In the words of the Steely Dan song; 'Yes Jack, I gave it back, the ring I could not own. Now, come my friend, I'll take your hand and lead you home.' You'll know what I mean, Street. PS, make sure one of the spare rooms is always made up for me.

Roussel dropped to his knees, almost in prayer. When he looked up, his smile was the width of his face. He pulled out his phone and dialled the number from memory.

'Hey Guilbeau,' he said. 'Get your drinking pants on, it's Powers Gold Label time, and have I got a tale for you!'

#

He'd decided to go straight to the office from the airport. He couldn't face going home and he was fairly sure the work would have built up while he was gone. What he was not expecting was the resounding cheer that sounded from below the *Welcome home Dale* banner that had been strung across the open plan space as he walked in.

He was sitting in the corner now; his back had been slapped and his hand had been shaken too many times to recall, and the two chocolate doughnuts were sitting uneasily in a pool of coffee in his otherwise empty stomach. He sipped his water and smiled warmly as Dodds approached.

'You ready to face the Boss now?' Dodds asked.

'Let's get it over with,' said Dale.

As the three of them sat down at Ray's small meeting table, Dale was surprised at how warmly he'd been greeted. But when he thought about it for a while, it made complete sense. Not only had his seemingly self-destructive career suicide been good for Dale's own prospects, but the expanding ripples had positively impacted his colleagues too. Both Ray and Dodds could now count the director of the CIA as a phone contact; you couldn't buy that kind of power and influence, especially where drug investigations were concerned.

'So, back on US time yet?' asked Ray as an icebreaker.

'It's not too bad coming this way,' said Dale. 'Your day just extends by a few hours. It's going the other way that's a killer. Oh, and before we go any further....'

He swung his rucksack up onto the table.

The bag had caused him days of anxiety; he had expected at any moment to feel a hand on his shoulder. He extracted all the documentation he'd removed from the briefcase, and placed it in the centre of the table. He'd also added the original file that had precipitated Street's involvement, so all the outstanding Storm documentation was in that one single pile in front of them.

Dale regarded it warily, as though it were an unexploded bomb or might spontaneously burst into flames.

'So that's it,' said Ray. 'That's what all the death and destruction has been about?'

It was just a pile of paper at the end of the day.

'That death and destruction is nothing to what would have happened if their collective plan had succeeded,' said Dale softly.

'True,' acknowledged Ray.

He watched curiously as Dale extracted an evidence bag from his pocket.

'What are you doing?' Ray asked suspiciously, as Dale started to pick up the bundle of documents.

'I'm tagging it as evidence,' said Dale.

'No you're not,' said Ray firmly, anchoring the pile to the table.

'Have we learned nothing from the past two weeks?' pleaded Dale.

'On the contrary,' said Ray, 'we've learnt a great deal. We've learnt that things are done for reasons that neither you nor I can comprehend. We may not like it; these guys may not get it right the whole time, but having met the director, I wouldn't like to do what he does.'

'But we came so close to a catastrophe,' argued Dale. 'Some controls need to be put in place.'

'We came close to a catastrophe,' echoed Ray, 'but we managed to avert it. Sometimes you can't make these decisions by committee.'

'So, what happens next time?' asked Dale. 'It's only a matter of time before someone's luck runs out.'

'We pray we are not involved at the time,' answered Ray. 'In the meantime, I suggest you forget it and enjoy your promotion and pay rise.'

'You're joking right?' said Dale suspiciously.

'No, I'm not,' said Ray. 'My superiors were unanimous; they think you rightly deserve it, for all the work you've put in on this problem.'

'Are you trying to buy me off?'

'No one is trying to buy you off Dale, but let me tell you this and it is not a threat by the way. If you breathe one word of this outside the small circle of people who are already in the know, then I guarantee one day, you will just disappear. In the UK, an army major started asking too many questions. He was shot and killed by *mysterious* terrorist elements.'

Ray paused, as if to accentuate the levity of the message.

'The man responsible for the leaking of Storm in the first place, a senior ranking CIA official, who I have no intention of naming by the way, just disappeared; gone. So my advice, and I'm including the both of you here, is to do what I've done. Chalk it down to experience, give thanks to God that you don't have to do that type of work yourself, and then get on with your life.'

Dale sat back and thought about what his boss had said. He could see Dodds ruminating on it as well. He thought about his informants, about the network of dealers and runners that expanded across his territory like a spider's web. He thought about all the good he would be able to do, and about how much better equipped he would now be to do his job. The boss was right; as far as he was concerned, *Storm* was now merely a representation of a geophysical disturbance; a violent weather system.

He heard the clink of glass, and was astonished to see Ray throw out three small shot glasses and a bottle of Jim Bean. He poured a healthy slug into each glass and then raised his own.

'To us,' he said.

'I'll drink to that,' responded Dodds.

'Amen,' said Dale, as the fiery liquid burned as strongly as his desire to get back to some real work.

#

She leant her elbows on the balcony railings, revelling in the warmth dissipated by the smooth mahogany balustrade. It was noon, when the day was at its hottest, but she loved the sun and relished the heat.

She looked down at herself. She was wearing a tasteful two-piece bikini. In a romance novel, her skin would have been described as alabaster. Indeed, it was what most of her clients told her they liked about her; it made her seem purer somehow.

This had always made her laugh, seeing as she was a prostitute; high class maybe, but a call girl none the less. Maybe they felt less guilt that way. No, she preferred to think of herself as pale. It covered a multitude of sins.

She had never been to Spain before; certainly never been to Marbella. Her images of Spain were tainted with visions of high-rise a la Benidorm and Torremolinos. She hadn't realised how classy Spain could be.

She looked around the exterior of the apartment, a term which was actually a bit of a misnomer. It was an enormous penthouse, the outside balcony space being larger than her small townhouse back home.

She thought about that word for a second; home.

She felt a presence behind her; hands gently placed over her eyes, and a whispered question.

'Guess who?'

'Prince Charming,' she answered, smiling.

'Close enough,' he replied, with a smile of his own.

'By rights, you should be dead,' she stated seriously.

'By rights, I think you're right,' he answered with feeling, 'although I have to say, I feel pretty good for a corpse.'

'They don't believe you're dead,' she said flatly.

'They might have initially,' he said. 'There were a lot of people there when it blew; a lot of bodies and body parts and a lot of rubble to sift through. But they will have confirmed me as missing by now; unlike those poor unfortunate souls.'

'Like Ben,' she said sadly.

'Like Ben,' he acknowledged, and they both bowed their heads for a few seconds in a silent mutual prayer.

'Why did he go back in?' she asked.

'Loyal to the end,' said David. 'He didn't want to leave without the documentation. We'd been planning all those months for it and I don't think he truly realised how dangerous the situation actually was. He was very much a man of numbers rather than a man of action.'

'So where does that leave you?' asked Sam.

'Well, the drug squad have a thorough file on me. They know the properties I own and at this stage they are probably also aware that less than twenty four hours after the explosion, I flew out from Cork to Fuengirola. They would also be acutely aware of where all my assets and holdings are, so on the face of it, I think they know exactly where I am. Will they bother to try and extradite me? Do you know what, I don't think they will? I think knowing I'm no longer around will be good enough for them and to be honest with you Sam, that's good enough for me too.'

'I had a horrible feeling of dread that night you left,' she said. 'I was convinced something bad was about to happen.'

'Something bad did happen,' he said sombrely. 'I lost my business partner and my best friend.'

'True,' she acknowledged. 'But I just can't shake the feeling; you know that one, the sick feeling in the pit of your stomach.'

'Sure it's not just Spanish tummy?' he asked.

'Maybe that's it,' she said, unconvinced.

'I love you Sam,' he said.

She didn't answer, but she held him a little tighter and said it silently to herself.

I think I love you too, David.

Two seconds later, the force of the explosion lifted the balcony area clean off the front of the penthouse, the rolling ball of fire incinerating them both instantly.

Ashes to ashes, dust to dust.

#

He looked out at the beautiful alpine landscape, rolling and twisting beyond the large picture window. Good; when you were paying the type of prices he was, the least you expected was a decent view.

He felt slight apprehension, but only slight. Money could buy a lot of things and he had been assured that pain medication was top of that list. He'd chosen the Bergmann clinic near Gstaad in Switzerland, not only because it was the best at what it did, which it undoubtedly was, but because it was beloved by Hollywood royalty. The actors, singers and rock stars, like him, had one thing they valued above all else; discretion.

As if to reinforce the point, there was a discreet knock at the door.

'Come,' he said.

A nurse and two orderlies entered the room.

'Are you ready?' asked the nurse, in flawless English.

He nodded and she gave him his pre-meds, two pills, and the orderlies grabbed each end of the bed, and wheeled him down to the anteroom outside the operating theatre.

The anaesthetist put a needle into his arm and asked him to count slowly to ten. He didn't even reach seven before he was out cold.

In the operating theatre, the surgeon and his assistant were studying two photographs.

'So he wants to go from this to this?' asked the assistant, pointing from one to the other. 'Why?'

'At this stage in my career, I don't ever question their motives,' said the surgeon honestly. 'I just bank their money and do a fantastic job, so they'll recommend me to their rich and flaky friends.'

'I mean,' the assistant pointed to the second picture. 'It's not like this guy is even good-looking or anything.'

'I know; I thought that initially,' said the surgeon, 'but look closely; the shape of the head, the sculpture of the bones. Forget about the flesh; that can be easily manipulated, but look at the bone structure. If I didn't know better, and to be honest I don't, I'd say these guys were related.'

#

'Thanks for coming to see me at such short notice,' he said.

I looked around the office and then back at him.

'I didn't really have a choice, did I?'

'I like to call it the management illusion of reality?' he said, laughing.

'What am I doing here, sir?' I asked.

'You see? That's what I like about you,' he said. 'You always get straight to the point; no fucking around. Okay, I'll extend the same courtesy to you. Bottom line is; we would like you to come and work for us.'

He corrected himself.

'I'd like you to come and work for me.'

'Well I'm flattered,' I said, 'but....'

He held up his hand.

'Don't give me an answer now,' he said. 'Think about it for a while, but while you do, think on this. You have all the skills we are looking for; aggressive, a good fighter, a marksman, decisive and a natural leader.'

'How long do I have?' I asked.

'Don't leave it too long,' he warned. 'I'm a patient man, but even my patience can be stretched.'

I didn't even bother asking him if that was a warning. He was the director of the CIA; it was flattering in a way.

'I'll be in touch,' I said. 'Very soon.'

'Goodbye Mr O'Neill,' he said, pumping my hand warmly. 'Or should I just say au revoir.'

#

Kate was waiting for me in the foyer. She smiled at me the same way she had that first time, and I felt the very same impact. I offered her my arm, as I had with Kathleen, and she linked it as we walked out into the warm sunshine.

'Okay, I've got one question?' she asked.

'Shoot,' I responded.

'Getting the guys to pass that note to me in the cells; how did you know that it would keep me safe; that I would think that way?'

'Easy,' I said. 'These people; people like Black Swan, look at things in black and white. If you're not with them, you're against them. The fact that you were prepared to pass information to him about my whereabouts, or where you suspected I'd be, automatically made you his ally and therefore protected. I also knew because of your background, that you would try and protect yourself; second nature.'

'I suppose there is some logic in there somewhere,' she said.

'Trust me,' I said. 'I thought about it for a long time.'

'I have so far,' she replied.

'What?' I asked, momentarily lost.

'Trusted you.'

'True,' I acknowledged.

'So where are we going?' she asked.

'New York, Midtown to be precise,' I said.

Her eyebrows rose.

'Really?' she said. 'Is that near Manhattan?'

'Right smack in the middle of it,' I replied.

'I'll miss Cork,' she said with a sigh.

'Strangely enough, I will too,' I said.

She looked down at her hand where it grasped my arm, and I felt the fingers tighten slightly.

'What'll we do for money?' she asked, suddenly serious.

'Oh don't you worry about money,' I said, placing my own hand over hers momentarily in a protective gesture. 'Besides, I have a job offer that I'm not going to be allowed to refuse.'

www.ingramcontent.com/pod-product-compliance
Lightning Source LLC
Chambersburg PA
CBHW070347260626
47161CB00001B/52